W.E.B. DU BOIS, author of *The Souls of Black Folk,* was born in 1868 in Massachusetts, educated at Fisk and Harvard universities, and taught at Wilberforce and Atlanta universities. A pioneer in sociology and historiography, he founded the Niagara Movement (1905), a forerunner of the NAACP (1909), and became the editor of the NAACP periodical *Crisis*. In 1961 he joined the Communist party and moved to Ghana, where he died in 1963.

FREDERICK DOUGLASS, author of *Narrative of the Life of Frederick Douglass, an American Slave,* was born in 1818 and grew up in Baltimore. He worked as a slave on a plantation before escaping, giving himself a new name, learning to write, and eventually lecturing with great success all over the North and in Britain, editing a newspaper, advising President Lincoln, and serving as a federal administrator and as U.S. minister and consul general to Haiti before his death in 1895.

HARRIET A. JACOBS, abolitionist, activist, feminist, and author of *Incidents in the Life of a Slave Girl: Written by Herself,* was born a slave in North Carolina around 1813. She was orphaned as a child, and when she was a teen had two children by a local white lawyer. In 1835 she faked an escape to the North, hiding in a nearby attic where she stayed for seven years until she went north in 1842. There she placed her daughter in a private school and her son in an apprenticeship as a printer, and published her famous account.

BOOKER T. WASHINGTON, author of *Up from Slavery,* was the greatest black educator of the nineteenth century. Born in 1856 in Virginia, he worked in the coal mines of West Virginia as a child. At sixteen, he went to the Hampton Institute in Virginia, where he worked his way through school as a janitor, and eventually returned as a teacher. In 1881 he founded Tuskegee Institute in Alabama, and became the most powerful black man in America, confidant of Carnegie and Rockefeller, and adviser to presidents until he died in 1915.

JAMES WELDON JOHNSON, author of *The Autobiography of an Ex-Colored Man,* was born in Florida in 1871, graduated from Atlanta University in 1894 and became the first black to be admitted to the bar in Duval County, Florida. He had a successful second career as a songwriter in New York, as well as writing poetry and essays, serving as consul to Venezuela and Nicaragua and field secretary of the NAACP, editing a newspaper, and teaching literature at Fisk University until his death in a car accident in 1938.

NTAM CLASSIC · A BANTAM CLASSIC · A BANTAM CLASSIC · A BANTAM CLASSIC · A BANTAM CLASSI

EARLY AFRICAN-AMERICAN CLASSICS

EDITED AND WITH AN INTRODUCTION BY

Anthony Appiah

BANTAM BOOKS
NEW YORK • TORONTO • LONDON • SYDNEY • AUCKLAND

EARLY AFRICAN-AMERICAN CLASSICS
A Bantam Classic Book / May 1990

PUBLISHING HISTORY
The Souls of Black Folk *first published 1903*
Narrative of the Life of Frederick Douglass, an American Slave *first published 1845*
Incidents in the Life of a Slave Girl: Written by Herself *first published 1861*
Up from Slavery *first published 1901*
The Autobiography of an Ex-Colored Man *first published 1912*

ISBN 0-553-21379-2

Published simultaneously in the United States and Canada

Bantam Books are published by Bantam Books, a division of Bantam Doubleday Dell Publishing Group, Inc. Its trademark, consisting of the words "Bantam Books" and the portrayal of a rooster, is Registered in U.S. Patent and Trademark Office and in other countries. Marca Registrada. Bantam Books, 1540 Broadway, New York, New York 10036.

PRINTED IN THE UNITED STATES OF AMERICA

0 9 8 7

CONTENTS

Introduction
by Anthony Appiah *vii*

Prologue: A Selection from *The Souls of Black Folk*
by W.E.B. Du Bois, 1903 *1*

Narrative of the Life of Frederick Douglass, an American Slave
by Frederick Douglass, 1845 *13*

Selections from *Incidents in the Life of a Slave Girl: Written by Herself*
by Harriet A. Jacobs, Edited by L. Maria Child, 1861 *111*

Selections from *Up from Slavery*
by Booker T. Washington, 1901 *317*

Selections from *The Autobiography of an Ex-Coloured Man*
by James Weldon Johnson, 1912 *457*

INTRODUCTION

Anthony Appiah

The "American Negro," W.E.B. Du Bois writes in the *Souls of Black Folk,*

> ever feels his twoness—an American, a Negro; two souls, two thoughts, two unreconciled strivings. . . .
>
> The history of the American Negro is the history of this strife,—this longing to attain self-conscious manhood, to merge his double self into a better and truer self. . . . He simply wishes to make it possible for a man to be both a Negro and an American. . . .

It is always important, then, to remember that African-American writing is American. The African-American classics gathered here—Frederick Douglass's 1845 *Narrative*, Harriet Jacobs's *Incidents in the Life of a Slave Girl*, Booker T. Washington's *Up from Slavery*, and James Weldon Johnson's *Autobiography of an Ex-Colored Man*—have an American literary and cultural context without which they cannot be understood. Indeed, as we shall see, the narratives of self-fashioning that make up this book are American in their broadest outlines and their minutest details. But it is, of course, crucial too to recall that they are the writings of black men and women. In this brief introduction, I should like to point to some of the major features of these four texts—some they share, some in which they differ—and to the cultural and literary contexts, both American, in general, and African-American in particular, that helped to form them.

> It is not too much to say that the popular literature of the Christian world, since the discovery of America, or, at least for the last two hundred years, has been anti-Negro.[1]

So wrote the West Indian black nationalist, Edward W. Blyden, in *Fraser's Magazine* in 1875; and we know all too well that a substantial part of the "anti-Negro" argument was that "Negro" men and women could not master those "sublimer" realms of literate culture and the arts that constituted the highest aspirations of a middle-class Christian culture. The "evidence" proffered for this proposition until the middle of the nineteenth century consisted in large part of the absence of any substantial body of writing by Africans and African-Americans: the few writings by black people of which most Euro-American thinkers were aware they dismissed as derivative or derisory.

Yet if we ask why so little published writing by African-Americans remains to us from before the middle of the nineteenth century, it cannot be out of place to remark that the great majority of black people in the New World until the Emancipation Proclamation were legally prohibited from learning to read and write. The literate slave who read defenses of slavery that assumed the incapacity of the Negro was thus in a double bind. He or she knew that writing—and particularly writing well—was the only effective way to refute this argument; but he or she also knew that writing was forbidden, often on pain—a pain the slave knew well—of the lash. The slaves-turned-writers—Douglass, Jacobs, even Washington—came to writing with the recognition that the very fact of their writing was an act of rebellion, made more substantial by its being published. It is worth noting that the title pages of the two works that were published before emancipation carry the emphatic stipulation "written by himself," "written by herself."

The major goal of these authors was to speak for black Americans, to America and, in particular, to white America. Because these narratives were addressed to an America that did not believe in the ability of the Negro, the authors thought of themselves, not only as witnesses to the condition of black people, but as exemplars—living, breathing, and, above all, writing refutations of the slanders of racism. Even though Johnson's *Autobiography* is a personal narrative that begins after slavery—"I was born," the narrator says, "in a little town of Georgia a few years after the close of the Civil War"—its primary goal was similar, perhaps even more ambitious because of the time in which he was writing. Johnson set out to show how African-Americans could now achieve new heights. He demonstrated—though not merely through the act of writing, but also through the character of his protagonist, who is a fine classical pianist and composer—the fact that black people were indeed capable of the highest achievement; while, at the same time, exposing, like his literary predecessors, the pain of the victims of racism.

Because the argument for racial oppression—whether it was slavery or segregation—depended crucially on the claim that black people could not contribute to high culture, every work by an African-American writer, writing *as* an African-American, was bound to be seen as an argument against that racial oppression. It was not just the achievements of a Douglass or a Jacobs or a Washington, but the fact that they wrote for themselves that mattered. This is why the question of authorship—whether these books were really written by the African-Americans who claimed to have written them—was so central to their reception at the time. That the events recounted in Douglass's *Narrative* and Washington's *Autobiography* are largely historical, those in Jacobs's account are lightly fictionalized to protect its author, and Johnson's is a work of fiction that does not correspond to the details of its author's life is, for these purposes, not the central issue.

To remark this common set of goals is by no means to deny what is distinctive in each of these narratives. Each protagonist is an exemplar in his or her own way; each offers a life with its own moral, and these various morals reflect the different times in which they were written and the different circumstances of their authors.

Because the intellectual incapacity of the Negro was supposed to show itself especially in the failures of African and African-American literary productivity, it was almost inevitable that the first African-American genre—the slave narrative—would be a form of autobiography. For autobiography aims above all to establish the existence of the author-protagonist as an autonomous agent, a person whose life is worthy of interest, whose experiences and choices matter to us as readers. The African-American writes him or herself into being, by claiming mastery of the privileged sphere of literary production.

Before the Civil War had ended what had come to be called the "peculiar institution," more than a hundred former slaves, men and women with a great variety of experiences and substantially differing literary talents, had written narratives recording their suffering as slaves. The slave narrative is a polemical genre; it makes no bones about it. Its aim is to persuade the reader of the evils of slavery: and unless we recall the real urgency of this objective—unless we remember, for example, that the Fugitive Slave Law was passed by Congress as late as 1850—we cannot fully appreciate the language that the finest of the narratives, the language of Douglass and Jacobs, brings to its polemical task. And nowhere is that language more masterfully handled than in the *Narrative* of Frederick Douglass.

Frederick Douglass was already an unusual person by the time he published the *Narrative of the Life of Frederick Douglass, An American Slave* in 1845. He went on, of course, to be one of the most famous Americans of his age. But by 1845, he had already escaped from slavery, taken a new name, and begun to lecture, with great success, to large (usually white) antislavery audiences all over the North. Born Frederick Augustus Washington Bailey in February 1818 at Holm Hill Farm in Talbot County, Maryland, Douglass was the child of a slave mother whom he was barely allowed to know and a white father, whose identity he merely suspected. Raised, until the age of eight, by his grandmother on a plantation, he was transferred to the family of Mr. and Mrs. Thomas Auld in the city of Baltimore, where Mrs. Auld began, against the laws of the state, to teach him to read. Though Thomas Auld forbade her to continue—because, he said, it would make Douglass unfit for slavery—Douglass carried on by himself, gleaning what he could from white playmates in the streets of Baltimore, and watching "ship carpenters, after hewing, and getting a piece of timber ready for use, write on the timber the name of that part of the ship for which it was intended."

At the age of sixteen, when his first master died, Douglass was returned to work as a field hand on a plantation, where he was sent to a "slave-breaker," because he was already displaying—in part as a result of the greater freedom he had experienced as an urban slave—the independence of spirit that was to lead him, finally, to escape from slavery. In one of the most powerful passages of his *Narrative,* Douglass describes how he finally resisted the beatings of Edward Covey, the slave-breaker: "You have seen how a man was made a slave," he writes; "you shall see how a slave was made a man."

When, after this episode, Douglass was returned to Baltimore, he was allowed to apprentice himself to a caulker in the shipyards, paying all of his wages to his master; but he also learned to write, apparently by copying the letters written by carpenters on timbers in the Baltimore shipyards.

> When a piece of timber was intended for the larboard side, it would be marked thus—"L." When a piece was for the starboard side, it would be marked thus—"S." . . . I soon learned the names of these letters. . . . I immediately commenced copying them.

Finally, on September 3, 1838, Douglass escaped, using forged papers written for him by Anna Murray,[2] a free black woman, who became, almost at once, his first wife. Douglass settled in New Bedford, Massachusetts, where he was hospitably received by Mr. Nathan Johnson who chose for him his new name of Douglass. Racial prejudice prevented Douglass from plying his trade as a caulker, and he made a living as a laborer. Three years later, much influenced by William Lloyd Garrison's antislavery weekly, *The Liberator,* Douglass attended a meeting of the Massachusetts Antislavery Society where he was asked to speak of his life as a slave.

We know that Douglass's account made a substantial impression, for the society took him on as a lecturer, paying him to travel the country speaking against slavery out of his experiences as a slave. The *Narrative* was, in essence, part of this antislavery work, but its publication allowed for the possibility that he would be recaptured and returned to his master. As a result, Douglass traveled to Britain to lecture against slavery, and there, too, he was extremely well received. While in England, British antislavery activists purchased Douglass from Auld: from then on, he was a free man, speaking and writing for his enslaved brothers and sisters.

Douglass went on to work as a lecturer, journalist, and editor, campaigning for the rights of blacks and women, publishing the *North Star* (which became *Frederick Douglass's Paper*) in Rochester, New York from 1847 to 1860. During the Civil War, he worked as an advisor to President Lincoln, campaigning to recruit free blacks and former slaves to the Union Army: his own two sons signed up for black regiments in Massachusetts. Throughout reconstruction, Douglass campaigned for the extension of full civil rights to the freedmen, and he served Republican administrations as assistant secretary to the Santo Domingo Commission, in 1871; as marshal and, later, recorder of deeds to the District of Columbia, from 1877 to 1886; and finally as U.S. minister and consul general to Haiti, from 1889 to 1891. Douglass died in Washington in 1895.

Though Douglass revised and extended his life story twice more in his life, publishing *My Bondage and My Freedom* in 1855 and the *Life and Times of Frederick Douglass* in 1882, it is the *Narrative* that occupies a special place in American and African-American letters. This is true in large part because of the power it derives from its extraordinary compression. In less than a hundred pages of vigorously eloquent English, Douglass both establishes the horrors of slavery and lays claim to his own life. The slave who was forbidden to write, claims writing as his occupation regardless of his master and the law. Even the more extravagant passages, whose grandiloquence will strike some contemporary tastes as excessive—the apostrophe to the "beautiful vessels, robed in purest white" on the Chesapeake stands out here—have a rigor that demands respect. The opposition between the sailing ships, "loosed from [their] moorings, . . . free . . . freedom's swift-winged angels" and Douglass "fast in chains, . . . a slave . . . confined in bands of iron" is more than a casual metaphor; it prepares the way for Douglass's escape through the shipyard to literacy and freedom.

And sometimes, as here in a passage that places the suffering of his grandmother in the wider context of the anguish of slave motherhood, Douglass writes sentences that could hardly be improved:

> The hearth is desolate. The unconscious children, who once sang and danced in her presence, are gone. She gropes her way in the darkness of age, for a drink of water. Instead of the voices of her children, she hears by day the moans of the dove, and by night the screams of the hideous owl. All is gloom.

If, in the end, there is one rhetorical feature above all that gives the *Narrative* its power, it is, surely, that it does not need to speak out against slavery: in recounting, in his own written words, the life of this singular slave, it made a case against slavery more powerful than a thousand appeals to abstract principle. As a correspondent to the *National Anti-Slavery Standard* wrote (in discussing Harriet Jacobs's *Incidents* in 1861): "They are the strongest witnesses who leave the summings up to the judge, and the verdict to the jury."[3]

Where Douglass's *Narrative* had begun "I was born in Tuckahoe, near Hillsborough . . ." Harriet Jacobs starts *Incidents in the Life of a Slave Girl* (published sixteen years later in 1861) with a direct address to the reader: "Reader, be assured this narrative is no fiction." And this more personal mode, with its appeal to an acknowledged reader, reflects the fact that Harriet Jacobs's experiences are those of an African-American woman. For Jacobs's writing draws not only on the traditions of the slave narrative genre but also on the—then still largely white—traditions of the sentimental novel, which is, of course, the exemplary genre of nineteenth century women's writing. And it is in this tradition that the book's opening is rooted. Jacobs writes at the end of her narrative (once more addressing the imagined reader):

> Reader, my story ends with freedom; not in the usual way, with marriage.

But whereas this is, indeed, "the usual way" of the slave narrative (which must end with freedom), it *is* the usual ending of the sentimental novel. And it is to the mores of the sentimental novel and its readers that Jacobs addresses the passages in which she excuses herself for what she euphemistically refers to as her "headlong plunge" into unwed motherhood.

> O virtuous reader! You never knew what it is to be a slave; to be entirely unprotected by law or custom; to have the laws reduce you to the condition of a chattel, entirely subject to the will of another. . . . I know I did wrong. . . . Still in looking back, calmly, on the events of my life, I feel that the slave woman ought not to be judged by the same standards as others.

What is clear in this passage, as in many others, is that *Incidents* is addressed to an audience of free, white women; and its language places the author, oddly, on the same side of the moral divide as these imagined readers, even as it describes an experience so radically different from theirs. In particular, whenever "Linda Brent" (as Jacobs called herself in the narrative) converses with a black person, her own voice remains that of a middle-class white speaker, while her interlocutor is trapped in the conventions of transcribing "Negro dialect." The result is sometimes, unintentionally, comical. Here is an exchange between Linda and Betty, the black woman servant of the white woman who first conceals Linda.

Linda has just told her that another of the servants had been trying to get into the room where she has been concealed.

> "Tut! tut! chile!" exclaimed Betty, "she ain't seen notin', nor hearn notin'. She only 'spects something. Dat's all. She wants to fine out who hab cut and make my gownd. But she won't nebber know. Dat's sartin. I'll get missis to fix her."
>
> I reflected a moment, and said, "Betty, I must leave here tonight."
>
> "Do as you tink best, poor chile," she replied. "I'se mighty 'fraid dat 'ere nigger vill pop on you some time."

If there is a black and a white voice in this exchange, the white voice is surely Linda's: and, bracketed by the energetic play of Betty's language, Linda sounds stilted, even prissy. What is explicitly true in Jacobs's narrative is implicitly true of Douglass's. The slave narrative is addressed to those who had it in their power to act against slavery: and they, of course, were white.

If *Incidents* does not always fully reconcile the conventions of slave narrative and sentimental novel, it surely reflects the tensions of trying to argue against slavery and the oppression of women at the same time. Indeed, the scholar Valerie Smith has suggested that we see the tensions in the narrative as exposing the inadequacies of each genre: of the (masculine) slave narrative as a medium for discussing women's rights, and of the (white) sentimental novel as a framework for addressing the specific condition of the black woman.[4] As Smith says: "Her story is not what is yielded up after one superimposes the story of (white) woman's experience over that of black (male) experience. Rather, her unique cultural experience requires her to question the assumptions of literary conventions."[5] If there is another central contrast between Jacobs's narrative and Douglass's, it is that for Douglass to be free is "to be a man." It is through an act of physical resistance—the fight with Covey—that Douglass begins his psychic escape from bondage. For Jacobs, on the other hand, freedom is, above all, freedom from sexual harassment, freedom to be a mother. While Douglass is preoccupied with his own liberation, which will enable him to struggle for the liberation of all slaves, Jacobs's concern is with her children. When she seeks to indict slavery, she often does it through expressions of concern for her young ones: "I would ten thousand times rather that my children should be the half-starved paupers of Ireland than to be the most pampered among the slaves of America."

Who, then, was the author of *Incidents*, the woman who called herself "Linda Brent," the slave mother who struggled mightily so that her children could be free?

Harriet Jacobs, abolitionist, activist, and feminist, was born a slave in Edenton, North Carolina. Like most slaves, she had no precise record of her birth, but she was probably born in 1813.[6] Orphaned as a child, she was willed by her first mistress (who died when Jacobs was eleven) to Matilda Norcom, the three-year-old daughter of a neighboring doctor's family. Dr. Norcom subjected her to persistent sexual harassment almost from the first, but she consistently resisted him. In her teens she had two children—a girl, Louisa Matilda, and a boy, Joseph—by a local white lawyer, and the protection of these children became her major preoccupation for much of the next two decades, eventually leading her to escape from slavery. In 1835, Jacobs was transferred from the house in Edenton to work at Auburn, one of Norcom's plantations, because she continued to refuse his proposal that he set her up as his "mistress." There she heard that he planned to move her children away from the house of her grandmother—a free woman, who plays an important role in *Incidents*—and decided that she must escape in order that they should not be subjected to plantation slavery.

In what is surely the most extraordinary episode in an extraordinary life, Jacobs then faked an escape to the North, disappearing, in fact, into an attic at her grandmother's house. There she remained for nearly seven years, able to watch her children grow. She arranged that the children should both be bought by their father, and that Louisa Matilda should be taken to Brooklyn where she could be educated; and she even wrote letters to be sent from New York and Boston in order to mislead Norcom as to her whereabouts. Finally, in 1842, she escaped to the North. She found her daughter in Brooklyn, arranged for her son to move to Boston with her brother, and worked as a nursemaid for a Mr. and Mrs. Willis.

During the next decade, Norcom came regularly to New York, seeking to recapture Jacobs, who was eventually forced to flee to Boston with Louisa Matilda, in October 1844. When Mrs. Willis died, her husband persuaded Jacobs to travel as his daughter's nurse to England. On her return—which brought the unhappy news that her son had been the victim of racial attacks in his apprenticeship as a printer and had shipped off to sea—she placed her daughter in a private school and moved to Rochester, where she worked in the antislavery reading room, and in the bookstore above the offices of Frederick Douglass's paper the *North Star*. It was during this period that she met and went to live with the Quaker abolitionists Amy and Isaac Post. Amy Post, abolitionist, feminist activist, and author, was to be her friend—and correspondent—for many years. It was also Post who first urged her to write her own story in order to strengthen the abolitionist cause.

In 1850, with the passage of the Fugitive Slave Law, Jacobs's freedom was again put at risk; and Matilda Norcom, now a married adult, threatened to seize Louisa Matilda if Jacobs did not return to slavery, on the (spurious) grounds that the sale of Louisa Matilda to her father had been illegal. In order to regularize her position and make sure that her children were secure, Mr. Willis and his second wife finally bought Harriet Jacobs in 1852—for three hundred dollars—and freed her. While continuing to work for the Willis's, she began, under Amy Post's promptings in their voluminous correspondence, to write the story of her life. Beginning with shorter pieces written for newspapers, she eventually composed the whole of *Incidents*.

Getting it published was something of a struggle. After trying a number of publishers, she found one that would publish the work . . . but only if it had an introduction by the well-known abolitionist author, Lydia Maria Child. So Jacobs made contact with Child, who agreed to a collaboration. Finally, towards the end of 1860, the Boston firm of Thayer and Eldridge agreed to a contract. But this firm went bankrupt a few months later. Somehow Jacobs managed to acquire the plates and to arrange for a printer to produce the volume for her. When *Incidents* first appeared, Harriet Jacobs had, in effect, published it herself.

The slave narratives are the first truly African-American genre.[7] (It can be argued that they are the first truly distinctively American genre.) The sophistication with which Douglass's *Narrative* handled the telling of the central episodes of an exemplary life make it a natural model for later African-American autobiography. As we have seen, the idea that the struggle for literacy lies at the heart of the struggle for freedom is an organizing principle of Douglass's book. There is no doubt that, in part because of Douglass, this theme is central to later African-American writing. And nowhere do we see this theme more strikingly developed than in the autobiography of Booker T. Washington, the greatest black educator of the nineteenth century.

Booker Taliaferro Washington, the author of *Up from Slavery* was born on April 5, 1856, in Franklin County, Virginia. Like Douglass, he was the son of a black slave woman and an unknown white man. After emancipation, his family moved to West Virginia, to the mining town of Malden, where he worked in various manual jobs, including a period in the coal mines. The hard-won schooling that Washington was able to get in Malden was rudimentary, but it inspired in him a deep longing for education that lead him to the Hampton Institute in Virginia at the age of sixteen, where he worked his way through school as a janitor. On graduation, Washington returned as a teacher to Malden, and, after a few months at a seminary in Washington, D.C., he returned to join the staff of Hampton as a teacher.

When, in 1881, the state of Alabama authorized the creation of a black school at Tuskegee (while neglecting to provide any financing for it), Hampton Institute principal, General Samuel C. Armstrong, whom Washington had impressed mightily, recommended that they ask his young colleague to head it. Working with the local community, both black and white, Washington built Tuskegee into the preeminent black-run college in the nation.

Washington's success at Tuskegee depended as much on his careful cultivation of his white neighbors as on the manifold successes of his black students. By insisting on training his students to work with their hands—Tuskegee was largely built by its earliest students—he managed not to threaten the world of white Alabamians. Washington's work did not challenge the established racial economy of an increasingly segregated South. His graduates were well-trained brickmakers and farmers and domestic servants; and they were also literate and numerate.

Building on the reputation he acquired as the founder of Tuskegee, and especially on his good relations with powerful white Alabamians, Washington gradually became the most powerful black man in America, the confidant of Andrew Carnegie and John D. Rockefeller, and advisor to Presidents Theodore Roosevelt and Taft. W.E.B. Du Bois wrote at the start of the third essay of *The Souls of Black Folk*: "Easily the most striking thing in the history of the Negro since 1876 is the ascendancy of Mr. Booker T. Washington."

Washington's story, as he tells it in *Up from Slavery*, is very much the story of the American self-made man. While Washington constantly records his dependence on a few others—and above all on General Samuel C. Armstrong—what one is most aware of is his own consistent struggle to achieve. Washington's struggle was, as we see again and again in his narrative, entirely *within* the segregated spaces that were codified in 1896 by the Supreme Court's decision, in *Plessy v. Ferguson*, to uphold the notion that segregation could create two communities "separate but equal." And he is constantly reminding his readers that the two communities can live and work side by side while remaining, as he said in the Atlanta Exposition Address of 1895, "[i]n all things purely social . . . as separate as the fingers, yet one hand in all things essential to mutual progress."

Contemporary readers may find Booker T. Washington's racial deference embarrassing. We may be less than enthusiastic about Washington's claim that many former slaves cared for their old masters, since he makes it in terms that oblige him to add:

> From some things that I have said one may get the idea that some of the slaves did not want freedom. This is not true.

But we can surely share his sense of pride in the extraordinary work he did in creating Tuskegee—as a black institution, dedicated to excellence—in the heart of the South as the promise of emancipation faded.

Indeed, if we reflect how much Washington achieved in the way of the building of black institutions in those unpromising times between the end of Reconstruction and the First World War, we may come to share the critic Houston A. Baker's conclusion that, in playing the "Uncle Tom" in carefully stage-managed displays of ritual racial deference, Washington was manipulating the white power structure to achieve black empowerment. A more than superficial reading of *Up from Slavery* will reveal key moments at which Washington allows his resistance to show through.

We see a brief—and exemplary—flash of this resistance when Washington, in discussing "the exact condition, mental and moral, of the coloured ministers in the South," observes that "[t]he picture painted was a rather black one—or, since I am black, shall I say 'white'?" At a moment when we least expect it, when Washington is acknowledging the deficiencies of black ministers of religion, his wit sharply reminds his white readers of the deal he is making with them: separate, yes, but equal; and equality means that he may use "white" as a term of derogation in symmetry with white uses of "black." Whenever Booker T. is caught "bowing and scraping" to "white folks," we should remember that he is also the man who wrote these words:

> From any point of view, I had rather be what I am, a member of the Negro race, than be able to claim membership with the most favored of any other race.

When Washington died in 1915, he had been the preeminent African-American for well more than a generation; and his connections, the empowerment that he bought at what some have thought too high a price, had allowed him to exercise substantial patronage. Among those he had helped along—by getting him employment in the United States consular service in Latin America—was the author of the last of our African-American classics of self-creation, James Weldon Johnson.

Johnson was born in Jacksonville, Florida, in 1871. His father was a headwaiter at a luxury hotel, and his mother a teacher at the Stanton School. Because his parents were relatively affluent, they were able to send him to college at Atlanta University, a black college, where he excelled. He studied music, touring New England with the Atlanta University Quartet during the summer vacation; did well in his studies and his sports; and delivered the commencement oration in 1894. After college he returned home to teach at the school where his mother had taught, while founding a newspaper, *The Daily American,* and studying for the Florida bar. In 1898 he became the first black person to be admitted to the bar in Duval County, Florida.

He went into partnership with Judson Wetmore, a college friend from his Atlanta days, who had gone to law school at the University of Michigan while "passing for white." Unsurprisingly, many have seen in Wetmore's experiences the germ of the idea for *The Autobiography of an Ex-Colored Man,* which records the life of a light-skinned African-American, who decides toward the end of the book to disappear into the white world, becoming "an ordinarily successful white man who has made a little money."

In the early years of the century, Johnson moved to New York City, where he had a second successful career as a songwriter, collaborating with his brother John in writing such classic popular songs as "Under the Bamboo Tree," and composing what is considered to be the black national anthem "Lift Every Voice and Sing," which remains, of course, as one of the classics of the African-American hymnology.

In the following years, he served under Roosevelt and Taft as a consul, first in Venezuela, from 1906 to 1909, then in Nicaragua, for the next three years. When he returned to the United States, Johnson became editor of *The New York Age,* the country's premier black newspaper in 1914. Two years later he became field secretary for the NAACP, recruiting members and starting branches around the nation; and in 1920 he started a decade of service as executive secretary of the organization. In 1930 he accepted a chair of creative literature at Fisk University, where he worked until he was killed in a tragic car accident in June 1938.

During all these years of public service, Johnson wrote a corpus of poetry and fiction that was one of the central monuments—and most profound influences—of the Harlem Renaissance: not only did he publish the *Autobiography,* written while he was in Nicaragua, in 1912; he also published scores of popular songs; *Fifty Years and Other Poems,* in 1917; *The Book of American Negro Poetry,* in 1922; *The Book of American Negro Spirituals,* in 1925; *Black Manhattan,* in 1930; and many profoundly influential essays, including, in 1920, a series of four pieces in *The Nation* exposing abuses in the American occupation of Haiti.

The preoccupations of Johnson's varied life are reflected throughout the *Autobiography:* in his concern for black folk-culture, which he describes; his love of music; and his deep political concern—epitomized in the discussions of the "Negro question" and the extraordinarily powerful description of a lynching that is the fulcrum of the plot. Johnson's protagonist, an African-American light-skinned enough to "pass" for white, responds to the Southern lynching by a flight northwards into whiteness. Nothing could more clearly embody Du Bois's recognition that the Negro in America is "two souls" than Johnson's extraordinary account of the life of a man who is able to live as an African-American among white people who do not recognize him as such.

Johnson's writing is often extremely vivid: the evocation of young love in the second chapter is sharply observed and masterfully written. And even though much of what he writes is explicitly addressed to racial politics, this work of fiction, unlike the more strictly biographical works of Douglass, Jacobs, and Washington, is able to explore questions of landscape—as at the beginning of chapter 4—that are, in an obvious sense, more purely literary, less tied to the central polemical intention of the work. If Johnson's work is so central to the work of black writers from the Harlem Renaissance on, it is in part because it begins the escape from the more strictly political motivations of the slave narrative and Washington's parable of elevation.

As Houston A. Baker, Jr. has observed, "the authentic geography of the American imagination can only be mapped by first surveying slave territory."[8] The slave narratives explore in the starkest circumstances the self-creation that is the central theme of American writing in the nineteenth century. Douglass's *Narrative* is surely the sublimest of the slave narratives. In Jacobs's rewriting of the genre into the structure of the sentimental novel, we find one of the earliest and strongest of the African-American women's voices that have come to be so central to our current literary culture. Washington seems to offer a dark-skinned rewriting of the nineteenth-century success story—but with an eye toward collective empowerment. And Johnson begins to write the story of African-American culture in the contemporary world. From slavery to freedom, from Douglass to Johnson, these African-American classics record the claim of African-American culture on America, the strivings in "*The Souls of Black Folk*"; which is why I have prefaced these narratives of soul-making with the first essay from Du Bois's great American classic.

NOTES

1. E.W. Blyden, *Christianity, Islam and the Negro Race* (1887), reprinted (Edinburgh: Edinburgh University Press, 1967), p. 17; from an essay in *Fraser's Magazine* in 1875.

2. You will notice that Douglass keeps this fact concealed in the 1845 narrative: he was still a fugitive and his wife's pass-writing had, of course, been illegal.

3. This letter is cited on page 25 of Jean Fagan Yellin's introduction to her scholarly edition of *Incidents in the Life of a Slave Girl* (Cambridge, MA: Harvard University Press, 1987).

4. See her introduction to the Schomburg Library edition of Linda Brent's *Incidents* (New York: Oxford University Press, 1988), p. 133.

5. Yellin, *op. cit.* pp. 37–38.

6. For a more detailed account, see Yellin's introduction to her edition of *Incidents (op. cit.)*.

7. This is not to deny its antecedents in slave narratives published in Britain in the eighteenth century. But by the Civil War, the slave narrative was the preeminent form of African-American writing.

8. Houston A. Baker, Jr., "Introduction" to the Penguin edition of Douglass's *Narrative* (New York, 1982), p. 13. And see his *The Journey Back* (Chicago: Chicago University Press, 1980).

PROLOGUE:

A Selection from *The Souls of Black Folk*

W.E.B. DU BOIS

1903

OF OUR SPIRITUAL STRIVINGS

O water, voice of my heart, crying in the sand,
All night long crying with a mournful cry,
As I lie and listen, and cannot understand
The voice of my heart in my side or the voice of the sea,
O water, crying for rest, is it I, is it I?
All night long the water is crying to me.

Unresting water, there shall never be rest
Till the last moon droop and the last tide fail,
And the fire of the end begin to burn in the west;
And the heart shall be weary and wonder and cry like the sea,
All life long crying without avail,
As the water all night long is crying to me.

ARTHUR SYMONS.

Between me and the other world there is ever an unasked question: unasked by some through feelings of delicacy;

by others through the difficulty of rightly framing it. All, nevertheless, flutter round it. They approach me in a half-hesitant sort of way, eye me curiously or compassionately, and then, instead of saying directly, How does it feel to be a problem? they say, I know an excellent colored man in my town; or, I fought at Mechanicsville; or, Do not these Southern outrages make your blood boil? At these I smile, or am interested, or reduce the boiling to a simmer, as the occasion may require. To the real question, How does it feel to be a problem? I answer seldom a word.

And yet, being a problem is a strange experience,—peculiar even for one who has never been anything else, save perhaps in babyhood and in Europe. It is in the early days of rollicking boyhood that the revelation first bursts upon one, all in a day, as it were. I remember well when the shadow swept across me. I was a little thing, away up in the hills of New England, where the dark Housatonic winds between Hoosac and Taghkanic to the sea. In a wee wooden schoolhouse, something put it into the boys' and girls' heads to buy gorgeous visiting-cards—ten cents a package—and exchange. The exchange was merry, till one girl, a tall newcomer, refused my card,—refused it peremptorily, with a glance. Then it dawned upon me with a certain suddenness that I was different from the others; or like, mayhap, in heart and life and longing, but shut out from their world by a vast veil. I had thereafter no desire to tear down that veil, to creep through; I held all beyond it in common contempt, and lived above it in a region of blue sky and great wandering shadows. That sky was bluest when I could beat my mates at examination-time, or beat them at a foot-race, or even beat their stringy heads. Alas, with the years all this fine contempt began to fade; for the words I longed for, and all their dazzling opportunities, were theirs, not mine. But they should not keep these prizes, I said; some, all, I would wrest from them. Just how I would do it I could never decide: by reading law, by healing the sick, by telling the wonderful tales that swam in my head,—some way. With other black boys the strife was not so fiercely sunny: their youth shrunk into tasteless sycophancy, or into silent hatred of the pale world about them and mocking distrust of everything white; or wasted itself in a bitter cry, Why did God make me an outcast and a stranger in mine own house? The shades of the prison-house closed round about us all: walls strait and stubborn to the whitest, but relentlessly narrow, tall, and unscalable to sons of night who must plod darkly on in resignation, or beat unavailing palms against the stone, or steadily, half hopelessly, watch the streak of blue above.

After the Egyptian and Indian, the Greek and Roman, the Teuton and Mongolian, the Negro is a sort of seventh son, born with a veil, and gifted with second-sight in this American world,—a world which yields him no true self-consciousness, but only lets him see himself through the revelation of the other world. It is a peculiar sensation, this double-consciousness, this sense of always looking at one's self through the eyes of others, of measuring one's soul by the tape of a world that looks on in amused contempt and pity. One ever feels his twoness,—an American, a Negro; two souls, two thoughts, two unreconciled strivings; two warring ideals in one dark body, whose dogged strength alone keeps it from being torn asunder.

The history of the American Negro is the history of this strife,—this longing to attain self-conscious manhood, to merge his double self into a better and truer self. In this merging he wishes neither of the older selves to be lost. He would not Africanize America, for America has too much to teach the world and Africa. He would not bleach his Negro soul in a flood of white Americanism, for he knows that Negro blood has a message for the world. He simply wishes to make it possible for a man to be both a Negro and an American, without being cursed and spit upon by his fellows, without having the doors of Opportunity closed roughly in his face.

This, then, is the end of his striving: to be a co-worker in the kingdom of culture, to escape both death and isolation, to husband and use his best powers and his latent genius. These powers of body and mind have in the past been strangely wasted, dispersed, or forgotten. The shadow of a mighty Negro past flits through the tale of Ethiopia the Shadowy and of Egypt the Sphinx. Through history, the powers of single black men flash here and there like falling stars, and die sometimes before the world has rightly gauged their brightness. Here in America, in the few days since Emancipation, the black man's turning hither and thither in hesitant and doubtful striving has often made his very strength to lose effectiveness, to seem like absence of power, like weakness. And yet it is not weakness,—it is the contradiction of double aims. The double-aimed struggle of the black artisan—on the one hand to escape white contempt for a nation of mere hewers of wood and drawers of water, and on the other hand to plough and nail and dig for a poverty-stricken horde—could only result in making him a poor craftsman, for he had but half a heart in either cause. By the poverty and ignorance of his people, the Negro minister or doctor was tempted toward quackery and demagogy; and by the criticism of the other world, toward ideals that made him ashamed of his lowly tasks. The would-be black *savant* was confronted by the paradox that the knowledge his people needed was a twice-told tale to his white neighbors, while the knowledge which would teach the white world was Greek to his own flesh and blood. The innate love of harmony and beauty that set the ruder souls of his people a-dancing and a-singing raised but confusion and doubt in the soul of the black artist; for the beauty revealed to him was the soul-beauty of a race which his larger audience despised, and he could not articulate the message of another people. This waste of double aims, this seeking to satisfy two unreconciled ideals, has wrought sad havoc with the courage and faith and deeds of ten thousand thousand people,—has sent them often wooing false gods and invoking false means of salvation, and at times has even seemed about to make them ashamed of themselves.

Away back in the days of bondage they thought to see in one divine event the end of all doubt and disappointment; few men ever worshipped Freedom with half such unquestioning faith as did the American Negro for two centuries. To him, so far as he thought and dreamed, slavery was indeed the sum of all villainies, the cause of all sorrow, the root of all prejudice; Emancipation was the key to a promised land of sweeter beauty than ever stretched before the eyes of wearied Israelites. In song and exhortation swelled one refrain—Liberty; in his tears and curses the God he implored had Freedom in his right hand. At last it came,—suddenly, fearfully, like a dream.

With one wild carnival of blood and passion came the message in his own plaintive cadences:—

> "Shout, O children!
> Shout, you're free!
> For God has bought your liberty!"

Years have passed away since then,—ten, twenty, forty; forty years of national life, forty years of renewal and development, and yet the swarthy spectre sits in its accustomed seat at the Nation's feast. In vain do we cry to this our vastest social problem:—

> "Take any shape but that, and my firm nerves
> Shall never tremble!"

The Nation has not yet found peace from its sins; the freedman has not yet found in freedom his promised land. Whatever of good may have come in these years of change, the shadow of a deep disappointment rests upon the Negro people,—a disappointment all the more bitter because the unattained ideal was unbounded save by the simple ignorance of a lowly people.

The first decade was merely a prolongation of the vain search for freedom, the boon that seemed ever barely to elude their grasp,—like a tantalizing will-o'-the-wisp, maddening and misleading the headless host. The holocaust of war, the terrors of the Ku-Klux Klan, the lies of carpet-baggers, the disorganization of industry, and the contradictory advice of friends and foes, left the bewildered serf with no new watchword beyond the old cry for freedom. As the time flew, however, he began to grasp a new idea. The ideal of liberty demanded for its attainment powerful means, and these the Fifteenth Amendment gave him. The ballot, which before he had looked upon as a visible sign of freedom, he now regarded as the chief means of gaining and perfecting the liberty with which war had partially endowed him. And why not? Had not votes made war and emancipated millions? Had not votes enfranchised the freedmen? Was anything impossible to a power that had done all this? A million black men started with renewed zeal to vote themselves into the kingdom. So the decade flew away, the revolution of 1876 came, and left the half-free serf weary, wondering, but still inspired. Slowly but steadily, in the following years, a new vision began gradually to replace the dream of political power,—a powerful movement, the rise of another ideal to guide the unguided, another pillar of fire by night after a clouded day. It was the ideal of "book-learning"; the curiosity, born of compulsory ignorance, to know and test the power of the cabalistic letters of the white man, the longing to know. Here at last seemed to have been discovered the mountain path to Canaan; longer than the highway of Emancipation and law, steep and rugged, but straight, leading to heights high enough to overlook life.

Up the new path the advance guard toiled, slowly, heavily, doggedly; only those who have watched and guided the faltering feet, the misty minds, the dull understandings, of the dark pupils of these schools know how faithfully, how piteously, this people strove to learn. It was weary work. The cold statistician wrote down the inches of progress here and there, noted also where here and there a foot had slipped or some one had fallen. To the tired climbers, the horizon was ever dark, the mists were often cold, the Canaan was always dim and far away. If, however, the vistas disclosed as yet no goal, no resting-place, little but flattery and criticism, the journey at least gave leisure for reflection and self-examination; it changed the child of Emancipation to the youth with dawning self-consciousness, self-realization, self-respect. In those sombre forests of his striving his own soul rose before him, and he saw himself,—darkly as through a veil; and yet he saw in himself some faint revelation of his power, of his mission. He began to have a dim feeling that, to attain his place in the world, he must be himself, and not another. For the first time he sought to analyze the burden he bore upon his back, that dead-weight of social degradation partially masked behind a half-named Negro problem. He felt his poverty; without a cent, without a home, without land, tools, or savings, he had entered into competition with rich, landed, skilled neighbors. To be a poor man is hard, but to be a poor race in a land of dollars is the very bottom of hardships. He felt the weight of his ignorance,—not simply of letters, but of life, of business, of the humanities; the accumulated sloth and shirking and awkwardness of decades and centuries shackled his hands and feet. Nor was his burden all poverty and ignorance. The red stain of bastardy, which two centuries of systematic legal defilement of Negro women had stamped upon his race, meant not only the loss of ancient African chastity, but also the hereditary weight of a mass of corruption from white adulterers, threatening almost the obliteration of the Negro home.

A people thus handicapped ought not to be asked to race with the world, but rather allowed to give all its time and thought to its own social problems. But alas! while sociologists gleefully count his bastards and his prostitutes, the very soul of the toiling, sweating black man is darkened by the shadow of a vast despair. Men call the shadow prejudice, and learnedly explain it as the natural defence of culture against barbarism, learning against ignorance, purity against crime, the "higher" against the "lower" races. To which the Negro cries Amen! and swears that to so much of this strange prejudice as is founded on just homage to civilization, culture, righteousness, and progress, he humbly bows and meekly does obeisance. But before that nameless prejudice that leaps beyond all this he stands helpless, dismayed, and well-nigh speechless; before that personal disrespect and mockery, the ridicule and systematic humiliation, the distortion of fact and wanton license of fancy, the cynical ignoring of the better and the boisterous welcoming of the worse, the all-pervading desire to inculcate disdain for everything black, from Toussaint to the devil,—before this there rises a sickening despair that would disarm and discourage any nation save that black host to whom "discouragement" is an unwritten word.

But the facing of so vast a prejudice could not but bring the inevitable self-questioning, self-disparagement, and lowering of ideals which ever accompany repression and breed in an atmosphere of contempt and hate. Whisperings and portents came borne upon the four winds: Lo! we are diseased and dying, cried the dark hosts; we cannot write, our voting is vain; what need of education, since we must always cook and serve? And the Nation echoed and enforced this self-criticism, saying: Be content to be servants, and nothing more; what need of higher culture for half-men? Away with the black man's ballot, by force or fraud,—and behold the suicide of a race! Nevertheless, out of the evil came something of good,—the more careful adjustment of education to real life, the clearer perception of the Negroes' social responsibilities, and the sobering realization of the meaning of progress.

So dawned the time of *Sturm und Drang:* storm and stress to-day rocks our little boat on the mad waters of the worldsea; there is within and without the sound of conflict, the burning of body and rending of soul; inspiration strives with doubt, and faith with vain questionings. The bright ideals of the past,—physical freedom, political power, the training of brains and the training of hands,—all these in turn have waxed and waned, until even the last grows dim and overcast. Are they all wrong,—all false? No, not that, but each alone was oversimple and incomplete,—the dreams of a credulous race-childhood, or the fond imaginings of the other world which does not know and does not want to know our power. To be really true, all these ideals must be melted and welded into one. The training of the schools we need to-day more than ever,—the training of deft hands, quick eyes and ears, and above all the broader, deeper, higher culture of gifted minds and pure hearts. The power of the ballot we need in sheer self-defence,—else what shall save us from a second slavery? Freedom, too, the long-sought, we still seek,—the freedom of life and limb, the freedom to work and think, the freedom to love and aspire. Work, culture, liberty,—all these we need, not singly but together, not successively but together, each growing and aiding each, and all striving toward that vaster ideal that swims before the Negro people, the ideal of human brotherhood, gained through the unifying ideal of Race; the ideal of fostering and developing the traits and talents of the Negro, not in opposition to or contempt for other races, but rather in large conformity to the greater ideals of the American Republic, in order that some day on American soil two world-races may give each to each those characteristics both so sadly lack. We the darker ones come even now not altogether empty-handed: there are to-day no truer exponents of the pure human spirit of the Declaration of Independence than the American Negroes; there is no true American music but the wild sweet melodies of the Negro slave; the American fairy tales and folklore are Indian and African; and, all in all, we black men seem the sole oasis of simple faith and reverence in a dusty desert of dollars and smartness. Will America be poorer if she replace her brutal dyspeptic blundering with light-hearted but determined Negro humility? or her coarse and cruel wit with loving jovial good-humor? or her vulgar music with the soul of the Sorrow Songs?

Merely a concrete test of the underlying principles of the great republic is the Negro Problem, and the spiritual striving of the freedmen's sons is the travail of souls whose burden is almost beyond the measure of their strength, but who bear it in the name of an historic race, in the name of this the land of their fathers' fathers, and in the name of human opportunity.

And now what I have briefly sketched in large outline let me on coming pages tell again in many ways, with loving emphasis and deeper detail, that men may listen to the striving in the souls of black folk.

Narrative of the Life of Frederick Douglass, an American Slave

FREDERICK DOUGLASS

1845

CHAPTER I

I was born in Tuckahoe, near Hillsborough, and about twelve miles from Easton, in Talbot county, Maryland. I have no accurate knowledge of my age, never having seen any authentic record containing it. By far the larger part of the slaves know as little of their ages as horses know of theirs, and it is the wish of most masters within my knowledge to keep their slaves thus ignorant. I do not remember to have ever met a slave who could tell of his birthday. They seldom come nearer to it than planting-time, harvest-time, cherry-time, spring-time, or fall-time. A want of information concerning my own was a source of unhappiness to me even during childhood. The white children could tell their ages. I could not tell why I ought to be deprived of the same privilege. I was not allowed to make any inquiries of my master concerning it. He deemed all such inquiries on the part of a slave improper and impertinent, and evidence of a restless spirit. The nearest estimate I can give makes me now between twenty-seven and twenty-eight years of age. I come to this, from hearing my master say, some time during 1835, I was about seventeen years old.

My mother was named Harriet Bailey. She was the daughter of Isaac and Betsey Bailey, both colored, and quite dark. My mother was of a darker complexion than either my grandmother or grandfather.

My father was a white man. He was admitted to be such by all I ever heard speak of my parentage. The opinion was also whispered that my master was my father; but of the correctness of this opinion, I know nothing; the means of knowing was withheld from me. My mother and I were separated when I was but an infant—before I knew her as my mother. It is a common custom, in the part of Maryland from which I ran away, to part children from their mothers at a very early age. Frequently, before the child has reached its twelfth month, its mother is taken from it, and hired out on some farm a considerable distance off, and the child is placed under the care of an old woman, too old for field labor. For what this separation is done, I do not know, unless it be to hinder the development of the child's affection toward its mother, and to blunt and destroy the natural affection of the mother for the child. This is the inevitable result.

I never saw my mother, to know her as such, more than four or five times in my life; and each of those times was very short in duration, and at night. She was hired by a Mr. Stewart, who lived about twelve miles from my home. She made her journeys to see me in the night, travelling the whole distance on foot, after the performance of her day's work. She was a field hand, and a whipping is the penalty of not being in the field at sunrise, unless a slave has special permission from his or her master to the contrary—a permission which they seldom get, and one that gives to him that gives it the proud name of being a kind master. I do not recollect of ever seeing my mother by the light of day. She was with me in the night. She would lie down with me, and get me to sleep, but long before I waked she was gone. Very little communication ever took place between us. Death soon ended what little we could have while she lived, and with it her hardships and suffering. She died when I was about seven years old, on one of my master's farms, near Lee's Mill. I was not allowed to be present during her illness, at her death, or burial. She was gone long before I knew any thing about it. Never having enjoyed, to any considerable extent, her soothing presence, her tender and watchful care, I received the tidings of her death with much the same emotions I should have probably felt at the death of a stranger.

Called thus suddenly away, she left me without the slightest intimation of who my father was. The whisper that my master was my father, may or may not be true; and, true or false, it is of but little consequence to my purpose whilst the fact remains, in all its glaring odiousness, that slaveholders have ordained, and by law established, that the children of slave women shall in all cases follow the condition of their mothers; and this is done too obviously to administer to their own lusts, and make a gratification of their wicked desires profitable as well as pleasurable; for by this cunning arrangement, the slaveholder, in cases not a few, sustains to his slaves the double relation of master and father.

I know of such cases; and it is worthy of remark that such slaves invariably suffer greater hardships, and have more to contend with, than others. They are, in the first place, a constant offence to their mistress. She is ever disposed to find fault with them; they can seldom do any thing to please her; she is never better pleased than when she sees them under the lash, especially when she suspects her husband of showing to his mulatto children favors which he withholds from his black slaves. The master is frequently compelled to sell this class of his slaves, out of deference to the feelings of his white wife; and, cruel as the deed may strike any one to be, for a man to sell his own children to human flesh-mongers, it is often the dictate of humanity for him to do so; for, unless he does this, he must not only whip them himself, but must stand by and see one white son tie up his brother, of but few shades darker complexion than himself, and ply the gory lash to his naked back; and if he lisp one word of disapproval, it is set down to his parental partiality, and only makes a bad matter worse, both for himself and the slave whom he would protect and defend.

Every year brings with it multitudes of this class of slaves. It was doubtless in consequence of a knowledge of this fact, that one great statesman of the south predicted the downfall of slavery by the inevitable laws of population. Whether this prophecy is ever fulfilled or not, it is nevertheless plain that a very different-looking class of people are springing up at the south, and are now held in slavery, from those originally brought to this country from Africa; and if their increase will do no other good, it will do away the force of the argument, that God cursed Ham, and therefore American slavery is right. If the lineal descendants of Ham are alone to be scripturally enslaved, it is certain that slavery at the south must soon become unscriptural; for thousands are ushered into the world, annually, who, like myself, owe their existence to white fathers, and those fathers most frequently their own masters.

I have had two masters. My first master's name was Anthony. I do not remember his first name. He was generally called Captain Anthony—a title which, I presume, he acquired by sailing a craft on the Chesapeake Bay. He was not considered a rich slaveholder. He owned two or three farms, and about thirty slaves. His farms and slaves were under the care of an overseer. The overseer's name was Plummer. Mr. Plummer was a miserable drunkard, a profane swearer, and a savage monster. He always went armed with a cowskin and a heavy cudgel. I have known him to cut and slash the women's heads so horribly, that even master would be enraged at his cruelty, and would threaten to whip him if he did not mind himself. Master, however, was not a humane slaveholder. It required extraordinary barbarity on the part of an overseer to affect him. He was a cruel man, hardened by a long life of slaveholding. He would at times seem to take great pleasure in whipping a slave. I have often been awakened at the dawn of day by the most heart-rending shrieks of an own aunt of mine, whom he used to tie up to a joist, and whip upon her naked back till she was literally covered with blood. No words, no tears, no prayers, from his gory victim, seemed to move his iron heart from its bloody purpose. The louder she screamed, the harder he whipped; and where the blood ran fastest, there he whipped longest. He would whip her to make her scream, and whip her to make her hush; and not until overcome by fatigue, would he cease to swing the blood-clotted cowskin. I remember the first time I ever witnessed this horrible exhibition. I was quite a child, but I well remember it. I never shall forget it whilst I remember any thing. It was the first of a long series of such outrages, of which I was doomed to be a witness and a participant. It struck me with awful force. It was the blood-stained gate, the entrance to the hell of slavery, through which I was about to pass. It was a most terrible spectacle. I wish I could commit to paper the feelings with which I beheld it.

This occurrence took place very soon after I went to live with my old master, and under the following circumstances. Aunt Hester went out one night,—where or for what I do not know,—and happened to be absent when my master desired her presence. He had ordered her not to go out evenings, and warned her that she must never let him catch her in company with a young man, who was paying attention to her belonging to Colonel Lloyd. The young man's name was Ned Roberts, generally called Lloyd's Ned. Why master was so careful of her, may be safely left to conjecture. She was a woman of noble form, and of graceful proportions, having very few equals, and fewer superiors, in personal appearance, among the colored or white women of our neighborhood.

Aunt Hester had not only disobeyed his orders in going out, but had been found in company with Lloyd's Ned; which circumstance, I found, from what he said while whipping her, was the chief offence. Had he been a man of pure morals himself, he might have been thought interested in protecting the innocence of my aunt; but those who knew him will not suspect him of any such virtue. Before he commenced whipping Aunt Hester, he took her into the kitchen, and stripped her from neck to waist, leaving her neck, shoulders, and back, entirely naked. He then told her to cross her hands, calling her at the same time a d——d b——h. After crossing her hands, he tied them with a strong rope, and led her to a stool under a large hook in the joist, put in for the purpose. He made her get upon the stool, and tied her hands to the hook. She now stood fair for his infernal purpose. Her arms were stretched up at their full length, so that she stood upon the ends of her toes. He then said to her, "Now, you d——d b——h. I'll learn you how to disobey my orders!" and after rolling up his sleeves, he commenced to lay on the heavy cowskin, and soon the warm, red blood (amid heartrending shrieks from her, and horrid oaths from him) came dripping to the floor. I was so terrified and horror-stricken at the sight, that I hid myself in a closet, and dared not venture out till long after the bloody transaction was over. I expected it would be my turn next. It was all new to me. I had never seen any thing like it before. I had always lived with my grandmother on the outskirts of the plantation, where she was put to raise the children of the younger women. I had therefore been, until now, out of the way of the bloody scenes that often occurred on the plantation.

CHAPTER II

My master's family consisted of two sons, Andrew and Richard; one daughter, Lucretia, and her husband, Captain Thomas Auld. They lived in one house, upon the home plantation of Colonel Edward Lloyd. My master was Colonel Lloyd's clerk and superintendent. He was what might be called the overseer of the overseers. I spent two years of childhood on this plantation in my old master's family. It was here that I witnessed the bloody transaction recorded in the first chapter; and as I received my first impressions of slavery on this plantation, I will give some description of it, and of slavery as it there existed. The plantation is about twelve miles north of Easton, in Talbot county, and is situated on the border of Miles River. The principal products raised upon it were tobacco, corn, and wheat. These were raised in great abundance; so that, with the products of this and the other farms belonging to him, he was able to keep in almost constant employment a large sloop, in carrying them to market at Baltimore. This sloop was named Sally Lloyd, in honor of one of the colonel's daughters. My master's son-in-law, Captain Auld, was master of the vessel; she was otherwise manned by the colonel's own slaves. Their names were Peter, Isaac, Rich, and Jake.

These were esteemed very highly by the other slaves, and looked upon as the privileged ones of the plantation; for it was no small affair, in the eyes of the slaves, to be allowed to see Baltimore.

Colonel Lloyd kept from three to four hundred slaves on his home plantation, and owned a large number more on the neighboring farms belonging to him. The names of the farms nearest to the home plantation were Wye Town and New Design. "Wye Town" was under the overseership of a man named Noah Willis. New Design was under the overseership of a Mr. Townsend. The overseers of these, and all the rest of the farms, numbering over twenty, received advice and direction from the managers of the home plantation. This was the great business place. It was the seat of government for the whole twenty farms. All disputes among the overseers were settled here. If a slave was convicted of any high misdemeanor, became unmanageable, or evinced a determination to run away, he was brought immediately here, severely whipped, put on board the sloop, carried to Baltimore, and sold to Austin Woolfolk, or some other slave-trader, as a warning to the slaves remaining.

Here, too, the slaves of all the other farms received their monthly allowance of food, and their yearly clothing. The men and women slaves received, as their monthly allowance of food, eight pounds of pork, or its equivalent in fish, and one bushel of corn meal. Their yearly clothing consisted of two coarse linen shirts, one pair of linen trousers, like the shirts, one jacket, one pair of trousers for winter, made of coarse negro cloth, one pair of stockings, and one pair of shoes; the whole of which could not have cost more than seven dollars. The allowance of the slave children was given to their mothers, or the old women having the care of them. The children unable to work in the field had neither shoes, stockings, jackets, nor trousers, given to them; their clothing consisted of two coarse linen shirts per year. When these failed them, they went naked until the next allowance-day. Children from seven to ten years old, of both sexes, almost naked, might be seen at all seasons of the year.

There were no beds given the slaves, unless one coarse blanket be considered such, and none but the men and women had these. This, however, is not considered a very great privation. They find less difficulty from the want of beds, than from the want of time to sleep; for when their day's work in the field is done, the most of them having their washing, mending, and cooking to do, and having few or none of the ordinary facilities for doing either of these, very many of their sleeping hours are consumed in preparing for the field the coming day; and when this is done, old and young, male and female, married and single, drop down side by side, on one common bed,—the cold, damp floor,—each covering himself or herself with their miserable blankets; and here they sleep till they are summoned to the field by the driver's horn. At the sound of this, all must rise, and be off to the field. There must be no halting; every one must be at his or her post; and woe betides them who hear not this morning summons to the field; for if they are not awakened by the sense of hearing, they are by the sense of feeling: no age nor sex finds any favor. Mr. Severe, the overseer, used to stand by the door of the quarter, armed with a large hickory stick and heavy cowskin, ready to whip any one who was so unfortunate as not to hear, or, from any other cause, was prevented from being ready to start for the field at the sound of the horn.

Mr. Severe was rightly named: he was a cruel man. I have seen him whip a woman, causing the blood to run half an hour at the time; and this, too, in the midst of her crying children, pleading for their mother's release. He seemed to take pleasure in manifesting his fiendish barbarity. Added to his cruelty, he was a profane swearer. It was enough to chill the blood and stiffen the hair of an ordinary man to hear him talk. Scarce a sentence escaped him but that was commenced or concluded by some horrid oath. The field was the place to witness his cruelty and profanity. His presence made it both the field of blood and of blasphemy. From the rising till the going down of the sun, he was cursing, raving, cutting, and slashing among the slaves of the field, in the most frightful manner. His career was short. He died very soon after I went to Colonel Lloyd's; and he died as he lived, uttering, with his dying groans, bitter curses and horrid oaths. His death was regarded by the slaves as the result of a merciful providence.

Mr. Severe's place was filled by a Mr. Hopkins. He was a very different man. He was less cruel, less profane, and made less noise, than Mr. Severe. His course was characterized by no extraordinary demonstrations of cruelty. He whipped, but seemed to take no pleasure in it. He was called by the slaves a good overseer.

The home plantation of Colonel Lloyd wore the appearance of a country village. All the mechanical operations for all the farms were performed here. The shoemaking and mending, the blacksmithing, cartwrighting, coopering, weaving, and grain-grinding, were all performed by the slaves on the home plantation. The whole place wore a business-like aspect very unlike the neighboring farms. The number of houses, too, conspired to give it advantage over the neighboring farms. It was called by the slaves the *Great House Farm*. Few privileges were esteemed higher, by the slaves of the out-farms, than that of being selected to do errands at the Great House Farm. It was associated in their minds with greatness. A representative could not be prouder of his election to a seat in the American Congress, than a slave on one of the out-farms would be of his election to do errands at the Great House Farm. They regarded it as evidence of great confidence reposed in them by their overseers; and it was on this account, as well as a constant desire to be out of the field from under the driver's lash, that they esteemed it a high privilege, one worth careful living for. He was called the smartest and most trusty fellow, who had this honor conferred upon him the most frequently. The competitors for this office sought as diligently to please their overseers, as the office-seekers in the political parties seek to please and deceive the people. The same traits of character might be seen in Colonel Lloyd's slaves, as are seen in the slaves of the political parties.

The slaves selected to go to the Great House Farm, for the monthly allowance for themselves and their fellow-slaves, were peculiarly enthusiastic. While on their way, they would make the dense old woods, for miles around, reverberate with their wild songs, revealing at once the highest joy and the deepest sadness. They would compose and sing as they went along, consulting neither time nor tune. The thought that came up, came out—if not in the word, in the sound;—and as frequently in the one as in the other. They would sometimes sing the most pathetic sentiment in the most rapturous tone, and the most rapturous sentiment in the most pathetic tone. Into all of their songs they would manage to weave something of the Great House Farm. Especially would they do this, when leaving home. They would then sing most exultingly the following words:—

"I am going away to the Great House Farm!
O, yea! O, yea! O!"

This they would sing, as a chorus, to words which to many would seem unmeaning jargon, but which, nevertheless, were full of meaning to themselves. I have sometimes thought that the mere hearing of those songs would do more to impress some minds with the horrible character of slavery, than the reading of whole volumes of philosophy on the subject could do.

I did not, when a slave, understand the deep meaning of those rude and apparently incoherent songs. I was myself within the circle; so that I neither saw nor heard as those without might see and hear. They told a tale of woe which was then altogether beyond my feeble comprehension; they were tones loud, long, and deep; they breathed the prayer and complaint of souls boiling over with the bitterest anguish. Every tone was a testimony against slavery, and a prayer to God for deliverance from chains. The hearing of those wild notes always depressed my spirit, and filled me with ineffable sadness. I have frequently found myself in tears while hearing them. The mere recurrence to those songs, even now, afflicts me; and while I am writing these lines, an expression of feeling has already found its way down my cheek. To those songs I trace my first glimmering conception of the dehumanizing character of slavery. I can never get rid of that conception. Those songs still follow me, to deepen my hatred of slavery, and quicken my sympathies for my brethren in bonds. If any one wishes to be impressed with the soul-killing effects of slavery, let him go to Colonel Lloyd's plantation, and, on allowance-day, place himself in the deep pine woods, and there let him, in silence, analyze the sounds that shall pass through the chambers of his soul,—and if he is not thus impressed, it will only be because "there is no flesh in his obdurate heart."

I have often been utterly astonished, since I came to the north, to find persons who could speak of the singing, among slaves, as evidence of their contentment and happiness. It is impossible to conceive of a greater mistake. Slaves sing most when they are most unhappy. The songs of the slave represent the sorrows of his heart; and he is relieved by them, only as an aching heart is relieved by its tears. At least, such is my experience. I have often sung to drown my sorrow, but seldom to express my happiness. Crying for joy, and singing for joy, were alike uncommon to me while in the jaws of slavery. The singing of a man cast away upon a desolate island might be as appropriately considered as evidence of contentment and happiness, as the singing of a slave; the songs of the one and of the other are prompted by the same emotion.

CHAPTER III

Colonel Lloyd kept a large and finely cultivated garden, which afforded almost constant employment for four men, besides the chief gardener, (Mr. M'Durmond.) This garden was probably the greatest attraction of the place. During the summer months, people came from far and near—from Baltimore, Easton, and Annapolis—to see it. It abounded in fruits of almost every description, from the hardy apple of the north to the delicate orange of the south. This garden was not the least source of trouble on the plantation. Its excellent fruit was quite a temptation to the hungry swarms of boys, as well as the older slaves, belonging to the colonel, few of whom had the virtue or the vice to resist it. Scarcely a day passed, during the summer, but that some slave had to take the lash for stealing fruit. The colonel had to resort to all kinds of stratagems to keep his slaves out of the garden. The last and most successful one was that of tarring his fence all around; after which, if a slave was caught with any tar upon his person, it was deemed sufficient proof that he had either been into the garden, or had tried to get in. In either case, he was severely whipped by the chief gardener. This plan worked well; the slaves became as fearful of tar as of the lash. They seemed to realize the impossibility of touching *tar* without being defiled.

The colonel also kept a splendid riding equipage. His stable and carriage-house presented the appearance of some of our large city livery establishments. His horses were of the finest form and noblest blood. His carriage-house contained three splendid coaches, three or four gigs, besides dearborns and barouches of the most fashionable style.

This establishment was under the care of two slaves—old Barney and young Barney—father and son. To attend to this establishment was their sole work. But it was by no means an easy employment; for in nothing was Colonel Lloyd more particular than in the management of his horses. The slightest inattention to these was unpardonable, and was visited upon those, under whose care they were placed, with the severest punishment; no excuse could shield them, if the colonel only suspected any want of attention to his horses—a supposition which he frequently indulged, and one which, of course, made the office of old and young Barney a very trying one. They never knew when they were safe from punishment. They were frequently whipped when least deserving, and escaped whipping when most deserving it. Every thing depended upon the looks of the horses, and the state of Colonel Lloyd's own mind when his horses were brought to him for use. If a horse did not move fast enough, or hold his head high enough, it was owing to some fault of his keepers. It was painful to stand near the stable-door, and hear the various complaints against the keepers when a horse was taken out for use. "This horse has not had proper attention. He has not been sufficiently rubbed and curried, or he has not been properly fed; his food was too wet or too dry; he got it too soon or too late; he was too hot or too cold; he had too much hay, and not enough of grain; or he had too much grain, and not enough of hay; instead of old Barney's attending to the horse, he had very improperly left it to his son." To all these complaints, no matter how unjust, the slave must answer never a word. Colonel Lloyd could not brook any contradiction from a slave. When he spoke, a slave must stand, listen, and tremble; and such was literally the case. I have seen Colonel Lloyd make old Barney, a man between fifty and sixty years of age, uncover his bald head, kneel down upon the cold, damp ground, and receive upon his naked and toil worn shoulders more than thirty lashes at the time. Colonel Lloyd had three sons—Edward, Murray, and Daniel,—and three sons-in-law, Mr. Winder, Mr. Nicholson, and Mr. Lowndes. All of these lived at the Great House Farm, and enjoyed the luxury of whipping the servants when they pleased, from old Barney down to William Wilkes, the coach-driver. I have seen Winder make one of the house-servants stand off from him a suitable distance to be touched with the end of his whip, and at every stroke raise great ridges upon his back.

To describe the wealth of Colonel Lloyd would be almost equal to describing the riches of Job. He kept from ten to fifteen house-servants. He was said to own a thousand slaves, and I think this estimate quite within the truth. Colonel Lloyd owned so many that he did not know them when he saw them; nor did all the slaves of the out-farms know him. It is reported of him, that, while riding along the road one day, he met a colored man, and addressed him in the usual manner of speaking to colored people on the public highways of the south: "Well, boy, whom do you belong to?" "To Colonel Lloyd," replied the slave. "Well, does the colonel treat you well?" "No, sir," was the ready reply. "What, does he work you too hard?" "Yes, sir." "Well, don't he give you enough to eat?" "Yes, sir, he gives me enough, such as it is."

The colonel, after ascertaining where the slave belonged, rode on; the man also went on about his business, not dreaming that he had been conversing with his master. He thought, said, and heard nothing more of the matter, until two or three weeks afterwards. The poor man was then informed by his overseer that, for having found fault with his master, he was now to be sold to a Georgia trader. He was immediately chained and handcuffed; and thus, without a moment's warning, he was snatched away, and forever sundered, from his family and friends, by a hand more unrelenting than death. This is the penalty of telling the truth, of telling the simple truth, in answer to a series of plain questions.

It is partly in consequence of such facts, that slaves, when inquired of as to their condition and the character of their masters, almost universally say they are contented, and that their masters are kind. The slaveholders have been known to send in spies among their slaves, to ascertain their views and feelings in regard to their condition. The frequency of this has had the effect to establish among the slaves the maxim, that a still tongue makes a wise head. They suppress the truth rather than take the consequences of telling it, and in so doing prove themselves a part of the human family. If they have any thing to say of their masters, it is generally in their masters' favor, especially when speaking to an untried man. I have been frequently asked, when a slave, if I had a kind master, and do not remember ever to have given a negative answer; nor did I, in pursuing this course, consider myself as uttering what was absolutely false; for I always measured the kindness of my master by the standard of kindness set up among slaveholders around us. Moreover, slaves are like other people, and imbibe prejudices quite common to others. They think their own better than that of others. Many, under the influence of this prejudice, think their own masters are better than the masters of other slaves; and this, too, in some cases, when the very reverse is true. Indeed, it is not uncommon for slaves even to fall out and quarrel among themselves about the relative goodness of their masters, each contending for the superior goodness of his own over that of the others. At the very same time, they mutually execrate their masters when viewed separately. It was so on our plantation. When Colonel Lloyd's slaves met the slaves of Jacob Jepson, they seldom parted without a quarrel about their masters; Colonel Lloyd's slaves contending that he was the richest, and Mr. Jepson's slaves that he was the smartest, and most of a man. Colonel Lloyd's slaves would boast his ability to buy and sell Jacob Jepson. Mr. Jepson's slaves would boast his ability to whip Colonel Lloyd. These quarrels would almost always end in a fight between the parties, and those that whipped were supposed to have gained the point at issue. They seemed to think that the greatness of their masters was transferable to themselves. It was considered as being bad enough to be a slave; but to be a poor man's slave was deemed a disgrace indeed!

CHAPTER IV

Mr. Hopkins remained but a short time in the office of overseer. Why his career was so short, I do not know, but suppose he lacked the necessary severity to suit Colonel Lloyd. Mr. Hopkins was succeeded by Mr. Austin Gore, a man possessing, in an eminent degree, all those traits of character indispensable to what is called a first-rate overseer. Mr. Gore had served Colonel Lloyd, in the capacity of overseer, upon one of the out-farms, and had shown himself worthy of the high station of overseer upon the home or Great House Farm.

Mr. Gore was proud, ambitious, and persevering. He was artful, cruel, and obdurate. He was just the man for such a place, and it was just the place for such a man. It afforded scope for the full exercise of all his powers, and he seemed to be perfectly at home in it. He was one of those who could torture the slightest look, word, or gesture, on the part of the slave, into impudence, and would treat it accordingly. There must be no answering back to him; no explanation was allowed a slave, showing himself to have been wrongfully accused. Mr. Gore acted fully up to the maxim laid down by slaveholders,—"It is better that a dozen slaves suffer under the lash, than that the overseer should be convicted, in the presence of the slaves, of having been at fault." No matter how innocent a slave might be—it availed him nothing, when accused by Mr. Gore of any misdemeanor. To be accused was to be convicted, and to be convicted was to be punished; the one always following the other with immutable certainty. To escape punishment was to escape accusation; and few slaves had the fortune to do either, under the overseership of Mr. Gore. He was just proud enough to demand the most debasing homage of the slave, and quite servile enough to crouch, himself, at the feet of the master. He was ambitious enough to be contented with nothing short of the highest rank of overseers, and persevering enough to reach the height of his ambition. He was cruel enough to inflict the severest punishment, artful enough to descend to the lowest trickery, and obdurate enough to be insensible to the voice of a reproving conscience. He was, of all the overseers, the most dreaded by the slaves. His presence was painful; his eye flashed confusion; and seldom was his sharp, shrill voice heard, without producing horror and trembling in their ranks.

Mr. Gore was a grave man, and, though a young man, he indulged in no jokes, said no funny words, seldom smiled. His words were in perfect keeping with his looks, and his looks were in perfect keeping with his words. Overseers will sometimes indulge in a witty word, even with the slaves; not so with Mr. Gore. He spoke but to command, and commanded but to be obeyed; he dealt sparingly with his words, and bountifully with his whip, never using the former where the latter would answer as well. When he whipped, he seemed to do so from a sense of duty, and feared no consequences. He did nothing reluctantly, no matter how disagreeable; always at his post, never inconsistent. He never promised but to fulfil. He was, in a word, a man of the most inflexible firmness and stone-like coolness.

His savage barbarity was equalled only by the consummate coolness with which he committed the grossest and most savage deeds upon the slaves under his charge. Mr. Gore once undertook to whip one of Colonel Lloyd's slaves, by the name of Demby. He had given Demby but few stripes, when, to get rid of the scourging, he ran and plunged himself into a creek, and stood there at the depth of his shoulders, refusing to come out. Mr. Gore told him that he would give him three calls, and that, if he did not come out at the third call, he would shoot him. The first call was given. Demby made no response, but stood his ground. The second and third calls were given with the same result. Mr. Gore then, without consultation or deliberation with any one, not even giving Demby an additional call, raised his musket to his face, taking deadly aim at his standing victim, and in an instant poor Demby was no more. His mangled body sank out of sight, and blood and brains marked the water where he had stood.

A thrill of horror flashed through every soul upon the plantation, excepting Mr. Gore. He alone seemed cool and collected. He was asked by Colonel Lloyd and my old master, why he resorted to this extraordinary expedient. His reply was (as well as I can remember) that Demby had become unmanageable. He was setting a dangerous example to the other slaves,—one which, if suffered to pass without some such demonstration on his part, would finally lead to the total subversion of all rule and order upon the plantation. He argued that if one slave refused to be corrected, and escaped with his life, the other slaves would soon copy the example; the result of which would be, the freedom of the slaves, and the enslavement of the whites. Mr. Gore's defence was satisfactory. He was continued in his station as overseer upon the home plantation. His fame as an overseer went abroad. His horrid crime was not even submitted to judicial investigation. It was committed in the presence of slaves, and they of course could neither institute a suit nor testify against him; and thus the guilty perpetrator of one of the bloodiest and most foul murders goes unwhipped of justice, and uncensured by the community in which he lives. Mr. Gore lived in St. Michael's, Talbot county, Maryland, when I left there; and if he is still alive, he very probably lives there now; and if so, he is now, as he was then, as highly esteemed and as much respected as though his guilty soul had not been stained with his brother's blood.

I speak advisedly when I say this,—that killing a slave, or any colored person, in Talbot county, Maryland, is not treated as a crime, either by the courts or the community.

Mr. Thomas Lanman, of St. Michael's, killed two slaves, one of whom he killed with a hatchet, by knocking his brains out. He used to boast of the commission of the awful and bloody deed. I have heard him do so laughingly, saying, among other things, that he was the only benefactor of his country in the company, and that when others would do as much as he had done, we should be relieved of "the d——d niggers."

The wife of Mr. Giles Hick [sic], living but a short distance from where I used to live, murdered my wife's cousin, a young girl between fifteen and sixteen years of age, mangling her person in the most horrible manner, breaking her nose and breastbone with a stick, so that the poor girl expired in a few hours afterward. She was immediately buried, but had not been in her untimely grave but a few hours before she was taken up and examined by the coroner, who decided that she had come to her death by severe beating. The offence for which this girl was thus murdered was this:—She had been sent that night to mind Mrs. Hick's baby, and during the night she fell asleep, and the baby cried. She, having lost her rest for several nights previous, did not hear the crying. They were both in the room with Mrs. Hicks. Mrs. Hicks, finding the girl slow to move, jumped from her bed, seized an oak stick of wood by the fireplace, and with it broke the girl's nose and breastbone, and thus ended her life. I will not say that this most horrid murder produced no sensation in the community. It did produce sensation, but not enough to bring the murderess to punishment. There was a warrant issued for her arrest, but it was never served. Thus she escaped not only punishment, but even the pain of being arraigned before a court for her horrid crime.

Whilst I am detailing bloody deeds which took place during my stay on Colonel Lloyd's plantation, I will briefly narrate another, which occurred about the same time as the murder of Demby by Mr. Gore.

Colonel Lloyd's slaves were in the habit of spending a part of their nights and Sundays in fishing for oysters, and in this way made up the deficiency of their scanty allowance. An old man belonging to Colonel Lloyd, while thus engaged, happened to get beyond the limits of Colonel Lloyd's, and on the premises of Mr. Beal Bondly. At this trespass, Mr. Bondly took offence, and with his musket came down to the shore, and blew its deadly contents into the poor old man.

Mr. Bondly came over to see Colonel Lloyd the next day, whether to pay him for his property, or to justify himself in what he had done, I know not. At any rate, this whole fiendish transaction was soon hushed up. There was very little said about it at all, and nothing done. It was a common saying, even among little white boys, that it was worth a half-cent to kill a "nigger," and a half-cent to bury one.

CHAPTER V

As to my own treatment while I lived on Colonel Lloyd's plantation, it was very similar to that of the other slave children. I was not old enough to work in the field, and there being little else than field work to do, I had a great deal of leisure time. The most I had to do was to drive up the cows at evening, keep the fowls out of the garden, keep the front yard clean, and run of errands for my old master's daughter, Mrs. Lucretia Auld. The most of my leisure time I spent in helping Master Daniel Lloyd in finding his birds, after he had shot them. My connection with Master Daniel was of some advantage to me. He became quite attached to me, and was a sort of protector of me. He would not allow the older boys to impose upon me, and would divide his cakes with me.

I was seldom whipped by my old master, and suffered little from any thing else than hunger and cold. I suffered much from hunger, but much more from cold. In hottest summer and coldest winter, I was kept almost naked—no shoes, no stockings, no jacket, no trousers, nothing on but a coarse tow linen shirt, reaching only to my knees. I had no bed. I must have perished with cold, but that, the coldest nights, I used to steal a bag which was used for carrying corn to the mill. I would crawl into this bag, and there sleep on the cold, damp, clay floor, with my head in and feet out. My feet have been so cracked with the frost, that the pen with which I am writing might be laid in the gashes.

We were not regularly allowanced. Our food was coarse corn meal boiled. This was called *mush*. It was put into a large wooden tray or trough, and set down upon the ground. The children were then called, like so many pigs, and like so many pigs they would come and devour the mush; some with oystershells, others with pieces of shingle, some with naked hands, and none with spoons. He that ate fastest got most; he that was strongest secured the best place; and few left the trough satisfied.

I was probably between seven and eight years old when I left Colonel Lloyd's plantation. I left it with joy. I shall never forget the ecstasy with which I received the intelligence that my old master (Anthony) had determined to let me go to Baltimore, to live with Mr. Hugh Auld, brother to my old master's son-in-law, Captain Thomas Auld. I received this information about three days before my departure. They were three of the happiest days I ever enjoyed. I spent the most part of all these three days in the creek, washing off the plantation scurf, and preparing myself for my departure.

The pride of appearance which this would indicate was not my own. I spent the time in washing, not so much because I wished to, but because Mrs. Lucretia had told me I must get all the dead skin off my feet and knees before I could go to Baltimore; for the people in Baltimore were very cleanly, and would laugh at me if I looked dirty. Besides, she was going to give me a pair of trousers, which I should not put on unless I got all the dirt off me. The thought of owning a pair of trousers was great indeed! It was almost a sufficient motive, not only to make me take off what would be called by pig-drovers the mange, but the skin itself. I went at it in good earnest, working for the first time with the hope of reward.

The ties that ordinarily bind children to their homes were all suspended in my case. I found no severe trial in my departure. My home was charmless; it was not home to me; on parting from it, I could not feel that I was leaving any thing which I could have enjoyed by staying.

My mother was dead, my grandmother lived far off, so that I seldom saw her. I had two sisters and one brother, that lived in the same house with me; but the early separation of us from our mother had well nigh blotted the fact of our relationship from our memories. I looked for home elsewhere, and was confident of finding none which I should relish less than the one which I was leaving. If, however, I found in my new home hardship, hunger, whipping, and nakedness, I had the consolation that I should not have escaped any one of them by staying. Having already had more than a taste of them in the house of my old master, and having endured them there, I very naturally inferred my ability to endure them elsewhere, and especially at Baltimore; for I had something of the feeling about Baltimore that is expressed in the proverb, that "being hanged in England is preferable to dying a natural death in Ireland." I had the strongest desire to see Baltimore. Cousin Tom, though not fluent in speech, had inspired me with that desire by his eloquent description of the place. I could never point out any thing at the Great House, no matter how beautiful or powerful, but that he had seen something at Baltimore far exceeding, both in beauty and strength, the object which I pointed out to him. Even the Great House itself, with all its pictures, was far inferior to many buildings in Baltimore. So strong was my desire, that I thought a gratification of it would fully compensate for whatever loss of comforts I should sustain by the exchange. I left without a regret, and with the highest hopes of future happiness.

We sailed out of Miles River for Baltimore on a Saturday morning. I remember only the day of the week, for at that time I had no knowledge of the days of the month, nor the months of the year. On setting sail, I walked aft, and gave to Colonel Lloyd's plantation what I hoped would be the last look. I then placed myself in the bows of the sloop, and there spent the remainder of the day in looking ahead, interesting myself in what was in the distance rather than in things near by or behind.

In the afternoon of that day, we reached Annapolis, the capital of the State. We stopped but a few moments, so that I had no time to go on shore. It was the first large town that I had ever seen, and though it would look small compared with some of our New England factory villages, I thought it a wonderful place for its size—more imposing even than the Great House Farm!

We arrived at Baltimore early on Sunday morning, landing at Smith's Wharf, not far from Bowley's Wharf. We had on board the sloop a large flock of sheep; and after aiding in driving them to the slaughterhouse of Mr. Curtis on Louden Slater's Hill, I was conducted by Rich, one of the hands belonging on board of the sloop, to my new home in Alliciana Street, near Mr. Gardner's shipyard, on Fells Point.

Mr. and Mrs. Auld were both at home, and met me at the door with their little son Thomas, to take care of whom I had been given. And here I saw what I had never seen before; it was a white face beaming with the most kindly emotions; it was the face of my new mistress, Sophia Auld. I wish I could describe the rapture that flashed through my soul as I beheld it. It was a new and strange sight to me, brightening up my pathway with the light of happiness. Little Thomas was told, there was his Freddy,—and I was told to take care of little Thomas; and thus I entered upon the duties of my new home with the most cheering prospect ahead.

I look upon my departure from Colonel Lloyd's plantation as one of the most interesting events of my life. It is possible, and even quite probable, that but for the mere circumstance of being removed from that plantation to Baltimore, I should have to-day, instead of being here seated by my own table, in the enjoyment of freedom and the happiness of home, writing this Narrative, been confined in the galling chains of slavery. Going to live at Baltimore laid the foundation, and opened the gateway, to all my subsequent prosperity. I have ever regarded it as the first plain manifestation of that kind providence which has ever since attended me, and marked my life with so many favors. I regarded the selection of myself as being somewhat remarkable. There were a number of slave children that might have been sent from the plantation to Baltimore. There were those younger, those older, and those of the same age. I was chosen from among them all, and was the first, last, and only choice.

I may be deemed superstitious, and even egotistical, in regarding this event as a special interposition of divine Providence in my favor. But I should be false to the earliest sentiments of my soul, if I suppressed the opinion. I prefer to be true to myself, even at the hazard of incurring the ridicule of others, rather than to be false, and incur my own abhorrence. From my earliest recollection, I date the entertainment of a deep conviction that slavery would not always be able to hold me within its foul embrace; and in the darkest hours of my career in slavery, this living word of faith and spirit of hope departed not from me, but remained like ministering angels to cheer me through the gloom. This good spirit was from God, and to him I offer thanksgiving and praise.

CHAPTER VI

My new mistress proved to be all she appeared when I first met her at the door,—a woman of the kindest heart and finest feelings. She had never had a slave under her control previously to myself, and prior to her marriage she had been dependent upon her own industry for a living. She was by trade a weaver; and by constant application to her business, she had been in a good degree preserved from the blighting and dehumanizing effects of slavery. I was utterly astonished at her goodness. I scarcely knew how to behave towards her. She was entirely unlike any other white woman I had ever seen. I could not approach her as I was accustomed to approach other white ladies. My early instruction was all out of place. The crouching servility, usually so acceptable a quality in a slave, did not answer when manifested toward her. Her favor was not gained by it; she seemed to be disturbed by it. She did not deem it impudent or unmannerly for a slave to look her in the face. The meanest slave was put fully at ease in her presence, and none left without feeling better for having seen her. Her face was made of heavenly smiles and her voice of tranquil music.

But, alas! this kind heart had but a short time to remain such. The fatal poison of irresponsible power was already in her hands, and soon commenced its infernal work. That cheerful eye, under the influence of slavery, soon became red with rage; that voice, made all of sweet accord, changed to one of harsh and horrid discord; and that angelic face gave place to that of a demon.

Very soon after I went to live with Mr. and Mrs. Auld, she very kindly commenced to teach me the A, B, C. After I had learned this, she assisted me in learning to spell words of three or four letters. Just at this point of my progress, Mr. Auld found out what was going on, and at once forbade Mrs. Auld to instruct me further, telling her, among other things, that it was unlawful, as well as unsafe, to teach a slave to read. To use his own words, further, he said, "If you give a nigger an inch, he will take an ell. A nigger should know nothing but to obey his master—to do as he is told to do. Learning would *spoil* the best nigger in the world. Now," said he, "if you teach that nigger (speaking of myself) how to read, there would be no keeping him. It would forever unfit him to be a slave. He would at once become unmanageable, and of no value to his master. As to himself, it could do him no good, but a great deal of harm. It would make him discontented and unhappy." These words sank deep into my heart, stirred up sentiments within that lay slumbering, and called into existence an entirely new train of thought. It was a new and special revelation, explaining dark and mysterious things, with which my youthful understanding had struggled, but struggled in vain. I now understood what had been to me a most perplexing difficulty—to wit, the white man's power to enslave the black man. It was a grand achievement, and I prized it highly. From that moment, I understood the pathway from slavery to freedom. It was just what I wanted, and I got it at a time when I the least expected it. Whilst I was saddened by the thought of losing the aid of my kind mistress, I was gladdened by the invaluable instruction which, by the merest accident, I had gained from my master. Though conscious of the difficulty of learning without a teacher, I set out with high hope, and a fixed purpose, at whatever cost of trouble, to learn how to read. The very decided manner with which he spoke, and strove to impress his wife with the evil consequences of giving me instruction, served to convince me that he was deeply sensible of the truths he was uttering. It gave me the best assurance that I might rely with the utmost confidence on the results which, he said, would flow from teaching me to read. What he most dreaded, that I most desired. What he most loved, that I most hated. That which to him was a great evil, to be carefully shunned, was to me a great good, to be diligently sought; and the argument which he so warmly urged, against my learning to read, only served to inspire me with a desire and determination to learn. In learning to read, I owe almost as much to the bitter opposition of my master, as to the kindly aid of my mistress. I acknowledge the benefit of both.

I had resided but a short time in Baltimore before I observed a marked difference, in the treatment of slaves, from that which I had witnessed in the country. A city slave is almost a freeman, compared with a slave on the plantation. He is much better fed and clothed, and enjoys privileges altogether unknown to the slave on the plantation. There is a vestige of decency, a sense of shame, that does much to curb and check those outbreaks of atrocious cruelty so commonly enacted upon the plantation. He is a desperate slaveholder, who will shock the humanity of his nonslaveholding neighbors with the cries of his lacerated slave. Few are willing to incur the odium attaching to the reputation of being a cruel master; and above all things, they would not be known as not giving a slave enough to eat. Every city slaveholder is anxious to have it known of him, that he feeds his slaves well; and it is due to them to say, that most of them do give their slaves enough to eat. There are, however, some painful exceptions to this rule. Directly opposite to us, on Philpot Street, lived Mr. Thomas Hamilton. He owned two slaves. Their names were Henrietta and Mary. Henrietta was about twenty-two years of age, Mary was about fourteen; and of all the mangled and emaciated creatures I ever looked upon, these two were the most so. His heart must be harder than stone, that could look upon these unmoved. The head, neck, and shoulders of Mary were literally cut to pieces. I have frequently felt her head, and found it nearly covered with festering sores, caused by the lash of her cruel mistress. I do not know that her master ever whipped her, but I have been an eye-witness to the cruelty of Mrs. Hamilton. I used to be in Mr. Hamilton's house nearly every day. Mrs. Hamilton used to sit in a large chair in the middle of the room, with a heavy cowskin always by her side, and scarce an hour passed during the day but was marked by the blood of one of these slaves. The girls seldom passed her without her saying, "Move faster, you *black gip!*" at the same time giving them a blow with the cowskin over the head or shoulders, often drawing the blood. She would then say, "Take that, you *black gip!*"—continuing, "If you don't move faster, I'll move you!" Added to the cruel lashings to which these slaves were subjected, they were kept nearly half-starved. They seldom knew what it was to eat a full meal. I have seen Mary contending with the pigs for the offal thrown into the street. So much was Mary kicked and cut to pieces, that she was oftener called "*pecked*" than by her name.

CHAPTER VII

I lived in Master Hugh's family about seven years. During this time, I succeeded in learning to read and write. In accomplishing this, I was compelled to resort to various stratagems. I had no regular teacher. My mistress, who had kindly commenced to instruct me, had, in compliance with the advice and direction of her husband, not only ceased to instruct, but had set her face against my being instructed by any one else. It is due, however, to my mistress to say of her, that she did not adopt this course of treatment immediately. She at first lacked the depravity indispensable to shutting me up in mental darkness. It was at least necessary for her to have some training in the exercise of irresponsible power, to make her equal to the task of treating me as though I were a brute.

My mistress was, as I have said, a kind and tender-hearted woman; and in the simplicity of her soul she commenced, when I first went to live with her, to treat me as she supposed one human being ought to treat another. In entering upon the duties of a slaveholder, she did not seem to perceive that I sustained to her the relation of a mere chattel, and that for her to treat me as a human being was not only wrong, but dangerously so. Slavery proved as injurious to her as it did to me. When I went there, she was a pious, warm, and tender-hearted woman. There was no sorrow or suffering for which she had not a tear. She had bread for the hungry, clothes for the naked, and comfort for every mourner that came within her reach. Slavery soon proved its ability to divest her of these heavenly qualities. Under its influence, the tender heart became stone, and the lamblike disposition gave way to one of tiger-like fierceness. The first step in her downward course was in her ceasing to instruct me. She now commenced to practise her husband's precepts. She finally became even more violent in her opposition than her husband himself. She was not satisfied with simply doing as well as he had commanded; she seemed anxious to do better. Nothing seemed to make her more angry than to see me with a newspaper. She seemed to think that here lay the danger. I have had her rush at me with a face made all up of fury, and snatch from me a newspaper, in a manner that fully revealed her apprehension. She was an apt woman; and a little experience soon demonstrated, to her satisfaction, that education and slavery were incompatible with each other.

From this time I was most narrowly watched. If I was in a separate room any considerable length of time, I was sure to be suspected of having a book, and was at once called to give an account of myself. All this, however, was too late. The first step had been taken. Mistress, in teaching me the alphabet, had given me the *inch,* and no precaution could prevent me from taking the *ell.*

The plan which I adopted, and the one by which I was most successful, was that of making friends of all the little white boys whom I met in the street. As many of these as I could, I converted into teachers. With their kindly aid, obtained at different times and in different places, I finally succeeded in learning to read. When I was sent on errands, I always took my book with me, and by going one part of my errand quickly, I found time to get a lesson before my return. I used also to carry bread with me, enough of which was always in the house, and to which I was always welcome; for I was much better off in this regard than many of the poor white children in our neighborhood. This bread I used to bestow upon the hungry little urchins, who, in return, would give me that more valuable bread of knowledge. I am strongly tempted to give the names of two or three of those little boys, as a testimonial of the gratitude and affection I bear them; but prudence forbids;—not that it would injure me, but it might embarrass them; for it is almost an unpardonable offence to teach slaves to read in this Christian country. It is enough to say of the dear little fellows, that they lived on Philpot Street, very near Durgin and Bailey's ship-yard. I used to talk this matter of slavery over with them. I would sometimes say to them, I wished I could be as free as they would be when they got to be men. "You will be free as soon as you are twenty-one, *but I am a slave for life!* Have not I as good a right to be free as you have?" These words used to trouble them; they would express for me the liveliest sympathy, and console me with the hope that something would occur by which I might be free.

I was now about twelve years old, and the thought of being *a slave for life* began to bear heavily upon my heart. Just about this time, I got hold of a book entitled "The Columbian Orator." Every opportunity I got, I used to read this book. Among much of other interesting matter, I found in it a dialogue between a master and his slave. The slave was represented as having run away from his master three times. The dialogue represented the conversation which took place between them, when the slave was retaken the third time. In this dialogue, the whole argument in behalf of slavery was brought forward by the master, all of which was disposed of by the slave. The slave was made to say some very smart as well as impressive things in reply to his master—things which had the desired though unexpected effect; for the conversation resulted in the voluntary emancipation of the slave on the part of the master.

In the same book, I met with one of Sheridan's mighty speeches on and in behalf of Catholic emancipation. These were choice documents to me. I read them over and over again with unabated interest. They gave tongue to interesting thoughts of my own soul, which had frequently flashed through my mind, and died away for want of utterance. The moral which I gained from the dialogue was the power of truth over the conscience of even a slaveholder. What I got from Sheridan was a bold denunciation of slavery, and a powerful vindication of human rights. The reading of these documents enabled me to utter my thoughts, and to meet the arguments brought forward to sustain slavery; but while they relieved me of one difficulty, they brought on another even more painful than the one of which I was relieved. The more I read, the more I was led to abhor and detest my enslavers. I could regard them in no other light than a band of successful robbers, who had left their homes, and gone to Africa, and stolen us from our homes, and in a strange land reduced us to slavery. I loathed them as being the meanest as well as the most wicked of men. As I read and contemplated the subject, behold! that very discontentment which Master Hugh had predicted would follow my learning to read had already come, to torment and sting my soul to unutterable anguish. As I writhed under it, I would at times feel that learning to read had been a curse rather than a blessing. It had given me a view of my wretched condition, without the remedy. It opened my eyes to the horrible pit, but to no ladder upon which to get out. In moments of agony, I envied my fellow-slaves for their stupidity. I have often wished myself a beast. I preferred the condition of the meanest reptile to my own. Any thing, no matter what, to get rid of thinking! It was this everlasting thinking of my condition that tormented me. There was no getting rid of it. It was pressed upon me by every object within sight or hearing, animate or inanimate. The silver trump of freedom had roused my soul to eternal wakefulness. Freedom now appeared, to disappear no more forever. It was heard in every sound, and seen in every thing. It was ever present to torment me with a sense of my wretched condition. I saw nothing without seeing it, I heard nothing without hearing it, and felt nothing without feeling it. It looked from every star, it smiled in every calm, breathed in every wind, and moved in every storm.

I often found myself regretting my own existence, and wishing myself dead; and but for the hope of being free, I have no doubt but that I should have killed myself, or done something for which I should have been killed. While in this state of mind, I was eager to hear any one speak of slavery. I was a ready listener. Every little while, I could hear something about the abolitionists. It was some time before I found what the word meant. It was always used in such conditions as to make it an interesting word to me. If a slave ran away and succeeded in getting clear, or if a slave killed his master, set fire to a barn, or did any thing very wrong in the mind of a slaveholder, it was spoken of as the fruit of *abolition*. Hearing the word in this connection very often, I set about learning what it meant. The dictionary afforded me little or no help. I found it was "the act of abolishing"; but then I did not know what was to be abolished. Here I was perplexed. I did not dare to ask any one about its meaning, for I was satisfied that it was something they wanted me to know very little about. After a patient waiting, I got one of our city papers, containing an account of the number of petitions from the north, praying for the abolition of slavery in the District of Columbia, and of the slave trade between the States. From this time I understood the words *abolition* and *abolitionist,* and always drew near when that word was spoken, expecting to hear something of importance to myself and fellow-slaves. The light broke in upon me by degrees. I went one day down on the wharf of Mr. Waters; and seeing two Irishmen unloading a scow of stone, I went, unasked, and helped them. When we had finished, one of them came to me and asked me if I were a slave. I told him I was. He asked, "Are ye a slave for life?" I told him that I was. The good Irishman seemed to be deeply affected by the statement. He said to the other that it was a pity so fine a little fellow as myself should be a slave for life. He said it was a shame to hold me. They both advised me to run away to the north; that I should find friends there, and that I should be free. I pretended not to be interested in what they said, and treated them as if I did not understand them; for I feared they might be treacherous. White men have been known to encourage slaves to escape, and then, to get the reward, catch them and return them to their masters. I was afraid that these seemingly good men might use me so; but I nevertheless remembered their advice, and from that time I resolved to run away. I looked forward to a time at which it would be safe for me to escape. I was too young to think of doing so immediately; besides, I wished to learn how to write, as I might have occasion to write my own pass. I consoled myself with the hope that I should one day find a good chance. Meanwhile, I would learn to write.

The idea as to how I might learn to write was suggested to me by being in Durgin and Bailey's ship-yard, and frequently seeing the ship carpenters, after hewing, and getting a piece of timber ready for use, write on the timber the name of that part of the ship for which it was intended. When a piece of timber was intended for the larboard side, it would be marked thus—"L." When a piece was for the starboard side, it would be marked thus—"S." A piece for the larboard side forward, would be marked thus—"L.F." When a piece was for starboard side forward, it would be marked thus—"S.F." For larboard aft, it would be marked thus—"L.A." For starboard aft, it would be marked thus—"S.A." I soon learned the names of these letters, and for what they were intended when placed upon a piece of timber in the ship-yard. I immediately commenced copying them, and in a short time was able to make the four letters named. After that, when I met with any boy who I knew could write, I would tell him I could write as well as he. The next word would be, "I don't believe you. Let me see you try it." I would then make the letters which I had been so fortunate as to learn, and ask him to beat that. In this way I got a good many lessons in writing, which it is quite possible I should never have gotten in any other way. During this time, my copy-book was the board fence, brick wall, and pavement; my pen and ink was a lump of chalk. With these, I learned mainly how to write. I then commenced and continued copying the Italics in Webster's Spelling Book, until I could make them all without looking on the book. By this time, my little Master Thomas had gone to school, and learned how to write, and had written over a number of copy-books. These had been brought home, and shown to some of our near neighbors, and then laid aside. My mistress used to go to class meeting at the Wilk Street meetinghouse every Monday afternoon, and leave me to take care of the house. When left thus, I used to spend the time in writing in the spaces left in Master Thomas's copy-book, copying what he had written. I continued to do this until I could write a hand very similar to that of Master Thomas. Thus, after a long, tedious effort for years, I finally succeeded in learning how to write.

CHAPTER VIII

In a very short time after I went to live at Baltimore, my old master's youngest son Richard died; and in about three years and six months after his death, my old master, Captain Anthony, died, leaving only his son, Andrew, and daughter, Lucretia, to share his estate. He died while on a visit to see his daughter at Hillsborough. Cut off thus unexpectedly, he left no will as to the disposal of his property. It was therefore necessary to have a valuation of the property, that it might be equally divided between Mrs. Lucretia and Master Andrew. I was immediately sent for, to be valued with the other property. Here again my feelings rose up in detestation of slavery. I had now a new conception of my degraded condition. Prior to this, I had become, if not insensible to my lot, at least partly so. I left Baltimore with a young heart overborne with sadness, and a soul full of apprehension. I took passage with Captain Rowe, in the schooner Wild Cat, and, after a sail of about twenty-four hours, I found myself near the place of my birth. I had now been absent from it almost, if not quite, five years. I, however, remembered the place very well. I was only about five years old when I left it, to go and live with my old master on Colonel Lloyd's plantation; so that I was now between ten and eleven years old.

We were all ranked together at the valuation. Men and women, old and young, married and single, were ranked with horses, sheep, and swine. There were horses and men, cattle and women, pigs and children, all holding the same rank in the scale of being, and were all subjected to the same narrow examination. Silvery-headed age and sprightly youth, maids and matrons, had to undergo the same indelicate inspection. At this moment, I saw more clearly than ever the brutalizing effects of slavery upon both slave and slaveholder.

After the valuation, then came the division. I have no language to express the high excitement and deep anxiety which were felt among us poor slaves during this time. Our fate for life was now to be decided. We had no more voice in that decision than the brutes among whom we were ranked. A single word from the white men was enough—against all our wishes, prayers, and entreaties—to sunder forever the dearest friends, dearest kindred, and strongest ties known to human beings. In addition to the pain of separation, there was the horrid dread of falling into the hands of Master Andrew. He was known to us all as being a most cruel wretch,—a common drunkard, who had, by his reckless mismanagement and profligate dissipation, already wasted a large portion of his father's property. We all felt that we might as well be sold at once to the Georgia traders, as to pass into his hands; for we knew that that would be our inevitable condition,—a condition held by us all in the utmost horror and dread.

I suffered more anxiety than most of my fellowslaves. I had known what it was to be kindly treated; they had known nothing of the kind. They had seen little or nothing of the world. They were in very deed men and women of sorrow, and acquainted with grief. Their backs had been made familiar with the bloody lash, so that they had become callous; mine was yet tender; for while at Baltimore I got few whippings, and few slaves could boast of a kinder master and mistress than myself; and the thought of passing out of their hands into those of Master Andrew—a man who, but a few days before, to give me a sample of his bloody disposition, took my little brother by the throat, threw him on the ground, and with the heel of his boot stamped upon his head till the blood gushed from his nose and ears—was well calculated to make me anxious as to my fate. After he had committed this savage outrage upon my brother, he turned to me, and said that was the way he meant to serve me one of these days,—meaning, I suppose, when I came into his possession.

Thanks to a kind Providence, I fell to the portion of Mrs. Lucretia, and was sent immediately back to Baltimore, to live again in the family of Master Hugh. Their joy at my return equalled their sorrow at my departure. It was a glad day to me. I had escaped a worse than lion's jaws. I was absent from Baltimore, for the purpose of valuation and division, just about one month, and it seemed to have been six.

Very soon after my return to Baltimore, my mistress, Lucretia, died, leaving her husband and one child, Amanda; and in a very short time after her death, Master Andrew died. Now all the property of my old master, slaves included, was in the hands of strangers,—strangers who had had nothing to do with accumulating it. Not a slave was left free. All remained slaves, from the youngest to the oldest. If any one thing in my experience, more than another, served to deepen my conviction of the infernal character of slavery, and to fill me with unutterable loathing of slaveholders, it was their base ingratitude to my poor old grandmother. She had served my old master faithfully from youth to old age. She had been the source of all his wealth; she had peopled his plantation with slaves; she had become a great grandmother in his service. She had rocked him in infancy, attended him in childhood, served him through life, and at his death wiped from his icy brow the cold death-sweat, and closed his eyes forever. She was nevertheless left a slave—a slave for life—a slave in the hands of strangers; and in their hands she saw her children, her grandchildren, and her great-grandchildren, divided, like so many sheep, without being gratified with the small privilege of a single word, as to their or her own destiny. And, to cap the climax of their base ingratitude and fiendish barbarity, my grandmother, who was now very old, having outlived my old master and all his children, having seen the beginning and end of all of them, and her present owners finding she was of but little value, her frame already racked with the pains of old age, and complete helplessness fast stealing over her once active limbs, they took her to the woods, built her a little hut, put up a little mud-chimney, and then made her welcome to the privilege of supporting herself there in perfect loneliness; thus virtually turning her out to die! If my poor old grandmother now lives, she lives to suffer in utter loneliness; she lives to remember and mourn over the loss of children, the loss of grandchildren, and the loss of great-grandchildren. They are, in the language of the slave's poet, Whittier,—

> "Gone, gone, sold and gone
> To the rice swamp dank and lone,
> Where the slave-whip ceaseless swings,
> Where the noisome insect stings,
> Where the fever-demon strews
> Poison with the falling dews,
> Where the sickly sunbeams glare
> Through the hot and misty air:—
>   Gone, gone, sold and gone
>   To the rice swamp dank and lone,
>   From Virginia hills and waters—
>   Woe is me, my stolen daughters!"

The hearth is desolate. The children, the unconscious children, who once sang and danced in her presence, are gone. She gropes her way, in the darkness of age, for a drink of water. Instead of the voices of her children, she hears by day the moans of the dove, and by night the screams of the hideous owl. All is gloom. The grave is at the door. And now, when weighed down by the pains and aches of old age, when the head inclines to the feet, when the beginning and ending of human existence meet, and helpless infancy and painful old age combine together—at this time, this most needful time, the time for the exercise of that tenderness and affection which children only can exercise towards a declining parent—my poor old grandmother, the devoted mother of twelve children, is left all alone, in yonder little hut, before a few dim embers. She stands—she sits—she staggers—she falls—she groans—she dies—and there are none of her children or grandchildren present, to wipe from her wrinkled brow the cold sweat of death, or to place beneath the sod her fallen remains. Will not a righteous God visit for these things?

In about two years after the death of Mrs. Lucretia, Master Thomas married his second wife. Her name was Rowena Hamilton. She was the eldest daughter of Mr. William Hamilton. Master now lived in St. Michael's. Not long after his marriage, a misunderstanding took place between himself and Master Hugh; and as a means of punishing his brother, he took me from him to live with himself at St. Michael's. Here I underwent another most painful separation. It, however, was not so severe as the one I dreaded at the division of property; for, during this interval, a great change had taken place in Master Hugh and his once kind and affectionate wife. The influence of brandy upon him, and of slavery upon her, had effected a disastrous change in the characters of both; so that, as far as they were concerned, I thought I had little to lose by the change. But it was not to them that I was attached. It was to those little Baltimore boys that I felt the strongest attachment. I had received many good lessons from them, and was still receiving them, and the thought of leaving them was painful indeed. I was leaving, too, without the hope of ever being allowed to return. Master Thomas had said he would never let me return again. The barrier betwixt himself and brother he considered impassable.

I then had to regret that I did not at least make the attempt to carry out my resolution to run away; for the chances of success are tenfold greater from the city than from the country.

I sailed from Baltimore for St. Michael's in the sloop Amanda, Captain Edward Dodson. On my passage, I paid particular attention to the direction which the steamboats took to go to Philadelphia. I found, instead of going down, on reaching North Point they went up the bay, in a north-easterly direction. I deemed this knowledge of the utmost importance. My determination to run away was again revived. I resolved to wait only so long as the offering of a favorable opportunity. When that came, I was determined to be off.

CHAPTER IX

I have now reached a period of my life when I can give dates. I left Baltimore, and went to live with Master Thomas Auld, at St. Michael's, in March, 1832. It was now more than seven years since I lived with him in the family of my old master, on Colonel Lloyd's plantation. We of course were now almost entire strangers to each other. He was to me a new master, and I to him a new slave. I was ignorant of his temper and disposition; he was equally so of mine. A very short time, however, brought us into full acquaintance with each other. I was made acquainted with his wife not less than with himself. They were well matched, being equally mean and cruel. I was now, for the first time during a space of more than seven years, made to feel the painful gnawings of hunger—a something which I had not experienced before since I left Colonel Lloyd's plantation. It went hard enough with me then, when I could look back to no period at which I had enjoyed a sufficiency. It was tenfold harder after living in Master Hugh's family, where I had always had enough to eat, and of that which was good. I have said Master Thomas was a mean man. He was so. Not to give a slave enough to eat, is regarded as the most aggravated development of meanness even among slaveholders. The rule is, no matter how coarse the food, only let there be enough of it. This is the theory; and in the part of Maryland from which I came, it is the general practice,—though there are many exceptions. Master Thomas gave us enough of neither coarse nor fine food. There were four slaves of us in the kitchen—my sister Eliza, my aunt Priscilla, Henny, and myself; and we were allowed less than a half of a bushel of corn-meal per week, and very little else, either in the shape of meat or vegetables. It was not enough for us to subsist upon. We were therefore reduced to the wretched necessity of living at the expense of our neighbors. This we did by begging and stealing, whichever came handy in the time of need, the one being considered as legitimate as the other. A great many times have we poor creatures been nearly perishing with hunger, when food in abundance lay mouldering in the safe and smoke-house, and our pious mistress was aware of the fact; and yet that mistress and her husband would kneel every morning, and pray that God would bless them in basket and store!

Bad as all slaveholders are, we seldom meet one destitute of every element of character commanding respect. My master was one of this rare sort. I do not know of one single noble act ever performed by him. The leading trait in his character was meanness; and if there were any other element in his nature, it was made subject to this. He was mean; and, like most other mean men, he lacked the ability to conceal his meanness. Captain Auld was not born a slaveholder. He had been a poor man, master only of a Bay craft. He came into possession of all his slaves by marriage; and of all men, adopted slaveholders are the worst. He was cruel, but cowardly. He commanded without firmness. In the enforcement of his rules, he was at times rigid, and at times lax. At times, he spoke to his slaves with the firmness of Napoleon and the fury of a demon; at other times, he might well be mistaken for an inquirer who had lost his way. He did nothing of himself. He might have passed for a lion, but for his ears. In all things noble which he attempted, his own meanness shone most conspicuous. His airs, words, and actions, were the airs, words, and actions of born slaveholders, and, being assumed, were awkward enough. He was not even a good imitator. He possessed all the disposition to deceive, but wanted the power. Having no resources within himself, he was compelled to be the copyist of many, and being such, he was forever the victim of inconsistency; and of consequence he was an object of contempt, and was held as such even by his slaves. The luxury of having slaves of his own to wait upon him was something new and unprepared for. He was a slaveholder without the ability to hold slaves. He found himself incapable of managing his slaves either by force, fear, or fraud. We seldom called him "master"; we generally called him "Captain Auld," and were hardly disposed to title him at all. I doubt not that our conduct had much to do with making him appear awkward, and of consequence fretful. Our want of reverence for him must have perplexed him greatly. He wished to have us call him master, but lacked the firmness necessary to command us to do so. His wife used to insist upon our calling him so, but to no purpose. In August, 1832, my master attended a Methodist camp-meeting held in the Bay-side, Talbot county, and there experienced religion. I indulged a faint hope that his conversion would lead him to emancipate his slaves, and that, if he did not do this, it would, at any rate, make him more kind and humane. I was disappointed in both these respects. It neither made him to be humane to his slaves, nor to emancipate them. If it had any effect on his character, it made him more cruel and hateful in all his ways; for I believe him to have been a much worse man after his conversion than before. Prior to his conversion, he relied upon his own depravity to shield and sustain him in his savage barbarity; but after his conversion, he found religious sanction and support for his slaveholding cruelty. He made the greatest pretensions to piety. His house was the house of prayer. He prayed morning, noon, and night. He very soon distinguished himself among his brethren, and was soon made a class-leader and exhorter. His activity in revivals was great, and he proved himself an instrument in the hands of the church in converting many souls. His house was the preachers' home. They used to take great pleasure in coming there to put up; for while he starved us, he stuffed them. We have had three or four preachers there at a time. The names of those who used to come most frequently while I lived there, were Mr. Storks, Mr. Ewery,

Mr. Humphry, and Mr. Hickey. I have also seen Mr. George Cookman at our house. We slaves loved Mr. Cookman. We believed him to be a good man. We thought him instrumental in getting Mr. Samuel Harrison, a very rich slaveholder, to emancipate his slaves; and by some means got the impression that he was laboring to effect the emancipation of all the slaves. When he was at our house, we were sure to be called in to prayers. When the others were there, we were sometimes called in and sometimes not. Mr. Cookman took more notice of us than either of the other ministers. He could not come among us without betraying his sympathy for us, and, stupid as we were, we had the sagacity to see it.

While I lived with my master in St. Michael's, there was a white young man, a Mr. Wilson, who proposed to keep a Sabbath school for the instruction of such slaves as might be disposed to learn to read the New Testament. We met but three times, when Mr. West and Mr. Fairbanks, both class-leaders, with many others, came upon us with sticks and other missiles, drove us off, and forbade us to meet again. Thus ended our little Sabbath school in the pious town of St. Michael's.

I have said my master found religious sanction for his cruelty. As an example, I will state one of many facts going to prove the charge. I have seen him tie up a lame young woman, and whip her with a heavy cowskin upon her naked shoulders, causing the warm red blood to drip; and, in justification of the bloody deed, he would quote this passage of Scripture—"He that knoweth his master's will, and doeth it not, shall be beaten with many stripes."

Master would keep this lacerated young woman tied up in this horrid situation four or five hours at a time. I have known him to tie her up early in the morning, and whip her before breakfast; leave her, go to his store, return at dinner, and whip her again, cutting her in the places already made raw with his cruel lash. The secret of master's cruelty toward "Henny" is found in the fact of her being almost helpless. When quite a child, she fell into the fire, and burned herself horribly. Her hands were so burnt that she never got the use of them. She could do very little but bear heavy burdens. She was to master a bill of expense; and as he was a mean man, she was a constant offence to him. He seemed desirous of getting the poor girl out of existence. He gave her away once to his sister; but, being a poor gift, she was not disposed to keep her. Finally, my benevolent master, to use his own words, "set her adrift to take care of herself." Here was a recently-converted man, holding on upon the mother, and at the same time turning out her helpless child, to starve and die! Master Thomas was one of the many pious slaveholders who hold slaves for the very charitable purpose of taking care of them.

My master and myself had quite a number of differences. He found me unsuitable to his purpose. My city life, he said, had had a very pernicious effect upon me. It had almost ruined me for every good purpose, and fitted me for every thing which was bad. One of my greatest faults was that of letting his horse run away, and go down to his father-in-law's farm, which was about five miles from St. Michael's. I would then have to go after it. My reason for this kind of carelessness, or carefulness, was, that I could always get something to eat when I went there. Master William Hamilton, my master's father-in-law, always gave his slaves enough to eat. I never left there hungry, no matter how great the need of my speedy return. Master Thomas at length said he would stand it no longer. I had lived with him nine months, during which time he had given me a number of severe whippings, all to no good purpose. He resolved to put me out, as he said, to be broken; and, for this purpose, he let me for one year to a man named Edward Covey. Mr. Covey was a poor man, a farm-renter. He rented the place upon which he lived, as also the hands with which he tilled it. Mr. Covey had acquired a very high reputation for breaking young slaves, and this reputation was of immense value to him. It enabled him to get his farm tilled with much less expense to himself than he could have had it done without such a reputation. Some slaveholders thought it not much loss to allow Mr. Covey to have their slaves one year, for the sake of the training to which they were subjected, without any other compensation. He could hire young help with great ease, in consequence of this reputation. Added to the natural good qualities of Mr. Covey, he was a professor of religion—a pious soul—a member and a class-leader in the Methodist church. All of this added weight to his reputation as a "nigger-breaker." I was aware of all the facts, having been made acquainted with them by a young man who had lived there. I nevertheless made the change gladly; for I was sure of getting enough to eat, which is not the smallest consideration to a hungry man.

CHAPTER X

I left Master Thomas's house, and went to live with Mr. Covey, on the 1st of January, 1833. I was now, for the first time in my life, a field hand. In my new employment, I found myself even more awkward than a country boy appeared to be in a large city. I had been at my new home but one week before Mr. Covey gave me a very severe whipping, cutting my back, causing the blood to run, and raising ridges on my flesh as large as my little finger. The details of this affair are as follows: Mr. Covey sent me, very early in the morning of one of our coldest days in the month of January, to the woods, to get a load of wood. He gave me a team of unbroken oxen. He told me which was the in-hand ox, and which the off-hand one. He then tied the end of a large rope around the horns of the in-hand ox, and gave me the other end of it, and told me, if the oxen started to run, that I must hold on upon the rope. I had never driven oxen before, and of course I was very awkward. I, however, succeeded in getting to the edge of the woods with little difficulty; but I had got a very few rods into the woods, when the oxen took fright, and started full tilt, carrying the cart against trees, and over stumps, in the most frightful manner. I expected every moment that my brains would be dashed out against the trees. After running thus for a considerable distance, they finally upset the cart, dashing it with great force against a tree, and threw themselves into a dense thicket. How I escaped death, I do not know. There I was, entirely alone, in a thick wood, in a place new to me. My cart was upset and shattered, my oxen were entangled among the young trees, and there was none to help me. After a long spell of effort, I succeeded in getting my cart righted, my oxen disentangled, and again yoked to the cart. I now proceeded with my team to the place where I had, the day before, been chopping wood, and loaded my cart pretty heavily, thinking in this way to tame my oxen. I then proceeded on my way home. I had now consumed one half of the day. I got out of the woods safely, and now felt out of danger. I stopped my oxen to open the woods gate; and just as I did so, before I could get hold of my ox-rope, the oxen again started, rushed through the gate, catching it between the wheel and the body of the cart, tearing it to pieces, and coming within a few inches of crushing me against the gate-post. Thus twice, in one short day, I escaped death by the merest chance. On my return, I told Mr. Covey what had happened, and how it happened. He ordered me to return to the woods again immediately. I did so, and he followed on after me. Just as I got into the woods, he came up and told me to stop my cart, and that he would teach me how to trifle away my time, and break gates. He then went to a large gum-tree, and with his axe cut three large switches, and, after trimming them up neatly with his pocket-knife, he ordered me to take off my clothes. I made him no answer, but stood with my clothes on. He repeated his order. I still made him no answer, nor did I move to strip myself. Upon this he rushed at me with the fierceness of a tiger, tore off my clothes, and lashed me till he had worn out his switches, cutting me so savagely as to leave the marks visible for a long time after. This whipping was the first of a number just like it, and for similar offences.

I lived with Mr. Covey one year. During the first six months, of that year, scarce a week passed without his whipping me. I was seldom free from a sore back. My awkwardness was almost always his excuse for whipping me. We were worked fully up to the point of endurance.

Long before day we were up, our horses fed, and by the first approach of day we were off to the field with our hoes and ploughing teams. Mr. Covey gave us enough to eat, but scarce time to eat it. We were often less than five minutes taking our meals. We were often in the field from the first approach of day till its last lingering ray had left us; and at saving-fodder time, midnight often caught us in the field binding blades.

Covey would be out with us. The way he used to stand it, was this. He would spend the most of his afternoons in bed. He would then come out fresh in the evening, ready to urge us on with his words, example, and frequently with the whip. Mr. Covey was one of the few slaveholders who could and did work with his hands. He was a hard-working man. He knew by himself just what a man or a boy could do. There was no deceiving him. His work went on in his absence almost as well as in his presence; and he had the faculty of making us feel that he was ever present with us. This he did by surprising us. He seldom approached the spot where we were at work openly, if he could do it secretly. He always aimed at taking us by surprise. Such was his cunning, that we used to call him, among ourselves, "the snake." When we were at work in the cornfield, he would sometimes crawl on his hands and knees to avoid detection, and all at once he would rise nearly in our midst, and scream out, "Ha, ha! Come, come! Dash on, dash on!" This being his mode of attack, it was never safe to stop a single minute. His comings were like a thief in the night. He appeared to us as being ever at hand. He was under every tree, behind every stump, in every bush, and at every window, on the plantation. He would sometimes mount his horse, as if bound to St. Michael's, a distance of seven miles, and in half an hour afterwards you would see him coiled up in the corner of the wood-fence, watching every motion of the slaves. He would, for this purpose, leave his horse tied up in the woods. Again, he would sometimes walk up to us, and give us orders as though he was upon the point of starting on a long journey, turn his back upon us, and make as though he was going to the house to get ready; and, before he would get half way thither, he would turn short and crawl into a fence-corner, or behind some tree, and there watch us till the going down of the sun.

Mr. Covey's *forte* consisted in his power to deceive. His life was devoted to planning and perpetrating the grossest deceptions. Every thing he possessed in the shape of learning or religion, he made conform to his disposition to deceive. He seemed to think himself equal to deceiving the Almighty. He would make a short prayer in the morning, and a long prayer at night; and, strange as it may seem, few men would at times appear more devotional than he. The exercises of his family devotions were always commenced with singing; and, as he was a very poor singer himself, the duty of raising the hymn generally came upon me. He would read his hymn, and nod at me to commence. I would at times do so; at others, I would not. My non-compliance would almost always produce much confusion. To show himself independent of me, he would start and stagger through with his hymn in the most discordant manner. In this state of mind, he prayed with more than ordinary spirit. Poor man! such was his disposition, and success at deceiving, I do verily believe that he sometimes deceived himself into the solemn belief, that he was a sincere worshipper of the most high God; and this, too, at a time when he may be said to have been guilty of compelling his woman slave to commit the sin of adultery. The facts in the case are these: Mr. Covey was a poor man; he was just commencing in life; he was only able to buy one slave; and, shocking as is the fact, he bought her, as he said, for a *breeder*. This woman was named Caroline. Mr. Covey bought her from Mr. Thomas Lowe, about six miles from St. Michael's. She was a large, able-bodied woman, about twenty years old. She had already given birth to one child, which proved her to be just what he wanted. After buying her, he hired a married man of Mr. Samuel Harrison, to live with him one year; and him he used to fasten up with her every night! The result was, that, at the end of the year, the miserable woman gave birth to twins. At this result Mr. Covey seemed to be highly pleased, both with the man and the wretched woman. Such was his joy, and that of his wife, that nothing they could do for Caroline during her confinement was too good, or too hard, to be done. The children were regarded as being quite an addition to his wealth.

If at any one time of my life more than another, I was made to drink the bitterest dregs of slavery, that time was during the first six months of my stay with Mr. Covey. We were worked in all weathers. It was never too hot or too cold; it could never rain, blow, hail, or snow, too hard for us to work in the field. Work, work, work, was scarcely more the order of the day than of the night. The longest days were too short for him, and the shortest nights too long for him. I was somewhat unmanageable when I first went there, but a few months of this discipline tamed me. Mr. Covey succeeded in breaking me. I was broken in body, soul, and spirit. My natural elasticity was crushed, my intellect languished, the disposition to read departed, the cheerful spark that lingered about my eye died; the dark night of slavery closed in upon me; and behold a man transformed into a brute!

Sunday was my only leisure time. I spent this in a sort of beast-like stupor, between sleep and wake, under some large tree. At times I would rise up, a flash of energetic freedom would dart through my soul, accompanied with a faint beam of hope, that flickered for a moment, and then vanished. I sank down again, mourning over my wretched condition. I was sometimes prompted to take my life, and that of Covey, but was prevented by a combination of hope and fear. My sufferings on this plantation seem now like a dream rather than a stern reality.

Our house stood within a few rods of the Chesapeake Bay, whose broad bosom was ever white with sails from every quarter of the habitable globe. Those beautiful vessels, robed in purest white, so delightful to the eye of freemen, were to me so many shrouded ghosts, to terrify and torment me with thoughts of my wretched condition. I have often, in the deep stillness of a summer's Sabbath, stood all alone upon the lofty banks of that noble bay, and traced, with saddened heart and tearful eye, the countless number of sails moving off to the mighty ocean. The sight of these always affected me powerfully. My thoughts would compel utterance; and there, with no audience but the Almighty, I would pour out my soul's complaint, in my rude way, with an apostrophe to the moving multitude of ships:—

"You are loosed from your moorings, and are free; I am fast in my chains, and am a slave! You move merrily before the gentle gale, and I sadly before the bloody whip! You are freedom's swift-winged angels, that fly round the world; I am confined in bands of iron! O that I were free! O, that I were on one of your gallant decks, and under your protecting wing! Alas! betwixt me and you, the turbid waters roll. Go on, go on. O that I could also go! Could I but swim! If I could fly! O, why was I born a man, of whom to make a brute! The glad ship is gone; she hides in the dim distance. I am left in the hottest hell of unending slavery. O God, save me! God, deliver me! Let me be free! Is there any God? Why am I a slave? I will run away. I will not stand it. Get caught, or get clear, I'll try it. I had as well die with ague as the fever. I have only one life to lose. I had as well be killed running as die standing. Only think of it; one hundred miles straight north, and I am free! Try it? Yes! God helping me, I will. It cannot be that I shall live and die a slave. I will take to the water. This very bay shall bear me into freedom. The steamboats steered in a north-east course from North Point. I will do the same; and when I get to the head of the bay, I will turn my canoe adrift, and walk straight through Delaware into Pennsylvania. When I get there, I shall not be required to have a pass; I can travel without being disturbed. Let but the first opportunity offer, and, come what will, I am off. Meanwhile, I will try to bear up under the yoke. I am not the only slave in the world. Why should I fret? I can bear as much as any of them. Besides, I am but a boy, and all boys are bound to some one. It may be that my misery in slavery will only increase my happiness when I get free. There is a better day coming."

Thus I used to think, and thus I used to speak to myself; goaded almost to madness at one moment, and at the next reconciling myself to my wretched lot.

I have already intimated that my condition was much worse, during the first six months of my stay at Mr. Covey's, than in the last six. The circumstances leading to the change in Mr. Covey's course toward me form an epoch in my humble history. You have seen how a man was made a slave; you shall see how a slave was made a man. On one of the hottest days of the month of August, 1833, Bill Smith, William Hughes, a slave named Eli, and myself, were engaged in fanning wheat. Hughes was clearing the fanned wheat from before the fan, Eli was turning, Smith was feeding, and I was carrying wheat to the fan. The work was simple, requiring strength rather than intellect; yet, to one entirely unused to such work, it came very hard. About three o'clock of that day, I broke down; my strength failed me; I was seized with a violent aching of the head, attended with extreme dizziness; I trembled in every limb. Finding what was coming, I nerved myself up, feeling it would never do to stop work. I stood as long as I could stagger to the hopper with grain. When I could stand no longer, I fell, and felt as if held down by an immense weight. The fan of course stopped; every one had his own work to do; and no one could do the work of the other, and have his own go on at the same time.

Mr. Covey was at the house, about one hundred yards from the treading-yard where we were fanning. On hearing the fan stop, he left immediately, and came to the spot where we were. He hastily inquired what the matter was. Bill answered that I was sick, and there was no one to bring wheat to the fan. I had by this time crawled away under the side of the post and rail-fence by which the yard was enclosed, hoping to find relief by getting out of the sun. He then asked where I was. He was told by one of the hands. He came to the spot, and, after looking at me awhile, asked me what was the matter. I told him as well as I could, for I scarce had strength to speak. He then gave me a savage kick in the side, and told me to get up. I tried to do so, but fell back in the attempt. He gave me another kick, and again told me to rise. I again tried, and succeeded in gaining my feet; but, stooping to get the tub with which I was feeding the fan, I again staggered and fell. While down in this situation, Mr. Covey took up the hickory slat with which Hughes had been striking off the half-bushel measure, and with it gave me a heavy blow upon the head, making a large wound, and the blood ran freely; and with this again told me to get up. I made no effort to comply, having now made up my mind to let him do his worst. In a short time after receiving this blow, my head grew better. Mr. Covey had now left me to my fate. At this moment I resolved, for the first time, to go to my master, enter a complaint, and ask his protection. In order to [do] this, I must that afternoon walk seven miles; and this, under the circumstances, was truly a severe undertaking. I was exceedingly feeble; made so as much by the kicks and blows which I received, as by the severe fit of sickness to which I had been subjected. I, however, watched my chance, while Covey was looking in an opposite direction, and started for St. Michael's. I succeeded in getting a considerable distance on my way to the woods, when Covey discovered me, and called after me to come back, threatening what he would do if I did not come. I disregarded both his calls and his threats, and made my way to the woods as fast as my feeble state would allow; and thinking I might be overhauled by him if I kept the road, I walked through the woods, keeping far enough from the road to avoid detection, and near enough to prevent losing my way. I had not gone far before my little strength again failed me. I could go no farther. I fell down, and lay for a considerable time. The blood was yet oozing from the wound on my head. For a time I thought I should bleed to death; and think now that I should have done so, but that the blood so matted my hair as to stop the wound. After lying there about three quarters of an hour, I nerved myself up again, and started on my way, through bogs and briers, barefooted and bareheaded, tearing my feet sometimes at nearly every step; and after a journey of about seven miles, occupying some five hours to perform it, I arrived at master's store. I then presented an appearance enough to affect any but a heart of iron. From the crown of my head to my feet, I was covered with blood. My hair was all clotted with dust and blood; my shirt was stiff with blood. My legs and feet were torn in sundry places with briers and thorns, and were also covered with blood. I suppose I looked like a man who had escaped a den of wild beasts, and barely escaped them. In this state I appeared before my master, humbly entreating him to interpose his authority for my protection. I told him all the circumstances as well as I could, and it seemed, as I spoke, at times to affect him. He would then walk the floor, and seek to justify Covey by saying he expected I deserved it. He asked me what I wanted. I told him, to let me get a new home; that as sure as I lived with Mr. Covey again, I should live with but to die with him; that Covey would surely kill me; he was in a fair way for it. Master Thomas ridiculed the idea that there was any danger of Mr. Covey's killing me, and said that he knew Mr. Covey; that he was a good man, and that he could not think of taking me from him; that, should he do so, he would lose the whole year's wages; that I belonged to Mr. Covey for one year, and that I must go back to him, come what might; and that I must not trouble him with any more stories, or that he would himself *get hold of me*. After threatening me thus, he gave me a very large dose of salts, telling me that I might remain in St. Michael's that night, (it being quite late,) but that I must be off back to Mr. Covey's early in the morning; and that if I did not, he would *get hold of me*, which meant that he would whip me. I remained all night, and, according to his orders, I started off to Covey's in the morning, (Saturday morning,) wearied in body and broken in spirit. I got no supper that night, or breakfast that morning. I reached Covey's about nine o'clock; and just as I was getting over the fence that divided Mrs. Kemp's fields from ours, out ran Covey with his cowskin, to give me another whipping. Before he could reach me, I succeeded in getting to the cornfield; and as the corn was very high, it afforded me the means of hiding. He seemed very angry, and searched for me a long time. My behavior was altogether unaccountable. He finally gave up the chase, thinking, I suppose, that I must come home for something to eat; he would give himself no further trouble in looking for me. I spent that day mostly in the woods, having the alternative before me,—to go home and be whipped to death, or stay in the woods and be starved to death. That night, I fell in with Sandy Jenkins, a slave with whom I was somewhat acquainted. Sandy had a free wife who lived about four miles from Mr. Covey's; and it being Saturday, he was on his way to see her. I told him my circumstances, and he very kindly invited me to go home with him. I went home with him, and talked this whole matter over, and got his advice as to what course it was best for me to pursue. I found Sandy an old adviser. He told me, with great solemnity, I must go back to Covey;

but that before I went, I must go with him into another part of the woods, where there was a certain *root*, which, if I would take some of it with me, carrying it *always on my right side*, would render it impossible for Mr. Covey, or any other white man, to whip me. He said he had carried it for years; and since he had done so, he had never received a blow, and never expected to while he carried it. I at first rejected the idea, that the simple carrying of a root in my pocket would have any such effect as he had said, and was not disposed to take it; but Sandy impressed the necessity with much earnestness, telling me it could do no harm, if it did no good. To please him, I at length took the root, and, according to his direction, carried it upon my right side. This was Sunday morning. I immediately started for home; and upon entering the yard gate, out came Mr. Covey on his way to meeting. He spoke to me very kindly, bade me drive the pigs from a lot near by, and passed on towards the church. Now, this singular conduct of Mr. Covey really made me begin to think that there was something in the *root* which Sandy had given me; and had it been on any other day than Sunday, I could have attributed the conduct to no other cause than the influence of that root; and as it was, I was half inclined to think the *root* to be something more than I at first had taken it to be. All went well till Monday morning. On this morning, the virtue of the *root* was fully tested. Long before daylight, I was called to go and rub, curry, and feed, the horses. I obeyed, and was glad to obey. But whilst thus engaged, whilst in the act of throwing down some blades from the loft, Mr. Covey entered the stable with a long rope; and just as I was half out of the loft, he caught hold of my legs, and was about tying me. As soon as I found what he was up to, I gave a sudden spring, and as I did so, he holding to my legs, I was brought sprawling on the stable floor. Mr. Covey seemed now to think he had me, and could do what he pleased; but at this moment—from whence came the spirit I don't know—I resolved to fight; and, suiting my action to the resolution, I seized Covey hard by the throat; and as I did so, I rose. He held on to me, and I to him. My resistance was so entirely unexpected, that Covey seemed taken all aback. He trembled like a leaf. This gave me assurance, and I held him uneasy, causing the blood to run where I touched him with the ends of my fingers. Mr. Covey soon called out to Hughes for help. Hughes came, and, while Covey held me, attempted to tie my right hand. While he was in the act of doing so, I watched my chance, and gave him a heavy kick close under the ribs. This kick fairly sickened Hughes, so that he left me in the hands of Mr. Covey. This kick had the effect of not only weakening Hughes, but Covey also. When he saw Hughes bending over with pain, his courage quailed. He asked me if I meant to persist in my resistance. I told him I did, come what might; that he had used me like a brute for six months, and that I was determined to be used so no longer. With that, he strove to drag me to a stick that was lying just out of the stable door. He meant to knock me down. But just as he was leaning over to get the stick, I seized him with both hands by the collar, and brought him by a sudden snatch to the ground. By this time, Bill came. Covey called upon him for assistance. Bill wanted to know what he could do. Covey said, "Take hold of him, take hold of him!" Bill said his master hired him out to work, and not to help to whip me; so he left Covey and myself to fight our own battle out. We were at it for nearly two hours. Covey at length let me go, puffing and blowing at a great rate, saying that if I had not resisted, he would not have whipped me half so much. The truth was, that he had not whipped me at all. I considered him as getting entirely the worst end of the bargain; for he had drawn no blood from me, but I had from him. The whole six months afterwards, that I spent with Mr. Covey, he never laid the weight of his finger upon me in anger. He would occasionally say, he didn't want to get hold of me again. "No," thought I, "you need not; for you will come off worse than you did before."

This battle with Mr. Covey was the turning-point in my career as a slave. It rekindled the few expiring embers of freedom, and revived within me a sense of my own manhood. It recalled the departed self-confidence, and inspired me again with a determination to be free. The gratification afforded by the triumph was a full compensation for whatever else might follow, even death itself. He only can understand the deep satisfaction which I experienced, who has himself repelled by force the bloody arm of slavery. I felt as I never felt before. It was a glorious resurrection, from the tomb of slavery, to the heaven of freedom. My long-crushed spirit rose, cowardice departed, bold defiance took its place; and I now resolved that, however long I might remain a slave in form, the day had passed forever when I could be a slave in fact. I did not hesitate to let it be known of me, that the white man who expected to succeed in whipping, must also succeed in killing me.

From this time I was never again what might be called fairly whipped, though I remained a slave four years afterwards. I had several fights, but was never whipped.

It was for a long time a matter of surprise to me why Mr. Covey did not immediately have me taken by the constable to the whipping-post, and there regularly whipped for the crime of raising my hand against a white man in defence of myself. And the only explanation I can now think of does not entirely satisfy me; but such as it is, I will give it. Mr. Covey enjoyed the most unbounded reputation for being a first-rate overseer and negro-breaker. It was of considerable importance to him. That reputation was at stake; and had he sent me—a boy about sixteen years old—to the public whipping-post, his reputation would have been lost; so, to save his reputation, he suffered me to go unpunished.

My term of actual service to Mr. Edward Covey ended on Christmas day, 1833. The days between Christmas and New Year's day are allowed as holidays; and, accordingly, we were not required to perform any labor, more than to feed and take care of the stock. This time we regarded as our own, by the grace of our masters; and we therefore used or abused it nearly as we pleased. Those of us who had families at a distance, were generally allowed to spend the whole six days in their society. This time, however, was spent in various ways. The staid, sober, thinking and industrious ones of our number would employ themselves in making cornbrooms, mats, horse-collars, and baskets; and another class of us would spend the time in hunting opossums, hares, and coons. But by far the larger part engaged in such sports and merriments as playing ball, wrestling, running foot-races, fiddling, dancing, and drinking whisky; and this latter mode of spending the time was by far the most agreeable to the feelings of our masters. A slave who would work during the holidays was considered by our masters as scarcely deserving them. He was regarded as one who rejected the favor of his master. It was deemed a disgrace not to get drunk at Christmas; and he was regarded as lazy indeed, who had not provided himself with the necessary means, during the year, to get whisky enough to last him through Christmas.

From what I know of the effect of these holidays upon the slave, I believe them to be among the most effective means in the hands of the slaveholder in keeping down the spirit of insurrection. Were the slaveholders at once to abandon this practice, I have not the slightest doubt it would lead to an immediate insurrection among the slaves. These holidays serve as conductors, or safety-valves, to carry off the rebellious spirit of enslaved humanity. But for these, the slave would be forced up to the wildest desperation; and woe betide the slaveholder, the day he ventures to remove or hinder the operation of those conductors! I warn him that, in such an event, a spirit will go forth in their midst, more to be dreaded than the most appalling earthquake.

The holidays are part and parcel of the gross fraud, wrong, and inhumanity of slavery. They are professedly a custom established by the benevolence of the slaveholders; but I undertake to say, it is the result of selfishness, and one of the grossest frauds committed upon the downtrodden slave. They do not give the slaves this time because they would not like to have their work during its continuance, but because they know it would be unsafe to deprive them of it. This will be seen by the fact, that the slaveholders like to have their slaves spend those days just in such a manner as to make them as glad of their ending as of their beginning. Their object seems to be, to disgust their slaves with freedom, by plunging them into the lowest depths of dissipation. For instance, the slaveholders not only like to see the slave drink of his own accord, but will adopt various plans to make him drunk. One plan is, to make bets on their slaves, as to who can drink the most whisky without getting drunk; and in this way they succeed in getting whole multitudes to drink to excess. Thus, when the slave asks for virtuous freedom, the cunning slaveholder, knowing his ignorance, cheats him with a dose of vicious dissipation, artfully labelled with the name of liberty. The most of us used to drink it down, and the result was just what might be supposed: many of us were led to think that there was little to choose between liberty and slavery. We felt, and very properly too, that we had almost as well be slaves to man as to rum. So, when the holidays ended, we staggered up from the filth of our wallowing, took a long breath, and marched to the field,—feeling, upon the whole, rather glad to go, from what our master had deceived us into a belief was freedom, back to the arms of slavery.

I have said that this mode of treatment is a part of the whole system of fraud and inhumanity of slavery. It is so. The mode here adopted to disgust the slave with freedom, by allowing him to see only the abuse of it, is carried out in other things. For instance, a slave loves molasses; he steals some. His master, in many cases, goes off to town, and buys a large quantity; he returns, takes his whip, and commands the slave to eat the molasses, until the poor fellow is made sick at the very mention of it. The same mode is sometimes adopted to make the slaves refrain from asking for more food than their regular allowance. A slave runs through his allowance, and applies for more. His master is enraged at him; but, not willing to send him off without food, gives him more than is necessary, and compels him to eat it within a given time. Then, if he complains that he cannot eat it, he is said to be satisfied neither full nor fasting, and is whipped for being hard to please! I have an abundance of such illustrations of the same principle, drawn from my own observation, but think the cases I have cited sufficient. The practice is a very common one.

On the first of January, 1834, I left Mr. Covey, and went to live with Mr. William Freeland, who lived about three miles from St. Michael's. I soon found Mr. Freeland a very different man from Mr. Covey. Though not rich, he was what would be called an educated southern gentleman. Mr. Covey, as I have shown, was a well-trained negro-breaker and slave-driver. The former (slaveholder though he was) seemed to possess some regard for honor, some reverence for justice, and some respect for humanity. The latter seemed totally insensible to all such sentiments. Mr. Freeland had many of the faults peculiar to slaveholders, such as being very passionate and fretful; but I must do him the justice to say, that he was exceedingly free from those degrading vices to which Mr. Covey was constantly addicted. The one was open and frank, and we always knew where to find him. The other was a most artful deceiver, and could be understood only by such as were skilful enough to detect his cunningly-devised frauds. Another advantage I gained in my new master was, he made no pretensions to, or profession of, religion; and this, in my opinion, was truly a great advantage. I assert most unhesitatingly, that the religion of the south is a mere covering for the most horrid crimes,—a justifier of the most appalling barbarity,—a sanctifier of the most hateful frauds,—and a dark shelter under, which the darkest, foulest, grossest, and most infernal deeds of slaveholders find the strongest protection. Were I to be again reduced to the chains of slavery, next to that enslavement, I should regard being the slave of a religious master the greatest calamity that could befall me. For of all slaveholders with whom I have ever met, religious slaveholders are the worst. I have ever found them the meanest and basest, the most cruel and cowardly, of all others. It was my unhappy lot not only to belong to a religious slaveholder, but to live in a community of such religionists. Very near Mr. Freeland lived the Rev. Daniel Weeden, and in the same neighborhood lived the Rev. Rigby Hopkins. These were members and ministers in the Reformed Methodist Church. Mr. Weeden owned, among others, a woman slave, whose name I have forgotten. This woman's back, for weeks, was kept literally raw, made so by the lash of this merciless, *religious* wretch. He used to hire hands. His maxim was, Behave well or behave ill, it is the duty of a master occasionally to whip a slave, to remind him of his master's authority. Such was his theory, and such his practice.

Mr. Hopkins was even worse than Mr. Weeden. His chief boast was his ability to manage slaves. The peculiar feature of his government was that of whipping slaves in advance of deserving it. He always managed to have one or more of his slaves to whip every Monday morning. He did this to alarm their fears, and strike terror into those who escaped. His plan was to whip for the smallest offences, to prevent the commission of large ones. Mr. Hopkins could always find some excuse for whipping a slave. It would astonish one, unaccustomed to a slave-holding life, to see with what wonderful ease a slave-holder can find things, of which to make occasion to whip a slave. A mere look, word, or motion,—a mistake, accident, or want of power,—are all matters for which a slave may be whipped at any time. Does a slave look dissatisfied? It is said, he has the devil in him, and it must be whipped out. Does he speak loudly when spoken to by his master? Then he is getting high-minded, and should be taken down a button-hole lower. Does he forget to pull off his hat at the approach of a white person? Then he is wanting in reverence, and should be whipped for it. Does he ever venture to vindicate his conduct, when censured for it? Then he is guilty of impudence,—one of the greatest crimes of which a slave can be guilty. Does he ever venture to suggest a different mode of doing things from that pointed out by his master? He is indeed presumptuous, and getting above himself; and nothing less than a flogging will do for him. Does he, while ploughing, break a plough,—or, while hoeing, break a hoe? It is owing to his carelessness, and for it a slave must always be whipped. Mr. Hopkins could always find something of this sort to justify the use of the lash, and he seldom failed to embrace such opportunities. There was not a man in the whole county, with whom the slaves who had the getting their own home, would not prefer to live, rather than with this Rev. Mr. Hopkins. And yet there was not a man any where round, who made higher professions of religion, or was more active in revivals,—more attentive to the class, love-feast, prayer and preaching meetings, or more devotional in his family,—that prayed earlier, later, louder, and longer,—than this same reverend slave-driver, Rigby Hopkins.

But to return to Mr. Freeland, and to my experience while in his employment. He, like Mr. Covey, gave us enough to eat; but, unlike Mr. Covey, he also gave us sufficient time to take our meals. He worked us hard, but always between sunrise and sunset. He required a good deal of work to be done, but gave us good tools with which to work. His farm was large, but he employed hands enough to work it, and with ease, compared with many of his neighbors. My treatment, while in his employment, was heavenly, compared with what I experienced at the hands of Mr. Edward Covey.

Mr. Freeland was himself the owner of but two slaves. Their names were Henry Harris and John Harris. The rest of his hands he hired. These consisted of myself, Sandy Jenkins,* and Handy Caldwell. Henry and John were quite intelligent, and in a very little while after I went there, I succeeded in creating in them a strong desire to learn how to read. This desire soon sprang up in the others also. They very soon mustered up some old spelling-books, and nothing would do but that I must keep a Sabbath school. I agreed to do so, and accordingly devoted my Sundays to teaching these my loved fellow-slaves how to read. Neither of them knew his letters when I went there. Some of the slaves of the neighboring farms found what was going on, and also availed themselves of this little opportunity to learn to read. It was understood, among all who came, that there must be as little display about it as possible. It was necessary to keep our religious masters at St. Michael's unacquainted with the fact, that, instead of spending the Sabbath in wrestling, boxing, and drinking whisky, we were trying to learn how to read the will of God; for they had much rather see us engaged in those degrading sports, than to see us behaving like intellectual, moral, and accountable beings. My blood boils as I think of the bloody manner in which Messrs. Wright Fairbanks and Garrison West, both class-leaders, in connection with many others, rushed in upon us with sticks and stones, and broke up our virtuous little Sabbath school, at St. Michael's—all calling themselves Christians! humble followers of the Lord Jesus Christ! But I am again digressing.

I held my Sabbath school at the house of a free colored man, whose name I deem it imprudent to mention; for should it be known, it might embarrass him greatly,

*This is the same man who gave me the roots to prevent my being whipped by Mr. Covey. He was "a clever soul." We used frequently to talk about the fight with Covey, and as often as we did so, he would claim my success as the result of the roots which he gave me. This superstition is very common among the more ignorant slaves. A slave seldom dies but that his death is attributed to trickery.

though the crime of holding the school was committed ten years ago. I had at one time over forty scholars, and those of the right sort, ardently desiring to learn. They were of all ages, though mostly men and women. I look back to those Sundays with an amount of pleasure not to be expressed. They were great days to my soul. The work of instructing my dear fellow-slaves was the sweetest engagement with which I was ever blessed. We loved each other, and to leave them at the close of the Sabbath was a severe cross indeed. When I think that these precious souls are to-day shut up in the prison-house of slavery, my feelings overcome me, and I am almost ready to ask, "Does a righteous God govern the universe? and for what does he hold the thunders in his right hand, if not to smite the oppressor, and deliver the spoiled out of the hand of the spoiler?" These dear souls came not to Sabbath school because it was popular to do so, nor did I teach them because it was reputable to be thus engaged. Every moment they spent in that school, they were liable to be taken up, and given thirty-nine lashes. They came because they wished to learn. Their minds had been starved by their cruel masters. They had been shut up in mental darkness. I taught them, because it was the delight of my soul to be doing something that looked like bettering the condition of my race. I kept up my school nearly the whole year I lived with Mr. Freeland; and, beside my Sabbath school, I devoted three evenings in the week, during the winter, to teaching the slaves at home. And I have the happiness to know, that several of those who came to Sabbath school learned how to read; and that one, at least, is now free through my agency.

The year passed off smoothly. It seemed only about half as long as the year which preceded it. I went through it without receiving a single blow. I will give Mr. Freeland the credit of being the best master I ever had, *till I became my own master*. For the ease with which I passed the year, I was, however, somewhat indebted to the society of my fellow-slaves. They were noble souls; they not only possessed loving hearts, but brave ones. We were linked and interlinked with each other. I loved them with a love stronger than any thing I have experienced since. It is sometimes said that we slaves do not love and confide in each other. In answer to this assertion, I can say, I never loved any or confided in any people more than my fellow-slaves, and especially those with whom I lived at Mr. Freeland's. I believe we would have died for each other. We never undertook to do any thing, of any importance, without a mutual consultation. We never moved separately. We were one; and as much so by our tempers and dispositions, as by the mutual hardships to which we were necessarily subjected by our condition as slaves.

At the close of the year 1834, Mr. Freeland again hired me of my master, for the year 1835. But, by this time, I began to want to live *upon free land* as well as *with Freeland;* and I was no longer content, therefore, to live with him or any other slaveholder. I began, with the commencement of the year, to prepare myself for a final struggle, which should decide my fate one way or the other. My tendency was upward. I was fast approaching manhood, and year after year had passed, and I was still a slave. These thoughts roused me—I must do something. I therefore resolved that 1835 should not pass without witnessing an attempt, on my part, to secure my liberty. But I was not willing to cherish this determination alone. My fellow-slaves were dear to me. I was anxious to have them participate with me in this, my life-giving determination. I therefore, though with great prudence, commenced early to ascertain their views and feelings in regard to their condition, and to imbue their minds with thoughts of freedom. I bent myself to devising ways and means for our escape, and meanwhile strove, on all fitting occasions, to impress them with the gross fraud and inhumanity of slavery. I went first to Henry, next to John, then to the others. I found, in them all, warm hearts and noble spirits. They were ready to hear, and ready to act when a feasible plan should be proposed. This was what I wanted. I talked to them of our want of manhood, if we submitted to our enslavement without at least one noble effort to be free. We met often, and consulted frequently, and told our hopes and fears, recounted the difficulties, real and imagined, which we should be called on to meet. At times we were almost disposed to give up, and try to content ourselves with our wretched lot; at others, we were firm and unbending in our determination to go. Whenever we suggested any plan, there was shrinking—the odds were fearful. Our path was beset with the greatest obstacles; and if we succeeded in gaining the end of it, our right to be free was yet questionable—we were yet liable to be returned to bondage. We could see no spot, this side of the ocean, where we could be free. We knew nothing about Canada. Our knowledge of the north did not extend farther than New York; and to go there, and be forever harassed with the frightful liability of being returned to slavery—with the certainty of being treated tenfold worse than before—the thought was truly a horrible one, and one which it was not easy to overcome. The case sometimes stood thus: At every gate through which we were to pass, we saw a watchman—at every ferry a guard—on every bridge a sentinel—and in every wood a patrol. We were hemmed in upon every side. Here were the difficulties, real or imagined—the good to be sought, and the evil to be shunned. On the one hand, there stood slavery, a stern reality, glaring frightfully upon us,—its robes already crimsoned with the blood of millions, and even now feasting itself greedily upon our own flesh. On the other hand, away back in the dim distance, under the flickering light of the north star, behind some craggy hill or snow-covered mountain, stood a doubtful freedom—half frozen—beckoning us to come and share its hospitality. This in itself was sometimes enough to stagger us; but when we permitted ourselves to survey the road, we were frequently appalled. Upon either side we saw grim death, assuming the most horrid shapes. Now it was starvation, causing us to eat our own flesh;—now we were contending with the waves, and were drowned;—now we were overtaken, and torn to pieces by the fangs of the terrible bloodhound. We were stung by scorpions, chased by wild beasts, bitten by snakes, and finally, after having nearly reached the desired spot,—after swimming rivers, encountering wild beasts, sleeping in the woods, suffering hunger and nakedness,—we were overtaken by our pursuers, and, in our resistance, we were shot dead upon the spot! I say, this picture sometimes appalled us, and made us

> "rather bear those ills we had,
> Than fly to others, that we knew not of."

In coming to a fixed determination to run away, we did more than Patrick Henry, when he resolved upon liberty or death. With us it was a doubtful liberty at most, and almost certain death if we failed. For my part, I should prefer death to hopeless bondage.

Sandy, one of our number, gave up the notion, but still encouraged us. Our company then consisted of Henry Harris, John Harris, Henry Bailey, Charles Roberts, and myself. Henry Bailey was my uncle, and belonged to my master. Charles married my aunt: he belonged to my master's father-in-law, Mr. William Hamilton.

The plan we finally concluded upon was, to get a large canoe belonging to Mr. Hamilton, and upon the Saturday night previous to Easter holidays, paddle directly up the Chesapeake Bay. On our arrival at the head of the bay, a distance of seventy or eighty miles from where we lived, it was our purpose to turn our canoe adrift, and follow the guidance of the north star till we got beyond the limits of Maryland. Our reason for taking the water route was, that we were less liable to be suspected as runaways; we hoped to be regarded as fishermen; whereas, if we should take the land route, we should be subjected to interruptions of almost every kind. Any one having a white face, and being so disposed, could stop us, and subject us to examination.

The week before our intended start, I wrote several protections, one for each of us. As well as I can remember, they were in the following words, to wit:—

> "This is to certify that I, the undersigned, have given the bearer, my servant, full liberty to go to Baltimore, and spend the Easter holidays. Written with mine own hand, &c., 1835.
>
> "WILLIAM HAMILTON,
>
> "Near St. Michael's, in Talbot county, Maryland."

We were not going to Baltimore; but, in going up the bay, we went toward Baltimore, and these protections were only intended to protect us while on the bay.

As the time drew near for our departure, our anxiety became more and more intense. It was truly a matter of life and death with us. The strength of our determination was about to be fully tested. At this time, I was very active in explaining every difficulty, removing every doubt, dispelling every fear, and inspiring all with the firmness indispensable to success in our undertaking; assuring them that half was gained the instant we made the move; we had talked long enough; we were now ready to move; if not now, we never should be; and if we did not intend to move now, we had as well fold our arms, sit down, and acknowledge ourselves fit only to be slaves. This, none of us were prepared to acknowledge. Every man stood firm; and at our last meeting, we pledged ourselves afresh, in the most solemn manner, that, at the time appointed, we would certainly start in pursuit of freedom. This was in the middle of the week, at the end of which we were to be off. We went, as usual, to our several fields of labor, but with bosoms highly agitated with thoughts of our truly hazardous undertaking. We tried to conceal our feelings as much as possible; and I think we succeeded very well.

After a painful waiting, the Saturday morning, whose night was to witness our departure, came. I hailed it with joy, bring what of sadness it might. Friday night was a sleepless one for me. I probably felt more anxious than the rest, because I was, by common consent, at the head of the whole affair. The responsibility of success or failure lay heavily upon me. The glory of the one, and the confusion of the other, were alike mine. The first two hours of that morning were such as I never experienced before, and hope never to again. Early in the morning, we went, as usual, to the field. We were spreading manure; and all at once, while thus engaged, I was overwhelmed with an indescribable feeling, in the fulness of which I turned to Sandy, who was near by, and said, "We are betrayed!" "Well," said he, "that thought has this moment struck me." We said no more. I was never more certain of any thing.

The horn was blown as usual, and we went up from the field to the house for breakfast. I went for the form, more than for want of any thing to eat that morning. Just as I got to the house, in looking out at the lane gate, I saw four white men, with two colored men. The white men were on horseback, and the colored ones were walking behind, as if tied. I watched them a few moments till they got up to our lane gate. Here they halted, and tied the colored men to the gate-post. I was not yet certain as to what the matter was. In a few moments, in rode Mr. Hamilton, with a speed betokening great excitement. He came to the door, and inquired if Master William was in. He was told he was at the barn. Mr. Hamilton, without dismounting, rode up to the barn with extraordinary speed. In a few moments, he and Mr. Freeland returned to the house. By this time, the three constables rode up, and in great haste dismounted, tied their horses, and met Master William and Mr. Hamilton returning from the barn; and after talking awhile, they all walked up to the kitchen door. There was no one in the kitchen but myself and John. Henry and Sandy were up at the barn. Mr. Freeland put his head in at the door, and called me by name, saying, there were some gentlemen at the door who wished to see me. I stepped to the door, and inquired what they wanted. They at once seized me, and, without giving me any satisfaction, tied me—lashing my hands closely together. I insisted upon knowing what the matter was. They at length said, that they had learned I had been in a "scrape," and that I was to be examined before my master; and if their information proved false, I should not be hurt.

In a few moments, they succeeded in tying John. They then turned to Henry, who had by this time returned, and commanded him to cross his hands. "I won't!" said Henry, in a firm tone, indicating his readiness to meet the consequences of his refusal. "Won't you?" said Tom Graham, the constable. "No, I won't!" said Henry, in a still stronger tone. With this, two of the constables pulled out their shining pistols, and swore, by their Creator, that they would make him cross his hands or kill him. Each cocked his pistol, and, with fingers on the trigger, walked up to Henry, saying, at the same time, if he did not cross his hands, they would blow his damned heart out. "Shoot me, shoot me!" said Henry; "you can't kill me but once. Shoot, shoot,—and be damned! *I won't be tied!*" This he said in a tone of loud defiance; and at the same time, with a motion as quick as lightning, he with one single stroke dashed the pistols from the hand of each constable. As he did this, all hands fell upon him, and, after beating him some time, they finally overpowered him, and got him tied.

During the scuffle, I managed, I know not how, to get my pass out, and, without being discovered, put it into the fire. We were all now tied; and just as we were to leave for Easton jail, Betsy Freeland, mother of William Freeland, came to the door with her hands full of biscuits, and divided them between Henry and John. She then delivered herself of a speech, to the following effect:—addressing herself to me, she said, "*You devil! You yellow devil!* it was you that put it into the heads of Henry and John to run away. But for you, you long-legged mulatto devil! Henry nor John would never have thought of such a thing." I made no reply, and was immediately hurried off towards St. Michael's. Just a moment previous to the scuffle with Henry, Mr. Hamilton suggested the propriety of making a search for the protections which he had understood Frederick had written for himself and the rest. But, just at the moment he was about carrying his proposal into effect, his aid was needed in helping to tie Henry; and the excitement attending the scuffle caused them either to forget, or to deem it unsafe, under the circumstances, to search. So we were not yet convicted of the intention to run away.

When we got about half way to St. Michael's, while the constables having us in charge were looking ahead, Henry inquired of me what he should do with his pass. I told him to eat it with his biscuit, and own nothing; and we passed the word around, "*Own nothing;*" and "*Own nothing!*" said we all. Our confidence in each other was unshaken. We were resolved to succeed or fail together, after the calamity had befallen us as much as before. We were now prepared for any thing. We were to be dragged that morning fifteen miles behind horses, and then to be placed in the Easton jail. When we reached St. Michael's, we underwent a sort of examination. We all denied that we ever intended to run away. We did this more to bring out the evidence against us, than from any hope of getting clear of being sold; for, as I have said, we were ready for that. The fact was, we cared but little where we went, so we went together. Our greatest concern was about separation. We dreaded that more than any thing this side of death. We found the evidence against us to be the testimony of one person; our master would not tell who it was; but we came to a unanimous decision among ourselves as to who their informant was. We were sent off to the jail at Easton. When we got there, we were delivered up to the sheriff, Mr. Joseph Graham, and by him placed in jail. Henry, John, and myself, were placed in one room together—Charles, and Henry Bailey, in another. Their object in separating us was to hinder concert.

We had been in jail scarcely twenty minutes, when a swarm of slave traders, and agents for slave traders, flocked into jail to look at us, and to ascertain if we were for sale. Such a set of beings I never saw before! I felt myself surrounded by so many fiends from perdition. A band of pirates never looked more like their father, the devil. They laughed and grinned over us, saying, "Ah, my boys! we have got you, haven't we?" And after taunting us in various ways, they one by one went into an examination of us, with intent to ascertain our value. They would impudently ask us if we would not like to have them for our masters. We would make them no answer, and leave them to find out as best they could. Then they would curse and swear at us, telling us that they could take the devil out of us in a very little while, if we were only in their hands.

While in jail, we found ourselves in much more comfortable quarters than we expected when we went there. We did not get much to eat, nor that which was very good; but we had a good clean room, from the windows of which we could see what was going on in the street, which was very much better than though we had been placed in one of the dark, damp cells. Upon the whole, we got along very well, so far as the jail and its keeper were concerned. Immediately after the holidays were over, contrary to all our expectations, Mr. Hamilton and Mr. Freeland came up to Easton, and took Charles, the two Henrys, and John, out of jail, and carried them home, leaving me alone. I regarded this separation as a final one. It caused me more pain than any thing else in the whole transaction. I was ready for any thing rather than separation. I supposed that they had consulted together, and had decided that, as I was the whole cause of the intention of the others to run away, it was hard to make the innocent suffer with the guilty; and that they had, therefore, concluded to take the others home, and sell me, as a warning to the others that remained. It is due to the noble Henry to say, he seemed almost as reluctant at leaving the prison as at leaving home to come to the prison. But we knew we should, in all probability, be separated, if we were sold; and since he was in their hands, he concluded to go peaceably home.

I was now left to my fate. I was all alone, and within the walls of a stone prison. But a few days before, and I was full of hope. I expected to have been safe in a land of freedom; but now I was covered with gloom, sunk down to the utmost despair. I thought the possibility of freedom was gone. I was kept in this way about one week, at the end of which, Captain Auld, my master, to my surprise and utter astonishment, came up, and took me out, with the intention of sending me, with a gentleman of his acquaintance, into Alabama. But, from some cause or other, he did not send me to Alabama, but concluded to send me back to Baltimore, to live again with his brother Hugh, and to learn a trade.

Thus, after an absence of three years and one month, I was once more permitted to return to my old home at Baltimore. My master sent me away, because there existed against me a very great prejudice in the community, and he feared I might be killed.

In a few weeks after I went to Baltimore, Master Hugh hired me to Mr. William Gardner, an extensive shipbuilder, on Fell's Point. I was put there to learn how to calk. It, however, proved a very unfavorable place for the accomplishment of this object. Mr. Gardner was engaged that spring in building two large man-of-war brigs, professedly for the Mexican government. The vessels were to be launched in the July of that year, and in failure thereof, Mr. Gardner was to lose a considerable sum; so that when I entered, all was hurry. There was no time to learn any thing. Every man had to do that which he knew how to do. In entering the ship-yard, my orders from Mr. Gardner were, to do whatever the carpenters commanded me to do. This was placing me at the beck and call of about seventy-five men. I was to regard all these as masters. Their word was to be my law. My situation was a most trying one. At times I needed a dozen pair of hands. I was called a dozen ways in the space of a single minute. Three or four voices would strike my ear at the same moment. It was—"Fred., come help me to cant this timber here."—"Fred., come carry this timber yonder."—"Fred., bring that roller here."—"Fred., go get a fresh can of water."—"Fred., come help saw off the end of this timber."—"Fred., go quick, and get the crowbar."—"Fred., hold on the end of this fall."—"Fred., go to the blacksmith's shop, and get a new punch."—"Hurra, Fred.! run and bring me a cold chisel."—"I say, Fred., bear a hand, and get up a fire as quick as lightning under that steam-box."—"Halloo, nigger! come, turn this grindstone."—"Come, come! move, move! and *bowse* this timber forward."—"I say, darky, blast your eyes, why don't you heat up some pitch?"—"Halloo! halloo! halloo!" (Three voices at the same time.) "Come here!—Go there!—Hold on where you are! Damn you, if you move, I'll knock your brains out!"

This was my school for eight months; and I might have remained there longer, but for a most horrid fight I had with four of the white apprentices, in which my left eye was nearly knocked out, and I was horribly mangled in other respects. The facts in the case were these: Until a very little while after I went there, white and black ship-carpenters worked side by side, and no one seemed to see any impropriety in it. All hands seemed to be very well satisfied. Many of the black carpenters were freemen. Things seemed to be going on very well. All at once, the white carpenters knocked off, and said they would not work with free colored workmen. Their reason for this, as alleged, was, that if free colored carpenters were encouraged, they would soon take the trade into their own hands, and poor white men would be thrown out of employment. They therefore felt called upon at once to put a stop to it. And, taking advantage of Mr. Gardner's necessities, they broke off, swearing they would work no longer, unless he would discharge his black carpenters. Now, though this did not extend to me in form, it did reach me in fact. My fellow-apprentices very soon began to feel it degrading to them to work with me. They began to put on airs, and talk about the "niggers" taking the country, saying we all ought to be killed; and, being encouraged by the journeymen, they commenced making my condition as hard as they could, by hectoring me around, and sometimes striking me. I, of course, kept the vow I made after the fight with Mr. Covey, and struck back again, regardless of consequences; and while I kept them from combining, I succeeded very well; for I could whip the whole of them, taking them separately. They, however, at length combined, and came upon me, armed with sticks, stones, and heavy handspikes. One came in front with a half brick. There was one at each side of me, and one behind me. While I was attending to those in front, and on either side, the one behind ran up with the handspike, and struck me a heavy blow upon the head. It stunned me. I fell, and with this they all ran upon me, and fell to beating me with their fists. I let them lay on for a while, gathering strength. In an instant, I gave a sudden surge, and rose to my hands and knees. Just as I did that, one of their number gave me, with his heavy boot, a powerful kick in the left eye. My eyeball seemed to have burst. When they saw my eye closed, and badly swollen, they left me. With this I seized the handspike, and for a time pursued them. But here the carpenters interfered, and I thought I might as well give it up. It was impossible to stand my hand against so many. All this took place in sight of not less than fifty white ship-carpenters, and not one interposed a friendly word; but some cried, "Kill the damned nigger! Kill him! kill him! He struck a white person." I found my only chance for life was in flight. I succeeded in getting away without an additional blow, and barely so; for to strike a white man is death by Lynch law,—and that was the law in Mr. Gardner's ship-yard; nor is there much of any other out of Mr. Gardner's ship-yard.

I went directly home, and told the story of my wrongs to Master Hugh; and I am happy to say of him, irreligious as he was, his conduct was heavenly, compared with that of his brother Thomas under similar circumstances. He listened attentively to my narration of the circumstances leading to the savage outrage, and gave many proofs of his strong indignation at it. The heart of my once over-kind mistress was again melted into pity. My puffed-out eye and blood-covered face moved her to tears. She took a chair by me, washed the blood from my face, and, with a mother's tenderness, bound up my head, covering the wounded eye with a lean piece of fresh beef. It was almost compensation for my suffering to witness, once more, a manifestation of kindness from this, my once affectionate old mistress. Master Hugh was very much enraged. He gave expression to his feelings by pouring out curses upon the heads of those who did the deed. As soon as I got a little the better of my bruises, he took me with him to Esquire Watson's, on Bond Street, to see what could be done about the matter. Mr. Watson inquired who saw the assault committed. Master Hugh told him it was done in Mr. Gardner's ship-yard, at midday, where there were a large company of men at work. "As to that," he said, "the deed was done, and there was no question as to who did it." His answer was, he could do nothing in the case, unless some white man would come forward and testify. He could issue no warrant on my word. If I had been killed in the presence of a thousand colored people, their testimony combined would have been insufficient to have arrested one of the murderers. Master Hugh, for once, was compelled to say this state of things was too bad. Of course, it was impossible to get any white man to volunteer his testimony in my behalf, and against the white young men. Even those who may have sympathized with me were not prepared to do this. It required a degree of courage unknown to them to do so; for just at that time, the slightest manifestation of humanity toward a colored person was denounced as abolitionism, and that name subjected its bearer to frightful liabilities. The watchwords of the bloody-minded in that region, and in those days, were, "Damn the abolitionists!" and "Damn the niggers!" There was nothing done, and probably nothing would have been done if I had been killed. Such was, and such remains, the state of things in the Christian city of Baltimore.

Master Hugh, finding he could get no redress, refused to let me go back again to Mr. Gardner. He kept me himself, and his wife dressed my wound till I was again restored to health. He then took me into the ship-yard of which he was foreman, in the employment of Mr. Walter Price. There I was immediately set to calking, and very soon learned the art of using my mallet and irons. In the course of one year from the time I left Mr. Gardner's, I was able to command the highest wages given to the most experienced calkers. I was now of some importance to my master. I was bringing him from six to seven dollars per week. I sometimes brought him nine dollars per week: my wages were a dollar and a half a day. After learning how to calk, I sought my own employment, made my own contracts, and collected the money which I earned. My pathway became much more smooth than before; my condition was now much more comfortable. When I could get no calking to do, I did nothing. During these leisure times, those old notions about freedom would steal over me again. When in Mr. Gardner's employment, I was kept in such a perpetual whirl of excitement, I could think of nothing, scarcely, but my life; and in thinking of my life, I almost forgot my liberty. I have observed this in my experience of slavery,—that whenever my condition was improved, instead of its increasing my contentment, it only increased my desire to be free, and set me to thinking of plans to gain my freedom. I have found that, to make a contented slave, it is necessary to make a thoughtless one. It is necessary to darken his moral and mental vision, and, as far as possible, to annihilate the power of reason. He must be able to detect no inconsistencies in slavery; he must be made to feel that slavery is right; and he can be brought to that only when he ceases to be a man.

I was now getting, as I have said, one dollar and fifty cents per day. I contracted for it; I earned it; it was paid to me; it was rightfully my own; yet, upon each returning Saturday night, I was compelled to deliver every cent of that money to Master Hugh. And why? Not because he earned it,—not because he had any hand in earning it,—not because I owed it to him,—nor because he possessed the slightest shadow of a right to it; but solely because he had the power to compel me to give it up. The right of the grim-visaged pirate upon the high seas is exactly the same.

CHAPTER XI

I now come to that part of my life during which I planned, and finally succeeded in making, my escape from slavery. But before narrating any of the peculiar circumstances, I deem it proper to make known my intention not to state all the facts connected with the transaction. My reasons for pursuing this course may be understood from the following: First, were I to give a minute statement of all the facts, it is not only possible, but quite probable, that others would thereby be involved in the most embarrassing difficulties. Secondly, such a statement would most undoubtedly induce greater vigilance on the part of slaveholders than has existed heretofore among them; which would, of course, be the means of guarding a door whereby some dear brother bondman might escape his galling chains. I deeply regret the necessity that impels me to suppress any thing of importance connected with my experience in slavery. It would afford me great pleasure indeed, as well as materially add to the interest of my narrative, were I at liberty to gratify a curiosity, which I know exists in the minds of many, by an accurate statement of all the facts pertaining to my most fortunate escape. But I must deprive myself of this pleasure, and the curious of the gratification which such a statement would afford. I would allow myself to suffer under the greatest imputations which evil-minded men might suggest, rather than exculpate myself, and thereby run the hazard of closing the slightest avenue by which a brother slave might clear himself of the chains and fetters of slavery.

I have never approved of the very public manner in which some of our western friends have conducted what they call the *underground railroad,* but which, I think, by their open declarations, has been made most emphatically the *upperground railroad.* I honor those good men and women for their noble daring, and applaud them for willingly subjecting themselves to bloody persecution, by openly avowing their participation in the escape of slaves. I, however, can see very little good resulting from such a course, either to themselves or the slaves escaping; while, upon the other hand, I see and feel assured that those open declarations are a positive evil to the slaves remaining, who are seeking to escape. They do nothing towards enlightening the slave, whilst they do much towards enlightening the master. They stimulate him to greater watchfulness, and enhance his power to capture his slave. We owe something to the slaves south of the line as well as to those north of it; and in aiding the latter on their way to freedom, we should be careful to do nothing which would be likely to hinder the former from escaping from slavery. I would keep the merciless slaveholder profoundly ignorant of the means of flight adopted by the slave. I would leave him to imagine himself surrounded by myriads of invisible tormentors, ever ready to snatch from his infernal grasp his trembling prey. Let him be left to feel his way in the dark; let darkness commensurate with his crime hover over him; and let him feel that at every step he takes, in pursuit of the flying bondman, he is running the frightful risk of having his hot brains dashed out by an invisible agency. Let us render the tyrant no aid; let us not hold the light by which he can trace the footprints of our flying brother. But enough of this. I will now proceed to the statement of those facts, connected with my escape, for which I am alone responsible, and for which no one can be made to suffer but myself.

In the early part of the year 1838, I became quite

restless. I could see no reason why I should, at the end of each week, pour the reward of my toil into the purse of my master. When I carried to him my weekly wages, he would, after counting the money, look me in the face with a robber-like fierceness, and ask, "Is this all?" He was satisfied with nothing less than the last cent. He would, however, when I made him six dollars, sometimes give me six cents, to encourage me. It had the opposite effect. I regarded it as a sort of admission of my right to the whole. The fact that he gave me any part of my wages was proof, to my mind, that he believed me entitled to the whole of them. I always felt worse for having received any thing; for I feared that the giving me a few cents would ease his conscience, and make him feel himself to be a pretty honorable sort of robber. My discontent grew upon me. I was ever on the look-out for means of escape; and, finding no direct means, I determined to try to hire my time, with a view of getting money with which to make my escape. In the spring of 1838, when Master Thomas came to Baltimore to purchase his spring goods, I got an opportunity, and applied to him to allow me to hire my time. He unhesitatingly refused my request, and told me this was another stratagem by which to escape. He told me I could go nowhere but that he could get me; and that, in the event of my running away, he should spare no pains in his efforts to catch me. He exhorted me to content myself, and be obedient. He told me, if I would be happy, I must lay out no plans for the future. He said, if I behaved myself properly, he would take care of me. Indeed, he advised me to complete thoughtlessness of the future, and taught me to depend solely upon him for happiness. He seemed to see fully the pressing necessity of setting aside my intellectual nature, in order to contentment in slavery. But in spite of him, and even in spite of myself, I continued to think, and to think about the injustice of my enslavement, and the means of escape.

About two months after this, I applied to Master Hugh for the privilege of hiring my time. He was not acquainted with the fact that I had applied to Master Thomas, and had been refused. He too, at first, seemed disposed to refuse; but, after some reflection, he granted me the privilege, and proposed the following terms: I was to be allowed all my time, make all contracts with those for whom I worked, and find my own employment; and, in return for this liberty, I was to pay him three dollars at the end of each week; find myself in calking tools, and in board and clothing. My board was two dollars and a half per week. This, with the wear and tear of clothing and calking tools, made my regular expenses about six dollars per week. This amount I was compelled to make up, or relinquish the privilege of hiring my time. Rain or shine, work or no work, at the end of each week the money must be forthcoming, or I must give up my privilege. This arrangement, it will be perceived, was decidedly in my master's favor. It relieved him of all need of looking after me. His money was sure. He received all the benefits of slaveholding without its evils; while I endured all the evils of a slave, and suffered all the care and anxiety of a freeman. I found it a hard bargain. But, hard as it was, I thought it better than the old mode of getting along. It was a step towards freedom to be allowed to bear the responsibilities of a freeman, and I was determined to hold on upon it. I bent myself to the work of making money. I was ready to work at night as well as day, and by the most untiring perseverance and industry, I made enough to meet my expenses, and lay up a little money every week. I went on thus from May till August. Master Hugh then refused to allow me to hire my time longer. The ground for his refusal was a failure on my part, one Saturday night, to pay him for my week's time. This failure was occasioned by my attending a camp meeting about ten miles from Baltimore. During the week, I had entered into an engagement with a number of young friends to start from Baltimore to the camp ground early Saturday evening; and being detained by my employer, I was unable to get down to Master Hugh's without disappointing the company. I knew that Master Hugh was in no special need of the money that night. I therefore decided to go to camp meeting, and upon my return pay him the three dollars. I staid [sic] at the camp meeting one day longer than I intended when I left. But as soon as I returned, I called upon him to pay him what he considered his due. I found him very angry; he could scarce restrain his wrath. He said he had a great mind to give me a severe whipping. He wished to know how I dared go out of the city without asking his permission. I told him I hired my time, and while I paid him the price which he asked for it, I did not know that I was bound to ask him when and where I should go. This reply troubled him; and, after reflecting a few moments, he turned to me, and said I should hire my time no longer; that the next thing he should know of, I would be running away. Upon the same plea, he told me to bring my tools and clothing home forthwith. I did so; but instead of seeking work, as I had been accustomed to do previously to hiring my time, I spent the whole week without the performance of a single stroke of work. I did this in retaliation. Saturday night, he called upon me as usual for my week's wages. I told him I had no wages; I had done no work that week. Here we were upon the point of coming to blows. He raved, and swore his determination to get hold of me. I did not allow myself a single word; but was resolved, if he laid the weight of his hand upon me, it should be blow for blow. He did not strike me, but told me that he would find me in constant employment in future. I thought the matter over during the next day, Sunday, and finally resolved upon the third day of September, as the day upon which I would make a second attempt to secure my freedom. I now had three weeks during which to prepare for my journey. Early on Monday morning, before Master Hugh had time to make any engagement for me, I went out and got employment of Mr. Butler, at his ship-yard near the draw-bridge, upon what is called the City Block, thus making it unnecessary for him to seek employment for me. At the end of the week, I brought him between eight and nine dollars. He seemed very well pleased, and asked me why I did not do the same the week before. He little knew what my plans were. My object in working steadily was to remove any suspicion he might entertain of my intent to run away; and in this I succeeded admirably. I suppose he thought I was never better satisfied with my condition than at the very time during which I was planning my escape. The second week passed, and again I carried him my full wages; and so well pleased was he, that he gave me twenty-five cents, (quite a large sum for a slaveholder to give a slave,) and bade me to make a good use of it. I told him I would.

Things went on without very smoothly indeed, but

within there was trouble. It is impossible for me to describe my feelings as the time of my contemplated start drew near. I had a number of warm-hearted friends in Baltimore,—friends that I loved almost as I did my life,—and the thought of being separated from them forever was painful beyond expression. It is my opinion that thousands would escape from slavery, who now remain, but for the strong cords of affection that bind them to their friends. The thought of leaving my friends was decidedly the most painful thought with which I had to contend. The love of them was my tender point, and shook my decision more than all things else. Besides the pain of separation, the dread and apprehension of a failure exceeded what I had experienced at my first attempt. The appalling defeat I then sustained returned to torment me. I felt assured that, if I failed in this attempt, my case would be a hopeless one—it would seal my fate as a slave forever. I could not hope to get off with any thing less than the severest punishment, and being placed beyond the means of escape. It required no very vivid imagination to depict the most frightful scenes through which I should have to pass, in case I failed. The wretchedness of slavery, and the blessedness of freedom, were perpetually before me. It was life and death with me. But I remained firm, and, according to my resolution, on the third day of September, 1838, I left my chains, and succeeded in reaching New York without the slightest interruption of any kind. How I did so,—what means I adopted,—what direction I travelled, and by what mode of conveyance,—I must leave unexplained, for the reasons before mentioned.

I have been frequently asked how I felt when I found myself in a free State. I have never been able to answer the question with any satisfaction to myself. It was a moment of the highest excitement I ever experienced. I suppose I felt as one may imagine the unarmed mariner to feel when he is rescued by a friendly man-of-war from the pursuit of a pirate. In writing to a dear friend, immediately after my arrival at New York, I said I felt like one who had escaped a den of hungry lions. This state of mind, however, very soon subsided; and I was again seized with a feeling of great insecurity and loneliness. I was yet liable to be taken back, and subjected to all the tortures of slavery. This in itself was enough to damp the ardor of my enthusiasm. But the loneliness overcame me. There I was in the midst of thousands, and yet a perfect stranger; without home and without friends, in the midst of thousands of my own brethren—children of a common Father, and yet I dared not to unfold to any one of them my sad condition. I was afraid to speak to any one for fear of speaking to the wrong one, and thereby falling into the hands of money-loving kidnappers, whose business it was to lie in wait for the panting fugitive, as the ferocious beasts of the forest lie in wait for their prey. The motto which I adopted when I started from slavery was this—"Trust no man!" I saw in every white man an enemy, and in almost every colored man cause for distrust. It was a most painful situation; and, to understand it, one must needs experience it, or imagine himself in similar circumstances. Let him be a fugitive slave in a strange land—a land given up to be the hunting-ground for slaveholders—whose inhabitants are legalized kidnappers—where he is every moment subjected to the terrible liability of being seized upon by his fellow-men, as the hideous crocodile seizes upon his prey!—I say, let him place himself in my situation—without home or friends—without money or credit—wanting shelter, and no one to give it—wanting bread, and no money to buy it,—and at the same time let him feel that he is pursued by merciless men-hunters, and in total darkness as to what to do, where to go, or where to stay,—perfectly helpless both as to the means of defence and means of escape,—in the midst of plenty, yet suffering the terrible gnawings of hunger,—in the midst of houses, yet having no home,—among fellow-men, yet feeling as if in the midst of wild beasts, whose greediness to swallow the trembling and half-famished fugitive is only equalled by that with which the monsters of the deep swallow up the helpless fish upon which they subsist,—I say, let him be placed in this most trying situation,—the situation in which I was placed,—then, and not till then, will he fully appreciate the hardships of, and know how to sympathize with, the toil-worn and whip-scarred fugitive slave.

Thank Heaven, I remained but a short time in this distressed situation. I was relieved from it by the humane hand of Mr. DAVID RUGGLES, whose vigilance, kindness, and perseverance, I shall never forget. I am glad of an opportunity to express, as far as words can, the love and gratitude I bear him. Mr. Ruggles is now afflicted with blindness, and is himself in need of the same kind offices which he was once so forward in the performance of toward others. I had been in New York but a few days, when Mr. Ruggles sought me out, and very kindly took me to his boarding-house at the corner of Church and Lespenard Streets. Mr. Ruggles was then very deeply engaged in the memorable *Darg* case, as well as attending to a number of other fugitive slaves, devising ways and means for their successful escape; and, though watched and hemmed in on almost every side, he seemed to be more than a match for his enemies.

Very soon after I went to Mr. Ruggles, he wished to know of me where I wanted to go; as he deemed it unsafe for me to remain in New York. I told him I was a calker, and should like to go where I could get work. I thought of going to Canada; but he decided against it, and in favor of my going to New Bedford, thinking I should be able to get work there at my trade. At this time, Anna,* my intended wife, came on; for I wrote to her immediately after my arrival at New York, (notwithstanding my homeless, houseless, and helpless condition,) informing her of my successful flight, and wishing her to come on forthwith. In a few days after her arrival, Mr. Ruggles called in the Rev. J. W. C. Pennington, who, in the presence of Mr. Ruggles, Mrs. Michaels, and two or three others, performed the marriage ceremony, and gave us a certificate, of which the following is an exact copy:—

> "THIS may certify that I joined together in holy matrimony Frederick Johnson† and Anna Murray, as man and wife, in the presence of Mr. David Ruggles and Mrs. Michaels.
>
> "JAMES W. C. PENNINGTON.
>
> "*New York, Sept.* 15, 1838."

Upon receiving this certificate, and a five-dollar bill from Mr. Ruggles, I shouldered one part of our baggage,

*She was free.

†I had changed my name from Frederick *Bailey* to that of *Johnson.*

and Anna took up the other, and we set out forthwith to take passage on board of the steamboat John W. Richmond for Newport, on our way to New Bedford. Mr. Ruggles gave me a letter to a Mr. Shaw in Newport, and told me, in case my money did not serve me to New Bedford, to stop in Newport and obtain further assistance; but upon our arrival at Newport, we were so anxious to get to a place of safety, that, notwithstanding we lacked the necessary money to pay our fare, we decided to take seats in the stage, and promise to pay when we got to New Bedford. We were encouraged to do this by two excellent gentlemen, residents of New Bedford, whose names I afterward ascertained to be Joseph Ricketson and William C. Taber. They seemed at once to understand our circumstances, and gave us such assurance of their friendliness as put us fully at ease in their presence. It was good indeed to meet with such friends, at such a time. Upon reaching New Bedford, we were directed to the house of Mr. Nathan Johnson, by whom we were kindly received, and hospitably provided for. Both Mr. and Mrs. Johnson took a deep and lively interest in our welfare. They proved themselves quite worthy of the name of abolitionists. When the stage-driver found us unable to pay our fare, he held on upon our baggage as security for the debt. I had but to mention the fact to Mr. Johnson, and he forthwith advanced the money.

We now began to feel a degree of safety, and to prepare ourselves for the duties and responsibilities of a life of freedom. On the morning after our arrival at New Bedford, while at the breakfast-table, the question arose as to what name I should be called by. The name given me by my mother was, "Frederick Augustus Washington Bailey." I, however, had dispensed with the two middle names long before I left Maryland so that I was generally known by the name of "Frederick Bailey." I started from Baltimore bearing the name of "Stanley." When I got to New York, I again changed my name to "Frederick Johnson," and thought that would be the last change. But when I got to New Bedford, I found it necessary again to change my name. The reason of this necessity was, that there were so many Johnsons in New Bedford, it was already quite difficult to distinguish between them. I gave

Mr. Johnson the privilege of choosing me a name, but told him he must not take from me the name of "Frederick." I must hold on to that, to preserve a sense of my identity. Mr. Johnson had just been reading the "Lady of the Lake," and at once suggested that my name be "Douglass." From that time until now I have been called "Frederick Douglass"; and as I am more widely known by that name than by either of the others, I shall continue to use it as my own.

I was quite disappointed at the general appearance of things in New Bedford. The impression which I had received respecting the character and condition of the people of the north, I found to be singularly erroneous. I had very strangely supposed, while in slavery, that few of the comforts, and scarcely any of the luxuries, of life were enjoyed at the north, compared with what were enjoyed by the slaveholders of the south. I probably came to this conclusion from the fact that northern people owned no slaves. I supposed that they were about upon a level with the non-slaveholding population of the south. I knew *they* were exceedingly poor, and I had been accustomed to regard their poverty as the necessary consequence of their being non-slaveholders. I had somehow imbibed the opinion that, in the absence of slaves, there could be no wealth, and very little refinement. And upon coming to the north, I expected to meet with a rough, hard-handed, and uncultivated population, living in the most Spartan-like simplicity, knowing nothing of the ease, luxury, pomp, and grandeur of southern slaveholders. Such being my conjectures, any one acquainted with the appearance of New Bedford may very readily infer how palpably I must have seen my mistake.

In the afternoon of the day when I reached New Bedford, I visited the wharves, to take a view of the shipping. Here I found myself surrounded with the strongest proofs of wealth. Lying at the wharves, and riding in the stream, I saw many ships of the finest model, in the best order, and of the largest size. Upon the right and left, I was walled in by granite warehouses of the widest dimensions, stowed to their utmost capacity with the necessaries and comforts of life. Added to this, almost every body seemed to be at work, but noiselessly so, compared with what I had been accustomed to in

Baltimore. There were no loud songs heard from those engaged in loading and unloading ships. I heard no deep oaths or horrid curses on the laborer. I saw no whipping of men; but all seemed to go smoothly on. Every man appeared to understand his work, and went at it with a sober, yet cheerful earnestness, which betokened the deep interest which he felt in what he was doing, as well as a sense of his own dignity as a man. To me this looked exceedingly strange. From the wharves I strolled around and over the town, gazing with wonder and admiration at the splendid churches, beautiful dwellings, and finely-cultivated gardens; evincing an amount of wealth, comfort, taste, and refinement, such as I had never seen in any part of slaveholding Maryland.

Every thing looked clean, new, and beautiful. I saw few or no dilapidated houses, with poverty-stricken inmates; no half-naked children and barefooted women, such as I had been accustomed to see in Hillsborough, Easton, St. Michael's, and Baltimore. The people looked more able, stronger, healthier, and happier, than those of Maryland. I was for once made glad by a view of extreme wealth, without being saddened by seeing extreme poverty. But the most astonishing as well as the most interesting thing to me was the condition of the colored people, a great many of whom, like myself, had escaped thither as a refuge from the hunters of men. I found many, who had not been seven years out of their chains, living in finer houses, and evidently enjoying more of the comforts of life, than the average of slaveholders in Maryland. I will venture to assert that my friend Mr. Nathan Johnson (of whom I can say with a grateful heart, "I was hungry, and he gave me meat; I was thirsty, and he gave me drink; I was a stranger, and he took me in") lived in a neater house; dined at a better table; took, paid for, and read, more newspapers; better understood the moral, religious, and political character of the nation,—than nine tenths of the slaveholders in Talbot county Maryland. Yet Mr. Johnson was a working man. His hands were hardened by toil, and not his alone, but those also of Mrs. Johnson. I found the colored people much more spirited than I had supposed they would be. I found among them a determination to protect each other from the blood-thirsty kidnapper, at all hazards. Soon after my arrival, I was told of a circumstance which illustrated their spirit. A colored man and a fugitive slave were on unfriendly terms. The former was heard to threaten the latter with informing his master of his whereabouts. Straightway a meeting was called among the colored people, under the stereotyped notice, "Business of importance!" The betrayer was invited to attend. The people came at the appointed hour, and organized the meeting by appointing a very religious old gentleman as president, who, I believe, made a prayer, after which he addressed the meeting as follows: *"Friends, we have got him here, and I would recommend that you young men just take him outside the door, and kill him!"* With this, a number of them bolted at him; but they were intercepted by some more timid than themselves, and the betrayer escaped their vengeance, and has not been seen in New Bedford since. I believe there have been no more such threats, and should there be hereafter, I doubt not that death would be the consequence.

I found employment, the third day after my arrival, in stowing a sloop with a load of oil. It was new, dirty, and hard work for me; but I went at it with a glad heart and a willing hand. I was now my own master. It was a happy moment, the rapture of which can be understood only by those who have been slaves. It was the first work, the reward of which was to be entirely my own. There was no Master Hugh standing ready, the moment I earned the money, to rob me of it. I worked that day with a pleasure I had never before experienced. I was at work for myself and newly-married wife. It was to me the starting-point of a new existence. When I got through with that job, I went in pursuit of a job of calking; but such was the strength of prejudice against color, among the white calkers, that they refused to work with me, and of course I could get no employment.* Finding my trade of no immediate benefit, I threw off my calking habiliments, and prepared myself to do any kind of work I could get to do. Mr. Johnson kindly let me have his wood-horse and saw, and I very soon found myself a plenty of work. There was no work too hard—none too dirty. I was ready

*I am told that colored persons can now get employment at calking in New Bedford—a result of anti-slavery effort.

to saw wood, shovel coal, carry the hod, sweep the chimney, or roll oil casks,—all of which I did for nearly three years in New Bedford, before I became known to the anti-slavery world.

In about four months after I went to New Bedford, there came a young man to me, and inquired if I did not wish to take the "Liberator." I told him I did; but, just having made my escape from slavery, I remarked that I was unable to pay for it then. I, however, finally became a subscriber to it. The paper came, and I read it from week to week with such feelings as it would be quite idle for me to attempt to describe. The paper became my meat and my drink. My soul was set all on fire. Its sympathy for my brethren in bonds—its scathing denunciations of slaveholders—its faithful exposures of slavery—and its powerful attacks upon the upholders of the institution—sent a thrill of joy through my soul, such as I had never felt before!

I had not long been a reader of the "Liberator," before I got a pretty correct idea of the principles, measures and spirit of the anti-slavery reform. I took right hold of the cause. I could do but little; but what I could, I did with a joyful heart, and never felt happier than when in an anti-slavery meeting. I seldom had much to say at the meetings, because what I wanted to say was said so much better by others. But, while attending an anti-slavery convention at Nantucket, on the 11th of August, 1841, I felt strongly moved to speak, and was at the same time much urged to do so by Mr. William C. Coffin, a gentleman who had heard me speak in the colored people's meeting at New Bedford. It was a severe cross, and I took it up reluctantly. The truth was, I felt myself a slave, and the idea of speaking to white people weighed me down. I spoke but a few moments, when I felt a degree of freedom, and said what I desired with considerable ease. From that time until now, I have been engaged in pleading the cause of my brethren—with what success, and with what devotion, I leave those acquainted with my labors to decide.

APPENDIX

I find, since reading over the foregoing Narrative that I have, in several instances, spoken in such a tone and manner, respecting religion, as may possibly lead those unacquainted with my religious views to suppose me an opponent of all religion. To remove the liability of such misapprehension, I deem it proper to append the following brief explanation. What I have said respecting and against religion, I mean strictly to apply to the *slaveholding religion* of this land, and with no possible reference to Christianity proper; for, between the Christianity of this land, and the Christianity of Christ, I recognize the widest possible difference—so wide, that to receive the one as good, pure, and holy, is of necessity to reject the other as bad, corrupt, and wicked. To be the friend of the one, is of necessity to be the enemy of the other. I love the pure, peaceable, and impartial Christianity of Christ: I therefore hate the corrupt, slaveholding, women-whipping, cradle-plundering, partial and hypocritical Christianity of this land. Indeed, I can see no reason, but the most deceitful one, for calling the religion of this land Christianity. I look upon it as the climax of all misnomers, the boldest of all frauds, and the grossest of all libels. Never was there a clearer case of "stealing the livery of the court of heaven to serve the devil in." I am filled with unutterable loathing when I contemplate the religious pomp and show, together with the horrible inconsistencies, which every where surround me. We have men-stealers for ministers, women-whippers for missionaries, and cradle-plunderers for church members. The man who wields the blood-clotted cowskin during the week fills the pulpit on Sunday, and claims to be a minister of the meek and lowly Jesus. The man who robs me of my earnings at the end of each week meets me as a class-leader on Sunday morning, to show me the way of life, and the path of salvation. He who sells my sister, for purposes of prostitution, stands forth as the pious advocate of purity. He who proclaims it a religious duty to read the Bible denies me the right of learning to read the name of the God who made me. He who is the religious advocate of marriage robs whole millions of its sacred influence, and leaves them to the ravages of wholesale pollution. The warm defender of the sacredness of the family relation is the same that scatters whole families,—sundering husbands and wives, parents and children, sisters and brothers,—leaving the hut vacant, and the hearth desolate. We see the thief preaching against theft, and the adulterer against adultery. We have men sold to build churches, women sold to support the gospel, and babes sold to purchase Bibles for the *poor heathen! all for the glory of God and the good of souls!* The slave auctioneer's bell and the church-going bell chime in with each other, and the bitter cries of the heart-broken slave are drowned in the religious shouts of his pious master. Revivals of religion and revivals in the slave-trade go hand in hand together. The slave prison and the church stand near each other. The clanking of fetters and the rattling of chains in the prison, and the pious psalm and solemn prayer in the church, may be heard at the same time. The dealers in the bodies and souls of men erect their stand in the presence of the pulpit, and they mutually help each other. The dealer gives his blood-stained gold to support the pulpit, and the pulpit, in return, covers his infernal business with the garb of Christianity. Here we have religion and robbery the allies of each other—devils dressed in angels' robes, and hell presenting the semblance of paradise.

"Just God! and these are they,
  Who minister at thine altar, God of right!
Men who their hands, with prayer and blessing, lay
  On Israel's ark of light.

"What! preach, and kidnap men?
  Give thanks, and rob thy own afflicted poor?
Talk of thy glorious liberty, and then
  Bolt hard the captive's door?

"What! servants of thy own
  Merciful Son, who came to seek and save
The homeless and the outcast, fettering down
  The tasked and plundered slave!

"Pilate and Herod friends!
  Chief priests and rulers, as of old, combine!
Just God and holy! is that church which lends
  Strength to the spoiler thine?"

The Christianity of America is a Christianity, of whose votaries it may be as truly said, as it was of the ancient scribes and Pharisees, "They bind heavy burdens, and grievous to be borne, and lay them on men's shoulders, but they themselves will not move them with one of their fingers. All their works they do for to be seen of men.——They love the uppermost rooms at feasts, and the chief seats in the synagogues, ... and to be called of men, Rabbi, Rabbi.——But woe unto you, scribes and Pharisees, hypocrites! for ye shut up the kingdom of heaven against men; for ye neither go in yourselves, neither suffer ye them that are entering to go in. Ye devour widows' houses, and for a pretence make long prayers; therefore ye shall receive the greater damnation. Ye compass sea and land to make one proselyte, and when he is made, ye make him twofold more the child of hell than yourselves.——Woe unto you, scribes and Pharisees, hypocrites! for ye pay tithe of mint, and anise, and cumin, and have omitted the weightier matters of the law, judgment, mercy, and faith; these ought ye to have done, and not to leave the other undone. Ye blind guides! which strain at a gnat, and swallow a camel. Woe unto you, scribes and Pharisees, hypocrites! for ye make clean the outside of the cup and of the platter; but within, they are full of extortion and excess.——Woe unto you, scribes and Pharisees, hypocrites! for ye are like unto whited sepulchres, which indeed appear beautiful outward, but are within full of dead men's bones, and of all uncleanness. Even so ye also outwardly appear righteous unto men, but within ye are full of hypocrisy and iniquity."

Dark and terrible as is this picture, I hold it to be strictly true of the overwhelming mass of professed Christians in America. They strain at a gnat, and swallow a camel. Could any thing be more true of our churches? They would be shocked at the proposition of fellowshipping a *sheep*-stealer; and at the same time they hug to their communion a *man*-stealer, and brand me with being an infidel, if I find fault with them for it. They attend with Pharisaical strictness to the outward forms of religion, and at the same time neglect the weightier matters of the law, judgment, mercy, and faith. They are always ready to sacrifice, but seldom to show mercy. They are they who are represented as professing to love God whom they have not seen, whilst they hate their brother whom they have seen. They love the heathen on the other side of the globe. They can pray for him, pay money to have the Bible put into his hand, and missionaries to instruct him; while they despise and totally neglect the heathen at their own doors.

Such is, very briefly, my view of the religion of this land; and to avoid any misunderstanding, growing out of the use of general terms, I mean, by the religion of this land, that which is revealed in the words, deeds, and actions, of those bodies, north and south, calling themselves Christian churches, and yet in union with slaveholders. It is against religion, as presented by these bodies, that I have felt it my duty to testify.

I conclude these remarks by copying the following portrait of the religion of the south, (which is, by communion and fellowship, the religion of the north,) which I soberly affirm is "true to the life," and without caricature or the slightest exaggeration. It is said to have been drawn, several years before the present anti-slavery agitation began, by a northern Methodist preacher, who, while residing at the south, had an opportunity to see slaveholding morals, manners, and piety, with his own eyes. "Shall I not visit for these things? saith the Lord. Shall not my soul be avenged on such a nation as this?"

"A PARODY.

"Come, saints and sinners, hear me tell
How pious priests whip Jack and Nell,
And women buy and children sell,
And preach all sinners down to hell,
And sing of heavenly union.

"They'll bleat and baa, dona like goats,
Gorge down black sheep, and strain at motes,
Array their backs in fine black coats,
Then seize their negroes by their throats,
And choke, for heavenly union.

"They'll church you if you sip a dram,
And damn you if you steal a lamb;
Yet rob old Tony, Doll, and Sam,
Of human rights, and bread and ham;
Kidnapper's heavenly union.

"They'll loudly talk of Christ's reward,
And bind his image with a cord,
And scold, and swing the lash abhorred,
And sell their brother in the Lord
To handcuffed heavenly union.

"They'll read and sing a sacred song,
And make a prayer both loud and long,
And teach the right and do the wrong,
Hailing the brother, sister throng,
With words of heavenly union.

"We wonder how such saints can sing,
Or praise the Lord upon the wing,
Who roar, and scold, and whip, and sting,
And to their slaves and mammon cling,
In guilty conscience union.

"They'll raise tobacco, corn, and rye,
And drive, and thieve, and cheat, and lie,
And lay up treasures in the sky,
By making switch and cowskin fly,
In hope of heavenly union.

"They'll crack old Tony on the skull,
And preach and roar like Bashan bull,
Or braying ass, of mischief full,
Then seize old Jacob by the wool,
And pull for heavenly union.

"A roaring, ranting, sleek man-thief,
Who lived on mutton, veal, and beef,
Yet never would afford relief
To needy, sable sons of grief,
Was big with heavenly union.

" 'Love not the world,' the preacher said,
And winked his eye, and shook his head;
He seized on Tom, and Dick, and Ned,
Cut short their meat, and clothes, and bread,
Yet still loved heavenly union.

"Another preacher whining spoke
Of One whose heart for sinners broke;
He tied old Nanny to an oak,
And drew the blood at every stroke,
And prayed for heavenly union.

"Two others oped their iron jaws,
And waved their children-stealing paws;
There sat their children in gewgaws;
By stinting negroes' backs and maws,
They kept up heavenly union.

"All good from Jack another takes,
And entertains their flirts and rakes,
Who dress as sleek as glossy snakes,
And cram their mouths with sweetened cakes;
And this goes down for union."

Sincerely and earnestly hoping that this little book may do something toward throwing light on the American slave system, and hastening the glad day of deliverance to the millions of my brethren in bonds—faithfully relying upon the power of truth, love, and justice, for success in my humble efforts—and solemnly pledging my self anew to the sacred cause,—I subscribe myself,

FREDERICK DOUGLASS.

Lynn, *Mass., April* 28, 1845.

Selections from *Incidents in the Life of a Slave Girl*

WRITTEN BY HERSELF
HARRIET A. JACOBS
EDITED BY L. MARIA CHILD

1861

PREFACE BY THE AUTHOR

Reader, be assured this narrative is no fiction. I am aware that some of my adventures may seem incredible; but they are, nevertheless, strictly true. I have not exaggerated the wrongs inflicted by Slavery; on the contrary, my descriptions fall far short of the facts. I have concealed the names of places, and given persons fictitious names. I had no motive for secrecy on my own account, but I deemed it kind and considerate towards others to pursue this course.

I wish I were more competent to the task I have undertaken. But I trust my readers will excuse deficiencies in consideration of circumstances. I was born and reared in Slavery; and I remained in a Slave State twenty-seven years. Since I have been at the North, it has been necessary for me to work diligently for my own support, and the education of my children. This has not left me much leisure to make up for the loss of early opportunities to improve myself; and it has compelled me to write these pages at irregular intervals, whenever I could snatch an hour from household duties.

When I first arrived in Philadelphia, Bishop Paine advised me to publish a sketch of my life, but I told him I was altogether incompetent to such an undertaking.

Though I have improved my mind somewhat since that time, I still remain of the same opinion; but I trust my motives will excuse what might otherwise seem presumptuous. I have not written my experiences in order to attract attention to myself; on the contrary, it would have been more pleasant to me to have been silent about my own history. Neither do I care to excite sympathy for my own sufferings. But I do earnestly desire to arouse the women of the North to a realizing sense of the condition of two millions of women at the South, still in bondage, suffering what I suffered, and most of them far worse. I want to add my testimony to that of abler pens to convince the people of the Free States what Slavery really is. Only by experience can any one realize how deep, and dark, and foul is that pit of abominations. May the blessing of God rest on this imperfect effort in behalf of my persecuted people!

LINDA BRENT.

INTRODUCTION BY THE EDITOR

The author of the following autobiography is personally known to me, and her conversation and manners inspire me with confidence. During the last seventeen years, she has lived the greater part of the time with a distinguished family in New York, and has so deported herself as to be highly esteemed by them. This fact is sufficient, without further credentials of her character. I believe those who know her will not be disposed to doubt her veracity, though some incidents in her story are more romantic than fiction.

At her request, I have revised her manuscript; but such changes as I have made have been mainly for purposes of condensation and orderly arrangement. I have not added any thing to the incidents, or changed the import of her very pertinent remarks. With trifling exceptions, both the ideas and the language are her own. I pruned excrescences a little, but otherwise I had no reason for changing her lively and dramatic way of telling her own story. The names of both persons and places are known to me; but for good reasons I suppress them.

It will naturally excite surprise that a woman reared in Slavery should be able to write so well. But circumstances will explain this. In the first place, nature endowed her with quick perceptions. Secondly, the mistress, with whom she lived till she was twelve years old, was a kind, considerate friend, who taught her to read and spell. Thirdly, she was placed in favorable circumstances after she came to the North; having frequent intercourse with intelligent persons, who felt a friendly interest in her welfare, and were disposed to give her opportunities for self-improvement.

I am well aware that many will accuse me of indecorum for presenting these pages to the public; for the experiences of this intelligent and much-injured woman belong to a class which some call delicate subjects, and others indelicate. This peculiar phase of Slavery has generally been kept veiled; but the public ought to be made acquainted with its monstrous features, and I willingly take the responsibility of presenting them with the veil withdrawn. I do this for the sake of my sisters in bondage, who are suffering wrongs so foul, that our ears are too delicate to listen to them. I do it with the hope of arousing conscientious and reflecting women at the North to a sense of their duty in the exertion of moral influence on the question of Slavery, on all possible occasions. I do it with the hope that every man who reads this narrative will swear solemnly before God that, so far as he has power to prevent it, no fugitive from Slavery shall ever be sent back to suffer in that loathsome den of corruption and cruelty.

L. MARIA CHILD.

CHAPTER I

Childhood

I was born a slave; but I never knew it till six years of happy childhood had passed away. My father was a carpenter, and considered so intelligent and skilful in his trade, that, when buildings out of the common line were to be erected, he was sent for from long distances, to be head workman. On condition of paying his mistress two hundred dollars a year, and supporting himself, he was allowed to work at his trade, and manage his own affairs. His strongest wish was to purchase his children; but, though he several times offered his hard earnings for that purpose, he never succeeded. In complexion my parents were a light shade of brownish yellow, and were termed mulattoes. They lived together in a comfortable home; and, though we were all slaves, I was so fondly shielded that I never dreamed I was a piece of merchandise, trusted to them for safe keeping, and liable to be demanded of them at any moment. I had one brother, William, who was two years younger than myself—a bright, affectionate child. I had also a great treasure in my maternal grandmother, who was a remarkable woman in many respects. She was the daughter of a planter in South Carolina, who, at his death, left her mother and his three children free, with money to go to St. Augustine, where they had relatives. It was during the Revolutionary War; and they were captured on their passage, carried back, and sold to different purchasers. Such was the story my grandmother used to tell me; but I do not remember all the particulars. She was a little girl when she was captured and sold to the keeper of a large hotel. I have often heard her tell how hard she fared during childhood. But as she grew older she evinced so much intelligence, and was so faithful, that her master and mistress could not help seeing it was for their interest to take care of such a valuable piece of property. She became an indispensable personage in the household, officiating in all capacities, from cook and wet nurse to seamstress. She was much praised for her cooking; and her nice crackers became so famous in the neighborhood that many people were desirous of obtaining them. In consequence of numerous requests of this kind, she asked permission of her mistress to bake crackers at night, after all the household work was done; and she obtained leave to do it, provided she would clothe herself and her children from the profits. Upon these terms, after working hard all day for her mistress, she began her midnight bakings, assisted by her two oldest children. The business proved profitable; and each year she laid by a little, which was saved for a fund to purchase her children. Her master died, and the property was divided among his heirs. The widow had her dower in the hotel, which she continued to keep open. My grandmother remained in her service as a slave; but her children were divided among her master's children. As she had five, Benjamin, the youngest one, was sold, in order that each heir might have an equal portion of dollars and cents. There was so little difference in our ages that he seemed more like my brother than my uncle. He was a bright, handsome lad, nearly white; for he inherited the complexion my grandmother had derived from Anglo-Saxon ancestors. Though only ten years old, seven hundred and twenty dollars were paid for him. His sale was a terrible blow to my grandmother; but she was naturally hopeful, and she went to work with renewed energy, trusting in time to be able to purchase some of her children. She had laid up three hundred dollars, which her mistress one day begged as a loan, promising to pay her soon. The reader probably knows that no promise or writing given to a slave is legally binding; for, according to Southern laws, a slave, *being* property, can *hold* no property. When my grandmother lent her hard earnings to her mistress, she trusted solely to her honor. The honor of a slaveholder to a slave!

To this good grandmother I was indebted for many comforts. My brother Willie and I often received portions of the crackers, cakes, and preserves, she made to sell; and after we ceased to be children we were indebted to her for many more important services.

Such were the unusually fortunate circumstances of my early childhood. When I was six years old, my mother died; and then, for the first time, I learned, by the talk around me, that I was a slave. My mother's mistress was the daughter of my grandmother's mistress. She was the foster sister of my mother; they were both nourished at my grandmother's breast. In fact, my mother had been weaned at three months old, that the babe of the mistress might obtain sufficient food. They played together as children; and, when they became women, my mother was a most faithful servant to her whiter foster sister. On her death-bed her mistress promised that her children should never suffer for any thing; and during her lifetime she kept her word. They all spoke kindly of my dead mother, who had been a slave merely in name, but in nature was noble and womanly. I grieved for her, and my young mind was troubled with the thought who would now take care of me and my little brother. I was told that my home was now to be with her mistress; and I found it a happy one. No toilsome or disagreeable duties were imposed upon me. My mistress was so kind to me that I was always glad to do her bidding, and proud to labor for her as much as my young years would permit. I would sit by her side for hours, sewing diligently, with a heart as free from care as that of any free-born white child. When she thought I was tired, she would send me out to run and jump; and away I bounded, to gather berries or flowers to decorate her room. Those were happy days—too happy to last. The slave child had no thought for the morrow; but there came that blight, which too surely waits on every human being born to be a chattel.

When I was nearly twelve years old, my kind mistress

sickened and died. As I saw the cheek grow paler, and the eye more glassy, how earnestly I prayed in my heart that she might live! I loved her; for she had been almost like a mother to me. My prayers were not answered. She died, and they buried her in the little churchyard, where, day after day, my tears fell upon her grave.

I was sent to spend a week with my grandmother. I was now old enough to begin to think of the future; and again and again I asked myself what they would do with me. I felt sure I should never find another mistress so kind as the one who was gone. She had promised my dying mother that her children should never suffer for any thing; and when I remembered that, and recalled her many proofs of attachment to me, I could not help having some hopes that she had left me free. My friends were almost certain it would be so. They thought she would be sure to do it, on account of my mother's love and faithful service. But, alas! we all know that the memory of a faithful slave does not avail much to save her children from the auction block.

After a brief period of suspense, the will of my mistress was read, and we learned that she had bequeathed me to her sister's daughter, a child of five years old. So vanished our hopes. My mistress had taught me the precepts of God's Word: "Thou shalt love thy neighbor as thyself." "Whatsoever ye would that men should do unto you, do ye even so unto them." But I was her slave, and I suppose she did not recognize me as her neighbor. I would give much to blot out from my memory that one great wrong. As a child, I loved my mistress; and, looking back on the happy days I spent with her, I try to think with less bitterness of this act of injustice. While I was with her, she taught me to read and spell; and for this privilege, which so rarely falls to the lot of a slave, I bless her memory.

She possessed but few slaves; and at her death those were all distributed among her relatives. Five of them were my grandmother's children, and had shared the same milk that nourished her mother's children. Notwithstanding my grandmother's long and faithful service to her owners, not one of her children escaped the auction block. These God-breathing machines are no more, in the sight of their masters, than the cotton they plant, or the horses they tend.

CHAPTER II

The New Master and Mistress

Dr. Flint, a physician in the neighborhood, had married the sister of my mistress, and I was now the property of their little daughter. It was not without murmuring that I prepared for my new home; and what added to my unhappiness, was the fact that my brother William was purchased by the same family. My father, by his nature, as well as by the habit of transacting business as a skilful mechanic, had more of the feelings of a freeman than is common among slaves. My brother was a spirited boy; and being brought up under such influences, he early detested the name of master and mistress. One day, when his father and his mistress had happened to call him at the same time, he hesitated between the two; being perplexed to know which had the strongest claim upon his obedience. He finally concluded to go to his mistress. When my father reproved him for it, he said, "You both called me, and I didn't know which I ought to go to first."

"You are *my* child," replied our father, "and when I call you, you should come immediately, if you have to pass through fire and water."

Poor Willie! He was now to learn his first lesson of obedience to a master. Grandmother tried to cheer us with hopeful words, and they found an echo in the credulous hearts of youth.

When we entered our new home we encountered cold looks, cold words, and cold treatment. We were glad when the night came. On my narrow bed I moaned and wept, I felt so desolate and alone.

I had been there nearly a year, when a dear little friend of mine was buried. I heard her mother sob, as the clods fell on the coffin of her only child, and I turned away from the grave, feeling thankful that I still had something left to love. I met my grandmother, who said, "Come with me, Linda;" and from her tone I knew that something sad had happened. She led me apart from the people, and then said, "My child, your father is dead." Dead! How could I believe it? He had died so suddenly I had not even heard that he was sick. I went home with my grandmother. My heart rebelled against God, who had taken from me mother, father, mistress, and friend. The good grandmother tried to comfort me. "Who knows the ways of God?" said she. "Perhaps they have been kindly taken from the evil days to come." Years afterwards I often thought of this. She promised to be a mother to her grandchildren, so far as she might be permitted to do so; and strengthened by her love, I returned to my master's. I thought I should be allowed to go to my father's house the next morning; but I was ordered to go for flowers, that my mistress's house might be decorated for an evening party. I spent the day gathering flowers and weaving them into festoons, while the dead body of my father was lying within a mile of me. What cared my owners for that? he was merely a piece of property. Moreover, they thought he had spoiled his children, by teaching them to feel that they were human beings. This was blasphemous doctrine for a slave to teach; presumptuous in him, and dangerous to the masters.

The next day I followed his remains to a humble grave beside that of my dear mother. There were those who knew my father's worth, and respected his memory.

My home now seemed more dreary than ever. The laugh of the little slave-children sounded harsh and cruel. It was selfish to feel so about the joy of others. My brother moved about with a very grave face. I tried to comfort him, by saying, "Take courage, Willie; brighter days will come by and by."

"You don't know any thing about it, Linda," he replied. "We shall have to stay here all our days; we shall never be free."

I argued that we were growing older and stronger, and that perhaps we might, before long, be allowed to hire our own time, and then we could earn money to buy our freedom. William declared this was much easier to say than to do; moreover, he did not intend to *buy* his freedom. We held daily controversies upon this subject.

Little attention was paid to the slaves' meals in Dr. Flint's house. If they could catch a bit of food while it was going, well and good. I gave myself no trouble on that score, for on my various errands I passed my grandmother's house, where there was always something to spare for me. I was frequently threatened with punishment if I stopped there; and my grandmother, to avoid detaining me, often stood at the gate with something for my breakfast or dinner. I was indebted to *her* for all my comforts, spiritual or temporal. It was *her* labor that supplied my scanty wardrobe. I have a vivid recollection of the linsey-woolsey dress given me every winter by Mrs. Flint. How I hated it! It was one of the badges of slavery.

While my grandmother was thus helping to support me from her hard earnings, the three hundred dollars she had lent her mistress were never repaid. When her mistress died, her son-in-law, Dr. Flint, was appointed executor. When grandmother applied to him for payment, he said the estate was insolvent, and the law prohibited payment. It did not, however, prohibit him from retaining the silver candelabra, which had been purchased with that money. I presume they will be handed down in the family, from generation to generation.

My grandmother's mistress had always promised her that, at her death, she should be free; and it was said that in her will she made good the promise. But when the estate was settled, Dr. Flint told the faithful old servant that, under existing circumstances, it was necessary she should be sold.

On the appointed day, the customary advertisement

was posted up, proclaiming that there would be a "public sale of negroes, horses, &c." Dr. Flint called to tell my grandmother that he was unwilling to wound her feelings by putting her up at auction, and that he would prefer to dispose of her at private sale. My grandmother saw through his hypocrisy; she understood very well that he was ashamed of the job. She was a very spirited woman, and if he was base enough to sell her, when her mistress intended she should be free, she was determined the public should know it. She had for a long time supplied many families with crackers and preserves; consequently, "Aunt Marthy," as she was called, was generally known, and every body who knew her respected her intelligence and good character. Her long and faithful service in the family was also well known, and the intention of her mistress to leave her free. When the day of sale came, she took her place among the chattels, and at the first call she sprang upon the auction-block. Many voices called out, "Shame! Shame! Who is going to sell *you*, aunt Marthy? Don't stand there! That is no place for *you*." Without saying a word, she quietly awaited her fate. No one bid for her. At last, a feeble voice said, "Fifty dollars." It came from a maiden lady, seventy years old, the sister of my grandmother's deceased mistress. She had lived forty years under the same roof with my grandmother; she knew how faithfully she had served her owners, and how cruelly she had been defrauded of her rights; and she resolved to protect her. The auctioneer waited for a higher bid; but her wishes were respected; no one bid above her. She could neither read nor write; and when the bill of sale was made out, she signed it with a cross. But what consequence was that, when she had a big heart overflowing with human kindness? She gave the old servant her freedom.

At that time, my grandmother was just fifty years old. Laborious years had passed since then; and now my brother and I were slaves to the man who had defrauded her of her money, and tried to defraud her of her freedom. One of my mother's sisters, called Aunt Nancy, was also a slave in his family. She was a kind, good aunt to me; and supplied the place of both housekeeper and waiting maid to her mistress. She was, in fact, at the beginning and end of every thing.

Mrs. Flint, like many southern women, was totally

deficient in energy. She had not strength to superintend her household affairs; but her nerves were so strong, that she could sit in her easy chair and see a woman whipped, till the blood trickled from every stroke of the lash. She was a member of the church; but partaking of the Lord's supper did not seem to put her in a Christian frame of mind. If dinner was not served at the exact time on that particular Sunday, she would station herself in the kitchen, and wait till it was dished, and then spit in all the kettles and pans that had been used for cooking. She did this to prevent the cook and her children from eking out their meagre fare with the remains of the gravy and other scrapings. The slaves could get nothing to eat except what she chose to give them. Provisions were weighed out by the pound and ounce, three times a day. I can assure you she gave them no chance to eat wheat bread from her flour barrel. She knew how many biscuits a quart of flour would make, and exactly what size they ought to be.

Dr. Flint was an epicure. The cook never sent a dinner to his table without fear and trembling; for if there happened to be a dish not to his liking, he would either order her to be whipped, or compel her to eat every mouthful of it in his presence. The poor, hungry creature might not have objected to eating it; but she did object to having her master cram it down her throat till she choked.

They had a pet dog, that was a nuisance in the house. The cook was ordered to make some Indian mush for him. He refused to eat, and when his head was held over it, the froth flowed from his mouth into the basin. He died a few minutes after. When Dr. Flint came in, he said the mush had not been well cooked, and that was the reason the animal would not eat it. He sent for the cook, and compelled her to eat it. He thought that the woman's stomach was stronger than the dog's; but her sufferings afterwards proved that he was mistaken. This poor woman endured many cruelties from her master and mistress; sometimes she was locked up, away from her nursing baby, for a whole day and night.

When I had been in the family a few weeks, one of the plantation slaves was brought to town, by order of his master. It was near night when he arrived, and Dr. Flint ordered him to be taken to the work house, and tied up to the joist, so that his feet would just escape the ground. In that situation he was to wait till the doctor had taken his tea. I shall never forget that night. Never before, in my life, had I heard hundreds of blows fall, in succession, on a human being. His piteous groans, and his "O, pray don't, massa," rang in my ear for months afterwards. There were many conjectures as to the cause of this terrible punishment. Some said master accused him of stealing corn; others said the slave had quarrelled with his wife, in presence of the overseer, and had accused his master of being the father of her child. They were both black, and the child was very fair.

I went into the work house next morning, and saw the cowhide still wet with blood, and the boards all covered with gore. The poor man lived, and continued to quarrel with his wife. A few months afterwards Dr. Flint handed them both over to a slavetrader. The guilty man put their value into his pocket, and had the satisfaction of knowing that they were out of sight and hearing. When the mother was delivered into the trader's hands, she said, "You *promised* to treat me well." To which he replied, "You have let your tongue run too far; damn you!" She had forgotten that it was a crime for a slave to tell who was the father of her child.

From others than the master persecution also comes in such cases. I once saw a young slave girl dying soon after the birth of a child nearly white. In her agony she cried out, "O Lord, come and take me!" Her mistress stood by, and mocked at her like an incarnate fiend. "You suffer, do you?" she exclaimed. "I am glad of it. You deserve it all, and more too."

The girl's mother said, "The baby is dead, thank God; and I hope my poor child will soon be in heaven, too."

"Heaven!" retorted the mistress. "There is no such place for the like of her and her bastard."

The poor mother turned away, sobbing. Her dying daughter called her, feebly, and as she bent over her, I heard her say, "Don't grieve so, mother; God knows all about it; and HE will have mercy upon me."

Her sufferings, afterwards, became so intense, that her mistress felt unable to stay; but when she left the room, the scornful smile was still on her lips. Seven children called her mother. The poor black woman had but the one child, whose eyes she saw closing in death, while she thanked God for taking her away from the greater bitterness of life.

CHAPTER

III

The Slaves' New Year's Day

Dr. Flint owned a fine residence in town, several farms, and about fifty slaves, besides hiring a number by the year.

Hiring-day at the south takes place on the 1st of January. On the 2d, the slaves are expected to go to their new masters. On a farm, they work until the corn and cotton are laid. They then have two holidays. Some masters give them a good dinner under the trees. This over, they work until Christmas eve. If no heavy charges are meantime brought against them, they are given four or five holidays, whichever the master or overseer may think proper. Then comes New Year's eve; and they gather together their little alls, or more properly speaking, their little nothings, and wait anxiously for the dawning of day. At the appointed hour the grounds are thronged with men, women, and children, waiting, like criminals, to hear their doom pronounced. The slave is sure to know who is the most humane, or cruel master, within forty miles of him.

It is easy to find out, on that day, who clothes and feeds his slaves well; for he is surrounded by a crowd, begging, "Please, massa, hire me this year. I will work *very* hard, massa."

If a slave is unwilling to go with his new master, he is

whipped, or locked up in jail, until he consents to go, and promises not to run away during the year. Should he chance to change his mind, thinking it justifiable to violate an extorted promise, woe unto him if he is caught! The whip is used till the blood flows at his feet; and his stiffened limbs are put in chains, to be dragged in the field for days and days!

If he lives until the next year, perhaps the same man will hire him again, without even giving him an opportunity of going to the hiring-ground. After those for hire are disposed of, those for sale are called up.

O, you happy free women, contrast *your* New Year's day with that of the poor bond-woman! With you it is a pleasant season, and the light of the day is blessed. Friendly wishes meet you every where, and gifts are showered upon you. Even hearts that have been estranged from you soften at this season, and lips that have been silent echo back, "I wish you a happy New Year." Children bring their little offerings, and raise their rosy lips for a caress. They are your own, and no hand but that of death can take them from you.

But to the slave mother New Year's day comes laden with peculiar sorrows. She sits on her cold cabin floor, watching the children who may all be torn from her the next morning; and often does she wish that she and they might die before the day dawns. She may be an ignorant creature, degraded by the system that has brutalized her from childhood; but she has a mother's instincts, and is capable of feeling a mother's agonies.

On one of these sale days, I saw a mother lead seven children to the auction-block. She knew that *some* of them would be taken from her; but they took *all*. The children were sold to a slave-trader, and their mother was bought by a man in her own town. Before night her children were all far away. She begged the trader to tell her where he intended to take them; this he refused to do. How *could* he, when he knew he would sell them, one by one, wherever he could command the highest price? I met that mother in the street, and her wild, haggard face lives to-day in my mind. She wrung her hands in anguish, and exclaimed, "Gone! All gone! Why *don't* God kill me?" I had no words wherewith to comfort her. Instances of this kind are of daily, yea, of hourly occurrence.

Slaveholders have a method, peculiar to their institution, of getting rid of *old* slaves, whose lives have been worn out in their service. I knew an old woman, who for seventy years faithfully served her master. She had become almost helpless, from hard labor and disease. Her owners moved to Alabama, and the old black woman was left to be sold to any body who would give twenty dollars for her.

CHAPTER V

The Trials of Girlhood

During the first years of my service in Dr. Flint's family, I was accustomed to share some indulgences with the children of my mistress. Though this seemed to me no more than right, I was grateful for it, and tried to merit the kindness by the faithful discharge of my duties. But I now entered on my fifteenth year—a sad epoch in the life of a slave girl. My master began to whisper foul words in my ear. Young as I was, I could not remain ignorant of their import. I tried to treat them with indifference or contempt. The master's age, my extreme youth, and the fear that his conduct would be reported to my grandmother, made him bear this treatment for many months. He was a crafty man, and resorted to many means to accomplish his purposes. Sometimes he had stormy, terrific ways, that made his victims tremble; sometimes he assumed a gentleness that he thought must surely subdue. Of the two, I preferred his stormy moods, although they left me trembling. He tried his utmost to corrupt the pure principles my grandmother had instilled. He peopled my young mind with unclean images, such as only a vile monster could think of. I turned from him with disgust and hatred. But he was my master. I was compelled to live under the same roof with him—where I saw a man forty years my senior daily violating the most sacred commandments of nature. He told me I was his property; that I must be subject to his will in all things. My soul revolted against the mean tyranny. But where could I turn for protection? No matter whether the slave girl be as black as ebony or as fair as her mistress. In either case, there is no shadow of law to protect her from insult, from violence, or even from death; all these are inflicted by fiends who bear the shape of men. The mistress, who ought to protect the helpless victim, has no other feelings towards her but those of jealousy and rage. The degradation, the wrongs, the vices, that grow out of slavery, are more than I can describe. They are greater than you would willingly believe. Surely, if you credited one half the truths that are told you concerning the helpless millions suffering in this cruel bondage, you at the north would not help to tighten the yoke. You surely would refuse to do for the master, on your own soil, the mean and cruel work which trained bloodhounds and the lowest class of whites do for him at the south.

Every where the years bring to all enough of sin and sorrow; but in slavery the very dawn of life is darkened by these shadows. Even the little child, who is accustomed to wait on her mistress and her children, will learn, before she is twelve years old, why it is that her mistress hates such and such a one among the slaves. Perhaps the child's own mother is among those hated ones. She listens to violent outbreaks of jealous passion, and cannot help understanding what is the cause. She will become prematurely knowing in evil things. Soon she will learn to tremble when she hears her master's footfall. She will be compelled to realize that she is no longer a child. If God has bestowed beauty upon her, it will prove her greatest curse. That which commands admiration in the white woman only hastens the degradation of the female slave. I know that some are too much brutalized by slavery to feel the humiliation of their position; but many slaves feel it most acutely, and shrink from the memory of it. I cannot tell how much I suffered in the presence of these wrongs, nor how I am still pained by the retrospect. My master met me at every turn, reminding me that I belonged to him, and swearing by heaven and earth that he would compel me to submit to him. If I went out for a breath of fresh air, after a day of unwearied toil, his footsteps dogged me. If I knelt by my mother's grave, his dark shadow fell on me even there. The light heart which nature had given me became heavy with sad forebodings. The other slaves in my master's house noticed the change. Many of them pitied me; but none dared to ask the cause. They had no need to inquire. They knew too well the guilty practices under that roof; and they were aware that to speak of them was an offence that never went unpunished.

I longed for some one to confide in. I would have given the world to have laid my head on my grandmother's faithful bosom, and told her all my troubles. But Dr. Flint swore he would kill me, if I was not as silent as the grave. Then, although my grandmother was all in all to me, I feared her as well as loved her. I had been accustomed to look up to her with a respect bordering upon awe. I was very young, and felt shamefaced about telling her such impure things, especially as I knew her to be very strict on such subjects. Moreover, she was a woman of a high spirit. She was usually very quiet in her demeanor; but if her indignation was once roused, it was not very easily quelled. I had been told that she once chased a white gentleman with a loaded pistol, because he insulted one of her daughters. I dreaded the consequences of a violent outbreak; and both pride and fear kept me silent. But though I did not confide in my grandmother, and even evaded her vigilant watchfulness and inquiry, her presence in the neighborhood was some protection to me. Though she had been a slave, Dr. Flint was afraid of her. He dreaded her scorching rebukes. Moreover, she was known and patronized by many people; and he did not wish to have his villainy made public. It was lucky for me that I did not live on a distant plantation, but in a town not so large that the inhabitants were ignorant of each other's affairs. Bad as the laws and customs in a slaveholding community, the doctor, as a professional man, deemed it prudent to keep up some outward show of decency.

O, what days and nights of fear and sorrow that man caused me! Reader, it is not to awaken sympathy for myself that I am telling you truthfully what I suffered in slavery. I do it to kindle a flame of compassion in your hearts for my sisters who are still in bondage, suffering as I once suffered.

I once saw two beautiful children playing together. One was a fair white child; the other was her slave, and also her sister. When I saw them embracing each other, and heard their joyous laughter, I turned sadly away from the lovely sight. I foresaw the inevitable blight that would fall on the little slave's heart. I knew how soon her laughter would be changed to sighs. The fair child grew up to be a still fairer woman. From childhood to womanhood her pathway was blooming with flowers, and overarched by a sunny sky. Scarcely one day of her life had been clouded when the sun rose on her happy bridal morning.

How had those years dealt with her slave sister, the little playmate of her childhood? She, also, was very beautiful; but the flowers and sunshine of love were not for her. She drank the cup of sin, and shame, and misery, whereof her persecuted race are compelled to drink.

In view of these things, why are ye silent, ye free men and women of the north? Why do your tongues falter in maintenance of the right? Would that I had more ability! But my heart is so full, and my pen is so weak! There are noble men and women who plead for us, striving to help those who cannot help themselves. God bless them! God give them strength and courage to go on! God bless those, every where, who are laboring to advance the cause of humanity!

CHAPTER VI

The Jealous Mistress

I would ten thousand times rather that my children should be the half-starved paupers of Ireland than to be the most pampered among the slaves of America. I would rather drudge out my life on a cotton plantation, till the grave opened to give me rest, than to live with an unprincipled master and a jealous mistress. The felon's home in a penitentiary is preferable. He may repent, and turn from the error of his ways, and so find peace; but it is not so with a favorite slave. She is not allowed to have any pride of character. It is deemed a crime in her to wish to be virtuous.

Mrs. Flint possessed the key to her husband's character before I was born. She might have used this knowledge to counsel and to screen the young and the innocent among her slaves; but for them she had no sympathy. They were the objects of her constant suspicion and malevolence. She watched her husband with unceasing vigilance; but he was well practised in means to evade it. What he could not find opportunity to say in words he manifested in signs. He invented more than were ever thought of in a deaf and dumb asylum. I let them pass, as if I did not understand what he meant; and many were the curses and threats bestowed on me for my stupidity.

One day he caught me teaching myself to write. He frowned, as if he was not well pleased; but I suppose he came to the conclusion that such an accomplishment might help to advance his favorite scheme. Before long, notes were often slipped into my hand. I would return them, saying, "I can't read them, sir." "Can't you?" he replied; "then I must read them to you." He always finished the reading by asking, "Do you understand?" Sometimes he would complain of the heat of the tea room, and order his supper to be placed on a small table in the piazza. He would seat himself there with a well-satisfied smile, and tell me to stand by and brush away the flies. He would eat very slowly, pausing between the mouthfuls. These intervals were employed in describing the happiness I was so foolishly throwing away, and in threatening me with the penalty that finally awaited my stubborn disobedience. He boasted much of the forbearance he had exercised towards me, and reminded me that there was a limit to his patience. When I succeeded in avoiding opportunities for him to talk to me at home, I was ordered to come to his office, to do some errand. When there, I was obliged to stand and listen to such language as he saw fit to address to me. Sometimes I so openly expressed my contempt for him that he would become violently enraged, and I wondered why he did not strike me. Circumstanced as he was, he probably thought it was better policy to be forbearing. But the state of things grew worse and worse daily. In desperation I told him that I must and would apply to my grandmother for protection. He threatened me with death, and worse than death, if I made any complaint to her. Strange to say, I did not despair. I was naturally of a buoyant disposition, and always I had a hope of somehow getting out of his clutches. Like many a poor, simple slave before me, I trusted that some threads of joy would yet be woven into my dark destiny.

I had entered my sixteenth year, and every day it became more apparent that my presence was intolerable to Mrs. Flint. Angry words frequently passed between her and her husband. He had never punished me himself, and he would not allow any body else to punish me. In that respect, she was never satisfied; but, in her angry moods, no terms were too vile for her to bestow upon me. Yet I, whom she detested so bitterly, had far more pity for her than he had, whose duty it was to make her life happy. I never wronged her, or wished to wrong her; and one word of kindness from her would have brought me to her feet.

After repeated quarrels between the doctor and his wife, he announced his intention to take his youngest daughter, then four years old, to sleep in his apartment. It was necessary that a servant should sleep in the same room, to be on hand if the child stirred. I was selected for that office, and informed for what purpose that arrangement had been made. By managing to keep within sight of people, as much as possible, during the day time, I had hitherto succeeded in eluding my master, though a razor was often held to my throat to force me to change this line of policy. At night I slept by the side of my great aunt, where I felt safe. He was too prudent to come into her room. She was an old woman, and had been in the family many years. Moreover, as a married man, and a professional man, he deemed it necessary to save appearances in some degree. But he resolved to remove the obstacle in the way of his scheme; and he thought he had planned it so that he should evade suspicion. He was well aware how much I prized my refuge by the side of my old aunt, and he determined to dispossess me of it. The first night the doctor had the little child in his room alone. The next morning, I was ordered to take my station as nurse the following night. A kind Providence interposed in my favor. During the day Mrs. Flint heard of this new arrangement, and a storm followed. I rejoiced to hear it rage.

After a while my mistress sent for me to come to her room. Her first question was, "Did you know you were to sleep in the doctor's room?"

"Yes, ma'am."

"Who told you?"

"My master."

"Will you answer truly all the questions I ask?"

"Yes, ma'am."

"Tell me, then, as you hope to be forgiven, are you innocent of what I have accused you?"

"I am."

She handed me a Bible, and said, "Lay your hand on

your heart, kiss this holy book, and swear before God that you tell me the truth."

I took the oath she required, and I did it with a clear conscience.

"You have taken God's holy word to testify your innocence," said she. "If you have deceived me, beware! Now take this stool, sit down, look me directly in the face, and tell me all that has passed between your master and you."

I did as she ordered. As I went on with my account her color changed frequently, she wept, and sometimes groaned. She spoke in tones so sad, that I was touched by her grief. The tears came to my eyes; but I was soon convinced that her emotions arose from anger and wounded pride. She felt that her marriage vows were desecrated, her dignity insulted; but she had no compassion for the poor victim of her husband's perfidy. She pitied herself as a martyr; but she was incapable of feeling for the condition of shame and misery in which her unfortunate, helpless slave was placed.

Yet perhaps she had some touch of feeling for me; for when the conference was ended, she spoke kindly, and promised to protect me. I should have been much comforted by this assurance if I could have had confidence in it; but my experiences in slavery had filled me with distrust. She was not a very refined woman, and had not much control over her passions. I was an object of her jealousy, and, consequently, of her hatred; and I knew I could not expect kindness or confidence from her under the circumstances in which I was placed. I could not blame her. Slaveholders' wives feel as other women would under similar circumstances. The fire of her temper kindled from small sparks, and now the flame became so intense that the doctor was obliged to give up his intended arrangement.

I knew I had ignited the torch, and I expected to suffer for it afterwards; but I felt too thankful to my mistress for the timely aid she rendered me to care much about that. She now took me to sleep in a room adjoining her own. There I was an object of her especial care, though not of her especial comfort, for she spent many a sleepless night to watch over me. Sometimes I woke up, and found her bending over me. At other times she whispered in my ear, as though it was her husband who was speaking to me, and listened to hear what I would answer. If she startled me, on such occasions, she would glide stealthily away; and the next morning she would tell me I had been talking in my sleep, and ask who I was talking to. At last, I began to be fearful for my life. It had been often threatened; and you can imagine, better than I can describe, what an unpleasant sensation it must produce to wake up in the dead of night and find a jealous woman bending over you. Terrible as this experience was, I had fears that it would give place to one more terrible.

My mistress grew weary of her vigils; they did not prove satisfactory. She changed her tactics. She now tried the trick of accusing my master of crime, in my presence, and gave my name as the author of the accusation. To my utter astonishment, he replied, "I don't believe it: but if she did acknowledge it, you tortured her into exposing me." Tortured into exposing him! Truly, Satan had no difficulty in distinguishing the color of his soul! I understood his object in making this false representation. It was to show me that I gained nothing by seeking the protection of my mistress; that the power was still all in his own hands. I pitied Mrs. Flint. She was a second wife, many years the junior of her husband; and the hoary-headed miscreant was enough to try the patience of a wiser and better woman. She was completely foiled, and knew not how to proceed. She would gladly have had me flogged for my supposed false oath; but, as I have already stated, the doctor never allowed any one to whip me. The old sinner was politic. The application of the lash might have led to remarks that would have exposed him in the eyes of his children and grandchildren. How often did I rejoice that I lived in a town where all the inhabitants knew each other! If I had been on a remote plantation, or lost among the multitude of a crowded city, I should not be a living woman at this day.

The secrets of slavery are concealed like those of the Inquisition. My master was, to my knowledge, the father of eleven slaves. But did the mothers dare to tell who was the father of their children? Did the other slaves dare to allude to it, except in whispers among themselves? No, indeed! They knew too well the terrible consequences.

My grandmother could not avoid seeing things which

excited her suspicions. She was uneasy about me, and tried various ways to buy me; but the neverchanging answer was always repeated: "Linda does not belong to *me*. She is my daughter's property, and I have no legal right to sell her." The conscientious man! He was too scrupulous to *sell* me; but he had no scruples whatever about committing a much greater wrong against the helpless young girl placed under his guardianship, as his daughter's property. Sometimes my persecutor would ask me whether I would like to be sold. I told him I would rather be sold to any body than to lead such a life as I did. On such occasions he would assume the air of a very injured individual, and reproach me for my ingratitude. "Did I not take you into the house, and make you the companion of my own children?" he would say. "Have I ever treated you like a negro? I have never allowed you to be punished, not even to please your mistress. And this is the recompense I get, you ungrateful girl!" I answered that he had reasons of his own for screening me from punishment, and that the course he pursued made my mistress hate me and persecute me. If I wept, he would say, "Poor child! Don't cry! don't cry! I will make peace for you with your mistress. Only let me arrange matters in my own way. Poor, foolish girl! you don't know what is for your own good. I would cherish you. I would make a lady of you. Now go, and think of all I have promised you."

I did think of it.

Reader, I draw no imaginary pictures of southern homes. I am telling you the plain truth. Yet when victims make their escape from this wild beast of Slavery, northerners consent to act the part of bloodhounds, and hunt the poor fugitive back into his den, "full of dead men's bones, and all uncleanness." Nay, more, they are not only willing, but proud, to give their daughters in marriage to slaveholders. The poor girls have romantic notions of a sunny clime, and of the flowering vines that all the year round shade a happy home. To what disappointments are they destined! The young wife soon learns that the husband in whose hands she has placed her happiness pays no regard to his marriage vows. Children of every shade of complexion play with her own fair babies, and too well she knows that they are born unto him of his own household. Jealousy and hatred enter the flowery home, and it is ravaged of its loveliness.

Southern women often marry a man knowing that he is the father of many little slaves. They do not trouble themselves about it. They regard such children as property, as marketable as the pigs on the plantation; and it is seldom that they do not make them aware of this by passing them into the slavetrader's hands as soon as possible, and thus getting them out of their sight. I am glad to say there are some honorable exceptions.

I have myself known two southern wives who exhorted their husbands to free those slaves towards whom they stood in a "parental relation;" and their request was granted. These husbands blushed before the superior nobleness of their wives' natures. Though they had only counselled them to do that which it was their duty to do, it commanded their respect, and rendered their conduct more exemplary. Concealment was at an end, and confidence took the place of distrust.

Though this bad institution deadens the moral sense, even in white women, to a fearful extent, it is not altogether extinct. I have heard southern ladies say of Mr. Such a one, "He not only thinks it no disgrace to be the father of those little niggers, but he is not ashamed to call himself their master. I declare, such things ought not to be tolerated in any decent society!"

CHAPTER VII

The Lover

Why does the slave ever love? Why allow the tendrils of the heart to twine around objects which may at any moment be wrenched away by the hand of violence? When separations come by the hand of death, the pious soul can bow in resignation, and say, "Not my will, but thine be done, O Lord!" But when the ruthless hand of man strikes the blow, regardless of the misery he causes, it is hard to be submissive. I did not reason thus when I was a young girl. Youth will be youth. I loved, and I indulged the hope that the dark clouds around me would turn out a bright lining. I forgot that in the land of my birth the shadows are too dense for light to penetrate. A land

> "Where laughter is not mirth; nor thought the mind;
> Nor words a language; nor e'en men mankind.
> Where cries reply to curses, shrieks to blows,
> And each is tortured in his separate hell."

There was in the neighborhood a young colored carpenter; a free-born man. We had been well acquainted in childhood, and frequently met together afterwards. We became mutually attached, and he proposed to marry me. I loved him with all the ardor of a young girl's first love. But when I reflected that I was a slave, and that the laws gave no sanction to the marriage of such, my heart sank within me. My lover wanted to buy me; but I knew that Dr. Flint was too wilful and arbitrary a man to consent to that arrangement. From him, I was sure of experiencing all sorts of opposition, and I had nothing to hope from my mistress. She would have been delighted to have got rid of me, but not in that way. It would have relieved her mind of a burden if she could have seen me sold to some distant state, but if I was married near home I should be just as much in her husband's power as I had previously been,—for the husband of a slave has no power to protect her. Moreover, my mistress, like many others, seemed to think that slaves had no right to any family ties of their own; that they were created merely to wait upon the family of the mistress. I once heard her abuse a young slave girl, who told her that a colored man wanted to make her his wife. "I will have you peeled and pickled, my lady," said she, "if I ever hear you mention that subject again. Do you suppose that I will have you tending *my* children with the children of that nigger?" The girl to whom she said this had a mulatto child, of course not acknowledged by its father. The poor black man who loved her would have been proud to acknowledge his helpless offspring.

Many and anxious were the thoughts I revolved in my mind. I was at a loss what to do. Above all things, I was desirous to spare my lover the insults that had cut so deeply into my own soul. I talked with my grandmother about it, and partly told her my fears. I did not dare to tell her the worst. She had long suspected all was not right, and if I confirmed her suspicions I knew a storm would rise that would prove the overthrow of all my hopes.

This love-dream had been my support through many trials; and I could not bear to run the risk of having it suddenly dissipated. There was a lady in the neighborhood, a particular friend of Dr. Flint's, who often visited the house. I had a great respect for her, and she had always manifested a friendly interest in me. Grandmother thought she would have great influence with the doctor. I went to this lady, and told her my story. I told her I was aware that my lover's being a free-born man would prove a great objection; but he wanted to buy me; and if Dr. Flint would consent to that arrangement, I felt sure he would be willing to pay any reasonable price. She knew that Mrs. Flint disliked me; therefore, I ventured to suggest that perhaps my mistress would approve of my being sold, as that would rid her of me. The lady listened with kindly sympathy, and promised to do her utmost to promote my wishes. She had an interview with the doctor, and I believe she pleaded my cause earnestly; but it was all to no purpose.

How I dreaded my master now! Every minute I expected to be summoned to his presence; but the day passed, and I heard nothing from him. The next morning, a message was brought to me: "Master wants you in his study." I found the door ajar, and I stood a moment gazing at the hateful man who claimed a right to rule me, body and soul. I entered, and tried to appear calm. I did not want him to know how my heart was bleeding. He looked fixedly at me, with an expression which seemed to say, "I have half a mind to kill you on the spot." At last he broke the silence, and that was a relief to both of us.

"So you want to be married, do you?" said he, "and to a free nigger."

"Yes, sir."

"Well, I'll soon convince you whether I am your master, or the nigger fellow you honor so highly. If you *must* have a husband, you may take up with one of my slaves."

What a situation I should be in, as the wife of one of *his* slaves, even if my heart had been interested!

I replied, "Don't you suppose, sir, that a slave can have some preference about marrying? Do you suppose that all men are alike to her?"

"Do you love this nigger?" said he, abruptly.

"Yes, sir."

"How dare you tell me so!" he exclaimed, in great wrath. After a slight pause, he added, "I supposed you thought more of yourself; that you felt above the insults of such puppies."

I replied, "If he is a puppy I am a puppy, for we are both of the negro race. It is right and honorable for us to love each other. The man you call a puppy never insulted me, sir; and he would not love me if he did not believe me to be a virtuous woman."

He sprang upon me like a tiger, and gave me a stunning blow. It was the first time he had ever struck me; and fear did not enable me to control my anger. When I had recovered a little from the effects, I exclaimed, "You have struck me for answering you honestly. How I despise you!"

There was silence for some minutes. Perhaps he was deciding what should be my punishment; or, perhaps, he wanted to give me time to reflect on what I had said, and to whom I had said it. Finally, he asked, "Do you know what you have said?"

"Yes, sir; but your treatment drove me to it."

"Do you know that I have a right to do as I like with you,—that I can kill you, if I please?"

"You have tried to kill me, and I wish you had; but you have no right to do as you like with me."

"Silence!" he exclaimed, in a thundering voice. "By heavens, girl, you forget yourself too far! Are you mad? If you are, I will soon bring you to your senses. Do you think any other master would bear what I have borne from you this morning? Many masters would have killed you on the spot. How would you like to be sent to jail for your insolence?"

"I know I have been disrespectful, sir," I replied; "but you drove me to it; I couldn't help it. As for the jail, there would be more peace for me there than there is here."

"You deserve to go there," said he, "and to be under such treatment, that you would forget the meaning of the word *peace*. It would do you good. It would take some of your high notions out of you. But I am not ready to send you there yet, notwithstanding your ingratitude for all my kindness and forbearance. You have been the plague of my life. I have wanted to make you happy, and I have been repaid with the basest ingratitude; but though you have proved yourself incapable of appreciating my kindness, I will be lenient towards you, Linda. I will give you one more chance to redeem your character. If you behave yourself and do as I require, I will forgive you and treat you as I always have done; but if you disobey me, I will punish you as I would the meanest slave on my plantation. Never let me hear that fellow's name mentioned again. If I ever know of your speaking to him, I will cowhide you both; and if I catch him lurking about my premises, I will shoot him as soon as I would a dog. Do you hear what I say? I'll teach you a lesson about marriage and free niggers! Now go, and let this be the last time I have occasion to speak to you on this subject."

Reader, did you ever hate? I hope not. I never did but once; and I trust I never shall again. Somebody has called it "the atmosphere of hell;" and I believe it is so.

For a fortnight the doctor did not speak to me. He thought to mortify me; to make me feel that I had disgraced myself by receiving the honorable addresses of a respectable colored man, in preference to the base proposals of a white man. But though his lips disdained to address me, his eyes were very loquacious. No animal ever watched its prey more narrowly than he watched me. He knew that I could write, though he had failed to make me read his letters; and he was now troubled lest I should exchange letters with another man. After a while he became weary of silence; and I was sorry for it. One morning, as he passed through the hall, to leave the house, he contrived to thrust a note into my hand. I thought I had better read it, and spare myself the vexation of having him read it to me. It expressed regret for the blow he had given me, and reminded me that I myself was wholly to blame for it. He hoped I had become convinced of the injury I was doing myself by incurring his displeasure. He wrote that he had made up his mind to go to Louisiana; that he should take several slaves with him, and intended I should be one of the number. My mistress would remain where she was; therefore I should have nothing to fear from that quarter. If I merited kindness from him, he assured me that it would be lavishly bestowed. He begged me to think over the matter, and answer the following day.

The next morning I was called to carry a pair of scissors to his room. I laid them on the table, with the letter beside them. He thought it was my answer, and did not call me back. I went as usual to attend my young mistress to and from school. He met me in the street, and ordered me to stop at his office on my way back. When I entered, he showed me his letter, and asked me why I had not answered it. I replied, "I am your daughter's property, and it is in your power to send me, or take me, wherever you please." He said he was very glad to find me so willing to go, and that we should start early in the autumn. He had a large practice in the town, and I rather thought he had made up the story merely to frighten me. However that might be, I was determined that I would never go to Louisiana with him.

Summer passed away, and early in the autumn Dr. Flint's eldest son was sent to Louisiana to examine the country, with a view to emigrating. That news did not disturb me. I knew very well that I should not be sent with *him*. That I had not been taken to the plantation before this time, was owing to the fact that his son was there. He was jealous of his son; and jealousy of the overseer had kept him from punishing me by sending me into the fields to work. Is it strange that I was not proud of these protectors? As for the overseer, he was a man for whom I had less respect than I had for a bloodhound.

Young Mr. Flint did not bring back a favorable report of Louisiana, and I heard no more of that scheme. Soon after this, my lover met me at the corner of the street, and I stopped to speak to him. Looking up, I saw my master watching us from his window. I hurried home, trembling with fear. I was sent for, immediately, to go to his room. He met me with a blow. "When is mistress to be married?" said he, in a sneering tone. A shower of oaths and imprecations followed. How thankful I was that my lover was a free man! that my tyrant had no power to flog him for speaking to me in the street!

Again and again I revolved in my mind how all this would end. There was no hope that the doctor would consent to sell me on any terms. He had an iron will, and was determined to keep me, and to conquer me. My lover was an intelligent and religious man. Even if he could have obtained permission to marry me while I was a slave, the marriage would give him no power to protect me from my master. It would have made him miserable to witness the insults I should have been subjected to. And then, if we had children, I knew they must "follow the condition of the mother." What a terrible blight that would be on the heart of a free, intelligent father! For *his* sake, I felt that I ought not to link his fate with my own unhappy destiny. He was going to Savannah to see about a little property left him by an uncle; and hard as it was to bring my feelings to it, I earnestly entreated him not to come back. I advised him to go to the Free States, where his tongue would not be tied, and where his intelligence would be of more avail to him. He left me, still hoping the day would come when I could be bought. With me the lamp of hope had gone out. The dream of my girlhood was over. I felt lonely and desolate.

Still I was not stripped of all. I still had my good grandmother, and my affectionate brother. When he put his arms round my neck, and looked into my eyes, as if to read there the troubles I dared not tell, I felt that I still had something to love. But even that pleasant emotion was chilled by the reflection that he might be torn from me at any moment, by some sudden freak of my master. If he had known how we love each other, I think he would have exulted in separating us. We often planned together how we could get to the north. But, as William remarked, such things are easier said than done. My movements were very closely watched, and we had no means of getting any money to defray our expenses. As for grandmother, she was strongly opposed to her children's undertaking any such project. She had not forgotten poor Benjamin's sufferings, and she was afraid that if another child tried to escape, he would have a similar or a worse fate. To me, nothing seemed more dreadful than my present life. I said to myself, "William *must* be free. He shall go to the north, and I will follow him." Many a slave sister has formed the same plans.

CHAPTER X

A Perilous Passage in the Slave Girl's Life

After my lover went away, Dr. Flint contrived a new plan. He seemed to have an idea that my fear of my mistress was his greatest obstacle. In the blandest tones, he told me that he was going to build a small house for me, in a secluded place, four miles away from the town. I shuddered; but I was constrained to listen, while he talked of his intention to give me a home of my own, and to make a lady of me. Hitherto, I had escaped my dreaded fate, by being in the midst of people. My grandmother had already had high words with my master about me. She had told him pretty plainly what she thought of his character, and there was considerable gossip in the neighborhood about our affairs, to which the open-mouthed jealousy of Mrs. Flint contributed not a little. When my master said he was going to build a house for me, and that he could do it with little trouble and expense, I was in hopes something would happen to frustrate his scheme; but I soon heard that the house was actually begun. I vowed before my Maker that I would never enter it. I had rather toil on the plantation from dawn till dark; I had rather live and die in jail, than drag on, from day to day, through such a living death. I was determined that the master, whom I so hated and loathed, who had blighted the prospects of my youth, and made my life a desert, should not, after my long struggle with him, succeed at last in trampling his victim under his feet. I would do any thing, every thing, for the sake of defeating him. What *could* I do? I thought and thought, till I became desperate, and made a plunge into the abyss.

And now, reader, I come to a period in my unhappy life, which I would gladly forget if I could. The remembrance fills me with sorrow and shame. It pains me to tell you of it; but I have promised to tell you the truth, and I will do it honestly, let it cost me what it may. I will not try to screen myself behind the plea of compulsion from a master; for it was not so. Neither can I plead ignorance or thoughtlessness. For years; my master had done his utmost to pollute my mind with foul images, and to destroy the pure principles inculcated by my grandmother, and the good mistress of my childhood. The influences of slavery had had the same effect on me that they had on other young girls; they had made me prematurely knowing, concerning the evil ways of the world. I knew what I did, and I did it with deliberate calculation.

But, O, ye happy women, whose purity has been sheltered from childhood, who have been free to choose the objects of your affection, whose homes are protected by law, do not judge the poor desolate slave girl too severely! If slavery had been abolished, I, also, could have married the man of my choice; I could have had a home shielded by the laws; and I should have been spared the painful task of confessing what I am now about to relate; but all my prospects had been blighted by slavery. I wanted to keep myself pure; and, under the most adverse circumstances, I tried hard to preserve my self-respect; but I was struggling alone in the powerful grasp of the demon Slavery; and the monster proved too strong for me. I felt as if I was forsaken by God and man; as if all my efforts must be frustrated; and I became reckless in my despair.

I have told you that Dr. Flint's persecutions and his wife's jealousy had given rise to some gossip in the neighborhood. Among others, it chanced that a white unmarried gentleman had obtained some knowledge of the circumstances in which I was placed. He knew my grandmother, and often spoke to me in the street. He became interested for me, and asked questions about my master, which I answered in part. He expressed a great deal of sympathy, and a wish to aid me. He constantly sought opportunities to see me, and wrote to me frequently. I was a poor slave girl, only fifteen years old.

So much attention from a superior person was, of course, flattering; for human nature is the same in all. I also felt grateful for his sympathy, and encouraged by his kind words. It seemed to me a great thing to have such a friend. By degrees, a more tender feeling crept into my heart. He was an educated and eloquent gentleman; too eloquent, alas, for the poor slave girl who trusted in him. Of course I saw whither all this was tending. I knew the impassable gulf between us; but to be an object of interest to a man who is not married, and who is not her master, is agreeable to the pride and feelings of a slave, if her miserable situation has left her any pride or sentiment. It seems less degrading to give one's self, than to submit to compulsion. There is something akin to freedom in having a lover who has no control over you, except that which he gains by kindness and attachment. A master may treat you as rudely as he pleases, and you dare not speak; moreover, the wrong does not seem so great with an unmarried man, as with one who has a wife to be made unhappy. There may be sophistry in all this; but the condition of a slave confuses all principles of morality, and, in fact, renders the practice of them impossible.

When I found that my master had actually begun to build the lonely cottage, other feelings mixed with those I have described. Revenge, and calculations of interest, were added to flattered vanity and sincere gratitude for kindness. I knew nothing would enrage Dr. Flint so much as to know that I favored another; and it was something to triumph over my tyrant even in that small way. I thought he would revenge himself by selling me, and I was sure my friend, Mr. Sands, would buy me. He was a man of more generosity and feeling than my master, and I thought my freedom could be easily obtained from him. The crisis of my fate now came so near that I was desperate. I shuddered to think of being the mother of children that should be owned by my old tyrant. I knew that as soon as a new fancy took him, his victims were sold far off to get rid of them; especially if they had children. I had seen several women sold, with his babies at the breast. He never allowed his offspring by slaves to remain long in sight of himself and his wife. Of a man who was not my master I could ask to have my children well supported; and in this case, I felt confident I should obtain the boon. I also felt quite sure that they would be made free. With all these thoughts revolving in my mind, and seeing no other way of escaping the doom I so much dreaded, I made a headlong plunge. Pity me, and pardon me, O virtuous reader! You never knew what it is to be a slave; to be entirely unprotected by law or custom; to have the laws reduce you to the condition of a chattel, entirely subject to the will of another. You never exhausted your ingenuity in avoiding the snares, and eluding the power of a hated tyrant; you never shuddered at the sound of his footsteps, and trembled within hearing of his voice. I know I did wrong. No one can feel it more sensibly than I do. The painful and humiliating memory will haunt me to my dying day. Still, in looking back, calmly, on the events of my life, I feel that the slave woman ought not to be judged by the same standard as others.

The months passed on. I had many unhappy hours. I secretly mourned over the sorrow I was bringing on my grandmother, who had so tried to shield me from harm. I knew that I was the greatest comfort of her old age, and that it was a source of pride to her that I had not degraded myself, like most of the slaves. I wanted to confess to her that I was no longer worthy of her love; but I could not utter the dreaded words.

As for Dr. Flint, I had a feeling of satisfaction and triumph in the thought of telling *him*. From time to time he told me of his intended arrangements, and I was silent. At last, he came and told me the cottage was completed, and ordered me to go to it. I told him I would never enter it. He said, "I have heard enough of such talk as that. You shall go, if you are carried by force; and you shall remain there."

I replied, "I will never go there. In a few months I shall be a mother."

He stood and looked at me in dumb amazement, and left the house without a word. I thought I should be happy in my triumph over him. But now that the truth was out, and my relatives would hear of it, I felt wretched. Humble as were their circumstances, they had pride in my good character. Now, how could I look them in the face? My self-respect was gone! I had resolved that I would be virtuous, though I was a slave. I had said, "Let the storm beat! I will brave it till I die." And now, how humiliated I felt!

I went to my grandmother. My lips moved to make confession, but the words stuck in my throat. I sat down in the shade of a tree at her door and began to sew. I think she saw something unusual was the matter with me. The mother of slaves is very watchful. She knows there is no security for her children. After they have entered their teens she lives in daily expectation of trouble. This leads to many questions. If the girl is of a sensitive nature, timidity keeps her from answering truthfully, and this well-meant course has a tendency to drive her from maternal counsels. Presently, in came my mistress, like a mad woman, and accused me concerning her husband. My grandmother, whose suspicions had been previously awakened, believed what she said. She exclaimed, "O Linda! has it come to this? I had rather see you dead than to see you as you now are. You are a disgrace to your dead mother." She tore from my fingers my mother's wedding ring and her silver thimble. "Go away!" she exclaimed, "and never come to my house, again." Her reproaches fell so hot and heavy, that they left me no chance to answer. Bitter tears, such as the eyes never shed but once, were my only answer. I rose from my seat, but fell back again, sobbing. She did not speak to me; but the tears were running down her furrowed cheeks, and they scorched me like fire. She had always been so kind to me! *So* kind! How I longed to throw myself at her feet, and tell her all the truth! But she had ordered me to go, and never to come there again. After a few minutes, I mustered strength, and started to obey her. With what feelings did I now close that little gate, which I used to open with such an eager hand in my childhood! It closed upon me with a sound I never heard before.

Where could I go? I was afraid to return to my master's. I walked on recklessly, not caring where I went, or what would become of me. When I had gone four or five miles, fatigue compelled me to stop. I sat down on the stump of an old tree. The stars were shining through the boughs above me. How they mocked me, with their bright, calm light! The hours passed by, and as I sat there alone a chilliness and deadly sickness came over me. I sank on the ground. My mind was full of horrid thoughts. I prayed to die; but the prayer was not answered. At last, with great effort I roused myself, and walked some distance further, to the house of a woman who had been a friend of my mother. When I told her why I was there, she spoke soothingly to me; but I could not be comforted. I thought I could bear my shame if I could only be reconciled to my grandmother. I longed to open my heart to her. I thought if she could know the real state of the case, and all I had been bearing for years, she would perhaps judge me less harshly. My friend advised me to send for her. I did so; but days of agonizing suspense passed before she came. Had she utterly forsaken me? No. She came at last. I knelt before her, and told her the things that had poisoned my life; how long I had been persecuted; that I saw no way of escape; and in an hour of extremity I had become desperate. She listened in silence. I told her I would bear any thing and do any thing, if in time I had hopes of obtaining her forgiveness. I begged of her to pity me, for my dead mother's sake. And she did pity me. She did not say, "I forgive you;" but she looked at me lovingly, with her eyes full of tears. She laid her old hand gently on my head, and murmured, "Poor child! Poor child!"

CHAPTER XI

The New Tie to Life

I returned to my good grandmother's house. She had an interview with Mr. Sands. When she asked him why he could not have left her one ewe lamb,—whether there were not plenty of slaves who did not care about character,—he made no answer; but he spoke kind and encouraging words. He promised to care for my child, and to buy me, be the conditions what they might.

I had not seen Dr. Flint for five days. I had never seen him since I made the avowal to him. He talked of the disgrace I had brought on myself; how I had sinned against my master, and mortified my old grandmother. He intimated that if I had accepted his proposals, he, as a physician, could have saved me from exposure. He even condescended to pity me. Could he have offered wormwood more bitter? He, whose persecutions had been the cause of my sin!

"Linda," said he, "though you have been criminal towards me, I feel for you, and I can pardon you if you obey my wishes. Tell me whether the fellow you wanted to marry is the father of your child. If you deceive me, you shall feel the fires of hell."

I did not feel as proud as I had done. My strongest weapon with him was gone. I was lowered in my own estimation, and had resolved to bear his abuse in silence. But when he spoke contemptuously of the lover who had always treated me honorably; when I remembered that but for *him* I might have been a virtuous, free, and happy wife, I lost my patience. "I have sinned against God and myself," I replied; "but not against you."

He clinched his teeth, and muttered, "Curse you!" He came towards me, with ill-suppressed rage, and exclaimed, "You obstinate girl! I could grind your bones to powder! You have thrown yourself away on some worthless rascal. You are weak-minded, and have been easily persuaded by those who don't care a straw for you. The future will settle accounts between us. You are blinded now; but hereafter you will be convinced that your master was your best friend. My lenity towards you is a proof of it. I might have punished you in many ways. I might have had you whipped till you fell dead under the lash. But I wanted you to live; I would have bettered your condition. Others cannot do it. You are my slave. Your mistress, disgusted by your conduct, forbids you to return to the house; therefore I leave you here for the present; but I shall see you often. I will call tomorrow."

He came with frowning brows, that showed a dissatisfied state of mind. After asking about my health, he inquired whether my board was paid, and who visited me. He then went on to say that he had neglected his duty; that as a physician there were certain things that he ought to have explained to me. Then followed talk such as would have made the most shameless blush. He ordered me to stand up before him. I obeyed. "I command you," said he, "to tell me whether the father of your child is white or black." I hesitated. "Answer me this instant!" he exclaimed. I did answer. He sprang upon me like a wolf, and grabbed my arm as if he would have broken it. "Do you love him?" said he, in a hissing tone.

"I am thankful that I do not despise him," I replied.

He raised his hand to strike me; but it fell again. I don't know what arrested the blow. He sat down, with lips tightly compressed. At last he spoke. "I came here," said he, "to make you a friendly proposition; but your ingratitude chafes me beyond endurance. You turn aside all my good intentions towards you. I don't know what it is that keeps me from killing you.'' Again he rose, as if he had a mind to strike me.

But he resumed. ''On one condition I will forgive your insolence and crime. You must henceforth have no communication of any kind with the father of your child. You must not ask any thing from him, or receive any thing from him. I will take care of you and your child. You had better promise this at once, and not wait till you are deserted by him. This is the last act of mercy I shall show towards you.''

I said something about being unwilling to have my child supported by a man who had cursed it and me also. He rejoined, that a woman who had sunk to my level had no right to expect any thing else. He asked, for the last time, would I accept his kindness? I answered that I would not.

''Very well,'' said he; ''then take the consequences of your wayward course. Never look to me for help. You are my slave, and shall always be my slave. I will never sell you, that you may depend upon.''

Hope died away in my heart as he closed the door after him. I had calculated that in his rage he would sell me to a slave-trader; and I knew the father of my child was on the watch to buy me.

About this time my uncle Phillip was expected to return from a voyage. The day before his departure I had officiated as bridesmaid to a young friend. My heart was then ill at ease, but my smiling countenance did not betray it. Only a year had passed; but what fearful changes it had wrought! My heart had grown gray in misery. Lives that flash in sunshine, and lives that are born in tears, receive their hue from circumstances. None of us know what a year may bring forth.

I felt no joy when they told me my uncle had come. He wanted to see me, though he knew what had happened. I shrank from him at first; but at last consented that he should come to my room. He received me as he always had done. O, how my heart smote me when I felt his tears on my burning cheeks! The words of my grandmother came to my mind,—''Perhaps your mother and father are taken from the evil days to come.'' My disappointed heart could now praise God that it was so. But why, thought I, did my relatives ever cherish hopes for me? What was there to save me from the usual fate of slave girls? Many more beautiful and more intelligent than I had experienced a similar fate, or a far worse one. How could they hope that I should escape?

My uncle's stay was short, and I was not sorry for it. I was too ill in mind and body to enjoy my friends as I had done. For some weeks I was unable to leave my bed. I could not have any doctor but my master, and I would not have him sent for. At last, alarmed by my increasing illness, they sent for him. I was very weak and nervous; and as soon as he entered the room, I began to scream. They told him my state was very critical. He had no wish to hasten me out of the world, and he withdrew.

When my babe was born, they said it was premature. It weighed only four pounds; but God let it live. I heard the doctor say I could not survive till morning. I had often prayed for death; but now I did not want to die, unless my child could die too. Many weeks passed before I was able to leave my bed. I was a mere wreck of my former self. For a year there was scarcely a day when I was free from chills and fever. My babe also was sickly. His little limbs were often racked with pain. Dr. Flint continued his visits, to look after my health; and he did not fail to remind me that my child was an addition to his stock of slaves.

I felt too feeble to dispute with him, and listened to his remarks in silence. His visits were less frequent; but his busy spirit could not remain quiet. He employed my brother in his office, and he was made the medium of frequent notes and messages to me. William was a bright lad, and of much use to the doctor. He had learned to put up medicines, to leech, cup, and bleed. He had taught himself to read and spell. I was proud of my brother; and the old doctor suspected as much. One day, when I had not seen him for several weeks, I heard his steps approaching the door. I dreaded the encounter, and hid myself. He inquired for me, of course; but I was nowhere to be found. He went to his office, and despatched William with a note. The color mounted to my brother's face when he gave it to me; and he said, "Don't you hate me, Linda, for bringing you these things?" I told him I could not blame him; he was a slave, and obliged to obey his master's will. The note ordered me to come to his office. I went. He demanded to know where I was when he called. I told him I was at home. He flew into a passion, and said he knew better. Then he launched out upon his usual themes,—my crimes against him, and my ingratitude for his forbearance. The laws were laid down to me anew, and I was dismissed. I felt humiliated that my brother should stand by, and listen to such language as would be addressed only to a slave. Poor boy! He was powerless to defend me; but I saw the tears, which he vainly strove to keep back. This manifestation of feeling irritated the doctor. William could do nothing to please him. One morning he did not arrive at the office so early as usual; and that circumstance afforded his master an opportunity to vent his spleen. He was put in jail. The next day my brother sent a trader to the doctor, with a request to be sold. His master was greatly incensed at what he called his insolence. He said he had put him there to reflect upon his bad conduct, and he certainly was not giving any evidence of repentance. For two days he harassed himself to find somebody to do his office work; but every thing went wrong without William. He was released, and ordered to take his old stand, with many threats, if he was not careful about his future behavior.

As the months passed on, my boy improved in health. When he was a year old, they called him beautiful. The little vine was taking deep root in my existence, though its clinging fondness excited a mixture of love and pain. When I was most sorely oppressed I found a solace in his smiles. I loved to watch his infant slumbers; but always there was a dark cloud over my enjoyment. I could never forget that he was a slave. Sometimes I wished that he might die in infancy. God tried me. My darling became very ill. The bright eyes grew dull, and the little feet and hands were so icy cold that I thought death had already touched them. I had prayed for his death, but never so earnestly as I now prayed for his life; and my prayer was heard. Alas, what mockery it is for a slave mother to try to pray back her dying child to life! Death is better than slavery. It was a sad thought that I had no name to give my child. His father caressed him and treated him kindly, whenever he had a chance to see him. He was not unwilling that he should bear his name; but he had no legal claim to it; and if I had bestowed it upon him, my master would have regarded it as a new crime, a new piece of insolence, and would, perhaps, revenge it on the boy. O, the serpent of Slavery has many and poisonous fangs!

CHAPTER XII

Fear of Insurrection

Not far from this time Nat Turner's insurrection broke out; and the news threw our town into great commotion. Strange that they should be alarmed, when their slaves were so "contented and happy"! But so it was.

It was always the custom to have a muster every year. On that occasion every white man shouldered his musket. The citizens and the so-called country gentlemen wore military uniforms. The poor whites took their places in the ranks in every-day dress, some without shoes, some without hats. This grand occasion had already passed; and when the slaves were told there was to be another muster, they were surprised and rejoiced. Poor creatures! They thought it was going to be a holiday. I was informed of the true state of affairs, and imparted it to the few I could trust. Most gladly would I have proclaimed it to every slave; but I dared not. All could not be relied on. Mighty is the power of the torturing lash.

By sunrise, people were pouring in from every quarter within twenty miles of the town. I knew the houses were to be searched; and I expected it would be done by country bullies and the poor whites. I knew nothing annoyed them so much as to see colored people living in comfort and respectability; so I made arrangements for them with especial care. I arranged every thing in my grandmother's house as neatly as possible. I put white quilts on the beds, and decorated some of the rooms with flowers. When all was arranged, I sat down at the window to watch. Far as my eye could reach, it rested on a motley crowd of soldiers. Drums and fifes were discoursing martial music. The men were divided into companies of sixteen, each headed by a captain. Orders were given, and the wild scouts rushed in every direction, wherever a colored face was to be found.

It was a grand opportunity for the low whites, who had no negroes of their own to scourge. They exulted in such a chance to exercise a little brief authority, and show their subserviency to the slaveholders; not reflecting that the power which trampled on the colored people also kept themselves in poverty, ignorance, and moral degradation. Those who never witnessed such scenes can hardly believe what I know was inflicted at this time on innocent men, women, and children, against whom there was not the slightest ground for suspicion. Colored people and slaves who lived in remote parts of the town suffered in an especial manner. In some cases the searchers scattered powder and shot among their clothes, and then sent other parties to find them, and bring them forward as proof that they were plotting insurrection. Every where men, women, and children were whipped till the blood stood in puddles at their feet. Some received five hundred lashes; others were tied hands and feet, and tortured with a bucking paddle, which blisters the skin terribly. The dwellings of the colored people, unless they happened to be protected by some influential white person, who was nigh at hand, were robbed of clothing and every thing else the marauders thought worth carrying away. All day long these unfeeling wretches went round, like a troop of demons, terrifying and tormenting the helpless. At night, they formed themselves into patrol bands, and went wherever they chose among the colored people, acting out their brutal will. Many women hid themselves in woods and swamps, to keep out of their way. If any of the husbands or fathers told of these outrages, they were tied up to the public whipping post, and cruelly scourged for telling lies about white men. The consternation was universal. No two people that had the slightest tinge of color in their faces dared to be seen talking together.

I entertained no positive fears about our household, because we were in the midst of white families who would protect us. We were ready to receive the soldiers whenever they came. It was not long before we heard the tramp of feet and the sound of voices. The door was rudely pushed open; and in they tumbled, like a pack of hungry wolves. They snatched at every thing within their reach. Every box, trunk, closet, and corner underwent a thorough examination. A box in one of the drawers containing some silver change was eagerly pounced upon. When I stepped forward to take it from them, one of the soldiers turned and said angrily, "What d'ye foller us fur? D'ye s'pose white folks is come to steal?"

I replied, "You have come to search; but you have searched that box, and I will take it, if you please."

At that moment I saw a white gentleman who was friendly to us; and I called to him, and asked him to have the goodness to come in and stay till the search was over. He readily complied. His entrance into the house brought in the captain of the company, whose business it was to guard the outside of the house, and see that none of the inmates left it. This officer was Mr. Litch, the wealthy slaveholder whom I mentioned, in the account of neighboring planters, as being notorious for his cruelty. He felt above soiling his hands with the search. He merely gave orders; and, if a bit of writing was discovered, it was carried to him by his ignorant followers, who were unable to read.

My grandmother had a large trunk of bedding and table cloths. When that was opened, there was a great shout of surprise; and one exclaimed, "Where'd the damned niggers git all dis sheet an' table clarf?"

My grandmother, emboldened by the presence of our white protector, said, "You may be sure we didn't pilfer 'em from *your* houses."

"Look here, mammy," said a grim-looking fellow without any coat, "you seem to feel mighty gran' 'cause you got all them 'ere fixens. White folks oughter have 'em all."

His remarks were interrupted by a chorus of voices

shouting, "We's got 'em! We's got 'em! Dis 'ere yaller gal's got letters!"

There was a general rush for the supposed letter, which, upon examination, proved to be some verses written to me by a friend. In packing away my things, I had overlooked them. When their captain informed them of their contents, they seemed much disappointed. He inquired of me who wrote them. I told him it was one of my friends. "Can you read them?" he asked. When I told him I could, he swore, and raved, and tore the paper into bits. "Bring me all your letters!" said he, in a commanding tone. I told him I had none. "Don't be afraid," he continued, in an insinuating way. "Bring them all to me. Nobody shall do you any harm." Seeing I did not move to obey him, his pleasant tone changed to oaths and threats. "Who writes to you? half free niggers?" inquired he. I replied, "O, no; most of my letters are from white people. Some request me to burn them after they are read, and some I destroy without reading."

An exclamation of surprise from some of the company put a stop to our conversation. Some silver spoons which ornamented an old-fashioned buffet had just been discovered. My grandmother was in the habit of preserving fruit for many ladies in the town, and of preparing suppers for parties; consequently she had many jars of preserves. The closet that contained these was next invaded, and the contents tasted. One of them, who was helping himself freely, tapped his neighbor on the shoulder, and said, "Wal done! Don't wonder de niggers want to kill all de white folks, when dey live on 'sarves" [meaning preserves]. I stretched out my hand to take the jar, saying, "You were not sent here to search for sweetmeats."

"And what *were* we sent for?" said the captain, bristling up to me. I evaded the question.

The search of the house was completed, and nothing found to condemn us. They next proceeded to the garden, and knocked about every bush and vine, with no better success. The captain called his men together, and, after a short consultation, the order to march was given. As they passed out of the gate, the captain turned back, and pronounced a malediction on the house. He said it ought to be burned to the ground, and each of its inmates receive thirty-nine lashes. We came out of this affair very fortunately; not losing any thing except some wearing apparel.

Towards evening the turbulence increased. The soldiers, stimulated by drink, committed still greater cruelties. Shrieks and shouts continually rent the air. Not daring to go to the door, I peeped under the window curtain. I saw a mob dragging along a number of colored people, each white man, with his musket upraised, threatening instant death if they did not stop their shrieks. Among the prisoners was a respectable old colored minister. They had found a few parcels of shot in his house, which his wife had for years used to balance her scales. For this they were going to shoot him on Court House Green. What a spectacle was that for a civilized country! A rabble, staggering under intoxication, assuming to be the administrators of justice!

The better class of the community exerted their influence to save the innocent, persecuted people; and in several instances they succeeded, by keeping them shut up in jail till the excitement abated. At last the white citizens found that their own property was not safe from the lawless rabble they had summoned to protect them. They rallied the drunken swarm, drove them back into the country, and set a guard over the town.

The next day, the town patrols were commissioned to search colored people that lived out of the city; and the most shocking outrages were committed with perfect impunity. Every day for a fortnight, if I looked out, I saw horsemen with some poor panting negro tied to their saddles, and compelled by the lash to keep up with their speed, till they arrived at the jail yard. Those who had been whipped too unmercifully to walk were washed with brine, tossed into a cart, and carried to jail. One black man, who had not fortitude to endure scourging, promised to give information about the conspiracy. But it turned out that he knew nothing at all. He had not even heard the name of Nat Turner. The poor fellow had, however, made up a story, which augmented his own sufferings and those of the colored people.

The day patrol continued for some weeks, and at sundown a night guard was substituted. Nothing at all was proved against the colored people, bond or free. The wrath of the slaveholders was somewhat appeased by the capture of Nat Turner. The imprisoned were released. The slaves were sent to their masters, and the free were permitted to return to their ravaged homes. Visiting was strictly forbidden on the plantations. The slaves begged the privilege of again meeting at their little church in the woods, with their burying ground around it. It was built by the colored people, and they had no higher happiness than to meet there and sing hymns together, and pour out their hearts in spontaneous prayer. Their request was denied, and the church was demolished. They were permitted to attend the white churches, a certain portion of the galleries being appropriated to their use. There, when every body else had partaken of the communion, and the benediction had been pronounced, the minister said, "Come down, now, my colored friends." They obeyed the summons, and partook of the bread and wine, in commemoration of the meek and lowly Jesus, who said, "God is your Father, and all ye are brethren."

CHAPTER

XIII

The Church and Slavery

After the alarm caused by Nat Turner's insurrection had subsided, the slaveholders came to the conclusion that it would be well to give the slaves enough of religious instruction to keep them from murdering their masters. The Episcopal clergyman offered to hold a separate service on Sundays for their benefit. His colored members were very few, and also very respectable—a fact which I presume had some weight with him. The difficulty was to decide on a suitable place for them to worship. The Methodist and Baptist churches admitted them in the afternoon; but their carpets and cushions were not so costly as those at the Episcopal church. It was at last decided that they should meet at the house of a free colored man, who was a member.

I was invited to attend, because I could read. Sunday evening came, and, trusting to the cover of night, I ventured out. I rarely ventured out by daylight, for I always went with fear, expecting at every turn to encounter Dr. Flint, who was sure to turn me back, or order me to his office to inquire where I got my bonnet, or some other article of dress. When the Rev. Mr. Pike came, there were some twenty persons present. The reverend gentleman knelt in prayer, then seated himself, and requested all present, who could read, to open their books, while he gave out the portions he wished them to repeat or respond to.

His text was, "Servants, be obedient to them that are your masters according to the flesh, with fear and trembling, in singleness of your heart, as unto Christ."

Pious Mr. Pike brushed up his hair till it stood upright, and, in deep, solemn tones, began: "Hearken, ye servants! Give strict heed unto my words. You are rebellious sinners. Your hearts are filled with all manner of evil. 'Tis the devil who tempts you. God is angry with you, and will surely punish you, if you don't forsake your wicked ways. You that live in town are eye-servants behind your master's back. Instead of serving your masters faithfully, which is pleasing in the sight of your heavenly Master, you are idle, and shirk your work. God sees you. You tell lies. God hears you. Instead of being engaged in worshipping him, you are hidden away somewhere, feasting on your master's substance; tossing coffee-grounds with some wicked fortuneteller, or cutting cards with another old hag. Your masters may not find you out, but God sees you, and will punish you. O, the depravity of your hearts! When your master's work is done, are you quietly together, thinking of the goodness of God to such sinful creatures? No; you are quarrelling, and tying up little bags of roots to bury under the doorsteps to poison each other with. God sees you. You men steal away to every grog shop to sell your master's corn, that you may buy rum to drink. God sees you. You sneak into the back streets, or among the bushes, to pitch coppers. Although your masters may not find you out, God sees you; and he will punish you. You must forsake your sinful ways, and be faithful servants. Obey your old master and your young master—your old mistress and your young mistress. If you disobey your earthly master, you offend your heavenly Master. You must obey God's commandments. When you go from here, don't stop at the corners of the streets to talk, but go directly home, and let your master and mistress see that you have come."

The benediction was pronounced. We went home, highly amused at brother Pike's gospel teaching, and we determined to hear him again. I went the next Sabbath evening, and heard pretty much a repetition of the last discourse. At the close of the meeting, Mr. Pike informed us that he found it very inconvenient to meet at the friend's house, and he should be glad to see us, every Sunday evening, at his own kitchen.

I went home with the feeling that I had heard the Reverend Mr. Pike for the last time. Some of his members repaired to his house, and found that the kitchen sported two tallow candles; the first time, I am sure, since its present occupant owned it, for the servants never had any thing but pine knots. It was so long before the reverend gentleman descended from his comfortable parlor that the slaves left, and went to enjoy a Methodist shout. They never seem so happy as when shouting and singing at religious meetings. Many of them are sincere, and nearer to the gate of heaven than sanctimonious Mr. Pike, and other longfaced Christians, who see wounded Samaritans, and pass by on the other side.

The slaves generally compose their own songs and hymns; and they do not trouble their heads much about the measure. They often sing the following verses:

"Old Satan is one busy ole man;
He rolls dem blocks all in my way;
But Jesus is my bosom friend;
He rolls dem blocks away.

"If I had died when I was young,
Den how my stam'ring tongue would have sung;
But I am ole, and now I stand
A narrow chance for to tread dat heavenly land."

I well remember one occasion when I attended a Methodist class meeting. I went with a burdened spirit, and happened to sit next a poor, bereaved mother, whose heart was still heavier than mine. The class leader was the town constable—a man who bought and sold slaves, who whipped his brethren and sisters of the church at the public whipping post, in jail or out of jail. He was ready to perform that Christian office any where for fifty cents. This white-faced, black-hearted brother came near us, and said to the stricken woman, "Sister, can't you tell us how the Lord deals with your soul? Do you love him as you did formerly?"

She rose to her feet, and said, in piteous tones, "My Lord and Master, help me! My load is more than I can bear. God has hid himself from me, and I am left in darkness and misery." Then, striking her breast, she continued, "I can't tell you what is in here! They've got all my children. Last week they took the last one. God only knows where they've sold her. They let me have her sixteen years, and then—— O! O! Pray for her brothers and sisters! I've got nothing to live for now. God make my time short!"

She sat down, quivering in every limb. I saw that constable class leader become crimson in the face with suppressed laughter, while he held up his handkerchief, that those who were weeping for the poor woman's calamity might not see his merriment. Then, with assumed gravity, he said to the bereaved mother, "Sister, pray to the Lord that every dispensation of his divine will may be sanctified to the good of your poor needy soul!"

The congregation struck up a hymn, and sung as though they were as free as the birds that warbled round us,—

"Ole Satan thought he had a mighty aim;
He missed my soul, and caught my sins.
Cry Amen, cry Amen, cry Amen to God!

"He took my sins upon his back;
Went muttering and grumbling down to hell.
Cry Amen, cry Amen, cry Amen to God!

"Ole Satan's church is here below.
Up to God's free church I hope to go.
Cry Amen, cry Amen, cry Amen to God!"

Precious are such moments to the poor slaves. If you were to hear them at such times, you might think they were happy. But can that hour of singing and shouting sustain them through the dreary week, toiling without wages, under constant dread of the lash?

The Episcopal clergyman, who, ever since my earliest recollection, had been a sort of god among the slaveholders, concluded, as his family was large, that he must go where money was more abundant. A very different clergyman took his place. The change was very agreeable to the colored people, who said, "God has sent us a good man this time." They loved him, and their children followed him for a smile or a kind word. Even the slaveholders felt his influence. He brought to the rectory five slaves. His wife taught them to read and write, and to be useful to her and themselves. As soon as he was settled, he turned his attention to the needy slaves around him. He urged upon his parishioners the duty of having a meeting expressly for them every Sunday, with a sermon adapted to their comprehension. After much argument and importunity, it was finally agreed that they might occupy the gallery of the church on Sunday evenings. Many colored people, hitherto unaccustomed to attend church, now gladly went to hear the gospel preached. The sermons were simple, and they understood them. Moreover, it was the first time they had ever been addressed as human beings. It was not long before his white parishioners began to be dissatisfied. He was accused of preaching better sermons to the negroes than he did to them. He honestly confessed that he bestowed more pains upon those sermons than upon any others; for the slaves were reared in such ignorance that it was a difficult task to adapt himself to their comprehension. Dissensions arose in the parish. Some wanted he should preach to them in the evening, and to the slaves in the afternoon. In the midst of these disputings his wife died, after a very short illness. Her slaves gathered round her dying bed in great sorrow. She said, "I have tried to do you good and promote your happiness; and if I have failed, it has not been for want of interest in your welfare. Do not weep for me; but prepare for the new duties that lie before you. I leave you all free. May we meet in a better world." Her liberated slaves were sent away, with funds to establish them comfortably. The colored people will long bless the memory of that truly Christian woman. Soon after her death her husband preached his farewell sermon, and many tears were shed at his departure.

Several years after, he passed through our town and preached to his former congregation. In his afternoon sermon he addressed the colored people. "My friends," said he, "it affords me great happiness to have an opportunity of speaking to you again. For two years I have been striving to do something for the colored people of my own parish; but nothing is yet accomplished. I have not even preached a sermon to them. Try to live according to the word of God, my friends. Your skin is darker than mine; but God judges men by their hearts, not by the color of their skins." This was strange doctrine from a southern pulpit. It was very offensive to slaveholders. They said he and his wife had made fools of their slaves, and that he preached like a fool to the negroes.

I knew an old black man, whose piety and childlike trust in God were beautiful to witness. At fifty-three years old he joined the Baptist church. He had a most earnest desire to learn to read. He thought he should know how to serve God better if he could only read the Bible. He came to me, and begged me to teach him. He said he could not pay me, for he had no money; but he would bring me nice fruit when the season for it came. I asked him if he didn't know it was contrary to law; and that slaves were whipped and imprisoned for teaching each other to read. This brought the tears into his eyes. "Don't be troubled, uncle Fred," said I. "I have no thoughts of refusing to teach you. I only told you of the law, that you might know the danger, and be on your guard." He thought he could plan to come three times a week without its being suspected. I selected a quiet nook, where no intruder was likely to penetrate, and there I taught him his A, B, C. Considering his age, his progress was astonishing. As soon as he could spell in two syllables he wanted to spell out words in the Bible. The happy smile that illuminated his face put joy into my heart. After spelling out a few words, he paused, and said, "Honey, it 'pears when I can read dis good book I shall be nearer to God. White man is got all de sense. He can larn easy. It ain't easy for ole black man like me. I only wants to read dis book, dat I may know how to live; den I hab no fear 'bout dying."

I tried to encourage him by speaking of the rapid progress he had made. "Hab patience, child," he replied. "I larns slow."

I had no need of patience. His gratitude, and the happiness I imparted, were more than a recompense for all my trouble.

At the end of six months he had read through the New Testament, and could find any text in it. One day, when he had recited unusually well, I said, "Uncle Fred, how do you manage to get your lessons so well?"

"Lord bress you, chile," he replied. "You nebber gibs me a lesson dat I don't pray to God to help me to understan' what I spells and what I reads. And he *does* help me, chile. Bress his holy name!"

There are thousands, who, like good uncle Fred, are thirsting for the water of life; but the law forbids it, and the churches withhold it. They send the Bible to heathen abroad, and neglect the heathen at home. I am glad that missionaries go out to the dark corners of the earth; but I ask them not to overlook the dark corners at home. Talk to American slaveholders as you talk to savages in Africa. Tell *them* it is wrong to traffic in men. Tell them it is sinful to sell their own children, and atrocious to violate their own daughters. Tell them that all men are brethren, and that man has no right to shut out the light of knowledge from his brother. Tell them they are answerable to God for sealing up the Fountain of Life from souls that are thirsting for it.

There are men who would gladly undertake such missionary work as this; but, alas! their number is small. They are hated by the south, and would be driven from its soil, or dragged to prison to die, as others have been before them. The field is ripe for the harvest, and awaits the reapers. Perhaps the great grandchildren of uncle Fred may have freely imparted to them the divine treasures, which he sought by stealth, at the risk of the prison and the scourge.

Are doctors of divinity blind, or are they hypocrites? I suppose some are the one, and some the other; but I think if they felt the interest in the poor and the lowly, that they ought to feel, they would not be so *easily* blinded. A clergyman who goes to the south, for the first time, has usually some feeling, however vague, that slavery is wrong. The slaveholder suspects this, and plays his game accordingly. He makes himself as agreeable as possible; talks on theology, and other kindred topics. The reverend gentleman is asked to invoke a blessing on a table loaded with luxuries. After dinner he walks round the premises, and sees the beautiful groves and flowering vines, and the comfortable huts of favored household slaves. The southerner invites him to talk with these slaves. He asks them if they want to be free, and they say, "O, no, massa." This is sufficient to satisfy him. He comes home to publish a "South-Side View of Slavery," and to complain of the exaggerations of abolitionists. He assures people that he has been to the south, and seen slavery for himself; that it is a beautiful "patriarchal institution;" that the slaves don't want their freedom; that they have hallelujah meetings, and other religious privileges.

What does *he* know of the half-starved wretches toiling from dawn till dark on the plantations? of mothers shrieking for their children, torn from their arms by slave traders? of young girls dragged down into moral filth? of pools of blood around the whipping post? of hounds trained to tear human flesh? of men screwed into cotton gins to die? The slaveholder showed him none of these things, and the slaves dared not tell of them if he had asked them.

There is a great difference between Christianity and religion at the south. If a man goes to the communion table, and pays money into the treasury of the church, no matter if it be the price of blood, he is called religious. If a pastor has offspring by a woman not his wife, the church dismiss him, if she is a white woman; but if she is colored, it does not hinder his continuing to be their good shepherd.

When I was told that Dr. Flint had joined the Episcopal church, I was much surprised. I supposed that religion had a purifying effect on the character of men; but the worst persecutions I endured from him were after he was a communicant. The conversation of the doctor, the day after he had been confirmed, certainly gave *me* no indication that he had "renounced the devil and all his works." In answer to some of his usual talk, I reminded him that he had just joined the church. "Yes, Linda," said he. "It was proper for me to do so. I am getting on in years, and my position in society requires it, and it puts an end to all the damned slang. You would do well to join the church, too, Linda."

"There are sinners enough in it already," rejoined I.

"If I could be allowed to live like a Christian, I should be glad."

"You can do what I require; and if you are faithful to me, you will be as virtuous as my wife," he replied.

I answered that the Bible didn't say so.

His voice became hoarse with rage. "How dare you preach to me about your infernal Bible!" he exclaimed. "What right have you, who are my negro, to talk to me about what you would like, and what you wouldn't like? I am your master, and you shall obey me."

No wonder the slaves sing,—

> "Ole Satan's church is here below;
> Up to God's free church I hope to go."

CHAPTER

XIV

Another Link to Life

I had not returned to my master's house since the birth of my child. The old man raved to have me thus removed from his immediate power; but his wife vowed, by all that was good and great, she would kill me if I came back; and he did not doubt her word. Sometimes he would stay away for a season. Then he would come and renew the old threadbare discourse about his forbearance and my ingratitude. He labored, most unnecessarily, to convince me that I had lowered myself. The venomous old reprobate had no need of descanting on that theme. I felt humiliated enough. My unconscious babe was the ever-present witness of my shame. I listened with silent contempt when he talked about my having forfeited *his* good opinion; but I shed bitter tears that I was no longer worthy of being respected by the good and pure. Alas! slavery still held me in its poisonous grasp. There was no chance for me to be respectable. There was no prospect of being able to lead a better life.

Sometimes, when my master found that I still refused to accept what he called his kind offers, he would threaten to sell my child. "Perhaps that will humble you," said he.

Humble *me!* Was I not already in the dust? But his

threat lacerated my heart. I knew the law gave him power to fulfil it; for slaveholders have been cunning enough to enact that "the child shall follow the condition of the *mother*," not of the *father;* thus taking care that licentiousness shall not interfere with avarice. This reflection made me clasp my innocent babe all the more firmly to my heart. Horrid visions passed through my mind when I thought of his liability to fall into the slave trader's hands. I wept over him, and said, "O my child! perhaps they will leave you in some cold cabin to die, and then throw you into a hole, as if you were a dog."

When Dr. Flint learned that I was again to be a mother, he was exasperated beyond measure. He rushed from the house, and returned with a pair of shears. I had a fine head of hair; and he often railed about my pride of arranging it nicely. He cut every hair close to my head, storming and swearing all the time. I replied to some of his abuse, and he struck me. Some months before, he had pitched me down stairs in a fit of passion; and the injury I received was so serious that I was unable to turn myself in bed for many days. He then said, "Linda, I swear by God I will never raise my hand against you again;" but I knew that he would forget his promise.

After he discovered my situation, he was like a restless spirit from the pit. He came every day; and I was subjected to such insults as no pen can describe. I would not describe them if I could; they were too low, too revolting. I tried to keep them from my grandmother's knowledge as much as I could. I knew she had enough to sadden her life, without having my troubles to bear. When she saw the doctor treat me with violence, and heard him utter oaths terrible enough to palsy a man's tongue, she could not always hold her peace. It was natural and motherlike that she should try to defend me; but it only made matters worse.

When they told me my new-born babe was a girl, my heart was heavier than it had ever been before. Slavery is terrible for men; but it is far more terrible for women. Superadded to the burden common to all, *they* have wrongs, and sufferings, and mortifications peculiarly their own.

Dr. Flint had sworn that he would make me suffer, to my last day, for this new crime against *him*, as he called it; and as long as he had me in his power he kept his word. On the fourth day after the birth of my babe, he entered my room suddenly, and commanded me to rise and bring my baby to him. The nurse who took care of me had gone out of the room to prepare some nourishment, and I was alone. There was no alternative. I rose, took up my babe, and crossed the room to where he sat. "Now stand there," said he, "till I tell you to go back!" My child bore a strong resemblance to her father, and to the deceased Mrs. Sands, her grandmother. He noticed this; and while I stood before him, trembling with weakness, he heaped upon me and my little one every vile epithet he could think of. Even the grandmother in her grave did not escape his curses. In the midst of his vituperations I fainted at his feet. This recalled him to his senses. He took the baby from my arms, laid it on the bed, dashed cold water in my face, took me up, and shook me violently, to restore my consciousness before any one entered the room. Just then my grandmother came in, and he hurried out of the house. I suffered in consequence of this treatment; but I begged my friends to let me die, rather than send for the doctor. There was nothing I dreaded so much as his presence. My life was spared; and I was glad for the sake of my little ones. Had it not been for these ties to life, I should have been glad to be released by death, though I had lived only nineteen years.

Always it gave me a pang that my children had no lawful claim to a name. Their father offered his; but, if I had wished to accept the offer, I dared not while my master lived. Moreover, I knew it would not be accepted at their baptism. A Christian name they were at least entitled to; and we resolved to call my boy for our dear good Benjamin, who had gone far away from us.

My grandmother belonged to the church; and she was very desirous of having the children christened. I knew Dr. Flint would forbid it, and I did not venture to attempt it. But chance favored me. He was called to visit a patient out of town, and was obliged to be absent during Sunday. "Now is the time," said my grandmother; "we will take the children to church, and have them christened."

When I entered the church, recollections of my mother came over me, and I felt subdued in spirit. There she had presented me for baptism, without any reason to feel ashamed. She had been married, and had such legal rights as slavery allows to a slave. The vows had at least been sacred to *her,* and she had never violated them. I was glad she was not alive, to know under what different circumstances her grandchildren were presented for baptism. Why had my lot been so different from my mother's? *Her* master had died when she was a child; and she remained with her mistress till she married. She was never in the power of any master; and thus she escaped one class of the evils that generally fall upon slaves.

When my baby was about to be christened, the former mistress of my father stepped up to me, and proposed to give it her Christian name. To this I added the surname of my father, who had himself no legal right to it; for my grandfather on the paternal side was a white gentleman. What tangled skeins are the genealogies of slavery! I loved my father; but it mortified me to be obliged to bestow his name on my children.

When we left the church, my father's old mistress invited me to go home with her. She clasped a gold chain around my baby's neck. I thanked her for this kindness; but I did not like the emblem. I wanted no chain to be fastened on my daughter, not even if its links were of gold. How earnestly I prayed that she might never feel the weight of slavery's chain, whose iron entereth into the soul!

CHAPTER XV

Continued Persecutions

My children grew finely; and Dr. Flint would often say to me, with an exulting smile, "These brats will bring me a handsome sum of money one of these days."

I thought to myself that, God being my helper, they should never pass into his hands. It seemed to me I would rather see them killed than have them given up to his power. The money for the freedom of myself and my children could be obtained; but I derived no advantage from that circumstance. Dr. Flint loved money, but he loved power more. After much discussion, my friends resolved on making another trial. There was a slaveholder about to leave for Texas, and he was commissioned to buy me. He was to begin with nine hundred dollars, and go up to twelve. My master refused his offers. "Sir," said he, "she don't belong to me. She is my daughter's property, and I have no right to sell her. I mistrust that you come from her paramour. If so, you may tell him that he cannot buy her for any money; neither can he buy her children."

The doctor came to see me the next day, and my heart beat quicker as he entered. I never had seen the old man tread with so majestic a step. He seated himself and looked at me with withering scorn. My children had learned to be afraid of him. The little one would shut her eyes and hide her face on my shoulder whenever she saw him; and Benny, who was now nearly five years old, often inquired, "What makes that bad man come here so many times? Does he want to hurt us?" I would clasp the dear boy in my arms, trusting that he would be free before he was old enough to solve the problem. And now, as the doctor sat there so grim and silent, the child left his play and came and nestled up by me. At last my tormentor spoke. "So you are left in disgust, are you?" said he. "It is no more than I expected. You remember I told you years ago that you would be treated so. So he is tired of you? Ha! ha! ha! The virtuous madam don't like to hear about it, does she? Ha! ha! ha!" There was a sting in his calling me virtuous madam. I no longer had the power of answering him as I had formerly done. He continued: "So it seems you are trying to get up another intrigue. Your new paramour came to me, and offered to buy you; but you may be assured you will not succeed. You are mine; and you shall be mine for life. There lives no human being that can take you out of slavery. I would have done it; but you rejected my kind offer."

I told him I did not wish to get up any intrigue; that I had never seen the man who offered to buy me.

"Do you tell me I lie?" exclaimed he, dragging me from my chair. "Will you say again that you never saw that man?"

I answered, "I do say so."

He clinched my arm with a volley of oaths. Ben began to scream, and I told him to go to his grandmother.

"Don't you stir a step, you little wretch!" said he. The child drew nearer to me, and put his arms round me, as if he wanted to protect me. This was too much for my enraged master. He caught him up and hurled him across the room. I thought he was dead, and rushed towards him to take him up.

"Not yet!" exclaimed the doctor. "Let him lie there till he comes to."

"Let me go! Let me go!" I screamed, "or I will raise the whole house." I struggled and got away; but he clinched me again. Somebody opened the door, and he released me. I picked up my insensible child, and when I turned my tormentor was gone. Anxiously I bent over the little form, so pale and still; and when the brown eyes at last opened, I don't know whether I was very happy.

All the doctor's former persecutions were renewed. He came morning, noon, and night. No jealous lover ever watched a rival more closely than he watched me and the unknown slaveholder, with whom he accused me of wishing to get up an intrigue. When my grandmother was out of the way he searched every room to find him.

In one of his visits, he happened to find a young girl, whom he had sold to a trader a few days previous. His statement was, that he sold her because she had been too familiar with the overseer. She had had a bitter life with him, and was glad to be sold. She had no mother, and no near ties. She had been torn from all her family years before. A few friends had entered into bonds for her safety, if the trader would allow her to spend with them the time that intervened between her sale and the gathering up of his human stock. Such a favor was rarely granted. It saved the trader the expense of board and jail fees, and though the amount was small, it was a weighty consideration in a slave-trader's mind.

Dr. Flint always had an aversion to meeting slaves after he had sold them. He ordered Rose out of the house; but he was no longer her master, and she took no notice of him. For once the crushed Rose was the conqueror. His gray eyes flashed angrily upon her; but that was the extent of his power. "How came this girl here?" he exclaimed. "What right had you to allow it, when you knew I had sold her?"

I answered "This is my grandmother's house, and Rose came to see her. I have no right to turn any body out of doors, that comes here for honest purposes."

He gave me the blow that would have fallen upon Rose if she had still been his slave. My grandmother's attention had been attracted by loud voices, and she entered in time to see a second blow dealt. She was not a woman to let such an outrage, in her own house, go unrebuked. The doctor undertook to explain that I had been insolent. Her indignant feelings rose higher and higher, and finally boiled over in words. "Get out of my house!" she exclaimed. "Go home, and take care of your wife and children, and you will have enough to do, without watching my family."

He threw the birth of my children in her face, and accused her of sanctioning the life I was leading. She told him I was living with her by compulsion of his wife; that he needn't accuse her, for he was the one to blame; he was the one who had caused all the trouble. She grew more and more excited as she went on. "I tell you what, Dr. Flint," said she, "you ain't got many more years to live, and you'd better be saying your prayers. It will take 'em all, and more too, to wash the dirt off your soul."

"Do you know whom you are talking to?" he exclaimed.

She replied, "Yes, I know very well who I am talking to."

He left the house in a great rage. I looked at my grandmother. Our eyes met. Their angry expression had passed away, but she looked sorrowful and weary—weary of incessant strife. I wondered that it did not lessen her love for me; but if it did she never showed it. She was always kind, always ready to sympathize with my troubles. There might have been peace and contentment in that humble home if it had not been for the demon Slavery.

The winter passed undisturbed by the doctor. The beautiful spring came; and when Nature resumes her loveliness, the human soul is apt to revive also. My drooping hopes came to life again with the flowers. I was dreaming of freedom again; more for my children's sake than my own. I planned and I planned. Obstacles hit against plans. There seemed no way of overcoming them; and yet I hoped.

Back came the wily doctor. I was not at home when he called. A friend had invited me to a small party, and to gratify her I went. To my great consternation, a messenger came in haste to say that Dr. Flint was at my grandmother's, and insisted on seeing me. They did not tell him where I was, or he would have come and raised a disturbance in my friend's house. They sent me a dark wrapper; I threw it on and hurried home. My speed did not save me; the doctor had gone away in anger. I dreaded the morning, but I could not delay it; it came, warm and bright. At an early hour the doctor came and asked me where I had been last night. I told him. He did not believe me, and sent to my friend's house to ascertain the facts. He came in the afternoon to assure me he was satisfied that I had spoken the truth. He seemed to be in a facetious mood, and I expected some jeers were coming. "I suppose you need some recreation," said he, "but I am surprised at your being there, among those negroes. It was not the place for *you*. Are you *allowed* to visit such people?"

I understood this covert fling at the white gentleman who was my friend; but I merely replied, "I went to visit my friends, and any company they keep is good enough for me."

He went on to say, "I have seen very little of you of late, but my interest in you is unchanged. When I said I would have no more mercy on you I was rash. I recall my words. Linda, you desire freedom for yourself and your children, and you can obtain it only through me. If you agree to what I am about to propose, you and they shall be free. There must be no communication of any kind between you and their father. I will procure a cottage, where you and the children can live together. Your labor shall be light, such as sewing for my family. Think what is offered you, Linda—a home and freedom! Let the past be forgotten. If I have been harsh with you at times, your wilfulness drove me to it. You know I exact obedience from my own children, and I consider you as yet a child."

He paused for an answer, but I remained silent.

"Why don't you speak?" said he. "What more do you wait for?"

"Nothing, sir."

"Then you accept my offer?"

"No, sir."

His anger was ready to break loose; but he succeeded in curbing it, and replied, "You have answered without thought. But I must let you know there are two sides to my proposition; if you reject the bright side, you will be obliged to take the dark one. You must either accept my offer, or you and your children shall be sent to your young master's plantation, there to remain till your young mistress is married; and your children shall fare like the rest of the negro children. I give you a week to consider of it."

He was shrewd; but I knew he was not to be trusted. I told him I was ready to give my answer now.

"I will not receive it now," he replied. "You act too much from impulse. Remember that you and your children can be free a week from to-day if you choose."

On what a monstrous chance hung the destiny of my children! I knew that my master's offer was a snare, and that if I entered it escape would be impossible. As for his promise, I knew him so well that I was sure if he gave me free papers, they would be so managed as to have no legal value. The alternative was inevitable. I resolved to go to the plantation. But then I thought how completely I should be in his power, and the prospect was appalling. Even if I should kneel before him, and implore him to spare me, for the sake of my children, I knew he would spurn me with his foot, and my weakness would be his triumph.

Before the week expired, I heard that young Mr. Flint was about to be married to a lady of his own stamp. I foresaw the position I should occupy in his establishment. I had once been sent to the plantation for punishment, and fear of the son had induced the father to recall me very soon. My mind was made up; I was resolved that I would foil my master and save my children, or I would perish in the attempt. I kept my plans to myself; I knew that friends would try to dissuade me from them, and I would not wound their feelings by rejecting their advice.

On the decisive day the doctor came, and said he hoped I had made a wise choice.

"I am ready to go to the plantation, sir," I replied.

"Have you thought how important your decision is to your children?" said he.

I told him I had.

"Very well. Go to the plantation, and my curse go with you," he replied. "Your boy shall be put to work, and he shall soon be sold; and your girl shall be raised for the purpose of selling well. Go your own ways!" He left the room with curses, not to be repeated.

As I stood rooted to the spot, my grandmother came and said, "Linda, child, what did you tell him?"

I answered that I was going to the plantation.

"*Must* you go?" said she. "Can't something be done to stop it?"

I told her it was useless to try; but she begged me not to give up. She said she would go to the doctor, and remind him how long and how faithfully she had served in the family, and how she had taken her own baby from her breast to nourish his wife. She would tell him I had been out of the family so long they would not miss me; that she would pay them for my time, and the money would procure a woman who had more strength for the situation than I had. I begged her not to go; but she persisted in saying, "He will listen to *me*, Linda." She went, and was treated as I expected. He coolly listened to what she said, but denied her request. He told her that what he did was for my good, that my feelings were entirely above my situation, and that on the plantation I would receive treatment that was suitable to my behavior.

My grandmother was much cast down. I had my secret hopes; but I must fight my battle alone. I had a woman's pride, and a mother's love for my children; and I resolved that out of the darkness of this hour a brighter dawn should rise for them. My master had power and law on his side; I had a determined will. There is might in each.

CHAPTER XVI

Scenes at the Plantation

Early the next morning I left my grandmother's with my youngest child. My boy was ill, and I left him behind. I had many sad thoughts as the old wagon jolted on. Hitherto, I had suffered alone; now, my little one was to be treated as a slave. As we drew near the great house, I thought of the time when I was formerly sent there out of revenge. I wondered for what purpose I was now sent. I could not tell. I resolved to obey orders so far as duty required; but within myself, I determined to make my stay as short as possible. Mr. Flint was waiting to receive us, and told me to follow him up stairs to receive orders for the day. My little Ellen was left below in the kitchen. It was a change for her, who had always been so carefully tended. My young master said she might amuse herself in the yard. This was kind of him, since the child was hateful to his sight. My task was to fit up the house for the reception of the bride. In the midst of sheets, table-cloths, towels, drapery, and carpeting, my head was as busy planning, as were my fingers with the needle. At noon I was allowed to go to Ellen. She had sobbed herself to sleep. I heard Mr. Flint say to a neighbor, "I've got her down here, and I'll soon take the town notions out of her head. My father is partly to blame for her nonsense.

He ought to have broke her in long ago." The remark was made within my hearing, and it would have been quite as manly to have made it to my face. He *had* said things to my face which might, or might not, have surprised his neighbor if he had known of them. He was "a chip of the old block."

I resolved to give him no cause to accuse me of being too much of a lady, so far as work was concerned. I worked day and night, with wretchedness before me. When I lay down beside my child, I felt how much easier it would be to see her die than to see her master beat her about, as I daily saw him beat other little ones. The spirit of the mothers was so crushed by the lash, that they stood by, without courage to remonstrate. How much more must I suffer, before I should be "broke in" to that degree?

I wished to appear as contented as possible. Sometimes I had an opportunity to send a few lines home; and this brought up recollections that made it difficult, for a time, to seem calm and indifferent to my lot. Notwithstanding my efforts, I saw that Mr. Flint regarded me with a suspicious eye. Ellen broke down under the trials of her new life. Separated from me, with no one to look after her, she wandered about, and in a few days cried herself sick. One day, she sat under the window where I was at work, crying that weary cry which makes a mother's heart bleed. I was obliged to steel myself to bear it. After a while it ceased. I looked out, and she was gone. As it was near noon, I ventured to go down in search of her. The great house was raised two feet above the ground. I looked under it, and saw her about midway, fast asleep. I crept under and drew her out. As I held her in my arms, I thought how well it would be for her if she never waked up; and I uttered my thought aloud. I was startled to hear some one say, "Did you speak to me?" I looked up, and saw Mr. Flint standing beside me. He said nothing further, but turned, frowning, away. That night he sent Ellen a biscuit and a cup of sweetened milk. This generosity surprised me. I learned afterwards, that in the afternoon he had killed a large snake, which crept from under the house; and I supposed that incident had prompted his unusual kindness.

The next morning the old cart was loaded with shingles

for town. I put Ellen into it, and sent her to her grandmother. Mr. Flint said I ought to have asked his permission. I told him the child was sick, and required attention which I had no time to give. He let it pass; for he was aware that I had accomplished much work in a little time.

I had been three weeks on the plantation, when I planned a visit home. It must be at night, after everybody was in bed. I was six miles from town, and the road was very dreary. I was to go with a young man, who, I knew, often stole to town to see his mother. One night, when all was quiet, we started. Fear gave speed to our steps, and we were not long in performing the journey. I arrived at my grandmother's. Her bed room was on the first floor, and the window was open, the weather being warm. I spoke to her and she awoke. She let me in and closed the window, lest some late passerby should see me. A light was brought, and the whole household gathered round me, some smiling and some crying. I went to look at my children, and thanked God for their happy sleep. The tears fell as I leaned over them. As I moved to leave, Benny stirred. I turned back, and whispered, "Mother is here." After digging at his eyes with his little fist, they opened, and he sat up in bed, looking at me curiously. Having satisfied himself that it was I, he exclaimed, "O mother! you ain't dead, are you? They didn't cut off your head at the plantation, did they?"

My time was up too soon, and my guide was waiting for me. I laid Benny back in his bed, and dried his tears by a promise to come again soon. Rapidly we retraced our steps back to the plantation. About half way we were met by a company of four patrols. Luckily we heard their horses' hoofs before they came in sight, and we had time to hide behind a large tree. They passed, hallooing and shouting in a manner that indicated a recent carousal. How thankful we were that they had not their dogs with them! We hastened our footsteps, and when we arrived on the plantation we heard the sound of the hand-mill. The slaves were grinding their corn. We were safely in the house before the horn summoned them to their labor. I divided my little parcel of food with my guide, knowing that he had lost the chance of grinding his corn, and must toil all day in the field.

Mr. Flint often took an inspection of the house, to see

that no one was idle. The entire management of the work was trusted to me, because he knew nothing about it; and rather than hire a superintendent he contented himself with my arrangements. He had often urged upon his father the necessity of having me at the plantation to take charge of his affairs, and make clothes for the slaves; but the old man knew him too well to consent to that arrangement.

When I had been working a month at the plantation, the great aunt of Mr. Flint came to make him a visit. This was the good old lady who paid fifty dollars for my grandmother, for the purpose of making her free, when she stood in the auction block. My grandmother loved this old lady, whom we all called Miss Fanny. She often came to take tea with us. On such occasions the table was spread with a snow-white cloth, and the china cups and silver spoons were taken from the old-fashioned buffet. There were hot muffins, tea rusks, and delicious sweetmeats. My grandmother kept two cows, and the fresh cream was Miss Fanny's delight. She invariably declared that it was the best in town. The old ladies had cosey times together. They would work and chat, and sometimes, while talking over old times, their spectacles would get dim with tears, and would have to be taken off and wiped. When Miss Fanny bade us good by, her bag was filled with grandmother's best cakes, and she was urged to come again soon.

There had been a time when Dr. Flint's wife came to take tea with us, and when her children were also sent to have a feast of "Aunt Marthy's" nice cooking. But after I became an object of her jealousy and spite, she was angry with grandmother for giving a shelter to me and my children. She would not even speak to her in the street. This wounded my grandmother's feelings, for she could not retain ill will against the woman whom she had nourished with her milk when a babe. The doctor's wife would gladly have prevented our intercourse with Miss Fanny if she could have done it, but fortunately she was not dependent on the bounty of the Flints. She had enough to be independent; and that is more than can ever be gained from charity, however lavish it may be.

Miss Fanny was endeared to me by many recollections, and I was rejoiced to see her at the plantation. The warmth of her large, loyal heart made the house seem pleasanter while she was in it. She staid a week, and I had many talks with her. She said her principal object in coming was to see how I was treated, and whether any thing could be done for me. She inquired whether she could help me in any way. I told her I believed not. She condoled with me in her own peculiar way; saying she wished that I and all my grandmother's family were at rest in our graves, for not until then should she feel any peace about us. The good old soul did not dream that I was planning to bestow peace upon her, with regard to myself and my children; not by death, but by securing our freedom.

Again and again I had traversed those dreary twelve miles, to and from the town; and all the way, I was meditating upon some means of escape for myself and my children. My friends had made every effort that ingenuity could devise to effect our purchase, but all their plans had proved abortive. Dr. Flint was suspicious, and determined not to loosen his grasp upon us. I could have made my escape alone; but it was more for my helpless children than for myself that I longed for freedom. Though the boon would have been precious to me, above all price, I would not have taken it at the expense of leaving them in slavery. Every trial I endured, every sacrifice I made for their sakes, drew them closer to my heart, and gave me fresh courage to beat back the dark waves that rolled and rolled over me in a seemingly endless night of storms.

The six weeks were nearly completed, when Mr. Flint's bride was expected to take possession of her new home. The arrangements were all completed, and Mr. Flint said I had done well. He expected to leave home on Saturday, and return with his bride the following Wednesday. After receiving various orders from him, I ventured to ask permission to spend Sunday in town. It was granted; for which favor I was thankful. It was the first I had ever asked of him, and I intended it should be the last. It needed more than one night to accomplish the project I had in view; but the whole of Sunday would give me an opportunity. I spent the Sabbath with my grandmother. A calmer, more beautiful day never came down out of heaven. To me it was a day of conflicting emotions.

Perhaps it was the last day I should ever spend under that dear, old sheltering roof! Perhaps these were the last talks I should ever have with the faithful old friend of my whole life! Perhaps it was the last time I and my children should be together! Well, better so, I thought, than that they should be slaves. I knew the doom that awaited my fair baby in slavery, and I determined to save her from it, or perish in the attempt. I went to make this vow at the graves of my poor parents, in the burying-ground of slaves. "There the wicked cease from troubling, and there the weary be at rest. There the prisoners rest together; they hear not the voice of the oppressor; the servant is free from his master." I knelt by the graves of my parents, and thanked God, as I had often done before, that they had not lived to witness my trials, or to mourn over my sins. I had received my mother's blessing when she died; and in many an hour of tribulation I had seemed to hear her voice, sometimes chiding me, sometimes whispering loving words into my wounded heart. I have shed many and bitter tears, to think that when I am gone from my children they cannot remember me with such entire satisfaction as I remembered my mother.

The graveyard was in the woods, and twilight was coming on. Nothing broke the death-like stillness except the occasional twitter of a bird. My spirit was overawed by the solemnity of the scene. For more than ten years I had frequented this spot, but never had it seemed to me so sacred as now. A black stump, at the head of my mother's grave, was all that remained of a tree my father had planted. His grave was marked by a small wooden board, bearing his name, the letters of which were nearly obliterated. I knelt down and kissed them, and poured forth a prayer to God for guidance and support in the perilous step I was about to take. As I passed the wreck of the old meeting house, where, before Nat Turner's time, the slaves had been allowed to meet for worship, I seemed to hear my father's voice come from it, bidding me not to tarry till I reached freedom or the grave. I rushed on with renovated hopes. My trust in God had been strengthened by that prayer among the graves.

My plan was to conceal myself at the house of a friend, and remain there a few weeks till the search was over. My hope was that the doctor would get discouraged, and, for fear of losing my value, and also of subsequently finding my children among the missing, he would consent to sell us; and I knew somebody would buy us. I had done all in my power to make my children comfortable during the time I expected to be separated from them. I was packing my things, when grandmother came into the room, and asked what I was doing, "I am putting my things in order," I replied. I tried to look and speak cheerfully; but her watchful eye detected something beneath the surface. She drew me towards her, and asked me to sit down. She looked earnestly at me, and said, "Linda, do you want to kill your old grandmother? Do you mean to leave your little, helpless children? I am old now, and cannot do for your babies as I once did for you."

I replied, that if I went away, perhaps their father would be able to secure their freedom.

"Ah, my child," said she, "don't trust too much to him. Stand by your own children, and suffer with them till death. Nobody respects a mother who forsakes her children; and if you leave them, you will never have a happy moment. If you go, you will make me miserable the short time I have to live. You would be taken and brought back, and your sufferings would be dreadful. Remember poor Benjamin. Do give it up, Linda. Try to bear a little longer. Things may turn out better than we expect."

My courage failed me, in view of the sorrow I should bring on that faithful, loving old heart. I promised that I would try longer, and that I would take nothing out of her house without her knowledge.

Whenever the children climbed on my knee, or laid their heads on my lap, she would say, "Poor little souls! what would you do without a mother? She don't love you as I do." And she would hug them to her own bosom, as if to reproach me for my want of affection; but she knew all the while that I loved them better than my life. I slept with her that night, and it was the last time. The memory of it haunted me for many a year.

On Monday I returned to the plantation, and busied myself with preparations for the important day. Wednesday came. It was a beautiful day, and the faces of the slaves were as bright as the sunshine. The poor creatures were merry. They were expecting little presents from the bride, and hoping for better times under her administration. I had no such hopes for them. I knew that the young wives of slaveholders often thought their authority and importance would be best established and maintained by cruelty; and what I had heard of young Mrs. Flint gave me no reason to expect that her rule over them would be less severe than that of the master and overseer. Truly, the colored race are the most cheerful and forgiving people on the face of the earth. That their masters sleep in safety is owing to their superabundance of heart; and yet they look upon their sufferings with less pity than they would bestow on those of a horse or a dog.

I stood at the door with others to receive the bridegroom and bride. She was a handsome, delicate-looking girl, and her face flushed with emotion at sight of her new home. I thought it likely that visions of a happy future were rising before her. It made me sad; for I knew how soon clouds would come over her sunshine. She examined every part of the house, and told me she was delighted with the arrangements I had made. I was afraid old Mrs. Flint had tried to prejudice her against me, and I did my best to please her.

All passed off smoothly for me until dinner time arrived. I did not mind the embarrassment of waiting on a dinner party, for the first time in my life, half so much as I did the meeting with Dr. Flint and his wife, who would be among the guests. It was a mystery to me why Mrs. Flint had not made her appearance at the plantation during all the time I was putting the house in order. I had not met her, face to face, for five years, and I had no wish to see her now. She was a praying woman, and, doubtless, considered my present position a special answer to her prayers. Nothing could please her better than to see me humbled and trampled upon. I was just where she would have me—in the power of a hard, unprincipled master. She did not speak to me when she took her seat at table; but her satisfied, triumphant smile, when I handed her plate, was more eloquent than words. The old doctor was not so quiet in his demonstrations. He ordered me here and there, and spoke with peculiar emphasis when he said, "your *mistress*." I was drilled like a disgraced soldier. When all was over, and the last key turned, I sought my pillow, thankful that God had appointed a season of rest for the weary.

The next day my new mistress began her housekeeping. I was not exactly appointed maid of all work; but I was to do whatever I was told. Monday evening came. It was always a busy time. On that night the slaves received their weekly allowance of food. Three pounds of meat, a peck of corn, and perhaps a dozen herring were allowed to each man. Women received a pound and a half of meat, a peck of corn, and the same number of herring. Children over twelve years old had half the allowance of the women. The meat was cut and weighed by the foreman of the field hands, and piled on planks before the meat house. Then the second foreman went behind the building, and when the first foreman called out, "Who takes this piece of meat?" he answered by calling somebody's name. This method was resorted to as means of preventing partiality in distributing the meat. The young mistress came out to see how things were done on her plantation, and she soon gave a specimen of her character. Among those in waiting for their allowance was a very old slave, who had faithfully served the Flint family through three generations. When he hobbled up to get his bit of meat, the mistress said he was too old to have any allowance; that when niggers were too old to work, they ought to be fed on grass. Poor old man! He suffered much before he found rest in the grave.

My mistress and I got along very well together. At the end of a week, old Mr. Flint made us another visit, and was closeted a long time with her daughter-in-law. I had my suspicions what was the subject of the conference. The old doctor's wife had been informed that I could leave the plantation on one condition, and she was very desirous to keep me there. If she had trusted me, as I deserved to be trusted by her, she would have had no fears of my accepting that condition. When she entered her carriage to return home, she said to young Mrs. Flint, "Don't neglect to send for them as quick as possible." My heart was on the watch all the time, and I at once concluded that she spoke of my children. The doctor came the next day, and as I entered the room to spread the tea table, I heard him say, "Don't wait any longer. Send for them to-morrow." I saw through the plan. They thought my children's being there would fetter me to the spot, and that it was a good place to break us all in to abject submission to our lot as slaves. After the doctor left, a gentleman called, who had always manifested friendly feelings towards my grandmother and her family. Mr. Flint carried him over the plantation to show him the results of labor performed by men and women who were unpaid, miserably clothed, and half famished. The cotton crop was all they thought of. It was duly admired, and the gentleman returned with specimens to show his friends. I was ordered to carry water to wash his hands. As I did so, he said, "Linda, how do you like your new home?" I told him I liked it as well as I expected. He replied, "They don't think you are contented, and to-morrow they are going to bring your children to be with you. I am sorry for you, Linda. I hope they will treat you kindly." I hurried from the room, unable to thank him. My suspicions were correct. My children were to be brought to the plantation to be "broke in."

To this day I feel grateful to the gentleman who gave me this timely information. It nerved me to immediate action.

CHAPTER

XVII

The Flight

Mr. Flint was hard pushed for house servants, and rather than lose me he had restrained his malice. I did my work faithfully, though not, of course, with a willing mind. They were evidently afraid I should leave them. Mr. Flint wished that I should sleep in the great house instead of the servants' quarters. His wife agreed to the proposition, but said I mustn't bring my bed into the house, because it would scatter feathers on her carpet. I knew when I went there that they would never think of such a thing as furnishing a bed of any kind for me and my little one. I therefore carried my own bed, and now I was forbidden to use it. I did as I was ordered. But now that I was certain my children were to be put in their power, in order to give them a stronger hold on me, I resolved to leave them that night. I remembered the grief this step would bring upon my dear old grandmother, and nothing less than the freedom of my children would have induced me to disregard her advice. I went about my evening work with trembling steps. Mr. Flint twice called from his chamber door to inquire why the house was not locked up. I replied that I had not done my work. "You have had time enough to do it," said he. "Take care how you answer me!"

I shut all the windows, locked all the doors, and went up to the third story, to wait till midnight. How long those hours seemed, and how fervently I prayed that God would not forsake me in this hour of utmost need! I was about to risk every thing on the throw of a die; and if I failed, O what would become of me and my poor children? They would be made to suffer for my fault.

At half past twelve I stole softly down stairs. I stopped on the second floor, thinking I heard a noise. I felt my way down into the parlor, and looked out of the window. The night was so intensely dark that I could see nothing. I raised the window very softly and jumped out. Large drops of rain were falling, and the darkness bewildered me. I dropped on my knees, and breathed a short prayer to God for guidance and protection. I groped my way to the road, and rushed towards the town with almost lightning speed. I arrived at my grandmother's house, but dared not see her. She would say, "Linda, you are killing me;" and I knew that would unnerve me. I tapped softly at the window of a room, occupied by a woman, who had lived in the house several years. I knew she was a faithful friend, and could be trusted with my secret. I tapped several times before she heard me. At last she raised the window, and I whispered, "Sally, I have run away. Let me in, quick." She opened the door softly, and said in low tones. "For God's sake, don't. Your grandmother is trying to buy you and de chillern. Mr. Sands was here last week. He told her he was going away on business, but he wanted her to go ahead about buying you and de chillern, and he would help her all he could. Don't run away, Linda. Your grandmother is all bowed down wid trouble now."

I replied, "Sally, they are going to carry my children to the plantation to-morrow; and they will never sell them to any body so long as they have me in their power. Now, would you advise me to go back?"

"No, chile, no," answered she. "When dey finds you is gone, dey won't want de plague ob de chillern; but where is you going to hide? Dey knows ebery inch ob dis house."

I told her I had a hiding-place, and that was all it was best for her to know. I asked her to go into my room as soon as it was light, and take all my clothes out of my trunk, and pack them in hers; for I knew Mr. Flint and the constable would be there early to search my room. I feared the sight of my children would be too much for my full heart; but I could not go out into the uncertain future without one last look. I bent over the bed where lay my little Benny and baby Ellen. Poor little ones! fatherless and motherless! Memories of their father came over me. He wanted to be kind to them; but they were not all to him, as they were to my womanly heart. I knelt and prayed for the innocent little sleepers. I kissed them lightly, and turned away.

As I was about to open the street door, Sally laid her hand on my shoulder, and said, "Linda, is you gwine all alone? Let me call your uncle."

"No, Sally," I replied, "I want no one to be brought into trouble on my account."

I went forth into the darkness and rain. I ran on till I came to the house of the friend who was to conceal me.

Early the next morning Mr. Flint was at my grandmother's inquiring for me. She told him she had not seen me, and supposed I was at the plantation. He watched her face narrowly, and said, "Don't you know any thing about her running off?" She assured him that she did not. He went on to say, "Last night she ran off without the least provocation. We had treated her very kindly. My wife liked her. She will soon be found and brought back. Are her children with you?" when told that they were, he said, "I am very glad to hear that. If they are here, she cannot be far off. If I find out that any of my niggers have had any thing to do with this damned business, I'll give 'em five hundred lashes." As he started to go to his father's, he turned round and added, persuasively, "Let her be brought back, and she shall have her children to live with her."

The tidings made the old doctor rave and storm at a furious rate. It was a busy day for them. My grandmother's house was searched from top to bottom. As my trunk was empty, they concluded I had taken my clothes with me. Before ten o'clock every vessel northward bound was thoroughly examined, and the law against harboring fugitives was read to all on board. At night a watch was set over the town. Knowing how distressed my grandmother would be, I wanted to send her a message; but it could not be done. Every one who went in or out of her house was closely watched. The doctor said he would take my children, unless she became responsible for them; which of course she willingly did. The next day was spent in searching. Before night, the following advertisement was posted at every corner, and in every public place for miles round:—

> "$300 Reward! Ran away from the subscriber, an intelligent, bright, mulatto girl, named Linda, 21 years of age. Five feet four inches high. Dark eyes, and black hair inclined to curl; but it can be made straight. Has a decayed spot on a front tooth. She can read and write, and in all probability will try to get to the Free States. All persons are forbidden, under penalty of the law, to harbor or employ said slave. $150 will be given to whoever takes her in the state, and $300 if taken out of the state and delivered to me, or lodged in jail.
>
> Dr. Flint.

CHAPTER XVIII

Months of Peril

The search for me was kept up with more perseverance than I had anticipated. I began to think that escape was impossible. I was in great anxiety lest I should implicate the friend who harbored me. I knew the consequences would be frightful; and much as I dreaded being caught, even that seemed better than causing an innocent person to suffer for kindness to me. A week had passed in terrible suspense, when my pursuers came into such close vicinity that I concluded they had tracked me to my hiding-place. I flew out of the house, and concealed myself in a thicket of bushes. There I remained in an agony of fear for two hours. Suddenly, a reptile of some kind seized my leg. In my fright, I struck a blow which loosened its hold, but I could not tell whether I had killed it; it was so dark, I could not see what it was; I only knew it was something cold and slimy. The pain I felt soon indicated that the bite was poisonous. I was compelled to leave my place of concealment, and I groped my way back into the house. The pain had become intense, and my friend was startled by my look of anguish. I asked her to prepare a poultice of warm ashes and vinegar, and I applied it to my leg, which was already much swollen. The application gave me some relief, but the swelling did not abate. The dread of being disabled was greater than the physical pain I endured. My friend asked an old woman, who doctored among the slaves, what was good for the bite of a snake or a lizard. She told her to steep a dozen coppers in vinegar, over night, and apply the cankered vinegar to the inflamed part.*

I had succeeded in cautiously conveying some messages to my relatives. They were harshly threatened, and despairing of my having a chance to escape, they advised me to return to my master, ask his forgiveness, and let him make an example of me. But such counsel had no influence with me. When I started upon this hazardous undertaking, I had resolved that, come what would, there should be no turning back. "Give me liberty, or give me death," was my motto. When my friend contrived to make known to my relatives the painful situation I had been in for twenty-four hours, they said no more about my going back to my master. Something must be done, and that speedily; but where to turn for help, they knew not. God in his mercy raised up "a friend in need."

Among the ladies who were acquainted with my grandmother, was one who had known her from childhood, and always been very friendly to her. She had also known my mother and her children, and felt interested for them. At this crisis of affairs she called to see my grandmother, as she not unfrequently did. She observed the sad and troubled expression of her face, and asked if she knew where Linda was, and whether she was safe. My grandmother shook her head, without answering. "Come, Aunt Martha," said the kind lady, "tell me all about it. Perhaps I can do something to help you." The husband of this lady held many slaves, and bought and sold slaves. She also held a number in her own name; but she treated them kindly, and would never allow any of them to be sold. She was unlike the majority of slaveholders' wives. My grandmother looked earnestly at her. Something in the expression of her face said "Trust me!" and she did

*The poison of a snake is a powerful acid, and is counteracted by powerful alkalies, such as potash, ammonia, &c. The Indians are accustomed to apply wet ashes, or plunge the limb into strong lye. White men, employed to lay out railroads in snaky places, often carry ammonia with them as an antidote.—Editor.

trust her. She listened attentively to the details of my story, and sat thinking for a while. At last she said, "Aunt Martha, I pity you both. If you think there is any chance of Linda's getting to the Free States, I will conceal her for a time. But first you must solemnly promise that my name shall never be mentioned. If such a thing should become known, it would ruin me and my family. No one in my house must know of it, except the cook. She is so faithful that I would trust my own life with her; and I know she likes Linda. It is a great risk; but I trust no harm will come of it. Get word to Linda to be ready as soon as it is dark, before the patrols are out. I will send the housemaids on errands, and Betty shall go to meet Linda." The place where we were to meet was designated and agreed upon. My grandmother was unable to thank the lady for this noble deed; overcome by her emotions, she sank on her knees and sobbed like a child.

I received a message to leave my friend's house at such an hour, and go to a certain place where a friend would be waiting for me. As a matter of prudence no names were mentioned. I had no means of conjecturing who I was to meet, or where I was going. I did not like to move thus blindfolded, but I had no choice. It would not do for me to remain where I was. I disguised myself, summoned up courage to meet the worst, and went to the appointed place. My friend Betty was there; she was the last person I expected to see. We hurried along in silence. The pain in my leg was so intense that it seemed as if I should drop; but fear gave me strength. We reached the house and entered unobserved. Her first words were: "Honey, now you is safe. Dem devils ain't coming to search *dis* house. When I get you into missis' safe place, I will bring some nice hot supper. I specs you need it after all dis skeering." Betty's vocation led her to think eating the most important thing in life. She did not realize that my heart was too full for me to care much about supper.

The mistress came to meet us, and led me up stairs to a small room over her sleeping apartment. "You will be safe here, Linda," said she; "I keep this room to store away things that are out of use. The girls are not accustomed to be sent to it, and they will not suspect any thing unless they hear some noise. I always keep it locked, and Betty shall take care of the key. But you must be very careful, for my sake as well as your own; and you must never tell my secret; for it would ruin me and my family. I will keep the girls busy in the morning, that Betty may have a chance to bring your breakfast; but it will not do for her to come to you again till night. I will come to see you sometimes. Keep up your courage. I hope this state of things will not last long." Betty came with the "nice hot supper," and the mistress hastened down stairs to keep things straight till she returned. How my heart overflowed with gratitude! Words choked in my throat; but I could have kissed the feet of my benefactress. For that deed of Christian womanhood, may God forever bless her!

I went to sleep that night with the feeling that I was for the present the most fortunate slave in town. Morning came and filled my little cell with light. I thanked the heavenly Father for this safe retreat. Opposite my window was a pile of feather beds. On the top of these I could lie perfectly concealed, and command a view of the street through which Dr. Flint passed to his office. Anxious as I was, I felt a gleam of satisfaction when I saw him. Thus far I had outwitted him, and I triumphed over it. Who can blame slaves for being cunning? They are constantly compelled to resort to it. It is the only weapon of the weak and oppressed against the strength of their tyrants.

I was daily hoping to hear that my master had sold my children; for I knew who was on the watch to buy them. But Dr. Flint cared even more for revenge than he did for money. My brother William, and the good aunt who had served in his family twenty years, and my little Benny, and Ellen, who was a little over two years old, were thrust into jail, as a means of compelling my relatives to give some information about me. He swore my grandmother should never see one of them again till I was brought back. They kept these facts from me for several days. When I heard that my little ones were in a loathsome jail, my first impulse was to go to them. I was encountering dangers for the sake of freeing them, and must I be the cause of their death? The thought was agonizing. My benefactress tried to soothe me by telling me that my aunt would take good care of the children while they remained in jail. But it added to my pain to think that the good old aunt, who had always been so kind to her sister's orphan children, should be shut up in prison for no other crime than loving them. I suppose my friends feared a reckless movement on my part, knowing, as they did, that my life was bound up in my children. I received a note from my brother William. It was scarcely legible, and ran thus: "Wherever you are, dear sister, I beg of you not to come here. We are all much better off than you are. If you come, you will ruin us all. They would force you to tell where you had been, or they would kill you. Take the advice of your friends; if not for the sake of me and your children, at least for the sake of those you would ruin."

Poor William! He also must suffer for being my brother. I took his advice and kept quiet. My aunt was taken out of jail at the end of a month, because Mrs. Flint could not spare her any longer. She was tired of being her own housekeeper. It was quite too fatiguing to order her dinner and eat it too. My children remained in jail, where brother William did all he could for their comfort. Betty went to see them sometimes, and brought me tidings. She was not permitted to enter the jail; but William would hold them up to the grated window while she chatted with them. When she repeated their prattle, and told me how they wanted to see their ma, my tears would flow. Old Betty would exclaim, "Lors, chile! what's you crying 'bout? Dem young uns vil kill you dead. Don't be so chick'n hearted! If you does, you vil nebber git thro' dis world."

Good old soul! She had gone through the world childless. She had never had little ones to clasp their arms round her neck; she had never seen their soft eyes looking into hers; no sweet little voices had called her mother; she had never pressed her own infants to her heart, with the feeling that even in fetters there was something to live for. How could she realize my feelings? Betty's husband loved children dearly, and wondered why God had denied them to him. He expressed great sorrow when he came to Betty with the tidings that Ellen had been taken out of jail and carried to Dr. Flint's. She had the measles a short time before they carried her to jail, and the disease had left her eyes affected. The doctor had taken her home to attend to them. My children had always been afraid of the doctor and his wife. They had never been inside of their house. Poor little Ellen cried all day to be carried back to prison. The instincts of childhood are true. She knew she was loved in the jail. Her screams and sobs annoyed Mrs. Flint. Before night she called one of the slaves, and said, "Here, Bill, carry this brat back to the jail. I can't stand her noise. If she would be quiet I should like to keep the little minx. She would make a handy waiting-maid for my daughter by and by. But if she staid here, with her white face, I suppose I should either kill her or spoil her. I hope the doctor will sell them as far as wind and water can carry them. As for their mother, her ladyship will find out yet what she gets by running away. She hasn't so much feeling for her children as a cow has for its calf. If she had, she would have come back long ago, to get them out of jail, and save all this expense and trouble. The good-for-nothing hussy! When she is caught, she shall stay in jail, in irons, for one six months, and then be sold to a sugar plantation. I shall see her broke in yet. What do you stand there for, Bill? Why don't you go off with the brat? Mind, now, that you don't let any of the niggers speak to her in the street!"

When these remarks were reported to me, I smiled at Mrs. Flint's saying that she should either kill my child or spoil her. I thought to myself there was very little danger of the latter. I have always considered it as one of God's special providences that Ellen screamed till she was carried back to jail.

That same night Dr. Flint was called to a patient, and did not return till near morning. Passing my grandmother's, he saw a light in the house, and thought to himself, "Perhaps this has something to do with Linda." He knocked, and the door was opened. "What calls you up so early?" said he. "I saw your light, and I thought I would just stop and tell you that I have found out where Linda is. I know where to put my hands on her, and I shall have her before twelve o'clock." When he had turned away, my grandmother and my uncle looked anxiously at each other. They did not know whether or not it was merely one of the doctor's tricks to frighten them. In their uncertainty, they thought it was best to have a message conveyed to my friend Betty. Unwilling to alarm her mistress, Betty resolved to dispose of me herself. She came to me, and told me to rise and dress quickly. We hurried down stairs, and across the yard, into the kitchen. She locked the door, and lifted up a plank in the floor. A buffalo skin and a bit of carpet were spread for me to lie on, and a quilt thrown over me. "Stay dar," said she, "till I sees if dey know 'bout you. Dey say dey vil put thar hans on you afore twelve o'clock. If dey *did* know whar you are, dey won't know *now*. Dey'll be disapinted dis time. Dat's all I got to say. If dey comes rummagin 'mong *my* tings, dey'll get one bressed sarssin from dis 'ere nigger." In my shallow bed I had but just room enough to bring my hands to my face to keep the dust out of my eyes; for Betty walked over me twenty times in an hour, passing from the dresser to the fireplace. When she was alone, I could hear her pronouncing anathemas over Dr. Flint and all his tribe, every now and then saying, with a chuckling laugh, "Dis nigger's too cute for 'em dis time." When the housemaids were about, she had sly ways of drawing them out, that I might hear what they would say. She would repeat stories she had heard about my being in this or that, or the other place. To which they would answer, that I was not fool enough to be staying round there; that I was in Philadelphia or New York before this time. When all were abed and asleep, Betty raised the plank, and said, "Come out, chile; come out. Dey don't know nottin 'bout you. 'Twas only white folks' lies, to skeer de niggers."

Some days after this adventure I had a much worse fright. As I sat very still in my retreat above stairs, cheerful visions floated through my mind. I thought Dr. Flint would soon get discouraged, and would be willing to sell my children, when he lost all hopes of making them the means of my discovery. I knew who was ready to buy them. Suddenly I heard a voice that chilled my blood. The sound was too familiar to me, it had been too dreadful, for me not to recognize at once my old master. He was in the house, and I at once concluded he had come to seize me. I looked around in terror. There was no way of escape. The voice receded. I supposed the constable was with him, and they were searching the house. In my alarm I did not forget the trouble I was bringing on my generous benefactress. It seemed as if I were born to bring sorrow on all who befriended me, and that was the bitterest drop in the bitter cup of my life. After a while I heard approaching footsteps; the key was turned in my door. I braced myself against the wall to keep from falling. I ventured to look up, and there stood my kind benefactress alone. I was too much overcome to speak, and sunk down upon the floor.

"I thought you would hear your master's voice," she said; "and knowing you would be terrified, I came to tell you there is nothing to fear. You may even indulge in a laugh at the old gentleman's expense. He is so sure you are in New York, that he came to borrow five hundred dollars to go in pursuit of you. My sister had some money to loan on interest. He has obtained it, and proposes to start for New York to-night. So, for the present, you see you are safe. The doctor will merely lighten his pocket hunting after the bird he has left behind."

CHAPTER XIX

The Children Sold

The doctor came back from New York, of course without accomplishing his purpose. He had expended considerable money, and was rather disheartened. My brother and the children had now been in jail two months, and that also was some expense. My friends thought it was a favorable time to work on his discouraged feelings. Mr. Sands sent a speculator to offer him nine hundred dollars for my brother William, and eight hundred for the two children. These were high prices, as slaves were then selling; but the offer was rejected. If it had been merely a question of money, the doctor would have sold any boy of Benny's age for two hundred dollars; but he could not bear to give up the power of revenge. But he was hard pressed for money, and he revolved the matter in his mind. He knew that if he could keep Ellen till she was fifteen, he could sell her for a high price; but I presume he reflected that she might die, or might be stolen away. At all events, he came to the conclusion that he had better accept the slave-trader's offer. Meeting him in the street, he inquired when he would leave town. "To-day, at ten o'clock," he replied. "Ah, do you go so soon?" said the doctor; "I have been reflecting upon your proposition, and I have concluded to let you have the three negroes if you will say nineteen hundred dollars." After some parley, the trader agreed to his terms. He wanted the bill of sale drawn up and signed immediately, as he had a great deal to attend to during the short time he remained in town. The doctor went to the jail and told William he would take him back into his service if he would promise to behave himself; but he replied that he would rather be sold. "And you *shall* be sold, you ungrateful rascal!" exclaimed the doctor. In less than an hour the money was paid, the papers were signed, sealed, and delivered, and my brother and children were in the hands of the trader.

It was a hurried transaction; and after it was over, the doctor's characteristic caution returned. He went back to the speculator, and said, "Sir, I have come to lay you under obligations of a thousand dollars not to sell any of those negroes in this state." "You come too late," replied the trader; "our bargain is closed." He had, in fact, already sold them to Mr. Sands, but he did not mention it. The doctor required him to put irons on "that rascal, Bill," and to pass through the back streets when he took his gang out of town. The trader was privately instructed to concede to his wishes. My good old aunt went to the jail to bid the children good by, supposing them to be the speculator's property, and that she should never see them again. As she held Benny in her lap, he said, "Aunt Nancy, I want to show you something." He led her to the door and showed her a long row of marks, saying, "Uncle Will taught me to count. I have made a mark for every day I have been here, and it is sixty days. It is a long time; and the speculator is going to take me and Ellen away. He's a bad man. It's wrong for him to take grandmother's children. I want to go to my mother."

My grandmother was told that the children would be restored to her, but she was requested to act as if they were really to be sent away. Accordingly, she made up a bundle of clothes and went to the jail. When she arrived, she found William handcuffed among the gang, and the children in the trader's cart. The scene seemed too much like reality. She was afraid there might have been some deception or mistake. She fainted, and was carried home.

When the wagon stopped at the hotel, several gentlemen came out and proposed to purchase William, but the trader refused their offers, without stating that he was already sold. And now came the trying hour for that drove of human beings, driven away like cattle, to be sold they knew not where. Husbands were torn from wives, parents from children, never to look upon each other again this side the grave. There was wringing of hands and cries of despair.

Dr. Flint had the supreme satisfaction of seeing the wagon leave town, and Mrs. Flint had the gratification of supposing that my children were going "as far as wind and water would carry them." According to agreement, my uncle followed the wagon some miles, until they came to an old farm house. There the trader took the irons from William, and as he did so, he said, "You are a damned clever fellow. I should like to own you myself. Them gentlemen that wanted to buy you said you was a bright, honest chap, and I must git you a good home. I guess your old master will swear to-morrow, and call himself an old fool for selling the children. I reckon he'll never git their mammy back agin. I expect she's made tracks for the north. Good by, old boy. Remember, I have done you a good turn. You must thank me by coaxing all the pretty gals to go with me next fall. That's going to be my last trip. This trading in niggers is a bad business for a fellow that's got any heart. Move on, you fellows!" And the gang went on, God alone knows where.

Much as I despise and detest the class of slave-traders, whom I regard as the vilest wretches on earth, I must do this man the justice to say that he seemed to have some feeling. He took a fancy to William in the jail, and wanted to buy him. When he heard the story of my children, he was willing to aid them in getting out of Dr. Flint's power, even without charging the customary fee.

My uncle procured a wagon and carried William and the children back to town. Great was the joy in my grandmother's house! The curtains were closed, and the candles lighted. The happy grandmother cuddled the little ones to her bosom. They hugged her, and kissed her, and clapped their hands, and shouted. She knelt down and poured forth one of her heartfelt prayers of thanksgiving to God. The father was present for a while; and though such a "parental relation" as existed between him and my children takes slight hold of the hearts or consciences of slaveholders, it must be that he experienced some moments of pure joy in witnessing the happiness he had imparted.

I had no share in the rejoicings of that evening. The events of the day had not come to my knowledge. And now I will tell you something that happened to me; though you will, perhaps, think it illustrates the superstition of slaves. I sat in my usual place on the floor near the window, where I could hear much that was said in the street without being seen. The family had retired for the night, and all was still. I sat there thinking of my children, when I heard a low strain of music. A band of serenaders were under the window, playing "Home, sweet home." I listened till the sounds did not seem like music, but like the moaning of children. It seemed as if my heart would burst. I rose from my sitting posture, and knelt. A streak of moonlight was on the floor before me, and in the midst of it appeared the forms of my two children. They vanished; but I had seen them distinctly. Some will call it a dream, others a vision. I know not how to account for it, but it made a strong impression on my mind, and I felt certain something had happened to my little ones.

I had not seen Betty since morning. Now I heard her softly turning the key. As soon as she entered, I clung to her, and begged her to let me know whether my children were dead, or whether they were sold; for I had seen their spirits in my room, and I was sure something had happened to them. "Lor, chile," said she, putting her arms round me, "you's got de highsterics. I'll sleep wid you to-night, 'cause you'll make a noise, and ruin missis. Something has stirred you up mightily. When you is done cryin, I'll talk wid you. De chillern is well, and mighty happy. I seed 'em myself. Does dat satisfy you? Dar, chile, be still! Somebody vill hear you." I tried to obey her. She lay down, and was soon sound asleep; but no sleep would come to my eyelids.

At dawn, Betty was up and off to the kitchen. The hours passed on, and the vision of the night keep constantly recurring to my thoughts. After a while I heard the voices of two women in the entry. In one of them I recognized the housemaid. The other said to her, "Did you know Linda Brent's children was sold to the speculator yesterday. They say ole massa Flint was mighty glad to see 'em drove out of town; but they say they've come back agin. I 'spect it's all their daddy's doings. They say he's bought William too. Lor! how it will take hold of ole massa Flint! I'm going roun' to aunt Marthy's to see 'bout it."

I bit my lips till the blood came to keep from crying out. Were my children with their grandmother, or had the speculator carried them off? The suspense was dreadful. Would Betty *never* come, and tell me the truth about it? At last she came, and I eagerly repeated what I had overheard. Her face was one broad, bright smile. "Lor, you foolish ting!" said she. "I'se gwine to tell you all 'bout it. De gals is eating thar breakfast, and missus tole me to let her tell you; but, poor creeter! t'aint right to keep you waitin', and I'se gwine to tell you. Brudder, chillern, all is bought by de daddy! I'se laugh more dan nuff, tinking 'bout ole massa Flint. Lor, how he *vill* swar! He's got ketched dis time, any how; but I must be getting out o' dis, or dem gals will come and ketch *me*."

Betty went off laughing; and I said to myself, "Can it be true that my children are free? I have not suffered for them in vain. Thank God!"

Great surprise was expressed when it was known that my children had returned to their grandmother's. The news spread through the town, and many a kind word was bestowed on the little ones.

Dr. Flint went to my grandmother's to ascertain who was the owner of my children, and she informed him. "I expected as much," said he. "I am glad to hear it. I have had news from Linda lately, and I shall soon have her. You need never expect to see *her* free. She shall be my slave as long as I live, and when I am dead she shall be the slave of my children. If I ever find out that you or Phillip had any thing to do with her running off I'll kill him. And if I meet William in the street, and he presumes to look at me, I'll flog him within an inch of his life. Keep those brats out of my sight!"

As he turned to leave, my grandmother said something to remind him of his own doings. He looked back upon her, as if he would have been glad to strike her to the ground.

I had my season of joy and thanksgiving. It was the

first time since my childhood that I had experienced any real happiness. I heard of the old doctor's threats, but they no longer had the same power to trouble me. The darkest cloud that hung over my life had rolled away. Whatever slavery might do to me, it could not shackle my children. If I fell a sacrifice, my little ones were saved. It was well for me that my simple heart believed all that had been promised for their welfare. It is always better to trust than to doubt.

CHAPTER

XX

New Perils

The doctor, more exasperated than ever, again tried to revenge himself on my relatives. He arrested uncle Phillip on the charge of having aided my flight. He was carried before a court, and swore truly that he knew nothing of my intention to escape, and that he had not seen me since I left my master's plantation. The doctor then demanded that he should give bail for five hundred dollars that he would have nothing to do with me. Several gentlemen offered to be security for him; but Mr. Sands told him he had better go back to jail, and he would see that he came out without giving bail.

The news of his arrest was carried to my grandmother, who conveyed it to Betty. In the kindness of her heart, she again stowed me away under the floor; and as she walked back and forth, in the performance of her culinary duties, she talked apparently to herself, but with the intention that I should hear what was going on. I hoped that my uncle's imprisonment would last but few days; still I was anxious. I thought it likely Dr. Flint would do his utmost to taunt and insult him, and I was afraid my uncle might lose control of himself, and retort in some way that would be construed into a punishable offence; and I was well aware that in court his word would not be taken against any white man's. The search for me was renewed. Something had excited suspicions that I was in the vicinity. They searched the house I was in. I heard their steps and their voices. At night, when all were asleep, Betty came to release me from my place of confinement. The fright I had undergone, the constrained posture, and the dampness of the ground, made me ill for several days. My uncle was soon after taken out of prison; but the movements of all my relatives, and of all our friends, were very closely watched.

We all saw that I could not remain where I was much longer. I had already staid longer than was intended, and I knew my presence must be a source of perpetual anxiety to my kind benefactress. During this time, my friends had laid many plans for my escape, but the extreme vigilance of my persecutors made it impossible to carry them into effect.

One morning I was much startled by hearing somebody trying to get into my room. Several keys were tried, but none fitted. I instantly conjectured it was one of the housemaids; and I concluded she must either have heard some noise in the room, or have noticed the entrance of Betty. When my friend came, at her usual time, I told her what had happened. "I knows who it was," said she. " 'Pend upon it, 'twas dat Jenny. Dat nigger allers got de debble in her." I suggested that she might have seen or heard something that excited her curiosity.

"Tut! tut! chile!" exclaimed Betty, "she ain't seen notin', nor hearn notin'. She only 'spects something. Dat's all. She wants to fine out who hab cut and make my gownd. But she won't nebber know. Dat's sartin. I'll git missis to fix her."

I reflected a moment, and said, "Betty, I must leave here tonight."

"Do as you tink best, poor chile," she replied. "I'se mighty 'fraid dat 'ere nigger vill pop on you sometime."

She reported the incident to her mistress, and received orders to keep Jenny busy in the kitchen till she could see my uncle Phillip. He told her he would send a friend for me that very evening. She told him she hoped I was going to the north, for it was very dangerous for me to remain any where in the vicinity. Alas, it was not an easy thing, for one in my situation, to go to the north. In order to leave the coast quite clear for me, she went into the country to spend the day with her brother, and took Jenny with her. She was afraid to come and bid me good by, but she left a kind message with Betty. I heard her carriage roll from the door, and I never again saw her who had so generously befriended the poor, trembling fugitive! Though she was a slaveholder, to this day my heart blesses her!

I had not the slightest idea where I was going. Betty brought me a suit of sailor's clothes—jacket, trowsers, and tarpaulin hat. She gave me a small bundle, saying I might need it where I was going. In cheery tones, she exclaimed, "I'se *so* glad you is gwine to free parts! Don't forget ole Betty. P'raps I'll come 'long by and by."

I tried to tell her how grateful I felt for all her kindness, but she interrupted me. "I don't want no tanks, honey. I'se glad I could help you, and I hope de good Lord vill open de path for you. I'se gwine wid you to de lower gate. Put your hands in your pockets, and walk ricketty, like de sailors."

I performed to her satisfaction. At the gate I found Peter, a young colored man, waiting for me. I had known him for years. He had been an apprentice to my father, and had always borne a good character. I was not afraid to trust to him. Betty bade me a hurried good by, and we walked off. "Take courage, Linda," said my friend Peter. "I've got a dagger, and no man shall take you from me, unless he passed over my dead body."

It was a long time since I had taken a walk out of doors, and the fresh air revived me. It was also pleasant to hear a human voice speaking to me above a whisper. I passed several people whom I know, but they did not recognize me in my disguise. I prayed internally that, for Peter's sake, as well as my own, nothing might occur to bring out his dagger. We walked on till we came to the wharf. My aunt Nancy's husband was a seafaring man, and it had been deemed necessary to let him into our secret. He took me into his boat, rowed out to a vessel not far distant, and hoisted me on board. We three were the only occupants of the vessel. I now ventured to ask what they proposed to do with me. They said I was to remain on board till near dawn, and then they would hide me in Snaky Swamp, till my uncle Phillip had prepared a place of concealment for me. If the vessel had been bound north, it would have been no avail to me, for it would certainly have been searched. About four o'clock, we were again seated in the boat, and rowed three miles to the swamp. My fear of snakes had been increased by the venomous bite I had received, and I dreaded to enter this hiding-place. But I was in no situation to choose, and I gratefully accepted the best that my poor, persecuted friends could do for me.

Peter landed first, and with a large knife cut a path through bamboos and briers of all descriptions. He came back, took me in his arms, and carried me to a seat made among the bamboos. Before we reached it, we were covered with hundreds of mosquitos. In an hour's time they had so poisoned my flesh that I was a pitiful sight to behold. As the light increased, I saw snake after snake crawling round us. I had been accustomed to the sight of snakes all my life, but these were larger than any I had ever seen. To this day I shudder when I remember that morning. As evening approached, the number of snakes increased so much that we were continually obliged to thrash them with sticks to keep them from crawling over us. The bamboos were so high and so thick that it was impossible to see beyond a very short distance. Just before it became dark we procured a seat nearer to the entrance of the swamp, being fearful of losing our way back to the boat. It was not long before we heard the paddle of oars, and the low whistle, which had been agreed upon as a signal. We made haste to enter the boat, and were rowed back to the vessel. I passed a wretched night; for the heat of the swamp, the mosquitos, and the constant terror of snakes, had brought on a burning fever. I had just dropped asleep, when they came and told me it was time to go back to that horrid swamp. I could scarcely summon courage to rise. But even those large, venomous snakes were less dreadful to my imagination than the white men in that community called civilized. This time Peter took a quantity of tobacco to burn, to keep off the mosquitos. It produced the desired effect on them, but gave me nausea and severe headache. At dark we returned to the vessel. I had been so sick during the day, that Peter declared I should go home that night, if the devil himself was on patrol. They told me a place of concealment had been provided for me at my grandmother's. I could not imagine how it was possible to hide me in her house, every nook and corner of which was known to the Flint family. They told me to wait and see. We were rowed ashore, and went boldly through the streets, to my grandmother's. I wore my sailor's clothes, and had blackened my face with charcoal. I passed several people whom I knew. The father of my children came so near that I brushed against his arm; but he had no idea who it was.

"You must make the most of this walk," said my friend Peter, "for you may not have another very soon."

I thought his voice sounded sad. It was kind of him to conceal from me what a dismal hole was to be my home for a long, long time.

CHAPTER

XXI

The Loophole of Retreat

A small shed had been added to my grandmother's house years ago. Some boards were laid across the joists at the top, and between these boards and the roof was a very small garret, never occupied by any thing but rats and mice. It was a pent roof, covered with nothing but shingles, according to the southern custom for such buildings. The garret was only nine feet long and seven wide. The highest part was three feet high, and sloped down abruptly to the loose board floor. There was no admission for either light or air. My uncle Phillip, who was a carpenter, had very skilfully made a concealed trap-door, which communicated with the storeroom. He had been doing this while I was waiting in the swamp. The storeroom opened upon a piazza. To this hole I was conveyed as soon as I entered the house. The air was stifling; the darkness total. A bed had been spread on the floor. I could sleep quite comfortably on one side; but the slope was so sudden that I could not turn on the other without hitting the roof. The rats and mice ran over my bed; but I was weary, and I slept such sleep as the wretched may, when a tempest has passed over them. Morning came. I knew it only by the noises I heard; for in my small den day and night were all the same. I suffered for air even more than for light. But I was not comfortless. I heard the voices of my children. There was joy and there was sadness in the sound. It made my tears flow. How I longed to speak to them! I was eager to look on their faces; but there was no hole, no crack, through which I could peep. This continued darkness was oppressive. It seemed horrible to sit or lie in a cramped position day after day, without one gleam of light. Yet I would have chosen this, rather than my lot as a slave, though white people considered it an easy one; and it was so compared with the fate of others. I was never cruelly over-worked; I was never lacerated with the whip from head to foot; I was never so beaten and bruised that I could not turn from one side to the other; I never had my heel-strings cut to prevent my running away; I was never chained to a log and forced to drag it about, while I toiled in the fields from morning till night; I was never branded with hot iron, or torn by bloodhounds. On the contrary, I had always been kindly treated, and tenderly cared for, until I came into the hands of Dr. Flint. I had never wished for freedom till then. But though my life in slavery was comparatively devoid of hardships, God pity the woman who is compelled to lead such a life!

My food was passed up to me through the trap-door my uncle had contrived; and my grandmother, my uncle Phillip, and aunt Nancy would seize such opportunities as they could, to mount up there and chat with me at the opening. But of course this was not safe in the daytime. It must all be done in darkness. It was impossible for me to move in an erect position, but I crawled about my den for exercise. One day I hit my head against something, and found it was a gimlet. My uncle had left it sticking there when he made the trap-door. I was as rejoiced as Robinson Crusoe could have been at finding such a treasure. It put a lucky thought into my head. I said to myself, "Now I will have some light. Now I will see my children." I did not dare to begin my work during the daytime, for fear of attracting attention. But I groped round; and having found the side next the street, where I could frequently see my children, I stuck the gimlet in and waited for evening. I bored three rows of holes, one above another; then I bored out the interstices between. I thus succeeded in making one hole about an inch long and an inch broad. I sat by it till late into the night, to enjoy the little whiff of air that floated in. In the morning I watched for my children. The first person I saw in the street was Dr. Flint. I had a shuddering, superstitious feeling that it was a bad omen. Several familiar faces passed by. At last I heard the merry laugh of children, and presently two sweet little faces were looking up at me, as though they knew I was there, and were conscious of the joy they imparted. How I longed to *tell* them I was there!

My condition was now a little improved. But for weeks I was tormented by hundreds of little red insects, fine as a needle's point, that pierced through my skin, and produced an intolerable burning. The good grandmother gave me herb teas and cooling medicines, and finally I got rid of them. The heat of my den was intense, for nothing but thin shingles protected me from the scorching summer's sun. But I had my consolations. Through my peeping-hole I could watch the children, and when they were near enough, I could hear their talk. Aunt Nancy brought me all the news she could hear at Dr. Flint's. From her I learned that the doctor had written to New York to a colored woman, who had been born and raised in our neighborhood, and had breathed his contaminating atmosphere. He offered her a reward if she could find out any thing about me. I know not what was the nature of her reply; but he soon after started for New York in haste, saying to his family that he had business of importance to transact. I peeped at him as he passed on his way to the steamboat. It was a satisfaction to have miles of land and water between us, even for a little while; and it was a still greater satisfaction to know that he believed me to be in the Free States. My little den seemed less dreary than it had done. He returned, as he did from his former journey to New York, without obtaining any satisfactory information. When he passed our house next morning, Benny was standing at the gate. He had heard them say that he had gone to find me, and he called out, "Dr. Flint, did you bring my mother home? I want to see her." The doctor stamped his foot at him in a rage, and exclaimed, "Get out of the way, you little damned rascal! If you don't, I'll cut off your head."

Benny ran terrified into the house, saying, "You can't

put me in jail again. I don't belong to you now." It was well that the wind carried the words away from the doctor's ear. I told my grandmother of it, when we had our next conference at the trap-door; and begged of her not to allow the children to be impertinent to the irascible old man.

Autumn came, with a pleasant abatement of heat. My eyes had become accustomed to the dim light, and by holding my book or work in a certain position near the aperture I contrived to read and sew. That was a great relief to the tedious monotony of my life. But when winter came, the cold penetrated through the thin shingle roof, and I was dreadfully chilled. The winters there are not so long, or so severe, as in northern latitudes; but the houses are not built to shelter from cold, and my little den was peculiarly comfortless. The kind grandmother brought me bed-clothes and warm drinks. Often I was obliged to lie in bed all day to keep comfortable; but with all my precautions, my shoulders and feet were frostbitten. O, those long, gloomy days, with no object for my eye to rest upon, and no thoughts to occupy my mind, except the dreary past and the uncertain future! I was thankful when there came a day sufficiently mild for me to wrap myself up and sit at the loophole to watch the passers by. Southerners have the habit of stopping and talking in the streets, and I heard many conversations not intended to meet my ears. I heard slave-hunters planning how to catch some poor fugitive. Several times I heard allusions to Dr. Flint, myself, and the history of my children, who, perhaps, were playing near the gate. One would say, "I wouldn't move my little finger to catch her, as old Flint's property." Another would say, "I'll catch *any* nigger for the reward. A man ought to have what belongs to him, if he *is* a damned brute." The opinion was often expressed that I was in the Free States. Very rarely did any one suggest that I might be in the vicinity. Had the least suspicion rested on my grandmother's house, it would have been burned to the ground. But it was the last place they thought of. Yet there was no place, where slavery existed, that could have afforded me so good a place of concealment.

Dr. Flint and his family repeatedly tried to coax and bribe my children to tell something they had heard said about me. One day the doctor took them into a shop, and offered them some bright little silver pieces and gay handkerchiefs if they would tell where their mother was. Ellen shrank away from him, and would not speak; but Benny spoke up, and said, "Dr. Flint, I don't know where my mother is. I guess she's in New York; and when you go there again, I wish you'd ask her to come home, for I want to see her; but if you put her in jail, or tell her you'll cut her head off, I'll tell her to go right back."

CHAPTER

XXII

Christmas Festivities

Christmas was approaching. Grandmother brought me materials, and I busied myself making some new garments and little playthings for my children. Were it not that hiring day is near at hand, and many families are fearfully looking forward to the probability of separation in a few days, Christmas might be a happy season for the poor slaves. Even slave mothers try to gladden the hearts of their little ones on that occasion. Benny and Ellen had their Christmas stockings filled. Their imprisoned mother could not have the privilege of witnessing their surprise and joy. But I had the pleasure of peeping at them as they went into the street with their new suits on. I heard Benny ask a little playmate whether Santa Claus brought him any thing. "Yes," replied the boy; "but Santa Claus ain't a real man. It's the children's mothers that put things into the stockings." "No, that can't be," replied Benny, "for Santa Claus brought Ellen and me these new clothes, and my mother has been gone this long time."

How I longed to tell him that his mother made those garments, and that many a tear fell on them while she worked!

Every child rises early on Christmas morning to see the Johnkannaus. Without them, Christmas would be shorn of its greatest attraction. They consist of companies of slaves from the plantations, generally of the lower class. Two athletic men, in calico wrappers, have a net thrown over them, covered with all manner of bright-colored stripes. Cows' tails are fastened to their backs, and their heads are decorated with horns. A box, covered with sheepskin, is called the gumbo box. A dozen beat on this, while others strike triangles and jawbones, to which bands of dancers keep time. For a month previous they are composing songs, which are sung on this occasion. These companies, of a hundred each, turn out early in the morning, and are allowed to go round till twelve o'clock, begging for contributions. Not a door is left unvisited where there is the least chance of obtaining a penny or a glass of rum. They do not drink while they are out, but carry the rum home in jugs, to have a carousal. These Christmas donations frequently amount to twenty or thirty dollars. It is seldom that any white man or child refuses to give them a trifle. If he does, they regale his ears with the following song:—

"Poor massa, so dey say;
Down in de heel, so dey say;
Got no money, so dey say;
Not one shillin, so dey say;
God A'mighty bress you, so dey say."

Christmas is a day of feasting, both with white and colored people. Slaves, who are lucky enough to have a few shillings, are sure to spend them for good eating; and many a turkey and pig is captured, without saying, "By your leave, sir." Those who cannot obtain these, cook a 'possum, or a raccoon, from which savory dishes can be made. My grandmother raised poultry and pigs for sale; and it was her established custom to have both a turkey and a pig roasted for Christmas dinner.

On this occasion, I was warned to keep extremely quiet, because two guests had been invited. One was the town constable, and the other was a free colored man, who tried to pass himself off for white, and who was always ready to do any mean work for the sake of currying favor with white people. My grandmother had a motive for inviting them. She managed to take them all over the house. All the rooms on the lower floor were thrown open for them to pass in and out; and after dinner, they were invited up stairs to look at a fine mocking bird my uncle had just brought home. There, too, the rooms were all thrown open, that they might look in. When I heard them talking on the piazza, my heart almost stood still. I knew this colored man had spent many nights hunting for me. Every body knew he had the blood of a slave father in his veins; but for the sake of passing himself off for white, he was ready to kiss the slaveholders' feet. How I despised him! As for the constable, he wore no false colors. The duties of his office were despicable, but he was superior to his companion, inasmuch as he did not pretend to be what he was not. Any white man, who could raise money enough to buy a slave, would have considered himself degraded by being a constable; but the office enabled its possessor to exercise authority. If he found any slave out after nine o'clock, he could whip him as much as he liked; and that was a privilege to be coveted. When the guests were ready to depart, my grandmother gave each of them some of her nice pudding, as a present for their wives. Through my peep-hole I saw them go out of the gate, and I was glad when it closed after them. So passed the first Christmas in my den.

CHAPTER XXIV

The Candidate for Congress

The summer had nearly ended, when Dr. Flint made a third visit to New York, in search of me. Two candidates were running for Congress, and he returned in season to vote. The father of my children was the Whig candidate. The doctor had hitherto been a stanch Whig; but now he exerted all his energies for the defeat of Mr. Sands. He invited large parties of men to dine in the shade of his trees, and supplied them with plenty of rum and brandy. If any poor fellow drowned his wits in the bowl, and, in the openness of his convivial heart, proclaimed that he did not mean to vote the Democratic ticket, he was shoved into the street without ceremony.

The doctor expended his liquor in vain. Mr. Sands was elected; an event which occasioned me some anxious thoughts. He had not emancipated my children, and if he should die they would be at the mercy of his heirs. Two little voices, that frequently met my ear, seemed to plead with me not to let their father depart without striving to make their freedom secure. Years had passed since I had spoken to him. I had not even seen him since the night I passed him, unrecognized, in my disguise of a sailor. I supposed he would call before he left, to say something to my grandmother concerning the children, and I resolved what course to take.

The day before his departure for Washington I made arrangements, towards evening, to get from my hiding-place into the storeroom below. I found myself so stiff and clumsy that it was with great difficulty I could hitch from one resting place to another. When I reached the storeroom my ankles gave way under me, and I sank exhausted on the floor. It seemed as if I could never use my limbs again. But the purpose I had in view roused all the strength I had. I crawled on my hands and knees to the window, and, screened behind a barrel, I waited for his coming. The clock struck nine, and I knew the steamboat would leave between ten and eleven. My hopes were failing. But presently I heard his voice, saying to some one, "Wait for me a moment. I wish to see aunt Martha." When he came out, as he passed the window, I said, "Stop one moment, and let me speak for my children." He started, hesitated, and then passed on, and went out of the gate. I closed the shutter I had partially opened, and sank down behind the barrel. I had suffered much; but seldom had I experienced a keener pang than I then felt. Had my children, then, become of so little consequence to him? And had he so little feeling for their wretched mother that he would not listen a moment while she pleaded for them? Painful memories were so busy within me, that I forgot I had not hooked the shutter, till I heard some one opening it. I looked up. He had come back. "Who called me?" said he, in a low tone. "I did," I replied. "Oh, Linda," said he, "I knew your voice; but I was afraid to answer, lest my friend should hear me. Why do you come here? Is it possible you risk yourself in this house? They are mad to allow it. I shall expect to hear that you are all ruined." I did not wish to implicate him, by letting him know my place of concealment; so I merely said, "I thought you would come to bid grandmother good by, and so I came here to speak a few words to you about emancipating my children. Many changes may take place during the six months you are gone to Washington, and it does not seem right for you to expose them to the risk of such changes. I want nothing for myself; all I ask is, that you will free my children, or authorize some friend to do it, before you go."

He promised he would do it, and also expressed a readiness to make any arrangements whereby I could be purchased.

I heard footsteps approaching, and closed the shutter hastily. I wanted to crawl back to my den, without letting the family know what I had done; for I knew they would deem it very imprudent. But he stepped back into the house, to tell my grandmother that he had spoken with me at the storeroom window, and to beg of her not to allow me to remain in the house over night. He said it was the height of madness for me to be there; that we should certainly all be ruined. Luckily, he was in too much of a hurry to wait for a reply, or the dear old woman would surely have told him all.

I tried to go back to my den, but found it more difficult to go up than I had to come down. Now that my mission was fulfilled, the little strength that had supported me through it was gone, and I sank helpless on the floor. My grandmother, alarmed at the risk I had run, came into the storeroom in the dark, and locked the door behind her. "Linda," she whispered, "where are you?"

"I am here by the window," I replied. "I *couldn't* have him go away without emancipating the children. Who knows what may happen?"

"Come, come, child," said she, "it won't do for you to stay here another minute. You've done wrong; but I can't blame you, poor thing!"

I told her I could not return without assistance, and she must call my uncle. Uncle Phillip came, and pity prevented him from scolding me. He carried me back to my dungeon, laid me tenderly on the bed, gave me some medicine, and asked me if there was any thing more he could do. Then he went away, and I was left with my own thoughts—starless as the midnight darkness around me.

My friends feared I should become a cripple for life; and I was so weary of my long imprisonment that, had it not been for the hope of serving my children, I should have been thankful to die; but, for their sakes, I was willing to bear on.

CHAPTER XXV

Competition in Cunning

Dr. Flint had not given me up. Every now and then he would say to my grandmother that I would yet come back, and voluntarily surrender myself; and that when I did, I could be purchased by my relatives, or any one who wished to buy me. I knew his cunning nature too well not to perceive that this was a trap laid for me; and so all my friends understood it. I resolved to match my cunning against his cunning. In order to make him believe that I was in New York, I resolved to write him a letter dated from that place. I sent for my friend Peter, and asked him if he knew any trustworthy seafaring person, who would carry such a letter to New York, and put it in thc post office there. He said he knew one that he would trust with his own life to the ends of the world. I reminded him that it was a hazardous thing for him to undertake. He said he knew it, but he was willing to do any thing to help me. I expressed a wish for a New York paper, to ascertain the names of some of the streets. He run his hand into his pocket, and said, "Here is half a one, that was round a cap I bought off a pedler yesterday." I told him the letter would be ready the next evening. He bade me good by, adding, "Keep up your spirits, Linda; brighter days will come by and by."

My uncle Phillip kept watch over the gate until our brief interview was over. Early the next morning, I seated myself near the little aperture to examine the newspaper. It was a piece of the New York Herald; and, for once, the paper that systematically abuses the colored people, was made to render them a service. Having obtained what information I wanted concerning streets and numbers, I wrote two letters, one to my grandmother, the other to Dr. Flint. I reminded him how he, a gray-headed man, had treated a helpless child, who had been placed in his power, and what years of misery he had brought upon her. To my grandmother, I expressed a wish to have my children sent to me at the north, where I could teach them to respect themselves, and set them a virtuous example; which a slave mother was not allowed to do at the south. I asked her to direct her answer to a certain street in Boston, as I did not live in New York, though I went there sometimes. I dated these letters ahead, to allow for the time it would take to carry them, and sent a memorandum of the date to the messenger. When my friend came for the letters, I said, "God bless and reward you, Peter, for this disinterested kindness. Pray be careful. If you are detected, both you and I will have to suffer dreadfully. I have not a relative who would dare to do it for me." He replied, "You may trust to me, Linda. I don't forget that your father was my best friend, and I will be a friend to his children so long as God lets me live."

It was necessary to tell my grandmother what I had done, in order that she might be ready for the letter, and prepared to hear what Dr. Flint might say about my being at the north. She was sadly troubled. She felt sure mischief would come of it. I also told my plan to aunt Nancy, in order that she might report to us what was said at Dr. Flint's house. I whispered it to her through a crack, and she whispered back, "I hope it will succeed. I shan't mind being a slave all *my* life, if I can only see you and the children free."

I had directed that my letters should be put into the New York post office on the 20th of the month. On the evening of the 24th my aunt came to say that Dr. Flint and his wife had been talking in a low voice about a letter he had received, and that when he went to his office he promised to bring it when he came to tea. So I concluded I should hear my letter read the next morning. I told my grandmother Dr. Flint would be sure to come, and asked her to have him sit near a certain door, and leave it open, that I might hear what he said. The next morning I took my station within sound of that door, and remained motionless as a statue. It was not long before I heard the gate slam, and the well-known footsteps enter the house. He seated himself in the chair that was placed for him, and said, "Well, Martha, I've brought you a letter from Linda. She has sent me a letter, also. I know exactly where to find her; but I don't choose to go to Boston for her. I had rather she would come back of her own accord, in a respectable manner. Her uncle Phillip is the best person to go for her. With *him,* she would feel perfectly free to act. I am willing to pay his expenses going and returning. She shall be sold to her friends. Her children are free; at least I suppose they are; and when you obtain her freedom, you'll make a happy family. I suppose, Martha, you have no objection to my reading to you the letter Linda has written to you."

He broke the seal, and I heard him read it. The old villain! He had suppressed the letter I wrote to grandmother, and prepared a substitute of his own, the purport of which was as follows:—

> "Dear Grandmother: I have long wanted to write to you; but the disgraceful manner in which I left you and my children made me ashamed to do it. If you knew how much I have suffered since I ran away, you would pity and forgive me. I have purchased freedom at a dear rate. If any arrangement could be made for me to return to the south without being a slave, I would gladly come. If not, I beg of you to send my children to the north. I cannot live any longer without them. Let me know in time, and I will meet them in New York or Philadelphia, whichever place best suits my uncle's convenience. Write as soon as possible to your unhappy daughter.
>
> Linda."

"It is very much as I expected it would be," said the old hypocrite, rising to go. "You see the foolish girl has repented of her rashness, and wants to return. We must help her to do it, Martha. Talk with Phillip about it. If he will go for her, she will trust to him, and come back. I should like an answer tomorrow. Good morning, Martha."

As he stepped out on the piazza, he stumbled over my little girl. "Ah, Ellen, is that you?" he said, in his most gracious manner. "I didn't see you. How do you do?"

"Pretty well, sir," she replied. "I heard you tell grandmother that my mother is coming home. I want to see her."

"Yes, Ellen, I am going to bring her home very soon," rejoined he; "and you shall see her as much as you like, you little curly-headed nigger."

This was as good as a comedy to me, who had heard it all; but grandmother was frightened and distressed, because the doctor wanted my uncle to go for me.

The next evening Dr. Flint called to talk the matter over. My uncle told him that from what he had heard of Massachusetts, he judged he should be mobbed if he went there after a runaway slave. "All stuff and nonsense, Phillip!" replied the doctor. "Do you suppose I want you to kick up a row in Boston? The business can all be done quietly. Linda writes that she wants to come back. You are her relative, and she would trust *you*. The case would be different if I went. She might object to coming with *me;* and the damned abolitionists, if they knew I was her master, would not believe me, if I told them she had begged to go back. They would get up a row; and I should not like to see Linda dragged through the streets like a common negro. She has been very ungrateful to me for all my kindness; but I forgive her, and want to act the part of a friend towards her. I have no wish to hold her as my slave. Her friends can buy her as soon as she arrives here."

Finding that his arguments failed to convince my uncle, the doctor "let the cat out of the bag," by saying that he had written to the mayor of Boston, to ascertain whether there was a person of my description at the street and number from which my letter was dated. He had omitted this date in the letter he had made up to read to my grandmother. If I had dated from New York, the old man would probably have made another journey to that city. But even in that dark region, where knowledge is so carefully excluded from the slave, I had heard enough about Massachusetts to come to the conclusion that slaveholders did not consider it a comfortable place to go to in search of a runaway. That was before the Fugitive Slave Law was passed; before Massachusetts had consented to become a "nigger hunter" for the south.

My grandmother, who had become skittish by seeing her family always in danger, came to me with a very distressed countenance, and said, "What will you do if the mayor of Boston sends him word that you haven't been there? Then he will suspect the letter was a trick; and maybe he'll find out something about it, and we shall all get into trouble. O Linda, I wish you had never sent the letters."

"Don't worry yourself, grandmother," said I. "The mayor of Boston won't trouble himself to hunt niggers for Dr. Flint. The letters will do good in the end. I shall get out of this dark hole some time or other."

"I hope you will, child," replied the good, patient old friend. "You have been here a long time; almost five years; but whenever you do go, it will break your old grandmother's heart. I should be expecting every day to hear that you were brought back in irons and put in jail. God help you, poor child! Let us be thankful that some time or other we shall go 'where the wicked cease from troubling, and the weary are at rest.' " My heart responded, Amen.

The fact that Dr. Flint had written to the mayor of Boston convinced me that he believed my letter to be genuine, and of course that he had no suspicion of my being any where in the vicinity. It was a great object to keep up this delusion, for it made me and my friends feel less anxious, and it would be very convenient whenever there was a chance to escape. I resolved, therefore, to continue to write letters from the north from time to time.

Two or three weeks passed, and as no news came from the mayor of Boston, grandmother began to listen to my entreaty to be allowed to leave my cell, sometimes, and exercise my limbs to prevent my becoming a cripple. I was allowed to slip down into the small storeroom, early in the morning, and remain there a little while. The room was all filled up with barrels, except a small open space under my trap-door. This faced the door, the upper part of which was of glass, and purposely left uncurtained, that the curious might look in. The air of this place was close; but it was so much better than the atmosphere of my cell, that I dreaded to return. I came down as soon as it was light, and remained till eight o'clock, when people began to be about, and there was danger that some one might come on the piazza. I had tried various applications to bring warmth and feeling into my limbs, but without avail. They were so numb and stiff that it was a painful effort to move; and had my enemies come upon me during the first mornings I tried to exercise them a little in the small unoccupied space of the storeroom, it would have been impossible for me to have escaped.

CHAPTER XXVI

Important Era in My Brother's Life

I missed the company and kind attentions of my brother William, who had gone to Washington with his master, Mr. Sands. We received several letters from him, written without any allusions to me, but expressed in such a manner that I knew he did not forget me. I disguised my hand, and wrote to him in the same manner. It was a long session; and when it closed, William wrote to inform us that Mr. Sands was going to the north, to be gone some time, and that he was to accompany him. I knew that his master had promised to give him his freedom, but no time had been specified. Would William trust to a slave's chances? I remembered how we used to talk together, in our young days, about obtaining our freedom, and I thought it very doubtful whether he would come back to us.

Grandmother received a letter from Mr. Sands, saying that William had proved a most faithful servant, and he would also say a valued friend; that no mother had ever trained a better boy. He said he had travelled through the Northern States and Canada; and though the abolitionists had tried to decoy him away, they had never succeeded. He ended by saying they should be at home shortly.

We expected letters from William, describing the novelties of his journey, but none came. In time, it was reported that Mr. Sands would return late in the autumn, accompanied by a bride. Still no letters from William. I felt almost sure I should never see him again on southern soil; but had he no word of comfort to send to his friends at home? to the poor captive in her dungeon? My thoughts wandered through the dark past, and over the uncertain future. Alone in my cell, where no eye but God's could see me, I wept bitter tears. How earnestly I prayed to him to restore me to my children, and enable me to be a useful woman and a good mother!

At last the day arrived for the return of the travellers. Grandmother had made loving preparations to welcome her absent boy back to the old hearthstone. When the dinner table was laid, William's plate occupied its old place. The stage coach went by empty. My grandmother waited dinner. She thought perhaps he was necessarily detained by his master. In my prison I listened anxiously, expecting every moment to hear my dear brother's voice and step. In the course of the afternoon a lad was sent by Mr. Sands to tell grandmother that William did not return with him; that the abolitionists had decoyed him away. But he begged her not to feel troubled about it, for he felt confident she would see William in a few days. As soon as he had time to reflect he would come back, for he could never expect to be so well off at the north as he had been with him.

If you had seen the tears, and heard the sobs, you would have thought the messenger had brought tidings of death instead of freedom. Poor old grandmother felt that she should never see her darling boy again. And I was selfish. I thought more of what I had lost, than of what my brother had gained. A new anxiety began to trouble me. Mr. Sands had expended a good deal of money, and would naturally feel irritated by the loss he had incurred. I greatly feared this might injure the prospects of my children, who were now becoming valuable property. I longed to have their emancipation made certain. The more so, because their master and father was now married. I was too familiar with slavery not to know that promises made to slaves, though with kind intentions, and sincere at the time, depend upon many contingencies for their fulfilment.

Much as I wished William to be free, the step he had taken made me sad and anxious. The following Sabbath was calm and clear; so beautiful that it seemed like a Sabbath in the eternal world. My grandmother brought the children out on the piazza, that I might hear their voices. She thought it would comfort me in my despondency; and it did. They chatted merrily, as only children can. Benny said, "Grandmother, do you think uncle Will has gone for good? Won't he ever come back again? May be he'll find mother. If he does, *won't* she be glad to see him! Why don't you and uncle Phillip, and all of us, go and live where mother is? I should like it; wouldn't you, Ellen?"

"Yes, I should like it," replied Ellen; "but how could we find her? Do you know the place, grandmother? I don't remember how mother looked—do you, Benny?"

Benny was just beginning to describe me when they were interrupted by an old slave woman, a near neighbor, named Aggie. This poor creature had witnessed the sale of her children, and seen them carried off to parts unknown, without any hopes of ever hearing from them again. She saw that my grandmother had been weeping, and she said, in a sympathizing tone, "What's the matter, aunt Marthy?"

"O Aggie," she replied, "it seems as if I shouldn't have any of my children or grandchildren left to hand me a drink when I'm dying, and lay my old body in the ground. My boy didn't come back with Mr. Sands. He staid at the north."

Poor old Aggie clapped her hands for joy. "Is *dat* what you's crying fur?" she exclaimed. "Git down on your knees and bress de Lord! I don't know whar my poor chillern is, and I nebber 'spect to know. You don't know whar poor Linda's gone to; but you *do* know whar her brudder is. He's in free parts; and dat's de right place. Don't murmur at de Lord's doings, but git down on your knees and tank him for his goodness."

My selfishness was rebuked by what poor Aggie said. She rejoiced over the escape of one who was merely her fellow-bondman, while his own sister was only thinking what his good fortune might cost her children. I knelt and prayed God to forgive me; and I thanked him from my heart, that one of my family was saved from the grasp of slavery.

It was not long before we received a letter from William. He wrote that Mr. Sands had always treated him kindly, and that he had tried to do his duty to him faithfully. But ever since he was a boy, he had longed to be free; and he had already gone through enough to convince him he had better not lose the chance that offered. He concluded by saying, "Don't worry about me, dear grandmother. I shall think of you always; and it will spur me on to work hard and try to do right. When I have earned money enough to give you a home, perhaps you will come to the north, and we can all live happy together."

Mr. Sands told my uncle Phillip the particulars about William's leaving him. He said, "I trusted him as if he were my own brother, and treated him as kindly. The abolitionists talked to him in several places; but I had no idea they could tempt him. However, I don't blame William. He's young and inconsiderate, and those Northern rascals decoyed him. I must confess the scamp was very bold about it. I met him coming down the steps of the Astor House with his trunk on his shoulder, and I asked him where he was going. He said he was going to change his old trunk. I told him it was rather shabby, and asked if he didn't need some money. He said, No, thanked me, and went off. He did not return so soon as I expected; but I waited patiently. At last I went to see if our trunks were packed, ready for our journey. I found them locked, and a sealed note on the table informed me where I could find the keys. The fellow even tried to be religious. He wrote that he hoped God would always bless me, and reward me for my kindness; that he was not unwilling to serve me; but he wanted to be a free man; and that if I thought he did wrong, he hoped I would forgive him. I intended to give him his freedom in five years. He might have trusted me. He has shown himself ungrateful; but I shall not go for him, or send for him. I feel confident that he will soon return to me."

I afterwards heard an account of the affair from William himself. He had not been urged away by abolitionists. He needed no information they could give him about slavery to stimulate his desire for freedom. He looked his hands, and remembered that they were once in irons. What security had he that they would not be so again? Mr. Sands was kind to him; but he might indefinitely postponc the promise he had made to give him his freedom. He might come under pecuniary embarrassments, and his property be seized by creditors; or he might die, without making any arrangements in his favor. He had too often known such accidents to happen to slaves who had kind masters, and he wisely resolved to make sure of the present opportunity to own himself. He was scrupulous about taking any money from his master on false pretences; so he sold his best clothes to pay for his passage to Boston. The slaveholders pronounced him a base, ungratcful wretch, for thus requiting his master's indulgence. What would *they* have done under similar circumstances?

When Dr. Flint's family heard that William had deserted Mr. Sands, they chuckled greatly over the news. Mrs. Flint made her usual manifestations of Christian feeling, by saying, "I'm glad of it. I hope he'll never get him again. I like to see people paid back in their own coin. I reckon Linda's children will have to pay for it. I should be glad to see them in the speculator's hands again, for I'm tired of seeing those little niggers march about the streets."

CHAPTER

XXVII

New Destination for the Children

Mrs. Flint proclaimed her intention of informing Mrs. Sands who was the father of my children. She likewise proposed to tell her what an artful devil I was; that I had made a great deal of trouble in her family; that when Mr. Sands was at the north, she didn't doubt I had followed him in disguise, and persuaded William to run away. She had some reason to entertain such an idea; for I had written from the north, from time to time, and I dated my letters from various places. Many of them fell into Dr. Flint's hands, as I expected they would; and he must have come to the conclusion that I travelled about a good deal. He kept a close watch over my children, thinking they would eventually lead to my detection.

A new and unexpected trial was in store for me. One day, when Mr. Sands and his wife were walking in the street, they met Benny. The lady took a fancy to him, and exclaimed, "What a pretty little negro! Whom does he belong to?"

Benny did not hear the answer; but he came home very indignant with the stranger lady, because she had called him a negro. A few days afterwards, Mr. Sands called on my grandmother, and told her he wanted her to take the children to his house. He said he had informed his wife of his relation to them, and told her they were motherless; and she wanted to see them.

When he had gone, my grandmother came and asked what I would do. The question seemed a mockery. What *could* I do? They were Mr. Sand's slaves, and their mother was a slave, whom he had represented to be dead. Perhaps he thought I was. I was too much pained and puzzled to come to any decision; and the children were carried without my knowledge.

Mrs. Sands had a sister from Illinois staying with her. This lady, who had no children of her own, was so much pleased with Ellen, that she offered to adopt her, and bring her up as she would a daughter. Mrs. Sands wanted to take Benjamin. When grandmother reported this to me, I was tried almost beyond endurance. Was this all I was to gain by what I had suffered for the sake of having my children free? True, the prospect *seemed* fair; but I knew too well how lightly slaveholders held such "parental relations." If pecuniary troubles should come, or if the new wife required more money than could conveniently be spared, my children might be thought of as a convenient means of raising funds. I had no trust in thee, O Slavery! Never should I know peace till my children were emancipated with all due formalities of law.

I was too proud to ask Mr. Sands to do any thing for my own benefit; but I could bring myself to become a supplicant for my children. I resolved to remind him of the promise he had made me, and to throw myself upon his honor for the performance of it. I persuaded my grandmother to go to him, and tell him I was not dead, and that I earnestly entreated him to keep the promise he had made me; that I had heard of the recent proposals concerning my children, and did not feel easy to accept them; that he had promised to emancipate them, and it was time for him to redeem his pledge. I knew there was some risk in thus betraying that I was in the vicinity; but what will not a mother do for her children? He received the message with surprise, and said, "The children are free. I have never intended to claim them as slaves. Linda may decide their fate. In my opinion, they had better be sent to the north. I don't think they are quite safe here. Dr. Flint boasts that they are still in his power. He says they were his daughter's property, and as she was not of age when they were sold, the contract is not legally binding."

So, then, after all I had endured for their sakes, my poor children were between two fires; between my old master and their new master! And I was powerless. There was no protecting arm of the law for me to invoke. Mr. Sands proposed that Ellen should go, for the present, to some of his relatives, who had removed to Brooklyn, Long Island. It was promised that she should be well taken care of, and sent to school. I consented to it, as the best arrangement I could make for her. My grandmother, of course, negotiated it all; and Mrs. Sands knew of no other person in the transaction. She proposed that they should take Ellen with them to Washington, and keep her till they had a good chance of sending her, with friends, to Brooklyn. She had an infant daughter. I had had a glimpse of it, as the nurse passed with it in her arms. It was not a pleasant thought to me, that the bondwoman's child should tend her free-born sister; but there was no alternative. Ellen was made ready for the journey. O, how it tried my heart to send her away, so young alone, among strangers! Without a mother's love to shelter her from the storms of life; almost without a memory of a mother! I doubted whether she and Benny would have for me the natural affection that children feel for a parent. I thought to myself that I might perhaps never see my daughter again, and I had a great desire that she should look upon me, before she went, that she might take my image with her in her memory. It seemed to me cruel to have her brought to my dungeon. It was sorrow enough for her young heart to know that her mother was a victim of slavery, without seeing the wretched hiding-place to which it had driven her. I begged permission to pass the last night in one of the open chambers, with my little girl. They thought I was crazy to think of trusting such a young child with my perilous secret. I told them I had watched her character, and I felt sure she would not betray me; that I was determined to have an interview, and if they would not facilitate it, I would take my own way to obtain it. They remonstrated against the rashness of such a proceeding; but finding they could not change my purpose, they yielded. I slipped through the trap-door into the storeroom, and my uncle kept watch at the gate, while I passed into the piazza and went up stairs, to the room I used to occupy. It was more than five years since I had seen it; and how the memories crowded on me! There I had taken shelter when my mistress drove me from her house; there came my old tyrant, to mock, insult, and curse me; there my children were first laid in my arms; there I had watched over them, each day with a deeper and sadder love; there I had knelt to God, in anguish of heart, to forgive the wrong I had done. How vividly it all came back! And after this long, gloomy interval, I stood there such a wreck!

In the midst of these meditations, I heard footsteps on the stairs. The door opened, and my uncle Phillip came in, leading Ellen by the hand. I put my arms round her, and said, "Ellen, my dear child, I am your mother." She drew back a little, and looked at me; then, with sweet confidence, she laid her cheek against mine, and I folded her to the heart that had been so long desolated. She was the first to speak. Raising her head, she said, inquiringly, "You really *are* my mother?" I told her I really was; that during all the long time she had not seen me, I had loved her most tenderly; and that now she was going away, I wanted to see her and talk with her, that she might remember me. With a sob in her voice, she said, "I'm glad you've come to see me; but why didn't you ever come before? Benny and I have wanted so much to see you! He remembers you, and sometimes he tells me about you. Why didn't you come home when Dr. Flint went to bring you?"

I answered, "I couldn't come before, dear. But now that I am with you, tell me whether you like to go away." "I don't know," said she, crying. "Grandmother says I ought not to cry; that I am going to a good place, where I can learn to read and write, and that by and by I can write her a letter. But I shan't have Benny, or grandmother, or uncle Phillip, or any body to love me. Can't you go with me? O, *do* go, dear mother!"

I told her I couldn't go now; but sometime I would come to her, and then she and Benny and I would live together, and have happy times. She wanted to run and bring Benny to see me now. I told her he was going to the north, before long, with uncle Phillip, and then I would come to see him before he went away. I asked if she would like to have me stay all night and sleep with her. "O, yes," she replied. Then, turning to her uncle, she said, pleadingly, "*May* I stay? Please, uncle! She is my own mother." He laid his hand on her head, and said, solemnly, "Ellen, this is the secret you have promised grandmother never to tell. If you ever speak of it to any body, they will never let you see your grandmother again, and your mother can never come to Brooklyn." "Uncle," she replied, "I will never tell." He told her she might stay with me; and when he had gone, I took her in my arms and told her I was a slave, and that was the reason she must never say she had seen me. I exhorted her to be a good child, to try to please the people where she was going, and that God would raise her up friends. I told her to say her prayers, and remember always to pray for her poor mother, and that God would permit us to meet again. She wept, and I did not check her tears. Perhaps she would never again have a chance to pour her tears into a mother's bosom. All night she nestled in my arms, and I had no inclination to slumber. The moments were too precious to lose any of them. Once, when I thought she was asleep, I kissed her forehead softly, and she said, "I am not asleep, dear mother."

Before dawn they came to take me back to my den. I drew aside the window curtain, to take a last look of my child. The moonlight shone on her face, and I bent over her, as I had done years before, that wretched night when I ran away. I hugged her close to my throbbing heart; and tears, too sad for such young eyes to shed, flowed down her cheeks, as she gave her last kiss, and whispered in my ear, "Mother, I will never tell." And she never did.

When I got back to my den, I threw myself on the bed and wept there alone in the darkness. It seemed as if my heart would burst. When the time for Ellen's departure grew nigh, I could hear neighbors and friends saying to her, "Good by, Ellen. I hope your poor mother will find you out. *Won't* you be glad to see her!" She replied, "Yes, ma'am;" and they little dreamed of the weighty secret that weighed down her young heart. She was an affectionate child, but naturally very reserved, except with those she loved, and I felt secure that my secret would be safe with her. I heard the gate close after her, with such feelings as only a slave mother can experience.

During the day my meditations were very sad. Sometimes I feared I had been very selfish not to give up all claim to her, and let her go to Illinois, to be adopted by Mrs. Sands's sister. It was my experience of slavery that decided me against it. I feared that circumstances might arise that would cause her to be sent back. I felt confident that I should go to New York myself; and then I should be able to watch over her, and in some degree protect her.

Dr. Flint's family knew nothing of the proposed arrangement till after Ellen was gone, and the news displeased them greatly. Mrs. Flint called on Mrs. Sands's sister to inquire into the matter. She expressed her opinion very freely as to the respect Mr. Sands showed for his wife, and for his own character, in acknowledging those "young niggers." And as for sending Ellen away, she pronounced it to be just as much stealing as it would be for him to come and take a piece of furniture out of her parlor. She said her daughter was not of age to sign the bill of sale, and the children were her property; and when she became of age, or was married, she could take them, wherever she could lay hands on them.

Miss Emily Flint, the little girl to whom I had been bequeathed, was now in her sixteenth year. Her mother considered it all right and honorable for her, or her future husband, to steal my children; but she did not understand how any body could hold up their heads in respectable society, after they had purchased their own children, as Mr. Sands had done. Dr. Flint said very little. Perhaps he thought that Benny would be less likely to be sent away if he kept quiet. One of my letters, that fell into his hands, was dated from Canada; and he seldom spoke of me now. This state of things enabled me to slip down into the storeroom more frequently, where I could stand upright, and move my limbs more freely.

Days, weeks, and months passed, and there came no news of Ellen. I sent a letter to Brooklyn, written in my grandmother's name, to inquire whether she had arrived there. Answer was returned that she had not. I wrote to her in Washington; but no notice was taken of it. There was one person there, who ought to have had some sympathy with the anxiety of the child's friends at home; but the links of such relations as she had formed with me, are easily broken and cast away as rubbish. Yet how protectingly and persuasively he once talked to the poor, helpless slave girl! And how entirely I trusted him! But now suspicions darkened my mind. Was my child dead, or had they deceived me, and sold her?

If the secret memoirs of many members of Congress should be published, curious details would be unfolded. I once saw a letter from a member of Congress to a slave, who was the mother of six of his children. He wrote to request that she would send her children away from the great house before his return, as he expected to be accompanied by friends. The woman could not read, and was obliged to employ another to read the letter. The existence of the colored children did not trouble this gentleman, it was only the fear that friends might recognize in their features a resemblance to him.

At the end of six months, a letter came to my grandmother, from Brooklyn. It was written by a young lady in the family, and announced that Ellen had just arrived. It contained the following message from her: "I do try to do just as you told me to, and I pray for you every night and morning." I understood that these words were meant for me; and they were a balsam to my heart. The writer closed her letter by saying, "Ellen is a nice little girl, and we shall like to have her with us. My cousin, Mr. Sands, has given her to me, to be my little waiting maid. I shall send her to school, and I hope some day she will write to you herself." This letter perplexed and troubled me. Had my child's father merely placed her there till she was old enough to support herself? Or had he given her to his cousin, as a piece of property? If the last idea was correct, his cousins might return to the south at any time, and hold Ellen as a slave. I tried to put away from me the painful thought that such a foul wrong could have been done to us. I said to myself, "Surely there must be *some* justice in man;" then I remembered, with a sigh, how slavery perverted all the natural feelings of the human heart. It gave me a pang to look on my light-hearted boy. He believed himself free; and to have him brought under the yoke of slavery, would be more than I could bear. How I longed to have him safely out of the reach of its power!

CHAPTER XXIX

Preparations for Escape

I hardly expect that the reader will credit me, when I affirm that I lived in that little dismal hole, almost deprived of light and air, and with no space to move my limbs, for nearly seven years. But it is a fact; and to me a sad one, even now; for my body still suffers from the effects of that long imprisonment, to say nothing of my soul. Members of my family, now living in New York and Boston, can testify to the truth of what I say.

Countless were the nights that I sat late at the little loophole scarcely large enough to give me a glimpse of one twinkling star. There, I heard the patrols and slave-hunters conferring together about the capture of runaways, well knowing how rejoiced they would be to catch me.

Season after season, year after year, I peeped at my children's faces, and heard their sweet voices, with a heart yearning all the while to say, "Your mother is here." Sometimes it appeared to me as if ages had rolled away since I entered upon that gloomy, monotonous existence. At times, I was stupefied and listless; at other times I became very impatient to know when these dark years would end, and I should again be allowed to feel the sunshine, and breathe the pure air.

After Ellen left us, this feeling increased. Mr. Sands had agreed that Benny might go to the north whenever his uncle Phillip could go with him; and I was anxious to be there also, to watch over my children, and protect them so far as I was able. Moreover, I was likely to be drowned out of my den, if I remained much longer; for the slight.roof was getting badly out of repair, and uncle Phillip was afraid to remove the shingles, lest some one should get a glimpse of me. When storms occurred in the night, they spread mats and bits of carpet, which in the morning appeared to have been laid out to dry; but to cover the roof in the daytime might have attracted attention. Consequently, my clothes and bedding were often drenched; a process by which the pains and aches in my cramped and stiffened limbs were greatly increased. I revolved various plans of escape in my mind, which I sometimes imparted to my grandmother, when she came to whisper with me at the trap-door. The kind-hearted old woman had an intense sympathy for runaways. She had known too much of the cruelties inflicted on those who were captured. Her memory always flew back at once to the sufferings of her bright and handsome son, Benjamin, the youngest and dearest of her flock. So, whenever I alluded to the subject, she would groan out, "O, don't think of it, child. You'll break my heart." I had no good old aunt Nancy now to encourage me; but my brother William and my children were continually beckoning me to the north.

And now I must go back a few months in my story. I have stated that the first of January was the time for selling slaves, or leasing them out to new masters. If time were counted by heart-throbs, the poor slaves might reckon years of suffering during that festival so joyous to the free. On the New Year's day preceding my aunt's death, one of my friends, named Fanny, was to be sold at auction, to pay her master's debts. My thoughts were with her during all the day, and at night I anxiously inquired what had been her fate. I was told that she had ben sold to one master, and her four little girls to another master, far distant; that she had escaped from her purchaser, and was not to be found. Her mother was the old Aggie I have spoken of. She lived in a small tenement belonging to my grandmother, and built on the same lot with her own house. Her dwelling was searched and watched, and that brought the patrols so near me that I was obliged to keep very close in my den. The hunters were somehow eluded; and not long afterwards Benny accidentally caught sight of Fanny in her mother's hut. He told his grandmother, who charged him never to speak of it, explaining to him the frightful consequences; and he never betrayed the trust. Aggie little dreamed that my grandmother knew where her daughter was concealed, and that the stooping form of her old neighbor was bending under a similar burden of anxiety and fear; but these dangerous secrets deepened the sympathy between the two old persecuted mothers.

My friend Fanny and I remained many weeks hidden within call of each other; but she was unconscious of the fact. I longed to have her share my den, which seemed a more secure retreat than her own; but I had brought so much trouble on my grandmother, that it seemed wrong to ask her to incur greater risks. My restlessness increased. I had lived too long in bodily pain and anguish of spirit. Always I was in dread that by some accident, or some contrivance, slavery would succeed in snatching my children from me. This thought drove me nearly frantic, and I determined to steer for the North Star at all hazards. At this crisis, Providence opened an unexpected way for me to escape. My friend Peter came one evening, and asked to speak with me. "Your day has come, Linda," said he. "I have found a chance for you to go to the Free States. You have a fortnight to decide." The news seemed too good to be true; but Peter explained his arrangements, and told me all that was necessary was for me to say I would go. I was going to answer him with a joyful yes, when the thought of Benny came to my mind. I told him the temptation was exceedingly strong, but I was terribly afraid of Dr. Flint's alleged power over my child, and that I could not go and leave him behind. Peter remonstrated earnestly. He said such a good chance might never occur again; that Benny was free, and could be sent to me; and that for the sake of my children's welfare I ought not to hesitate a moment. I told him I would consult with uncle Phillip. My uncle rejoiced in the plan, and bade me go by all means. He promised, if his life was spared, that he would either bring or send my son to me as soon as I reached a place of safety. I resolved to go, but thought nothing had better be said to my grandmother till very near the time of departure. But my uncle thought she would feel it more keenly if I left her so suddenly. "I will reason with her," said he, "and convince her how necessary it is, not only for your sake, but for hers also. You cannot be blind to the fact that she is sinking under her burdens." I was not blind to it. I knew that my concealment was an ever-present source of anxiety, and that the older she grew the more nervously fearful she was of discovery. My uncle talked with her, and finally succeeded in persuading her that it was absolutely necessary for me to seize the chance so unexpectedly offered.

The anticipation of being a free woman proved almost too much for my weak frame. The excitement stimulated me, and at the same time bewildered me. I made busy preparations for my journey, and for my son to follow me. I resolved to have an interview with him before I went, that I might give him cautions and advice, and tell him how anxiously I should be waiting for him at the north. Grandmother stole up to me as often as possible to whisper words of counsel. She insisted upon my writing to Dr. Flint, as soon as I arrived in the Free States, and asking him to sell me to her. She said she would sacrifice her house, and all she had in the world, for the sake of having me safe with my children in any part of the world. If she could only live to know *that* she could die in peace. I promised the dear old faithful friend that I would write to her as soon as I arrived, and put the letter in a safe way to reach her; but in my own mind I resolved that not another cent of her hard earnings should be spent to pay rapacious slaveholders for what they called their property. And even if I had not been unwilling to buy what I had already a right to possess, common humanity would have prevented me from accepting the generous offer, at the expense of turning my aged relative out of house and home, when she was trembling on the brink of the grave.

I was to escape in a vessel; but I forbear to mention any further particulars. I was in readiness, but the vessel was unexpectedly detained several days. Meantime, news came to town of a most horrible murder committed on a fugitive slave, named James. Charity, the mother of this unfortunate young man, had been an old acquaintance of ours. I have told the shocking particulars of his death, in my description of some of the neighboring slaveholders. My grandmother, always nervously sensitive about runaways, was terribly frightened. She felt sure that a similar fate awaited me, if I did not desist from my enterprise. She sobbed, and groaned, and entreated me not to go. Her excessive fear was somewhat contagious, and my heart was not proof against her extreme agony. I was grievously disappointed, but I promised to relinquish my project.

When my friend Peter was apprised of this, he was both disappointed and vexed. He said, that judging from our past experience, it would be a long time before I had such another chance to throw away. I told him it need not be thrown away; that I had a friend concealed near by, who would be glad enough to take the place that had been provided for me. I told him about poor Fanny, and the kind-hearted, noble fellow, who never turned his back upon any body in distress, white or black, expressed his readiness to help her. Aggie was much surprised when she found that we knew her secret. She was rejoiced to hear of such a chance for Fanny, and arrangements were made for her to go on board the vessel the next night. They both supposed that I had long been at the north, therefore my name was not mentioned in the transaction. Fanny was carried on board at the appointed time, and stowed away in a very small cabin. This accommodation had been purchased at a price that would pay for a voyage to England. But when one proposes to go to fine old England, they stop to calculate whether they can afford the cost of the pleasure; while in making a bargain to escape from slavery, the trembling victim is ready to say, "Take all I have, only don't betray me!"

The next morning I peeped through my loophole, and saw that it was dark and cloudy. At night I received news that the wind was ahead, and the vessel had not sailed. I was exceedingly anxious about Fanny, and Peter too, who was running a tremendous risk at my instigation. Next day the wind and weather remained the same. Poor Fanny had been half dead with fright when they carried her on board, and I could readily imagine how she must be suffering now. Grandmother came often to my den, to say how thankful she was I did not go. On the third morning she rapped for me to come down to the storeroom. The poor old sufferer was breaking down under her weight of trouble. She was easily flurried now. I found her in a nervous, excited state, but I was not aware that she had forgotten to lock the door behind her, as usual. She was exceedingly worried about the detention of the vessel. She was afraid all would be discovered, and then Fanny, and Peter, and I, would all be tortured to death, and Phillip would be utterly ruined, and her house would be torn down. Poor Peter! If he should die such a horrible death as the poor slave James had lately done, and all for his kindness in trying to help me, how dreadful it would be for us all! Alas, the thought was familiar to me, and had sent many a sharp pang through my heart. I tried to suppress my own anxiety, and speak soothingly to her. She brought in some allusion to aunt Nancy, the dear daughter she had recently buried, and then she lost all control of herself. As she stood there, trembling and sobbing, a voice from the piazza called out, "Whar is you, aunt Marthy?" Grandmother was startled, and in her agitation opened the door, without thinking of me. In stepped Jenny, the mischievous housemaid, who had tried to enter my room, when I was concealed in the house of my white benefactress. "I's bin huntin ebery whar for you, aunt Marthy," said she. "My missis wants you to send her some crackers." I had slunk down behind a barrel, which entirely screened me, but I imagined that Jenny was looking directly at the spot, and my heart beat violently. My grandmother immediately thought what she had done, and went out quickly with Jenny to count the crackers locking the door after her. She returned to me, in a few minutes, the perfect picture of despair. "Poor child!" she exclaimed, "my carelessness has ruined you. The boat ain't gone yet. Get ready immediately, and go with Fanny. I ain't got another word to say against it now; for there's no telling what may happen this day."

Uncle Phillip was sent for, and he agreed with his mother in thinking that Jenny would inform Dr. Flint in less than twenty-four hours. He advised getting me on board the boat, if possible; if not, I had better keep very still in my den, where they could not find me without tearing the house down. He said it would not do for him to move in the matter, because suspicion would be immediately excited; but he promised to communicate with Peter. I felt reluctant to apply to him again, having implicated him too much already; but there seemed to be no alternative. Vexed as Peter had been by my indecision, he was true to his generous nature, and said at once that he would do his best to help me, trusting I should show myself a stronger woman this time.

He immediately proceeded to the wharf, and found that the wind had shifted, and the vessel was slowly beating down stream. On some pretext of urgent necessity, he offered two boatman a dollar apiece to catch up with her. He was of lighter complexion than the boatmen he hired, and when the captain saw them coming so rapidly, he thought officers were pursuing his vessel in search of the runaway slave he had on board. They hoisted sails, but the boat gained upon them, and the indefatigable Peter sprang on board.

The captain at once recognized him. When he told his errand, the captain replied, "Why, the woman's here already; and I've put her where you or the devil would have a tough job to find her."

"But it is another woman I want to bring," said Peter. "*She* is in great distress, too, and you shall be paid any thing within reason, if you'll stop and take her."

"What's her name?" inquired the captain.

"Linda," he replied.

"That's the name of the woman already here," rejoined the captain. "By George! I believe you mean to betray me."

"O!" exclaimed Peter, "God knows I wouldn't harm a hair of your head. I am too grateful to you. But there really *is* another woman in great danger. Do have the humanity to stop and take her!"

After a while they came to an understanding. Fanny, not dreaming I was any where about in that region, had assumed my name, though she had called herself Johnson. "Linda is a common name," said Peter, "and the woman I want to bring is Linda Brent."

The captain agreed to wait at a certain place till evening, being handsomely paid for his detention.

Of course, the day was an anxious one for us all. But we concluded that if Jenny had seen me, she would be too wise to let her mistress know of it; and that she probably would not get a chance to see Dr. Flint's family till evening, for I knew very well what were the rules in that household. I afterwards believe that she did not see me; for nothing ever came of it, and she was one of those base characters that would have jumped to betray a suffering fellow being for the sake of thirty pieces of silver.

I made all my arrangements to go on board as soon as it was dusk. The intervening time I resolved to spend with my son. I had not spoken to him for seven years, though I had been under the same roof, and seen him every day, when I was well enough to sit at the loophole. I did not dare to venture beyond the storeroom; so they brought him there, and locked us up together, in a place concealed from the piazza door. It was an agitating interview for both of us. After we had talked and wept together for a little while, he said, "Mother, I'm glad you're going away. I wish I could go with you. I knew you was here; and I have been *so* afraid they would come and catch you!"

I was greatly surprised, and asked him how he had found it out.

He replied, "I was standing under the eaves, one day, before Ellen went away, and I heard somebody cough up over the wood shed. I don't know what made me think it was you, but I did think so. I missed Ellen, the night before she went away; and grandmother brought her back into the room in the night; and I thought maybe she'd been to see *you*, before she went, for I heard grandmother whisper to her, 'Now go to sleep; and remember never to tell.' "

I asked him if he ever mentioned his suspicions to his sister. He said he never did; but after he heard the cough, if he saw her playing with other children on that side of the house, he always tried to coax her round to the other side, for fear they would hear me cough, too. He said he had kept a close lookout for Dr. Flint, and if he saw him speak to a constable, or a patrol, he always told grandmother. I now recollected that I had seen him manifest uneasiness, when people were on that side of the house, and I had at the time been puzzled to conjecture a motive for his actions. Such prudence may seem extraordinary in a boy of twelve years, but slaves, being surrounded by mysteries, deceptions, and dangers, early learn to be suspicious and watchful, and prematurely cautious and cunning. He had never asked a question of grandmother, or uncle Phillip, and I had often heard him chime in with other children, when they spoke of my being at the north.

I told him I was now really going to the Free States, and if he was a good, honest boy, and a loving child to his dear old grandmother, the Lord would bless him, and bring him to me, and we and Ellen would live together. He began to tell me that grandmother had not eaten any thing all day. While he was speaking, the door was unlocked, and she came in with a small bag of money, which she wanted me to take. I begged her to keep a part of it, at least, to pay for Benny's being sent to the north; but she insisted, while her tears were falling fast, that I should take the whole. "You may be sick among strangers," she said, "and they would send you to the poorhouse to die." Ah, that good grandmother!

For the last time I went up to my nook. Its desolate appearance no longer chilled me, for the light of hope had risen in my soul. Yet, even with the blessed prospect of freedom before me, I felt very sad at leaving forever that old homestead, where I had been sheltered so long by the dear old grandmother; where I had dreamed my first young dream of love; and where, after that had faded away, my children came to twine themselves so closely round my desolate heart. As the hour approached for me to leave, I again descended to the storeroom. My grandmother and Benny were there. She took me by the hand, and said, "Linda, let us pray." We knelt down together, with my child pressed to my heart, and my other arm round the faithful, loving old friend I was about to leave forever. On no other occasion has it ever been my lot to listen to so fervent a supplication for mercy and protection. It thrilled through my heart, and inspired me with trust in God.

Peter was waiting for me in the street. I was soon by his side, faint in body, but strong of purpose. I did not look back upon the old place, though I felt that I should never see it again.

CHAPTER

XXX

Northward Bound

I never could tell how we reached the wharf. My brain was all of a whirl, and my limbs tottered under me. At an appointed place we met my uncle Phillip, who had started before us on a different route, that he might reach the wharf first, and give us timely warning if there was any danger. A row-boat was in readiness. As I was about to step in, I felt something pull me gently, and turning round I saw Benny, looking pale and anxious. He whispered in my ear, "I've been peeping into the doctor's window, and he's at home. Good by, mother. Don't cry; I'll come." He hastened away. I clasped the hand of my good uncle, to whom I owed so much, and of Peter, the brave, generous friend who had volunteered to run such terrible risks to secure my safety. To this day I remember how his bright face beamed with joy, when he told me he had discovered a safe method for me to escape. Yet that intelligent, enterprising, noble-hearted man was a chattel! liable, by the laws of a country that calls itself civilized, to be sold with horses and pigs! We parted in silence. Our hearts were all too full for words!

Swiftly the boat glided over the water. After a while, one of the sailors said, "Don't be down-hearted, madam. We will take you safely to your husband, in ——." At first I could not imagine what he meant; but I had presence of mind to think that it probably referred to something the captain had told him; so I thanked him, and said I hoped we should have pleasant weather.

When I entered the vessel the captain came forward to meet me. He was an elderly man, with a pleasant countenance. He showed me to a little box of a cabin, where sat my friend Fanny. She started as if she had seen a spectre. She gazed on me in utter astonishment, and exclaimed, "Linda, can this be *you?* or is it your ghost?" When we were locked in each other's arms, my overwrought feelings could no longer be restrained. My sobs reached the ears of the captain, who came and very kindly reminded us, that for his safety, as well as our own, it would be prudent for us not to attract any attention. He said that when there was a sail in sight he wished us to keep below; but at other times, he had no objection to our being on deck. He assured us that he would keep a good lookout, and if we acted prudently, he thought we should be in no danger. He had represented us as women going to meet our husbands in ———. We thanked him, and promised to observe carefully all the directions he gave us.

Fanny and I now talked by ourselves, low and quietly, in our little cabin. She told me of the sufferings she had gone through in making her escape, and of her terrors while she was concealed in her mother's house. Above all, she dwelt on the agony of separation from all her children on that dreadful auction day. She could scarcely credit me, when I told her of the place where I had passed nearly seven years. "We have the same sorrows," said I. "No," replied she, "you are going to see your children soon, and there is no hope that I shall ever even hear from mine."

The vessel was soon under way, but we made slow progress. The wind was against us. I should not have cared for this, if we had been out of sight of the town; but until there were miles of water between us and our enemies, we were filled with constant apprehensions that the constables would come on board. Neither could I feel quite at ease with the captain and his men. I was an entire stranger to that class of people, and I had heard that sailors were rough, and sometimes cruel. We were so completely in their power, that if they were bad men, our situation would be dreadful. Now that the captain was paid for our passage, might he not be tempted to make more money by giving us up to those who claimed us as property? I was naturally of a confiding disposition, but slavery had made me suspicious of every body. Fanny did not share my distrust of the captain or his men. She said she was afraid at first, but she had been on board three days while the vessel lay in the dock, and nobody had betrayed her, or treated her otherwise than kindly.

The captain soon came to advise us to go on deck for fresh air. His friendly and respectful manner, combined with Fanny's testimony, reassured me, and we went with him. He placed us in a comfortable seat, and occasionally entered into conversation. He told us he was a Southerner by birth, and had spent the greater part of his life in the Slave States, and that he had recently lost a brother who traded in slaves. "But," said he, "it is a pitiable and degrading business, and I always felt ashamed to acknowledge my brother in connection with it." As we passed Snaky Swamp, he pointed to it, and said, "There is a slave territory that defies all the laws." I thought of the terrible days I had spent there, and though it was not called Dismal Swamp, it made me feel very dismal as I looked at it.

I shall never forget that night. The balmy air of spring was so refreshing! And how shall I describe my sensations when we were fairly sailing on Chesapeake Bay? O, the beautiful sunshine! the exhilarating beeze! and I could enjoy them without fear or restraint. I had never realized what grand things air and sunlight are till I had been deprived of them.

Ten days after we left land we were approaching Philadelphia. The captain said we should arrive there in the night, but he thought we had better wait till morning, and go on shore in broad daylight, as the best way to avoid suspicion.

I replied, "You know best. But will you stay on board and protect us?"

He saw that I was suspicious, and he said he was sorry, now that he had brought us to the end of our voyage, to find I had so little confidence in him. Oh, if he had ever been a slave he would have known how difficult it was to trust a white man. He assured us that we might sleep through the night without fear; that he would take care we were not left unprotected. Be it said to the honor of this captain, Southerner as he was, that if Fanny and I had been white ladies, and our passage lawfully engaged, he could not have treated us more respectfully. My intelligent friend, Peter, had rightly estimated the character of the man to whose honor he had intrusted us.

The next morning I was on deck as soon as the day dawned. I called Fanny to see the sun rise, for the first time in our lives, on free soil; for such I *then* believed it to be. We watched the reddening sky, and saw the great orb come up slowly out of the water, as it seemed. Soon the waves began to sparkle, and every thing caught the beautiful glow. Before us lay the city of strangers. We looked at each other, and the eyes of both were moistened with tears. We had escaped from slavery, and we supposed ourselves to be safe from the hunters. But we were alone in the world, and we had left dear ties behind us; ties cruelly sundered by the demon Slavery.

CHAPTER XXXI

Incidents in Philadelphia

I had heard that the poor slave had many friends at the north. I trusted we should find some of them. Meantime, we would take it for granted that all were friends, till they proved to the contrary. I sought out the kind captain, thanked him for his attentions, and told him I should never cease to be grateful for the service he had rendered us. I gave him a message to the friends I had left at home, and he promised to deliver it. We were placed in a row-boat, and in about fifteen minutes were landed on a wood wharf in Philadelphia. As I stood looking round, the friendly captain touched me on the shoulder, and said, "There is a respectable-looking colored man behind you. I will speak to him about the New York trains, and tell him you wish to go directly on." I thanked him, and asked him to direct me to some shops where I could buy gloves and veils. He did so, and said he would talk with the colored man till I returned. I made what haste I could. Constant exercise on board the vessel, and frequent rubbing with salt water, had nearly restored the use of my limbs. The noise of the great city confused me, but I found the shops, and bought some double veils and gloves for Fanny and myself. The shopman told me they were so many levies. I had never heard the word before, but I did not tell him so. I thought if he knew I was a stranger he might ask me where I came from. I gave him a gold piece, and when he returned the change, I counted it, and found out how much a levy was. I made my way back to the wharf, where the captain introduced me to the colored man, as the Rev. Jeremiah Durham, minister of Bethel church. He took me by the hand, as if I had been an old friend. He told us we were too late for the morning cars to New York, and must wait until the evening, or the next morning. He invited me to go home with him, assuring me that his wife would give me a cordial welcome; and for my friend he would provide a home with one of his neighbors. I thanked him for so much kindness to strangers, and told him if I must be detained, I should like to hunt up some people who formerly went from our part of the country. Mr. Durham insisted that I should dine with him, and then he would assist me in finding my friends. The sailors came to bid us good by. I shook their hardy hands, with tears in my eyes. They had all been kind to us, and they had rendered us a greater service than they could possibly conceive of.

I had never seen so large a city, or been in contact with so many people in the streets. It seemed as if those who passed looked at us with an expression of curiosity. My face was so blistered and peeled, by sitting on deck, in wind and sunshine, that I thought they could not easily decide to what nation I had belonged.

Mrs. Durham met me with a kindly welcome, without asking any questions. I was tired, and her friendly manner was a sweet refreshment. God bless her! I was sure that she had comforted other weary hearts, before I received her sympathy. She was surrounded by her husband and children, in a home made sacred by protecting laws. I thought of my own children, and sighed.

After dinner Mr. Durham went with me in quest of the friends I had spoken of. They went from my native town, and I anticipated much pleasure in looking on familiar faces. They were not at home, and we retraced our steps through streets delightfully clean. On the way, Mr. Durham observed that I had spoken to him of a daughter I expected to meet; that he was surprised, for I looked so young he had taken me for a single woman. He was approaching a subject on which I was extremely sensitive. He would ask about my husband next, I thought, and if I answered him truly, what would he think of me? I told him I had two children, one in New York the other at the south. He asked some further questions, and I frankly told him some of the most important events of my life. It was painful for me to do it; but I would not deceive him. If he was desirous of being my friend, I thought he ought to know how far I was worthy of it. "Excuse me, if I have tried your feelings," said he. "I did not question you from idle curiosity. I wanted to understand your situation, in order to know whether I could be of any service to you, or your little girl. Your straight-forward answers do you credit; but don't answer every body so openly. It might give some heartless people a pretext for treating you with contempt."

That word *contempt* burned me like coals of fire. I replied, "God alone knows how I have suffered; and He, I trust, will forgive me. If I am permitted to have my children, I intend to be a good mother, and to live in such a manner that people cannot treat me with contempt."

"I respect your sentiments," said he. "Place your trust in God, and be governed by good principles, and you will not fail to find friends."

When we reached home, I went to my room, glad to shut out the world for a while. The words he had spoken made an indelible impression upon me. They brought up great shadows from the mournful past. In the midst of my meditations I was startled by a knock at the door. Mrs. Durham entered, her face all beaming with kindness, to say that there was an anti-slavery friend down stairs, who would like to see me. I overcame my dread of encountering strangers, and went with her. Many questions were asked concerning my experiences, and my escape from slavery; but I observed how careful they all were not to say any thing that might wound my feelings. How gratifying this was, can be fully understood only by those who have been accustomed to be treated as if they were not included within the pale of human beings. The anti-slavery friend had come to inquire into my plans, and to offer assistance, if needed. Fanny was comfortably established, for the present, with a friend of Mr. Durham. The Anti-Slavery Society agreed to pay her expenses to New York. The same was offered to me, but I declined to accept it; telling them that my grandmother had given me sufficient to pay my expenses to the end of my journey. We were urged to remain in Philadelphia a few days, until some suitable escort could be found for us. I gladly accepted the proposition, for I had a dread of meeting slaveholders, and some dread also of railroads. I had never entered a railroad car in my life, and it seemed to me quite an important event.

That night I sought my pillow with feelings I had never carried to it before. I verily believed myself to be a free woman. I was wakeful for a long time, and I had no sooner fallen asleep, than I was roused by fire-bells. I jumped up, and hurried on my clothes. Where I came from, every body hastened to dress themselves on such occasions. The white people thought a great fire might be used as a good opportunity for insurrection, and that it was best to be in readiness; and the colored people were ordered out to labor in extinguishing the flames. There was but one engine in our town, and colored women and children were often required to drag it to the river's edge and fill it. Mrs. Durham's daughter slept in the same room with me, and seeing that she slept through all the din, I thought it was my duty to wake her. "What's the matter?" said she, rubbing her eyes.

"They're screaming fire in the streets, and the bells are ringing," I replied.

"What of that?" said she, drowsily. "We are used to it. We never get up, without the fire is very near. What good would it do?"

I was quite surprised that it was not necessary for us to go and help fill the engine. I was an ignorant child, just beginning to learn how things went on in great cities.

At daylight, I heard women crying fresh fish, berries, radishes, and various other things. All this was new to me. I dressed myself at an early hour, and sat at the window to watch that unknown tide of life. Philadelphia seemed to me a wonderfully great place. At the breakfast table, my idea of going out to drag the engine was laughed over, and I joined in the mirth.

I went to see Fanny, and found her so well contented among her new friends that she was in no haste to leave. I was also very happy with my kind hostess. She had had advantages for education, and was vastly my superior.

Every day, almost every hour, I was adding to my little stock of knowledge. She took me out to see the city as much as she deemed prudent. One day she took me to an artist's room, and showed me the portraits of some of her children. I had never seen any paintings of colored people before, and they seemed to me beautiful.

At the end of five days, one of Mrs. Durham's friends offered to accompany us to New York the following morning. As I held the hand of my good hostess in a parting clasp, I longed to know whether her husband had repeated to her what I had told him. I supposed he had, but she never made any allusion to it. I presume it was the delicate silence of womanly sympathy.

When Mr. Durham handed us our tickets, he said, "I am afraid you will have a disagreeable ride; but I could not procure tickets for the first class cars."

Supposing I had not given him money enough, I offered more. "O, no," said he, "they could not be had for any money. They don't allow colored people to go in the first-class cars."

This was the first chill to my enthusiasm about the Free States. Colored people were allowed to ride in a filthy box, behind white people, at the south, but there they were not required to pay for the privilege. It made me sad to find how the north aped the customs of slavery.

We were stowed away in a large, rough car, with windows on each side, too high for us to look out without standing up. It was crowded with people, apparently of all nations. There were plenty of beds and cradles, containing screaming and kicking babies. Every other man had a cigar or pipe in his mouth, and jugs of whiskey were handed round freely. The fumes of the whiskey and the dense tobacco smoke were sickening to my senses, and my mind was equally nauseated by the coarse jokes and ribald songs around me. It was a very disagreeable ride. Since that time there has been some improvement in these matters.

CHAPTER XXXII

The Meeting of Mother and Daughter

When we arrived in New York, I was half crazed by the crowd of coachmen calling out, "Carriage, ma'am?" We bargained with one to take us to Sullivan Street for twelve shillings. A burly Irishman stepped up and said, "I'll tak' ye for sax shllings." The reduction of half the price was an object to us, and we asked if he could take us right away. "Troth an I will, ladies," he replied. I noticed that the hackmen smiled at each other, and I inquired whether his conveyance was decent. "Yes, it's dacent it is, marm. Devil a bit would I be after takin' ladies in a cab that was not dacent." We gave him our checks. He went for the baggage, and soon reappeared, saying, "This way, if you plase, ladies." We followed, and found our trunks on a truck, and we were invited to take our seats on them. We told him that was not what we bargained for, and he must take the trunks off. He swore they should not be touched till we had paid him six shillings. In our situation it was not prudent to attract attention, and I was about to pay him what he required, when a man near by shook his head for me not to do it. After a great ado we got rid of the Irishman, and had our trunks fastened on a hack. We had been recommended to a boarding-house in Sullivan Street, and thither we drove. There Fanny and I separated. The Anti-Slavery Society provided a home for her, and I afterwards heard of her in prosperous circumstances. I sent for an old friend from my part of the country, who had for some time been doing business in New York. He came immediately. I told him I wanted to go to my daughter, and asked him to aid me in procuring an interview.

I cautioned him not to let it be known to the family that I had just arrived from the south, because they supposed I had been at the north seven years. He told me there was a colored woman in Brooklyn who came from the same town I did, and I had better go to her house, and have my daughter meet me there. I accepted the proposition thankfully, and he agreed to escort me to Brooklyn. We crossed Fulton ferry, went up Myrtle Avenue, and stopped at the house he designated. I was just about to enter, when two girls passed. My friend called my attention to them. I turned, and recognized in the eldest, Sarah, the daughter of a woman who used to live with my grandmother, but who had left the south years ago. Surprised and rejoiced at this unexpected meeting, I threw my arms round her, and inquired concerning her mother.

"You take no notice of the other girl," said my friend. I turned, and there stood my Ellen! I pressed her to my heart, then held her away from me to take a look at her. She had changed a good deal in the two years since I parted from her. Signs of neglect could be discerned by eyes less observing than a mother's. My friend invited us all to go into the house; but Ellen said she had been sent on an errand, which she would do as quickly as possible, and go home and ask Mrs. Hobbs to let her come and see me. It was agreed that I should send for her the next day. Her companion, Sarah, hastened to tell her mother of my arrival. When I entered the house, I found the mistress of it absent, and I waited for her return. Before I saw her, I heard her saying, "Where is Linda Brent? I used to know her father and mother." Soon Sarah came with her mother. So there was quite a company of us, all from my grandmother's neighborhood. These friends gathered round me and questioned me eagerly. They laughed, they cried, and they shouted. They thanked God that I had got away from my persecutors and was safe on Long Island.

It was a day of great excitement. How different from the silent days I had passed in my dreary den!

The next morning was Sunday. My first waking thoughts were occupied with the note that I was to send to Mrs. Hobbs, the lady with whom Ellen lived. That I had recently come into that vicinity was evident; otherwise I should have sooner inquired for my daughter. It would not do to let them know I had just arrived from the south, for that would involve the suspicion of my having been harbored there, and might bring trouble, if not ruin, on several people.

I liked a straightforward course, and am always reluctant to resort to subterfuges. So far as my ways have been crooked, I charge them all upon slavery. It was that system of violence and wrong which now left me no alternative but to enact a falsehood. I began my note by stating that I had recently arrived from Canada, and was very desirous to have my daughter come to see me. She came and brought a message from Mrs. Hobbs, inviting me to her house, and assuring me that I need not have any fears. The conversation I had with my child did not leave my mind at ease. When I asked if she was well treated, she answered yes; but there was no heartiness in the tone, and it seemed to me that she said it from an unwillingness to have me troubled on her account. Before she left me, she asked very earnestly, "Mother, when will you take me to live with you?" It made me sad to think that I could not give her a home till I went to work and earned the means; and that might take me a long time. When she was placed with Mrs. Hobbs, the agreement was that she should be sent to school. She had been there two years, and was now nine years old, and she scarcely knew her letters. There was no excuse for this, for there were good public schools in Brooklyn, to which she could have been sent without expense.

She staid with me till dark, and I went home with her. I was received in a friendly manner by the family, and all agreed in saying that Ellen was a useful, good girl. Mrs. Hobbs looked me coolly in the face, and said, "I suppose you know that my cousin, Mr. Sands, has *given* her to my eldest daughter. She will make a nice waiting-maid for her when she grows up." I did not answer a word. How *could* she, who knew by experience the strength of a mother's love, and who was perfectly aware of the relation Mr. Sands bore to my children,—how *could* she look me in the face, while she thrust such a dagger into my heart?

I was no longer surprised that they had kept her in such a state of ignorance. Mr. Hobbs had formerly been wealthy, but he had failed, and afterwards obtained a subordinate situation in the Custom House. Perhaps they expected to return to the south some day; and Ellen's knowledge was quite sufficient for a slave's condition. I was impatient to go to work and earn money, that I might change the uncertain position of my children. Mr. Sands had not kept his promise to emancipate them. I had also been deceived about Ellen. What security had I with regard to Benjamin? I felt that I had none.

I returned to my friend's house in an uneasy state of mind. In order to protect my children, it was necessary that I should own myself. I called myself free, and sometimes felt so; but I knew I was insecure. I sat down that night and wrote a civil letter to Dr. Flint, asking him to state the lowest terms on which he would sell me; and as I belonged by law to his daughter, I wrote to her also, making a similar request.

Since my arrival at the north I had not been unmindful of my dear brother William. I had made diligent inquiries for him, and having heard of him in Boston, I went thither. When I arrived there, I found he had gone to New Bedford. I wrote to that place, and was informed he had gone on a whaling voyage, and would not return for some months. I went back to New York to get employment near Ellen. I received an answer from Dr. Flint, which gave me no encouragement. He advised me to return and submit myself to my rightful owners, and then any request I might make would be granted. I lent this letter to a friend, who lost it; otherwise I would present a copy to my readers.

CHAPTER XXXIII

A Home Found

My greatest anxiety now was to obtain employment. My health was greatly improved, though my limbs continued to trouble me with swelling whenever I walked much. The greatest difficulty in my way was, that those who employed strangers required a recommendation; and in my peculiar position, I could, of course, obtain no certificates from the families I had so faithfully served.

One day an acquaintance told me of a lady who wanted a nurse for her babe, and I immediately applied for the situation. The lady told me she preferred to have one who had been a mother, and accustomed to the care of infants. I told her I had nursed two babes of my own. She asked me many questions, but, to my great relief, did not require a recommendation from my former employers. She told me she was an English woman, and that was a pleasant circumstance to me, because I had heard they had less prejudice against color than Americans entertained. It was agreed that we should try each other for a week. The trial proved satisfactory to both parties, and I was engaged for a month.

The heavenly Father had been most merciful to me in leading me to this place. Mrs. Bruce was a kind and gentle lady, and proved a true and sympathizing friend.

Before the stipulated month expired, the necessity of passing up and down stairs frequently, caused my limbs to swell so painfully, that I became unable to perform my duties. Many ladies would have thoughtlessly discharged me; but Mrs. Bruce made arrangements to save me steps, and employed a physician to attend upon me. I had not yet told her that I was a fugitive slave. She noticed that I was often sad, and kindly inquired the cause. I spoke of being separated from my children, and from relatives who were dear to me; but I did not mention the constant feeling of insecurity which oppressed my spirits. I longed for some one to confide in; but I had been so deceived by white people, that I had lost all confidence in them. If they spoke kind words to me, I thought it was for some selfish purpose. I had entered this family with the distrustful feelings I had brought with me out of slavery; but ere six months had passed, I found that the gentle deportment of Mrs. Bruce and the smiles of her lovely babe were thawing my chilled heart. My narrow mind also began to expand under the influences of her intelligent conversation, and the opportunities for reading, which were gladly allowed me whenever I had leisure from my duties. I gradually became more energetic and more cheerful.

The old feeling of insecurity, especially with regard to my children, often threw its dark shadow across my sunshine. Mrs. Bruce offered me a home for Ellen; but pleasant as it would have been, I did not dare to accept it, for fear of offending the Hobbs family. Their knowledge of my precarious situation placed me in their power; and I felt that it was important for me to keep on the right side of them, till, by dint of labor and economy, I could make a home for my children. I was far from feeling satisfied with Ellen's situation. She was not well cared for. She sometimes came to New York to visit me; but she generally brought a request from Mrs. Hobbs that I would buy her a pair of shoes, or some article of clothing. This was accompanied by a promise of payment when Mr. Hobb's salary at the Custom House became due; but some how or other the pay-day never came. Thus many dollars of my earnings were expended to keep my child comfortably clothed. That, however, was a slight trouble, compared with the fear that their pecuniary embarrassments might induce them to sell my precious young daughter. I knew they were in constant communication with Southerners, and had frequent opportunities to do it. I have stated that when Dr. Flint put Ellen in jail, at two years old, she had an inflammation of the eyes, occasioned by measles. This disease still troubled her; and kind Mrs. Bruce proposed that she should come to New York for a while, to be under the care of Dr. Elliott, a well known oculist. It did not occur to me that there was any thing improper in a mother's making such a request; but Mrs. Hobbs was very angry, and refused to let her go. Situated as I was, it was not politic to insist upon it. I made no complaint, but I longed to be entirely free to act a mother's part towards my children. The next time I went over to Brooklyn, Mrs. Hobbs, as if to apologize for her anger, told me she had employed her own physician to attend to Ellen's eyes, and that she had refused my request because she did not consider it safe to trust her in New York. I accepted the explanation in silence; but she had told me that my child *belonged* to her daughter, and I suspected that her real motive was a fear of my conveying her property away from her. Perhaps I did her injustice; but my knowledge of Southerners made it difficult for me to feel otherwise.

Sweet and bitter were mixed in the cup of my life, and I was thankful that it had ceased to be entirely bitter. I loved Mrs. Bruce's babe. When it laughed and crowed in my face, and twined its little tender arms confidingly about my neck, it made me think of the time when Benny and Ellen were babies, and my wounded heart was soothed. One bright morning, as I stood at the window, tossing baby in my arms, my attention was attracted by a young man in sailor's dress, who was closely observing every house as he passed. I looked at him earnestly. Could it be my brother William? It *must* be he—and yet, how changed! I placed the baby safely, flew down stairs, opened the front door, beckoned to the sailor, and in less than a minute I was clasped in my brother's arms. How much we had to tell each other! How we laughed, and how we cried, over each other's adventures! I took him to Brooklyn, and again saw him with Ellen, the dear child whom he had loved and tended so carefully, while I was shut up in my miserable den. He staid in New York a week. His old feelings of affection for me and Ellen were as lively as ever. There are no bonds so strong as those which are formed by suffering together.

CHAPTER XXXIV

The Old Enemy Again

My young mistress, Miss Emily Flint, did not return any answer to my letter requesting her to consent to my being sold. But after a while, I received a reply, which purported to be written by her younger brother. In order rightly to enjoy the contents of this letter, the reader must bear in mind that the Flint family supposed I had been at the north many years. They had no idea that I knew of the doctor's three excursions to New York in search of me; that I had heard his voice, when he came to borrow five hundred dollars for that purpose; and that I had seen him pass on his way to the steamboat. Neither were they aware that all the particulars of aunt Nancy's death and burial were conveyed to me at the time they occurred. I have kept the letter, of which I herewith subjoin a copy:—

> "Your letter to sister was received a few days ago. I gather from it that you are desirous of returning to your native place, among your friends and relatives. We were all gratified with the contents of your letter; and let me assure you that if any members of the family have had any feeling of resentment towards you, they feel

it no longer. We all sympathize with you in your unfortunate condition, and are ready to do all in our power to make you contented and happy. It is difficult for you to return home as a free person. If you were purchased by your grandmother, it is doubtful whether you would be permitted to remain, although it would be lawful for you to do so. If a servant should be allowed to purchase herself, after absenting herself so long from her owners, and return free, it would have an injurious effect. From your letter, I think your situation must be hard and uncomfortable. Come home. You have it in your power to be reinstated in our affections. We would receive you with open arms and tears of joy. You need not apprehend any unkind treatment, as we have not put ourselves to any trouble or expense to get you. Had we done so, perhaps we should feel otherwise. You know my sister was always attached to you, and that you were never treated as a slave. You were never put to hard work, nor exposed to field labor. On the contrary, you were taken into the house, and treated as one of us, and almost as free; and we, at least, felt that you were above disgracing yourself by running away. Believing you may be induced to come home voluntarily has induced me to write for my sister. The family will be rejoiced to see you; and your poor old grandmother expressed a great desire to have you come, when she heard your letter read. In her old age she needs the consolation of having her children round her. Doubtless you have heard of the death of your aunt. She was a faithful servant, and a faithful member of the Episcopal church. In her Christian life she taught us how to live—and, O, too high the price of knowledge, she taught us how to die! Could you have seen us round her death bed, with her mother, all mingling our tears in one common stream, you would have thought the same heartfelt tie existed between a master and his servant, as between a mother and her child. But this subject is too painful to dwell upon. I must bring my letter to a close. If you are contented to stay away from your old grandmother, your child, and the friends who love you, stay where you are. We shall never trouble ourselves to apprehend you. But should you prefer to come home, we will do all that we can to make you happy. If you do not wish to remain in the family, I know that father, by our persuasion, will be induced to let you be purchased by any person you may choose in our community. You will please answer this as soon as possible, and let us know your decision. Sister sends much love to you. In the mean time believe me your sincere friend and well wisher."

This letter was signed by Emily's brother, who was as yet a mere lad. I knew, by the style, that it was not written by a person of his age, and though the writing was disguised, I had been made too unhappy by it, in former years, not to recognize at once the hand of Dr. Flint. O, the hypocrisy of slaveholders! Did the old fox suppose I was goose enough to go into such a trap? Verily, he relied too much on "the stupidity of the African race." I did not return the family of Flints any thanks for their cordial invitation—a remissness for which I was, no doubt, charged with base ingratitude.

Not long afterwards I received a letter from one of my friends at the south, informing me that Dr. Flint was about to visit the north. The letter had been delayed, and I supposed he might be already on the way. Mrs. Bruce did not know I was a fugitive. I told her that important business called me to Boston, where my brother then was, and asked permission to bring a friend to supply my place as nurse, for a fortnight. I started on my journey immediately; and as soon as I arrived, I wrote to my grandmother that if Benny came, he must be sent to Boston. I knew she was only waiting for a good chance to send him north, and, fortunately, she had the legal power to do so, without asking leave of any body. She was a free woman; and when my children were purchased, Mr. Sands preferred to have the bill of sale drawn up in her name. It was conjectured that he advanced the money, but it was not known. At the south, a gentleman may have a shoal of colored children without any disgrace; but if he is known to purchase them, with the view of setting them free, the example is thought to be dangerous to their "peculiar institution," and he becomes unpopular.

There was a good opportunity to send Benny in a vessel coming directly to New York. He was put on board with a letter to a friend, who was requested to see him off to Boston. Early one morning, there was a loud rap at my door, and in rushed Benjamin, all out of breath. "O mother!" he exclaimed, "here I am! I run all the way; and I come all alone. How d'you do?"

O reader, can you imagine my joy? No, you cannot, unless you have been a slave mother. Benjamin rattled away as fast as his tongue could go. "Mother, why don't you bring Ellen here? I went over to Brooklyn to see her, and she felt very bad when I bid her good by. She said, 'O Ben, I wish I was going too.' I thought she'd know ever so much; but she don't know so much as I do; for I can read; and she can't. And, mother, I lost all my clothes coming. What can I do to get some more? I 'spose free boys can get along here at the north as well as white boys."

I did not like to tell the sanguine, happy little fellow how much he was mistaken. I took him to a tailor, and procured a change of clothes. The rest of the day was spent in mutual asking and answering questions, with the wish constantly repeated that the good old grandmother was with us, and frequent injunctions from Benny to write to her immediately, and be sure to tell her every thing about his voyage, and his journey to Boston.

Dr. Flint made his visit to New York, and made every exertion to call upon me, and invite me to return with him; but not being able to ascertain where I was, his hospitable intentions were frustrated, and the affectionate family, who were waiting for me with "open arms," were doomed to disappointment.

As soon as I knew he was safely at home, I placed Benjamin in the care of my brother William, and returned to Mrs. Bruce. There I remained through the winter and spring, endeavoring to perform my duties faithfully, and finding a good degree of happiness in the attractions of baby Mary, the considerate kindness of her excellent mother, and occasional interviews with my darling daughter.

But when summer came, the old feeling of insecurity haunted me. It was necessary for me to take little Mary out daily, for exercise and fresh air, and the city was swarming with Southerners, some of whom might recognize me. Hot weather brings out snakes and slaveholders, and I like one class of the venomous creatures as little as I do the other. What a comfort it is, to be free to *say* so!

CHAPTER XXXV

Prejudice Against Color

It was a relief to my mind to see preparations for leaving the city. We went to Albany in the steamboat Knickerbocker. When the gong sounded for tea, Mrs. Bruce said, "Linda, it is late, and you and baby had better come to the table with me." I replied, "I know it is time baby had her supper, but I had rather not go with you, if you please. I am afraid of being insulted." "O no, not if you are with *me,*" she said. I saw several white nurses go with their ladies, and I ventured to do the same. We were at the extreme end of the table. I was no sooner seated, than a gruff voice said, "Get up! You know you are not allowed to sit here." I looked up, and, to my astonishment and indignation, saw that the speaker was a colored man. If his office required him to enforce the by-laws of the boat, he might, at least, have done it politely. I replied, "I shall not get up, unless the captain comes and takes me up." No cup of tea was offered me, but Mrs. Bruce handed me hers and called for another. I looked to see whether the other nurses were treated in a similar manner. They were all properly waited on.

Next morning, when we stopped at Troy for breakfast, every body was making a rush for the table. Mrs. Bruce said, "Take my arm, Linda, and we'll go in together."

The landlord heard her, and said, "Madam, will you allow your nurse and baby to take breakfast with my family?" I knew this was to be attributed to my complexion; but he spoke courteously, and therefore I did not mind it.

At Saratoga we found the United States Hotel crowded, and Mr. Bruce took one of the cottages belonging to the hotel. I had thought, with gladness, of going to the quiet of the country, where I should meet few people, but here I found myself in the midst of a swarm of Southerners. I looked round me with fear and trembling, dreading to see some one who would recognize me. I was rejoiced to find that we were to stay but a short time.

We soon returned to New York, to make arrangements for spending the remainder of the summer at Rockaway. While the laundress was putting the clothes in order, I took an opportunity to go over to Brooklyn to see Ellen. I met her going to a grocery store, and the first words she said, were, "O, mother, don't go to Mrs. Hobbs's. Her brother, Mr. Thorne has come from the south, and may be he'll tell where you are." I accepted the warning. I told her I was going away with Mrs. Bruce the next day, and would try to see her when I came back.

Being in servitude to the Anglo-Saxon race, I was not put into a "Jim Crow car," on our way to Rockaway, neither was I invited to ride through the streets on the top of trunks in a truck; but every where I found the same manifestations of that cruel prejudice, which so discourages the feelings, and represses the energies of the colored people. We reached Rockaway before dark, and put up at the Pavilion—a large hotel, beautifully situated by the sea-side—a great resort of the fashionable world. Thirty or forty nurses were there, of a great variety of nations. Some of the ladies had colored waiting-maids and coachmen, but I was the only nurse tinged with the blood of Africa. When the tea bell rang, I took little Mary and followed the other nurses. Supper was served in a long hall. A young man, who had the ordering of things, took the circuit of the table two or three times, and finally pointed me to a seat at the lower end of it. As there was but one chair, I sat down and took the child in my lap. Whereupon the young man came to me and said, in the blandest manner possible, "Will you please to seat the little girl in the chair, and stand behind it and feed her? After they have done, you will be shown to the kitchen, where you will have a good supper."

This was the climax! I found it hard to preserve my self-control, when I looked round, and saw women who were nurses, as I was, and only one shade lighter in complexion, eyeing me with a defiant look, as if my presence were a contamination. However, I said nothing. I quietly took the child in my arms, went to our room, and refused to go to the table again. Mr. Bruce ordered meals to be sent to the room for little Mary and I. This answered for a few days; but the waiters of the establishment were white, and they soon began to complain, saying they were not hired to wait on negroes. The landlord requested Mr. Bruce to send me down to my meals, because his servants rebelled against bringing them up, and the colored servants of other boarders were dissatisfied because all were not treated alike.

My answer was that the colored servants ought to be dissatisfied with *themselves,* for not having too much self-respect to submit to such treatment; that there was no difference in the price of board for colored and white servants, and there was no justification for difference of treatment. I staid a month after this, and finding I was resolved to stand up for my rights, they concluded to treat me well. Let every colored man and woman do this, and eventually we shall cease to be trampled under foot by our oppressors.

CHAPTER XXXVI

The Hairbreadth Escape

After we returned to New York, I took the earliest opportunity to go and see Ellen. I asked to have her called down stairs; for I supposed Mrs. Hobbs's southern brother might still be there, and I was desirous to avoid seeing him, if possible. But Mrs. Hobbs came to the kitchen, and insisted on my going up stairs. "My brother wants to see you," said she, "and he is sorry you seem to shun him. He knows you are living in New York. He told me to say to you that he owes thanks to good old aunt Martha for too many little acts of kindness for him to be base enough to betray her grandchild."

This Mr. Thorne had become poor and reckless long before he left the south, and such persons had much rather go to one of the faithful old slaves to borrow a dollar, or get a good dinner, than to go to one whom they consider an equal. It was such acts of kindness as these for which he professed to feel grateful to my grandmother. I wished he had kept at a distance, but as he was here, and knew where I was, I concluded there was nothing to be gained by trying to avoid him; on the contrary, it might be the means of exciting his ill will. I followed his sister up stairs. He met me in a very friendly manner, congratulated me on my escape from slavery, and I hoped I had a good place, where I felt happy.

I continued to visit Ellen as often as I could. She, good thoughtful child, never forgot my hazardous situation, but always kept a vigilant lookout for my safety. She never made any complaint about her own inconveniences and troubles; but a mother's observing eye easily perceived that she was not happy. On the occasion of one of my visits I found her unusually serious. When I asked her what was the matter, she said nothing was the matter. But I insisted upon knowing what made her look so very grave. Finally, I ascertained that she felt troubled about the dissipation that was continually going on in the house. She was sent to the store very often for rum and brandy, and she felt ashamed to ask for it so often; and Mr. Hobbs and Mr. Thorne drank a great deal, and their hands trembled so that they had to call her to pour out the liquor for them. "But for all that," said she, "Mr. Hobbs is good to me, and I can't help liking him. I feel sorry for him." I tried to comfort her, by telling her that I had laid up a hundred dollars, and that before long I hoped to be able to give her and Benjamin a home, and send them to school. She was always desirous not to add to my troubles more than she could help, and I did not discover till years afterwards that Mr. Thorne's intemperance was not the only annoyance she suffered from him. Though he professed too much gratitude to my grandmother to injure any of her descendants, he had poured vile language into the ears of her innocent great-grandchild.

I usually went to Brooklyn to spend Sunday afternoon. One Sunday, I found Ellen anxiously waiting for me near the house. "O, mother," said she, "I've been waiting for you this long time. I'm afraid Mr. Thorne has written to tell Dr. Flint where you are. Make haste and come in. Mrs. Hobbs will tell you all about it!"

The story was soon told. While the children were playing in the grape-vine arbor, the day before, Mr. Thorne came out with a letter in his hand, which he tore up and scattered about. Ellen was sweeping the yard at the time, and having her mind full of suspicions of him, she picked up the pieces and carried them to the children, saying, "I wonder who Mr. Thorne has been writing to."

"I'm sure I don't know, and don't care," replied the oldest of the children; "and I don't see how it concerns you."

"But it does concern me," replied Ellen; "for I'm afraid he's been writing to the south about my mother."

They laughed at her, and called her a silly thing, but good-naturedly put the fragments of writing together, in order to read them to her. They were no sooner arranged, than the little girl exclaimed, "I declare, Ellen, I believe you are right."

The contents of Mr. Thorne's letter, as nearly as I can remember, were as follows: "I have seen your slave, Linda, and conversed with her. She can be taken very easily, if you manage prudently. There are enough of us here to swear to her identity as your property. I am a patriot, a lover of my country, and I do this as an act of justice to the laws." He concluded by informing the doctor of the street and number where I lived. The children carried the pieces to Mrs. Hobbs, who immediately went to her brother's room for an explanation. He was not to be found. The servants said they saw him go out with a letter in his hand, and they supposed he had gone to the post office. The natural inference was, that he had sent to Dr. Flint a copy of those fragments. When he returned, his sister accused him of it, and he did not deny the charge. He went immediately to his room, and the next morning he was missing. He had gone over to New York, before any of the family were astir.

It was evident that I had no time to lose; and I hastened back to the city with a heavy heart. Again I was to be torn from a comfortable home, and all my plans for the welfare of my children were to be frustrated by that demon Slavery! I now regretted that I never told Mrs. Bruce my story. I had not concealed it merely on account of being a fugitive; that would have made her anxious, but it would have excited sympathy in her kind heart. I valued her good opinion, and I was afraid of losing it, if I told her all the particulars of my sad story. But now I felt that it was necessary for her to know how I was situated. I had once left her abruptly, without explaining the reason, and it would not be proper to do it again. I went home resolved to tell her in the morning. But the sadness of my face attracted her attention, and, in answer to her kind inquiries, I poured out my full heart to her, before bed time. She listened with true womanly sympathy, and told me she would do all she could to protect me. How my heart blessed her!

Early the next morning, Judge Vanderpool and Lawyer Hopper were consulted. They said I had better leave the city at once, as the risk would be great if the case came to trial. Mrs. Bruce took me in a carriage to the house of one of her friends, where she assured me I should be safe until my brother could arrive, which would be in a few days. In the interval my thoughts were much occupied with Ellen. She was mine by birth, and she was also mine by Southern law, since my grandmother held the bill of sale that made her so. I did not feel that she was safe unless I had her with me. Mrs. Hobbs, who felt badly about her brother's treachery, yielded to my entreaties, on condition that she should return in ten days. I avoided making any promise. She came to me clad in very thin garments, all outgrown, and with a school satchel on her arm, containing a few articles. It was late in October, and I knew the child must suffer; and not daring to go out in the streets to purchase any thing, I took off my own flannel skirt and converted it into one for her. Kind Mrs. Bruce came to bid me good by, and when she saw that I had taken off my clothing for my child, the tears came to her eyes. She said, "Wait for me, Linda," and went out. She soon returned with a nice warm shawl and hood for Ellen. Truly, of such souls as hers are the kingdom of heaven.

My brother reached New York on Wednesday. Lawyer Hopper advised us to go to Boston by the Stonington route, as there was less Southern travel in that direction. Mrs. Bruce directed her servants to tell all inquirers that I formerly lived there, but had gone from the city.

We reached the steamboat Rhode Island in safety. That boat employed colored hands, but I knew that colored passengers were not admitted to the cabin. I was very desirous for the seclusion of the cabin, not only on account of exposure to the night air, but also to avoid observation. Lawyer Hopper was waiting on board for us. He spoke to the stewardess, and asked, as a particular favor, that she would treat us well. He said to me, "Go and speak to the captain yourself by and by. Take your little girl with you, and I am sure that he will not let her sleep on deck." With these kind words and a shake of the hand he departed.

The boat was soon on her way, bearing me rapidly from the friendly home where I had hoped to find security and rest. My brother had left me to purchase the tickets, thinking that I might have better success than he would. When the stewardess came to me, I paid what she asked, and she gave me three tickets with clipped corners. In the most unsophisticated manner I said, "You have made a mistake; I asked you for cabin tickets. I cannot possibly consent to sleep on deck with my little daughter." She assured me there was no mistake. She said on some of the routes colored people were allowed to sleep in the cabin, but not on this route, which was much travelled by the wealthy. I asked her to show me to the captain's office, and she said she would after tea. When the time came, I took Ellen by the hand and went to the captain, politely requesting him to change our tickets, as we should be very uncomfortable on deck. He said it was contrary to their custom, but he would see that we had berths below; he would also try to obtain comfortable seats for us in the cars; of that he was not certain, but he would speak to the conductor about it, when the boat arrived. I thanked him, and returned to the ladies' cabin. He came afterwards and told me that the conductor of the cars was on board, that he had spoken to him, and he had promised to take care of us. I was very much surprised at receiving so much kindness. I don't know whether the pleasing face of my little girl had won his heart, or whether the stewardess inferred from Lawyer Hopper's manner that I was a fugitive, and had pleaded with him in my behalf.

When the boat arrived at Stonington, the conductor kept his promise, and showed us to seats in the first car, nearest the engine. He asked us to take seats next to the door, but as he passed through, we ventured to move on toward the other end of the car. No incivility was offered us, and we reached Boston in safety.

The day after my arrival was one of the happiest of my life. I felt as if I was beyond the reach of the bloodhounds; and, for the first time during many years, I had both my children together with me. They greatly enjoyed their reunion, and laughed and chatted merrily. I watched them with a swelling heart. Their every motion delighted me.

I could not feel safe in New York, and I accepted the offer of a friend, that we should share expenses and keep house together. I represented to Mrs. Hobbs that Ellen must have some schooling, and must remain with me for that purpose. She felt ashamed of being unable to read or spell at her age, so instead of sending her to school with Benny, I instructed her myself till she was fitted to enter an intermediate school. The winter passed pleasantly, while I was busy with my needle, and my children with their books.

CHAPTER XXXVII

A Visit to England

In the spring, sad news came to me. Mrs. Bruce was dead. Never again, in this world, should I see her gentle face, or hear her sympathizing voice. I had lost an excellent friend, and little Mary had lost a tender mother. Mr. Bruce wished the child to visit some of her mother's relatives in England, and he was desirous that I should take charge of her. The little motherless one was accustomed to me, and attached to me, and I thought she would be happier in my care than in that of a stranger. I could also earn more in this way than I could by my needle. So I put Benny to a trade, and left Ellen to remain in the house with my friend and go to school.

We sailed from New York, and arrived in Liverpool after a pleasant voyage of twelve days. We proceeded directly to London, and took lodgings at the Adelaide Hotel. The supper seemed to me less luxurious than those I had seen in American hotels; but my situation was indescribably more pleasant. For the first time in my life I was in a place where I was treated according to my deportment, without reference to my complexion. I felt as if a great millstone had been lifted from my breast. Ensconced in a pleasant room, with my dear little charge,

I laid my head on my pillow, for the first time, with the delightful consciousness of pure, unadulterated freedom.

As I had constant care of the child, I had little opportunity to see the wonders of that great city; but I watched the tide of life that flowed through the streets, and found it a strange contrast to the stagnation in our Southern towns. Mr. Bruce took his little daughter to spend some days with friends in Oxford Crescent, and of course it was necessary for me to accompany her. I had heard much of the systematic method of English education, and I was very desirous that my dear Mary should steer straight in the midst of so much propriety. I closely observed her little playmates and their nurses, being ready to take any lessons in the science of good management. The children were more rosy than American children, but I did not see that they differed materially in other respects. They were like all children— sometimes docile and sometimes wayward.

We next went to Steventon, in Berkshire. It was a small town, said to be the poorest in the county. I saw men working in the fields for six shillings, and seven shillings, a week, and women for sixpence, and sevenpence, a day, out of which they boarded themselves. Of course they lived in the most primitive manner; it could not be otherwise, where a woman's wages for an entire day were not sufficient to buy a pound of meat. They paid very low rents, and their clothes were made of the cheapest fabrics, though much better than could have been procured in the United States for the same money. I had heard much about the oppression of the poor in Europe. The people I saw around me were, many of them, among the poorest poor. But when I visited them in their little thatched cottages, I felt that the condition of even the meanest and most ignorant among them was vastly superior to the condition of the most favored slaves in America. They labored hard; but they were not ordered out to toil while the stars were in the sky, and driven and slashed by an overseer, through heat and cold, till the stars shone out again. Their homes were very humble; but they were protected by law. No insolent patrols could come, in the dead of night, and flog them at their pleasure. The father, when he closed his cottage door, felt safe with his family around him. No master or overseer could come and take from him his wife, or his daughter. They must separate to earn their living; but the parents knew where their children were going, and could communicate with them by letters. The relations of husband and wife, parent and child, were too sacred for the richest noble in the land to violate with impunity. Much was being done to enlighten these poor people. Schools were established among them, and benevolent societies were active in efforts to ameliorate their condition. There was no law forbidding them to learn to read and write; and if they helped each other in spelling out the Bible, they were in no danger of thirty-nine lashes, as was the case with myself and poor, pious, old uncle Fred. I repeat that the most ignorant and the most destitute of these peasants was a thousand fold better off than the most pampered American slave.

I do not deny that the poor are oppressed in Europe. I am not disposed to paint their condition so rose-colored as the Hon. Miss Murray paints the condition of the slaves in the United States. A small portion of *my* experience would enable her to read her own pages with anointed eyes. If she were to lay aside her title, and instead of visiting among the fashionable, become domesticated, as a poor governess, on some plantation in Louisiana or Alabama, she would see and hear things that would make her tell quite a different story.

My visit to England is a memorable event in my life, from the fact of my having there received strong religious impressions. The contemptuous manner in which the communion had been administered to colored people, in my native place; the church membership of Dr. Flint, and others like him; and the buying and selling of slaves, by professed ministers of the gospel, had given me a prejudice against the Episcopal church. The whole service seemed to me a mockery and a sham. But my home in Steventon was in the family of a clergyman, who was a true disciple of Jesus. The beauty of his daily life inspired me with faith in the genuineness of Christian professions. Grace entered my heart, and I knelt at the communion table, I trust, in true humility of soul.

I remained abroad ten months, which was much longer than I had anticipated. During all that time, I never saw the slightest symptom of prejudice against color. Indeed, I entirely forgot it, till the time came for us to return to America.

CHAPTER

XXXVIII

Renewed Invitations to Go South

We had a tedious winter passage, and from the distance spectres seemed to rise up on the shores of the United States. It is a sad feeling to be afraid of one's native country. We arrived in New York safely, and I hastened to Boston to look after my children. I found Ellen well, and improving at her school; but Benny was not there to welcome me. He had been left at a good place to learn a trade, and for several months every thing worked well. He was liked by the master, and was a favorite with his fellow-apprentices; but one day they accidentally discovered a fact they had never before suspected—that he was colored! This at once transformed him into a different being. Some of the apprentices were Americans, others American-born Irish; and it was offensive to their dignity to have a "nigger" among them, after they had been told that he *was* a "nigger." They began by treating him with silent scorn, and finding that he returned the same, they resorted to insults and abuse. He was too spirited a boy to stand that, and he went off. Being desirous to do something to support himself, and having no one to advise him, he shipped for a whaling voyage. When I received these tidings I shed many tears, and bitterly reproached myself for having left him so long. But I had done it for the best, and now all I could do was to pray to the heavenly Father to guide and protect him.

Not long after my return, I received the following letter from Miss Emily Flint, now Mrs. Dodge:

> "In this you will recognize the hand of your friend and mistress. Having heard that you had gone with a family to Europe, I have waited to hear of your return to write to you. I should have answered the letter you wrote to me long since, but as I could not then act independently of my father, I knew there could be nothing done satisfactory to you. There were persons here who were willing to buy you and run the risk of getting you. To this I would not consent. I have always been attached to you, and would not like to see you the slave of another, or have unkind treatment. I am married now, and can protect you. My husband expects to move to Virginia this spring, where we think of settling. I am very anxious that you should come and live with me. If you are not willing to come, you may purchase yourself; but I should prefer having you live with me. If you come, you may, if you like, spend a month with your grandmother and friends, then come to me in Norfolk, Virginia. Think this over, and write as soon as possible, and let me know the conclusion. Hoping that your children are well, I remain your friend and mistress."

Of course I did not write to return thanks for this cordial invitation. I felt insulted to be thought stupid enough to be caught by such professions.

> " 'Come up into my parlor,' said the spider to the fly;
> ' 'Tis the prettiest little parlor that ever you did spy.' "

It was plain that Dr. Flint's family were apprised of my movements, since they knew of my voyage to Europe. I expected to have further trouble from them; but having eluded them thus far, I hoped to be as successful in future. The money I had earned, I was desirous to devote to the education of my children, and to secure a home for them. It seemed not only hard, but unjust, to pay for myself. I could not possibly regard myself as a piece of property. Moreover, I had worked many years without wages, and during that time had been obliged to depend on my grandmother for many comforts in food and clothing. My children certainly belonged to me; but though Dr. Flint had incured no expense for their support, he had received a large sum of money for them. I knew the law would decide that I was his property, and would probably still give his daughter a claim to my children; but I regarded such laws as the regulations of robbers, who had no rights that I was bound to respect.

The Fugitive Slave Law had not then passed. The judges of Massachusetts had not then stooped under chains to enter her courts of justice, so called. I knew my old master was rather skittish of Massachusetts. I relied on her love of freedom, and felt safe on her soil. I am now aware that I honored the old Commonwealth beyond her deserts.

CHAPTER XXXIX

The Confession

For two years my daughter and I supported ourselves comfortably in Boston. At the end of that time, my brother William offered to send Ellen to a boarding school. It required a great effort for me to consent to part with her, for I had few near ties, and it was her presence that made my two little rooms seem home-like. But my judgment prevailed over my selfish feelings. I made preparations for her departure. During the two years we had lived together I had often resolved to tell her something about her father; but I had never been able to muster sufficient courage. I had a shrinking dread of diminishing my child's love. I knew she must have curiosity on the subject, but she had never asked a question. She was always very careful not to say any thing to remind me of my troubles. Now that she was going from me, I thought if I should die before she returned, she might hear my story from some one who did not understand the palliating circumstances; and that if she were entirely ignorant on the subject, her sensitive nature might receive a rude shock.

When we retired for the night, she said, "Mother, it is very hard to leave you alone. I am almost sorry I am going, though I do want to improve myself. But you will write to me often; won't you, mother?"

I did not throw my arms round her. I did not answer her. But in a calm, solemn way, for it cost me great effort, I said, "Listen to me, Ellen; I have something to tell you!" I recounted my early sufferings in slavery, and told her how nearly they had crushed me. I began to tell her how they had driven me into a great sin, when she clasped me in her arms, and exclaimed. "Oh, don't, mother! Please don't tell me any more."

I said, "But, my child, I want you to know about your father."

"I know all about it, mother," she replied; "I am nothing to my father, and he is nothing to me. All my love is for you. I was with him five months in Washington, and he never cared for me. He never spoke to me as he did to his little Fanny. I knew all the time he was my father, for Fanny's nurse told me so; but she said I must never tell any body, and I never did. I used to wish he would take me in his arms and kiss me, as he did Fanny; or that he would sometimes smile at me, as he did at her. I thought if he was my own father, he ought to love me. I was a little girl then, and didn't know any better. But now I never think any thing about my father. All my love is for you." She hugged me closer as she spoke, and I thanked God that the knowledge I had so much dreaded to impart had not diminished the affection of my child. I had not the slightest idea she knew that portion of my history. If I had, I should have spoken to her long before; for my pent-up feelings had often longed to pour themselves out to some one I could trust. But I loved the dear girl better for the delicacy she had manifested towards her unfortunate mother.

The next morning, she and her uncle started on their journey to the village in New York, where she was to be placed at school. It seemed as if all the sunshine had gone away. My little room was dreadfully lonely. I was thankful when a message came from a lady, accustomed to employ me, requesting me to come and sew in her family for several weeks. On my return, I found a letter from brother William. He thought of opening an anti-slavery reading room in Rochester, and combining with it the sale of some books and stationery; and he wanted me to unite with him. We tried it, but it was not successful. We found warm anti-slavery friends there, but the feeling was not general enough to support such an establishment. I passed nearly a year in the family of Isaac and Amy Post, practical believers in the Christian doctrine of human brotherhood. They measured a man's worth by his character, not by his complexion. The memory of those beloved and honored friends will remain with me to my latest hour.

CHAPTER XL

The Fugitive Slave Law

My brother, being disappointed in his project, concluded to go to California; and it was agreed that Benjamin should go with him. Ellen liked her school, and was a great favorite there. They did not know her history, and she did not tell it, because she had no desire to make capital out of their sympathy. But when it was accidentally discovered that her mother was a fugitive slave, every method was used to increase her advantages and diminish her expenses.

I was alone again. It was necessary for me to be earning money, and I preferred that it should be among those who knew me. On my return from Rochester, I called at the house of Mr. Bruce, to see Mary, the darling little babe that had thawed my heart, when it was freezing into a cheerless distrust of all my fellow-beings. She was growing a tall girl now, but I loved her always. Mr. Bruce had married again, and it was proposed that I should become nurse to a new infant. I had but one hesitation, and that was my feeling of insecurity in New York, now greatly increased by the passage of the Fugitive Slave Law. However, I resolved to try the experiment. I was again fortunate in my employer. The new Mrs. Bruce was an American, brought up under aristocratic influences, and still living in the midst of them; but if she had any prejudice against color, I was never made aware of it; and as for the system of slavery, she had a most hearty dislike of it. No sophistry of Southerners could blind her to its enormity. She was a person of excellent principles and a noble heart. To me, from that hour to the present, she has been a true and sympathizing friend. Blessings be with her and hers!

About the time that I reëntered the Bruce family, an event occurred of disastrous import to the colored people. The slave Hamlin, the first fugitive that came under the new law, was given up by the bloodhounds of the north to the bloodhounds of the south. It was the beginning of a reign of terror to the colored population. The great city rushed on in its whirl of excitement, taking no note of the "short and simple annals of the poor." But while fashionables were listening to the thrilling voice of Jenny Lind in Metropolitan Hall, the thrilling voices of poor hunted colored people went up, in an agony of supplication, to the Lord, from Zion's church. Many families, who had lived in the city for twenty years, fled from it now. Many a poor washerwoman, who, by hard labor, had made herself a comfortable home, was obliged to sacrifice her furniture, bid a hurried farewell to friends, and seek her fortune among strangers in Canada. Many a wife discovered a secret she had never known before—that her husband was a fugitive, and must leave her to insure his own safety. Worse still, many a husband discovered that his wife had fled from slavery years ago, and as "the child follows the condition of its mother," the children of his love were liable to be seized and carried into slavery. Every where, in those humble homes, there was consternation and anguish. But what cared the legislators of the "dominant race" for the blood they were crushing out of trampled hearts?

When my brother William spent his last evening with me, before he went to California, we talked nearly all the time of the distress brought on our oppressed people by the passage of this iniquitous law; and never had I seen him manifest such bitterness of spirit, such stern hostility to our oppressors. He was himself free from the operation of the law; for he did not run from any Slaveholding State, being brought into the Free States by his master.

But I was subject to it; and so were hundreds of intelligent and industrious people all around us. I seldom ventured into the streets; and when it was necessary to do an errand for Mrs. Bruce, or any of the family, I went as much as possible through back streets and by-ways. What a disgrace to a city calling itself free, that inhabitants, guiltless of offence, and seeking to perform their duties conscientiously, should be condemned to live in such incessant fear, and have nowhere to turn for protection! This state of things, of course, gave rise to many impromptu vigilance committees. Every colored person, and every friend of their persecuted race, kept their eyes wide open. Every evening I examined the newspapers carefully, to see what Southerners had put up at the hotels. I did this for my own sake, thinking my young mistress and her husband might be among the list; I wished also to give information to others, if necessary; for if many were "running to and fro," I resolved that "knowledge should be increased."

This brings up one of my Southern reminiscences, which I will here briefly relate. I was somewhat acquainted with a slave named Luke, who belonged to a wealthy man in our vicinity. His master died, leaving a son and daughter heirs to his large fortune. In the division of the slaves, Luke was included in the son's portion. This young man became a prey to the vices growing out of the "patriarchal institution," and when he went to the north, to complete his education, he carried his vices with him. He was brought home, deprived of the use of his limbs, by excessive dissipation. Luke was appointed to wait upon his bed-ridden master, whose despotic habits were greatly increased by exasperation at his own helplessness. He kept a cowhide beside him, and, for the most trivial occurrence, he would order his attendant to bare his back, and kneel beside the couch, while he whipped him till his strength was exhausted. Some days he was not allowed to wear any thing but his shirt, in order to be in readiness to be flogged. A day seldom passed without his receiving more or less blows. If the slightest resistance was offered, the town constable was sent for to execute the punishment, and Luke learned from experience how much more the constable's strong arm was to be dreaded than the comparatively feeble one of his master. The arm of his tyrant grew weaker, and was finally palsied; and then the constable's services were in constant requisition. The fact that he was entirely dependent on Luke's care, and was obliged to be tended like an infant, instead of inspiring any gratitude or compassion towards his poor slave, seemed only to increase his irritability and cruelty. As he lay there on his bed, a mere degraded wreck of manhood, he took into his head the strangest freaks of despotism; and if Luke hesitated to submit to his orders, the constable was immediately sent for. Some of these freaks were of a nature too filthy to be repeated. When I fled from the house of bondage, I left poor Luke still chained to the bedside of this cruel and disgusting wretch.

One day, when I had been requested to do an errand for Mrs. Bruce, I was hurrying through back streets, as usual, when I saw a young man approaching, whose face was familiar to me. As he came nearer, I recognized Luke. I always rejoiced to see or hear of any one who had escaped from the black pit; but, remembering this poor fellow's extreme hardships, I was peculiarly glad to see him on Northern soil, though I no longer called it *free* soil. I well remembered what a desolate feeling it was to be alone among strangers, and I went up to him and greeted him cordially. At first, he did not know me; but when I mentioned my name, he remembered all about me. I told him of the Fugitive Slave Law, and asked him if he did not know that New York was a city of kidnappers.

He replied, "De risk ain't so bad for me, as 'tis fur you. 'Cause I runned away from de speculator, and you runned away from de massa. Dem speculators vont spen dar money to come here for a runaway, if dey ain't sartin sure to put dar hans right on him. An I tell you I's tuk good car 'bout dat. I had too hard times down dar, to let 'em ketch dis nigger."

He then told me of the advice he had received, and the plans he had laid. I asked if he had money enough to take him to Canada. " 'Pend upon it, I hab," he replied. "I tuk car fur dat. I'd bin workin all my days fur dem cussed whites, an got no pay but kicks and cuffs. So I tought dis nigger had a right to money nuff to bring him to de Free States. Massa Henry he lib till ebery body vish him dead;

an ven he did die, I knowed de debbil would hab him, an vouldn't vant him to bring his money 'long too. So I tuk some of his bills, and put 'em in de pocket of his ole trousers. An ven he was buried, dis nigger ask fur dem ole trousers, an dey gub 'em to me." With a low, chuckling laugh, he added, "You see I didn't *steal* it; dey *gub* it to me. I tell you, I had mighty hard time to keep de speculator from findin it; but he didn't git it."

This is a fair specimen of how the moral sense is educated by slavery. When a man has his wages stolen from him, year after year, and the laws sanction and enforce the theft, how can he be expected to have more regard to honesty than has the man who robs him? I have become somewhat enlightened, but I confess that I agree with poor, ignorant, much-abused Luke, in thinking he had a *right* to that money, as a portion of his unpaid wages. He went to Canada forthwith, and I have not since heard from him.

All that winter I lived in a state of anxiety. When I took the children out to breathe the air, I closely observed the countenances of all I met. I dreaded the approach of summer, when snakes and slaveholders make their appearance. I was, in fact, a slave in New York, as subject to slave laws as I had been in a Slave State. Strange incongruity in a State called free!

Spring returned, and I received warning from the south that Dr. Flint knew of my return to my old place, and was making preparations to have me caught. I learned afterwards that my dress, and that of Mrs. Bruce's children, had been described to him by some of the Northern tools, which slaveholders employ for their base purposes, and then indulge in sneers at their cupidity and mean servility.

I immediately informed Mrs. Bruce of my danger, and she took prompt measures for my safety. My place as nurse could not be supplied immediately, and this generous, sympathizing lady proposed that I should carry her baby away. It was a comfort to me to have the child with me; for the heart is reluctant to be torn away from every object it loves. But how few mothers would have consented to have one of their own babes become a fugitive, for the sake of a poor, hunted nurse, on whom the legislators of the country had let loose the bloodhounds!

When I spoke of the sacrifice she was making, in depriving herself of her dear baby, she replied, "It is better for you to have baby with you, Linda; for if they get on your track, they will be obliged to bring the child to me; and then, if there is a possibility of saving you, you shall be saved."

This lady had a very wealthy relative, a benevolent gentleman in many respects, but aristocratic and proslavery. He remonstrated with her for harboring a fugitive slave; told her she was violating the laws of her country; and asked her if she was aware of the penalty. She replied, "I am very well aware of it. It is imprisonment and one thousand dollars fine. Shame on my country that it *is* so! I am ready to incur the penalty. I will go to the state's prison, rather than have any poor victim torn from *my* house, to be carried back to slavery."

The noble heart! The brave heart! The tears are in my eyes while I write of her. May the God of the helpless reward her for her sympathy with my persecuted people!

I was sent into New England, where I was sheltered by the wife of a senator, whom I shall always hold in grateful remembrance. This honorable gentleman would not have voted for the Fugitive Slave Law, as did the senator in "Uncle Tom's Cabin;" on the contrary, he was strongly opposed to it; but he was enough under its influence to be afraid of having me remain in his house many hours. So I was sent into the country, where I remained a month with the baby. When it was supposed that Dr. Flint's emissaries had lost track of me, and given up the pursuit for the present, I returned to New York.

CHAPTER XLI

Free at Last

Mrs. Bruce, and every member of her family, were exceedingly kind to me. I was thankful for the blessings of my lot, yet I could not always wear a cheerful countenance. I was doing harm to no one; on the contrary, I was doing all the good I could in my small way; yet I could never go out to breathe God's free air without trepidation at my heart. This seemed hard; and I could not think it was a right state of things in any civilized country.

From time to time I received news from my good old grandmother. She could not write; but she employed others to write for her. The following is an extract from one of her last letters:—

> "Dear Daughter: I cannot hope to see you again on earth; but I pray to God to unite us above, where pain will no more rack this feeble body of mine; where sorrow and parting from my children will be no more. God has promised these things if we are faithful unto the end. My age and feeble health deprive me of going to church now; but God is with me here at home. Thank your brother for his kindness. Give much

> love to him, and tell him to remember the Creator in the days of his youth, and strive to meet me in the Father's kingdom. Love to Ellen and Benjamin. Don't neglect him. Tell him for me, to be a good boy. Strive, my child, to train them for God's children. May he protect and provide for you, is the prayer of your loving old mother."

These letters both cheered and saddened me. I was always glad to have tidings from the kind, faithful old friend of my unhappy youth; but her messages of love made my heart yearn to see her before she died, and I mourned over the fact that it was impossible. Some months after I returned from my flight to New England, I received a letter from her, in which she wrote, "Dr. Flint is dead. He has left a distressed family. Poor old man! I hope he made his peace with God."

I remembered how he had defrauded my grandmother of the hard earnings she had loaned; how he had tried to cheat her out of the freedom her mistress had promised her, and how he had persecuted her children; and I thought to myself that she was a better Christian than I was, if she could entirely forgive him. I cannot say, with truth, that the news of my old master's death softened my feelings towards him. There are wrongs which even the grave does not bury. The man was odious to me while he lived, and his memory is odious now.

His departure from this world did not diminish my danger. He had threatened my grandmother that his heirs should hold me in slavery after he was gone; that I never should be free so long as a child of his survived. As for Mrs. Flint, I had seen her in deeper afflictions than I supposed the loss of her husband would be, for she had buried several children; yet I never saw any signs of softening in her heart. The doctor had died in embarrassed circumstances, and had little to will to his heirs, except such property as he was unable to grasp. I was well aware what I had to expect from the family of Flints; and my fears were confirmed by a letter from the south, warning me to be on my guard, because Mrs. Flint openly declared that her daughter could not afford to lose so valuable a slave as I was.

I kept close watch of the newspapers for arrivals; but one Saturday night, being much occupied, I forgot to examine the Evening Express as usual. I went down into the parlor for it, early in the morning, and found the boy about to kindle a fire with it. I took it from him and examined the list of arrivals. Reader, if you have never been a slave, you cannot imagine the acute sensation of suffering at my heart, when I read he names of Mr. and Mrs. Dodge, at a hotel in Courtland Street. It was a third-rate hotel, and that circumstance convinced me of the truth of what I had heard, that they were short of funds and had need of my value, as *they* valued me; and that was by dollars and cents. I hastened with the paper to Mrs. Bruce. Her heart and hand were always open to every one in distress, and she always warmly sympathized with mine. It was impossible to tell how near the enemy was. He might have passed and repassed the house while we were sleeping. He might at that moment be waiting to pounce upon me if I ventured out of doors. I had never seen the husband of my young mistress, and therefore I could not distinguish him from any other stranger. A carriage was hastily ordered; and, closely veiled, I followed Mrs. Bruce, taking the baby again with me into exile. After various turnings and crossings, and returnings, the carriage stopped at the house of one of Mrs. Bruce's friends, where I was kindly received. Mrs. Bruce returned immediately, to instruct the domestics what to say if any one came to inquire for me.

It was lucky for me that the evening paper was not burned up before I had a chance to examine the list of arrivals. It was not long after Mrs. Bruce's return to her house, before several people came to inquire for me. One inquired for me, another asked for my daughter Ellen, and another said he had a letter from my grandmother, which he was requested to deliver in person.

They were told, "She *has* lived here, but she has left."

"How long ago?"

"I don't know, sir."

"Do you know where she went?"

"I do not, sir." And the door was closed.

This Mr. Dodge, who claimed me as his property, was originally a Yankee pedler in the south; then he became a merchant, and finally a slaveholder. He managed to get introduced into what was called the first society, and married Miss Emily Flint. A quarrel arose between him and her brother, and the brother cowhided him. This led to a family feud, and he proposed to remove to Virginia. Dr. Flint left him no property, and his own means had become circumscribed, while a wife and children depended upon him for support. Under these circumstances, it was very natural that he should make an effort to put me into his pocket.

I had a colored friend, a man from my native place, in whom I had the most implicit confidence. I sent for him, and told him that Mr. and Mrs. Dodge had arrived in New York. I proposed that he should call upon them to make inquiries about his friends at the south, with whom Dr. Flint's family were well acquainted. He thought there was no impropriety in his doing so, and he consented. He went to the hotel, and knocked at the door of Mr. Dodge's room, which was opened by the gentleman himself, who gruffly inquired, "What brought you here? How came you to know I was in the city?"

"Your arrival was published in the evening papers, sir; and I called to ask Mrs. Dodge about my friends at home. I didn't suppose it would give any offence."

"Where's that negro girl, that belongs to my wife?"

"What girl, sir?"

"You know well enough. I mean Linda, that ran away from Dr. Flint's plantation, some years ago. I dare say you've seen her, and know where she is."

"Yes, sir, I've seen her, and know where she is. She is out of your reach, sir."

"Tell me where she is, or bring her to me, and I will give her a chance to buy her freedom."

"I don't think it would be of any use, sir. I have heard her say she would go to the ends of the earth, rather than pay any man or woman for her freedom, because she thinks she has a right to it. Besides, she couldn't do it, if she would, for she has spent her earnings to educate her children."

This made Mr. Dodge very angry, and some high words passed between them. My friend was afraid to come where I was; but in the course of the day I received a note from him. I supposed they had not come from the south, in the winter, for a pleasure excursion; and now the nature of their business was very plain.

Mrs. Bruce came to me and entreated me to leave the city the next morning. She said her house was watched, and it was possible that some clew to me might be obtained. I refused to take her advice. She pleaded with an earnest tenderness, that ought to have moved me; but I was in a bitter, disheartened mood. I was weary of flying from pillar to post. I had been chased during half my life, and it seemed as if the chase was never to end. There I sat, in that great city, guiltless of crime, yet not daring to worship God in any of the churches. I heard the bells ringing for afternoon service, and, with contemptuous sarcasm, I said, "Will the preachers take for their text, 'Proclaim liberty to the captive, and the opening of prison doors to them that are bound'? or will they preach from the text, 'Do unto others as ye would they should do unto you'?" Oppressed Poles and Hungarians could find a safe refuge in that city; John Mitchell was free to proclaim in the City Hall his desire for "a plantation well stocked with slaves;" but there I sat, an oppressed American, not daring to show my face. God forgive the black and bitter thoughts I indulged on that Sabbath day! The Scripture says, "Oppression makes even a wise man mad;" and I was not wise.

I had been told that Mr. Dodge said his wife had never signed away her right to my children, and if he could not get me, he would take them. This it was, more than any thing else, that roused such a tempest in my soul. Benjamin was with his uncle William in California, but my innocent young daughter had come to spend a vacation with me. I thought of what I had suffered in slavery at her age, and my heart was like a tiger's when a hunter tries to seize her young.

Dear Mrs. Bruce! I seem to see the expression of her face, as she turned away discouraged by my obstinate mood. Finding her expostulations unavailing, she sent Ellen to entreat me. When ten o'clock in the evening arrived and Ellen had not returned, this watchful and unwearied friend became anxious. She came to us in a carriage, bringing a well-filled trunk for my journey—trusting that by this time I would listen to reason. I yielded to her, as I ought to have done before.

The next day, baby and I set out in a heavy snow storm, bound for New England again. I received letters from the City of Iniquity, addressed to me under an assumed name. In a few days one came from Mrs. Bruce, informing me that my new master was still searching for me, and that she intended to put an end to this persecution by buying my freedom. I felt grateful for the kindness that prompted this offer, but the idea was not so pleasant to me as might have been expected. The more my mind had become enlightened, the more difficult it was for me to consider myself an article of property; and to pay money to those who had so grievously oppressed me seemed like taking from my sufferings the glory of triumph. I wrote to Mrs. Bruce, thanking her, but saying that being sold from one owner to another seemed too much like slavery; that such a great obligation could not be easily cancelled; and that I preferred to go to my brother in California.

Without my knowledge, Mrs. Bruce employed a gentleman in New York to enter into negotiations with Mr. Dodge. He proposed to pay three hundred dollars down, if Mr. Dodge would sell me, and enter into obligations to relinquish all claim to me or my children forever after. He who called himself my master said he scorned so small an offer for such a valuable servant. The gentleman replied, "You can do as you choose, sir. If you reject this offer you will never get any thing; for the woman has friends who will convey her and her children out of the country."

Mr. Dodge concluded that "half a loaf was better than no bread," and he agreed to the proffered terms. By the next mail I received this brief letter from Mrs. Bruce: "I am rejoiced to tell you that the money for your freedom has been paid to Mr. Dodge. Come home to-morrow. I long to see you and my sweet babe."

My brain reeled as I read these lines. A gentleman near me said, "It's true; I have seen the bill of sale." "The bill of sale!" Those words struck me like a blow. So I was *sold* at last! A human being *sold* in the free city of New York! The bill of sale is on record, and future generations will learn from it that women were articles of traffic in New York, late in the nineteenth century of the Christian religion. It may hereafter prove a useful document to antiquaries, who are seeking to measure the progress of civilization in the United States. I well know the value of that bit of paper; but much as I love freedom, I do not like to look upon it. I am deeply grateful to the generous friend who procured it, but I despise the miscreant who demanded payment for what never rightfully belonged to him or his.

I had objected to having my freedom bought, yet I must confess that when it was done I felt as if a heavy load had been lifted from my weary shoulders. When I rode home in the cars I was no longer afraid to unveil my face and look at people as they passed. I should have been glad to have met Daniel Dodge himself; to have had him seen me and known me, that he might have mourned over the untoward circumstances which compelled him to sell me for three hundred dollars.

When I reached home, the arms of my benefactress were thrown round me, and our tears mingled. As soon as she could speak, she said, "O Linda, I'm *so* glad it's all over! You wrote to me as if you thought you were going to be transferred from one owner to another. But I did not buy you for your services. I should have done just the same, if you had been going to sail for California tomorrow. I should, at least, have the satisfaction of knowing that you left me a free woman."

My heart was exceedingly full. I remembered how my poor father had tried to buy me, when I was a small child, and how he had been disappointed. I hoped his spirit was rejoicing over me now. I remembered how my good old grandmother had laid up her earnings to purchase me in later years, and how often her plans had been frustrated. How that faithful, loving old heart would leap for joy, if she could look on me and my children now that we were free! My relatives had been foiled in all their efforts, but God had raised me up a friend among strangers, who had bestowed on me the precious, long-desired boon. Friend! It is a common word, often lightly used. Like other good and beautiful things, it may be tarnished by careless handling; but when I speak of Mrs. Bruce as my friend, the word is sacred.

My grandmother lived to rejoice in my freedom; but not long after, a letter came with a black seal. She had gone "where the wicked cease from troubling, and the weary are at rest."

Time passed on, and a paper came to me from the south, containing an obituary notice of my uncle Phillip. It was the only case I ever knew of such an honor conferred upon a colored person. It was written by one of his friends, and contained these words: "Now that death has laid him low, they call him a good man and a useful citizen; but what are eulogies to the black man, when the world has faded from his vision? It does not require man's praise to obtain rest in God's kingdom." So they called a colored man a *citizen!* Strange words to be uttered in that region!

Reader, my story ends with freedom; not in the usual way, with marriage. I and my children are now free! We are as free from the power of slaveholders as are the white people of the north; and though that, according to my ideas, is not saying a great deal, it is a vast improvement in *my* condition. The dream of my life is not yet realized. I do not sit with my children in a home of my own. I still long for a hearthstone of my own, however humble. I wish it for my children's sake far more than for my own. But God so orders circumstances as to keep me with my friend Mrs. Bruce. Love, duty, gratitude, also bind me to her side. It is a privilege to serve her who pities my oppressed people, and who has bestowed the inestimable boon of freedom on me and my children.

It has been painful to me, in many ways, to recall the dreary years I passed in bondage. I would gladly forget them if I could. Yet the retrospection is not altogether without solace; for with those gloomy recollections come tender memories of my good old grandmother, like light, fleecy clouds floating over a dark and troubled sea.

APPENDIX

The following statement is from Amy Post, a member of the Society of Friends in the State of New York, well known and highly respected by friends of the poor and the oppressed. As has been already stated, in the preceding pages, the author of this volume spent some time under her hospitable roof.

L.M.C.

"The author of this book is my highly-esteemed friend. If its readers knew her as I know her, they could not fail to be deeply interested in her story. She was a beloved inmate of our family nearly the whole of the year 1849. She was introduced to us by her affectionate and conscientious brother, who had previously related to us some of the almost incredible events in his sister's life. I immediately became much interested in Linda; for her appearance was prepossessing, and her deportment indicated remarkable delicacy of feeling and purity of thought.

"As we became acquainted, she related to me, from time to time some of the incidents in her bitter experiences as a slave-woman. Though impelled by a natural craving for human sympathy, she passed through a baptism of suffering, even in recounting her trials to me, in private confidential conversations. The burden of these memories lay heavily upon her spirit—naturally virtuous and refined. I repeatedly urged her to consent to the publication of her narrative; for I felt that it would arouse people to a more earnest work for the disinthralment of millions still remaining in that soul-crushing condition, which was so unendurable to her. But her sensitive spirit shrank from publicity. She said, 'You know a woman can whisper her cruel wrongs in the ear of a dear friend much easier than she can record them for the world to read.' Even in talking with me, she wept so much, and seemed to suffer such mental agony, that I felt her story was too sacred to be drawn from her by inquisitive questions, and I left her free to tell as much, or as little, as she chose. Still, I urged upon her the duty of publishing her experience, for the sake of the good it might do; and, at last, she undertook the task.

"Having been a slave so large a portion of her life, she is unlearned; she is obliged to earn her living by her own labor, and she has worked untiringly to procure education for her children; several times she has been obliged to leave her employments, in order to fly from the man-hunters and woman-hunters of our land; but she pressed through all these obstacles and overcame them. After the labors of the day were over, she traced secretly and wearily, by the midnight lamp, a truthful record of her eventful life.

"This Empire State is a shabby place of refuge for the oppressed; but here, through anxiety, turmoil, and despair, the freedom of Linda and her children was finally secured, by the exertions of a generous friend. She was grateful for the boon; but the idea of having been *bought* was always galling to a spirit that could never acknowledge itself to be a chattel. She wrote to us thus, soon after the event: 'I thank you for your kind expressions in regard to my freedom; but the freedom I had before the money was paid was dearer to me. God gave me *that* freedom; but man put God's image in the scales with the paltry sum of three hundred dollars. I served for my liberty as faithfully as Jacob served for Rachel. At the end, he had large possessions; but I was robbed of my victory; I was obliged to resign my crown, to rid myself of a tyrant.

"Her story, as written by herself, cannot fail to interest the reader. It is a sad illustration of the condition of this country, which boasts of its civilization, while it sanctions laws and customs which make the experiences of the present more strange than any fictions of the past.

AMY POST.

"ROCHESTER, N.Y., Oct. 30th, 1859."

The following testimonial is from a man who is now a highly respectable colored citizen of Boston.

L.M.C

"This narrative contains some incidents so extraordinary, that, doubtless, many persons, under whose eyes it may chance to fall, will be ready to believe that it is colored highly, to serve a special purpose. But, however it may be regarded by the incredulous, I know that it is full of living truths. I have been well acquainted with the author from my boyhood. The circumstances recounted in her history are perfectly familiar to me. I knew of her treatment from her master; of the imprisonment of her children; of their sale and redemption; of her seven years' concealment; and of her subsequent escape to the North. I am now a resident of Boston, and am a living witness to the truth of this interesting narrative.

GEORGE W. LOWTHER."

Selections from *Up from Slavery*

BOOKER T. WASHINGTON

1901

CHAPTER I

A Slave Among Slaves

I was born a slave on a plantation in Franklin County, Virginia. I am not quite sure of the exact place or exact date of my birth, but at any rate I suspect I must have been born somewhere and at some time. As nearly as I have been able to learn, I was born near a cross-roads post-office called Hale's Ford, and the year was 1858 or 1859. I do not know the month or the day. The earliest impressions I can now recall are of the plantation and the slave quarters—the latter being the part of the plantation where the slaves had their cabins.

My life had its beginning in the midst of the most miserable, desolate, and discouraging surroundings. This was so, however, not because my owners were especially cruel, for they were not, as compared with many others. I was born in a typical log cabin, about fourteen by sixteen feet square. In this cabin I lived with my mother and a brother and sister till after the Civil War, when we were all declared free.

Of my ancestry I know almost nothing. In the slave quarters, and even later, I heard whispered conversations among the coloured people of the tortures which the slaves, including, no doubt, my ancestors on my mother's side, suffered in the middle passage of the slave ship while being conveyed from Africa to America. I have been unsuccessful in securing any information that would throw any accurate light upon the history of my family beyond my mother. She, I remember, had a half-brother and a half-sister. In the days of slavery not very much attention was given to family history and family records—that is, black family records. My mother, I suppose, attracted the attention of a purchaser who was afterward my owner and hers. Her addition to the slave family attracted about as much attention as the purchase of a new horse or cow. Of my father I know even less than of my mother. I do not even know his name. I have heard reports to the effect that he was a white man who lived on one of the near-by plantations. Whoever he was, I never heard of his taking the least interest in me or providing in any way for my rearing. But I do not find especial fault with him. He was simply another unfortunate victim of the institution which the Nation unhappily had engrafted upon it at that time.

The cabin was not only our living-place, but was also used as the kitchen for the plantation. My mother was the plantation cook. The cabin was without glass windows; it had only openings in the side which let in the light, and also the cold, chilly air of winter. There was a door to the cabin—that is, something that was called a door—but the uncertain hinges by which it was hung, and the large cracks in it, to say nothing of the fact that it was too small, made the room a very uncomfortable one. In addition to these openings there was, in the lower right-hand corner of the room, the "cat-hole,"—a contrivance which almost every mansion or cabin in Virginia possessed during the antebellum period. The "cat-hole" was a square opening, about seven by eight inches, provided for the purpose of letting the cat pass in and out of the house at will during the night. In the case of our particular cabin I could never understand the necessity for this convenience, since there were at least a half-dozen other places in the cabin that would have accommodated the cats. There was no wooden floor in our cabin, the naked earth being used as a floor. In the centre of the earthen floor there was a large, deep opening covered with boards, which was used as a place in which to store sweet potatoes during the winter. An impression of this potato-hole is very distinctly engraved upon my memory, because I recall that during the process of putting the potatoes in or taking them out I would often come into possession of one or two, which I roasted and thoroughly enjoyed. There was no cooking-stove on our plantation, and all the cooking for the whites and slaves my mother had to do over an open fireplace, mostly in pots and "skillets." While the poorly built cabin caused us to suffer with cold in the winter, the heat from the open fireplace in summer was equally trying.

The early years of my life, which were spent in the little cabin, were not very different from those of thousands of other slaves. My mother, of course, had little time in which to give attention to the training of her children during the day. She snatched a few moments for our care in the early morning before her work began, and at night after the day's work was done. One of my earliest recollections is that of my mother cooking a chicken late at night, and awakening her children for the purpose of feeding them. How or where she got it I do not know. I presume, however, it was procured from our owner's farm. Some people may call this theft. If such a thing were to happen now, I should condemn it as theft myself. But taking place at the time it did, and for the reason that it did, no one could ever make me believe that my mother was guilty of thieving. She was simply a victim of the system of slavery. I cannot remember having slept in a bed until after our family was declared free by the Emancipation Proclamation. Three children—John, my older brother, Amanda, my sister, and myself—had a pallet on the dirt floor, or, to be more correct, we slept in and on a bundle of filthy rags laid upon the dirt floor.

I was asked not long ago to tell something about the sports and pastimes that I engaged in during my youth. Until that question was asked it had never occurred to me that there was no period of my life that was devoted to play. From the time that I can remember anything, almost every day of my life has been occupied in some kind of labour; though I think I would now be a more useful man if I had had time for sports. During the period that I spent in slavery I was not large enough to be of much service, still I was occupied most of the time in cleaning the yards, carrying water to the men in the fields, or going to the mill, to which I used to take the corn, once a week, to be ground. The mill was about three miles from the plantation. This work I always dreaded. The heavy bag of corn would be thrown across the back of the horse, and the corn divided about evenly on each side; but in some way, almost without exception, on these trips, the corn would so shift as to become unbalanced and would fall off the horse, and often I would fall with it. As I was not strong enough to reload the corn upon the horse, I would have to wait, sometimes for many hours, till a chance passer-by came along who would help me out of my trouble. The hours while waiting for some one were usually spent in crying. The time consumed in this way made me late in reaching the mill, and by the time I got my corn ground and reached home it would be far into the night. The road was a lonely one, and often led through dense forests. I was always frightened. The woods were said to be full of soldiers who had deserted from the army, and I had been told that the first thing a deserter did to a Negro boy when he found him alone was to cut off his ears. Besides, when I was late in getting home I knew I would always get a severe scolding or a flogging.

I had no schooling whatever while I was a slave, though I remember on several occasions I went as far as the schoolhouse door with one of my young mistresses to carry her books. The picture of several dozen boys and girls in a schoolroom engaged in study made a deep impression upon me, and I had the feeling that to get into a schoolhouse and study in this way would be about the same as getting into paradise.

So far as I can now recall, the first knowledge that I got of the fact that we were slaves, and that freedom of the slaves was being discussed, was early one morning before day, when I was awakened by my mother kneeling over her children and fervently praying that Lincoln and his armies might be successful, and that one day she and her children might be free. In this connection I have never been able to understand how the slaves throughout the South, completely ignorant as were the masses so far as books or newspapers were concerned, were able to keep themselves so accurately and completely informed about the great National questions that were agitating the country. From the time that Garrison, Lovejoy, and others began to agitate for freedom, the slaves throughout the South kept in close touch with the progress of the movement. Though I was a mere child during the preparation for the Civil War and during the war itself, I now recall the many late-at-night whispered discussions that I heard my mother and the other slaves on the plantation indulge in. These discussions showed that they understood the situation, and that they kept themselves informed of events by what was termed the "grape-vine telegraph."

During the campaign when Lincoln was first a candidate for the Presidency, the slaves on our far-off plantation, miles from any railroad or large city or daily newspaper, knew what the issues involved were. When war was begun between the North and the South, every slave on our plantation felt and knew that, though other issues were discussed, the primal one was that of slavery. Even the most ignorant members of my race on the remote plantations felt in their hearts, with a certainty that admitted of no doubt, that the freedom of the slaves would be the one great result of the war, if the Northern armies conquered. Every success of the Federal armies and every defeat of the Confederate forces was watched with the keenest and most intense interest. Often the slaves got knowledge of the results of great battles before the white people received it. This news was usually gotten from the coloured man who was sent to the post office for the mail. In our case the post-office was about three miles from the plantation and the mail came once or twice a week. The man who was sent to the office would linger about the place long enough to get the drift of the conversation from the group of white people who naturally congregated there, after receiving their mail, to discuss the latest news. The mail-carrier on his way back to our master's house would as naturally retail the news that he had secured among the slaves, and in this way they often heard of important events before the white people at the "big house," as the master's house was called.

I cannot remember a single instance during my childhood or early boyhood when our entire family sat down to the table together, and God's blessing was asked, and the family ate a meal in a civilized manner. On the plantation in Virginia, and even later, meals were gotten by the children very much as dumb animals get theirs. It was a piece of bread here and a scrap of meat there. It was a cup of milk at one time and some potatoes at another. Sometimes a portion of our family would eat out of the skillet or pot, while some one else would eat from a tin plate held on the knees, and often using nothing but the hands with which to hold the food. When I had grown to sufficient size, I was required to go to the "big house" at meal-times to fan the flies from the table by means of a large set of paper fans operated by a pulley. Naturally much of the conversation of the white people turned upon the subject of freedom and the war, and I absorbed a good deal of it. I remember that at one time I saw two of my young mistresses and some lady visitors eating ginger-cakes, in the yard. At that time those cakes seemed to me to be absolutely the most tempting and desirable things that I had ever seen; and I then and there resolved that, if I ever got free, the height of my ambition would be reached if I could get to the point where I could secure and eat ginger-cakes in the way that I saw those ladies doing.

Of course as the war was prolonged the white people, in many cases, often found it difficult to secure food for themselves. I think the slaves felt the deprivation less than the whites, because the usual diet for the slaves was corn bread and pork, and these could be raised on the plantation, but coffee, tea, sugar, and other articles which the whites had been accustomed to use could not be raised on the plantation, and the conditions brought about by the war frequently made it impossible to secure these things. The whites were often in great straits. Parched corn was used for coffee, and a kind of black molasses was used instead of sugar. Many times nothing was used to sweeten the so-called tea and coffee.

The first pair of shoes that I recall wearing were wooden ones. They had rough leather on the top, but the bottoms, which were about an inch thick, were of wood. When I walked they made a fearful noise, and besides this they were very inconvenient, since there was no yielding to the natural pressure of the foot. In wearing them one presented an exceedingly awkward appearance. The most trying ordeal that I was forced to endure as a slave boy, however, was the wearing of a flax shirt. In the portion of Virginia where I lived it was common to use flax as part of the clothing for the slaves. That part of the flax from which our clothing was made was largely the refuse, which of course was the cheapest and roughest part. I can scarcely imagine any torture, except, perhaps, the pulling of a tooth, that is equal to that caused by putting on a new flax shirt for the first time. It is almost equal to the feeling that one would experience if he had a dozen or more chestnuts burrs, or a hundred small pin-points, in contact with his flesh. Even to this day I can recall accurately the tortures that I underwent when putting on one of these garments. The fact that my flesh was soft and tender added to the pain. But I had no choice. I had to wear the flax shirt or none; and had it been left to me to choose, I should have chosen to wear no covering. In connection with the flax shirt, my brother John, who is several years older than I am, performed one of the most generous acts that I ever heard of one slave relative doing for another. On several occasions when I was being forced to wear a new flax shirt, he generously agreed to put it on in my stead and wear it for several days, till it was "broken in." Until I had grown to be quite a youth this single garment was all that I wore.

One may get the idea from what I have said, that there was bitter feeling toward the white people on the part of my race, because of the fact that most of the white population was away fighting in a war which would result in keeping the Negro in slavery if the South was successful. In the case of the slaves on our place this was not true, and it was not true of any large portion of the slave population in the South where the Negro was treated with anything like decency. During the Civil War one of my young masters was killed, and two were severely wounded. I recall the feeling of sorrow which existed among the slaves when they heard of the death of "Mars' Billy." It was no sham sorrow but real. Some of the slaves had nursed "Mars' Billy"; others had played with him when he was a child. "Mars' Billy" had begged for mercy in the case of others when the overseer or master was thrashing them. The sorrow in the slave quarter was only second to that in the "big house." When the two young masters were brought home wounded, the sympathy of the slaves was shown in many ways. They were just as anxious to assist in the nursing as the family relatives of the wounded. Some of the slaves would even beg for the privilege of sitting up at night to nurse their wounded masters. This tenderness and sympathy on the part of those held in bondage was a result of their kindly and generous nature. In order to defend and protect the women and children who were left on the plantations when the white males went to war, the slaves would have laid down their lives. The slave who was selected to sleep in the "big house" during the absence of the males was considered to have the place of honour. Any one attempting to harm "young Mistress" or "old Mistress" during the night would have had to cross the dead body of the slave to do so. I do not know how many have noticed it, but I think that it will be found to be true that there are few instances, either in slavery or freedom, in which a member of my race has been known to betray a specific trust.

As a rule, not only did the members of my race entertain no feelings of bitterness against the whites before and during the war, but there are many instances of Negroes tenderly caring for their former masters and mistresses who for some reason have become poor and dependent since the war. I know of instances where the former masters of slaves have for years been supplied with money by their former slaves to keep them from suffering. I have known of still other cases in which the former slaves have assisted in the education of the descendants of their former owners. I know of a case on a large plantation in the South in which a young white man, the son of the former owner of the estate, has become so reduced in purse and self-control by reason of drink that he is a pitiable creature; and yet, notwithstanding the poverty of the coloured people themselves on this plantation, they have for years supplied this young white man with the necessities of life. One sends him a little coffee or sugar, another a little meat, and so on. Nothing that the coloured people possess is too good for the son of "old Mars' Tom," who will perhaps never be permitted to suffer while any remain on the place who knew directly or indirectly of "old Mars' Tom."

I have said that there are few instances of a member of

my race betraying a specific trust. One of the best illustrations of this which I know of is in the case of an ex-slave from Virginia whom I met not long ago in a little town in the state of Ohio. I found that this man had made a contract with his master, two or three years previous to the Emancipation Proclamation, to the effect that the slave was to be permitted to buy himself, by paying so much per year for his body; and while he was paying for himself, he was to be permitted to labour where and for whom he pleased. Finding that he could secure better wages in Ohio, he went there. When freedom came, he was still in debt to his master some three hundred dollars. Notwithstanding that the Emancipation Proclamation freed him from any obligation to his master, this black man walked the greater portion of the distance back to where his old master lived in Virginia, and placed the last dollar, with interest, in his hands. In talking to me about this, the man told me that he knew that he did not have to pay the debt, but that he had given his word to his master, and his word he had never broken. He felt that he could not enjoy his freedom till he had fulfilled his promise.

From some things that I have said one may get the idea that some of the slaves did not want freedom. This is not true. I have never seen one who did not want to be free, or one who would return to slavery.

I pity from the bottom of my heart any nation or body of people that is so unfortunate as to get entangled in the net of slavery. I have long since ceased to cherish any spirit of bitterness against the Southern white people on account of the enslavement of my race. No one section of our country was wholly responsible for its introduction, and, besides, it was recognized and protected for years by the General Government. Having once got its tentacles fastened on to the economic and social life of the Republic, it was no easy matter for the country to relieve itself of the institution. Then, when we rid ourselves of prejudice, or racial feeling, and look facts in the face, we must acknowledge that, notwithstanding the cruelty and moral wrong of slavery, the ten million Negroes inhabiting this country, who themselves or whose ancestors went through the school of American slavery, are in a stronger and more hopeful condition, materially, intellectually, morally, and religiously, than is true of an equal number of black people in any other portion of the globe. This is so to such an extent that Negroes in this country, who themselves or whose forefathers went through the school of slavery, are constantly returning to Africa as missionaries to enlighten those who remained in the fatherland. This I say, not to justify slavery—on the other hand, I condemn it as an institution, as we all know that in America it was established for selfish and financial reasons, and not from a missionary motive—but to call attention to a fact, and to show how Providence so often uses men and institutions to accomplish a purpose. When persons ask me in these days how, in the midst of what sometimes seem hopelessly discouraging conditions, I can have such faith in the future of my race in this country, I remind them of the wilderness through which and out of which, a good Providence has already led us.

Ever since I have been old enough to think for myself, I have entertained the idea that, notwithstanding the cruel wrongs inflicted upon us, the black man got nearly as much out of slavery as the white man did. The hurtful influences of the institution were not by any means confined to the Negro. This was fully illustrated by the life upon our own plantation. The whole machinery of slavery was so constructed as to cause labour, as a rule, to be looked upon as a badge of degradation, of inferiority. Hence labour was something that both races on the slave plantation sought to escape. The slave system on our place, in a large measure, took the spirit of self-reliance and self-help out of the white people. My old master had many boys and girls, but not one, so far as I know, ever mastered a single trade or special line of productive industry. The girls were not taught to cook, sew, or to take care of the house. All of this was left to the slaves. The slaves, of course, had little personal interest in the life of the plantation, and their ignorance prevented them from learning how to do things in the most improved and thorough manner. As a result of the system, fences were out of repair, gates were hanging half off the hinges, doors creaked, window-panes were out, plastering had fallen but was not replaced, weeds grew in the yard. As a rule, there was food for whites and blacks, but inside the house, and on the dining room table, there was wanting that delicacy and refinement of touch and finish which can make a home the most convenient, comfortable, and attractive place in the world. Withal there was a waste of food and other materials which was sad. When freedom came, the slaves were almost as well fitted to begin life anew as the master, except in the matter of book-learning and ownership of property. The slave owner and his sons had mastered no special industry. They unconsciously had inbibed the feeling that manual labour was not the proper thing for them. On the other hand, the slaves, in many cases, had mastered some handicraft, and none were ashamed, and few unwilling, to labour.

Finally the war closed, and the day of freedom came. It was a momentous and eventful day to all upon our plantation. We had been expecting it. Freedom was in the air, and had been for months. Deserting soldiers returning to their homes were to be seen every day. Others who had been discharged, or whose regiments had been paroled, were constantly passing near our place. The "grape-vine telegraph" was kept busy night and day. The news and mutterings of great events were swiftly carried from one plantation to another. In the fear of "Yankee" invasions, the silverware and other valuables were taken from the "big house," buried in the woods, and guarded by trusted slaves. Woe be to any one who would have attempted to disturb the buried treasure. The slaves would give the Yankee soldiers food, drink, clothing—anything but that which had been specifically intrusted to their care and honour. As the great day drew nearer, there was more singing in the slave quarters than usual. It was bolder, had more ring, and lasted later into the night. Most of the verses of the plantation songs had some reference to freedom. True, they had sung those same verses before, but they had been careful to explain that the "freedom" in these songs referred to the next world, and had no connection with life in this world. Now they gradually threw off the mask, and were not afraid to let it be known that the "freedom" in their songs meant freedom of the body in this world. The night before the eventful day, word was sent to the slave quarters to the effect that something unusual was going to take place at the "big house" the next morning. There was little, if any, sleep that night. All was excitement and expectancy. Early the next morning word was sent to all the slaves, old and young, to gather at the house. In company with my mother, brother, and sister, and a large number of other slaves, I went to the master's house. All of our master's family were either standing or seated on the veranda of the house, where they could see what was to take place and hear what was said. There was a feeling of deep interest, or perhaps sadness, on their faces, but not bitterness. As I now recall the impression they made upon me, they did not at the moment seem to be sad because of the loss of property, but rather because of parting with those whom they had reared and who were in many ways very close to them. The most distinct thing that I now recall in connection with the scene was that some man who seemed to be a stranger (a United States officer, I presume) made a little speech and then read a rather long paper—the Emancipation Proclamation, I think. After the reading we were told that we were all free, and could go when and where we pleased. My mother, who was standing by my side, leaned over and kissed her children, while tears of joy ran down her cheeks. She explained to us what it all meant, that this was the day for which she had been so long praying, but fearing that she would never live to see.

For some minutes there was great rejoicing, and thanksgiving, and wild scenes of ecstasy. But there was no feeling of bitterness. In fact, there was pity among the slaves for our former owners. The wild rejoicing on the part of the emancipated coloured people lasted but for a brief period, for I noticed that by the time they returned to their cabins there was a change in their feelings. The great responsibility of being free, of having charge of themselves, of having to think and plan for themselves and their children, seemed to take possession of them. It was very much like suddenly turning a youth of ten or twelve years out into the world to provide for himself. In a few hours the great questions with which the Anglo-Saxon race had been grappling for centuries had been thrown upon these people to be solved. These were the questions of a home, a living, the rearing of children, education, citizenship, and the establishment and support of churches. Was it any wonder that within a few hours the wild rejoicing ceased and a feeling of deep gloom seemed to pervade the slave quarters? To some it seemed that, now that they were in actual possession of it, freedom was a more serious thing than they had expected to find it. Some of the slaves were seventy or eighty years old; their best days were gone. They had no strength with which to earn a living in a strange place and among strange people, even if they had been sure where to find a new place of abode. To this class the problem seemed especially hard. Besides, deep down in their hearts there was a strange and peculiar attachment to "old Marster" and "old Missus," and to their children, which they found it hard to think of breaking off. With these they had spent in some cases nearly a half-century, and it was no light thing to think of parting. Gradually, one by one, stealthily at first, the older slaves began to wander from the slave quarters back to the "big house" to have a whispered conversation with their former owners as to the future.

CHAPTER II

Boyhood Days

After the coming of freedom there were two points upon which practically all the people on our place were agreed, and I find that this was generally true throughout the South: that they must change their names, and that they must leave the old plantation for at least a few days or weeks in order that they might really feel sure that they were free.

In some way a feeling got among the coloured people that it was far from proper for them to bear the surname of their former owners, and a great many of them took other surnames. This was one of the first signs of freedom. When they were slaves, a coloured person was simply called "John" or "Susan." There was seldom occasion for more than the use of the one name. If "John" or "Susan" belonged to a white man by the name of "Hatcher," sometimes he was called "John Hatcher," or as often "Hatcher's John." But there was a feeling that "John Hatcher" or "Hatcher's John" was not the proper title by which to denote a freeman; and so in many cases "John Hatcher" was changed to "John S. Lincoln" or "John S. Sherman," the initial "S" standing for no name, it being simply a part of what the coloured man proudly called his "entitles."

As I have stated, most of the coloured people left the old plantation for a short while at least, so as to be sure, it seemed, that they could leave and try their freedom on to see how it felt. After they had remained away for a time, many of the older slaves, especially, returned to their old homes and made some kind of contract with their former owners by which they remained on the estate.

My mother's husband, who was the stepfather of my brother John and myself, did not belong to the same owners as did my mother. In fact, he seldom came to our plantation. I remember seeing him there perhaps once a year, that being about Christmas time. In some way, during the war, by running away and following the Federal soldiers, it seems, he found his way into the new state of West Virginia. As soon as freedom was declared, he sent for my mother to come to the Kanawha Valley, in West Virginia. At that time a journey from Virginia over the mountains to West Virginia was rather a tedious and in some cases a painful undertaking. What little clothing and few household goods we had were placed in a cart, but the children walked the greater portion of the distance, which was several hundred miles.

I do not think any of us ever had been very far from the plantation, and the taking of a long journey into another state was quite an event. The parting from our former owners and the members of our own race on the plantation was a serious occasion. From the time of our parting till their death we kept up a correspondence with the older members of the family, and in later years we have kept in touch with those who were the younger members. We were several weeks making the trip, and most of the time we slept in the open air and did our cooking over a log fire out of doors. One night I recall that we camped near an abandoned log cabin, and my mother decided to build a fire in that for cooking, and afterward to make a "pallet" on the floor for our sleeping. Just as the fire had gotten well started a large black snake fully a yard and a half long dropped down the chimney and ran out on the floor. Of course we at once abandoned that cabin. Finally we reached our destination—a little town called Malden, which is about five miles from Charleston, the present capital of the state.

At that time salt-mining was the great industry in that part of West Virginia, and the little town of Malden was right in the midst of the salt-furnaces. My stepfather had already secured a job at a salt-furnace, and he had also secured a little cabin for us to live in. Our new house was no better than the one we had left on the old plantation in Virginia. In fact, in one respect it was worse. Notwithstanding the poor condition of our plantation cabin, we were at all times sure of pure air. Our new home was in the midst of a cluster of cabins crowded closely together, and as there were no sanitary regulations, the filth about the cabins was often intolerable. Some of our neighbours were coloured people, and some were the poorest and most ignorant and degraded white people. It was a motley mixture. Drinking, gambling, quarrels, fights, and shockingly immoral practices were frequent. All who lived in the little town were in one way or another connected with the salt business. Though I was a mere child, my stepfather put me and my brother at work in one of the furnaces. Often I began work as early as four o'clock in the morning.

The first thing I ever learned in the way of book knowledge was while working in this salt-furnace. Each saltpacker had his barrels marked with a certain number. The number allotted to my stepfather was "18." At the close of the day's work the boss of the packers would come around and put "18" on each of our barrels, and I soon learned to recognize that figure wherever I saw it, and after a while got to the point where I could make that figure, though I knew nothing about any other figures or letters.

From the time that I can remember having any thoughts about anything, I recall that I had an intense longing to learn to read. I determined, when quite a small child, that, if I accomplished nothing else in life, I would in some way get enough education to enable me to read common books and newspapers. Soon after we got settled in some manner in our new cabin in West Virginia, I induced my mother to get hold of a book for me. How or where she got it I do not know, but in some way she procured an old copy of Webster's "blue-back" spelling-book, which contained the alphabet, followed by such meaningless words as "ab," "ba," "ca," "da." I began at once to devour this book, and I think that it was the first one I ever had in my hands. I had learned from somebody that the way to begin to read was to learn the alphabet, so I tried in all the ways I could think of to learn it,—all of course without a teacher, for I could find no one to teach me. At that time there was not a single member of my race anywhere near us who could read, and I was too timid to approach any of the white people. In some way, within a few weeks, I mastered the greater portion of the alphabet. In all my efforts to learn to read my mother shared fully my ambition, and sympathized with me and aided me in every way that she could. Though she was totally ignorant, so far as mere book knowledge was concerned, she had high ambitions for her children, and a large fund of good, hard, common sense which seemed to enable her to meet and master every situation. If I have done anything in life worth attention, I feel sure that I inherited the disposition from my mother.

In the midst of my struggles and longing for an education, a young coloured boy who had learned to read in the state of Ohio came to Malden. As soon as the coloured people found out that he could read, a newspaper was secured, and at the close of nearly every day's work this young man would be surrounded by a group of men and women who were anxious to hear him read the news contained in the papers. How I used to envy this man! He seemed to me to be the one young man in all the world who ought to be satisfied with his attainments.

About this time the question of having some kind of a school opened for the coloured children in the village began to be discussed by members of the race. As it would be the first school for Negro children that had ever been opened in that part of Virginia, it was, of course, to be a great event, and the discussion excited the widest interest. The most perplexing question was where to find a teacher. The young man from Ohio who had learned to read the papers was considered, but his age was against him. In the midst of the discussion about a teacher, another young coloured man from Ohio, who had been a soldier, in some way found his way into town. It was soon learned that he possessed considerable education, and he was engaged by the coloured people to teach their first school. As yet no free schools had been started for coloured people in that section, hence each family agreed to pay a certain amount per month, with the understanding that the teacher was to "board 'round"—that is, spend a day with each family. This was not bad for the teacher, for each family tried to provide the very best on the day the teacher was to be its guest. I recall that I looked forward with an anxious appetite to the "teacher's day" at our little cabin.

This experience of a whole race beginning to go to school for the first time, presents one of the most interesting studies that has ever occurred in connection with the development of any race. Few people who were not right in the midst of the scenes can form any exact idea of the intense desire which the people of my race showed for an education. As I have stated, it was a whole race trying to go to school. Few were too young, and none too old, to make the attempt to learn. As fast as any kind of teachers could be secured, not only were day-schools filled, but night-schools as well. The great ambition of the older people was to try to learn to read the Bible before they died. With this end in view, men and women who were fifty or seventy-five years old would often be found in the night-school. Sunday-schools were formed soon after freedom, but the principal book studied in the Sunday-school was the spelling-book. Day-school, night-school, Sunday-school, were always crowded, and often many had to be turned away for want of room.

The opening of the school in the Kanawha Valley, however, brought to me one of the keenest disappointments that I ever experienced. I had been working in a salt-furnace for several months, and my stepfather had discovered that I had a financial value, and so, when the school opened, he decided that he could not spare me from my work. This decision seemed to cloud my every ambition. The disappointment was made all the more severe by reason of the fact that my place of work was where I could see the happy children passing to and from school, mornings and afternoons. Despite this disappointment, however, I determined that I would learn something, anyway. I applied myself with greater earnestness than ever to the mastering of what was in the "blue-back" speller.

My mother sympathized with me in my disappointment, and sought to comfort me in all the ways she could, and to help me find a way to learn. After a while I succeeded in making arrangements with the teacher to give me some lessons at night, after the day's work was done. These night lessons were so welcome that I think I learned more at night than the other children did during the day. My own experiences in the night-school gave me faith in the night-school idea, with which, in after years, I had to do both at Hampton and Tuskegee. But my boyish heart was still set upon going to the day-school, and I let no opportunity slip to push my case. Finally I won, and was permitted to go to the school in the day for a few months, with the understanding that I was to rise early in the morning and work in the furnace till nine o'clock, and return immediately after school closed in the afternoon for at least two more hours of work.

The schoolhouse was some distance from the furnace, and as I had to work till nine o'clock, and the school opened at nine, I found myself in a difficulty. School would always be begun before I reached it, and sometimes my class had recited. To get around this difficulty I yielded to a temptation for which most people, I suppose, will condemn me; but since it is a fact, I might as well state it. I have great faith in the power and influence of facts. It is seldom that anything is permanently gained by holding back a fact. There was a large clock in a little office in the furnace. This clock, of course, all the hundred or more workmen depended upon to regulate their hours of beginning and ending the day's work. I got the idea that the way for me to reach school on time was to move the clock hands from half-past eight up to the nine o'clock mark. This I found myself doing morning after morning, till the furnace "boss" discovered that something was wrong, and locked the clock in a case. I did not mean to inconvenience any body. I simply meant to reach that schoolhouse in time.

When, however, I found myself at the school for the first time, I also found myself confronted with two other difficulties. In the first place, I found that all of the other children wore hats or caps on their heads, and I had neither hat nor cap. In fact, I do not remember that up to the time of going to school I had ever worn any kind of covering upon my head, nor do I recall that either I or anybody else had even thought anything about the need of covering for my head. But, of course, when I saw how all the other boys were dressed, I began to feel quite uncomfortable. As usual, I put the case before my mother, and she explained to me that she had no money with which to buy a "store hat," which was a rather new institution at that time among the members of my race and was considered quite the thing for young and old to own, but that she would find a way to help me out of the difficulty. She accordingly got two pieces of "homespun" (jeans) and sewed them together, and I was soon the proud possessor of my first cap.

The lesson that my mother taught me in this has always remained with me, and I have tried as best I could to teach it to others. I have always felt proud, whenever I think of the incident, that my mother had strength of character enough not to be led into the temptation of seeming to be that which she was not—of trying to impress my schoolmates and others with the fact that she was able to buy me a "store hat" when she was not. I have always felt proud that she refused to go into debt for that which she did not have the money to pay for. Since that time I have owned many kinds of caps and hats, but never one of which I have felt so proud as of the cap made of the two pieces of cloth sewed together by my mother. I have noted the fact, but without satisfaction, I need not add, that several of the boys who began their careers with "store hats" and who were my schoolmates and used to join in the sport that was made of me because I had only a "homespun" cap, have ended their careers in the penitentiary, while others are not able now to buy any kind of hat.

My second difficulty was with regard to my name, or rather *a* name. From the time when I could remember anything, I had been called simply "Booker." Before going to school it had never occurred to me that it was needful or appropriate to have an additional name. When I heard the school-roll called, I noticed that all of the children had at least two names, and some of them indulged in what seemed to me the extravagance of having three. I was in deep perplexity, because I knew that the teacher would demand of me at least two names, and I had only one. By the time the occasion came for the enrolling of my name, an idea occurred to me which I thought would make me equal to the situation; and so, when the teacher asked me what my full name was, I calmly told him "Booker Washington," as if I had been called by that name all my life; and by that name I have since been known. Later in my life I found that my mother had given me the name of "Booker Taliaferro" soon after I was born, but in some way that part of my name seemed to disappear, and for a long while was forgotten, but as soon as I found out about it I revived it, and made my full name "Booker Taliaferro Washington." I think there are not many men in our country who have had the privilege of naming themselves in the way that I have.

More than once I have tried to picture myself in the position of a boy or man with an honoured and distinguished ancestry which I could trace back through a period of hundreds of years, and who had not only inherited a name, but fortune and a proud family homestead; and yet I have sometimes had the feeling that if I had inherited these, and had been a member of a more popular race, I should have been inclined to yield to the temptation of depending upon my ancestry and my colour to do that for me which I should do for myself. Years ago I resolved that because I had no ancestry myself I would leave a record of which my children would be proud, and which might encourage them to still higher effort.

The world should not pass judgment upon the Negro, and especially the Negro youth, too quickly or too harshly. The Negro boy has obstacles, discouragements, and temptations to battle with that are little known to those not situated as he is. When a white boy undertakes a task, it is taken for granted that he will succeed. On the other hand, people are usually surprised if the Negro boy does not fail. In a word, the Negro youth starts out with the presumption against him.

The influence of ancestry, however, is important in helping forward any individual or race, if too much reliance is not placed upon it. Those who constantly direct attention to the Negro youth's moral weaknesses, and compare his advancement with that of white youths, do not consider the influence of the memories which cling about the old family homesteads. I have no idea, as I have stated elsewhere, who my grandmother was. I have, or have had, uncles and aunts and cousins, but I have no knowledge as to where most of them are. My case will illustrate that of hundreds of thousands of black people in every part of our country. The very fact that the white boy is conscious that, if he fails in life, he will disgrace the whole family record, extending back through many generations, is of tremendous value in helping him to resist temptations. The fact that the individual has behind and surrounding him proud family history and connection serves as a stimulus to help him to overcome obstacles when striving for success.

The time that I was permitted to attend school during the day was short, and my attendance was irregular. It was not long before I had to stop attending day-school altogether, and devote all of my time again to work. I resorted to the night-school again. In fact, the greater part of the education I secured in my boyhood was gathered through the night-school after my day's work was done. I had difficulty often in securing a satisfactory teacher. Sometimes, after I had secured some one to teach me at night, I would find, much to my disappointment, that the teacher knew but little more than I did. Often I would have to walk several miles at night in order to recite my night-school lessons. There was never a time in my youth, no matter how dark and discouraging the days might be, when one resolve did not continually remain with me, and that was a determination to secure an education at any cost.

Soon after we moved to West Virginia, my mother adopted into our family, notwithstanding our poverty, an orphan boy, to whom afterward we gave the name of James B. Washington. He has ever since remained a member of the family.

After I had worked in the salt-furnace for some time, work was secured for me in a coal-mine which was operated mainly for the purpose of securing fuel for the salt-furnace. Work in the coal-mine I always dreaded. One reason for this was that any one who worked in a coal-mine was always unclean, at least while at work, and it was a very hard job to get one's skin clean after the day's work was over. Then it was fully a mile from the opening of the coal-mine to the face of the coal, and all, of course, was in the blackest darkness. I do not believe that one ever experiences anywhere else such darkness as he does in a coal-mine. The mine was divided into a large number of different "rooms" or departments, and, as I never was able to learn the location of all these "rooms," I many times found myself lost in the mine. To add to the horror of being lost, sometimes my light would go out, and then, if I did not happen to have a match, I would wander about in the darkness until by chance I found some one to give me a light. The work was not only hard, but it was dangerous. There was always the danger of being blown to pieces by a premature explosion of powder, or of being crushed by falling slate. Accidents from one or the other of these causes were frequently occurring, and this kept me in constant fear. Many children of the tenderest years were compelled then, as is now true I fear, in most coal-mining districts, to spend a large part of their lives in these coal-mines, with little opportunity to get an education; and, what is worse, I have often noted that, as a rule, young boys who begin life in a coal-mine are often physically and mentally dwarfed. They soon lose ambition to do anything else than to continue as a coal-miner.

In those days, and later as a young man, I used to try to picture in my imagination the feelings and ambitions of a white boy with absolutely no limit placed upon his aspirations and activities. I used to envy the white boy who had no obstacles placed in the way of his becoming a Congressman, Governor, Bishop, or President by reason of the accident of his birth or race. I used to picture the way that I would act under such circumstances; how I would begin at the bottom and keep rising until I reached the highest round of success.

In later years, I confess that I do not envy the white boy as I once did. I have learned that success is to be measured not so much by the position that one has reached in life as by the obstacles which he has overcome while trying to succeed. Looked at from this standpoint, I almost reach the conclusion that often the Negro boy's birth and connection with an unpopular race is an advantage, so far as real life is concerned. With few exceptions, the Negro youth must work harder and must perform his task even better than a white youth in order to secure recognition. But out of the hard and unusual struggle through which he is compelled to pass, he gets a strength, a confidence, that one misses whose pathway is comparatively smooth by reason of birth and race.

From any point of view, I had rather be what I am, a member of the Negro race, than be able to claim membership with the most favoured of any other race. I have always been made sad when I have heard members of any race claiming rights and privileges, or certain badges of distinction, on the ground simply that they were members of this or that race, regardless of their own individual worth or attainments. I have been made to feel sad for such persons because I am conscious of the fact that mere connection with what is known as a superior race will not permanently carry an individual forward unless he has individual worth, and mere connection with what is regarded as an inferior race will not finally hold an individual back if he possesses intrinsic, individual merit. Every persecuted individual and race should get much consolation out of the great human law, which is universal and eternal, that merit, no matter under what skin found, is in the long run, recognized and rewarded. This I have said here, not to call attention to myself as an individual, but to the race to which I am proud to belong.

CHAPTER III

The Struggle for an Education

One day, while at work in the coal-mine, I happened to overhear two miners talking about a great school for coloured people somewhere in Virginia. This was the first time that I had ever heard anything about any kind of school or college that was more pretentious than the little coloured school in our town.

In the darkness of the mine I noiselessly crept as close as I could to the two men who were talking. I heard one tell the other that not only was the school established for the members of my race, but that opportunities were provided by which poor but worthy students could work out all or a part of the cost of board, and at the same time be taught some trade or industry.

As they went on describing the school, it seemed to me that it must be the greatest place on earth, and not even Heaven presented more attractions for me at that time than did the Hampton Normal and Agricultural Institute in Virginia, about which these men were talking. I resolved at once to go to that school, although I had no idea where it was, or how many miles away, or how I was going to reach it; I remembered only that I was on fire constantly with one ambition, and that was to go to Hampton. This thought was with me day and night.

After hearing of the Hampton Institute, I continued to work for a few months longer in the coal-mine. While at work there, I heard of a vacant position in the household of General Lewis Ruffner, the owner of the salt-furnace and coal-mine. Mrs. Viola Ruffner, the wife of General Ruffner, was a "Yankee" woman from Vermont. Mrs. Ruffner had a reputation all through the vicinity for being very strict with her servants, and especially with the boys who tried to serve her. Few of them had remained with her more than two or three weeks. They all left with the same excuse: she was too strict. I decided, however, that I would rather try Mrs. Ruffner's house than remain in the coal-mine, and so my mother applied to her for the vacant position. I was hired at a salary of $5 per month.

I had heard so much about Mrs. Ruffner's severity that I was almost afraid to see her, and trembled when I went into her presence. I had not lived with her many weeks, however, before I began to understand her. I soon began to learn that, first of all, she wanted everything kept clean about her, that she wanted things done promptly and systematically, and that at the bottom of everything she wanted absolute honesty and frankness. Nothing must be sloven or slipshod; every door, every fence, must be kept in repair.

I cannot now recall how long I lived with Mrs. Ruffner before going to Hampton, but I think it must have been a year and a half. At any rate, I here repeat what I have said more than once before, that the lessons that I learned in the home of Mrs. Ruffner were as valuable to me as any education I have ever gotten anywhere since. Even to this day I never see bits of paper scattered around a house or in the street that I do not want to pick them up at once. I never see a filthy yard that I do not want to clean it, a paling off of a fence that I do not want to put it on, an unpainted or unwhitewashed house that I do not want to paint or whitewash it, or a button off one's clothes, or a grease-spot on them or on a floor, that I do not want to call attention to it.

From fearing Mrs. Ruffner I soon learned to look upon her as one of my best friends. When she found that she could trust me she did so implicitly. During the one or two winters that I was with her she gave me an opportunity to go to school for an hour in the day during a portion of the winter months, but most of my studying was done at night, sometimes alone, sometimes under some one whom I could hire to teach me. Mrs. Ruffner always encouraged and sympathized with me in all my efforts to get an education. It was while living with her that I began to get together my first library. I secured a dry-goods box, knocked out one side of it, put some shelves in it, and began putting into it every kind of book that I could get my hands upon, and called it my "library."

Notwithstanding my success at Mrs. Ruffner's I did not give up the idea of going to the Hampton Institute. In the fall of 1872 I determined to make an effort to get there, although, as I have stated, I had no definite idea of the direction in which Hampton was, or of what it would cost to go there. I do not think that any one thoroughly sympathized with me in my ambition to go to Hampton unless it was my mother, and she was troubled with a grave fear that I was starting out on a "wild-goose chase." At any rate, I got only a half-hearted consent from her that I might start. The small amount of money that I had earned had been consumed by my stepfather and the remainder of the family, with the exception of a very few dollars, and so I had very little with which to buy clothes and pay my travelling expenses. My brother John helped me all that he could, but of course that was not a great deal, for his work was in the coal-mine, where he did not earn much, and most of what he did earn went in the direction of paying the household expenses.

Perhaps the thing that touched and pleased me most in connection with my starting for Hampton was the interest that many of the older coloured people took in the matter. They had spent the best days of their lives in slavery, and hardly expected to live to see the time when they would see a member of their race leave home to attend a boarding-school. Some of these older people would give me a nickel, others a quarter, or a handkerchief.

Finally the great day came, and I started for Hampton. I had only a small, cheap satchel that contained what few articles of clothing I could get. My mother at the time was rather weak and broken in health. I hardly expected to see her again, and thus our parting was all the more sad. She, however, was very brave through it all. At that time there were no through trains connecting that part of

West Virginia with eastern Virginia. Trains ran only a portion of the way, and the remainder of the distance was travelled by stage-coaches.

The distance from Malden to Hampton is about five hundred miles. I had not been away from home many hours before it began to grow painfully evident that I did not have enough money to pay my fare to Hampton. One experience I shall long remember. I had been travelling over the mountains most of the afternoon in an old-fashioned stage-coach, when, late in the evening, the coach stopped for the night at a common, unpainted house called a hotel. All the other passengers except myself were whites. In my ignorance I supposed that the little hotel existed for the purpose of accommodating the passengers who travelled on the stage-coach. The difference that the colour of one's skin would make I had not thought anything about. After all the other passengers had been shown rooms and were getting ready for supper, I shyly presented myself before the man at the desk. It is true I had practically no money in my pocket with which to pay for bed or food, but I had hoped in some way to beg my way into the good graces of the landlord, for at that season in the mountains of Virginia the weather was cold, and I wanted to get indoors for the night. Without asking as to whether I had any money, the man at the desk firmly refused to even consider the matter of providing me with food or lodging. This was my first experience in finding out what the colour of my skin meant. In some way I managed to keep warm by walking about, and so got through the night. My whole soul was so bent upon reaching Hampton that I did not have time to cherish any bitterness toward the hotel-keeper.

By walking, begging rides both in wagons and in the cars, in some way, after a number of days, I reached the city of Richmond, Virginia, about eighty-two miles from Hampton. When I reached there, tired, hungry, and dirty, it was late in the night. I had never been in a large city, and this rather added to my misery. When I reached Richmond, I was completely out of money. I had not a single acquaintance in the place, and, being unused to city ways, I did not know where to go. I applied at several places for lodging, but they all wanted money, and that was what I did not have. Knowing nothing else better to do, I walked the streets. In doing this I passed by many food-stands where fried chicken and half-moon apple pies were piled high and made to present a most tempting apearance. At that time it seemed to me that I would have promised all that I expected to possess in the future to have gotten hold of one of those chicken legs or one of those pies. But I could not get either of these, nor anything else to eat.

I must have walked the streets till after midnight. At last I became so exhausted that I could walk no longer. I was tired, I was hungry, I was everything but discouraged. Just about the time when I reached extreme physical exhaustion, I came upon a portion of a street where the board sidewalk was considerably elevated. I waited for a few minutes, till I was sure that no passers-by could see me, and then crept under the sidewalk and lay for the night upon the ground, with my satchel of clothing for a pillow. Nearly all night I could hear the tramp of feet over my head. The next morning I found myself somewhat refreshed, but I was extremely hungry, because it had been a long time since I had had sufficient food. As soon as it became light enough for me to see my surroundings I noticed that I was near a large ship, and that this ship seemed to be unloading a cargo of pig iron. I went at once to the vessel and asked the captain to permit me to help unload the vessel in order to get money for food. The captain, a white man, who seemed to be kind-hearted, consented. I worked long enough to earn money for my breakfast, and it seems to me, as I remember it now, to have been about the best breakfast that I have ever eaten.

My work pleased the captain so well that he told me if I desired I could continue working for a small amount per day. This I was very glad to do. I continued working on this vessel for a number of days. After buying food with the small wages I received there was not much left to add to the amount I must get to pay my way to Hampton. In order to economize in every way possible, so as to be sure to reach Hampton in a reasonable time, I continued to sleep under the sidewalk that gave me shelter the first night I was in Richmond. Many years after that the coloured citizens of Richmond very kindly tendered me a reception at which there must have been two thousand people present. This reception was held not far from the spot where I slept the first night I spent in that city, and I must confess that my mind was more upon the sidewalk that first gave me shelter than upon the reception, agreeable and cordial as it was.

When I had saved what I considered enough money with which to reach Hampton, I thanked the captain of the vessel for his kindness, and started again. Without any unusual occurrence I reached Hampton, with a surplus of exactly fifty cents with which to begin my education. To me it had been a long, eventful journey; but the first sight of the large, three-story, brick school building seemed to have rewarded me for all that I had undergone in order to reach the place. If the people who gave the money to provide that building could appreciate the influence the sight of it had upon me, as well as upon thousands of other youths, they would feel all the more encouraged to make such gifts. It seemed to me to be the largest and most beautiful building I had ever seen. The sight of it seemed to give me a new life. I felt that a new kind of existence had now begun—that life would now have a new meaning. I felt that I had reached the promised land, and I resolved to let no obstacle prevent me from putting forth the highest effort to fit myself to accomplish the most good in the world.

As soon as possible after reaching the grounds of the Hampton Institute, I presented myself before the head teacher for assignment to a class. Having been so long without proper food, a bath and change of clothing, I did not, of course, make a very favourable impression upon her, and I could see at once that there were doubts in her mind about the wisdom of admitting me as a student. I felt that I could hardly blame her if she got the idea that I was a worthless loafer or tramp. For some time she did not refuse to admit me, neither did she decide in my favour, and I continued to linger about her, and to impress her in all the ways I could with my worthiness. In the meantime I saw her admitting other students, and that added greatly to my discomfort, for I felt, deep down in my heart, that I could do as well as they, if I could only get a chance to show what was in me.

After some hours had passed, the head teacher said to

me: "The adjoining recitation-room needs sweeping. Take the broom and sweep it."

It occurred to me at once that here was my chance. Never did I receive an order with more delight. I knew that I could sweep, for Mrs. Ruffner had thoroughly taught me how to do that when I lived with her.

I swept the recitation-room three times. Then I got a dusting-cloth and I dusted it four times. All the woodwork around the walls, every bench, table, and desk, I went over four times with my dusting-cloth. Besides, every piece of furniture had been moved and every closet and corner in the room had been thoroughly cleaned. I had the feeling that in a large measure my future depended upon the impression I made upon the teacher in the cleaning of that room. When I was through, I reported to the head teacher. She was a "Yankee" woman who knew just where to look for dirt. She went into the room and inspected the floor and closets; then she took her handkerchief and rubbed it on the woodwork about the walls, and over the table and benches. When she was unable to find one bit of dirt on the floor, or a particle of dust on any of the furniture, she quietly remarked, "I guess you will do to enter this institution."

I was one of the happiest souls on earth. The sweeping of that room was my college examination, and never did any youth pass an examination for entrance into Harvard or Yale that gave him more genuine satisfaction. I have passed several examinations since then, but I have always felt that this was the best one I ever passed.

I have spoken of my own experience in entering the Hampton Institute. Perhaps few, if any, had anything like the same experience that I had, but about that same period there were hundreds who found their way to Hampton and other institutions after experiencing something of the same difficulties that I went through. The young men and women were determined to secure an education at any cost.

The sweeping of the recitation-room in the manner that I did it seems to have paved the way for me to get through Hampton. Miss Mary F. Mackie, the head teacher, offered me a position as janitor. This, of course, I gladly accepted, because it was a place where I could work out nearly all the cost of my board. The work was hard and taxing, but I stuck to it. I had a large number of rooms to care for, and had to work late into the night, while at the same time I had to rise by four o'clock in the morning, in order to build the fires and have a little time in which to prepare my lessons. In all my career at Hampton, and ever since I have been out in the world, Miss Mary F. Mackie, the head teacher to whom I have referred, proved one of my strongest and most helpful friends. Her advice and encouragement were always helpful and strengthening to me in the darkest hour.

I have spoken of the impression that was made upon me by the buildings and general appearance of the Hampton Institute, but I have not spoken of that which made the greatest and most lasting impression upon me, and that was a great man—the noblest, rarest human being that it has ever been my privilege to meet. I refer to the late General Samuel C. Armstrong.

It has been my fortune to meet personally many of what are called great characters, both in Europe and America, but I do not hesitate to say that I never met any man who, in my estimation, was the equal of General Armstrong. Fresh from the degrading influences of the slave plantation and the coal-mines, it was a rare privilege for me to be permitted to come into direct contact with such a character as General Armstrong. I shall always remember that the first time I went into his presence he made the impression upon me of being a perfect man: I was made to feel that there was something about him that was superhuman. It was my privilege to know the General personally from the time I entered Hampton till he died, and the more I saw of him the greater he grew in my estimation. One might have removed from Hampton all the buildings, class-rooms, teachers, and industries, and given the men and women there the opportunity of coming into daily contact with General Armstrong, and that alone would have been a liberal education. The older I grow, the more I am convinced that there is no education which one can get from books and costly apparatus that is equal to that which can be gotten from contact with great men and women. Instead of studying books so constantly, how I wish that our schools and colleges might learn to study men and things!

General Armstrong spent two of the last six months of

his life in my home at Tuskegee. At that time he was paralyzed to the extent that he had lost control of his body and voice in a very large degree. Notwithstanding his affliction, he worked almost constantly night and day for the cause to which he had given his life. I never saw a man who so completely lost sight of himself. I do not believe he ever had a selfish thought. He was just as happy in trying to assist some other institution in the South as he was when working for Hampton. Although he fought the Southern white man in the Civil War, I never heard him utter a bitter word against him afterward. On the other hand, he was constantly seeking to find ways by which he could be of service to the Southern whites.

It would be difficult to describe the hold that he had upon the students at Hampton, or the faith they had in him. In fact, he was worshipped by his students. It never occurred to me that General Armstrong could fail in anything that he undertook. There is almost no request that he could have made that would not have been complied with. When he was a guest at my home in Alabama, and was so badly paralyzed that he had to be wheeled about in an invalid's chair, I recall that one of the General's former students had occasion to push his chair up a long, steep hill that taxed his strength to the utmost. When the top of the hill was reached, the former pupil, with a glow of happiness on his face, exclaimed, "I am so glad that I have been permitted to do something that was real hard for the General before he dies!" While I was a student at Hampton, the dormitories became so crowded that it was impossible to find room for all who wanted to be admitted. In order to help remedy the difficulty the General conceived the plan of putting up tents to be used as rooms. As soon as it became known that General Armstrong would be pleased if some of the older students would live in the tents during the winter, nearly every student in school volunteered to go.

I was one of the volunteers. The winter that we spent in those tents was an intensely cold one, and we suffered severely—how much I am sure General Armstrong never knew, because we made no complaints. It was enough for us to know that we were pleasing General Armstrong, and that we were making it possible for an additional number of students to secure an education. More than once, during a cold night, when a stiff gale would be blowing, our tent was lifted bodily, and we would find ourselves in the open air. The General would usually pay a visit to the tents early in the morning, and his earnest, cheerful, encouraging voice would dispel any feeling of despondency.

I have spoken of my admiration for General Armstrong, and yet he was but a type of that Christlike body of men and women who went into the Negro schools at the close of the war by the hundreds to assist in lifting up my race. The history of the world fails to show a higher, purer, and more unselfish class of men and women than those who found their way into those Negro schools.

Life at Hampton was a constant revelation to me; was constantly taking me into a new world. The matter of having meals at regular hours, of eating on a tablecloth, using a napkin, the use of the bathtub and of the toothbrush, as well as the use of sheets upon the bed, were all new to me.

I sometimes feel that almost the most valuable lesson I got at the Hampton Institute was in the use and value of the bath. I learned there for the first time some of its value, not only in keeping the body healthy, but in inspiring self-respect and promoting virtue. In all my travels in the South and elsewhere since leaving Hampton I have always in some way sought my daily bath. To get it sometimes when I have been the guest of my own people in a single-roomed cabin has not always been easy to do, except by slipping away to some stream in the woods. I have always tried to teach my people that some provision for bathing should be a part of every house.

For some time, while a student at Hampton, I possessed but a single pair of socks, but when I had worn these till they became soiled, I would wash them at night and hang them by the fire to dry, so that I might wear them again the next morning.

The charge for my board at Hampton was ten dollars per month. I was expected to pay a part of this in cash and to work out the remainder. To meet this cash payment, as I have stated, I had just fifty cents when I reached the institution. Aside from a very few dollars that my brother John was able to send me once in a while,

I had no money with which to pay my board. I was determined from the first to make my work as janitor so valuable that my services would be indispensable. This I succeeded in doing to such an extent that I was soon informed that I would be allowed the full cost of my board in return for my work. The cost of tuition was seventy dollars a year. This, of course, was wholly beyond my ability to provide. If I had been compelled to pay the seventy dollars for tuition, in addition to providing for my board, I would have been compelled to leave the Hampton school. General Armstrong, however, very kindly got Mr. S. Griffitts Morgan, of New Bedford, Mass., to defray the cost of my tuition during the whole time that I was at Hampton. After I finished the course at Hampton and had entered upon my lifework at Tuskegee, I had the pleasure of visiting Mr. Morgan several times.

After having been for a while at Hampton, I found myself in difficulty because I did not have books and clothing. Usually, however, I got around the trouble about books by borrowing from those who were more fortunate than myself. As to clothes, when I reached Hampton I had practically nothing. Everything that I possessed was in a small hand satchel. My anxiety about clothing was increased because of the fact that General Armstrong made a personal inspection of the young men in ranks, to see that their clothes were clean. Shoes had to be polished, there must be no buttons off the clothing, and no grease-spots. To wear one suit of clothes continually, while at work and in the schoolroom, and at the same time keep it clean, was rather a hard problem for me to solve. In some way I managed to get on till the teachers learned that I was in earnest and meant to succeed, and then some of them were kind enough to see that I was partly supplied with second-hand clothing that had been sent in barrels from the North. These barrels proved a blessing to hundreds of poor but deserving students. Without them I question whether I should ever have gotten through Hampton.

When I first went to Hampton I do not recall that I had ever slept in a bed that had two sheets on it. In those days there were not many buildings there, and room was very precious. There were seven other boys in the same room with me; most of them, however, students who had been there for some time. The sheets were quite a puzzle to me. The first night I slept under both of them, and the second night I slept on top of both of them; but by watching the other boys I learned my lesson in this, and have been trying to follow it ever since and to teach it to others.

I was among the youngest of the students who were in Hampton at that time. Most of the students were men and women—some as old as forty years of age. As I now recall the scene of my first year, I do not believe that one often has the opportunity of coming into contact with three or four hundred men and women who were so tremendously in earnest as these men and women were. Every hour was occupied in study or work. Nearly all had had enough actual contact with the world to teach them the need of education. Many of the older ones were, of course, too old to master the text-books very thoroughly, and it was often sad to watch their struggles; but they made up in earnestness much of what they lacked in books. Many of them were as poor as I was, and, besides having to wrestle with their books, they had to struggle with a poverty which prevented their having the necessities of life. Many of them had aged parents who were dependent upon them, and some of them were men who had wives whose support in some way they had to provide for.

The great and prevailing idea that seemed to take possession of every one was to prepare himself to lift up the people at his home. No one seemed to think of himself. And the officers and teachers, what a rare set of human beings they were! They worked for the students night and day, in season and out of season. They seemed happy only when they were helping the students in some manner. Whenever it is written—and I hope it will be—the part that the Yankee teachers played in the education of the Negroes immediately after the war will make one of the most thrilling parts of the history of this country. The time is not far distant when the whole South will appreciate this service in a way that it has not yet been able to do.

CHAPTER IV

Helping Others

At the end of my first year at Hampton I was confronted with another difficulty. Most of the students went home to spend their vacation. I had no money with which to go home, but I had to go somewhere. In those days very few students were permitted to remain at the school during vacation. It made me feel very sad and homesick to see the other students preparing to leave and starting for home. I not only had no money with which to go home, but I had none with which to go anywhere.

In some way, however, I had gotten hold of an extra, second-hand coat which I thought was a pretty valuable coat. This I decided to sell, in order to get a little money for travelling expenses. I had a good deal of boyish pride, and I tried to hide, as far as I could, from the other students the fact that I had no money and nowhere to go. I made it known to a few people in the town of Hampton that I had this coat to sell, and, after a good deal of persuading, one coloured man promised to come to my room to look the coat over and consider the matter of buying it. This cheered my drooping spirits considerably. Early the next morning the prospective customer appeared. After looking the garment over carefully, he asked me how much I wanted for it. I told him I thought it was worth three dollars. He seemed to agree with me as to price, but remarked in the most matter-of-fact way: "I tell you what I will do; I will take the coat, and I will pay you five cents, cash down, and pay you the rest of the money just as soon as I can get it." It is not hard to imagine what my feelings were at the time.

With this disappointment I gave up all hope of getting out of the town of Hampton for my vacation work. I wanted very much to go where I might secure work that would at least pay me enough to purchase some much-needed clothing and other necessities. In a few days practically all the students and teachers had left for their homes, and this served to depress my spirits even more.

After trying for several days in and near the town of Hampton, I finally secured work in a restaurant at Fortress Monroe. The wages, however, were very little more than my board. At night, and between meals, I found considerable time for study and reading; and in this direction I improved myself very much during the summer.

When I left school at the end of my first year, I owed the institution sixteen dollars that I had not been able to work out. It was my greatest ambition during the summer to save money enough with which to pay this debt. I felt that this was a debt of honour, and that I could hardly bring myself to the point of even trying to enter school again till it was paid. I economized in every way that I could think of—did my own washing, and went without necessary garments—but still I found my summer vacation ending and I did not have the sixteen dollars.

One day, during the last week of my stay in the restaurant, I found under one of the tables a crisp, new ten-dollar bill. I could hardly contain myself, I was so happy. As it was not my place of business I felt it to be the proper thing to show the money to the proprietor. This I did. He seemed as glad as I was, but he coolly explained to me that, as it was his place of business, he had a right to keep the money, and he proceeded to do so. This, I confess, was another pretty hard blow to me. I will not say that I became discouraged, for as I now look back over my life I do not recall that I ever became discouraged over anything that I set out to accomplish. I have begun everything with the idea that I could succeed, and I never had much patience with the multitudes of people who are always ready to explain why one cannot succeed. I have always had a high regard for the man who could tell me how to succeed. I determined to face the situation just as it was. At the end of the week I went to the treasurer of the Hampton Institute, General J. F. B. Marshall, and told him frankly my condition. To my gratification he told me that I could reënter the institution, and that he would trust me to pay the debt when I could. During the second year I continued to work as a janitor.

The education that I received at Hampton out of the text-books was but a small part of what I learned there. One of the things that impressed itself upon me deeply, the second year, was the unselfishness of the teachers. It was hard for me to understand how any individuals could bring themselves to the point where they could be so happy in working for others. Before the end of the year, I think I began learning that those who are happiest are those who do the most for others. This lesson I have tried to carry with me ever since.

I also learned a valuable lesson at Hampton by coming into contact with the best breeds of live stock and fowls. No student, I think, who has had the opportunity of doing this could go out into the world and content himself with the poorest grades.

Perhaps the most valuable thing that I got out of my second year was an understanding of the use and value of the Bible. Miss Nathalie Lord, one of the teachers, from Portland, Me., taught me how to use and love the Bible. Before this I had never cared a great deal about it, but now I learned to love to read the Bible, not only for the spiritual help which it gives, but on account of it as literature. The lessons taught me in this respect took such a hold upon me that at the present time, when I am at home, no matter how busy I am, I always make it a rule to read a chapter or a portion of a chapter in the morning, before beginning the work of the day.

Whatever ability I may have as a public speaker I owe in a measure to Miss Lord. When she found out that I had some inclination in this direction, she gave me private lessons in the matter of breathing, emphasis, and articulation. Simply to be able to talk in public for the sake of talking has never had the least attraction for me. In fact,

I consider that there is nothing so empty and unsatisfactory as mere abstract public speaking; but from my early childhood I have had a desire to do something to make the world better, and then to be able to speak to the world about that thing.

The debating societies at Hampton were a constant source of delight to me. These were held on Saturday evening; and during my whole life at Hampton I do not recall that I missed a single meeting. I not only attended the weekly debating society, but was instrumental in organizing an additional society. I noticed that between the time when supper was over and the time to begin evening study there were about twenty minutes which the young men usually spent in idle gossip. About twenty of us formed a society for the purpose of utilizing this time in debate or in practice in public speaking. Few persons ever derived more happiness or benefit from the use of twenty minutes of time than we did in this way.

At the end of my second year at Hampton, by the help of some money sent me by my mother and brother John, supplemented by a small gift from one of the teachers at Hampton, I was enabled to return to my home in Malden, West Virginia, to spend my vacation. When I reached home I found that the salt-furnaces were not running, and that the coal-mine was not being operated on account of the miners being out on a "strike." This was something which, it seemed, usually occurred whenever the men got two or three months ahead in their savings. During the strike, of course, they spent all that they had saved, and would often return to work in debt at the same wages, or would move to another mine at considerable expense. In either case, my observations convinced me that the miners were worse off at the end of a strike. Before the days of strikes in that section of the country, I knew miners who had considerable money in the bank, but as soon as the professional labour agitators got control, the savings of even the more thrifty ones began disappearing.

My mother and the other members of the family were, of course, much rejoiced to see me and to note the improvement that I had made during my two years' absence. The rejoicing on the part of all classes of the coloured people, and especially the older ones, over my return, was almost pathetic. I had to pay a visit to each family and take a meal with each, and at each place tell the story of my experiences at Hampton. In addition to this I had to speak before the church and Sunday-school, and at various other places. The thing that I was most in search of, though, work, I could not find. There was no work on account of the strike. I spent nearly the whole of the first month of my vacation in an effort to find something to do by which I could earn money to pay my way back to Hampton and save a little money to use after reaching there.

Toward the end of the first month, I went to a place a considerable distance from my home, to try to find employment. I did not succeed, and it was night before I got started on my return. When I had gotten within a mile or so of my home I was so completely tired out that I could not walk any farther, and I went into an old, abandoned house to spend the remainder of the night. About three o'clock in the morning my brother John found me asleep in this house, and broke to me, as gently as he could, the sad news that our dear mother had died during the night.

This seemed to me the saddest and blankest moment in my life. For several years my mother had not been in good health, but I had no idea, when I parted from her the previous day, that I should never see her alive again. Besides that, I had always had an intense desire to be with her when she did pass away. One of the chief ambitions which spurred me on at Hampton was that I might be able to get to be in a position in which I could better make my mother comfortable and happy. She had so often expressed the wish that she might be permitted to live to see her children educated and started out into the world.

In a very short time after the death of my mother our little home was in confusion. My sister Amanda, although she tried to do the best she could, was too young to know anything about keeping house, and my stepfather was not able to hire a housekeeper. Sometimes we had food cooked for us, and sometimes we did not. I remember that more than once a can of tomatoes and some crackers constituted a meal. Our clothing went uncared for, and everything about our home was soon in a tumble-down condition. It seems to me that this was the most dismal period of my life.

My good friend Mrs. Ruffner, to whom I have already referred, always made me welcome at her home, and assisted me in many ways during this trying period. Before the end of the vacation she gave me some work, and this, together with work in a coal-mine at some distance from my home, enabled me to earn a little money.

At one time it looked as if I would have to give up the idea of returning to Hampton, but my heart was so set on returning that I determined not to give up going back without a struggle. I was very anxious to secure some clothes for the winter, but in this I was disappointed, except for a few garments which my brother John secured for me. Notwithstanding my need for money and clothing, I was very happy in the fact that I had secured enough money to pay my travelling expenses back to Hampton.

Once there, I knew that I could make myself so useful as a janitor that I could in some way get through the school year.

Three weeks before the time for the opening of the term at Hampton, I was pleasantly surprised to receive a letter from my good friend Miss Mary F. Mackie, the lady principal, asking me to return to Hampton two weeks before the opening of the school, in order that I might assist her in cleaning the buildings and getting things in order for the new school year. This was just the opportunity I wanted. It gave me a chance to secure a credit in the treasurer's office. I started for Hampton at once.

During these two weeks I was taught a lesson which I shall never forget. Miss Mackie was a member of one of the oldest and most cultured families of the North, and yet for two weeks she worked by my side cleaning windows, dusting rooms, putting beds in order, and what not. She felt that things would not be in condition for the opening of school unless every window-pane was perfectly clean, and she took the greatest satisfaction in helping to clean them herself. The work which I have described she did every year that I was at Hampton.

It was hard for me at this time to understand how a woman of her education and social standing could take such delight in performing such service, in order to assist in the elevation of an unfortunate race. Ever since then I have had no patience with any school for my race in the South which did not teach its students the dignity of labour.

During my last year at Hampton every minute of my time that was not occupied with my duties as janitor was devoted to hard study. I was determined, if possible, to make such a record in my class as would cause me to be placed on the "honour roll" of Commencement speakers. This I was successful in doing. It was June of 1875 when I finished the regular course of study at Hampton. The greatest benefits that I got out of my life at the Hampton Institute, perhaps, may be classified under two heads:—

First was contact with a great man, General S. C. Armstrong, who, I repeat, was, in my opinion, the rarest, strongest, and most beautiful character that it has ever been my privilege to meet.

Second, at Hampton, for the first time, I learned what education was expected to do for an individual. Before going there I had a good deal of the then rather prevalent idea among our people that to secure an education meant to have a good, easy time, free from all necessity for manual labour. At Hampton I not only learned that it was not a disgrace to labour, but learned to love labour, not alone for its financial value, but for labour's own sake and for the independence and self-reliance which the ability to do something which the world wants done brings. At that institution I got my first taste of what it meant to live a life of unselfishness, my first knowledge of the fact that the happiest individuals are those who do the most to make others useful and happy.

I was completely out of money when I graduated. In company with other Hampton students, I secured a place as a table waiter in a summer hotel in Connecticut, and managed to borrow enough money with which to get there. I had not been in this hotel long before I found out that I knew practically nothing about waiting on a hotel table. The head waiter, however, supposed that I was an accomplished waiter. He soon gave me charge of a table at which there sat four or five wealthy and rather aristocratic people. My ignorance of how to wait upon them was so apparent that they scolded me in such a severe manner that I became frightened and left their table, leaving them sitting there without food. As a result of this

I was reduced from the position of waiter to that of a dish-carrier.

But I determined to learn the business of waiting, and did so within a few weeks and was restored to my former position. I have had the satisfaction of being a guest in this hotel several times since I was a waiter there.

At the close of the hotel season I returned to my former home in Malden, and was elected to teach the coloured school at that place. This was the beginning of one of the happiest periods of my life. I now felt that I had the opportunity to help the people of my home town to a higher life. I felt from the first that mere book education was not all that the young people of that town needed. I began my work at eight o'clock in the morning, and, as a rule, it did not end until ten o'clock at night. In addition to the usual routine of teaching, I taught the pupils to comb their hair, and to keep their hands and faces clean, as well as their clothing. I gave special attention to teaching them the proper use of the tooth-brush and the bath. In all my teaching I have watched carefully the influence of the tooth-brush, and I am convinced that there are few single agencies of civilization that are more far-reaching.

There were so many of the older boys and girls in the town, as well as men and women, who had to work in the daytime but still were craving an opportunity for some education, that I soon opened a night-school. From the first, this was crowded every night, being about as large as the school that I taught in the day. The efforts of some of the men and women, who in many cases were over fifty years of age, to learn, were in some cases very pathetic.

My day and night school work was not all that I undertook. I established a small reading-room and a debating society. On Sundays I taught two Sunday-schools, one in the town of Malden in the afternoon, and the other in the morning at a place three miles distant from Malden. In addition to this, I gave private lessons to several young men whom I was fitting to send to the Hampton Institute. Without regard to pay and with little thought of it, I taught any one who wanted to learn anything that I could teach him. I was supremely happy in the opportunity of being able to assist somebody else.

I did receive, however, a small salary from the public fund, for my work as a public-school teacher.

During the time that I was a student at Hampton my older brother, John, not only assisted me all that he could, but worked all of the time in the coal-mines in order to support the family. He willingly neglected his own education that he might help me. It was my earnest wish to help him to prepare to enter Hampton, and to save money to assist him in his expenses there. Both of these objects I was successful in accomplishing. In three years my brother finished the course at Hampton, and he is now holding the important position of Superintendent of Industries at Tuskegee. When he returned from Hampton, we both combined our efforts and savings to send our adopted brother, James, through the Hampton Institute. This we succeeded in doing, and he is now the postmaster at the Tuskegee Institute. The year 1877, which was my second year of teaching in Malden, I spent very much as I did the first.

It was while my home was at Malden that what was known as the "Ku Klux Klan" was in the height of its activity. The "Ku Klux" were bands of men who had joined themselves together for the purpose of regulating the conduct of the coloured people, especially with the object of preventing the members of the race from exercising any influence in politics. They corresponded somewhat to the "patrollers" of whom I used to hear a great deal during the days of slavery, when I was a small boy. The "patrollers" were bands of white men—usually young men—who were organized largely for the purpose of regulating the conduct of the slaves at night in such matters as preventing the slaves from going from one plantation to another without passes, and for preventing them from holding any kind of meetings without permission and without the presence at these meetings of at least one white man.

Like the "patrollers" the "Ku Klux" operated almost wholly at night. They were, however, more cruel than the "patrollers." Their objects, in the main, were to crush out the political aspirations of the Negroes, but they did not confine themselves to this, because schoolhouses as well as churches were burned by them, and many innocent persons were made to suffer. During this period not a few coloured people lost their lives.

As a young man, the acts of these lawless bands made a great impression upon me. I saw one open battle take place at Malden between some of the coloured and white people. There must have been not far from a hundred persons engaged on each side; many on both sides were seriously injured, among them being General Lewis Ruffner, the husband of my friend Mrs. Viola Ruffner. General Ruffner tried to defend the coloured people, and for this he was knocked down and so seriously wounded that he never completely recovered. It seemed to me as I watched this struggle between members of the two races, that there was no hope for our people in this country. The "Ku Klux" period was, I think, the darkest part of the Reconstruction days.

I have referred to this unpleasant part of the history of the South simply for the purpose of calling attention to the great change that has taken place since the days of the "Ku Klux." To-day there are no such organizations in the South, and the fact that such ever existed is almost forgotten by both races. There are few places in the South now where public sentiment would permit such organizations to exist.

CHAPTER V

The Reconstruction Period

The years from 1867 to 1878 I think may be called the period of Reconstruction. This included the time that I spent as a student at Hampton and as a teacher in West Virginia. During the whole of the Reconstruction period two ideas were constantly agitating the minds of the coloured people, or, at least, the minds of a large part of the race. One of these was the craze for Greek and Latin learning, and the other was a desire to hold office.

It could not have been expected that a people who had spent generations in slavery, and before that generations in the darkest heathenism, could at first form any proper conception of what an education meant. In every part of the South, during the Reconstruction period, schools, both day and night, were filled to overflowing with people of all ages and conditions, some being as far along in age as sixty and seventy years. The ambition to secure an education was most praiseworthy and encouraging. The idea, however, was too prevalent that, as soon as one secured a little education, in some unexplainable way he would be free from most of the hardships of the world, and, at any rate, could live without manual labour. There was a further feeling that a knowledge however little, of the Greek and Latin languages would make one a very superior human being, something bordering almost on the supernatural. I remember that the first coloured man whom I saw who knew something about foreign languages impressed me at that time as being a man of all others to be envied.

Naturally, most of our people who received some little education became teachers or preachers. While among these two classes there were many capable, earnest, godly men and women, still a large proportion took up teaching or preaching as an easy way to make a living. Many became teachers who could do little more than write their names. I remember there came into our neighbourhood one of this class, who was in search of a school to teach, and the question arose while he was there as to the shape of the earth and how he would teach the children concerning this subject. He explained his position in the matter by saying that he was prepared to teach that the earth was either flat or round, according to the preference of a majority of his patrons.

The ministry was the profession that suffered most—and still suffers, though there has been great improvement—on account of not only ignorant but in many cases immoral men who claimed that they were "called to preach." In the earlier days of freedom almost every coloured man who learned to read would receive "a call to preach" within a few days after he began reading. At my home in West Virginia the process of being called to the ministry was a very interesting one. Usually the "call" came when the individual was sitting in church. Without warning the one called would fall upon the floor as if struck by a bullet, and would lie there for hours, speechless and motionless. Then the news would spread all through the neighbourhood that this individual had received a "call." If he were inclined to resist the summons, he would fall or be made to fall a second or third time. In the end he always yielded to the call. While I wanted an education badly, I confess that in my youth I had a fear that when I had learned to read and write well I would receive one of these "calls"; but, for some reason, my call never came.

When we add the number of wholly ignorant men who preached or "exhorted" to that of those who possessed something of an education, it can be seen at a glance that the supply of ministers was large. In fact, some time ago I knew a certain church that had a total membership of about two hundred, and eighteen of that number were ministers. But, I repeat, in many communities in the South the character of the ministry is being improved, and I believe that within the next two or three decades a very large proportion of the unworthy ones will have disappeared. The "calls" to preach, I am glad to say, are not nearly so numerous now as they were formerly, and the calls to some industrial occupations are growing more numerous. The improvement that has taken place in the character of the teachers is even more marked than in the case of the ministers.

During the whole of the Reconstruction period our people throughout the South looked to the Federal Government for everything, very much as a child looks to its mother. This was not unnatural. The central government gave them freedom, and the whole Nation had been enriched for more than two centuries by the labour of the Negro. Even as a youth, and later in manhood, I had the feeling that it was cruelly wrong in the central government, at the beginning of our freedom, to fail to make some provision for the general education of our people in addition to what the states might do, so that the people would be the better prepared for the duties of citizenship.

It is easy to find fault, to remark what might have been done, and perhaps, after all, and under all the circumstances, those in charge of the conduct of affairs did the only thing that could be done at the time. Still, as I look back now over the entire period of our freedom, I cannot help feeling that it would have been wiser if some plan could have been put in operation which would have made the possession of a certain amount of education or property, or both, a test for the exercise of the franchise, and a way provided by which this test should be made to apply honestly and squarely to both the white and black races.

Though I was but little more than a youth during the period of Reconstruction, I had the feeling that mistakes were being made, and that things could not remain in the condition that they were in then very long. I felt that the Reconstruction policy, so far as it related to my race, was in a large measure on a false foundation, was artificial and forced. In many cases it seemed to me that the ignorance of my race was being used as a tool with which to help white men into office, and that there was an element in the North which wanted to punish the Southern white men by forcing the Negro into positions over the heads of the Southern whites. I felt that the Negro would be the one to suffer for this in the end. Besides, the general political agitation drew the attention of our people away from the more fundamental matters of perfecting themselves in the industries at their doors and in securing property.

The temptations to enter political life were so alluring that I came very near yielding to them at one time, but I was kept from doing so by the feeling that I would be helping in a more substantial way by assisting in the laying of the foundation of the race through a generous education of the hand, head, and heart. I saw coloured men who were members of the state legislatures, and county officers, who, in some cases, could not read or write, and whose morals were as weak as their education. Not long ago, when passing through the streets of a certain city in the South, I heard some brick-masons calling out, from the top of a two-story brick building on which they were working, for the "Governor" to "hurry up and bring up some more bricks." Several times I heard the command, "Hurry up, Governor!" "Hurry up, Governor!" My curiosity was aroused to such an extent that I made inquiry as to who the "Governor" was, and soon found that he was a coloured man who at one time had held the position of Lieutenant-Governor of his state.

But not all the coloured people who were in office during Reconstruction were unworthy of their positions, by any means. Some of them, like the late Senator B. K. Bruce, Governor Pinchback, and many others, were strong, upright, useful men. Neither were all the class designated as carpetbaggers dishonourable men. Some of them, like ex-Govenor Bullock, of Georgia, were men of high character and usefulness.

Of course the coloured people, so largely without education, and wholly without experience in government, made tremendous mistakes, just as any people similarly situated would have done. Many of the Southern whites have a feeling that, if the Negro is permitted to exercise his political rights now to any degree, the mistakes of the Reconstruction period will repeat themselves. I do not think this would be true, because the Negro is a much stronger and wiser man than he was thirty-five years ago, and he is fast learning the lesson that he cannot afford to act in a manner that will alienate his Southern white neighbours from him. More and more I am convinced that the final solution of the political end of our race problem will be for each state that finds it necessary to change the law bearing upon the franchise to make the law apply with absolute honesty, and without opportunity for double dealing or evasion, to both races alike. Any other course my daily observation in the South convinces me, will be unjust to the Negro, unjust to the white man, and unfair to the rest of the states in the Union, and will be, like slavery, a sin that at some time we shall have to pay for.

In the fall of 1878, after having taught school in Malden for two years, and after I had succeeded in preparing several of the young men and women, besides my two brothers, to enter the Hampton Institute, I decided to spend some months in study at Washington, D.C. I remained there for eight months. I derived a great deal of benefit from the studies which I pursued, and I came into contact with some strong men and women. At the institution I attended there was no industrial training given to the students, and I had an opportunity of comparing the influence of an institution with no industrial training with that of one like the Hampton Institute, that emphasized the industries. At this school I found the students, in most cases, had more money, were better dressed, wore the latest style of all manner of clothing and in some cases were more brilliant mentally. At Hampton it was a standing rule that, while the institution would be responsible for securing some one to pay the tuition for the students, the men and women themselves must provide for their own board, books, clothing, and room wholly by work, or partly by work and partly in cash. At the institution at which I now was, I found that a large proportion of the students by some means had their personal expenses paid for them. At Hampton the student was constantly making the effort through the industries to help himself, and that very effort was of immense value in character-building. The students at the other school seemed to be less self-dependent. They seemed to give more attention to mere outward appearances. In a word, they did not appear to me to be beginning at the bottom, on a real, solid foundation, to the extent that they were at Hampton. They knew more about Latin and Greek when they left school, but they seemed to know less about life and its conditions as they would meet it at their homes. Having lived for a number of years in the midst of comfortable surroundings, they were not as much inclined as the Hampton students to go into the country districts of the South, where there was little of comfort, to take up work for our people, and they were more inclined to yield to the temptation to become hotel waiters and Pullman-car porters as their life-work.

During the time I was a student in Washington the city was crowded with coloured people, many of whom had recently come from the South. A large proportion of these people had been drawn to Washington because they felt that they could lead a life of ease there. Others had secured minor government positions, and still another large class was there in the hope of securing Federal positions. A number of coloured men—some of them very strong and brilliant—were in the House of Representatives at that time, and one, the Hon. B. K. Bruce, was in the Senate. All this tended to make Washington an attractive place for members of the coloured race. Then, too, they knew that at all times they could have the protection of the law in the District of Columbia. The public schools in Washington for coloured people were better there than they were elsewhere. I took great interest in studying the life of our people there closely at that time. I found that while among them there was a large element of substantial, worthy citizens, there was also a superficiality about the life of a large class that greatly alarmed me. I saw young coloured men who were not earning more than four dollars a week spend two dollars or more for a buggy on Sunday to ride up and down Pennsylvania Avenue in order that they might try to convince the world that they were worth thousands. I saw other young men who received seventy-five or one hundred dollars per month from the Government, who were in debt at the end of every month. I saw men who but a few months previous were members of Congress, then without employment and in poverty. Among a large class there seemed to be a dependence upon the Government of every conceivable thing. The members of this class had little ambition to create a position for themselves, but wanted the Federal officials to create one for them. How many times I wished then, and have often wished since, that by some power of magic I might remove the great bulk of these people into the country districts and plant them upon the soil, upon the solid and never deceptive foundation of Mother Nature, where all nations and races that have ever succeeded have gotten their start,—a start that at first may be slow and toilsome, but one that nevertheless is real.

In Washington I saw girls whose mothers were earning their living by laundrying. These girls were taught by their mothers, in rather a crude way it is true, the industry of laundrying. Later these girls entered the public schools and remained there perhaps six or eight years. When the public-school course was finally finished, they wanted more costly dresses, more costly hats and shoes. In a word, while their wants had been increased, their ability to supply their wants had not been increased in the same degree. On the other hand, their six or eight years of book education had weaned them away from the occupation of their mothers. The result of this was in too many cases that the girls went to the bad. I often thought how much wiser it would have been to give these girls the same amount of mental training—and I favour any kind of training, whether in the languages or mathematics, that gives strength and culture to the mind—but at the same time to give them the most thorough training in the latest and best methods of laundrying and other kindred occupations.

CHAPTER VI

Black Race and Red Race

During the year that I spent in Washington, and for some little time before this there had been considerable agitation in the state of West Virginia over the question of moving the capital of the state from Wheeling to some other central point. As a result of this, the Legislature designated three cities to be voted upon by the citizens of the state as the permanent seat of government. Among these cities was Charleston, only five miles from Malden, my home. At the close of my school year in Washington I was very pleasantly surprised to receive, from a committee of white people in Charleston, an invitation to canvass the state in the interests of that city. This invitation I accepted, and spent nearly three months in speaking in various parts of the state. Charleston was successful in winning the prize, and is now the permanent seat of government.

The reputation that I made as a speaker during this campaign induced a number of persons to make an earnest effort to get me to enter political life, but I refused, still believing that I could find other service which would prove of more permanent value to my race. Even then I had a strong feeling that what our people most needed was to get a foundation in education, industry, and property, and for this I felt that they could better afford to strive than for political preferment. As for my individual self, it appeared to me to be reasonably certain that I could succeed in political life, but I had a feeling that it would be a rather selfish kind of success—individual success at the cost of failing to do my duty in assisting in laying a foundation for the masses.

As this period in the progress of our race a very large proportion of the young men who went to school or to college did so with the expressed determination to prepare themselves to be great lawyers, or Congressmen, and many of the women planned to become music teachers; but I had a reasonably fixed idea, even at that early period in my life, that there was need for something to be done to prepare the way for successful lawyers, Congressmen, and music teachers.

I felt that the conditions were a good deal like those of an old coloured man, during the days of slavery, who wanted to learn how to play on the guitar. In his desire to take guitar lessons he applied to one of his young masters to teach him, but the young man, not having much faith in the ability of the slave to master the guitar at his age, sought to discourage him by telling him: "Uncle Jake, I will give you guitar lessons; but, Jake, I will have to charge you three dollars for the first lesson, two dollars for the second lesson, and one dollar for the third lesson. But I will charge you only twenty-five cents for the last lesson."

Uncle Jake answered: "All right, boss, I hires you on dem terms. But boss! I wants yer to be sure an' give me dāt las' lesson first."

Soon after my work in connection with the removal of the capital was finished, I received an invitation which gave me great joy and which at the same time was a very pleasant surprise. This was a letter from General Armstrong, inviting me to return to Hampton at the next Commencement to deliver what was called the "post-graduate address." This was an honour which I had not dreamed of receiving. With much care I prepared the best address that I was capable of. I chose for my subject "The Force That Wins."

As I returned to Hampton for the purpose of delivering this address, I went over much of the same ground—

now, however, covered entirely by railroad—that I had traversed nearly six years before, when I first sought entrance into Hampton Institute as a student. Now I was able to ride the whole distance in the train. I was constantly contrasting this with my first journey to Hampton. I think I may say, without seeming egotism, that it is seldom that five years have wrought such a change in the life and aspirations of an individual.

At Hampton I received a warm welcome from teachers and students. I found that during my absence from Hampton the Institute each year had been getting closer to the real needs and conditions of our people; that the industrial teaching, as well as that of the academic department, had greatly improved. The plan of the school was not modelled after that of any other institution then in existence, but every improvement was made under the magnificent leadership of General Armstrong solely with the view of meeting and helping the needs of our people as they presented themselves at the time. Too often, it seems to me, in missionary and educational work among undeveloped races, people yield to the temptation of doing that which was done a hundred years before, or is being done in other communities a thousand miles away. The temptation often is to run each individual through a certain educational mould, regardless of the condition of the subject or the end to be accomplished. This was not so at Hampton Institute.

The address which I delivered on Commencement Day seems to have pleased every one, and many kind and encouraging words were spoken to me regarding it. Soon after my return to my home in West Virginia, where I had planned to continue teaching, I was again surprised to receive a letter from General Armstrong, asking me to return to Hampton, partly as a teacher and partly to pursue some supplementary studies. This was in the summer of 1879. Soon after I began my first teaching in West Virginia I had picked out four of the brightest and most promising of my pupils, in addition to my two brothers, to whom I have already referred, and had given them special attention, with the view of having them go to Hampton. They had gone there, and in each case the teachers had found them so well prepared that they entered advanced classes. This fact, it seems, led to my being called back to Hampton as a teacher. One of the young men that I sent to Hampton in this way is now Dr. Samuel E. Courtney, a successful physician in Boston, and a member of the School Board of that city.

About this time the experiment was being tried for the first time, by General Armstrong, of educating Indians at Hampton. Few people then had any confidence in the ability of the Indians to receive education and to profit by it. General Armstrong was anxious to try the experiment systematically on a large scale. He secured from the reservations in the Western states over one hundred wild and for the most part perfectly ignorant Indians, the greater proportion of whom were young men. The special work which the General desired me to do was to be a sort of "house father" to the Indian young men—that is, I was to live in the building with them and have the charge of their discipline, clothing, rooms, and so on. This was a very tempting offer, but I had become so much absorbed in my work in West Virginia that I dreaded to give it up. However, I tore myself away from it. I did not know how to refuse to perform any service that General Armstrong desired of me.

On going to Hampton, I took up my residence in a building with about seventy-five Indian youths. I was the only person in the building who was not a member of their race. At first I had a good deal of doubt about my ability to succeed. I knew that the average Indian felt himself above the white man, and, of course, he felt himself far above the Negro, largely on account of the fact of the Negro having submitted to slavery—a thing which the Indian would never do. The Indians, in the Indian Territory, owned a large number of slaves during the days of slavery. Aside from this, there was a general feeling that the attempt to educate and civilize the red men at Hampton would be a failure. All this made me proceed very cautiously, for I felt keenly the great responsibility. But I was determined to succeed. It was not long before I had the complete confidence of the Indians, and not only this, but I think I am safe in saying that I had their love and respect. I found that they were about like any other human beings; that they responded to kind treatment and resented ill-treatment. They were continually planning to do something that would add to my happiness and comfort. The things that they disliked most, I think, were to have their long hair cut, to give up wearing their blankets, and to cease smoking; but no white American ever thinks that any other race is wholly civilized until he wears the white man's clothes, eats the white man's food, speaks the white man's language, and professes the white man's religion.

When the difficulty of learning the English language was subtracted, I found that in the matter of learning trades and in mastering academic studies there was little difference between the coloured and Indian students. It was a constant delight to me to note the interest which the coloured students took in trying to help the Indians in every way possible. There were a few of the coloured students who felt that the Indians ought not to be admitted to Hampton, but these were in the minority. Whenever they were asked to do so, the Negro students gladly took the Indians as room-mates, in order that they might teach them to speak English and to acquire civilized habits.

I have often wondered if there was a white institution in this country whose students would have welcomed the incoming of more than a hundred companions of another race in the cordial way that these black students at Hampton welcomed the red ones. How often I have wanted to say to white students that they lift themselves up in proportion as they help to lift others, and the more unfortunate the race, and the lower in the scale of civilization, the more does one raise one's self by giving the assistance.

This reminds me of a conversation which I once had with the Hon. Frederick Douglass. At one time Mr. Douglass was travelling in the state of Pennsylvania, and was forced, on account of his colour, to ride in the baggage-car, in spite of the fact that he had paid the same price for his passage that the other passengers had paid. When some of the white passengers went into the baggage-car to console Mr. Douglass, and one of them said to him: "I am sorry, Mr. Douglass, that you have been degraded in this manner," Mr. Douglass straightened himself up on the box upon which he was sitting, and replied: "They cannot degrade Frederick Douglass. The soul that is within me no man can degrade. I am not the one that is being degraded on account of this treatment, but those who are inflicting it upon me."

In one part of our country, where the law demands the separation of the races on the railroad trains, I saw at one time a rather amusing instance which showed how difficult it sometimes is to know where the black begins and the white ends.

There was a man who was well known in his community as a Negro, but who was so white that even an expert would have hard work to classify him as a black man. This man was riding in the part of the train set aside for the coloured passengers. When the train conductor reached him, he showed at once that he was perplexed. If the man was a Negro, the conductor did not want to send him into the white people's coach; at the same time, if he was a white man, the conductor did not want to insult him by asking him if he was a Negro. The official looked him over carefully, examining his hair, eyes, nose, and hands, but still seemed puzzled. Finally, to solve the difficulty, he stooped over and peeped at the man's feet. When I saw the conductor examining the feet of the man in question, I said to myself, "That will settle it"; and so it did, for the trainman promptly decided that the passenger was a Negro, and let him remain where he was. I congratulated myself that my race was fortunate in not losing one of its members.

My experience has been that the time to test a true gentleman is to observe him when he is in contact with individuals of a race that is less fortunate than his own. This is illustrated in no better way than by observing the conduct of the old-school type of Southern gentleman when he is in contact with his former slaves or their descendants.

An example of what I mean is shown in a story told of George Washington, who, meeting a coloured man in the road once, who politely lifted his hat, lifted his own in return. Some of his white friends who saw the incident criticised Washington for his action. In reply to their criticism George Washington said: "Do you suppose that I am going to permit a poor, ignorant, coloured man to be more polite than I am?"

While I was in charge of the Indian boys at Hampton, I had one or two experiences which illustrate the curious workings of caste in America. One of the Indian boys was taken ill, and it became my duty to take him to Washington, deliver him over to the Secretary of the Interior, and get a receipt for him, in order that he might be returned to his Western reservation. At that time I was rather ignorant of the ways of the world. During my journey to Washington, on a steamboat, when the bell rang for dinner, I was careful to wait and not enter the dining room until after the greater part of the passengers had finished their meal. Then, with my charge, I went to the dining saloon. The man in charge politely informed me that the Indian could be served, but that I could not. I never could understand how he knew just where to draw the colour line, since the Indian and I were of about the same complexion. The steward, however, seemed to be an expert in this matter. I had been directed by the authorities at Hampton to stop at a certain hotel in Washington with my charge, but when I went to this hotel the clerk stated that he would be glad to receive the Indian into the house, but said that he could not accommodate me.

An illustration of something of this same feeling came under my observation afterward. I happened to find myself in a town in which so much excitement and indignation were being expressed that it seemed likely for a time that there would be a lynching. The occasion of the trouble was that a dark-skinned man had stopped at the local hotel. Investigation, however, developed the fact that this individual was a citizen of Morocco, and that while travelling in this country he spoke the English language. As soon as it was learned that he was not an American Negro, all the signs of indignation disappeared. The man who was the innocent cause of the excitement, though, found it prudent after that not to speak English.

At the end of my first year with the Indians there came another opening for me at Hampton, which, as I look back over my life now, seems to have come providentially, to help to prepare me for my work at Tuskegee later. General Armstrong had found out that there was quite a number of young coloured men and women who were intensely in earnest in wishing to get an education, but who were prevented from entering Hampton Institute because they were too poor to be able to pay any portion of the cost of their board, or even to supply themselves with books. He conceived the idea of starting a night-school in connection with the Institute, into which a limited number of the most promising of these young men and women would be received, on condition that they were to work for ten hours during the day, and attend school for two hours at night. They were to be paid something above the cost of their board for their work. The greater part of their earnings was to be reserved in the school's treasury as a fund to be drawn on to pay their board when they had become students in the day-school, after they had spent one or two years in the night-school. In this way they would obtain a start in their books and a knowledge of some trade or industry, in addition to the other far-reaching benefits of the institution.

General Armstrong asked me to take charge of the night-school, and I did so. At the beginning of this school there were about twelve strong, earnest men and women who entered the class. During the day the greater part of the young men worked in the school's sawmill, and the young women worked in the laundry. The work was not easy in either place, but in all my teaching I never taught pupils who gave me such genuine satisfaction as these did. They were good students, and mastered their work thoroughly. They were so much in earnest that only the ringing of the retiring-bell would make them stop studying, and often they would urge me to continue the lessons after the usual hour for going to bed had come.

These students showed so much earnestness both in their hard work during the day, as well as in their application to their studies at night, that I gave them the name of "The Plucky Class"— a name which soon grew popular and spread throughout the institution. After a student had been in the night-school long enough to prove what was in him, I gave him a printed certificate which read something like this:

"This is to certify that James Smith is a member of The Plucky Class of the Hampton Institute, and is in good and regular standing."

The students prized these certificates highly, and they added greatly to the popularity of the night-school. Within a few weeks this department had grown to such an extent that there were about twenty-five students in attendance. I have followed the course of many of these twenty-five men and women ever since then, and they are now holding important and useful positions in nearly every part of the South. The night-school at Hampton, which started with only twelve students, now numbers between three and four hundred, and is one of the permanent and most important features of the institution.

CHAPTER

VII

Early Days at Tuskegee

During the time that I had charge of the Indians and the night-school at Hampton, I pursued some studies myself, under the direction of the instructors there. One of these instructors was the Rev. Dr. H. B. Frissell, the present Principal of the Hampton Institute, General Armstrong's successor.

In May, 1881, near the close of my first year in teaching the night-school, in a way that I had not dared expect, the opportunity opened for me to begin my life-work. One night in the chapel, after the usual chapel exercises were over, General Armstrong referred to the fact that he had received a letter from some gentlemen in Alabama asking him to recommend some one to take charge of what was to be a normal school for the coloured people in the little town of Tuskegee in that state. These gentlemen seemed to take it for granted that no coloured man suitable for the position could be secured, and they were expecting the General to recommend a white man for the place. The next day General Armstrong sent for me to come to his office, and, much to my surprise, asked me if I thought I could fill the position in Alabama. I told him that I would be willing to try. Accordingly, he wrote to the people who had applied to him for the information, that he did not know of any white man to suggest, but if they would be willing to take a coloured man, he had one whom he could recommend. In this letter he gave them my name.

Several days passed before anything more was heard about the matter. Some time afterward, one Sunday evening during the chapel exercises, a messenger came in and handed the General a telegram. At the end of the exercises he read the telegram to the school. In substance, these were its words: "Booker T. Washington will suit us. Send him at once."

There was a great deal of joy expressed among the students and teachers, and I received very hearty congratulations. I began to get ready at once to go to Tuskegee. I went by way of my old home in West Virginia, where I remained for several days, after which I proceeded to Tuskegee. I found Tuskegee to be a town of about two thousand inhabitants, nearly one-half of whom were coloured. It was in what was known as the Black Belt of the South. In the county in which Tuskegee is situated the coloured people outnumbered the whites by about three to one. In some of the adjoining and near-by counties the proportion was not far from six coloured persons to one white.

I have often been asked to define the term "Black Belt." So far as I can learn, the term was first used to designate a part of the country which was distinguished by the colour of the soil. The part of the country possessing this thick, dark, and naturally rich soil was, of course, the part of the South where the slaves were most profitable, and consequently they were taken there in the largest numbers. Later and especially since the war, the term seems to be used wholly in a political sense—that is, to designate the counties where the black people outnumber the white.

Before going to Tuskegee I had expected to find there a building and all the necessary apparatus ready for me to begin teaching. To my disappointment, I found nothing of the kind. I did find, though, that which no costly building and apparatus can supply,—hundreds of hungry, earnest souls who wanted to secure knowledge.

Tuskegee seemed an ideal place for the school. It was in the midst of the great bulk of the Negro population, and was rather secluded, being five miles from the main line of railroad, with which it was connected by a short line. During the days of slavery, and since, the town had been a centre for the education of the white people. This was an added advantage, for the reason that I found the white people possessing a degree of culture and education that is not surpassed by many localities. While the coloured people were ignorant, they had not, as a rule degraded and weakened their bodies by vices such as are common to the lower class of people in the large cities. In general, I found the relations between the two races pleasant. For example, the largest, and I think at that time the only hardware store in the town was owned and operated jointly by a coloured man and a white man. This copartnership continued until the death of the white partner.

I found that about a year previous to my going to Tuskegee some of the coloured people who had heard something of the work of education being done at Hampton had applied to the state Legislature, through their representatives, for a small appropriation to be used in starting a normal school in Tuskegee. This request the Legislature had complied with to the extent of granting an annual appropriation of two thousand dollars. I soon learned however, that this money could be used only for the payment of the salaries of the instructors, and that there was no provision for securing land, buildings, or apparatus. The task before me did not seem a very encouraging one. It seemed much like making bricks without straw. The coloured people were overjoyed, and were constantly offering their services in any way in which they could be of assistance in getting the school started.

My first task was to find a place in which to open the school. After looking the town over with some care, the most suitable place that could be secured seemed to be a rather dilapidated shanty near the coloured Methodist church, together with the church itself as a sort of assembly-room. Both the church and the shanty were in about as bad condition as was possible. I recall that during the first months of school that I taught in this building it was in such poor repair that, whenever it rained, one of the older students would very kindly leave his lessons and hold an umbrella over me while I heard the recitations of the others. I remember, also, that on more than one occasion my landlady held an umbrella over me while I ate breakfast.

At the time I went to Alabama the coloured people were taking considerable interest in politics, and they were very anxious that I should become one of them politically, in every respect. They seemed to have a little distrust of strangers in this regard. I recall that one man, who seemed to have been designated by the others to look after my political destiny, came to me on several occasions and said, with a good deal of earnestness: "We wants you to be sure to vote jes' like we votes. We can't read de newspapers very much, but we knows how to vote, an' we wants you to vote jes' like we votes." He added: "We watches de white man, and we keeps watching de white man till we finds out which way de white man's gwine to vote; an' when we finds out which way de white man's gwine to vote, den we votes 'xactly de other way. Den we knows we's right."

I am glad to add, however, that at the present time the disposition to vote against the white man merely because he is white is largely disappearing, and the race is learning to vote from principle, for what the voter considers to be for the best interests of both races.

I reached Tuskegee, as I have said, early in June, 1881. The first month I spent in finding accommodations for the school, and in travelling through Alabama, examining into the actual life of the people, especially in the country districts, and in getting the school advertised among the class of people that I wanted to have attend it. The most of my travelling was done over the country roads, with a mule and a cart or a mule and a buggy wagon for conveyance. I ate and slept with the people, in their little cabins. I saw their farms, their schools, their churches. Since, in the case of the most of these visits, there had been no notice given in advance that a stranger was expected, I had the advantage of seeing the real, everyday life of the people.

In the plantation districts I found that, as a rule the whole family slept in one room, and that in addition to the immediate family there sometimes were relatives, or others not related to the family, who slept in the same room. On more than one occasion I went outside the house to get ready for bed, or to wait until the family had gone to sleep, either on the floor or in a special part of another's bed. Rarely was there any place provided in the cabin where one could bathe even the face and hands, but usually some provision was made for this outside the house, in the yard.

The common diet of the people was fat pork and corn bread. At times I have eaten in cabins where they had only corn bread and "black-eye peas" cooked in plain water. The people seemed to have no other idea than to live on this fat meat and corn bread,—the meat, and the meal of which the bread was made, having been bought at a high price at a store in town, notwithstanding the fact that the land all about the cabin homes could easily have been made to produce nearly every kind of garden vegetable that is raised anywhere in the country. Their one object seemed to be plant nothing but cotton; and in many cases cotton was planted up to the very door of the cabin.

In these cabin homes I often found sewing-machines which had been bought, or were being bought, on installments, frequently at a cost of as much as sixty dollars, or showy clocks for which the occupants of the cabins had paid twelve or fourteen dollars. I remember that on one occasion when I went into one of these cabins for dinner, when I sat down to the table for a meal with the four members of the family, I noticed that, while there were five of us at the table, there was but one fork for the five of us to use. Naturally there was an awkward pause on my part. In the opposite corner of that same cabin was an organ for which the people told me they were paying sixty dollars in monthly instalments. One fork, and a sixty-dollar organ!

In most cases the sewing-machine was not used, the clocks were so worthless that they did not keep correct time—and if they had, in nine cases out of ten there would have been no one in the family who could have told the time of day—while the organ, of course, was rarely used for want of a person who could play upon it.

In the case to which I have referred, where the family sat down to the table for the meal at which I was their guest, I could see plainly that this was an awkward and unusual proceeding, and was done in my honour. In most cases, when the family got up in the morning, for example, the wife would put a piece of meat in a frying-pan and put a lump of dough in a "skillet," as they called it. These utensils would be placed on the fire, and in ten or fifteen minutes breakfast would be ready. Frequently the husband would take his bread and meat in his hand and start for the field, eating as he walked. The mother would sit down in a corner and eat her breakfast, perhaps from a plate and perhaps directly from the "skillet" or frying-pan, while the children would eat their portion of the bread and meat while running about the yard. At certain seasons of the year, when meat was scarce, it was rarely that the children who were not old enough or strong enough to work in the fields would have the luxury of meat.

The breakfast over, and with practically no attention given to the house, the whole family would, as a general thing, proceed to the cotton-field. Every child that was large enough to carry a hoe was put to work, and the baby—for usually there was at least one baby—would be laid down at the end of the cotton row, so that its mother could give it a certain amount of attention when she had finished chopping her row. The noon meal and the supper were taken in much the same way as the breakfast.

All the days of the family would be spent after much this same routine, except Saturday and Sunday. On Saturday the whole family would spend at least half a day, and often a whole day, in town. The idea in going to town was, I suppose, to do shopping, but all the shopping that the whole family had money for could have been attended to in ten minutes by one person. Still, the whole family remained in town for most of the day, spending the greater part of the time in standing on the streets, the women, too often, sitting about somewhere smoking or dipping snuff. Sunday was usually spent in going to some big meeting. With few exceptions, I found that the crops were mortgaged in the counties where I went, and that the most of the coloured farmers were in debt. The state had not been able to build schoolhouses in the country districts, and, as a rule, the schools were taught in churches or in log cabins. More than once, while on my journeys, I found that there was no provision made in the house used for school purposes for heating the building during the winter, and consequently a fire had to be built in the yard, and teacher and pupils passed in and out of the house as they got cold or warm. With few exceptions, I found the teachers in these country schools to be miserably poor in preparation for their work, and poor in moral character. The schools were in session from three to five months. There was practically no apparatus in the schoolhouses, except that occasionally there was a rough blackboard. I recall that one day I went into a schoolhouse—or rather into an abandoned log cabin that was being used as a schoolhouse—and found five pupils who were studying a lesson from one book. Two of these, on the front seat, were using the book between them; behind these were two others peeping over the shoulders of the first two, and behind the four was a fifth little fellow who was peeping over the shoulders of all four.

What I have said concerning the character of the schoolhouses and teachers will also apply quite accurately as a description of the church buildings and the ministers.

I met some very interesting characters during my travels. As illustrating the peculiar mental processes of the country people, I remember that I asked one coloured man, who was about sixty years old, to tell me something of his history. He said that he had been born in Virginia, and sold into Alabama in 1845. I asked him how many were sold at the same time. He said "There were five of us; myself and brother and three mules."

In giving all these descriptions of what I saw during my month of travel in the country around Tuskegee, I wish my readers to keep in mind the fact that there were many encouraging exceptions to the conditions which I have described. I have stated in such plain words what I saw, mainly for the reason that later I want to emphasize the encouraging changes that have taken place in the community, not wholly by the work of the Tuskegee school but by that of other institutions as well.

CHAPTER X

A Harder Task than Making Bricks Without Straw

From the very beginning, at Tuskegee, I was determined to have the students do not only the agricultural and domestic work, but to have them erect their own buildings. My plan was to have them, while performing this service, taught the latest and best methods of labour, so that the school would not only get the benefit of their efforts, but the students themselves would be taught to see not only utility in labour, but beauty and dignity, would be taught, in fact, how to lift labour up from mere drudgery and toil, and would learn to love work for its own sake. My plan was not to teach them to work in the old way, but to show them how to make the forces of nature—air, water, steam, electricity, horse-power—assist them in their labour.

At first many advised against the experiment of having the buildings erected by the labour of the students, but I was determined to stick to it. I told those who doubted the wisdom of the plan that I knew that our first buildings would not be so comfortable or so complete in their finish as buildings erected by the experienced hands of outside workmen, but that in the teaching of civilization, self-help, and self-reliance, the erection of the buildings by the students themselves would more than compensate for any lack of comfort or fine finish.

I further told those who doubted the wisdom of this plan, that the majority of our students came to us in poverty, from the cabins of the cotton, sugar, and rice plantations of the South, and that while I knew it would please the students very much to place them at once in finely constructed buildings, I felt that it would be following out a more natural process of development to teach them how to construct their own buildings. Mistakes I knew would be made, but these mistakes would teach us valuable lessons for the future.

During the now nineteen years' existence of the Tuskegee school, the plan of having the buildings erected by student labour has been adhered to. In this time forty buildings, counting small and large, have been built, and all except four are almost wholly the product of student labour. As an additional result, hundreds of men are now scattered throughout the South who received their knowledge of mechanics while being taught how to erect these buildings. Skill and knowledge are now handed down from one set of students to another in this way, until at the present time a building of any description or size can be constructed wholly by our instructors and students, from the drawing of the plans to the putting in of the electric fixtures without going off the grounds for a single workman.

Not a few times, when a new student has been led into the temptation of marring the looks of some building by leadpencil marks or by the cuts of a jack-knife, I have heard an old student remind him. "Don't do that. That is our building. I helped put it up."

In the early days of the school I think my most trying experience was in the matter of brickmaking. As soon as we got the farm work reasonably well started, we directed our next efforts toward the industry of making bricks. We needed these for use in connection with the erection of our own buildings; but there was also another reason for establishing this industry. There was no brickyard in the town, and in addition to our own needs there was a demand for bricks in the general market.

I had always sympathized with the "Children of Israel," in their task of "making bricks without straw," but ours was the task of making bricks with no money and no experience.

In the first place, the work was hard and dirty, and it was difficult to get the students to help. When it came to brickmaking, their distaste for manual labour in connection with book education became especially manifest. It was not a pleasant task for one to stand in the mud-pit for hours, with the mud up to his knees. More than one man became disgusted and left the school.

We tried several locations before we opened up a pit that furnished brick clay. I had always supposed that brickmaking was very simple, but I soon found out by bitter experience that it required skill and knowledge, particularly in the burning of the bricks. After a good deal of effort we moulded about twenty-five thousand bricks, and put them into a kiln to be burned. This kiln turned out to be a failure, because it was not properly constructed or properly burned. We began at once, however, on a second kiln. This, for some reason, also proved a failure. The failure of this kiln made it still more difficult to get the students to take any part in the work. Several of the teachers, however, who had been trained in the industries at Hampton, volunteered their services, and in some way we succeeded in getting a third kiln ready for burning. The burning of a kiln required about a week. Toward the latter part of the week, when it seemed as if we were going to have a good many thousand bricks in a few hours, in the middle of the night the kiln fell. For the third time we had failed.

The failure of this last kiln left me without a single dollar with which to make another experiment. Most of the teachers advised the abandoning of the effort to make bricks. In the midst of my troubles I thought of a watch which had come into my possession years before. I took this watch to the city of Montgomery, which was not far distant, and placed it in a pawn-shop. I secured cash upon it to the amount of fifteen dollars, with which to renew the brickmaking experiment. I returned to Tuskegee, and, with the help of the fifteen dollars, rallied our rather demoralized and discouraged forces and began a fourth attempt to make bricks. This time, I am glad to say, we were successful. Before I got hold of any money, the time-limit on my watch had expired, and I have never seen it since; but I have never regretted the loss of it.

Brickmaking has now become such an important industry at the school that last season our students manufactured twelve hundred thousand of first-class bricks, of a quality suitable to be sold in any market. Aside from this, scores of young men have mastered the brickmaking trade—both the making of bricks by hand and by machinery—and are now engaged in this industry in many parts of the South.

The making of these bricks taught me an important lesson in regard to the relations of the two races in the South. Many white people who had had no contact with the school, and perhaps no sympathy with it, came to us to buy bricks because they found out that ours were good bricks. They discovered that we were supplying a real want in the community. The making of these bricks caused many of the white residents of the neighbourhood to begin to feel that the education of the Negro was not making him worthless, but that in educating our students we were adding something to the wealth and comfort of the community. As the people of the neighbourhood came to us to buy bricks, we got acquainted with them; they traded with us and we with them. Our business interests became intermingled. We had something which they wanted; they had something which we wanted. This, in a large measure, helped to lay the foundation for the pleasant relations that have continued to exist between us and the white people in that section, and which now extend throughout the South.

Wherever one of our brickmakers has gone in the South, we find that he has something to contribute to the well-being of the community into which he has gone; something that has made the community feel that, in a degree, it is indebted to him, and perhaps, to a certain extent, dependent upon him. In this way pleasant relations between the races have been stimulated.

My experience is that there is something in human nature which always makes an individual recognize and reward merit, no matter under what colour of skin merit is found. I have found, too, that it is the visible, the tangible, that goes a long ways in softening prejudices. The actual sight of a first-class house that a Negro has built is ten times more potent than pages of discussion about a house that he ought to build, or perhaps could build.

The same principle of industrial education has been carried out in the building of our own wagons, carts, and buggies, from the first. We now own and use on our farm and about the school dozens of these vehicles, and every one of them has been built by the hands of the students. Aside from this, we help supply the local market with these vehicles. The supplying of them to the people in the community has had the same effect as the supplying of bricks, and the man who learns at Tuskegee to build and repair wagons and carts is regarded as a benefactor by both races in the community where he goes. The people with whom he lives and works are going to think twice before they part with such a man.

The individual who can do something that the world wants done will, in the end, make his way regardless of his race. One man may go into a community prepared to supply the people there with an analysis of Greek sentences. The community may not at that time be prepared for, or feel the need of, Greek analysis, but it may feel its need of bricks and houses and wagons. If the man can supply the need for those, then, it will lead eventually to a demand for the first product, and with the demand will come the ability to appreciate it and to profit by it.

About the time that we succeeded in burning our first kiln of bricks we began facing in an emphasized form the objection of the students to being taught to work. By this time it had gotten to be pretty well advertised throughout the state that every student who came to Tuskegee, no matter what his financial ability might be, must learn some industry. Quite a number of letters came from parents protesting against their children engaging in labour while they were in the school. Other parents came to the school to protest in person. Most of the new students brought a written or a verbal request from their parents to the effect that they wanted their children taught nothing but books. The more books, the larger they were, and the longer the titles printed upon them, the better pleased the students and their parents seemed to be.

I gave little heed to these protests, except that I lost no

opportunity to go into as many parts of the state as I could, for the purpose of speaking to the parents, and showing them the value of industrial education. Besides, I talked to the students constantly on the subject. Notwithstanding the unpopularity of industrial work, the school continued to increase in numbers to such an extent that by the middle of the second year there was an attendance of about one hundred and fifty, representing almost all parts of the state of Alabama, and including a few from other states.

In the summer of 1882 Miss Davidson and I both went North and engaged in the work of raising funds for the completion of our new building. On my way North I stopped in New York to try to get a letter of recommendation from an officer of a missionary organization who had become somewhat acquainted with me a few years previous. This man not only refused to give me the letter, but advised me most earnestly to go back home at once, and not make an attempt to get money, for he was quite sure that I would never get more than enough to pay my travelling expenses. I thanked him for his advice, and proceeded on my journey.

The first place I went to in the North, was Northampton, Mass., where I spent nearly a half-day in looking for a coloured family with whom I could board, never dreaming that any hotel would admit me. I was greatly surprised when I found that I would have no trouble in being accommodated at a hotel.

We were successful in getting money enough so that on Thanksgiving Day of that year we held our first service in the chapel of Porter Hall, although the building was not completed.

In looking about for some one to preach the Thanksgiving sermon, I found one of the rarest men that it has ever been my privilege to know. This was the Rev. Robert C. Bedford, a white man from Wisconsin, who was then pastor of a little coloured Congregational church in Montgomery, Ala. Before going to Montgomery to look for some one to preach this sermon I had never heard of Mr. Bedford. He had never heard of me. He gladly consented to come to Tuskegee and hold the Thanksgiving service. It was the first service of the kind that the coloured people there had ever observed, and what a deep interest they manifested in it! The sight of the new building made it a day of Thanksgiving for them never to be forgotten.

Mr. Bedford consented to become one of the trustees of the school, and in that capacity, and as a worker for it, he has been connected with it for eighteen years. During this time he has borne the school upon his heart night and day, and is never so happy as when he is performing some service, no matter how humble, for it. He completely obliterates himself in everything, and looks only for permission to serve where service is most disagreeable, and where others would not be attracted. In all my relations with him he has seemed to me to approach as nearly to the spirit of the Master as almost any man I ever met.

A little later there came into the service of the school another man, quite young at the time, and fresh from Hampton, without whose service the school never could have become what it is. This was Mr. Warren Logan, who now for seventeen years has been the treasurer of the Institute, and the acting principal during my absence. He has always shown a degree of unselfishness and an amount of business tact, coupled with a clear judgment, that has kept the school in good condition no matter how long I have been absent from it. During all the financial stress through which the school has passed, his patience and faith in our ultimate success have not left him.

As soon as our first building was near enough to completion so that we could occupy a portion of it—which was near the middle of the second year of the school—we opened a boarding department. Students had begun coming from quite a distance, and in such increasing numbers that we felt more and more that we were merely skimming over the surface, in that we were not getting hold of the students in their home life.

We had nothing but the students and their appetites with which to begin a boarding department. No provision had been made in the new building for a kitchen and dining room; but we discovered that by digging out a large amount of earth from under the building we could make a partially lighted basement room that could be used for a kitchen and dining room. Again I called on the students to volunteer for work, this time to assist in digging out the basement. This they did, and in a few weeks we had a place to cook and eat in, although it was very rough and uncomfortable. Any one seeing the place now would never believe that it was once used for a dining room.

The most serious problem, though, was to get the boarding department started off in running order, with nothing to do with in the way of furniture, and with no money with which to buy anything. The merchants in the town would let us have what food we wanted on credit. In fact, in those earlier years I was constantly embarrassed because people seemed to have more faith in me than I had in myself. It was pretty hard to cook, however, without stoves, and awkward to eat without dishes. At first the cooking was done out-of-doors, in the old-fashioned, primitive style, in pots and skillets placed over a fire. Some of the carpenters' benches that had been used in the construction of the building were utilized for tables. As for dishes, there were too few to make it worth while to spend time in describing them.

No one connected with the boarding department seemed to have any idea that meals must be served at certain fixed and regular hours, and this was a source of great worry. Everything was so out of joint and so inconvenient that I feel safe in saying that for the first two weeks something was wrong at every meal. Either the meat was not done or had been burnt, or the salt had been left out of the bread, or the tea had been forgotten.

Early one morning I was standing near the dining-room door listening to the complaints of the students. The complaints that morning were especially emphatic and numerous, because the whole breakfast had been a failure. One of the girls who had failed to get any breakfast came out and went to the well to draw some water to drink to take the place of the breakfast which she had not been able to get. When she reached the well, she found that the rope was broken and that she could get no water. She turned from the well and said, in the most discouraged tone, not knowing that I was where I could hear her, "We can't even get water to drink at this school." I think no one remark ever came so near discouraging me as that one.

At another time, when Mr. Bedford—whom I have already spoken of as one of our trustees, and a devoted friend of the institution—was visiting the school, he was given a bedroom immediately over the dining room. Early in the morning he was awakened by a rather animated discussion between two boys in the dining room below. The discussion was over the question as to whose turn it was to use the coffee-cup that morning. One boy won the case by proving that for three mornings he had not had an opportunity to use the cup at all.

But gradually, by patience and hard work, we brought order out of chaos, just as will be true of any problem if we stick to it with patience and wisdom and earnest effort.

As I look back now over that part of our struggle, I am glad that we had it. I am glad that we endured all those discomforts and inconveniences. I am glad that our students had to dig out the place for their kitchen and dining room. I am glad that our first boarding-place was in that dismal, ill-lighted, and damp basement. Had we started in a fine, attractive, convenient room, I fear we would have "lost our heads" and become "stuck up." It means a great deal, I think, to start off on a foundation which one has made for one's self.

When our old students return to Tuskegee now, as they often do, and go into our large, beautiful, well-ventilated, and well-lighted dining room, and see tempting, well-cooked food—largely grown by the students themselves—and see tables, neat tablecloths and napkins, and vases of flowers upon the tables, and hear singing birds, and note that each meal is served exactly upon the minute, with no disorder, and with almost no complaint coming from the hundreds that now fill our dining room, they, too, often say to me that they are glad that we started as we did, and built ourselves up year by year, by a slow and natural process of growth.

CHAPTER

XIII

Two Thousand Miles for a Five-Minute Speech

Soon after the opening of our boarding department, quite a number of students who evidently were worthy, but who were so poor that they did not have any money to pay even the small charges at the school, began applying for admission. This class was composed of both men and women. It was a great trial to refuse admission to these applicants, and in 1884 we established a night-school to accommodate a few of them.

The night-school was organized on a plan similar to the one which I had helped to establish at Hampton. At first it was composed of about a dozen students. They were admitted to the night-school only when they had no money with which to pay any part of their board in the regular day-school. It was further required that they must work for ten hours during the day at some trade or industry, and study academic branches for two hours during the evening. This was the requirement for the first one or two years of their stay. They were to be paid something above the cost of their board, with the understanding that all of their earnings, except a very small part, were to be reserved in the school's treasury, to be used for paying their board in the regular day-school after they had entered that department. The night-school, started in this manner, has grown until there are at present four hundred and fifty-seven students enrolled in it alone.

There could hardly be a more severe test of a student's worth than this branch of the Institute's work. It is largely because it furnishes such a good opportunity to test the backbone of a student that I place such high value upon our night-school. Any one who is willing to work ten hours a day at the brick-yard, or in the laundry, through one or two years, in order that he or she may have the privilege of studying academic branches for two hours in the evening, has enough bottom to warrant being further educated.

After the student has left the night-school he enters the day-school, where he takes academic branches four days in a week, and works at his trade two days. Besides this he usually works at his trade during the three summer months. As a rule, after a student has succeeded in going through the night-school test, he finds a way to finish the regular course in industrial and academic training. No student, no matter how much money he may be able to command, is permitted to go through school without doing manual labour. In fact, the industrial work is now as popular as the academic branches. Some of the most successful men and women who have graduated from the institution obtained their start in the night-school.

While a great deal of stress is laid upon the industrial side of the work at Tuskegee, we do not neglect or overlook in any degree the religious and spiritual side. The school is strictly undenominational, but it is thoroughly Christian, and the spiritual training of the students is not neglected. Our preaching service, prayer-meetings, Sunday-school, Christian Endeavour Society, Young Men's Christian Association, and various missionary organizations, testify to this.

In 1885, Miss Olivia Davidson, to whom I have already referred as being largely responsible for the success of the school during its early history, and I were married. During our married life she continued to divide her time and strength between our home and the work for the school. She not only continued to work in the school at Tuskegee, but also kept up her habit of going North to secure funds. In 1889 she died, after four years of happy married life and eight years of hard and happy work for the school. She literally wore herself out in her never ceasing efforts in behalf of the work that she so dearly loved. During our married life there were born to us two bright, beautiful boys, Booker Taliaferro and Ernest Davidson. The older of these, Booker, has already mastered the brick-maker's trade at Tuskegee.

I have often been asked how I began the practice of public speaking. In answer I would say that I never planned to give any large part of my life to speaking in public. I have always had more of an ambition to *do* things than merely to talk *about* doing them. It seems that when I went North with General Armstrong to speak at the series of public meetings to which I have referred, the President of the National Educational Association, the Hon. Thomas W. Bicknell, was present at one of those meetings and heard me speak. A few days afterward he sent me an invitation to deliver an address at the next meeting of the Educational Association. This meeting was to be held in Madison, Wis. I accepted the invitation. This was, in a sense, the beginning of my public-speaking career.

On the evening that I spoke before the Association there must have been not far from four thousand persons present. Without my knowing it, there were a large number of people present from Alabama, and some from the town of Tuskegee. These white people afterward frankly told me that they went to this meeting expecting to hear the South roundly abused, but were pleasantly surprised to find that there was no word of abuse in my address. On the contrary, the South was given credit for all the praiseworthy things that it had done. A white lady who was teacher in a college in Tuskegee wrote back to the local paper that she was gratified, as well as surprised, to note the credit which I gave the white people of Tuskegee for their help in getting the school started. This address at Madison was the first that I had delivered that in any large measure dealt with the general problem of the races. Those who heard it seemed to be pleased with what I said and with the general position that I took.

When I first came to Tuskegee, I determined that I would make it my home, that I would take as much pride in the right actions of the people of the town as any white man could do, and that I would, at the same time, deplore the wrong-doing of the people as much as any white man. I determined never to say anything in a public address in the North that I would not be willing to say in the South. I early learned that it is a hard matter to convert an individual by abusing him, and that this is more often accomplished by giving credit for all the praiseworthy actions performed than by calling attention alone to all the evil done.

While pursuing this policy I have not failed, at the proper time and in the proper manner, to call attention in no uncertain terms, to the wrongs which any part of the South has been guilty of. I have found that there is a large element in the South that is quick to respond to straightforward, honest criticism of any wrong policy. As a rule, the place to criticise the South, when criticism is necessary, is in the South—not in Boston. A Boston man who came to Alabama to criticise Boston would not effect so much good, I think, as one who had his word of criticism to say in Boston.

In this address at Madison I took the ground that the policy to be pursued with reference to the races was, by every honourable means, to bring them together and to encourage the cultivation of friendly relations, instead of doing that which would embitter. I further contended that, in relation to his vote, the Negro should more and more consider the interests of the community in which he lived, rather than seek alone to please some one who lived a thousand miles away from him and from his interests.

In this address I said that the whole future of the Negro rested largely upon the question as to whether or not he should make himself, through his skill, intelligence, and character, of such undeniable value to the community in which he lived that the community could not dispense with his presence. I said that any individual who learned to do something better than anybody else—learned to do a common thing in an uncommon manner—had solved his problem, regardless of the colour of his skin, and that in proportion as the Negro learned to produce what other people wanted and must have, in the same proportion would he be respected.

I spoke of an instance where one of our graduates had

produced two hundred and sixty-six bushels of sweet potatoes from an acre of ground, in a community where the average production had been only forty-nine bushels to the acre. He had been able to do this by reason of his knowledge of the chemistry of the soil and by his knowledge of improved methods of agriculture. The white farmers in the neighbourhood respected him, and came to him for ideas regarding the raising of sweet potatoes. These white farmers honoured and respected him because he, by his skill and knowledge, had added something to the wealth and the comfort of the community in which he lived. I explained that my theory of education for the Negro would not, for example, confine him for all time to farm life—to the production of the best and the most sweet potatoes—but that, if he succeeded in this line of industry, he could lay the foundations upon which his children and grandchildren could grow to higher and more important things in life.

Such, in brief, were some of the views I advocated in this first address dealing with the broad question of the relations of the two races, and since that time I have not found any reason for changing my views on any important point.

In my early life I used to cherish a feeling of ill will toward any one who spoke in bitter terms against the Negro, or who advocated measures that tended to oppress the black man or take from him opportunities for growth in the most complete manner. Now, whenever I hear any one advocating measures that are meant to curtail the development of another, I pity the individual who would do this. I know that the one who makes this mistake does so because of his own lack of opportunity for the highest kind of growth. I pity him because I know that he is trying to stop the progress of the world, and because I know that in time the development and the ceaseless advance of humanity will make him ashamed of his weak and narrow position. One might as well try to stop the progress of a mighty railroad train by throwing his body across the track, as to try to stop the growth of the world in the direction of giving mankind more intelligence, more culture, more skill, more liberty, and in the direction of extending more sympathy and more brotherly kindness.

The address which I delivered at Madison, before the National Education Association, gave me a rather wide introduction in the North, and soon after that opportunities began offering themselves for me to address audiences there.

I was anxious, however, that the way might also be opened for me to speak directly to a representative Southern white audience. A partial opportunity of this kind, one that seemed to me might serve as an entering wedge, presented itself in 1893, when the international meeting of Christian Workers was held at Atlanta, Ga. When this invitation came to me, I had engagements in Boston that seemed to make it impossible for me to speak in Atlanta. Still, after looking over my list of dates and places carefully, I found that I could take a train from Boston that would get me into Atlanta about thirty minutes before my address was to be delivered, and that I could remain in that city about sixty minutes before taking another train for Boston. My invitation to speak in Atlanta stipulated that I was to confine my address to five minutes. The question, then, was whether or not I could put enough into a five-minute address to make it worth while for me to make such a trip.

I knew that the audience would be largely composed of the most influential class of white men and women, and that it would be a rare opportunity for me to let them know what we were trying to do at Tuskegee, as well as to speak to them about the relations of the races. So I decided to make the trip. I spoke for five minutes to an audience of two thousand people, composed mostly of Southern and Northern whites. What I said seemed to be received with favour and enthusiasm. The Atlanta papers of the next day commented in friendly terms on my address, and a good deal was said about it in different parts of the country. I felt that I had in some degree accomplished my object—that of getting a hearing from the dominant class of the South.

The demands made upon me for public addresses continued to increase, coming in about equal numbers from my own people and from Northern whites. I gave as much time to these addresses as I could spare from the immediate work at Tuskegee. Most of the addresses in the North were made for the direct purpose of getting funds with which to support the school. Those delivered before the coloured people had for their main object the impressing upon them of the importance of industrial and technical education in addition to academic and religious training.

I now come to that one of the incidents in my life which seems to have excited the greatest amount of interest, and which perhaps went further than anything else in giving me a reputation that in a sense might be called National. I refer to the address which I delivered at the opening of the Atlanta Cotton States and International Exposition, at Atlanta, Ga., September 18, 1895.

So much has been said and written about this incident, and so many questions have been asked me concerning the address, that perhaps I may be excused for taking up the matter with some detail. The five-minute address in Atlanta, which I came from Boston to deliver, was possibly the prime cause for an opportunity being given me to make the second address there. In the spring of 1895 I received a telegram from prominent citizens in Atlanta asking me to accompany a committee from that city to Washington for the purpose of appearing before a committee of Congress in the interest of securing Government help for the Exposition. The committee was composed of about twenty-five of the most prominent and most influential white men of Georgia. All the members of this committee were white men except Bishop Grant, Bishop Gaines, and myself. The mayor and several other city and state officials spoke before the committee. They were followed by the two coloured bishops. My name was the last on the list of speakers. I had never before appeared before such a committee, nor had I ever delivered any address in the capital of the Nation. I had many misgivings as to what I ought to say, and as to the impression that my address would make. While I cannot recall in detail what I said, I remember that I tried to impress upon the committee, with all the earnestness and plainness of any language that I could command, that if Congress wanted to do something which would assist in ridding the South of the race question and making friends between the two races, it should, in every proper way, encourage the material and intellectual growth of both races. I said that the Atlanta Exposition would present an opportunity for both races to show what advance they had made since freedom, and would at the same time afford encouragement to them to make still greater progress.

I tried to emphasize the fact that while the Negro should not be deprived by unfair means of the franchise, political agitation alone would not save him, and that back of the ballot he must have property, industry, skill, economy, intelligence, and character, and that no race without these elements could permanently succeed. I said that in granting the appropriation Congress could do something that would prove to be of real and lasting value to both races, and that it was the first great opportunity of the kind that had been presented since the close of the Civil War.

I spoke for fifteen or twenty minutes, and was surprised at the close of my address to receive the hearty congratulations of the Georgia committee and of the members of Congress who were present. The committee was unanimous in making a favourable report, and in a few days the bill passed Congress. With the passing of this bill the success of the Atlanta Exposition was assured.

Soon after this trip to Washington the directors of the Exposition decided that it would be a fitting recognition of the coloured race to erect a large and attractive building which should be devoted wholly to showing the progress of the Negro since freedom. It was further decided to have the building designed and erected wholly by Negro mechanics. This plan was carried out. In design, beauty, and general finish the Negro Building was equal to the others on the grounds.

After it was decided to have a separate Negro exhibit, the question arose as to who should take charge of it. The officials of the Exposition were anxious that I should assume this responsibility, but I declined to do so, on the plea that the work at Tuskegee at that time demanded my time and strength. Largely at my suggestion, Mr. I. Garland Penn, of Lynchburg, Va., was selected to be at the head of the Negro department. I gave him all the aid that I could. The Negro exhibit, as a whole, was large and creditable. The two exhibits in this department which attracted the greatest amount of attention were those from the Hampton Institute and the Tuskegee Institute.

The people who seemed to be the most surprised, as well as pleased, at what they saw in the Negro Building were the Southern white people.

As the day for the opening of the Exposition drew near, the Board of Directors began preparing the programme for the opening exercises. In the discussion from day to day of the various features of this programme, the question came up as to the advisability of putting a member of the Negro race on for one of the opening addresses, since the Negroes had been asked to take such a prominent part in the Exposition. It was argued, further, that such recognition would mark the good feeling prevailing between the two races. Of course there were those who were opposed to any such recognition of the rights of the Negro, but the Board of Directors, composed of men who represented the best and most progressive element in the South, had their way, and voted to invite a black man to speak on the opening day. The next thing was to decide upon the person who was thus to represent the Negro race. After the question had been canvassed for several days, the directors voted unanimously to ask me to deliver one of the opening-day addresses, and in a few days after that I received the official invitation.

The receiving of this invitation brought to me a sense of responsibility that it would be hard for any one not placed in my position to appreciate. What were my feelings when this invitation came to me? I remembered that I had been a slave; that my early years had been spent in the lowest depths of poverty and ignorance, and that I had had little opportunity to prepare me for such a responsibility as this. It was only a few years before that time that any white man in the audience might have claimed me as his slave; and it was easily possible that some of my former owners might be present to hear me speak.

I knew, too, that this was the first time in the entire history of the Negro that a member of my race had been asked to speak from the same platform with white Southern men and women on any important National occasion. I was asked now to speak to an audience composed of the wealth and culture of the white South, the representatives of my former masters. I knew, too, that while the greater part of my audience would be composed of Southern people, yet there would be present a large number of Northern whites, as well as a great many men and women of my own race.

I was determined to say nothing that I did not feel from the bottom of my heart to be true and right. When the invitation came to me, there was not one word of intimation as to what I should say or as to what I should omit. In this I felt that the Board of Directors had paid a tribute to me. They knew that by one sentence I could have blasted, in a large degree, the success of the Exposition. I was also painfully conscious of the fact that, while I must be true to my own race in my utterances, I had it in my power to make such an ill-timed address as would result in preventing any similar invitation being extended to a black man again for years to come. I was equally determined to be true to the North, as well as to the best element of the white South, in what I had to say.

The papers, North and South, had taken up the discussion of my coming speech, and as the time for it drew near this discussion became more and more widespread. Not a few of the Southern white papers were unfriendly to the idea of my speaking. From my own race I received many suggestions as to what I ought to say. I prepared myself as best I could for the address, but as the eighteenth of September drew nearer, the heavier my heart became, and the more I feared that my effort would prove a failure and a disappointment.

The invitation had come at a time when I was very busy with my school work, as it was the beginning of our school year. After preparing my address, I went through it, as I usually do with all those utterances which I consider particularly important, with Mrs. Washington, and she approved of what I intended to say. On the sixteenth of September, the day before I was to start for Atlanta, so many of the Tuskegee teachers expressed a desire to hear my address that I consented to read it to them in a body. When I had done so, and had heard their criticisms and comments, I felt somewhat relieved, since they seemed to think well of what I had to say.

On the morning of September 17, together with Mrs. Washington and my three children, I started for Atlanta. I felt a good deal as I suppose a man feels when he is on his way to the gallows. In passing through the town of

Tuskegee I met a white farmer who lived some distance out in the country. In a jesting manner this man said: "Washington, you have spoken before the Northern white people, the Negroes in the South, and to us country white people in the South; but in Atlanta, to-morrow, you will have before you the Northern whites, the Southern whites, and the Negroes all together. I am afraid that you have got yourself into a tight place." This farmer diagnosed the situation correctly, but his frank words did not add anything to my comfort.

In the course of the journey from Tuskegee to Atlanta both coloured and white people came to the train to point me out, and discussed with perfect freedom, in my hearing, what was going to take place the next day. We were met by a committee in Atlanta. Almost the first thing that I heard when I got off the train in that city was an expression something like this, from an old coloured man near by: "Dat's de man of my race what's gwine to make a speech at de Exposition to-morrow. I'se sho' gwine to hear him."

Atlanta was literally packed, at the time, with people from all parts of this country, and with representatives of foreign governments, as well as with military and civic organizations. The afternoon papers had forecasts of the next day's proceedings in flaring headlines. All this tended to add to my burden. I did not sleep much that night. The next morning, before day, I went carefully over what I intended to say. I also kneeled down and asked God's blessing upon my effort. Right here, perhaps, I ought to add that I make it a rule never to go before an audience, on any occasion, without asking the blessing of God upon what I want to say.

I always make it a rule to make especial preparation for each separate address. No two audiences are exactly alike. It is my aim to reach and talk to the heart of each individual audience, taking it into my confidence very much as I would a person. When I am speaking to an audience, I care little for how what I am saying is going to sound in the newspapers, or to another audience, or to an individual. At the time, the audience before me absorbs all my sympathy, thought, and energy.

Early in the morning a committee called to escort me to my place in the procession which was to march to the

Exposition grounds. In this procession were prominent coloured citizens in carriages, as well as several Negro military organizations. I noted that the Exposition officials seemed to go out of their way to see that all of the coloured people in the procession were properly placed and properly treated. The procession was about three hours in reaching the Exposition grounds, and during all of this time the sun was shining down upon us disagreeably hot. When we reached the grounds, the heat, together with my nervous anxiety, made me feel as if I were about ready to collapse, and to feel that my address was not going to be a success. When I entered the audience-room, I found it packed with humanity from bottom to top, and there were thousands outside who could not get in.

The room was very large, and well suited to public speaking. When I entered the room, there were vigorous cheers from the coloured portion of the audience, and faint cheers from some of the white people. I had been told, while I had been in Atlanta, that while many white people were going to be present to hear me speak, simply out of curiosity, and that others who would be present would be in full sympathy with me, there was a still larger element of the audience which would consist of those who were going to be present for the purpose of hearing me make a fool of myself, or, at least, of hearing me say some foolish thing, so that they could say to the officials who had invited me to speak, "I told you so!"

One of the trustees of the Tuskegee Institute, as well as my personal friend, Mr. William H. Baldwin, Jr. was at one time General Manager of the Southern Railroad, and happened to be in Atlanta on that day. He was so nervous about the kind of reception that I would have, and the effect that my speech would produce, that he could not persuade himself to go into the building, but walked back and forth in the grounds outside until the opening exercises were over.

CHAPTER

XIV

The Atlanta Exposition Address

The Atlanta Exposition, at which I had been asked to make an address as a representative of the Negro race, as stated in the last chapter, was opened with a short address from Governor Bullock. After other interesting exercises, including an invocation from Bishop Nelson, of Georgia, a dedicatory ode by Albert Howell, Jr., and addresses by the President of the Exposition and Mrs. Joseph Thompson, the President of the Woman's Board, Governor Bullock introduced me with the words, "We have with us to-day, a representative of Negro enterprise and Negro civilization."

When I arose to speak, there was considerable cheering, especially from the coloured people. As I remember it now, the thing that was uppermost in my mind was the desire to say something that would cement the friendship of the races and bring about hearty coöperation between them. So far as my outward surroundings were concerned, the only thing that I recall distinctly now is that when I got up, I saw thousands of eyes looking intently into my face. The following is the address which I delivered:—

MR. PRESIDENT AND GENTLEMEN OF THE BOARD OF DIRECTORS AND CITIZENS.

One-third of the population of the South is of the Negro race. No enterprise seeking the material, civil, or moral welfare of this section can disregard this element of our population and reach the highest success. I but convey to you, Mr. President and Directors, the sentiment of the masses of my race when I say that in no way have the value and manhood of the American Negro been more fittingly and generously recognized than by the managers of this magnificent Exposition at every stage of its progress. It is a recognition that will do more to cement the friendship of the two races than any occurrence since the dawn of our freedom.

Not only this, but the opportunity here afforded will awaken among us a new era of industrial progress. Ignorant and inexperienced, it is not strange that in the first years of our new life we began at the top instead of at the bottom; that a seat in Congress or the state legislature was more sought than real estate or industrial skill; that the political convention of stump speaking had more attractions than starting a dairy farm or truck garden.

A ship lost at sea for many days suddenly sighted a friendly vessel. From the mast of the unfortunate vessel was seen a signal, "Water, water; we die of thirst!" The answer from the friendly vessel at once came back, "Cast down your bucket where you are." A second time the signal, "Water, water; send us water!" ran up from the distressed vessel, and was answered, "Cast down your bucket where you are." And a third and fourth signal for water was answered, "Cast down your bucket where you are." The captain of the distressed vessel, at last heeding the injunction, cast down his bucket, and it came up full of fresh, sparkling water from the mouth of the Amazon River. To those of my race who depend on bettering their condition in a foreign land or who underestimate the importance of cultivating friendly relations with the Southern white man, who is their next-door neighbour, I would say: "Cast down your bucket where you are"—cast it down in making friends in every manly way of the people of all races by whom we are surrounded.

Cast it down in agriculture, mechanics, in commerce, in domestic service, and in the professions. And in this connection it is well to bear in mind that whatever other sins the South may be called to bear, when it comes to business, pure and simple, it is in the South that the Negro is given a man's chance in the commercial world, and in nothing is this Exposition more eloquent than in emphasizing this chance. Our greatest danger is that in the great leap from slavery to freedom we may overlook the fact that the masses of us are to live by the productions of our hands, and fail to keep in mind that we shall prosper in proportion as we learn to dignify and glorify common labour and put brains and skill into the common occupations of life; shall prosper in proportion as we learn to draw the line between the superficial and the substantial, the ornamental gewgaws of life and the useful. No race can prosper till it learns that there is as much dignity in tilling a field as in writing a poem. It is at the bottom of life we must begin, and not at the top. Nor should we permit our grievances to overshadow our opportunities.

To those of the white race who look to the incoming of those of foreign birth and strange tongue and habits for the prosperity of the South, were I permitted I would repeat what I say to my own race, "Cast down your bucket where you are." Cast it down among the eight millions of Negroes whose habits you know, whose fidelity and love you have tested in days when to have proved treacherous meant the ruin of your firesides. Cast down your bucket among these people who have, without strikes and labour wars, tilled your fields, cleared your forests, builded your railroads and cities, and brought forth treasures from the bowels of the earth, and helped make possible this magnificent representation of the progress of the South. Casting down your bucket among my people, helping and encouraging them as you are doing on these grounds, and to education of head, hand, and heart, you will find that they will buy your surplus land, make blossom the waste places in your fields, and run your factories. While doing this, you can be sure in the future, as in the past, that you and your families will be surrounded by the most patient, faithful, law-abiding, and unresentful people that the world has seen. As we have proved our loyalty to you in the past, in nursing your children, watching by the sick-bed of your mothers and fathers, and often following them with tear-dimmed eyes to their graves, so in the future, in our humble way, we shall stand by you with a devotion that no foreigner can approach, ready to lay down our lives, if need be, in defence of yours, interlacing our industrial, commercial, civil, and religious life with yours in a way that shall make the interests of both races one. In all things that are purely social we can be as separate as the fingers, yet one as the hand in all things essential to mutual progress.

There is no defence or security for any of us except in the highest intelligence and development of all. If anywhere there are efforts tending to curtail the fullest growth of the Negro, let these efforts be turned into stimulating, encouraging, and making him the most useful and intelligent citizen. Effort or means so invested will pay a thousand per cent interest. These efforts will be twice blessed—"blessing him that gives and him that takes."

There is no escape through law of man or God from the inevitable:—

The laws of changeless justice bind
Oppressor with oppressed;
And close as sin and suffering joined
We march to fate abreast.

Nearly sixteen millions of hands will aid you in pulling the load upward, or they will pull against you the load downward. We shall constitute one-third and more of the ignorance and crime of the South, or one-third its intelligence and progress; we shall contribute one-third to the business and industrial prosperity of the South, or we shall prove a veritable body of death, stagnating, depressing, retarding every effort to advance the body politic.

Gentlemen of the Exposition, as we present to you our humble effort at an exhibition of our progress, you must not expect overmuch. Starting thirty years ago with ownership here and there in a few quilts and pumpkins and chickens (gathered from miscellaneous sources), remember the path that has led from these to the inventions and production of agricultural implements, buggies, steam-engines, newspapers, books, statuary, carving, paintings, the management of drugstores and banks, has not been trodden without contact with thorns and thistles. While we take pride in what we exhibit as a result of our independent efforts, we do not for a moment forget that our part in this exhibition would fall far short of your expectations but for the constant help that has come to our educational life, not only from the Southern states, but especially from Northern philanthropists, who have made their gifts a constant stream of blessing and encouragement.

The wisest among my race understand that the agitation of questions of social equality is the extremest folly, and that progress in the enjoyment of all the privileges that will come to us must be the result of severe and constant struggle rather than of artificial forcing. No race that has anything to contribute to the markets of the world is long in any degree ostracized. It is important and right that all privileges of the law be ours, but it is vastly more important that we be prepared for the exercises of these privileges. The opportunity to earn a dollar in a factory just now is worth infinitely more than the opportunity to spend a dollar in an opera-house.

In conclusion, may I repeat that nothing in thirty years has given us more hope and encouragement, and drawn us so near to you of the white race, as this opportunity offered by the Exposition; and here bending, as it were, over the altar that represents the results of the struggles of your race and mine, both starting practically empty-handed three decades ago, I pledge that in your effort to work out the great and intricate problem which God has laid at the doors of the South, you shall have at all times the patient, sympathetic help of my race; only let this be constantly in mind, that, while from representations in these buildings of the product of field, of forest, of mine, of factory, letters, and art, much good will come, yet far above and beyond material benefits will be that higher good, that, let us pray God, will come, in a blotting out of sectional differences and racial animosities and suspicions, in a determination to administer absolute justice, in a willing obedience among all classes to the mandates of law. This, this, coupled with our material prosperity, will bring into our beloved South a new heaven and a new earth.

The first thing that I remember, after I had finished speaking, was that Governor Bullock rushed across the platform and took me by the hand, and that others did the same. I received so many and such hearty congratulations that I found it difficult to get out of the building. I did not appreciate to any degree, however, the impression which my address seemed to have made, until the next morning, when I went into the business part of the city. As soon as I was recognized, I was surprised to find myself pointed out and surrounded by a crowd of men who wished to shake hands with me. This was kept up on every street on to which I went, to an extent which embarrassed me so much that I went back to my boarding-place. The next morning I returned to Tuskegee. At the station in Atlanta, and at almost all of the stations at which the train stopped between that city and Tuskegee, I found a crowd of people anxious to shake hands with me.

The papers in all parts of the United States published the address in full, and for months afterward there were complimentary editorial references to it. Mr. Clark Howell, the editor of the Atlanta *Constitution*, telegraphed to a New York paper, among other words, the following, "I do not exaggerate when I say that Professor Booker T. Washington's address yesterday was one of the most notable speeches, both as to character and as to the warmth of its reception, ever delivered to a Southern audience. The address was a revelation. The whole speech is a platform upon which blacks and whites can stand with full justice to each other."

The Boston *Transcript* said editorially: "The speech of Booker T. Washington at the Atlanta Exposition, this week, seems to have dwarfed all the other proceedings and the Exposition itself. The sensation that it has caused in the press has never been equalled."

I very soon began receiving all kinds of propositions from lecture bureaus, and editors of magazines and papers, to take the lecture platform, and to write articles. One lecture bureau offered me fifty thousand dollars, or two hundred dollars a night and expenses, if I would place my services at its disposal for a given period. To all these communications I replied that my life-work was at Tuskegee; and that whenever I spoke it must be in the interests of the Tuskegee school and my race, and that I would enter into no arrangements that seemed to place a mere commercial value upon my services.

Some days after its delivery I sent a copy of my address to the President of the United States, the Hon. Grover Cleveland. I received from him the following autograph reply:—

GRAY GABLES, BUZZARD'S BAY, MASS.,
October 6, 1895.

BOOKER T. WASHINGTON, ESQ.

MY DEAR SIR:

I thank you for sending me a copy of your address delivered at the Atlanta Exposition.

I thank you with much enthusiasm for making the address. I have read it with intense interest, and I think the Exposition would be fully justified if it did not do more than furnish the opportunity for its delivery. Your words cannot fail to delight and encourage all who wish well for your race; and if our coloured fellow-citizens do not from your utterances gather new hope and form new determinations to gain every valuable advantage offered them by their citizenship, it will be strange indeed.

Yours very truly,
GROVER CLEVELAND.

Later I met Mr. Cleveland, for the first time, when, as President, he visited the Atlanta Exposition. At the request of myself and others he consented to spend an hour in the Negro Building, for the purpose of inspecting the Negro exhibit and of giving the coloured people in attendance an opportunity to shake hands with him. As soon as I met Mr. Cleveland I became impressed with his simplicity, greatness, and rugged honesty. I have met him many times since then, both at public functions and at his private residence in Princeton, and the more I see of him the more I admire him. When he visited the Negro Building in Atlanta he seemed to give himself up wholly, for that hour, to the coloured people. He seemed to be as careful to shake hands with some old coloured "auntie" clad partially in rags, and to take as much pleasure in doing so, as if he were greeting some millionaire. Many of the coloured people took advantage of the occasion to get him to write his name in a book or on a slip of paper. He was as careful and patient in doing this as if he were putting his signature to some great state document.

Mr. Cleveland has not only shown his friendship for me in many personal ways, but has always consented to do anything I have asked of him for our school. This he has done, whether it was to make a personal donation or to use his influence in securing the donations of others. Judging from my personal acquaintance with Mr. Cleveland, I do not believe that he is conscious of possessing any colour prejudice. He is too great for that. In my contact with people I find that, as a rule, it is only the little, narrow people who live for themselves, who never read good books, who do not travel, who never open up their souls in a way to permit them to come into contact with other souls—with the great outside world. No man whose vision is bounded by colour can come into contact with what is highest and best in the world. In meeting men, in many places, I have found that the happiest people are those who do the most for others; the most miserable are those who do the least. I have also found that few things, if any, are capable of making one so blind and narrow as race prejudice. I often say to our students, in the course of my talks to them on Sunday evenings in the chapel, that the longer I live and the more experience I have of the world, the more I am convinced that, after all, the one thing that is most worth living for—and dying for, if need be—is the opportunity of making some one else more happy and more useful.

The coloured people and the coloured newspapers at first seemed to be greatly pleased with the character of my Atlanta address, as well as with its reception. But after the first burst of enthusiasm began to die away, and the coloured people began reading the speech in cold type, some of them seemed to feel that they had been hypnotized. They seemed to feel that I had been too liberal in my remarks toward the Southern whites, and that I had not spoken out strongly enough for what they termed the "rights" of the race. For a while there was a reaction, so far as a certain element of my own race was concerned, but later these reactionary ones seemed to have been won over to my way of believing and acting.

While speaking of changes in public sentiment, I recall that about ten years after the school at Tuskegee was established, I had an experience that I shall never forget. Dr. Lyman Abbott, then the pastor of Plymouth Church, and also editor of the *Outlook* (then the *Christian Union*), asked me to write a letter for his paper giving my opinion of the exact condition, mental and moral, of the coloured ministers in the South, as based upon my observations. I wrote the letter, giving the exact facts as I conceived them to be. The picture painted was a rather black one—or, since I am black, shall I say "white"? It could not be otherwise with a race but a few years out of slavery, a race which had not had time or opportunity to produce a competent ministry.

What I said soon reached every Negro minister in the country, I think, and the letters of condemnation which I received from them were not few. I think that for a year after the publication of this article every association and every conference or religious body of any kind, of my race, that met, did not fail before adjourning to pass a resolution condemning me, or calling upon me to retract or modify what I had said. Many of these organizations went so far in their resolutions as to advise parents to cease sending their children to Tuskegee. One association even appointed a "missionary" whose duty it was to warn the people against sending their children to Tuskegee. This missionary had a son in the school, and I noticed that, whatever the "missionary" might have said or done with regard to others, he was careful not to take his son away from the institution. Many of the coloured papers, especially those that were the organs of religious bodies, joined in the general chorus of condemnation or demands for retraction.

During the whole time of the excitement, and through all the criticism, I did not utter a word of explanation or retraction. I knew that I was right, and that time and the sober second thought of the people would vindicate me. It was not long before the bishops and other church leaders began to make a careful investigation of the conditions of the ministry, and they found out that I was right. In fact, the oldest and most influential bishop in one branch of the Methodist Church said that my words were far too mild. Very soon public sentiment began making itself felt, in demanding a purifying of the ministry. While this is not yet complete by any means, I think I may say, without egotism, and I have been told by many of our most influential ministers, that my words had much to do with starting a demand for the placing of a higher type of men in the pulpit. I have had the satisfaction of having many who once condemned me thank me heartily for my frank words.

The change of the attitude of the Negro ministry, so far as regards myself, is so complete that at the present time I have no warmer friends among any class than I have among the clergymen. The improvement in the character and life of the Negro ministers is one of the most gratifying evidences of the progress of the race. My experience with them, as well as other events in my life, convince me that the thing to do, when one feels sure that he has said or done the right thing, and is condemned, is to stand still and keep quiet. If he is right, time will show it.

In the midst of the discussion which was going on concerning my Atlanta speech, I received the letter which I give below, from Dr. Gilman, the President of Johns Hopkins University, who had been made chairman of the judges of award in connection with the Atlanta Exposition:—

JOHNS HOPKINS UNIVERSITY, BALTIMORE,
President's Office, September 30, 1895.

DEAR MR. WASHINGTON:

Would it be agreeable to you to be one of the Judges of Award in the Department of Education at Atlanta? If so, I shall be glad to place your name upon the list. A line by telegraph will be welcomed.

Yours very truly,
D. C. GILMAN.

I think I was even more surprised to receive this invitation than I had been to receive the invitation to speak at the opening of the Exposition. It was to be a part of my duty, as one of the jurors, to pass not only upon the exhibits of the coloured schools, but also upon those of the white schools. I accepted the position, and spent a month in Atlanta in performance of the duties which it entailed. The board of jurors was a large one, consisting in all of sixty members. It was about equally divided between Southern white people and Northern white people. Among them were college presidents, leading scientists and men of letters, and specialists in many subjects. When the group of jurors to which I was assigned met for organization, Mr. Thomas Nelson Page, who was one of the number, moved that I be made secretary of that division, and the motion was unanimously adopted. Nearly half of our division were Southern people. In performing my duties in the inspection of the exhibits of white schools I was in every case treated with respect, and at the close of our labours I parted from my associates with regret.

I am often asked to express myself more freely than I do upon the political condition and the political future of my race. These recollections of my experience in Atlanta give me the opportunity to do so briefly. My own belief is, although I have never before said so in so many words, that the time will come when the Negro in the South will be accorded all the political rights which his ability, character, and material possessions entitle him to. I think, though, that the opportunity to freely exercise such political rights will not come in any large degree through outside or artificial forcing, but will be accorded to the Negro by the Southern white people themselves, and that they will protect him in the exercise of those rights. Just as soon as the South gets over the old feeling that it is being forced by "foreigners," or "aliens," to do something which it does not want to do, I believe that the change in the direction that I have indicated is going to begin. In fact, there are indications that it is already beginning in a slight degree.

Let me illustrate my meaning. Suppose that some months before the opening of the Atlanta Exposition there had been a general demand from the press and public platform outside the South that a Negro be given a place on the opening programme, and that a Negro be placed upon the board of jurors of award. Would any such recognition of the race have taken place? I do not think so. The Atlanta officials went as far as they did because they felt it to be a pleasure, as well as a duty, to reward what they considered merit in the Negro race. Say what we will, there is something in human nature which we cannot blot out, which makes one man, in the end, recognize and reward merit in another, regardless of colour or race.

I believe it is the duty of the Negro—as the greater part of the race is already doing—to deport himself modestly in regard to political claims, depending upon the slow but sure influences that proceed from the possession of property, intelligence, and high character for the full recognition of his political rights. I think that the according of the full exercise of political rights is going to be a matter of natural, slow growth, not an over-night, gourd-vine affair. I do not believe that the Negro should cease voting, for a man cannot learn the exercise of self-government by ceasing to vote any more than a boy can learn to swim by keeping out of the water, but I do believe that in his voting he should more and more be influenced by those of intelligence and character who are his next-door neighbours.

I know coloured men who, through the encouragement, help, and advice of Southern white people, have accumulated thousands of dollars' worth of property, but who, at the same time, would never think of going to those same persons for advice concerning the casting of their ballots. This, it seems to me, is unwise and unreasonable, and should cease. In saying this I do not mean that the Negro should truckle, or not vote from principle, for the instant he ceases to vote from principle he loses the confidence and respect of the Southern white man even.

I do not believe that any state should make a law that permits an ignorant and poverty-stricken white man to vote, and prevents a black man in the same condition from voting. Such a law is not only unjust, but it will react, as all unjust laws do, in time; for the effect of such a law is to encourage the Negro to secure education and property, and at the same time it encourages the white man to remain in ignorance and poverty. I believe that in time, through the operation of intelligence and friendly race relations, all cheating at the ballot box in the South will cease. It will become apparent that the white man who begins by cheating a Negro out of his ballot soon learns to cheat a white man out of his, and that the man who does this ends his career of dishonesty by the theft of property or by some equally serious crime. In my opinion, the time will come when the South will encourage all of its citizens to vote. It will see that it pays better, from every standpoint, to have healthy, vigorous life than to have that political stagnation which always results when one-half of the population has no share and no interest in the Government.

As a rule, I believe in universal, free suffrage, but I believe that in the South we are confronted with peculiar conditions that justify the protection of the ballot in many of the states, for a while at least, either by an educational test, a property test, or by both combined; but whatever tests are required, they should be made to apply with equal and exact justice to both races.

CHAPTER XVI

Europe

In 1893 I was married to Miss Margaret James Murray, a native of Mississippi, and a graduate of Fisk University, in Nashville, Tenn., who had come to Tuskegee, as a teacher several years before, and at the time we were married was filling the position of Lady Principal. Not only is Mrs. Washington completely one with me in the work directly connected with the school, relieving me of many burdens and perplexities, but aside from her work on the school grounds, she carries on a mothers' meeting in the town of Tuskegee, and a plantation work among the women, children, and men who live in a settlement connected with a large plantation about eight miles from Tuskegee. Both the mothers' meeting and the plantation work are carried on, not only with a view to helping those who are directly reached, but also for the purpose of furnishing object-lessons in these two kinds of work that may be followed by our students when they go out into the world for their own life-work.

Aside from these two enterprises, Mrs. Washington is also largely responsible for a woman's club at the school which brings together, twice a month, the women who live on the school grounds and those who live near, for the discussion of some important topic. She is also the

President of what is known as the Federation of Southern Coloured Women's Clubs, and is Chairman of the Executive Committee of the National Federation of Coloured Women's Clubs.

Portia, the oldest of my three children, has learned dress-making. She has unusual ability in instrumental music. Aside from her studies at Tuskegee, she has already begun to teach there.

Booker Taliaferro is my next oldest child. Young as he is, he has already nearly mastered the brickmason's trade. He began working at this trade when he was quite small, dividing his time between this and class work; and he has developed great skill in the trade and a fondness for it. He says that he is going to be an architect and brickmason. One of the most satisfactory letters that I have ever received from any one came to me from Booker, last summer. When I left home for the summer, I told him that he must work at his trade half of each day, and that the other half of the day he could spend as he pleased. When I had been away from home two weeks, I received the following letter from him:

> TUSKEGEE, ALABAMA.
>
> My dear Papa:
>
> Before you left home you told me to work at my trade half of each day. I like my work so much that I want to work at my trade all day. Besides, I want to earn all the money I can, so that when I go to another school I shall have money to pay my expenses.
>
> Your son,
> BOOKER.

My youngest child, Ernest Davidson Washington, says that he is going to be a physician. In addition to going to school, where he studies books and has manual training, he regularly spends a portion of his time in the office of our resident physician, and has already learned to do many of the duties which pertain to a doctor's office.

The thing in my life which brings me the keenest regret is that my work in connection with public affairs keeps me for so much of the time away from my family, where, of all places in the world, I delight to be. I always envy the individual whose life-work is so laid that he can spend his evenings at home. I have sometimes thought that people who have this rare privilege do not appreciate it as they should. It is such a rest and relief to get away from crowds of people, and handshaking, and travelling, and get home, even if it be for but a very brief while.

Another thing at Tuskegee out of which I get a great deal of pleasure and satisfaction is in the meeting with our students, and teachers, and their families, in the chapel for devotional exercises every evening at half-past eight, the last thing before retiring for the night. It is an inspiring sight when one stands on the platform there and sees before him eleven or twelve hundred earnest young men and women; and one cannot but feel that it is a privilege to help to guide them to a higher and more useful life.

In the spring of 1899 there came to me what I might describe as almost the greatest surprise of my life. Some good ladies in Boston arranged a public meeting in the interests of Tuskegee, to be held in the Hollis Street Theatre. This meeting was attended by large numbers of the best people of Boston, of both races. Bishop Lawrence presided. In addition to an address made by myself, Mr. Paul Lawrence Dunbar read from his poems, and Dr. W. E. B. Du Bois read an original sketch.

Some of those who attended this meeting noticed that I seemed unusually tired, and some little time after the close of the meeting, one of the ladies who had been interested in it asked me in a casual way if I had ever been to Europe. I replied that I never had. She asked me if I had ever thought of going, and I told her no; that it was something entirely beyond me. This conversation soon passed out of my mind, but a few days afterward I was informed that some friends in Boston, including Mr. Francis J. Garrison, had raised a sum of money sufficient to pay all the expenses of Mrs. Washington and myself during a three or four months' trip to Europe. It was added with emphasis that we *must* go. A year previous to this Mr. Garrison had attempted to get me to promise to go to Europe for a summer's rest, with the understanding that he would be responsible for raising the money among his friends for the expenses of the trip. At that time such a journey seemed so entirely foreign to anything that I should ever be able to undertake that I confess I did not give the matter very serious attention; but later Mr. Garrison joined his efforts to those of the ladies whom I have mentioned, and when their plans were made known to me Mr. Garrison not only had the route mapped out, but had, I believe, selected the steamer upon which we were to sail.

The whole thing was so sudden and so unexpected that I was completely taken off my feet. I had been at work steadily for eighteen years in connection with Tuskegee, and I had never thought of anything else but ending my life in that way. Each day the school seemed to depend upon me more largely for its daily expenses, and I told these Boston friends that, while I thanked them sincerely for their thoughtfulness and generosity, I could not go to Europe, for the reason that the school could not live financially while I was absent. They then informed me that Mr. Henry L. Higginson, and some other good friends who I know do not want their names made public, were then raising a sum of money which would be sufficient to keep the school in operation while I was away. At this point I was compelled to surrender. Every avenue of escape had been closed.

Deep down in my heart the whole thing seemed more like a dream than like reality, and for a long time it was difficult for me to make myself believe that I was actually going to Europe. I had been born and largely reared in the lowest depths of slavery, ignorance, and poverty. In my childhood I had suffered for want of a place to sleep, for lack of food, clothing, and shelter. I had not had the privilege of sitting down to a dining-table until I was quite well grown. Luxuries had always seemed to me to be something meant for white people, not for my race. I had always regarded Europe, and London, and Paris, much as I regard heaven. And now could it be that I was actually going to Europe? Such thoughts as these were constantly with me.

Two other thoughts troubled me a good deal. I feared that people who heard that Mrs. Washington and I were going to Europe might not know all the circumstances, and might get the idea that we had become, as some might say, "stuck up," and were trying to "show off." I recalled that from my youth I had heard it said that too often, when people of my race reached any degree of success, they were inclined to unduly exalt themselves; to try and ape the wealthy, and in so doing to lose their heads. The fear that people might think this of us haunted me a good deal. Then, too, I could not see how my conscience would permit me to spare the time from my work and be happy. It seemed mean and selfish in me to be taking a vacation while others were at work, and while there was so much that needed to be done. From the time I could remember, I had always been at work, and I did not see how I could spend three or four months in doing nothing. The fact was that I did not know how to take a vacation.

Mrs. Washington had much the same difficulty in getting away, but she was anxious to go because she thought that I needed the rest. There were many important National questions bearing upon the life of the race which were being agitated at that time, and this made it all the harder for us to decide to go. We finally gave our Boston friends our promise that we would go, and then they insisted that the date of our departure be set as soon as possible. So we decided upon May 10. My good friend Mr. Garrison kindly took charge of all the details necessary for the success of the trip, and he, as well as other friends, gave us a great number of letters of introduction to people in France and England, and made other arrangements for our comfort and convenience abroad. Good-bys were said at Tuskegee, and we were in New York May 9, ready to sail the next day. Our daughter Portia, who was then studying in South Framingham, Mass., came to New York to see us off. Mr. Scott, my secretary, came with me to New York, in order that I might clear up the last bit of business before I left. Other friends also came to New York to see us off. Just before we went on board the steamer another pleasant surprise came to us in the form of a letter from two generous ladies, stating that they had decided to give us the money with which to erect a new building to be used in properly housing all our industries for girls at Tuskegee.

We were to sail on the *Friesland*, of the Red Star Line, and a beautiful vessel she was. We went on board just before noon, the hour of sailing. I had never before been on board a large ocean steamer, and the feeling which took possession of me when I found myself there is rather hard to describe. It was a feeling, I think, of awe mingled with delight. We were agreeably surprised to find that the captain, as well as several of the other officers, not only knew who we were, but was expecting us and gave us a pleasant greeting. There were several passengers whom we knew, including Senator Sewell, of New Jersey, and Edward Marshall, the newspaper correspondent. I had just a little fear that we would not be treated civilly by some of the passengers. This fear was based upon what I had heard other people of my race, who had crossed the ocean, say about unpleasant experiences in crossing the ocean in American vessels. But in our case, from the captain down to the most humble servant, we were treated with the greatest kindness. Nor was this kindness confined to those who were connected with the steamer; it was shown by all the passengers also. There were not a few Southern men and women on board, and they were as cordial as those from other parts of the country.

As soon as the last good-bys were said, and the steamer had cut loose from the wharf, the load of care, anxiety, and responsibility which I had carried for eighteen years began to lift itself from my shoulders at the rate, it seemed to me, of a pound a minute. It was the first time in all those years that I had felt, even in a measure, free from care; and my feeling of relief it is hard to describe on paper. Added to this was the delightful anticipation of being in Europe soon. It all seemed more like a dream than like a reality.

Mr. Garrison had thoughtfully arranged to have us have one of the most comfortable rooms on the ship. The second or third day out I began to sleep, and I think that I slept at the rate of fifteen hours a day during the remainder of the ten days' passage. Then it was that I began to understand how tired I really was. These long sleeps I kept up for a month after we landed on the other side. It was such an unusual feeling to wake up in the morning and realize that I had no engagements; did not have to take a train at a certain hour; did not have an appointment to meet some one, or to make an address, at a certain hour. How different all this was from some of the experiences that I have been through when travelling, when I have sometimes slept in three different beds in a single night!

When Sunday came, the captain invited me to conduct the religious services, but, not being a minister, I declined. The passengers, however, began making requests that I deliver an address to them in the dining-saloon some time during the voyage, and this I consented to do. Senator Sewell presided at this meeting. After ten days of delightful weather, during which I was not seasick for a day, we landed at the interesting old city of Antwerp, in Belgium.

The next day after we landed happened to be one of those numberless holidays which the people of those countries are in the habit of observing. It was a bright, beautiful day. Our room in the hotel faced the main public square, and the sights there—the people coming in from the country with all kinds of beautiful flowers to sell, the women coming in with their dogs drawing large, brightly polished cans filled with milk, the people streaming into the cathedral—filled me with a sense of newness that I had never before experienced.

After spending some time in Antwerp, we were invited to go with a party of a half-dozen persons on a trip through Holland. This party included Edward Marshall and some American artists who had come over on the same steamer with us. We accepted the invitation, and enjoyed the trip greatly. I think it was all the more interesting and instructive because we went for most of the way on one of the slow, old-fashioned canal-boats. This gave us an opportunity of seeing and studying the real life of the people in the country districts. We went in this way as far as Rotterdam, and later went to The Hague, where the Peace Conference was then in session, and where we were kindly received by the American representatives.

The thing that impressed itself most on me in Holland was the thoroughness of the agriculture and the excellence of the Holstein cattle. I never knew, before visiting Holland, how much it was possible for people to get out of a small plot of ground. It seemed to me that absolutely no land was wasted. It was worth a trip to Holland, too, just to get a sight of three or four hundred fine Holstein cows grazing in one of those intensely green fields.

From Holland we went to Belgium, and made a hasty trip through that country, stopping at Brussels, where we visited the battlefield of Waterloo. From Belgium we went direct to Paris, where we found that Mr. Theodore Stanton, the son of Mrs. Elizabeth Cady Stanton, had kindly provided accommodations for us. We had barely got settled in Paris before an invitation came to me from the University Club of Paris to be its guest at a banquet which was soon to be given. The other guests were ex-President Benjamin Harrison and Archbishop Ireland, who were in Paris at the time. The American Ambassador, General Horace Porter, presided at the banquet. My address on this occasion seemed to give satisfaction to those who heard it. General Harrison kindly devoted a large portion of his remarks at dinner to myself and to the influence of the work at Tuskegee on the American race question. After my address at this banquet other invitations came to me, but I declined the most of them, knowing that if I accepted them all, the object of my visit would be defeated. I did, however, consent to deliver an address in the American chapel the following Sunday morning, and at this meeting General Harrison, General Porter, and other distinguished Americans were present.

Later we received a formal call from the American Ambassador, and were invited to attend a reception at his residence. At this reception we met many Americans, among them Justices Fuller and Harlan, of the United States Supreme Court. During our entire stay of a month in Paris, both the American Ambassador and his wife, as well as several other Americans, were very kind to us.

While in Paris we saw a good deal of the now famous American Negro painter, Mr. Henry C. Tanner, whom we had formerly known in America. It was very satisfactory to find how well known Mr. Tanner was in the field of art, and to note the high standing which all classes accorded to him. When we told some Americans that we were going to the Luxembourg Palace to see a painting by an American Negro, it was hard to convince them that a Negro had been thus honoured. I do not believe that they were really convinced of the fact until they saw the picture for themselves. My acquaintance with Mr. Tanner reënforced in my mind the truth which I am constantly trying to impress upon our students at Tuskegee—and on our people throughout the country, as far as I can reach them with my voice—that any man, regardless of colour, will be recognized and rewarded just in proportion as he learns to do something well—learns to do it better than some one else—however humble the thing may be. As I have said, I believe that my race will succeed in proportion as it learns to do a common thing in an uncommon manner; learns to do a thing so thoroughly that no one can improve upon what it has done; learns to make its services of indispensable value. This was the spirit that inspired me in my first effort at Hampton, when I was given the opportunity to sweep and dust that schoolroom. In a degree I felt that my whole future life depended upon the thoroughness with which I cleaned that room, and I was determined to do it so well that no one could find any fault with the job. Few people ever stopped, I found, when looking at his pictures, to inquire whether Mr. Tanner was a Negro painter, a French painter, or a German painter. They simply knew that he was able to produce something which the world wanted—a great painting—and the matter of his colour did not enter into their minds. When a Negro girl learns to cook, to wash dishes, to sew, to write a book, or a Negro boy learns to groom horses, or to grow sweet potatoes, or to produce butter, or to build a house, or to be able to practise medicine, as well or better than some one else, they will be rewarded regardless of race or colour. In the long run, the world is going to have the best, and any difference in race, religion, or previous history will not long keep the world from what it wants.

I think that the whole future of my race hinges on the question as to whether or not it can make itself of such indispensable value that the people in the town and the state where we reside will feel that our presence is necessary to the happiness and well-being of the community. No man who continues to add something to the material, intellectual, and moral well-being of the place in which he lives is long left without proper reward. This is a great human law which cannot be permanently nullified.

The love of pleasure and excitement which seems in a large measure to possess the French people impressed itself upon me. I think they are more noted in this respect than is true of the people of my own race. In point of morality and moral earnestness I do not believe that the French are ahead of my own race in America. Severe competition and the great stress of life have led them to learn to do things more thoroughly, and to exercise greater economy; but time, I think, will bring my race to the same point. In the matter of truth and high honour I do not believe that the average Frenchman is ahead of the American Negro; while so far as mercy and kindness to dumb animals go, I believe that my race is far ahead. In fact, when I left France, I had more faith in the future of the black man in America than I had ever possessed.

From Paris we went to London, and reached there early in July, just about the height of the London social season. Parliament was in session, and there was a great deal of gaiety. Mr. Garrison and other friends had provided us with a large number of letters of introduction, and they had also sent letters to other persons in different parts of the United Kingdom, apprising these people of our coming. Very soon after reaching London we were flooded with invitations to attend all manner of social functions, and a great many invitations came to me asking that I deliver public addresses. The most of these invitations I declined, for the reason that I wanted to rest. Neither were we able to accept more than a small proportion of the other invitations. The Rev. Dr. Brooke Herford and Mrs. Herford, whom I had known in Boston, consulted with the American Ambassador, the Hon. Joseph Choate, and arranged for me to speak at a public meeting to be held in Exeter Hall. Mr. Choate kindly consented to preside. The meeting was largely attended. There were many distinguished persons present, among them several members of Parliament, including Mr. James Bryce, who spoke at the meeting. What the American Ambassador said in introducing me, as well as a synopsis of what I said, was widely published in England and in the American papers at the time. Dr. and Mrs. Herford gave Mrs. Washington and myself a reception, at which we had the privilege of meeting some of the best people in England. Throughout our stay in London Ambassador Choate was most kind and attentive to us. At the Ambassador's reception I met, for the first time, Mark Twain.

We were the guests several times of Mrs. T. Fisher Unwin, the daughter of the English statesman, Richard Cobden. It seemed as if both Mr. and Mrs. Unwin could not do enough for our comfort and happiness. Later, for nearly a week, we were the guests of the daughter of John Bright, now Mrs. Clark, of Street, England. Both Mr. and Mrs. Clark, with their daughter, visited us at Tuskegee the next year. In Birmingham, England, we were the guests for several days of Mr. Joseph Sturge, whose father was a great abolitionist and friend of Whittier and Garrison. It was a great privilege to meet throughout England those who had known and honoured the late William Lloyd Garrison, the Hon. Frederick Douglass, and other abolitionists. The English abolitionists with whom we came in contact never seemed to tire of talking about these two Americans. Before going to England I had had no proper conception of the deep interest displayed by the abolitionists of England in the cause of freedom, nor did I realize the amount of substantial help given by them.

In Bristol, England, both Mrs. Washington and I spoke at the Women's Liberal Club. I was also the principal speaker at the Commencement exercises of the Royal College for the Blind. These exercises were held in the Crystal Palace, and the presiding officer was the late Duke of Westminster, who was said to be, I believe, the richest man in England, if not in the world. The Duke, as well as his wife and their daughter, seemed to be pleased with what I said, and thanked me heartily. Through the kindness of Lady Aberdeen, my wife and I were enabled to go with a party of those who were attending the International Congress of Women, then in session in London, to see Queen Victoria, at Windsor Castle, where, afterward, we were all the guests of her Majesty at tea. In our party was Miss Susan B. Anthony, and I was deeply impressed with the fact that one did not often get an opportunity to see, during the same hour, two women so remarkable in different ways as Susan B. Anthony and Queen Victoria.

In the House of Commons, which we visited several times, we met Sir Henry M. Stanley. I talked with him about Africa and its relation to the American Negro, and after my interview with him I became more convinced than ever that there was no hope of the American Negro's improving his condition by emigrating to Africa.

On various occasions Mrs. Washington and I were the guests of Englishmen in their country homes, where, I think, one sees the Englishman at his best. In one thing, at least, I feel sure that the English are ahead of Americans, and that is, that they have learned how to get more out of life. The home life of the English seems to me to be about as perfect as anything can be. Everything moves like clockwork. I was impressed, too, with the deference that the servants show to their "masters" and "mistresses,"—terms which I suppose would not be tolerated in America. The English servant expects, as a rule, to be nothing but a servant, and so he perfects himself in the art to a degree that no class of servants in America has yet reached. In our country, the servant expects to become, in a few years, a "master" himself. Which system is preferable? I will not venture an answer.

Another thing that impressed itself upon me throughout England was the high regard that all classes have for law and order, and the ease and thoroughness with which everything is done. The Englishmen, I found, took plenty of time for eating, as for everything else. I am not sure if, in the long run, they do not accomplish as much or more than rushing, nervous Americans do.

My visit to England gave me a higher regard for the nobility than I had had. I had no idea that they were so generally loved and respected by the masses, nor had I any correct conception of how much time and money they spent in works of philanthropy, and how much real heart they put into this work. My impression had been that they merely spent money freely and had a "good time."

It was hard for me to get accustomed to speaking to English audiences. The average Englishman is so serious, and is so tremendously in earnest about everything, that when I told a story that would have made an American audience roar with laughter, the Englishmen simply looked me straight in the face without even cracking a smile.

When the Englishman takes you into his heart and friendship, he binds you there as with cords of steel, and I do not believe that there are many other friendships that are so lasting or so satisfactory. Perhaps I can illustrate this point in no better way than by relating the following incident. Mrs. Washington and I were invited to attend a reception given by the Duke and Duchess of Sutherland, at Stafford House—said to be the finest house in London; I may add that I believe the Duchess of Sutherland is said to be the most beautiful woman in England. There must have been at least three hundred persons at this reception. Twice during the evening the Duchess sought us out for a conversation, and she asked me to write her when we got home, and tell her more about the work at Tuskegee. This I did. When Christmas came we were surprised and delighted to receive her photograph with her autograph on it. The correspondence has continued, and we now feel that in the Duchess of Sutherland we have one of our warmest friends.

After three months in Europe we sailed from Southampton in the steamship *St. Louis*. On this steamer there was a fine library that had been presented to the ship by the citizens of St. Louis, Mo. In this library I found a life of Frederick Douglass, which I began reading. I became especially interested in Mr. Douglass's description of the way he was treated on shipboard during his first or second visit to England. In this description he told how he was not permitted to enter the cabin, but had to confine himself to the deck of the ship. A few minutes after I had finished reading this description I was waited on by a committee of ladies and gentlemen with the request that I deliver an address at a concert which was to be given the following evening. And yet there are people who are bold enough to say that race feeling in America is not growing less intense! At this concert the Hon. Benjamin B. Odell, Jr., the present governor of New York, presided. I was never given a more cordial hearing anywhere. A large proportion of the passengers were Southern people. After the concert some of the passengers proposed that a subscription be raised to help the work at Tuskegee, and the money to support several scholarships was the result.

While we were in Paris I was very pleasantly surprised to receive the following invitation from the citizens of West Virginia and of the city near which I had spent my boyhood days:—

CHARLESTON, W. VA.,
May 16, 1899.

PROFESSOR BOOKER T. WASHINGTON,
PARIS, FRANCE

Dear Sir:

Many of our best citizens of West Virginia have united in liberal expressions of admiration and praise of your worth and work, and desire that on your return from Europe you should favour them with your presence and with the inspiration of your words. We most sincerely indorse this move, and on behalf of the citizens of Charleston extend to you our most cordial invitation to have you come to us, that we may honour you who have done so much by your life and work to honour us.

We are,
Very truly yours,
THE COMMON COUNCIL OF THE CITY OF CHARLESTON
By W. HERMAN SMITH, Mayor.

This invitation from the City Council of Charleston was accompanied by the following:—

PROFESSOR BOOKER T. WASHINGTON,
PARIS, FRANCE.

Dear Sir:

We, the citizens of Charleston and West Virginia, desire to express our pride in you and the splendid career that you have thus far accomplished, and ask that we be permitted to show our pride and interest in a substantial way.

Your recent visit to your old home in our midst awoke within us the keenest regret that we were not permitted to hear you and render some substantial aid to your work before you left for Europe.

In view of the foregoing, we earnestly invite you to share the hospitality of our city upon your return from Europe, and give us the opportunity to hear you and put ourselves in touch with your work in a way that will be most gratifying to yourself, and that we may receive the inspiration of your words and presence.

An early reply to this invitation, with an indication of the time you may reach our city, will greatly oblige,

Yours very respectfully,

The Charleston *Daily Gazette;* The *Daily Mail Tribune;* G. W. Atkinson, Governor; E. L. Boggs, Secretary to Governor; Wm. M. O. Dawson, Secretary of State; L. M. La Follette, Auditor; J. R. Trotter, Superintendent of Schools; E. W. Wilson, ex-Governor; W. A. MacCorkle, ex-Governor; John Q. Dickinson, President Kanawha Valley Bank; L. Prichard, President Charleston National Bank; Geo. S. Couch, President Kanawha National Bank; Ed. Reid, Cashier Kanawha National Bank; Geo. S. Laidley, Superintendent City Schools; L. E. McWhorter, President Board of Education; Chas. K. Payne, wholesale merchant; and many others.

This invitation coming as it did from the City Council, the state officers, and all the substantial citizens of both races of the community where I had spent my boyhood, and from which I had gone a few years before, unknown, in poverty and ignorance, in quest of an education, not only surprised me, but almost unmanned me. I could not understand what I had done to deserve it all.

I accepted the invitation, and at the appointed day was met at the railway station at Charleston by a committee headed by ex-Governor W. A. MacCorkle, and composed of men of both races. The public reception was held in the Opera-House at Charleston. The Governor of the state, the Hon. George W. Atkinson, presided, and an address of welcome was made by ex-Governor MacCorkle. A prominent part in the reception was taken by the coloured citizens. The Opera-House was filled with citizens of both races, and among the white people were many for whom I had worked when a boy. The next day Governor and Mrs. Atkinson gave me a public reception at the State House, which was attended by all classes.

Not long after this the coloured people in Atlanta,

Georgia, gave me a reception at which the Governor of the state presided, and a similar reception was given me in New Orleans, which was presided over by the Mayor of the city. Invitations came from many other places which I was not able to accept.

CHAPTER XVII

Last Words

Before going to Europe some events came into my life which were great surprises to me. In fact, my whole life has largely been one of surprises. I believe that any man's life will be filled with constant, unexpected encouragements of this kind if he makes up his mind to do his level best each day of his life—that is, tries to make each day reach as nearly as possible the high-water mark of pure, unselfish, useful living. I pity the man, black or white, who has never experienced the joy and satisfaction that come to one by reason of an effort to assist in making some one else more useful and more happy.

Six months before he died, and nearly a year after he had been stricken with paralysis, General Armstrong expressed a wish to visit Tuskegee again before he passed away. Notwithstanding the fact that he had lost the use of his limbs to such an extent that he was practically helpless, his wish was gratified, and he was brought to Tuskegee. The owners of the Tuskegee Railroad, white men living in the town, offered to run a special train without cost, out to the main station—Chehaw, five miles away—to meet him. He arrived on the school grounds about nine o'clock in the evening. Some one had suggested that we give the General a "pine-knot torchlight reception." This plan was carried out, and the moment that his carriage entered the school grounds he began passing between two lines of lighted and waving "fat pine" wood knots held by over a thousand students and teachers. The whole thing was so novel and surprising that the General was completely overcome with happiness. He remained a guest in my home for nearly two months, and, although almost wholly without the use of voice or limb, he spent nearly every hour in devising ways and means to help the South. Time and time again he said to me, during this visit, that it was not only the duty of the country to assist in elevating the Negro of the South, but the poor white man as well. At the end of his visit I resolved anew to devote myself more earnestly than ever to the cause which was so near his heart. I said that if a man in his condition was willing to think, work, and act, I should not be wanting in furthering in every possible way the wish of his heart.

The death of General Armstrong, a few weeks later, gave me the privilege of getting acquainted with one of the finest, most unselfish, and most attractive men that I have ever come in contact with. I refer to the Rev. Dr. Hollis B. Frissell, now the Principal of the Hampton Institute, and General Armstrong's successor. Under the clear, strong, and almost perfect leadership of Dr. Frissell, Hampton has had a career of prosperity and usefulness that is all that the General could have wished for. It seems to be the constant effort of Dr. Frissell to hide his own great personality behind that of General Armstrong—to make himself of "no reputation" for the sake of the cause.

More than once I have been asked what was the greatest surprise that ever came to me. I have little hesitation in answering that question. It was the following letter, which came to me one Sunday morning when I was sitting on the veranda of my home at Tuskegee, surrounded by my wife and three children:—

HARVARD UNIVERSITY, CAMBRIDGE,
May 28, 1896.

PRESIDENT BOOKER T. WASHINGTON,

MY DEAR SIR:

Harvard University desires to confer on you

> at the approaching Commencement an honorary degree; but it is our custom to confer degrees only on gentlemen who are present. Our Commencement occurs this year on June 24, and your presence would be desirable from about noon till about five o'clock in the afternoon. Would it be possible for you to be in Cambridge on that day?
>
> Believe me, with great regard,
>
> Very truly yours,
> CHARLES W. ELIOT.

This was a recognition that had never in the slightest manner entered into my mind, and it was hard for me to realize that I was to be honoured by a degree from the oldest and most renowned university in America. As I sat upon my veranda, with this letter in my hand, tears came into my eyes. My whole former life—my life as a slave on the plantation, my work in the coal-mine, the times when I was without food and clothing, when I made my bed under a sidewalk, my struggles for an education, the trying days I had had at Tuskegee, days when I did not know where to turn for a dollar to continue the work there, the ostracism and sometimes oppression of my race—all this passed before me and nearly overcame me.

I had never sought or cared for what the world calls fame. I have always looked upon fame as something to be used in accomplishing good. I have often said to my friends that if I can use whatever prominence may have come to me as an instrument with which to do good, I am content to have it. I care for it only as a means to be used for doing good, just as wealth may be used. The more I come into contact with wealthy people, the more I believe that they are growing in the direction of looking upon their money simply as an instrument which God has placed in their hand for doing good with. I never go to the office of Mr. John D. Rockefeller, who more than once has been generous to Tuskegee, without being reminded of this. The close, careful, and minute investigation that he always makes in order to be sure that every dollar that he gives will do the most good—an investigation that is just as searching as if he were investing money in a business enterprise—convinces me that the growth in this direction is most encouraging.

At nine o'clock, on the morning of June 24, I met President Eliot, the Board of Overseers of Harvard University, and the other guests, at the designated place on the university grounds, for the purpose of being escorted to Sanders Theatre, where the Commencement exercises were to be held and degrees conferred. Among others invited to be present for the purpose of receiving a degree at this time were General Nelson A. Miles, Dr. Bell, the inventor of the Bell telephone, Bishop Vincent, and the Rev. Minot J. Savage. We were placed in line immediately behind the President and the Board of Overseers, and directly afterward the Governor of Massachusetts, escorted by the Lancers, arrived and took his place in the line of march by the side of President Eliot. In the line there were also various other officers and professors, clad in cap and gown. In this order we marched to Sanders Theatre, where, after the usual Commencement exercise, came the conferring of the honorary degrees. This, it seems, is always considered the most interesting feature at Harvard. It is not known, until the individuals appear, upon whom the honorary degrees are to be conferred, and those receiving these honours are cheered by the students and others in proportion to their popularity. During the conferring of the degrees excitement and enthusiasm are at the highest pitch.

When my name was called, I rose, and President Eliot, in beautiful and strong English, conferred upon me the degree of Master of Arts. After these exercises were over, those who had received honorary degrees were invited to lunch with the President. After the lunch we were formed in line again, and were escorted by the Marshal of the day, who that year happened to be Bishop William Lawrence, through the grounds, where, at different points, those who had been honoured were called by name and received the Harvard yell. This march ended at Memorial Hall, where the alumni dinner was served. To see over a thousand strong men, representing all that is best in State, Church, business, and education, with the glow and enthusiasm of college loyalty and college pride,—which has, I think, a peculiar Harvard flavour,—is a sight that does not easily fade from memory.

Among the speakers after dinner were President Eliot, Governor Roger Wolcott, General Miles, Dr. Minot J. Savage, the Hon. Henry Cabot Lodge, and myself. When I was called upon, I said, among other things:—

> It would in some measure relieve my embarrassment if I could, even in a slight degree, feel myself worthy of the great honour which you do me to-day. Why you have called me from the Black Belt of the South, from among my humble people, to share in the honours of this occasion, is not for me to explain; and yet it may not be inappropriate for me to suggest that it seems to me that one of the most vital questions that touch our American life is how to bring the strong, wealthy, and learned into helpful touch with the poorest, most ignorant, and humblest, and at the same time make one appreciate the vitalizing, strengthening influence of the other. How shall we make the mansions on yon Beacon Street feel and see the need of the spirits in the lowliest cabin in Alabama cotton-fields or Louisiana sugar-bottoms? This problem Harvard University is solving, not by bringing itself down, but by bringing the masses up.
>
> If my life in the past has meant anything in the lifting up of my people and the bringing about of better relations between your race and mine, I assure you from this day it will mean doubly more. In the economy of God there is but one standard by which an individual can succeed—there is but one for a race. This country demands that every race shall measure itself by the American standard. By it a race must rise or fall, succeed or fail, and in the last analysis mere sentiment counts for little. During the next half-century and more, my race must continue passing through the severe American crucible. We are to be tested in our patience, our forbearance, our perseverance, our power to endure wrong, to withstand temptations, to economize, to acquire and use skill; in our ability to compete, to succeed in commerce, to disregard the

> superficial for the real, the appearance for the substance, to be great and yet small, learned and yet simple, high and yet the servant of all.

As this was the first time that a New England university had conferred an honorary degree upon a Negro, it was the occasion of much newspaper comment throughout the country. A correspondent of a New York paper said:—

> When the name of Booker T. Washington was called, and he arose to acknowledge and accept, there was such an outburst of applause as greeted no other name except that of the popular soldier patriot, General Miles. The applause was not studied and stiff, sympathetic and condoling; it was enthusiasm and admiration. Every part of the audience from pit to gallery joined in, and a glow covered the cheeks of those around me, proving sincere appreciation of the rising struggle of an ex-slave and the work he has accomplished for his race.

A Boston paper said, editorially:—

> In conferring the honorary degree of Master of Arts upon the Principal of Tuskegee Institute, Harvard University has honoured itself as well as the object of this distinction. The work which Professor Booker T. Washington has accomplished for the education, good citizenship and popular enlightenment in his chosen field of labour in the South entitles him to rank with our national benefactors. The university which can claim him on its list of sons, whether in regular course or *honoris causa,* may be proud.
>
> It has been mentioned that Mr. Washington is the first of his race to receive an honorary degree from a New England university. This, in itself, is a distinction. But the degree was not conferred because Mr. Washington is a coloured man, or because he was born in slavery, but because he has shown, by his work for the

> elevation of the people of the Black Belt of the south, a genius and a broad humanity which count for greatness in any man, whether his skin be white or black.

Another Boston paper said:—

> It is Harvard which, first among New England colleges, confers an honorary degree upon a black man. No one who has followed the history of Tuskegee and its work can fail to admire the courage, persistence, and splendid common sense of Booker T. Washington. Well may Harvard honour the ex-slave, the value of whose services, alike to his race and country, only the future can estimate.

The correspondent of the New York *Times* wrote:—

> All the speeches were enthusiastically received, but the coloured man carried off the oratorical honours, and the applause which broke out when he had finished was vociferous and long-continued.

Soon after I began work at Tuskegee I formed a resolution, in the secret of my heart, that I would try to build up a school that would be of so much service to the country that the President of the United States would one day come to see it. This was, I confess, rather a bold resolution, and for a number of years I kept it hidden in my own thoughts, not daring to share it with any one.

In November, 1897, I made the first move in this direction, and that was in securing a visit from a member of President McKinley's Cabinet, the Hon. James Wilson, Secretary of Agriculture. He came to deliver an address at the formal opening of the Slater-Armstrong Agricultural Building, our first large building to be used for the purpose of giving training to our students in agriculture and kindred branches.

In the fall of 1898 I heard that President McKinley was likely to visit Atlanta, Georgia, for the purpose of taking part in the Peace Jubilee exercises to be held there to commemorate the successful close of the Spanish-American war. At this time I had been hard at work, together with our teachers, for eighteen years, trying to build up a school that we thought would be of service to the Nation, and I determined to make a direct effort to secure a visit from the President and his Cabinet. I went to Washington, and I was not long in the city before I found my way to the White House. When I got there I found the waiting rooms full of people, and my heart began to sink, for I feared there would not be much chance of my seeing the President that day, if at all. But, at any rate, I got an opportunity to see Mr. J. Addison Porter, the secretary to the President, and explained to him my mission. Mr. Porter kindly sent my card directly to the President, and in a few minutes word came from Mr. McKinley that he would see me.

How any man can see so many people of all kinds, with all kinds of errands, and do so much hard work, and still keep himself calm, patient, and fresh for each visitor in the way that President McKinley does, I cannot understand. When I saw the President he kindly thanked me for the work which we were doing at Tuskegee for the interests of the country. I then told him, briefly, the object of my visit. I impressed upon him the fact that a visit from the Chief Executive of the Nation would not only encourage our students and teachers, but would help the entire race. He seemed interested, but did not make a promise to go to Tuskegee, for the reason that his plans about going to Atlanta were not then fully made; but he asked me to call the matter to his attention a few weeks later.

By the middle of the following month the President had definitely decided to attend the Peace Jubilee in Atlanta. I went to Washington again and saw him, with a view of getting him to extend his trip to Tuskegee. On this second visit Mr. Charles W. Hare, a prominent white citizen of Tuskegee, kindly volunteered to accompany me, to reënforce my invitation with one from the white people of Tuskegee and the vicinity.

Just previous to my going to Washington the second time, the country had been excited, and the coloured people greatly depressed, because of several severe race riots which had occurred at different points in the South.

As soon as I saw the President, I perceived that his heart was greatly burdened by reason of these race disturbances. Although there were many people waiting to see him, he detained me for some time, discussing the condition and prospects of the race. He remarked several times that he was determined to show his interest and faith in the race, not merely in words, but by acts. When I told him that I thought that at that time scarcely anything would go farther in giving hope and encouragement to the race than the fact that the President of the Nation would be willing to travel one hundred and forty miles out of his way to spend a day at a Negro institution, he seemed deeply impressed.

While I was with the President, a white citizen of Atlanta, a Democrat and an ex-slaveholder, came into the room, and the President asked his opinion as to the wisdom of his going to Tuskegee. Without hesitation the Atlanta man replied that it was the proper thing for him to do. This opinion was reënforced by that friend of the race, Dr. J. L. M. Curry. The President promised that he would visit our school on the 16th of December.

When it became known that the President was going to visit our school, the white citizens of the town of Tuskegee—a mile distant from the school—were as much pleased as were our students and teachers. The white people of the town, including both men and women, began arranging to decorate the town, and to form themselves into committees for the purpose of coöperating with the officers of our school in order that the distinguished visitor might have a fitting reception. I think I never realized before this how much the white people of Tuskegee and vicinity thought of our institution. During the days when we were preparing for the President's reception, dozens of these people came to me and said that, while they did not want to push themselves into prominence, if there was anything they could do to help, or to relieve me personally, I had but to intimate it and they would be only too glad to assist. In fact, the thing that touched me almost as deeply as the visit of the President itself was the deep pride which all classes of citizens in Alabama seemed to take in our work.

The morning of December 16th brought to the little city of Tuskegee such a crowd as it had never seen before.

With the President came Mrs. McKinley and all of the Cabinet officers but one; and most of them brought their wives or some members of their families. Several prominent generals came, including General Shafter and General Joseph Wheeler, who were recently returned from the Spanish-American war. There was also a host of newspaper correspondents. The Alabama Legislature was in session at Montgomery at this time. This body passed a resolution to adjourn for the purpose of visiting Tuskegee. Just before the arrival of the President's party the Legislature arrived, headed by the governor and other state officials.

The citizens of Tuskegee had decorated the town from the station to the school in a generous manner. In order to economize in the matter of time, we arranged to have the whole school pass in review before the President. Each student carried a stalk of sugar-cane with some open bolls of cotton fastened to the end of it. Following the students the work of all departments of the school passed in review, displayed on "floats" drawn by horses, mules, and oxen. On these floats we tried to exhibit not only the present work of the school, but to show the contrasts between the old methods of doing things and the new. As an example, we showed the old method of dairying in contrast with the improved methods, the old methods of tilling the soil in contrast with the new, the old methods of cooking and housekeeping in contrast with the new. These floats consumed an hour and a half of time in passing.

In his address in our large, new chapel, which the students had recently completed, the President said, among other things:—

> To meet you under such pleasant auspices and to have the opportunity of a personal observation of your work is indeed most gratifying. The Tuskegee Normal and Industrial Institute is ideal in its conception, and has already a large and growing reputation in the country, and is not unknown abroad. I congratulate all who are associated in this undertaking for the good work which it is doing in the education of its students

to lead lives of honour and usefulness, thus exalting the race for which it was established.

Nowhere, I think, could a more delightful location have been chosen for this unique educational experiment, which has attracted the attention and won the support even of conservative philanthropists in all sections of the country.

To speak of Tuskegee without paying special tribute to Booker T. Washington's genius and perseverance would be impossible. The inception of this noble enterprise was his, and he deserves high credit for it. His was the enthusiasm and enterprise which made its steady progress possible and established in the institution its present high standard of accomplishment. He has won a worthy reputation as one of the great leaders of his race, widely known and much respected at home and abroad as an accomplished educator, a great orator, and a true philanthropist.

The Hon. John D. Long, the Secretary of the Navy, said in part:—

I cannot make a speech to-day. My heart is too full—full of hope, admiration, and pride for my countrymen of both sections and both colours. I am filled with gratitude and admiration for your work, and from this time forward I shall have absolute confidence in your progress and in the solution of the problem in which you are engaged.

The problem, I say, has been solved. A picture has been presented to-day which should be put upon canvas with the pictures of Washington and Lincoln, and transmitted to future time and generations—a picture which the press of the country should spread broadcast over the land, a most dramatic picture, and that picture is this: The President of the United States standing on this platform on one side the Governor of Alabama, on the other, completing the trinity, a

> representative of a race only a few years ago in bondage, the coloured President of the Tuskegee Normal and Industrial Institute.
>
> God bless the President under whose majesty such a scene as that is presented to the American people. God bless the state of Alabama, which is showing that it can deal with this problem for itself. God bless the orator, philanthropist, and disciple of the Great Master—who, if he were on earth, would be doing the same work—Booker T. Washington.

Postmaster General Smith closed the address which he made with these words:—

> We have witnessed many spectacles within the last few days. We have seen the magnificent grandeur and the magnificent achievements of one of the great metropolitan cities of the South. We have seen heroes of the war pass by in procession. We have seen floral parades. But I am sure my colleagues will agree with me in saying that we have witnessed no spectacle more impressive and more encouraging, more inspiring for our future, than that which we have witnessed here this morning.

Some days after the President returned to Washington I received the letter which follows:—

> EXECUTIVE MANSION,
> *Washington, Dec. 23, 1899.*
>
> Dear Sir:
>
> By this mail I take pleasure in sending you engrossed copies of the souvenir of the visit of the President to your institution. These sheets bear the autographs of the President and the members of the Cabinet who accompanied him on the trip. Let me take this opportunity of congratulating you most heartily and sincerely upon the great success of the exercises provided for and entertainment furnished us under your

auspices during our visit to Tuskegee. Every feature of the programme was perfectly executed and was viewed or participated in with the heartiest satisfaction by every visitor present. The unique exhibition which you gave of your pupils engaged in their industrial vocations was not only artistic but thoroughly impressive. The tribute paid by the President and his Cabinet to your work was none too high, and forms a most encouraging augury, I think, for the future prosperity of your institution. I cannot close without assuring you that the modesty shown by yourself in the exercises was most favourably commented upon by all the members of our party.

With best wishes for the continued advance of your most useful and patriotic undertaking, kind personal regards and the compliments of the season, believe me, always,

Very sincerely yours,
JOHN ADDISON PORTER.
Secretary to the President.

TO PRESIDENT BOOKER T. WASHINGTON, Tuskegee
Normal and Industrial Institute, Tuskegee, Ala.

Twenty years have now passed since I made the first humble effort at Tuskegee, in a broken-down shanty and an old hen-house, without owning a dollar's worth of property, and with but one teacher and thirty students. At the present time the institution owns twenty-three hundred acres of land, one thousand of which are under cultivation each year, entirely by student labour. There are now upon the grounds, counting large and small, sixty-six buildings; and all except four of these have been almost wholly erected by the labour of our students. While the students are at work upon the land and in erecting buildings, they are taught, by competent instructors, the latest methods of agriculture and the trades connected with building.

There are in constant operation at the school, in connection with thorough academic and religious training, thirty industrial departments. All of these teach industries at which our men and women can find immediate employment as soon as they leave the institution. The only difficulty now is that the demand for our graduates from both white and black people in the South is so great that we cannot supply more than one-half the persons for whom applications come to us. Neither have we the buildings nor the money for current expenses to enable us to admit to the school more than one-half the young men and women who apply to us for admission.

In our industrial teaching we keep three things in mind: first, that the student shall be so educated that he shall be enabled to meet conditions as they exist *now,* in the part of the South where he lives—in a word, to be able to do the thing which the world wants done; second, that every student who graduates from the school shall have enough skill, coupled with intelligence and moral character, to enable him to make a living for himself and others; third, to send every graduate out feeling and knowing that labor is dignified and beautiful—to make each one love labour instead of trying to escape it. In addition to the agricultural training which we give to young men, and the training given to our girls in all the usual domestic employments, we now train a number of girls in agriculture each year. These girls are taught gardening, fruit-growing, dairying, bee-culture, and poultry-raising.

While the institution is in no sense denominational, we have a department known as the Phelps Hall Bible Training School, in which a number of students are prepared for the ministry and other forms of Christian work, especially work in the country districts. What is equally important, each one of these students works half of each day at some industry, in order to get skill and the love of work, so that when he goes out from the institution he is prepared to set the people with whom he goes to labour a proper example in the matter of industry.

The value of our property is now over $700,000. If we add to this our endowment fund, which at present is $1,000,000, the value of the total property is now $1,700,000. Aside from the need for more buildings and for money for current expenses, the endowment fund should be increased to at least $3,000,000. The annual current expenses are now about $150,000. The greater part of this I collect each year by going from door to door and from house to house. All of our property is free from mortgage, and is deeded to an undenominational board of trustees who have the control of the institution.

From thirty students the number has grown to fourteen hundred, coming from twenty-seven states and territories, from Africa, Cuba, Porto Rico, Jamaica, and other foreign countries. In our departments there are one hundred and ten officers and instructors; and if we add the families of our instructors, we have a constant population upon our grounds of not far from seventeen hundred people.

I have often been asked how we keep so large a body of people together, and at the same time keep them out of mischief. There are two answers: that the men and women who come to us for an education are in earnest; and that everybody is kept busy. The following outline of our daily work will testify to this:—

> 5 A.M., rising bell; 5:50 A.M., warning breakfast bell; 6 A.M., breakfast bell; 6:20 A.M., breakfast over; 6:20 to 6:50 A.M., rooms are cleaned; 6:50, work bell; 7:30, morning study hour; 8:20, morning school bell; 8:25, inspection of young men's toilet in ranks; 8:40, devotional exercises in chapel; 8:55, "five minutes with the daily news"; 9 A.M., class work begins; 12, class work closes; 12:15 P.M., dinner; 1 P.M., work bell; 1:30 P.M., class work begins; 3:30 P.M., class work ends; 5:30 P.M., bell to "knock off" work; 6 P.M., supper; 7:10 P.M., evening prayers; 7:30 P.M., evening study hour; 8:45 P.M., evening study hour closes; 9:20 P.M., warning retiring bell; 9:30 P.M., retiring bell.

We try to keep constantly in mind the fact that the worth of the school is to be judged by its graduates. Counting those who have finished the full course, together with those who have taken enough training to enable them to do reasonably good work, we can safely say that at least six thousand men and women from Tuskegee are now at work in different parts of the South; men and women who, by their own example or by direct effort, are showing the masses of our race how to improve their material, educational, and moral and religious life. What is equally important, they are exhibiting a degree of common sense and self-control which is causing better relations to exist between the races and is causing the Southern white man to learn to believe in the value of educating the men and women of my race. Aside from this, there is the influence that is constantly being exerted through the mothers' meeting and the plantation work conducted by Mrs. Washington.

Wherever our graduates go, the changes which soon begin to appear in the buying of land, improving homes, saving money, in education, and in high moral character are remarkable. Whole communities are fast being revolutionized through the instrumentality of these men and women.

Ten years ago I organized at Tuskegee the first Negro Conference. This is an annual gathering which now brings to the school eight or nine hundred representative men and women of the race, who come to spend a day in finding out what the actual industrial, mental, and moral conditions of the people are, and in forming plans for improvement. Out from this central Negro Conference at Tuskegee have grown numerous state and local conferences which are doing the same kind of work. As a result of the influence of these gatherings, one delegate reported at the last annual meeting that ten families in his community had bought and paid for homes. On the day following the annual Negro Conference, there is held the "Workers' Conference." This is composed of officers and teachers who are engaged in educational work in the larger institutions in the South. The Negro Conference furnishes a rare opportunity for these workers to study the real condition of the rank and file of the people.

In the summer of 1900, with the assistance of such prominent coloured men as Mr. T. Thomas Fortune, who has always upheld my hands in every effort, I organized the National Negro Business League, which held its first meeting in Boston, and brought together for the first time a large number of the coloured men who are engaged in various lines of trade or business in different parts of the United States. Thirty states were represented at our first meeting. Out of this national meeting grew state and local business leagues.

In addition to looking after the executive side of the work at Tuskegee, and raising the greater part of the money for the support of the school, I cannot seem to escape the duty of answering at least a part of the calls which come to me unsought to address Southern white audiences and audiences of my own race, as well as frequent gatherings in the North. As to how much of my time is spent in this way, the following clipping from a Buffalo (N.Y.) paper will tell. This has reference to an occasion when I spoke before the National Educational Association in that city.

> Booker T. Washington, the foremost educator among the coloured people of the world, was a very busy man from the time he arrived in the city the other night from the West and registered at the Iroquois. He had hardly removed the stains of travel when it was time to partake of supper. Then he held a public levee in the parlours of the Iroquois until eight o'clock. During that time he was greeted by over two hundred eminent teachers and educators from all parts of the United States. Shortly after eight o'clock he was driven in a carriage to Music Hall, and in one hour and a half he made two ringing addresses, to as many as five thousand people, on Negro education. Then Mr. Washington was taken in charge by a delegation of coloured citizens, headed by the Rev. Mr. Watkins, and hustled off to a small informal reception, arranged in honour of the visitor by the people of his race.

Nor can I, in addition to making these addresses, escape the duty of calling the attention of the South and of the country in general, through the medium of the press, to matters that pertain to the interests of both races. This, for example, I have done in regard to the evil habit of lynching. When the Louisiana State Constitutional Convention was in session, I wrote an open letter to that body pleading for justice for the races. In all such efforts I have received warm and hearty support from the

Southern newspapers, as well as from those in all other parts of the country.

Despite superficial and temporary signs which might lead one to entertain a contrary opinion, there was never a time when I felt more hopeful for the race than I do at the present. The great human law that in the end recognizes and rewards merit is everlasting and universal. The outside world does not know, neither can it appreciate, the struggle that is constantly going on in the hearts of both the Southern white people and their former slaves to free themselves from racial prejudice; and while both races are thus struggling they should have the sympathy, the support, and the forbearance of the rest of the world.

As I write the closing words of this autobiography I find myself—not by design—in the city of Richmond, Virginia: the city which only a few decades ago was the capital of the Southern Confederacy, and where, about twenty-five years ago, because of my poverty I slept night after night under a sidewalk.

This time I am in Richmond as the guest of the coloured people of the city; and came at their request to deliver an address last night to both races in the Academy of Music, the largest and finest audience room in the city. This was the first time that the coloured people had ever been permitted to use this hall. The day before I came, the City Council passed a vote to attend the meeting in a body to hear me speak. The state Legislature, including the House of Delegates and the Senate, also passed a unanimous vote to attend in a body. In the presence of hundreds of coloured people, many distinguished white citizens, the City Council, the state Legislature, and state officials, I delivered my message, which was one of hope and cheer; and from the bottom of my heart I thanked both races for this welcome back to the state that gave me birth.

Selections from *The Autobiography of an Ex-Coloured Man*

JAMES WELDON JOHNSON

1912

CHAPTER I

I know that in writing the following pages I am divulging the great secret of my life, the secret which for some years I have guarded far more carefully than any of my earthly possessions; and it is a curious study to me to analyse the motives which prompt me to do it. I feel that I am led by the same impulse which forces the un-found-out criminal to take somebody into his confidence, although he knows that the act is likely, even almost certain, to lead to his undoing. I know that I am playing with fire, and I feel the thrill which accompanies that most fascinating pastime; and, back of it all, I think I find a sort of savage and diabolical desire to gather up all the little tragedies of my life, and turn them into a practical joke on society.

And, too, I suffer a vague feeling of unsatisfaction, of regret, of almost remorse, from which I am seeking relief, and of which I shall speak in the last paragraph of this account.

I was born in a little town of Georgia a few years after the close of the Civil War. I shall not mention the name of the town, because there are people still living there who could be connected with this narrative. I have only a faint recollection of the place of my birth. At times I can close my eyes and call up in a dreamlike way things that seem to have happened ages ago in some other world. I can see in this half vision a little house—I am quite sure it was not a large one—I can remember that flowers grew in the front yard, and that around each bed of flowers was a hedge of varicoloured glass bottles stuck in the ground neck down. I remember that once, while playing round in the sand, I became curious to know whether or not the bottles grew as the flowers did, and I proceeded to dig them up to find out; the investigation brought me a terrific spanking, which indelibly fixed the incident in my mind. I can remember, too, that behind the house was a shed under which stood two or three wooden wash-tubs. These tubs were the earliest aversion of my life, for regularly on certain evenings I was plunged into one of them and scrubbed until my skin ached. I can remember to this day the pain caused by the strong, rank soap's getting into my eyes.

Back from the house a vegetable garden ran, perhaps seventy-five or one hundred feet; but to my childish fancy it was an endless territory. I can still recall the thrill of joy, excitement, and wonder it gave me to go on an exploring expedition through it, to find the blackberries, both ripe and green, that grew along the edge of the fence.

I remember with what pleasure I used to arrive at, and stand before, a little enclosure in which stood a patient cow chewing her cud, how I would occasionally offer her through the bars a piece of my bread and molasses, and how I would jerk back my hand in half fright if she made any motion to accept my offer.

I have a dim recollection of several people who moved in and about this little house, but I have a distinct mental image of only two: one, my mother; and the other, a tall man with a small, dark moustache. I remember that his shoes or boots were always shiny, and that he wore a gold chain and a great gold watch with which he was always willing to let me play. My admiration was almost equally divided between the watch and chain and the shoes. He used to come to the house evenings, perhaps two or three times a week; and it became my appointed duty whenever he came to bring him a pair of slippers and to put the shiny shoes in a particular corner; he often gave me in return for this service a bright coin, which my mother taught me to promptly drop in a little tin bank. I remember distinctly the last time this tall man came to the little house in Georgia; that evening before I went to bed he took me up in his arms and squeezed me very tightly; my mother stood behind his chair wiping tears from her eyes. I remember how I sat upon his knee and watched him laboriously drill a hole through a ten-dollar gold piece, and then tie the coin around my neck with a string. I have worn that gold piece around my neck the greater part of my life, and still possess it, but more than once I have wished that some other way had been found of attaching it to me besides putting a hole through it.

On the day after the coin was put around my neck my mother and I started on what seemed to me an endless journey. I knelt on the seat and watched through the train window the corn- and cotton-fields pass swiftly by until I fell asleep. When I full awoke, we were being driven through the streets of a large city—Savannah. I sat up and blinked at the bright lights. At Savannah we boarded a steamer which finally landed us in New York. From New York we went to a town in Connecticut, which became the home of my boyhood.

My mother and I lived together in a little cottage which seemed to me to be fitted up almost luxuriously; there were horse-hair covered chairs in the parlour, and a little square piano; there was a stairway with red carpet on it leading to a half second story; there were pictures on the walls, and a few books in a glass-doored case. My mother dressed me very neatly, and I developed that pride which well-dressed boys generally have. She was careful about my associates, and I myself was quite particular. As I look back now I can see that I was a perfect little aristocrat. My mother rarely went to anyone's house, but she did sewing, and there were a great many ladies coming to our cottage. If I was round they would generally call me, and ask me my name and age and tell my mother what a pretty boy I was. Some of them would pat me on the head and kiss me.

My mother was kept very busy with her sewing; sometimes she would have another woman helping her. I think she must have derived a fair income from her work. I know, too, that at least once each month she received a letter; I used to watch for the postman, get the letter, and run to her with it; whether she was busy or not, she would take it and instantly thrust it into her bosom. I never saw her read one of these letters. I knew later that they contained money and what was to her more than money. As busy as she generally was, she found time, however, to teach me my letters and figures and how to spell a number of easy words. Always on Sunday evenings she opened the little square piano and picked out hymns. I can recall now that whenever she played hymns from the book her *tempo* was always decidedly *largo*. Sometimes on other evenings, when she was not sewing, she would play simple accompaniments to some old Southern songs which she sang. In these songs she was freer, because she played them by ear. Those evenings on which she opened the little piano were the happiest hours of my childhood. Whenever she started toward the instrument, I used to follow her with all the interest and irrepressible joy that a pampered pet dog shows when a package is opened in which he knows there is a sweet bit for him. I used to stand by her side and often interrupt and annoy her by chiming in with strange harmonies which I found on either the high keys of the treble or the low keys of the bass. I remember that I had a particular fondness for the black keys. Always on such evenings, when the music was over, my mother would sit with me in her arms, often for a very long time. She would hold me close, softly crooning some old melody without words, all the while gently stroking her face against my head; many and many a night I thus fell asleep. I can see her now, her great dark eyes looking into the fire, to where? No one knew but her. The memory of that picture has more than once kept me from straying too far from the place of purity and safety in which her arms held me.

At a very early age I began to thump on the piano alone, and it was not long before I was able to pick out a few tunes. When I was seven years old, I could play by ear all of the hymns and songs that my mother knew. I had also learned the names of the notes in both clefs, but I preferred not to be hampered by notes. About this time several ladies for whom my mother sewed heard me play and they persuaded her that I should at once be put under a teacher; so arrangements were made for me to study the piano with a lady who was a fairly good musician; at the same time arrangements were made for me to study my books with this lady's daughter. My music teacher had no small difficulty at first in pinning me down to the notes. If she played my lesson over for me, I invariably attempted to reproduce the required sounds without the slightest recourse to the written characters. Her daughter, my other teacher, also had her worries. She found that, in reading, whenever I came to words that were difficult or unfamiliar, I was prone to bring my imagination to the rescue and read from the picture. She has laughingly told me, since then, that I would sometimes substitute whole sentences and even paragraphs from what meaning I thought the illustrations conveyed. She said she not only was sometimes amused at the fresh treatment I would give an author's subject, but, when I gave some new and sudden turn to the plot of the story, often grew interested and even excited in listening to hear what kind of a denouement I would bring about. But I am sure this was not due to dullness, for I made rapid progress in both my music and my books.

And so for a couple of years my life was divided between my music and my school-books. Music took up the greater part of my time. I had no playmates, but amused myself with games—some of them my own invention—which could be played alone. I knew a few boys whom I had met at the church which I attended with my mother, but I had formed no close friendships with any of them. Then, when I was nine years old, my mother decided to enter me in the public school, so all at once I found myself thrown among a crowd of boys of all sizes and kinds; some of them seemed to me like savages. I shall never forget the bewilderment, the pain, the heart-sickness, of that first day at school. I seemed to be the only stranger in the place; every other boy seemed to know every other boy. I was fortunate enough, however, to be assigned to a teacher who knew me; my mother made her dresses. She was one of the ladies who used to pat me on the head and kiss me. She had the tact to address a few words directly to me; this gave me a certain sort of standing in the class and put me somewhat at ease.

Within a few days I had made one staunch friend and

was on fairly good terms with most of the boys. I was shy of the girls, and remained so; even now a word or look from a pretty woman sets me all a-tremble. This friend I bound to me with hooks of steel in a very simple way. He was a big awkward boy with a face full of freckles and a head full of very red hair. He was perhaps fourteen years of age; that is, four or five years older than any other boy in the class. This seniority was due to the fact that he had spent twice the required amount of time in several of the preceding classes. I had not been at school many hours before I felt that "Red Head"—as I involuntarily called him—and I were to be friends. I do not doubt that this feeling was strengthened by the fact that I had been quick enough to see that a big, strong boy was a friend to be desired at a public school; and, perhaps, in spite of his dullness, "Red Head" had been able to discern that I could be of service to him. At any rate there was a simultaneous mutual attraction.

The teacher had strung the class promiscuously round the walls of the room for a sort of trial heat for places of rank; when the line was straightened out, I found that by skilful manoeuvring I had placed myself third and had piloted "Red Head" to the place next to me. The teacher began by giving us to spell the words corresponding to our order in the line. "Spell *first*." "Spell *second*." "Spell *third*." I rattled off: "T-h-i-r-d, third," in a way which said: "Why don't you give us something hard?" As the words went down the line, I could see how lucky I had been to get a good place together with an easy word. As young as I was, I felt impressed with the unfairness of the whole proceeding when I saw the tail-enders going down before *twelfth* and *twentieth*, and I felt sorry for those who had to spell such words in order to hold a low position. "Spell *fourth*." "Red Head," with his hands clutched tightly behind his back, began bravely: "F-o-r-t-h." Like a flash a score of hands went up, and the teacher began saying: "No snapping of fingers, no snapping of fingers." This was the first word missed, and it seemed to me that some of the scholars were about to lose their senses; some were dancing up and down on one foot with a hand above their heads, the fingers working furiously, and joy beaming all over their faces; others stood still, their hands raised not so high, their fingers working less rapidly, and their faces expressing not quite so much happiness; there were still others who did not move or raise their hands, but stood with great wrinkles on their foreheads, looking very thoughtful.

The whole thing was new to me, and I did not raise my hand, but slyly whispered the letter "u" to "Red Head" several times. "Second chance," said the teacher. The hands went down and the class became quiet. "Red Head," his face now red, after looking beseechingly at the ceiling, then pitiably at the floor, began very haltingly: "F-u——" Immediately an impulse to raise hands went through the class, but the teacher checked it, and poor "Red Head," though he knew that each letter he added only took him farther out of the way, went doggedly on and finished: "—r-t-h." The hand-raising was now repeated with more hubbub and excitement than at first. Those who before had not moved a finger were now waving their hands above their heads. "Red Head" felt that he was lost. He looked very big and foolish, and some of the scholars began to snicker. His helpless condition went straight to my heart, and gripped my sympathies. I felt that if he failed, it would in some way be my failure. I raised my hand, and, under cover of the excitement and the teacher's attempts to regain order, I hurriedly shot up into his ear twice, quite distinctly: "F-o-u-r-t-h, f-o-u-r-t-h." The teacher tapped on her desk and said: "Third and last chance." The hands came down, the silence became oppressive. "Red Head" began: "F——" Since that day I have waited anxiously for many a turn of the wheel of fortune, but never under greater tension than when I watched for the order in which those letters would fall from "Red's" lips—"o-u-r-t-h." A sigh of relief and disappointment went up from the class. Afterwards, through all our school-days, "Red Head" shared my wit and quickness and I benefited by his strength and dogged faithfulness.

There were some black and brown boys and girls in the school, and several of them were in my class. One of the boys strongly attracted my attention from the first day I saw him. His face was as black as night, but shone as though it were polished; he had sparkling eyes, and when he opened his mouth, he displayed glistening white teeth. It struck me at once as appropriate to call him "Shiny

Face," or "Shiny Eyes," or "Shiny Teeth," and I spoke of him often by one of these names to the other boys. These terms were finally merged into "Shiny," and to that name he answered good-naturedly during the balance of his public school days.

"Shiny" was considered without question to be the best speller, the best reader, the best penman—in a word, the best scholar, in the class. He was very quick to catch anything, but, nevertheless, studied hard; thus he possessed two powers very rarely combined in one boy. I saw him year after year, on up into the high school, win the majority of the prizes for punctuality, deportment, essay writing, and declamation. Yet it did not take me long to discover that, in spite of his standing as a scholar, he was in some way looked down upon.

The other black boys and girls were still more looked down upon. Some of the boys often spoke of them as "niggers." Sometimes on the way home from school a crowd would walk behind them repeating:

"Nigger, nigger, never die,
Black face and shiny eye."

On one such afternoon one of the black boys turned suddenly on his tormentors and hurled a slate; it struck one of the white boys in the mouth, cutting a slight gash in his lip. At sight of the blood the boy who had thrown the slate ran, and his companions quickly followed. We ran after them pelting them with stones until they separated in several directions. I was very much wrought up over the affair, and went home and told my mother how one of the "niggers" had struck a boy with a slate. I shall never forget how she turned on me. "Don't you ever use that word again," she said, "and don't you ever bother the coloured children at school. You ought to be ashamed of yourself." I did hang my head in shame, not because she had convinced me that I had done wrong, but because I was hurt by the first sharp word she had ever given me.

My school-days ran along very pleasantly. I stood well in my studies, not always so well with regard to my behaviour. I was never guilty of any serious misconduct, but my love of fun sometimes got me into trouble. I remember, however, that my sense of humour was so sly that most of the trouble usually fell on the head of the other fellow. My ability to play on the piano at school exercises was looked upon as little short of marvellous in a boy of my age. I was not chummy with many of my mates, but, on the whole, was about as popular as it is good for a boy to be.

One day near the end of my second term at school the principal came into our room and, after talking to the teacher, for some reason said: "I wish all of the white scholars to stand for a moment." I rose with the others. The teacher looked at me and, calling my name, said: "You sit down for the present, and rise with the others." I did not quite understand her, and questioned: "Ma'm?" She repeated, with a softer tone in her voice: "You sit down now, and rise with the others." I sat down dazed. I saw and heard nothing. When the others were asked to rise, I did not know it. When school was dismissed, I went out in a kind of stupor. A few of the white boys jeered me, saying: "Oh, you're a nigger too." I heard some black children say: "We knew he was coloured." "Shiny" said to them: "Come along, don't tease him," and thereby won my undying gratitude.

I hurried on as fast as I could, and had gone some distance before I perceived that "Red Head" was walking by my side. After a while he said to me: "Le' me carry your books." I gave him my strap without being able to answer. When we got to my gate, he said as he handed me my books: "Say, you know my big red agate? I can't shoot with it any more. I'm going to bring it to school for you tomorrow." I took my books and ran into the house. As I passed through the hallway, I saw that my mother was busy with one of her customers; I rushed up into my own little room, shut the door, and went quickly to where my looking-glass hung on the wall. For an instant I was afraid to look, but when I did, I looked long and earnestly. I had often heard people say to my mother: "What a pretty boy you have!" I was accustomed to hear remarks about my beauty; but now, for the first time, I became conscious of it and recognized it. I noticed the ivory whiteness of my skin, the beauty of my mouth, the size and liquid darkness of my eyes, and how the long, black lashes that fringed and shaded them produced an effect that was strangely fascinating even to me. I noticed the softness and glossiness of my dark hair that fell in waves over my temples, making my forehead appear whiter than it really was. How long I stood there gazing at my image I do not know. When I came out and reached the head of the stairs, I heard the lady who had been with my mother going out. I ran downstairs and rushed to where my mother was sitting, with a piece of work in her hands. I buried my head in her lap and blurted out: "Mother, mother, tell me, am I a nigger?" I could not see her face, but I knew the piece of work dropped to the floor and I felt her hands on my head. I looked up into her face and repeated: "Tell me, mother, am I a nigger?" There were tears in her eyes and I could see that she was suffering for me. And then it was that I looked at her critically for the first time. I had thought of her in a childish way only as the most beautiful woman in the world; now I looked at her searching for defects. I could see that her skin was almost brown, that her hair was not so soft as mine, and that she did differ in some way from the other ladies who came to the house; yet, even so, I could see that she was very beautiful, more beautiful than any of them. She must have felt that I was examining her, for she hid her face in my hair and said with difficulty: "No, my darling, you are not a nigger." She went on: "You are as good as anybody; if anyone calls you a nigger, don't notice them." But the more she talked, the less was I reassured, and I stopped her by saying: "Well, mother, am I white? Are you white?" She answered tremblingly: "No, I am not white, but you—your father is one of the greatest men in the country—the best blood of the South is in you——" This suddenly opened up in my heart a fresh chasm of misgiving and fear, and I almost fiercely demanded: "Who is my father? Where is he?" She stroked my hair and said: "I'll tell you about him some day." I sobbed: "I want to know now." She answered: "No, not now."

Perhaps it had to be done, but I have never forgiven the woman who did it so cruelly. It may be that she never knew that she gave me a sword-thrust that day in school which was years in healing.

CHAPTER II

Since I have grown older I have often gone back and tried to analyse the change that came into my life after that fateful day in school. There did come a radical change, and, young as I was, I felt fully conscious of it, though I did not fully comprehend it. Like my first spanking, it is one of the few incidents in my life that I can remember clearly. In the life of everyone there is a limited number of unhappy experiences which are not written upon the memory, but stamped there with a die; and in long years after, they can be called up in detail, and every emotion that was stirred by them can be lived through anew; these are the tragedies of life. We may grow to include some of them among the trivial incidents of childhood—a broken toy, a promise made to us which was not kept, a harsh, heart-piercing word—but these, too, as well as the bitter experiences and disappointments of mature years, are the tragedies of life.

And so I have often lived through that hour, that day, that week, in which was wrought the miracle of my transition from one world into another; for I did indeed pass into another world. From that time I looked out through other eyes, my thoughts were coloured, my words dictated, my actions limited by one dominating, all-pervading idea which constantly increased in force and weight until I finally realized in it a great, tangible fact.

And this is the dwarfing, warping, distorting influence which operates upon each and every coloured man in the United States. He is forced to take his outlook on all things, not from the view-point of a citizen, or a man, or even a human being, but from the view-point of a *coloured* man. It is wonderful to me that the race has progressed so broadly as it has, since most of its thought and all of its activity must run through the narrow neck of this one funnel.

And it is this, too, which makes the coloured people of this country, in reality, a mystery to the whites. It is a difficult thing for a white man to learn what a coloured man really thinks; because, generally, with the latter an additional and different light must be brought to bear on what he thinks; and his thoughts are often influenced by considerations so delicate and subtle that it would be impossible for him to confess or explain them to one of the opposite race. This gives to every coloured man, in proportion to his intellectuality, a sort of dual personality; there is one phase of him which is disclosed only in the freemasonry of his own race. I have often watched with interest and sometimes with amazement even ignorant coloured men under cover of broad grins and minstrel antics maintain this dualism in the presence of white men.

I believe it to be a fact that the coloured people of this country know and understand the white people better than the white people know and understand them.

I now think that this change which came into my life was at first more subjective than objective. I do not think my friends at school changed so much toward me as I did toward them. I grew reserved, I might say suspicious. I grew constantly more and more afraid of laying myself open to some injury to my feelings or my pride. I frequently saw or fancied some slight where, I am sure, none was intended. On the other hand, my friends and teachers were, if anything different, more considerate of me; but I can remember that it was against this very attitude in particular that my sensitiveness revolted. "Red" was the only one who did not so wound me; up to this day I recall with a swelling heart his clumsy efforts to make me understand that nothing could change his love for me.

I am sure that at this time the majority of my white school-mates did not understand or appreciate any differences between me and themselves; but there were a few who had evidently received instructions at home on the matter, and more than once they displayed their knowledge in word and action. As the years passed, I noticed that the most innocent and ignorant among the others grew in wisdom.

I myself would not have so clearly understood this difference had it not been for the presence of the other coloured children at school; I had learned what their status was, and now I learned that theirs was mine. I had had no particular like or dislike for these black and brown boys and girls; in fact, with the exception of "Shiny," they had occupied very little of my thought; but I do know that when the blow fell, I had a very strong aversion to being classed with them. So I became something of a solitary. "Red" and I remained inseparable, and there was between "Shiny" and me a sort of sympathetic bond, but my intercourse with the others was never entirely free from a feeling of constraint. I must add, however, that this feeling was confined almost entirely to my intercourse with boys and girls of about my own age; I did not experience it with my seniors. And when I grew to manhood, I found myself freer with elderly white people than with those near my own age.

I was now about eleven years old, but these emotions and impressions which I have just described could not have been stronger or more distinct at an older age. There were two immediate results of my forced loneliness: I began to find company in books, and greater pleasure in music. I made the former discovery through a big, gilt-bound, illustrated copy of the Bible, which used to lie in splendid neglect on the centre table in our little parlour. On top of the Bible lay a photograph album. I had often looked at the pictures in the album, and one day, after taking the larger book down and opening it on the floor, I was overjoyed to find that it contained what seemed to be an inexhaustible supply of pictures. I looked at these pictures many times; in fact, so often that I knew the story of each one without having to read the subject, and then, somehow, I picked up the thread of history on which are strung the trials and tribulations of the Hebrew children; this I followed with feverish interest and excitement. For a long time King David, with Samson a close second, stood at the head of my list of heroes; he was not displaced until I came to know Robert the Bruce. I read a good portion of the Old Testament, all that part treating of wars and rumours of wars, and then started in on the New. I became interested in the life of Christ, but became impatient and disappointed when I found that, notwithstanding the great power he possessed, he did not make use of it when, in my judgment, he most needed to do so. And so my first general impression of the Bible was what my later impression has been of a number of modern books, that the authors put their best work in the first part, and grew either exhausted or careless toward the end.

After reading the Bible, or those parts which held my attention, I began to explore the glass-doored bookcase which I have already mentioned. I found there *Pilgrim's Progress,* Peter Parley's *History of the United States,* Grimm's *Household Stories, Tales of a Grandfather,* a bound volume of an old English publication (I think it was called *The Mirror*), a little volume called *Familiar Science,* and somebody's *Natural Theology,* which last, of course, I could not read, but which, nevertheless, I tackled, with the result of gaining a permanent dislike for all kinds of theology. There were several other books of no particular name or merit, such as agents sell to people who know nothing of buying books. How my mother came by this little library which, considering all things, was so well suited to me I never sought to know. But she was far from being an ignorant woman and had herself, very likely, read the majority of these books, though I do not remember ever seeing her with a book in her hand, with the exception of the Episcopal Prayer-book. At any rate she encouraged in me the habit of reading, and when I had about exhausted those books in the little library which interested me, she began to buy books for me. She also regularly gave me money to buy a weekly paper which was then very popular for boys.

At this time I went in for music with an earnestness

worthy of maturer years; a change of teachers was largely responsible for this. I began now to take lessons of the organist of the church which I attended with my mother; he was a good teacher and quite a thorough musician. He was so skilful in his instruction and filled me with such enthusiasm that my progress—these are his words—was marvellous. I remember that when I was barely twelve years old I appeared on a program with a number of adults at an entertainment given for some charitable purpose, and carried off the honours. I did more, I brought upon myself through the local newspapers the handicapping title of "infant prodigy."

I can believe that I did astonish my audience, for I never played the piano like a child; that is, in the "one-two-three" style with accelerated motion. Neither did I depend upon mere brilliancy of technique, a trick by which children often surprise their listeners; but I always tried to interpret a piece of music; I always played with feeling. Very early I acquired that knack of using the pedals, which makes the piano a sympathetic, singing instrument, quite a different thing from the source of hard or blurred sounds it so generally is. I think this was due not entirely to natural artistic temperament, but largely to the fact that I did not begin to learn the piano by counting out exercises, but by trying to reproduce the quaint songs which my mother used to sing, with all their pathetic turns and cadences.

Even at a tender age, in playing I helped to express what I felt by some of the mannerisms which I afterwards observed in great performers; I had not copied them. I have often heard people speak of the mannerisms of musicians as affectations adopted for mere effect; in some cases they may be so; but a true artist can no more play upon the piano or violin without putting his whole body in accord with the emotions he is striving to express than a swallow can fly without being graceful. Often when playing I could not keep the tears which formed in my eyes from rolling down my cheeks. Sometimes at the end or even in the midst of a composition, as big a boy as I was, I would jump from the piano, and throw myself sobbing into my mother's arms. She, by her caresses and often her tears, only encouraged these fits of sentimental hysteria. Of course, to counteract this tendency to temperamental excesses I should have been out playing ball or in swimming with other boys of my age; but my mother didn't know that. There was only once when she was really firm with me, making me do what she considered was best; I did not want to return to school after the unpleasant episode which I have related, and she was inflexible.

I began my third term, and the days ran along as I have already indicated. I had been promoted twice, and had managed each time to pull "Red" along with me. I think the teachers came to consider me the only hope of his ever getting through school, and I believe they secretly conspired with me to bring about the desired end. At any rate, I know it became easier in each succeeding examination for me not only to assist "Red," but absolutely to do his work. It is strange how in some things honest people can be dishonest without the slightest compunction. I knew boys at school who were too honourable to tell a fib even when one would have been just the right thing, but could not resist the temptation to assist or receive assistance in an examination. I have long considered it the highest proof of honesty in a man to hand his street-car fare to the conductor who had overlooked it.

One afternoon after school, during my third term, I rushed home in a great hurry to get my dinner and go to my music teacher's. I was never reluctant about going there, but on this particular afternoon I was impetuous. The reason of this was I had been asked to play the accompaniment for a young lady who was to play a violin solo at a concert given by the young people of the church, and on this afternoon we were to have our first rehearsal. At that time playing accompaniments was the only thing in music I did not enjoy; later this feeling grew into positive dislike. I have never been a really good accompanist because my ideas of interpretation were always too strongly individual. I constantly forced my *accelerandos* and *rubatos* upon the soloist, often throwing the duet entirely out of gear.

Perhaps the reader has already guessed why I was so willing and anxious to play the accompaniment to this violin solo; if not—the violinist was a girl of seventeen or eighteen whom I had first heard play a short time before on a Sunday afternoon at a special service of some kind, and who had moved me to a degree which now I can hardly think of as possible. At present I do not think it was due to her wonderful playing, though I judge she must have been a very fair performer, but there was just the proper setting to produce the effect upon a boy such as I was; the half-dim church, the air of devotion on the part of the listeners, the heaving tremor of the organ under the clear wail of the violin, and she, her eyes almost closing, the escaping strands of her dark hair wildly framing her pale face, and her slender body swaying to the tones she called forth, all combined to fire my imagination and my heart with a passion, though boyish, yet strong and, somehow, lasting. I have tried to describe the scene; if I have succeeded, it is only half success, for words can only partially express what I wish to convey. Always in recalling that Sunday afternoon I am subconscious of a faint but distinct fragrance which, like some old memory-awakening perfume, rises and suffuses my whole imagination, inducing a state of reverie so airy as just to evade the powers of expression.

She was my first love, and I loved her as only a boy loves. I dreamed of her, I built air castles for her, she was the incarnation of each beautiful heroine I knew; when I played the piano, it was to her, not even music furnished an adequate outlet for my passion; I bought a new note-book and, to sing her praises, made my first and last attempts at poetry. I remember one day at school, after we had given in our note-books to have some exercises corrected, the teacher called me to her desk and said: "I couldn't correct your exercises because I found nothing in your book but a rhapsody on somebody's brown eyes." I had passed in the wrong note-book. I don't think I have felt greater embarrassment in my whole life than I did at that moment. I was ashamed not only that my teacher should see this nakedness of my heart, but that she should find out that I had any knowledge of such affairs. It did not then occur to me to be ashamed of the kind of poetry I had written.

Of course, the reader must know that all of this adoration was in secret; next to my great love for this young lady was the dread that in some way she would find it out. I did not know what some men never find out, that the woman who cannot discern when she is loved has never lived. It makes me laugh to think how successful I was in concealing it all; within a short time after our duet all of the friends of my dear one were referring to me as her "little sweetheart," or her "little beau," and she laughingly encouraged it. This did not entirely satisfy me; I wanted to be taken seriously. I had definitely made up my mind that I should never love another woman, and that if she deceived me I should do something desperate—the great difficulty was to think of something sufficiently desperate—and the heartless jade, how she led me on!

So I hurried home that afternoon, humming snatches of the violin part of the duet, my heart beating with pleasurable excitement over the fact that I was going to be near her, to have her attention placed directly upon me; that I was going to be of service to her, and in a way in which I could show myself to advantage—this last consideration has much to do with cheerful service.—The anticipation produced in me a sensation somewhat between bliss and fear. I rushed through the gate, took the three steps to the house at one bound, threw open the door, and was about to hang my cap on its accustomed peg of the hall rack when I noticed that that particular peg was occupied by a black derby hat. I stopped suddenly and gazed at this hat as though I had never seen an object of its description. I was still looking at it in open-eyed wonder when my mother, coming out of the parlour into the hallway, called me and said there was someone inside who wanted to see me. Feeling that I was being made a party to some kind of mystery, I went in with her, and there I saw a man standing leaning with one elbow on the mantel, his back partly turned toward the door. As I entered, he turned and I saw a tall, handsome, well-dressed gentleman of perhaps thirty-five; he advanced a step toward me with a smile on his face. I stopped and looked at him with the same feelings with which I had looked at the derby hat, except that they were greatly magnified. I looked at him from head to foot, but he was an absolute blank to me until my eyes rested on his slender, elegant polished shoes; then it seemed that indistinct and partly obliterated films of memory began, at first slowly, then rapidly, to unroll, forming a vague panorama of my childhood days in Georgia.

My mother broke the spell by calling me by name and saying: "This is your father."

"Father, father," that was the word which had been to me a source of doubt and perplexity ever since the interview with my mother on the subject. How often I had wondered about my father, who he was, what he was like, whether alive or dead, and, above all, why she would not tell me about him. More than once I had been on the point of recalling to her the promise she had made me, but I instinctively felt that she was happier for not telling me and that I was happier for not being told; yet I had not the slightest idea what the real truth was. And here he stood before me, just the kind of looking father I had wishfully pictured him to be; but I made no advance toward him; I stood there feeling embarrassed and foolish, not knowing what to say or do. I am not sure but that he felt pretty much the same. My mother stood at my side with one hand on my shoulder, almost pushing me forward, but I did not move. I can well remember the look of disappointment, even pain, on her face; and I can now understand that she could expect nothing else but that at the name "father" I should throw myself into his arms. But I could not rise to this dramatic, or, better, melodramatic, climax. Somehow I could not arouse any considerable feeling of need for a father. He broke the awkward tableau by saying: "Well, boy, aren't you glad to see me?" He evidently meant the words kindly enough, but I don't know what he could have said that would have had a worse effect; however, my good breeding came to my rescue, and I answered: "Yes, sir," and went to him and offered him my hand. He took my hand into one of his, and, with the other, stroked my head, saying that I had grown into a fine youngster. He asked me how old I was; which, of course, he must have done merely to say something more, or perhaps he did so as a test of my intelligence. I replied: "Twelve, sir." He then made the trite observation about the flight of time, and we lapsed into another awkward pause.

My mother was all in smiles; I believe that was one of the happiest moments of her life. Either to put me more at ease or to show me off, she asked me to play something for my father. There is only one thing in the world that can make music, at all times and under all circumstances, up to its general standard; that is a hand-organ, or one of its variations. I went to the piano and played something in a listless, half-hearted way. I simply was not in the mood. I was wondering, while playing, when my mother would dismiss me and let me go; but my father was so enthusiastic in his praise that he touched my vanity—which was great—and more than that; he displayed that sincere appreciation which always arouses an artist to his best effort, and, too, in an unexplainable manner, makes him feel like shedding tears. I showed my gratitude by playing for him a Chopin waltz with all the feeling that was in me. When I had finished, my mother's eyes were glistening with tears; my father stepped across the room, seized me in his arms, and squeezed me to his breast. I am certain that for that moment he was proud to be my father. He sat and held me standing between his knees while he talked to my mother. I, in the mean time, examined him with more curiosity, perhaps, than politeness. I interrupted the conversation by asking: "Mother, is he going to stay with us now?" I found it impossible to frame the word "father"; it was too new to me; so I asked the question through my mother. Without waiting for her to speak, my father answered: "I've got to go back to New York this afternoon, but I'm coming to see you again." I turned abruptly and went over to my mother, and almost in a whisper reminded her that I had an appointment which I should not miss; to my pleasant surprise she said that she would give me something to eat at once so that I might go. She went out of the room and I began to gather from off the piano the music I needed. When I had finished, my father, who had been watching me, asked: "Are you going?" I replied: "Yes, sir, I've got to go to practise for a concert." He spoke some words of advice to me about being a good boy and taking care of my mother when I grew up, and added that he was going to send me something nice from New York. My mother called, and I said good-bye to him and went out. I saw him only once after that.

I quickly swallowed down what my mother had put on the table for me, seized my cap and music, and hurried off to my teacher's house. On the way I could think of nothing but this new father, where he came from, where he had been, why he was here, and why he would not stay. In my mind I ran over the whole list of fathers I had become acquainted with in my reading, but I could not classify him. The thought did not cross my mind that he was different from me, and even if it had, the mystery would not thereby have been explained; for, notwithstanding my changed relations with most of my schoolmates, I had only a faint knowledge of prejudice and no idea at all how it ramified and affected our entire social organism. I felt, however, that there was something about the whole affair which had to be hid.

When I arrived, I found that she of the brown eyes had been rehearsing with my teacher and was on the point of leaving. My teacher, with some expressions of surprise, asked why I was late, and I stammered out the first deliberate lie of which I have any recollection. I told him that when I reached home from school, I found my mother quite sick, and that I had stayed with her awhile before coming. Then unnecessarily and gratuitously—to give my words force of conviction, I suppose—I added: "I don't think she'll be with us very long." In speaking these words I must have been comical; for I noticed that my teacher, instead of showing signs of anxiety or sorrow, half hid a smile. But how little did I know that in that lie I was speaking a prophecy!

She of the brown eyes unpacked her violin, and we went through the duet several times. I was soon lost to all other thoughts in the delights of music and love. I saw delights of love without reservation; for at no time of life is love so pure, so delicious, so poetic, so romantic, as it is in boyhood. A great deal has been said about the heart of a girl when she stands "where the brook and river meet," but what she feels is negative; more interesting is the heart of a boy when just at the budding dawn of manhood he stands looking wide-eyed into the long vistas opening before him; when he first becomes conscious of the awakening and quickening of strange desires and unknown powers; when what he sees and feels is still shadowy and mystical enough to be intangible, and, so, more beautiful; when his imagination is unsullied, and his faith new and whole—then it is that love wears a halo.

The man who has not loved before he was fourteen has missed a foretaste of Elysium.

When I reached home, it was quite dark and I found my mother without a light, sitting rocking in a chair, as she so often used to do in my childhood days, looking into the fire and singing softly to herself. I nestled close to her, and, with her arms round me, she haltingly told me who my father was—a great man, a fine gentleman—he loved me and loved her very much; he was going to make a great man of me. All she said was so limited by reserve and so coloured by her feelings that it was but half truth; and so I did not yet fully understand.

CHAPTER III

Perhaps I ought not pass on in this narrative without mentioning that the duet was a great success, so great that we were obliged to respond with two encores. It seemed to me that life could hold no greater joy than it contained when I took her hand and we stepped down to the front of the stage bowing to our enthusiastic audience. When we reached the little dressing-room, where the other performers were applauding as wildly as the audience, she impulsively threw both her arms round me and kissed me, while I struggled to get away.

One day a couple of weeks after my father had been to see us, a wagon drove up to our cottage loaded with a big box. I was about to tell the men on the wagon that they had made a mistake, when my mother, acting darkly wise, told them to bring their load in; she had them unpack the box, and quickly there was evolved from the boards, paper, and other packing-material a beautiful, brand-new, upright piano. Then she informed me that it was a present to me from my father. I at once sat down and ran my fingers over the keys; the full, mellow tone of the instrument was ravishing. I thought, almost remorsefully, of how I had left my father; but, even so, there momentarily crossed my mind a feeling of disappointment that the piano was not a grand. The new instrument greatly increased the pleasure of my hours of study and practice at home.

Shortly after this I was made a member of the boys' choir, it being found that I possessed a clear, strong soprano voice. I enjoyed the singing very much. About a year later I began the study of the pipe organ and the theory of music; and before I finished the grammar-school, I had written out several simple preludes for organ which won the admiration of my teacher, and which he did me the honour to play at services.

The older I grew, the more thought I gave to the question of my mother's and my position, and what was our exact relation to the world in general. My idea of the whole matter was rather hazy. My study of United States history had been confined to those periods which were designated in my book as "Discovery," "Colonial," "Revolutionary," and "Constitutional." I now began to study about the Civil War, but the story was told in such a condensed and skipping style that I gained from it very little real information. It is a marvel how children ever learn any history out of books of that sort. And, too, I began now to read the newspapers; I often saw articles which aroused my curiosity, but did not enlighten me. But one day I drew from the circulating library a book that cleared the whole mystery, a book that I read with the same feverish intensity with which I had read the old Bible stories, a book that gave me my first perspective of the life I was entering; that book was *Uncle Tom's Cabin*.

This work of Harriet Beecher Stowe has been the object of much unfavourable criticism. It has been assailed, not only as fiction of the most imaginative sort, but as being a direct misrepresentation. Several successful attempts have lately been made to displace the book from Northern school libraries. Its critics would brush it aside with the remark that there never was a Negro as good as Uncle Tom, nor a slave-holder as bad as Legree. For my part, I was never an admirer of Uncle Tom, nor of his type of goodness; but I believe that there were lots of old Negroes as foolishly good as he; the proof of which is that they knowingly stayed and worked the plantations that furnished sinews for the army which was fighting to keep them enslaved. But in these later years several cases have come to my personal knowledge in which old Negroes have died and left what was a considerable fortune to the descendants of their former masters. I do not think it takes any great stretch of the imagination to believe there was a fairly large class of slave-holders typified in Legree. And we must also remember that the author depicted a number of worthless if not vicious Negroes, and a slave-holder who was as much of a Christian and a gentleman as it was possible for one in his position to be; that she pictured the happy, singing, shuffling "darky" as well as the mother wailing for her child sold "down river."

I do not think it is claiming too much to say that *Uncle Tom's Cabin* was a fair and truthful panorama of slavery; however that may be, it opened my eyes as to who and what I was and what my country considered me; in fact, it gave me my bearing. But there was no shock; I took the whole revelation in a kind of stoical way. One of the greatest benefits I derived from reading the book was that I could afterwards talk frankly with my mother on all the questions which had been vaguely troubling my mind. As a result, she was entirely freed from reserve, and often herself brought up the subject, talking of things directly touching her life and mine and of things which had come down to her through the "old folks." What she told me interested and even fascinated me, and, what may seem strange, kindled in me a strong desire to see the South. She spoke to me quite frankly about herself, my father, and myself: she, the sewing girl of my father's mother; he, an impetuous young man home from college; I, the child of this unsanctioned love. She told me even the principal reason for our coming north. My father was about to be married to a young lady of another great Southern family. She did not neglect to add that another reason for our being in Connecticut was that he intended to give me an education and make a man of me. In none of her talks did she ever utter one word of complaint against my father. She always endeavoured to impress upon me how good he had been and still was, and that he was all to us that custom and the law would allow. She loved him; more, she worshipped him, and she died firmly believing that he loved her more than any other woman in the world. Perhaps she was right. Who knows?

All of these newly-awakened ideas and thoughts took the form of a definite aspiration on the day I graduated from the grammar-school. And what a day that was! The girls in white dresses, with fresh ribbons in their hair; the boys in new suits and creaky shoes; the great crowd of parents and friends; the flowers, the prizes and congratulations, made the day seem to me one of the greatest importance. I was on the program, and played a piano solo which was received by the audience with that amount of applause which I had come to look upon as being only the just due of my talent.

But the real enthusiasm was aroused by "Shiny." He was the principal speaker of the day, and well did he measure up to the honour. He made a striking picture, that thin little black boy standing on the platform, dressed in clothes that did not fit him any too well, his eyes burning with excitement, his shrill, musical voice vibrating in tones of appealing defiance, and his black face alight with such great intelligence and earnestness as to be positively handsome. What were his thoughts when he stepped forward and looked into that crowd of faces, all white with the exception of a score or so that were lost to view? I do not know, but I fancy he felt his loneliness. I think there must have rushed over him a feeling akin to that of a gladiator tossed into the arena and bade to fight for his life. I think that solitary little black figure standing there felt that for the particular time and place he bore the weight and responsibility of his race; that for him to fail meant general defeat; but he won, and nobly. His oration was Wendell Phillips's "Toussaint L'Ouverture," a speech which may now be classed as rhetorical—even, perhaps, bombastic; but as the words fell from "Shiny's" lips their effect was magical. How so young an orator could stir so great enthusiasm was to be wondered at. When, in the famous peroration, his voice, trembling with suppressed emotion, rose higher and higher and then rested on the name "Toussaint L'Ouverture," it was like touching an electric button which loosed the pent-up feelings of his listeners. They actually rose to him.

I have since known of coloured men who have been chosen as class orators in our leading universities, of others who have played on the varsity football and baseball teams, of coloured speakers who have addressed great white audiences. In each of these instances I believe the men were stirred by the same emotions which actuated "Shiny" on the day of his graduation; and, too, in each case where the efforts have reached any high standard of excellence they have been followed by the same phenomenon of enthusiasm. I think the explanation of the latter lies in what is a basic, though often dormant, principle of the Anglo-Saxon heart, love of fair play. "Shiny," it is true, was what is so common in his race, a natural orator; but I doubt that any white boy of equal talent could have wrought the same effect. The sight of that boy gallantly waging with puny, black arms so unequal a battle touched the deep springs in the hearts of his audience, and they were swept by a wave of sympathy and admiration.

But the effect upon me of "Shiny's" speech was double; I not only shared the enthusiasm of his audience, but he imparted to me some of his own enthusiasm. I felt leap within me pride that I was coloured; and I began to form wild dreams of bringing glory and honour to the Negro race. For days I could talk of nothing else with my mother except my ambitions to be a great man, a great coloured man, to reflect credit on the race and gain fame for myself. It was not until years after that I formulated a definite and feasible plan for realizing my dreams.

I entered the high school with my class, and still continued my study of the piano, the pipe organ, and the theory of music. I had to drop out of the boys' choir on account of a changing voice; this I regretted very much. As I grew older, my love for reading grew stronger. I read with studious interest everything I could find relating to coloured men who had gained prominence. My heroes had been King David, then Robert the Bruce; now Frederick Douglass was enshrined in the place of honour. When I learned that Alexandre Dumas was a coloured man, I re-read *Monte Cristo* and *The Three Guardsmen* with magnified pleasure. I lived between my music and books, on the whole a rather unwholesome life for a boy to lead. I dwelt in a world of imagination, of dreams and air castles—the kind of atmosphere that sometimes nourishes a genius, more often men unfitted for the practical struggles of life. I never played a game of ball, never went fishing or learned to swim; in fact, the only outdoor exercise in which I took any interest was skating. Nevertheless, though slender, I grew well formed and in perfect health. After I entered the high school, I began to notice the change in my mother's health, which I suppose had been going on for some years. She began to complain a little and to cough a great deal; she tried several remedies, and finally went to see a doctor; but though she was failing in health, she kept her spirits up. She still did a great deal of sewing, and in the busy seasons hired two women to help her. The purpose she had formed of having me go through college without financial worries kept her at work when she was not fit for it. I was so fortunate as to be able to organize a class of eight or ten beginners on the piano, and so start a separate little fund of my own. As the time for my graduation from the high school grew nearer, the plans for my college career became the chief subject of our talks. I sent for catalogues of all the prominent schools in the East and eagerly gathered all the information I could concerning them from different sources. My mother told me that my father wanted me to go to Harvard or Yale; she herself had a half desire for me to go to Atlanta University, and even had me write for a catalogue of that school. There were two reasons, however, that inclined her to my father's choice; the first, that at Harvard or Yale I should be near her; the second, that my father had promised to pay for a part of my college education.

Both "Shiny" and "Red" came to my house quite often of evenings, and we used to talk over our plans and prospects for the future. Sometimes I would play for them, and they seemed to enjoy the music very much. My mother often prepared sundry Southern dishes for them, which I am not sure but that they enjoyed more. "Shiny" had an uncle in Amherst, Mass., and he expected to live with him and work his way through Amherst College. "Red" declared that he had enough of school and that after he got his high school diploma, he would get a position in a bank. It was his ambition to become a banker and he felt sure of getting the opportunity through certain members of his family.

My mother barely had strength to attend the closing exercises of the high school when I graduated, and after that day she was seldom out of bed. She could no longer direct her work, and under the expense of medicines, doctors, and someone to look after her our college fund began to diminish rapidly. Many of her customers and some of the neighbours were very kind, and frequently brought her nourishment of one kind of another. My mother realized what I did not, that she was mortally ill, and she had me write a long letter to my father. For some time past she had heard from him only at irregular intervals; we never received an answer. In those last days I often sat at her bed-side and read to her until she fell asleep. Sometimes I would leave the parlour door open and play on the piano, just loud enough for the music to reach her. This she always enjoyed.

One night, near the end of July, after I had been watching beside her for some hours, I went into the parlour and, throwing myself into the big arm-chair, dozed off into a fitful sleep. I was suddenly aroused by one of the neighbours, who had come in to sit with her that night. She said: "Come to your mother at once." I hurried upstairs, and at the bedroom door met the woman who was acting as nurse. I noted with a dissolving heart the strange look of awe on her face. From my first glance at my mother I discerned the light of death upon her countenance. I fell upon my knees beside the bed and, burying my face in the sheets, sobbed convulsively. She died with the fingers of her left hand entwined in my hair.

I will not rake over this, one of the two sacred sorrows of my life; nor could I describe the feeling of unutterable loneliness that fell upon me. After the funeral I went to the house of my music teacher; he had kindly offered me the hospitality of his home for so long as I might need it. A few days later I moved my trunk, piano, my music, and most of my books to his home; the rest of my books I divided between "Shiny" and "Red." Some of the household effects I gave to "Shiny's" mother and to two or three of the neighbours who had been kind to us during my mother's illness; the others I sold. After settling up my little estate I found that, besides a good supply of clothes, a piano, some books and trinkets, I had about two hundred dollars in cash.

The question of what I was to do now confronted me. My teacher suggested a concert tour; but both of us realized that I was too old to be exploited as an infant prodigy and too young and inexperienced to go before the public as a finished artist. He, however, insisted that the people of the town would generously patronize a benefit concert; so he took up the matter and made arrangements for such an entertainment. A more than sufficient number of people with musical and elocutionary talent volunteered their services to make a program. Among these was my brown-eyed violinist. But our relations were not the same as they were when we had played our first duet together. A year or so after that time she had dealt me a crushing blow by getting married. I was partially avenged, however, by the fact that, though she was growing more beautiful, she was losing her ability to play the violin.

I was down on the program for one number. My selection might have appeared at that particular time as a bit of affectation, but I considered it deeply appropriate; I played Beethoven's "Sonata Pathétique." When I sat down at the piano and glanced into the faces of the several hundreds of people who were there solely on account of love or sympathy for me, emotions swelled in my heart which enabled me to play the "Pathétique" as I could never again play it. When the last tone died away, the few who began to applaud were hushed by the silence of the others; and for once I played without receiving an encore.

The benefit yielded me a little more than two hundred dollars, thus raising my cash capital to about four hundred dollars. I still held to my determination of going to college; so it was now a question of trying to squeeze through a year at Harvard or going to Atlanta, where the money I had would pay my actual expenses for at least two years. The peculiar fascination which the South held over my imagination and my limited capital decided me in favour of Atlanta University; so about the last of September I bade farewell to the friends and scenes of my boyhood and boarded a train for the south.

CHAPTER IV

The farther I got below Washington, the more disappointed I became in the appearance of the country. I peered through the car windows, looking in vain for the luxuriant semi-tropical scenery which I had pictured in my mind. I did not find the grass so green, nor the woods so beautiful, nor the flowers so plentiful, as they were in Connecticut. Instead, the red earth partly covered by tough, scrawny grass, the muddy, straggling roads, the cottages of unpainted pine boards, and the clay-daubed huts imparted a "burnt up" impression. Occasionally we ran through a little white and green village that was like an oasis in a desert.

When I reached Atlanta, my steadily increasing disappointment was not lessened. I found it a big, dull, red town. This dull red colour of that part of the South I was then seeing had much, I think, to do with the extreme depression of my spirits—no public squares, no fountains, dingy streetcars, and, with the exception of three or four principal thoroughfares, unpaved streets. It was raining when I arrived and some of these unpaved streets were absolutely impassable. Wheels sank to the hubs in red mire, and I actually stood for an hour and watched four or five men work to save a mule, which had stepped into a deep sink, from drowning, or, rather, suffocating in the mud. The Atlanta of today is a new city.

On the train I had talked with one of the Pullman-car porters, a bright young fellow who was himself a student, and told him that I was going to Atlanta to attend school. I had also asked him to tell me where I might stop for a day or two until the University opened. He said I might go with him to the place where he stopped during his "layovers" in Atlanta. I gladly accepted his offer and went with him along one of those muddy streets until we came to a rather rickety-looking frame-house, which we entered. The proprietor of the house was a big, fat, greasy-looking brown-skin man. When I asked him if he could give me accommodation, he wanted to know how long I would stay. I told him perhaps two days, not more than three. In reply he said: "Oh, dat's all right den," at the same time leading the way up a pair of creaky stairs. I followed him and the porter to a room, the door of which the proprietor opened while continuing, it seemed, his remark, "Oh, dat's all right den," by adding: "You kin sleep in dat cot in de corner der. Fifty cents, please." The porter interrupted by saying: "You needn't collect from him now, he's got a trunk." This seemed to satisfy the man, and he went down, leaving me and my porter friend in the room. I glanced round the apartment and saw that it contained a double bed and two cots, two wash-stands, three chairs, and a time-worn bureau, with a looking-glass that would have made Adonis appear hideous. I looked at the cot in which I was to sleep and suspected, not without good reasons, that I should not be the first to use the sheets and pillow-case since they had last come from the wash. When I thought of the clean, tidy, comfortable surroundings in which I had been reared, a wave of homesickness swept over me that made me feel faint. Had it not been for the presence of my companion, and that I knew this much of his history—that he was not yet quite twenty, just three years older than myself, and that he had been fighting his own way in the world, earning his own living and providing for his own education since he was fourteen—I should not have been able to stop the tears that were welling up in my eyes.

I asked him why it was that the proprietor of the house

seemed unwilling to accommodate me for more than a couple of days. He informed me that the man ran a lodging-house especially for Pullman porters, and, as their stays in town were not longer than one or two nights, it would interfere with his arrangements to have anyone stay longer. He went on to say: "You see this room is fixed up to accommodate four men at a time. Well, by keeping a sort of table of trips, in and out, of the men, and working them like checkers, he can accommodate fifteen or sixteen in each week and generally avoid having an empty bed. You happen to catch a bed that would have been empty for a couple of nights." I asked him where he was going to sleep. He answered: "I sleep in that other cot tonight; tomorrow night I go out." He went on to tell me that the man who kept the house did not serve meals, and that if I was hungry, we would go out and get something to eat.

We went into the street, and in passing the railroad station I hired a wagon to take my trunk to my lodging-place. We passed along until, finally, we turned into a street that stretched away, up and down hill, for a mile or two; and here I caught my first sight of coloured people in large numbers. I had seen little squads around the railroad stations on my way south, but here I saw a street crowded with them. They filled the shops and thronged the sidewalks and lined the curb. I asked my companion if all the coloured people in Atlanta lived in this street. He said they did not and assured me that the ones I saw were of the lower class. I felt relieved, in spite of the size of the lower class. The unkempt appearance, the shambling, slouching gait and loud talk and laughter of these people aroused in me a feeling of almost repulsion. Only one thing about them awoke a feeling of interest; that was their dialect. I had read some Negro dialect and had heard snatches of it on my journey down from Washington; but here I heard it in all of its fullness and freedom. I was particularly struck by the way in which it was punctuated by such exclamatory phrases as "Lawd a mussy!" "G'wan, man!" "Bless ma soul!" "Look heah, chile!" These people talked and laughed without restraint. In fact, they talked straight from their lungs and laughed from the pits of their stomachs. And this hearty laughter was often justified by the droll humour of some remark. I paused long enough to hear one man say to another: "W'at's de mattah wid you an' yo' fr'en' Sam?" and the other came back like a flash: "Ma fr'en'? He ma fr'en'? Man! I'd go to his funeral jes' de same as I'd go to a minstrel show." I have since learned that this ability to laugh heartily is, in part, the salvation of the American Negro; it does much to keep him from going the way of the Indian.

The business places of the street along which we were passing consisted chiefly of low bars, cheap dry-goods and notion stores, barber shops, and fish and bread restaurants. We, at length, turned down a pair of stairs that led to a basement and I found myself in an eating-house somewhat better than those I had seen in passing; but that did not mean much for its excellence. The place was smoky, the tables were covered with oilcloth, the floor with sawdust, and from the kitchen came a rancid odour of fish fried over several times, which almost nauseated me. I asked my companion if this was the place where we were to eat. He informed me that it was the place in town where a coloured man could get a meal. I then wanted to know why somebody didn't open a place where respectable coloured people who had money could be accommodated. He answered: "It wouldn't pay; all the respectable coloured people eat at home, and the few who travel generally have friends in the towns to which they go, who entertain them." He added: "Of course, you could go in any place in the city; they wouldn't know you from white."

I sat down with the porter at one of the tables, but was not hungry enough to eat with any relish what was put before me. The food was not badly cooked; but the iron knives and forks needed to be scrubbed, the plates and dishes and glasses needed to be washed and well dried. I minced over what I took on my plate while my companion ate. When we finished, we paid the waiter twenty cents each and went out. We walked round until the lights of the city were lit. Then the porter said that he must get to bed and have some rest, as he had not had six hours' sleep since he left Jersey City. I went back to our lodging-house with him.

When I awoke in the morning, there were, besides my new-found friend, two other men in the room, asleep in the double bed. I got up and dressed myself very quietly, so as not to awake anyone. I then drew from under the pillow my precious roll of greenbacks, took out a ten-dollar bill, and, very softly unlocking my trunk, put the remainder, about three hundred dollars, in the inside pocket of a coat near the bottom, glad of the opportunity to put it unobserved in a place of safety. When I had carefully locked my trunk, I tiptoed toward the door with the intention of going out to look for a decent restaurant where I might get something fit to eat. As I was easing the door open, my porter friend said with a yawn: "Hello! You're going out?" I answered him: "Yes." "Oh!" he yawned again, "I guess I've had enough sleep; wait a minute, I'll go with you." For the instant his friendship bored and embarrassed me. I had visions of another meal in the greasy restaurant of the day before. He must have divined my thoughts, for he went on to say: "I know a woman across town who takes a few boarders; I think we can go over there and get a good breakfast." With a feeling of mingled fears and doubts regarding what the breakfast might be, I waited until he had dressed himself.

When I saw the neat appearance of the cottage we entered, my fears vanished, and when I saw the woman who kept it, my doubts followed the same course. Scrupulously clean, in a spotless white apron and coloured head-handkerchief, her round face beaming with motherly kindness, she was picturesquely beautiful. She impressed me as one broad expanse of happiness and good nature. In a few minutes she was addressing me as "chile" and "honey." She made me feel as though I should like to lay my head on her capacious bosom and go to sleep.

And the breakfast, simple as it was, I could not have had at any restaurant in Atlanta at any price. There was fried chicken, as it is fried only in the South, hominy boiled to the consistency where it could be eaten with a fork, and biscuits so light and flaky that a fellow with any appetite at all would have no difficulty in disposing of eight or ten. When I had finished, I felt that I had experienced the realization of, at least, one of my dreams of Southern life.

During the meal we found out from our hostess, who had two boys in school, that Atlanta University opened on that very day. I had somehow mixed my dates. My friend the porter suggested that I go out to the University at once and offered to walk over and show me the way. We had to walk because, although the University was not more than twenty minutes' distance from the centre of the city, there were no street-cars running in that direction. My first sight of the school-grounds made me feel that I was not far from home; here the red hills had been terraced and covered with green grass; clean gravel walks, well shaded, led up to the buildings; indeed, it was a bit of New England transplanted. At the gate my companion said he would bid me good-bye, because it was likely that he would not see me again before his car went out. He told me that he would make two more trips to Atlanta and that he would come out and see me; that after his second trip he would leave the Pullman service for the winter and return to school in Nashville. We shook hands, I thanked him for all his kindness, and we said good-bye.

I walked up to a group of students and made some inquiries. They directed me to the president's office in the main building. The president gave me a cordial welcome; it was more than cordial; he talked to me, not as the official head of a college, but as though he were adopting me into what was his large family, personally to look after my general welfare as well as my education. He seemed especially pleased with the fact that I had come to them all the way from the North. He told me that I could have come to the school as soon as I had reached the city and that I had better move my trunk out at once. I gladly promised him that I would do so. He then called a boy and directed him to take me to the matron, and to show me round afterwards. I found the matron even more motherly than the president was fatherly. She had me register, which was in effect to sign a pledge to abstain from the use of intoxicating beverages, tobacco, and profane language while I was a student in the school. This act caused me no sacrifice, as, up to that time, I was free from all three habits. The boy who was with me then showed me about the grounds. I was especially interested in the industrial building.

The sounding of a bell, he told me, was the signal for the students to gather in the general assembly hall, and he asked me if I would go. Of course I would. There were between three and four hundred students and perhaps all of the teachers gathered in the room. I noticed that several of the latter were coloured. The president gave a talk addressed principally to new-comers; but I scarcely heard what he said, I was so much occupied in looking at those around me. They were of all types and colours, the more intelligent types predominating. The colours ranged from jet black to pure white, with light hair and eyes. Among the girls especially there were many so fair that it was difficult to believe that they had Negro blood in them. And, too, I could not help noticing that many of the girls, particularly those of the delicate brown shades, with black eyes and wavy dark hair, were decidedly pretty. Among the boys many of the blackest were fine specimens of young manhood, tall, straight, and muscular, with magnificent heads; these were the kind of boys who developed into the patriarchal "uncles" of the old slave regime.

When I left the University, it was with the determination to get my trunk and move out to the school before night. I walked back across the city with a light step and a light heart. I felt perfectly satisfied with life for the first time since my mother's death. In passing the railroad station I hired a wagon and rode with the driver as far as my stopping-place. I settled with my landlord and went upstairs to put away several articles I had left out. As soon as I opened my trunk, a dart of suspicion shot through my heart; the arrangement of things did not look familiar. I began to dig down excitedly to the bottom till I reached the coat in which I had concealed my treasure. My money was gone! Every single bill of it. I knew it was useless to do so, but I searched through every other coat, every pair of trousers, every vest, and even each pair of socks. When I had finished my fruitless search, I sat down dazed and heart-sick. I called the landlord up and informed him of my loss; he comforted me by saying that I ought to have better sense than to keep money in a trunk and that he was not responsible for his lodgers' personal effects. His cooling words brought me enough to my senses to cause me to look and see if anything else was missing. Several small articles were gone, among them a black and grey neck-tie of odd design upon which my heart was set; almost as much as the loss of my money I felt the loss of my tie.

After thinking for a while as best I could, I wisely decided to go at once back to the University and lay my troubles before the president. I rushed breathlessly back to the school. As I neared the grounds, the thought came across me, would not my story sound fishy? Would it not place me in the position of an impostor or beggar? What right had I to worry these busy people with the results of my carelessness? If the money could not be recovered, and I doubted that it could, what good would it do to tell them about it? The shame and embarrassment which the whole situation gave me caused me to stop at the gate. I paused, undecided, for a moment; then turned and slowly retraced my steps, and so changed the whole course of my life.

If the reader has never been in a strange city without money or friends, it is useless to try to describe what my feelings were; he could not understand. If he has been, it is equally useless, for he understands more than words could convey. When I reached my lodgings, I found in the room one of the porters who had slept there the night before. When he heard what misfortune had befallen me, he offered many words of sympathy and advice. He asked me how much money I had left. I told him that I had ten or twelve dollars in my pocket. He said: "That won't last you very long here, and you will hardly be able to find anything to do in Atlanta. I'll tell you what you do, go down to Jacksonville and you won't have any trouble to get a job in one of the big hotels there, or in St. Augustine." I thanked him, but intimated my doubts of being able to get to Jacksonville on the money I had. He reassured me by saying: "Oh, that's all right. You express your trunk on through, and I'll take you down in my closet." I thanked him again, not knowing then what it was to travel in a Pullman porter's closet. He put me under a deeper debt of gratitude by lending me fifteen dollars, which he said I could pay back after I had secured work. His generosity brought tears to my eyes, and I concluded that, after all, there were some kind hearts in the world.

I now forgot my troubles in the hurry and excitement of getting my trunk off in time to catch the train, which went out at seven o'clock. I even forgot that I hadn't eaten anything since morning. We got a wagon—the porter went with me—and took my trunk to the express office. My new friend then told me to come to the station at about a quarter of seven and walk straight to the car where I should see him standing, and not to lose my nerve. I found my role not so difficult to play as I thought it would be, because the train did not leave from the central station, but from a smaller one, where there were no gates and guards to pass. I followed directions, and the porter took me on his car and locked me in his closet. In a few minutes the train pulled out for Jacksonville.

I may live to be a hundred years old, but I shall never forget the agonies I suffered that night. I spent twelve hours doubled up in the porter's basket for soiled linen, not being able to straighten up on account of the shelves for clean linen just over my head. The air was hot and suffocating and the smell of damp towels and used linen was sickening. At each lurch of the car over the none too smooth track I was bumped and bruised against the narrow walls of my narrow compartment. I became acutely conscious of the fact that I had not eaten for hours. Then nausea took possession of me, and at one time I had grave doubts about reaching my destination alive. If I had the trip to make again, I should prefer to walk.

CHAPTER V

The next morning I got out of the car at Jacksonville with a stiff and aching body. I determined to ask no more porters, not even my benefactor, about stopping-places; so I found myself on the street not knowing where to go. I walked along listlessly until I met a coloured man who had the appearance of a preacher. I asked him if he could direct me to a respectable boarding-house for coloured people. He said that if I walked along with him in the direction he was going, he would show me such a place: I turned and walked at his side. He proved to be a minister, and asked me a great many direct questions about myself. I answered as many as I saw fit to answer; the others I evaded or ignored. At length we stopped in front of a frame-house, and my guide informed me that it was the place. A woman was standing in the doorway, and he called to her saying that he had brought her a new boarder. I thanked him for his trouble, and after he had urged upon me to attend his church while I was in the city, he went on his way.

I went in and found the house neat and not uncomfortable. The parlour was furnished with cane-bottomed chairs, each of which was adorned with a white crocheted tidy. The mantel over the fireplace had a white crocheted cover; a marble-topped centre table held a lamp, a photograph album and several trinkets, each of which was set upon a white crocheted mat. There was a cottage organ in a corner of the room, and I noted that the lamp-racks upon it were covered with white crocheted mats. There was a matting on the floor, but a white crocheted carpet would not have been out of keeping. I made arrangements with the landlady for my board and lodging; the amount was, I think, three dollars and a half a week. She was a rather fine-looking, stout, brown-skin woman of about forty years of age. Her husband was a light-coloured Cuban, a man about one half her size, and one whose age could not be guessed from his appearance. He was small in size, but a handsome black moustache and typical Spanish eyes redeemed him from insignificance.

I was in time for breakfast, and at the table I had the opportunity to see my fellow boarders. There were eight or ten of them. Two, as I afterwards learned, were coloured Americans. All of them were cigar-makers and worked in one of the large factories—cigar-making is one trade in which the colour line is not drawn. The conversation was carried on entirely in Spanish, and my ignorance of the language subjected me more to alarm than embarrassment. I had never heard such uproarious conversation; everybody talked at once, loud exclamations, rolling *"carambas,"* menacing gesticulations with knives, forks, and spoons. I looked every moment for the clash of blows. One man was emphasizing his remarks by flourishing a cup in his hand, seemingly forgetful of the fact that it was nearly full of hot coffee. He ended by emptying it over what was, relatively, the only quiet man at the table excepting myself, bringing from him a volley of language which made the others appear dumb by comparison. I soon learned that in all of this clatter of voices and table utensils they were discussing purely ordinary affairs and arguing about mere trifles, and that not the least ill feeling was aroused. It was not long before I enjoyed the spirited chatter and *badinage* at the table as much as I did my meals—and the meals were not bad.

I spent the afternoon in looking round the town. The streets were sandy, but were well shaded by fine oak-trees and far preferable to the clay roads of Atlanta. One or two public squares with green grass and trees gave the city a touch of freshness. That night after supper I spoke to my landlady and her husband about my intentions. They told me that the big winter hotels would not open within two months. It can easily be imagined what effect this news had on me. I spoke to them frankly about my financial condition and related the main fact of my misfortune in Atlanta. I modestly mentioned my ability to teach music and asked if there was any likelihood of my being able to get some scholars. My landlady suggested that I speak to the preacher who had shown me her house; she felt sure that through his influence I should be able to get up a class in piano. She added, however, that the coloured people were poor, and that the general price for music lessons was only twenty-five cents. I noticed that the thought of my teaching white pupils did not even remotely enter her mind. None of this information made my prospects look much brighter.

The husband, who up to this time had allowed the woman to do most of the talking, gave me the first bit of tangible hope; he said that he could get me a job as a "stripper" in the factory where he worked, and that if I succeeded in getting some music pupils, I could teach a couple of them every night, and so make a living until something better turned up. He went on to say that it would not be a bad thing for me to stay at the factory and learn my trade as a cigar-maker, and impressed on me that, for a young man knocking about the country, a trade was a handy thing to have. I determined to accept his offer and thanked him heartily. In fact, I became enthusiastic, not only because I saw a way out of my financial troubles, but also because I was eager and curious over the new experience I was about to enter. I wanted to know all about the cigar-making business. This narrowed the conversation down to the husband and myself, so the wife went in and left us talking.

He was what is called a *regalía* workman, and earned from thirty-five to forty dollars a week. He generally worked a sixty-dollar job; that is, he made cigars for which he was paid at the rate of sixty dollars per thousand. It was impossible for him to make a thousand in a week because he had to work very carefully and slowly. Each cigar was made entirely by hand. Each piece of filler and each wrapper had to be selected with care. He was able to make a bundle of one hundred cigars in a day, not one of which could be told from the others by any difference in size or shape, or even by any appreciable difference in weight. This was the acme of artistic skill in cigar-making. Workmen of this class were rare, never more than three or four in one factory, and it was never necessary for them to remain out of work. There were men who made two, three, and four hundred cigars of the cheaper grades in a day; they had to be very fast in order to make decent week's wages. Cigar-making was a rather independent trade; the men went to work when they pleased and knocked off when they felt like doing so. As a class the workmen were careless and improvident; some very rapid makers would not work more than three or four days out of the week, and there were others who never showed up at the factory on Mondays. "Strippers" were the boys who pulled the long stems from the tobacco leaves. After they had served at that work for a certain time they were given tables as apprentices.

All of this was interesting to me; and we drifted along in conversation until my companion struck the subject nearest his heart, the independence of Cuba. He was an exile from the island, and a prominent member of the Jacksonville Junta. Every week sums of money were collected from juntas all over the country. This money went to buy arms and ammunition for the insurgents. As the man sat there nervously smoking his long, "green" cigar, and telling me of the Gómezes, both the white one and the black one, of Macéo and Bandera, he grew positively eloquent. He also showed that he was a man of considerable education and reading. He spoke English excellently, and frequently surprised me by using words one would hardly expect from a foreigner. The first one of this class of words he employed almost shocked me, and I never forgot it; 'twas "ramify." We sat on the piazza until after ten o'clock. When we arose to go in to bed, it was with the understanding that I should start in the factory on the next day.

I began work the next morning seated at a barrel with another boy, who showed me how to strip the stems from the leaves, to smooth out each half leaf, and to put the "rights" together in one pile, and the "lefts" together in another pile on the edge of the barrel. My fingers, strong and sensitive from their long training, were well adapted to this kind of work, and within two weeks I was accounted the fastest "stripper" in the factory. At first the heavy odour of the tobacco almost sickened me, but when I became accustomed to it, I liked the smell. I was now earning four dollars a week, and was soon able to pick up a couple more by teaching a few scholars at night, whom I had secured through the good offices of the preacher I had met on my first morning in Jacksonville.

At the end of about three months, through my skill as a "stripper" and the influence of my landlord, I was advanced to a table and began to learn my trade; in fact, more than my trade; for I learned not only to make cigars, but also to smoke, to swear, and to speak Spanish. I discovered that I had a talent for languages as well as for music. The rapidity and ease with which I acquired Spanish astonished my associates. In a short time I was able not only to understand most of what was said at the table during meals, but to join in the conversation. I bought a method for learning the Spanish language, and with the aid of my landlord as a teacher, by constant practice with my fellow workmen, and by regularly reading the Cuban newspapers and finally some books of standard Spanish literature which were at the house, I was able in less than a year to speak like a native. In fact, it was my pride that I spoke better Spanish than many of the Cuban workmen at the factory.

After I had been in the factory a little over a year, I was repaid for all the effort I had put forth to learn Spanish by being selected as "reader." The "reader" is quite an institution in all cigar factories which employ Spanish-speaking workmen. He sits in the centre of the large room in which the cigar-makers work and reads to them for a certain number of hours each day all the important news from the papers and whatever else he may consider would be interesting. He often selects an exciting novel and reads it in daily instalments. He must, of course, have a good voice, but he must also have a reputation among the men for intelligence, for being well posted and having in his head a stock of varied information. He is generally the final authority on all arguments which arise, and in a cigar factory these arguments are many and frequent, ranging from the respective and relative merits of rival baseball clubs to the duration of the sun's light and energy—cigar-making is a trade in which talk does not interfere with the work. My position as "reader" not only released me from the rather monotonous work of rolling cigars, and gave me something more in accord with my tastes, but also added considerably to my income. I was now earning about twenty-five dollars a week, and was able to give up my peripatetic method of giving music lessons. I hired a piano and taught only those who could arrange to take their lessons where I lived. I finally gave up teaching entirely, as what I made scarcely paid for my time and trouble. I kept the piano, however, in order to keep up my own studies, and occasionally I played at some church concert or other charitable entertainment.

Through my music teaching and my not absolutely irregular attendance at church I became acquainted with the best class of coloured people in Jacksonville. This was really my entrance into the race. It was my initiation into what I have termed the freemasonry of the race. I had formulated a theory of what it was to be coloured; now I was getting the practice. The novelty of my position caused me to observe and consider things which, I think, entirely escaped the young men I associated with; or, at least, were so commonplace to them as not to attract their attention. And of many of the impressions which came to me then I have realized the full import only within the past few years, since I have had a broader knowledge of men and history, and a fuller comprehension of the tremendous struggle which is going on between the races in the South.

It is a struggle; for though the black man fights passively, he nevertheless fights; and his passive resistance is more effective at present than active resistance could possibly be. He bears the fury of the storm as does the willow-tree.

It is a struggle; for though the white man of the South may be too proud to admit it, he is, nevertheless, using in the contest his best energies; he is devoting to it the greater part of his thought and much of his endeavour. The South today stands panting and almost breathless from its exertions.

And how the scene of the struggle has shifted! The battle was first waged over the right of the Negro to be classed as a human being with a soul; later, as to whether he had sufficient intellect to master even the rudiments of learning; and today it is being fought out over his social recognition.

I said somewhere in the early part of this narrative that because the coloured man looked at everything through the prism of his relationship to society as a *coloured* man, and because most of his mental efforts ran through the narrow channel bounded by his rights and his wrongs, it was to be wondered at that he has progressed so broadly as he has. The same thing may be said of the white man of the South; most of his mental efforts run through one narrow channel; his life as a man and a citizen, many of his financial activities, and all of his political activities are impassably limited by the ever present "Negro question." I am sure it would be safe to wager that no group of Southern white men would get together and talk for sixty minutes without bringing up the "race question." If a Northern white man happened to be in the group, the time could be safely cut to thirty minutes. In this respect I consider the conditions of the whites more to be deplored than that of the blacks. Here, a truly great people, a people that produced a majority of the great historic Americans from Washington to Lincoln, now forced to use up its energies in a conflict as lamentable as it is violent.

I shall give the observations I made in Jacksonville as seen through the light of after years; and they apply generally to every Southern community. The coloured people may be said to be roughly divided into three classes, not so much in respect to themselves as in respect to their relations with the whites. There are those constituting what might be called the desperate class—the men who work in the lumber and turpentine camps, the ex-convicts, the bar-room loafers are all in this class. These men conform to the requirements of civilization much as a trained lion with low muttered growls goes through his stunts under the crack of the trainer's whip. They cherish a sullen hatred for all white men, and they value life as cheap. I have heard more than one of them say: "I'll go to hell for the first white man that bothers me." Many who have expressed that sentiment have kept their word, and it is that fact which gives such prominence to this class; for in numbers it is only a small proportion of the coloured people, but it often dominates public opinion concerning the whole race. Happily, this class represents the black people of the South far below their normal physical and moral condition, but in its increase lies the possibility of grave dangers. I am sure there is no more urgent work before the white South, not only for its present happiness, but for its future safety, than the decreasing of this class of blacks. And it is not at all a hopeless class; for these men are but the creatures of conditions, as much so as the slum and criminal elements of all the great cities of the world are creatures of conditions. Decreasing their number by shooting and burning them off will not be successful; for these men are truly desperate, and thoughts of death, however terrible, have little effect in deterring them from acts the result of hatred or degeneracy. This class of blacks hate everything covered by a white skin, and in return they are loathed by the whites. The whites regard them just about as a man would a vicious mule, a thing to be worked, driven, and beaten, and killed for kicking.

The second class, as regards the relation between blacks and whites, comprises the servants, the washerwomen, the waiters, the cooks, the coachmen, and all who are connected with the whites by domestic service. These may be generally characterized as simple, kindhearted, and faithful; not over-fine in their moral deductions, but intensely religious, and relatively—such matters can be judged only relatively—about as honest and wholesome in their lives as any other grade of society. Any white person is "good" who treats them kindly, and they love him for that kindness. In return, the white people with whom they have to do regard them with indulgent affection. They come into close daily contact with the whites, and may be called the connecting link between whites and blacks; in fact, it is through them that the whites know the rest of their coloured neighbours. Between this class of the blacks and the whites there is little or no friction.

The third class is composed of the independent workmen and tradesmen, and of the well-to-do and educated coloured people; and, strange, to say, for a directly opposite reason they are as far removed from the whites as the members of the first class I mentioned. These people live in a little world of their own; in fact, I concluded that if a coloured man wanted to separate himself from his white neighbours, he had but to acquire some money, education, and culture, and to live in accordance. For example, the proudest and fairest lady in the South could with propriety—and it is what she would most likely do—go to the cabin of Aunt Mary, her cook, if Aunt Mary was sick, and minister to her comfort with her own hands; but if Mary's daughter, Eliza, a girl who used to run round my lady's kitchen, but who has received an education and married a prosperous young coloured man, were at death's door, my lady would no more think of crossing the threshold of Eliza's cottage than she would of going into a bar-room for a drink.

I was walking down the street one day with a young man who was born in Jacksonville, but had been away to prepare himself for a professional life. We passed a young white man, and my companion said to me: "You see that young man? We grew up together; we have played, hunted, and fished together; we have even eaten and slept together; and now since I have come back home, he barely speaks to me." The fact that the whites of the South despise and ill-treat the desperate class of blacks is not only explainable according to the ancient laws of human nature, but it is not nearly so serious or important as the fact that as the progressive coloured people advance, they constantly widen the gulf between themselves and their white neighbours. I think that the white people somehow feel that coloured people who have education and money, who wear good clothes and live in comfortable houses, are "putting on airs," that they do these things for the sole purpose of "spiting the white folks," or are, at best, going through a sort of monkey-like imitation. Of course, such feelings can only cause irritation or breed disgust. It seems that the whites have not yet been able to realize and understand that these people in striving to better their physical and social surroundings in accordance with their financial and intellectual progress are simply obeying an impulse which is common to human nature the world over. I am in grave doubt as to whether the greater part of the friction in the South is caused by the whites' having a natural antipathy to Negroes as a race, or an acquired antipathy to Negroes in certain relations to themselves. However that may be, there is to my mind no more pathetic side of this many-sided question than the isolated position into which are forced the very coloured people who most need and who could best appreciate sympathetic co-operation; and their position grows tragic when the effort is made to couple them, whether or no, with the Negroes of the first class I mentioned.

This latter class of coloured people are well-disposed towards the whites, and always willing to meet them more than half-way. They, however, feel keenly any injustice or gross discrimination, and generally show their resentment. The effort is sometimes made to convey the impression that the better class of coloured people fight against riding in "Jim Crow" cars because they want to ride with white people or object to being with humbler members of their own race. The truth is they object to the humiliation of being forced to ride in a *particular* car, aside from the fact that that car is distinctly inferior, and that they are required to pay full first-class fare. To say that the whites are forced to ride in the superior car is less than a joke. And, too, odd as it may sound, refined coloured people get no more pleasure out of riding with offensive Negroes than anybody else would get.

I can realize more fully than I could years ago that the position of the advanced element of the coloured race is often very trying. They are the ones among the blacks who carry the entire weight of the race question; it worries the others very little, and I believe the only thing which at times sustains them is that they know that they are in the right. On the other hand, this class of coloured people get a good deal of pleasure out of life; their existence is far from being one long groan about their condition. Out of a chaos of ignorance and poverty they have evolved a social life of which they need not be ashamed. In cities where the professional and well-to-do class is large they have formed society—society as discriminating as the actual conditions will allow it to be; I should say, perhaps, society possessing discriminating tendencies which become rules as fast as actual conditions allow. This statement will, I know, sound preposterous, even ridiculous, to some persons; but as this class of coloured people is the least known of the race it is not surprising. These social circles are connected throughout the country, and a person in good standing in one city is readily accepted in another. One who is on the outside will often find it a difficult matter to get in. I know personally of one case in which money to the extent of thirty or forty thousand dollars and a fine house, not backed up by a good reputation, after several years of repeated effort, failed to gain entry for the possessor. These people have their dances and dinners and card parties, their musicals, and their literary societies. The women attend social affairs dressed in good taste, and the men in dress suits which they own; and the reader will make a mistake to confound these entertainments with the "Bellman's Balls" and "Whitewashers' Picnics" and "Lime-kiln Clubs" with which the humorous press of the country illustrates "Cullud Sassiety."

Jacksonville, when I was there, was a small town, and the number of educated and well-to-do coloured people was small; so this society phase of life did not equal what I have since seen in Boston, Washington, Richmond, and Nashville; and it is upon what I have more recently seen in these cities that I have made the observations just above. However, there were many comfortable and pleasant homes in Jacksonville to which I was often invited. I belonged to the literary society—at which we generally discussed the race question—and attended all of the church festivals and other charitable entertainments. In this way I passed three years which were not at all the least enjoyable of my life. In fact, my joy took such an exuberant turn that I fell in love with a young schoolteacher and began to have dreams of matrimonial bliss; but another turn in the course of my life brought these dreams to an end.

I do not wish to mislead my readers into thinking that I led a life in Jacksonville which would make copy for the hero of a Sunday-school library book. I was a hail fellow well met with all of the workmen at the factory, most of whom knew little and cared less about social distinctions. From their example I learned to be careless about money, and for that reason I constantly postponed and finally abandoned returning to Atlanta University. It seemed impossible for me to save as much as two hundred dollars. Several of the men at the factory were my intimate friends, and I frequently joined them in their pleasures. During the summer months we went almost every Monday on an excursion to a seaside resort called Pablo Beach. These excursions were always crowded. There was a dancing-pavilion, a great deal of drinking, and generally a fight or two to add to the excitement. I also contracted the cigar-maker's habit of riding round in a hack on Sunday afternoons. I sometimes went with my cigar-maker friends to public balls that were given at a large hall on one of the main streets. I learned to take a drink occasionally and paid for quite a number that my friends took; but strong liquors never appealed to my appetite. I drank them only when the company I was in required it, and suffered for it afterwards. On the whole, though I was a bit wild, I can't remember that I ever did anything disgraceful, or, as the usual standard for young men goes, anything to forfeit my claim to respectability.

At one of the first public balls I attended I saw the Pullman-car porter who had so kindly assisted me in getting to Jacksonville. I went immediately to one of my factory friends and borrowed fifteen dollars with which to repay the loan my benefactor had made me. After I had given him the money, and was thanking him, I noticed that he wore what was, at least, an exact duplicate of my lamented black and grey tie. It was somewhat worn, but distinct enough for me to trace the same odd design which had first attracted my eye. This was enough to arouse my strongest suspicions, but whether it was sufficient for the law to take cognizance of I did not consider. My astonishment and the ironical humour of the situation drove everything else out of my mind.

These balls were attended by a great variety of people. They were generally given by the waiters of some one of the big hotels, and were often patronized by a number of hotel guests who came to "see the sights." The crowd was always noisy, but good-natured; there was much quadrille-dancing, and a strong-lunged man called figures in a voice which did not confine itself to the limits of the hall. It is not worth the while for me to describe in detail how these people acted; they conducted themselves in about the same manner as I have seen other people at similar balls conduct themselves. When one has seen something of the world and human nature, one must conclude, after all, that between people in like stations of life there is very little difference the world over.

However, it was at one of these balls that I first saw the cake-walk. There was a contest for a gold watch, to be awarded to the hotel head-waiter receiving the greatest number of votes. There was some dancing while the votes were being counted. Then the floor was cleared for the cake-walk. A half-dozen guests from some of the hotels took seats on the stage to act as judges, and twelve or fourteen couples began to walk for a sure enough, highly decorated cake, which was in plain evidence. The spectators crowded about the space reserved for the contestants and watched them with interest and excitement. The couples did not walk round in a circle, but in a square, with the men on the inside. The fine points to be considered were the bearing of the men, the precision with which they turned the corners, the grace of the women, and the ease with which they swung round the pivots. The men walked with stately and soldierly step, and the women with considerable grace. The judges arrived at their decision by a process of elimination. The music and the walk continued for some minutes; then both were stopped while the judges conferred; when the walk began again, several couples were left out. In this way the contest was finally narrowed down to three or four couples. Then the excitement became intense; there was much partisan cheering as one couple or another would execute a turn in extra elegant style. When the cake was finally awarded, the spectators were about evenly divided between those who cheered the winners and those who muttered about the unfairness of the judges. This was the cake-walk in its original form, and it is what the coloured performers on the theatrical stage developed into the prancing movements now known all over the world, and which some Parisian critics pronounced the acme of poetic motion.

There are a great many coloured people who are ashamed of the cake-walk, but I think they ought to be proud of it. It is my opinion that the coloured people of this country have done four things which refute the oft-advanced theory that they are an absolutely inferior race, which demonstrate that they have originality and artistic conception, and, what is more, the power of creating that which can influence and appeal universally. The first two of these are the Uncle Remus stories, collected by Joel Chandler Harris, and the Jubilee songs, to which the Fisk singers made the public and the skilled musicians of both America and Europe listen. The other two are rag-time music and the cake-walk. No one who has travelled can question the world-conquering influence of rag-time, and I do not think it would be an exaggeration to say that in Europe the United States is popularly known better by rag-time than by anything else it has produced in a generation. In Paris they call it American music. The newspapers have already told how the practice of intricate cake-walk steps has taken up the time of European royalty and nobility. These are lower forms of art, but they give evidence of a power that will some day be applied to the higher forms. In this measure, at least, and aside from the number of prominent individuals the coloured people of the United States have produced, the race has been a world influence; and all of the Indians between Alaska and Patagonia haven't done as much.

Just when I was beginning to look upon Jacksonville as my permanent home and was beginning to plan about marrying the young school-teacher, raising a family, and working in a cigar factory the rest of my life, for some reason, which I do not now remember, the factory at which I worked was indefinitely shut down. Some of the men got work in other factories in town; some decided to go to Key West and Tampa, others made up their minds to go to New York for work. All at once a desire like a fever seized me to see the North again and I cast my lot with those bound for New York.

CHAPTER VI

We steamed up into New York harbor late one afternoon in spring. The last efforts of the sun were being put forth in turning the waters of the bay to glistening gold; the green islands on either side, in spite of their warlike mountings, looked calm and peaceful; the buildings of the town shone out in a reflected light which gave the city an air of enchantment; and, truly, it is an enchanted spot. New York City is the most fatally fascinating thing in America. She sits like a great witch at the gate of the country, showing her alluring white face and hiding her crooked hands and feet under the folds of her wide garments—constantly enticing thousands from far within, and tempting those who come from across the seas to go no farther. And all these become the victims of her caprice. Some she at once crushes beneath her cruel feet; others she condemns to a fate like that of galley-slaves; a few she favours and fondles, riding them high on the bubbles of fortune; then with a sudden breath she blows the bubbles out and laughs mockingly as she watches them fall.

Twice I had passed through it, but this was really my first visit to New York; and as I walked about that evening, I began to feel the dread power of the city; the crowds, the lights, the excitement, the gaiety, and all its subtler stimulating influences began to take effect upon me. My blood ran quicker and I felt that I was just beginning to live. To some natures this stimulant of life in a great city becomes a thing as binding and necessary as opium is to one addicted to the habit. It becomes their breath of life; they cannot exist outside of it; rather than be deprived of it they are content to suffer hunger, want, pain, and misery; they would not exchange even a ragged and wretched condition among the great crowd for any degree of comfort away from it.

As soon as we landed, four of us went directly to a lodging-house in Twenty-seventh Street, just west of Sixth Avenue. The house was run by a short, stout mulatto man, who was exceedingly talkative and inquisitive. In fifteen minutes he not only knew the history of the past life of each one of us, but had a clearer idea of what we intended to do in the future than we ourselves. He sought this information so much with an air of being very particular as to whom he admitted into his house that we tremblingly answered every question that he asked. When we had become located, we went out and got supper, then walked round until about ten o'clock. At that hour we met a couple of young fellows who lived in New York and were known to one of the members of our party. It was suggested we go to a certain place which was known by the proprietor's name. We turned into one of the cross streets and mounted the stoop of a house in about the middle of a block between Sixth and Seventh Avenues. One of the young men whom we had met rang a bell, and a man on the inside cracked the door a couple of inches; then opened it and let us in. We found ourselves in the hallway of what had once been a residence. The front parlour had been converted into a bar, and a half-dozen or so well-dressed men were in the room. We went in and after a general introduction had several rounds of beer. In the back parlour a crowd was sitting and standing round the walls of the room watching an exciting and noisy game of pool. I walked back and joined this crowd to watch the game, and principally to get away from the drinking party. The game was really interesting, the players being quite expert, and the excitement was heightened by the bets which were being made on the result. At times the antics and remarks of both players and spectators were amusing. When, at a critical point, a player missed a shot, he was deluged, by those financially interested in his making it, with a flood of epithets synonymous with "chump"; while from the others he would be jeered by such remarks as "Nigger, dat cue ain't no hoe-handle." I noticed that among this class of coloured men the word "nigger" was freely used in about the same sense as the word "fellow," and sometimes as a term of almost endearment; but I soon learned that its use was positively and absolutely prohibited to white men.

I stood watching this pool game until I was called by my friends, who were still in the bar-room, to go upstairs. On the second floor there were two large rooms. From the hall I looked into the one on the front. There was a large, round table in the centre, at which five or six men were seated playing poker. The air and conduct here were greatly in contrast to what I had just seen in the pool-room; these men were evidently the aristocrats of the place; they were well, perhaps a bit flashily, dressed and spoke in low modulated voices, frequently using the word "gentlemen"; in fact, they seemed to be practising a sort of Chesterfieldian politeness towards each other. I was watching these men with a great deal of interest and some degree of admiration when I was again called by the members of our party, and I followed them on to the back room. There was a door-keeper at this room, and we were admitted only after inspection. When we got inside, I saw a crowd of men of all ages and kinds grouped about an old billiard-table, regarding some of whom, in supposing them to be white, I made no mistake. At first I did not know what these men were doing; they were using terms that were strange to me. I could hear only a confusion of voices exclaiming: "Shoot the two!" "Shoot the four!" "Fate me! Fate me!" "I've got you fated!" "Twenty-five cents he don't run!" This was the ancient and terribly fascinating game of dice, popularly known as "craps." I myself had played pool in Jacksonville—it is a favourite game among cigar-makers—and I had seen others play cards; but here was something new. I edged my way in to the table and stood between one of my new-found New York friends and a tall, slender, black fellow, who was making side bets while the dice were at the other end of the table. My companion explained to me the principles of the game; and they are so simple that they hardly need to be explained twice. The dice came round the table until they reached the man on the other side of the tall, black fellow. He lost, and the latter said: "Gimme the bones." He threw a dollar on the table and said: "Shoot the dollar." His style of play was so strenuous that he had to be allowed plenty of room. He shook the dice high above his head, and each time he threw them on the table, he emitted a grunt such as men give when they are putting forth physical exertion with a rhythmic regularity. He frequently whirled completely round on his heels, throwing the dice the entire length of the table, and talking to them as though they were trained animals. He appealed to them in short singsong phrases. "Come, dice," he would say. "Little Phoebe," "Little Joe," " 'Way down yonder in the cornfield." Whether these mystic incantations were efficacious or not I could not say, but, at any rate, his luck was great, and he had what gamblers term "nerve." "Shoot the dollar!" "Shoot the two!" "Shoot the four!" "Shoot the eight!" came from his lips as quickly as the dice turned to his advantage. My companion asked me if I had ever played. I told him no. He said that I ought to try my luck: that everybody won at first. The tall man at my side was waving his arms in the air, exclaiming: "Shoot the sixteen!" "Shoot the sixteen!" "Fate me!" Whether it was my companion's suggestion or some latent dare-devil strain in my blood which suddenly sprang into activity I do not know; but with a thrill of excitement which went through my whole body I threw a twenty-dollar bill on the table and said in a trembling voice: "I fate you."

I could feel that I had gained the attention and respect of everybody in the room, every eye was fixed on me, and the widespread question, "Who is he?" went round. This was gratifying to a certain sense of vanity of which I have never been able to rid myself, and I felt that it was worth the money even if I lost. The tall man, with a whirl on his heels and a double grunt, threw the dice; four was the number which turned up. This is considered as a hard "point" to make. He redoubled his contortions and his grunts and his pleadings to the dice; but on his third or fourth throw the fateful seven turned up, and I had won.

My companion and all my friends shouted to me to follow up my luck. The fever was on me. I seized the dice. My hands were so hot that the bits of bone felt like pieces of ice. I shouted as loudly as I could: "Shoot it all!" but the blood was tingling so about my ears that I could not hear my own voice. I was soon "fated." I threw the dice—seven—I had won. "Shoot it all!" I cried again. There was a pause; the stake was more than one man cared to or could cover. I was finally "fated" by several men taking each a part of it. I then threw the dice again. Seven. I had won. "Shoot it all!" I shouted excitedly. After a short delay I was "fated." Again I rolled the dice. Eleven. Again I won. My friends now surrounded me and, much against my inclination, forced me to take down all of the money except five dollars. I tried my luck once more, and threw some small "point" which I failed to make, and the dice passed on to the next man.

In less than three minutes I had won more than two hundred dollars, a sum which afterwards cost me dearly. I was the hero of the moment and was soon surrounded by a group of men who expressed admiration for my "nerve" and predicted for me a brilliant future as a gambler. Although at the time I had no thought of becoming a gambler, I felt proud of my success. I felt a bit ashamed, too, that I had allowed my friends to persuade me to take down my money so soon. Another set of men also got round me and begged me for twenty-five or fifty cents to put them back into the game. I gave each of them something. I saw that several of them had on linen dusters, and as I looked about, I noticed that there were perhaps a dozen men in the room similarly clad. I asked the fellow who had been my prompter at the dice table why they dressed in such a manner. He told me that men who had lost all the money and jewellery they possessed, frequently, in an effort to recoup their losses, would gamble away all their outer clothing and even their shoes; and that the proprietor kept on hand a supply of linen dusters for all who were so unfortunate. My informant went on to say that sometimes a fellow would become almost completely dressed and then, by a turn of the dice, would be thrown back into a state of semi-nakedness. Some of them were virtually prisoners and unable to get into the streets for days at a time. They ate at the lunch counter, where their credit was good so long as they were fair gamblers and did not attempt to jump their debts, and they slept round in chairs. They importuned friends and winners to put them back in the game, and kept at it until fortune again smiled on them. I laughed heartily at this, not thinking the day was coming which would find me in the same ludicrous predicament.

On passing downstairs I was told that the third and top floor of the house was occupied by the proprietor. When we passed through the bar, I treated everybody in the room—and that was no small number, for eight or ten had followed us down. Then our party went out. It was now about a half past twelve, but my nerves were at such a tension that I could not endure the mere thought of going to bed. I asked if there was no other place to which we could go; our guides said yes, and suggested that we go to the "Club." We went to Sixth Avenue, walked two blocks, and turned to the west into another street. We stopped in front of a house with three stories and a basement. In the basement was a Chinese chop-suey restaurant. There was a red lantern at the iron gate to the areaway, inside of which the Chinaman's name was printed. We went up the steps of the stoop, rang the bell, and were admitted without any delay. From the outside the house bore a rather gloomy aspect, the windows being absolutely dark, but within, it was a veritable house of mirth. When we had passed through a small vestibule and reached the hallway, we heard mingled sounds of music and laughter, the clink of glasses, and the pop of bottles. We went into the main room and I was little prepared for what I saw. The brilliancy of the place, the display of diamond rings, scarf-pins, ear-rings, and breast-pins, the big rolls of money that were brought into evidence when drinks were paid for, and the air of gaiety that pervaded the place, all completely dazzled and dazed me. I felt positively giddy, and it was several minutes before I was able to make any clear and definite observations.

We at length secured places at a table in a corner of the room and, as soon as we could attract the attention of one of the busy waiters, ordered a round of drinks. When I had somewhat collected my senses, I realized that in a large back room into which the main room opened, there was a young fellow singing a song, accompanied on the piano by a short, thickset, dark man. After each verse he did some dance steps, which brought forth great applause and a shower of small coins at his feet. After the singer had responded to a rousing encore, the stout man at the piano began to run his fingers up and down the keyboard. This he did in a manner which indicated that he was master of a good deal of technique. Then he began to play; and such playing! I stopped talking to listen. It was music of a kind I had never heard before. It was music that demanded physical response, patting of the feet, drumming of the fingers, or nodding of the head in time with the beat. The barbaric harmonies, the audacious resolutions, often consisting of an abrupt jump from one key to another, the intricate rhythms in which the accents fell in the most unexpected places, but in which the beat was never lost, produced a most curious effect. And, too, the player—the dexterity of his left hand in making rapid octave runs and jumps was little short of marvellous; and with his right hand he frequently swept half the keyboard with clean-cut chromatics which he fitted in so nicely as never to fail to arouse in his listeners a sort of pleasant surprise at the accomplishment of the feat.

This was rag-time music, then a novelty in New York, and just growing to be a rage, which has not yet subsided. It was originated in the questionable resorts about Memphis and St. Louis by Negro piano-players who knew no more of the theory of music than they did of the theory of the universe, but were guided by natural musical instinct and talent. It made its way to Chicago, where it was popular some time before it reached New York. These players often improvised crude and, at times, vulgar words to fit the melodies. This was the beginning of the rag-time song. Several of these improvisations were taken down by white men, the words slightly altered, and published under the names of the arrangers. They sprang into immediate popularity and earned small fortunes, of which the Negro originators got only a few dollars. But I have learned that since that time a number of coloured men, of not only musical talent, but training, are writing out their own melodies and words and reaping the reward of their work. I have learned also that they have a large number of white imitators and adulterators.

American musicians, instead of investigating rag-time, attempt to ignore it, or dismiss it with a contemptuous word. But that has always been the course of scholasticism in every branch of art. Whatever new thing the *people* like is pooh-poohed; whatever is *popular* is spoken of as not worth the while. The fact is, nothing great or enduring, especially in music, has ever sprung full-fledged and unprecedented from the brain of any master; the best that he gives to the world he gathers from the hearts of the people, and runs it through the alembic of his genius. In spite of the bans which musicians and music teachers have placed upon it, the people still demand and enjoy rag-time. One thing cannot be denied; it is music which possesses at least one strong element of greatness: it appeals universally; not only the American, but the English, the French, and even the German people find delight in it. In fact, there is not a corner of the civilized world in which it is not known, and this proves its originality; for if it were an imitation, the people of Europe, anyhow, would not have found it a novelty. Anyone who doubts that there is a peculiar heel-tickling, smile-provoking, joy-awakening charm in rag-time needs only to hear a skilful performer play the genuine article to be convinced. I believe that it has its place as well as the music which draws from us sighs and tears.

I became so interested in both the music and the player that I left the table where I was sitting, and made my way through the hall into the back room, where I could see as well as hear. I talked to the piano-player between the musical numbers and found out that he was just a natural musician, never having taken a lesson in his life. Not only could he play almost anything he heard, but he could accompany singers in songs he had never heard. He had, by ear alone, composed some pieces, several of which he played over for me; each of them was properly proportioned and balanced. I began to wonder what this man with such a lavish natural endowment would have done had he been trained. Perhaps he wouldn't have done anything at all; he might have become, at best, a mediocre imitator of the great masters in what they have already done to a finish, or one of the modern innovators who strive after originality by seeing how cleverly they can dodge about through the rules of harmony and at the same time avoid melody. It is certain that he would not have been so delightful as he was in rag-time.

I sat by, watching and listening to this man until I was dragged away by my friends. The place was now almost deserted; only a few stragglers hung on, and they were all the worse for drink. My friends were well up in this class. We passed into the street; the lamps were pale against the sky; day was just breaking. We went home and got into bed. I fell into a fitful sort of sleep, with rag-time music ringing continually in my ears.

CHAPTER VIII

On the day following our night at the "Club" we slept until late in the afternoon; so late that beginning search for work was entirely out of the question. This did not cause me much worry, for I had more than three hundred dollars, and New York had impressed me as a place where there was lots of money and not much difficulty in getting it. It is needless to inform my readers that I did not long hold this opinion. We got out of the house about dark, went to a restaurant on Sixth Avenue and ate something, then walked round for a couple of hours. I finally suggested that we visit the same places we had been in the night before. Following my suggestion, we started first to the gambling-house. The man on the door let us in without any question; I accredited this to my success of the night before. We went straight to the "crap" room, and I at once made my way to a table, where I was rather flattered by the murmur of recognition which went round. I played it up and down luck for three or four hours; then, worn with nervous excitement, quit, having lost about fifty dollars. But I was so strongly possessed with the thought that I would make up my losses the next time I played that I left the place with a light heart.

When we got into the street our party was divided against itself; two were for going home at once and getting to bed. They gave as a reason that we were to get up early and look for jobs. I think the real reason was that they had each lost several dollars in the game. I lived to learn that in the world of sport all men win alike, but lose differently; and so gamblers are rated, not by the way in which they win, but by the way in which they lose. Some men lose with a careless smile, recognizing that losing is a part of the game; others curse their luck and rail at fortune; and others, still, lose sadly; after each such experience they are swept by a wave of reform; they resolve to stop gambling and be good. When in this frame of mind it would take very little persuasion to lead them into a prayer-meeting. Those in the first class are looked upon with admiration; those in the second class are merely commonplace; while those in the third are regarded with contempt. I believe these distinctions hold good in all the ventures of life. After some minutes one of my friends and I succeeded in convincing the other two that a while at the "Club" would put us all in better spirits; and they consented to go, on our promise not to stay longer than an hour. We found the place crowded, and the same sort of thing going on which we had seen the night before. I took a seat at once by the side of the piano-player, and was soon lost to everything except the novel charm of the music. I watched the performer with the idea of catching the trick, and during one of his intermissions I took his place at the piano and made an attempt to imitate him, but even my quick ear and ready fingers were unequal to the task on first trial.

We did not stay at the "Club" very long, but went home to bed in order to be up early the next day. We had no difficulty in finding work, and my third morning in New York found me at a table rolling cigars. I worked steadily for some weeks, at the same time spending my earnings between the "crap" game and the "Club." Making cigars became more and more irksome to me; perhaps my more congenial work as a "reader" had unfitted me for work at the table. And, too, the late hours I was keeping made such a sedentary occupation almost beyond the powers of will and endurance. I often found it hard to keep my eyes open and sometimes had to get up and move round to keep from falling asleep. I began to miss whole days from the factory, days on which I was compelled to stay at home and sleep.

My luck at the gambling-table was varied; sometimes I was fifty to a hundred dollars ahead, and at other times I had to borrow money from my fellow workmen to settle my room rent and pay for my meals. Each night after leaving the dice game I went to the "Club" to hear the music and watch the gaiety. If I had won, this was in accord with my mood; if I had lost, it made me forget. I at last realized that making cigars for a living and gambling for a living could not both be carried on at the same time, and I resolved to give up the cigar-making. This resolution led me into a life which held me bound more than a year. During that period my regular time for going to bed was somewhere between four and six o'clock in the mornings. I got up late in the afternoons, walked about a little, then went to the gambling-house or the "Club." My New York was limited to ten blocks; the boundaries were Sixth Avenue from Twenty-third to Thirty-third Streets, with the cross streets one block to the west. Central Park was a distant forest, and the lower part of the city a foreign land. I look back upon the life I then led with a shudder when I think what would have been had I not escaped it. But had I not escaped it, I should have been no more unfortunate than are many young coloured men who come to New York. During that dark period I became acquainted with a score of bright, intelligent young fellows who had come up to the great city with high hopes and ambitions and who had fallen under the spell of this under life, a spell they could not throw off. There was one popularly known as "the doctor"; he had had two years in the Harvard Medical School, but here he was, living this gas-light life, his will and moral sense so enervated and deadened that it was impossible for him to break away. I do not doubt that the same thing is going on now, but I have sympathy rather than censure for these victims, for I know how easy it is to slip into a slough from which it takes a herculean effort to leap.

I regret that I cannot contrast my views of life among coloured people of New York; but the truth is, during my entire stay in this city I did not become acquainted with a single respectable family. I knew that there were several coloured men worth a hundred or so thousand dollars each, and some families who proudly dated their free ancestry back a half-dozen generations. I also learned that in Brooklyn there lived quite a large colony in comfortable homes which they owned; but at no point did my life come in contact with theirs.

In my gambling-experiences I passed through all the states and conditions that a gambler is heir to. Some days found me able to peel ten- and twenty-dollar bills from a roll, and others found me clad in a linen duster and carpet slippers. I finally caught up another method of earning money, and so did not have to depend entirely upon the caprices of fortune at the gaming-table. Through continually listening to the music at the "Club," and through my own previous training, my natural talent and perseverance, I developed into a remarkable player of rag-time; indeed, I had the name at that time of being the best rag-time-player in New York. I brought all my knowledge of classic music to bear and, in so doing, achieved some novelties which pleased and even astonished my listeners. It was I who first made rag-time transcriptions of familiar classic selections. I used to play Mendelssohn's "Wedding March" in a manner that never failed to arouse enthusiasm among the patrons of the "Club." Very few nights passed during which I was not asked to play it. It was no secret that the great increase in slumming visitors was due to my playing. By mastering rag-time I gained several things: first of all, I gained the title of professor. I was known as "the professor" as long as I remained in that world. Then, too, I gained the means of earning a rather fair livelihood. This work took up much of my time and kept me almost entirely away from the gambling-table. Through it I also gained a friend who was the means by which I escaped from this lower world. And, finally, I secured a wedge which has opened to me more doors and made me a welcome guest than my playing of Beethoven and Chopin could ever have done.

The greater part of the money I now began to earn came through the friend to whom I alluded in the foregoing paragraph. Among the other white "slummers" there came into the "Club" one night a clean-cut, slender, but athletic-looking man, who would have been taken for a youth had it not been for the tinge of grey about his temples. He was clean-shaven and had regular features, and all of his movements bore the indefinable but unmistakable stamp of culture. He spoke to no one, but sat languidly puffing cigarettes and sipping a glass of beer. He was the centre of a great deal of attention; all of the old-timers were wondering who he was. When I had finished playing, he called a waiter and by him sent me a five-dollar bill. For about a month after that he was at the "Club" one or two nights each week, and each time after I had played, he gave me five dollars. One night he sent for me to come to his table; he asked me several questions about myself; then told me that he had an enagement which he wanted me to fill. He gave me a card containing his address and asked me to be there on a certain night.

I was on hand promptly and found that he was giving a dinner in his own apartments to a party of ladies and gentlemen and that I was expected to furnish the musical entertainment. When the grave, dignified man at the door let me in, the place struck me as being almost dark, my eyes had been so accustomed to the garish light of the "Club." He took my coat and hat, bade me take a seat, and went to tell his master that I had come. When my eyes were adjusted to the soft light, I saw that I was in the midst of elegance and luxury in a degree such as I had never seen; but not the elegance which makes one ill at ease. As I sank into a great chair, the subdued tone, the delicately sensuous harmony of my surroundings, drew from me a deep sigh of relief and comfort. How long the man was gone I do not know, but I was startled by a voice saying: "Come this way, if you please, sir," and I saw him standing by my chair. I had been asleep; and I awoke very much confused and a little ashamed, because I did not know how many times he may have called me. I followed him through into the dining-room, where the butler was putting the finishing touches to a table which already looked like a big jewel. The doorman turned me over to the butler, and I passed with the butler on back to where several waiters were busy polishing and assorting table utensils. Without being asked whether I was hungry or not, I was placed at a table and given something to eat. Before I had finished eating, I heard the laughter and talk of the guests who were arriving. Soon afterwards I was called in to begin my work.

I passed in to where the company was gathered and went directly to the piano. According to a suggestion from the host, I began with classic music. During the first number there was absolute quiet and appreciative attention, and when I had finished, I was given a round of generous applause. After that the talk and the laughter began to grow until the music was only an accompaniment to the chatter. This, however, did not disconcert me as it once would have done, for I had become accustomed to playing in the midst of uproarious noise. As the guests began to pay less attention to me, I was enabled to pay more to them. There were about a dozen of them. The men ranged in appearance from a girlish-looking youth to a big grizzled man whom everybody addressed as "Judge." None of the women appeared to be under thirty, but each of them struck me as being handsome. I was not long in finding out that they were all decidedly blasé. Several of the women smoked cigarettes, and with a careless grace which showed they were used to the habit. Occasionally a "Damn it!" escaped from the lips of some one of them, but in such a charming way as to rob it of all vulgarity. The most notable thing which I observed was that the reserve of the host increased in direct proportion with the hilarity of his guests. I thought that there was something going wrong which displeased him. I afterwards learned that it was his habitual manner on such occasions. He seemed to take cynical delight in watching and studying others indulging in excess. His guests were evidently accustomed to his rather non-participating attitude, for it did not seem in any degree to dampen their spirits.

When dinner was served, the piano was moved and the door left open, so that the company might hear the music while eating. At a word from the host I struck up one of my liveliest rag-time pieces. The effect was surprising, perhaps even to the host; the rag-time music came very near spoiling the party so far as eating the dinner was concerned. As soon as I began, the conversation suddenly stopped. It was a pleasure to me to watch the expression of astonishment and delight that grew on the faces of everybody. These were people—and they represented a large class—who were ever expecting to find happiness in novelty, each day restlessly exploring and exhausting every resource of this great city that might possibly furnish a new sensation or awaken a fresh emotion, and who were always grateful to anyone who aided them in their quest. Several of the women left the table and gathered about the piano. They watched my fingers and asked what kind of music it was that I was playing, where I had learned it, and a host of other questions. It was only by being repeatedly called back to the table that they were induced to finish their dinner. When the guests arose, I struck up my rag-time transcription of Mendelssohn's "Wedding March," playing it with terrific chromatic octave runs in the base. This raised everybody's spirit to the highest point of gaiety, and the whole company involuntarily and unconsciously did an impromptu cake-walk. From that time on until the time of leaving they kept me so busy that my arms ached. I obtained a little respite when the girlish-looking youth and one or two of the ladies sang several songs, but after each of these it was "back to rag-time."

In leaving, the guests were enthusiastic in telling the host that he had furnished them the most unusual entertainment they had ever enjoyed. When they had gone, my millionaire friend—for he was reported to be a millionaire—said to me with a smile: "Well, I have given them something they've never had before." After I had put on my coat and was ready to leave, he made me take a glass of wine; he then gave me a cigar and twenty dollars in bills. He told me that he would give me lots of work, his only stipulation being that I should not play any engagements such as I had just filled for him, except by his instructions. I readily accepted the proposition, for I was sure that I could not be the loser by such a contract.

I afterwards played for him at many dinners and parties of one kind or another. Occasionally he "loaned" me to some of his friends. And, too, I often played for him alone at his apartments. At such times he was quite a puzzle to me until I became accustomed to his manners. He would sometimes sit for three or four hours hearing me play, his eyes almost closed, making scarcely a motion except to light a fresh cigarette, and never commenting one way or another on the music. At first I sometimes thought he had fallen asleep and would pause in playing. The stopping of the music always aroused him enough to tell me to play this or that; and I soon learned that my task was not to be considered finished until he got up from his chair and said: "That will do." The man's powers of endurance in listening often exceeded mine in performing—yet I am not sure that he was always listening. At times I became so oppressed with fatigue and sleepiness that it took almost superhuman effort to keep my fingers going; in fact, I believe I sometimes did so while dozing. During such moments this man sitting there so mysteriously silent, almost hid in a cloud of heavy-scented smoke, filled me with a sort of unearthly terror. He seemed to be some grim, mute, but relentless tyrant, possessing over me a supernatural power which he used to drive me on mercilessly to exhaustion. But these feelings came very rarely; besides, he paid me so liberally I could forget much. There at length grew between us a familiar and warm relationship, and I am sure he had a decided personal liking for me. On my part, I looked upon him at that time as about all a man could wish to be.

The "Club" still remained my headquarters, and when I was not playing for my good patron, I was generally to be found there. However, I no longer depended on playing at the "Club" to earn my living; I rather took rank with the visiting celebrities and, occasionally, after being sufficiently urged, would favour my old and new admirers with a number or two. I say, without any egotistic pride, that among my admirers were several of the best-looking women who frequented the place, and who made no secret of the fact that they admired me as much as they did my playing. Among these was the "widow"; indeed, her attentions became so marked that one of my friends warned me to beware of her black companion, who was generally known as a "bad man." He said there was much more reason to be careful because the pair had lately quarrelled and had not been together at the "Club" for some nights. This warning greatly impressed me and I resolved to stop the affair before it should go any further; but the woman was so beautiful that my native galantry and delicacy would not allow me to repulse her;

my finer feelings entirely overcame my judgment. The warning also opened my eyes sufficiently to see that though my artistic temperament and skill made me interesting and attractive to the woman, she was, after all, using me only to excite the jealousy of her companion and revenge herself upon him. It was this surly, black despot who held sway over her deepest emotions.

One night, shortly afterwards, I went into the "Club" and saw the "widow" sitting at a table in company with another woman. She at once beckoned for me to come to her. I went, knowing that I was committing worse than folly. She ordered a quart of champagne and insisted that I sit down and drink with her. I took a chair on the opposite side of the table and began to sip a glass of the wine. Suddenly I noticed by an expression on the "widow's" face that something had occurred. I instinctively glanced round and saw that her companion had just entered. His ugly look completely frightened me. My back was turned to him, but by watching the "widow's" eyes I judged that he was pacing back and forth across the room. My feelings were far from being comfortable; I expected every moment to feel a blow on my head. She, too, was very nervous; she was trying hard to appear unconcerned, but could not succeed in hiding her real feelings. I decided that it was best to get out of such a predicament even at the expense of appearing cowardly, and I made a motion to rise. Just as I partly turned in my chair, I saw the black fellow approaching; he walked directly to our table and leaned over. The "widow" evidently feared he was going to strike her, and she threw back her head. Instead of striking her he whipped out a revolver and fired; the first shot went straight into her throat. There were other shots fired, but how many I do not know; for the first knowledge I had of my surroundings and actions was that I was rushing through the chop-suey restaurant into the street. Just which streets I followed when I got outside I do not know, but I think I must have gone towards Eighth Avenue, then down towards Twenty-third Street and across towards Fifth Avenue. I travelled, not by sight, but instinctively. I felt like one fleeing in a horrible nightmare.

How long and far I walked I cannot tell; but on Fifth Avenue, under a light, I passed a cab containing a solitary occupant, who called to me, and I recognized the voice and face of my millionaire friend. He stopped the cab and asked: "What on earth are you doing strolling in this part of the town?" For answer I got into the cab and related to him all that had happened. He reassured me by saying that no charge of any kind could be brought against me; then added: "But of course you don't want to be mixed up in such an affair." He directed the driver to turn round and go into the park, and then went on to say: "I decided last night that I'd got to Europe tomorrow. I think I'll take you along instead of Walter." Walter was his valet. It was settled that I should go to his apartments for the rest of the night and sail with him in the morning.

We drove round through the park, exchanging only an occasional word. The cool air somewhat calmed my nerves and I lay back and closed my eyes; but still I could see that beautiful white throat with the ugly wound. The jet of blood pulsing from it had placed an indelible red stain on my memory.

CHAPTER IX

I did not feel at ease until the ship was well out of New York harbour; and, notwithstanding the repeated reassurances of my millionaire friend and my own knowledge of the facts in the case, I somehow could not rid myself of the sentiment that I was, in a great degree, responsible for the "widow's" tragic end. We had brought most of the morning papers aboard with us, but my great fear of seeing my name in connection with the killing would not permit me to read the accounts, although, in one of the papers, I did look at the picture of the victim, which did not in the least resemble her. This morbid state of mind, together with sea-sickness, kept me miserable for three or four days. At the end of that time my spirits began to revive, and I took an interest in the ship, my fellow passengers, and the voyage in general. On the second or third day out we passed several spouting whales, but I could not arouse myself to make the effort to go to the other side of the ship to see them. A little later we ran in close proximity to a large iceberg. I was curious enough to get up and look at it, and I was fully repaid for my pains. The sun was shining full upon it, and it glistened like a mammoth diamond, cut with a million facets. As we passed, it constantly changed its shape; at each different angle of vision it assumed new and astonishing forms of beauty. I watched it through a pair of glasses, seeking to verify my early conception of an iceberg—in the geographies of my grammar-school days the pictures of icebergs always included a stranded polar bear, standing desolately upon one of the snowy crags. I looked for the bear, but if he was there, he refused to put himself on exhibition.

It was not, however, until the morning that we entered the harbour of Havre that I was able to shake off my gloom. Then the strange sights, the chatter in an unfamiliar tongue, and the excitement of landing and passing the customs officials caused me to forget completely the events of a few days before. Indeed, I grew so light-hearted that when I caught my first sight of the train which was to take us to Paris, I enjoyed a hearty laugh. The toy-looking engine, the stuffy little compartment cars, with tiny, old-fashioned wheels, struck me as being extremely funny. But before we reached Paris my respect for our train rose considerably. I found that the "tiny" engine made remarkably fast time, and that the old-fashioned wheels ran very smoothly. I even began to appreciate the "stuffy" cars for their privacy. As I watched the passing scenery from the car window, it seemed too beautiful to be real. The bright-coloured houses against the green background impressed me as the work of some idealistic painter. Before we arrived in Paris, there was awakened in my heart a love for France which continued to grow stronger, a love which today makes that country for me the one above all others to be desired.

We rolled into the station Saint Lazare about four o'clock in the afternoon and drove immediately to the Hôtel Continental. My benefactor, humouring my curiosity and enthusiasm, which seemed to please him very much, suggested that we take a short walk before dinner. We stepped out of the hotel and turned to the right into the rue de Rivoli. When the vista of the Place de la Concorde and the Champs Élysées suddenly burst on me, I could hardly credit my own eyes. I shall attempt no such supererogatory task as a description of Paris. I wish only to give briefly the impressions which that wonderful city made upon me. It impressed me as the perfect and perfectly beautiful city; and even after I had been there for some time, and seen not only its avenues and palaces, but its most squalid alleys and hovels, this impression was not weakened. Paris became for me a charmed spot, and whenever I have returned there, I have fallen under the spell, a spell which compels admiration for all of its manners and customs and justification of even its follies and sins.

We walked a short distance up the Champs Élysées and sat for a while in chairs along the sidewalk, watching the passing crowds on foot and in carriages. It was with reluctance that I went back to the hotel for dinner. After dinner we went to one of the summer theatres, and after the performance my friend took me to a large café on one of the Grands Boulevards. Here it was that I had my first glimpse of the French life of popular literature, so different from real French life. There were several hundred people, men and women, in the place drinking, smoking, talking, and listening to the music. My millionaire friend and I took seats at a table, where we sat smoking and watching the crowd. It was not long before we were joined by two or three good-looking, well-dressed young women. My friend talked to them in French and bought drinks for the whole party. I tried to recall my high-school French, but the effort availed me little. I could stammer out a few phrases, but, very naturally, could not understand a word that was said to me. We stayed at the café a couple of hours, then went back to the hotel. The next day we spent several hours in the shops and at the tailor's. I had no clothes except what I had been able to gather together at my benefactor's apartments the night before we sailed. He bought me the same kind of clothes which he himself wore, and that was the best; and he treated me in every way as he dressed me, as an equal, not as a servant. In fact, I don't think anyone could have guessed that such a relation existed. My duties were light and few, and he was a man full of life and vigour, who rather enjoyed doing things for himself. He kept me supplied with money far beyond what ordinary wages would have amounted to. For the first two weeks we were together almost constantly, seeing the sights, sights old to him, but from which he seemed to get new pleasure in showing them to me. During the day we took in the places of interest, and at night the theatres and cafés. This sort of life appealed to me as ideal, and I asked him one day how long he intended to stay in Paris. He answered: "Oh, until I get tired of it." I could not understand how that could ever happen. As it was, including several short trips to the Mediterranean, to Spain, to Brussels, and to Ostend, we did remain there fourteen or fifteen months. We stayed at the Hôtel Continental about two months of this time. Then my millionaire took apartments, hired a piano, and lived almost the same life he lived in New York. He entertained a great deal, some of the parties being a good deal more blasé than the New York ones. I played for the guests at all of them with an effect which to relate would be but a tiresome repetition to the reader. I played not only for the guests, but continued, as I used to do in New York, to play often for the host when he was alone. This man of the world, who grew weary of everything and was always searching for something new, appeared never to grow tired of my music; he seemed to take it as a drug. He fell into a habit which caused me no little annoyance; sometimes he would come in during the early hours of the morning and, finding me in bed asleep, would wake me up and ask me to play something. This, so far as I can remember, was my only hardship during my whole stay with him in Europe.

After the first few weeks spent in sight-seeing I had a great deal of time left to myself; my friend was often I did not know where. When not with him, I spent the day nosing about all the curious nooks and corners of Paris; of this I never grew tired. At night I usually went to some theatre, but always ended up at the big café on the Grands Boulevards. I wish the reader to know that it was not alone the gaiety which drew me there; aside from that I had a laudable purpose. I had purchased an English-French conversational dictionary, and I went there every night to take a language lesson. I used to get three or four of the young women who frequented the place at a table and buy beer and cigarettes for them. In return I received my lesson. I got more than my money's worth, for they actually compelled me to speak the language. This, together with reading the papers every day, enabled me within a few months to express myself fairly well, and, before I left Paris, to have more than an ordinary command of French. Of course, every person who goes to Paris could not dare to learn French in this manner, but I can think of no easier or quicker way of doing it. The acquiring of another foreign language awoke me to the fact that with a little effort I could secure an added accomplishment as fine and as valuable as music; so I determined to make myself as much of a linguist as possible. I bought a Spanish newspaper every day in order to freshen my memory of that language, and, for French, devised what was, so far as I knew, an original system of study. I compiled a list which I termed "Three hundred necessary words." These I thoroughly committed to memory, also the conjugation of the verbs which were included in the list. I studied these words over and over, much as children of a couple of generations ago studied the alphabet. I also practised a set of phrases like the following: "How?" "What did you say?" "What does the word——mean?" "I understand all you say except——." "Please repeat." "What do you call——?" "How do you say——?" These I called my working sentences. In an astonishingly short time I reached the point where the language taught itself—where I learned to speak merely by speaking. This point is the place which students taught foreign languages in our schools and colleges find great difficulty in reaching. I think the main trouble is that they learn too much of a language at a time. A French child with a vocabulary of two hundred words can express more spoken ideas than a student of French can with a knowledge of two thousand. A small vocabulary, the smaller the better, which embraces the common, everyday-used ideas, thoroughly mastered, is the key to a language. When that much is acquired the vocabulary can be increased simply by talking. And it is easy. Who cannot commit three hundred words to memory? Later I tried my method, if I may so term it, with German, and found that it worked in the same way.

I spent a good many evenings at the Opéra. The music there made me strangely reminiscent of my life in Connecticut; it was an atmosphere in which I caught a fresh breath of my boyhood days and early youth. Generally, in the morning after I had attended a performance, I would sit at the piano and for a couple of hours play the music which I used to play in my mother's little parlour.

One night I went to hear *Faust*. I got into my seat just as the lights went down for the first act. At the end of the act I noticed that my neighbour on the left was a young girl. I cannot describe her either as to feature, or colour of her hair, or of her eyes; she was so young, so fair, so ethereal, that I felt to stare at her would be a violation; yet I was distinctly conscious of her beauty. During the intermission she spoke English in a low voice to a gentleman and a lady who sat in the seats to her left, addressing them as father and mother. I held my program as though studying it, but listened to catch every sound of her voice. Her observations on the performance and the audience were so fresh and naïve as to be almost amusing. I gathered that she was just out of school, and that this was her first trip to Paris. I occasionally stole a glance at her, and each time I did so my heart leaped into my throat. Once I glanced beyond to the gentleman who sat next to her. My glance immediately turned into a stare. Yes, there he was, unmistakably, my father! looking hardly a day older than when I had seen him some ten years before. What a strange coincidence! What should I say to him? What would he say to me? Before I had recovered from my first surprise, there came another shock in the realization that the beautiful, tender girl at my side was my sister. Then all the springs of affection in my heart, stopped since my mother's death, burst out in fresh and terrible torrents, and I could have fallen at her feet and worshipped her. They were singing the second act, but I did not hear the music. Slowly the desolate loneliness of my position became clear to me. I knew that I could not speak, but I would have given a part of my life to touch her hand with mine and call her "sister." I sat through the opera until I could stand it no longer. I felt that I was suffocating. Valentine's love seemed like mockery, and I felt an almost uncontrollable impulse to rise up and scream to the audience: "Here, here in your very midst, is a tragedy, a real tragedy!" This impulse grew so strong that I became afraid of myself, and in the darkness of one of the scenes I stumbled out of the theatre. I walked aimlessly about for an hour or so, my feelings divided between a desire to weep and a desire to curse. I finally took a cab and went from café to café, and for one of the very few times in my life drank myself into a stupor.

It was unwelcome news for me when my benefactor—I could not think of him as employer—informed me that he was at last tired of Paris. This news gave me, I think, a passing doubt as to his sanity. I had enjoyed life in Paris, and, taking all things into consideration, enjoyed it wholesomely. One thing which greatly contributed to my enjoyment was the fact that I was an American. Americans are immensely popular in Paris; and this is not due solely to the fact that they spend lots of money there, for they spend just as much or more in London, and in the latter city they are merely tolerated because they do spend. The Londoner seems to think that Americans are people whose only claim to be classed as civilized is that they have money, and the regrettable thing about that is that the money is not English. But the French are more logical and freer from prejudices than the British; so the difference of attitude is easily explained. Only once in Paris did I have cause to blush for my American citizenship. I had become quite friendly with a young man from Luxemburg whom I had met at the big café. He was a stolid, slow-witted fellow, but, as we say, with a heart of gold. He and I grew attached to each other and were together frequently. He was a great admirer of the United States and never grew tired of talking to me about the country and asking for information. It was his intention to try his fortune there some day. One night he asked me in a tone of voice which indicated that he expected an authoritative denial of an ugly rumour: "Did they really burn a man alive in the United States?" I never knew what I stammered out to him as an answer. I should have felt relieved if I could even have said to him: "Well, only one."

When we arrived in London, my sadness at leaving Paris was turned into despair. After my long stay in the French capital, huge, ponderous, massive London seemed to me as ugly a thing as man could contrive to make. I thought of Paris as a beauty-spot on the face of the earth, and of London as a big freckle. But soon London's massiveness, I might say its very ugliness, began to impress me. I began to experience that sense of grandeur which one feels when he looks at a great mountain or a mighty river. Beside London Paris becomes a toy, a pretty plaything. And I must own that before I left the world's metropolis I discovered much there that was beautiful. The beauty in and about London is entirely different from that in and about Paris; and I could not but admit that the beauty of the French city seemed hand-made, artificial, as though set up for the photographer's camera, everything nicely adjusted so as not to spoil the picture; while that of the English city was rugged, natural, and fresh.

How these two cities typify the two peoples who built them! Even the sound of their names expresses a certain racial difference. Paris is the concrete expression of the gaiety, regard for symmetry, love of art, and, I might well add, of the morality of the French people. London stands for the conservatism, the solidarity, the utilitarianism, and, I might well add, the hypocrisy of the Anglo-Saxon. It may sound odd to speak of the morality of the French, if not of the hypocrisy of the English; but this seeming paradox impresses me as a deep truth. I saw many things in Paris which were immoral according to English standards, but the absence of hypocrisy, the absence of the spirit to do the thing if it might only be done in secret, robbed these very immoralities of the damning influence of the same evils in London. I have walked along the terrace cafés of Paris and seen hundreds of men and women sipping their wine and beer, without observing a sign of drunkenness. As they drank, they chatted and laughed and watched the passing crowds; the drinking seemed to be a secondary thing. This I have witnessed, not only in the cafés along the Grand Boulevards, but in the out-of-the-way places patronized by the working-classes. In London I have seen in the "pubs" men and women crowded in stuffy little compartments, drinking seemingly only for the pleasure of swallowing as much as they could hold. I have seen there women from eighteen to eighty, some in tatters, and some clutching babes in their arms, drinking the heavy English ales and whiskies served to them by women. In the whole scene, not one ray of brightness, not one flash of gaiety, only maudlin joviality or grim despair. And I have thought, if some men and women will drink—and it is certain that some will—is it not better that they do so under the open sky, in the fresh air, than huddled together in some close, smoky room? There is a sort of frankness about the evils of Paris which robs them of much of the seductiveness of things forbidden, and with that frankness goes a certain cleanliness of thought belonging to things not hidden. London will do whatever Paris does, provided exterior morals are not shocked. As a result, Paris has the appearance only of being the more immoral city. The difference may be summed up in this: Paris practises its sins as lightly as it does its religion, while London practises both very seriously.

I should not neglect to mention what impressed me most forcibly during my stay in London. It was not St. Paul's nor the British Museum nor Westminster Abbey. It was nothing more or less than the simple phrase "Thank you," or sometimes more elaborated, "Thank you very kindly, sir." I was continually surprised by the varied uses to which it was put; and, strange to say, its use as an expression of politeness seemed more limited than any other. One night I was in a cheap music-hall and accidentally bumped into a waiter who was carrying a tray-load of beer, almost bringing him to several shillings' worth of grief. To my amazement he righted himself and said: "Thank ye, sir," and left me wondering whether he meant that he thanked me for not completely spilling his beer, or that he would thank me for keeping out of his way.

I also found cause to wonder upon what ground the English acuse Americans of corrupting the language by introducing slang words. I think I heard more and more different kinds of slang during my few weeks' stay in London than in my whole "tenderloin" life in New York. But I suppose the English feel that the language is theirs, and that they may do with it as they please without at the same time allowing that privilege to others.

My millionaire was not so long in growing tired of London as of Paris. After a stay of six or eight weeks we went across into Holland. Amsterdam was a great surprise to me. I had always thought of Venice as the city of canals; it had never entered my mind that I should find similar conditions in a Dutch town. I don't suppose the comparison goes far beyond the fact that there are canals in both cities—I have never seen Venice—but Amsterdam struck me as being extremely picturesque. From Holland we went to Germany, where we spent five or six months, most of the time in Berlin. I found Berlin more to my taste than London, and occasionally I had to admit that in some things it was superior to Paris.

In Berlin I especially enjoyed the orchestral concerts, and I attended a large number of them. I formed the acquaintance of a good many musicians, several of whom spoke of my playing in high terms. It was in Berlin that my inspiration was renewed. One night my millionaire entertained a party of men composed of artists, musicians, writers, and, for aught I know, a count or two. They drank and smoked a great deal, talked art and music, and discussed, it seemed to me, everything that ever entered man's mind. I could only follow the general drift of what they were saying. When they discussed music, it was more interesting to me; for then some fellow would run excitedly to the piano and give a demonstration of his opinions, and another would follow quickly, doing the same. In this way, I learned that, regardless of what his specialty might be, every man in the party was a musician. I was at the same time impressed with the falsity of the general idea that Frenchmen are excitable and emotional, and that Germans are calm and phlegmatic. Frenchmen are merely gay and never overwhelmed by their emotions. When they talk loud and fast, it is merely talk, while Germans get worked up and red in the face when sustaining an opinion, and in heated discussions are likely to allow their emotions to sweep them off their feet.

My millionaire planned, in the midst of the discussion on music, to have me play the "new American music" and astonish everybody present. The result was that I was more astonished than anyone else. I went to the piano and played the most intricate rag-time piece I knew. Before there was time for anybody to express an opinion on what I had done, a big bespectacled, bushy-headed man rushed over, and, shoving me out of the chair, exclaimed: "Get up! Get up!" He seated himself at the piano, and, taking the theme of my rag-time, played it through first in straight chords; then varied and developed it through every known musical form. I sat amazed. I had been turning classic music into rag-time, a comparatively easy task; and this man had taken rag-time and made it classic. The thought came across me like a flash—It can be done, why can't I do it? From that moment my mind was made up. I clearly saw the way of carrying out the ambition I had formed when a boy.

I now lost interest in our trip. I thought: "Here I am a man, no longer a boy, and what am I doing but wasting my time and abusing my talent? What use am I making of my gifts? What future have I before me following my present course?" These thoughts made me feel remorseful and put me in a fever to get to work, to begin to do something. Of course I know now that I was not wasting time; that there was nothing I could have done at that age which would have benefited me more than going to Europe as I did. The desire to begin work grew stronger each day. I could think of nothing else. I made up my mind to go back into the very heart of the South, to live among the people, and drink in my inspiration firsthand. I gloated over the immense amount of material I had to work with, not only modern rag-time, but also the old slave songs—material which no one had yet touched.

The more decided and anxious I became to return to the United States, the more I dreaded the ordeal of breaking with my millionaire. Between this peculiar man and me there had grown a very strong bond of affection, backed up by a debt which each owed to the other. He had taken me from a terrible life in New York and, by giving me the opportunity of travelling and of coming in contact with the people with whom he associated, had made me a polished man of the world. On the other hand, I was his chief means of disposing of the thing which seemed to sum up all in life that he dreaded—time. As I remember him now, I can see that time was what he was always endeavouring to escape, to bridge over, to blot out; and it is not strange that some years later he did escape it for ever, by leaping into eternity.

For some weeks I waited for just the right moment in which to tell my patron of my decision. Those weeks were a trying time to me. I felt that I was playing the part of a traitor to my best friend. At length, one day he said to me: "Well, get ready for a long trip; we are going to Egypt, and then to Japan." The temptation was for an instant almost overwhelming, but I summoned determination enough to say: "I don't think I want to go." "What!" he exclaimed, "you want to go back to your dear Paris? You still think that the only spot on earth? Wait until you see Cairo and Tokyo, you may change your mind." "No," I stammered, "it is not because I want to go back to Paris. I want to go back to the United States." He wished to know my reason, and I told him, as best I could, my dreams, my ambition, and my decision. While I was talking, he watched me with a curious, almost cynical, smile growing on his lips. When I had finished he put his hand on my shoulder—this was the first physical expression of tender regard he had ever shown me—and looking at me in a big-brotherly way, said. "My boy, you are by blood, by appearance, by education, and by tastes a white man. Now, why do you want to throw your life away amidst the poverty and ignorance, in the hopeless struggle, of the black people of the United States? Then look at the terrible handicap you are placing on yourself by going home and working as a Negro composer; you can never be able to get the hearing for your work which it might deserve. I doubt that even a white musician of recognized ability could succeed there by working on the theory that American music should be based on Negro themes. Music is a universal art; anybody's music belongs to everybody; you can't limit it to race or country. Now, if you want to become a composer, why not stay right here in Europe? I will put you under the best teachers on the Continent. Then if you want to write music on Negro themes, why, go ahead and do it."

We talked for some time on music and the race question. On the latter subject I had never before heard him express any opinion. Between him and me no suggestion of racial differences had ever come up. I found that he was a man entirely free from prejudice, but he recognized that prejudice was a big stubborn entity which had to be taken into account. He went on to say: "This idea you have of making a Negro out of yourself is nothing more than a sentiment; and you do not realize the fearful import of what you intend to do. What kind of a Negro would you make now, especially in the South? If you had remained there, or perhaps even in your club in New York, you might have succeeded very well; but now you would be miserable. I can imagine no more dissatisfied human being than an educated, cultured, and refined coloured man in the United States. I have given more study to the race question in the United States than you may suppose, and I sympathize with the Negroes there; but what's the use? I can't right their wrongs, and neither can you; they must do that themselves. They are unfortunate in having wrongs to right, and you would be foolish to take their wrongs unnecessarily on your shoulders. Perhaps some day, through study and observation, you will come to see that evil is a force, and, like the physical and chemical forces, we cannot annihilate it; we may only change its form. We light upon one evil and hit it with all the might of our civilization, but only succeed in scattering it into a dozen other forms. We hit slavery through a great civil war. Did we destroy it? No, we only changed it into hatred between sections of the country: in the South, into political corruption and chicanery, the degradation of the blacks through peonage, unjust laws, unfair and cruel treatment; and the degradation of the whites by their resorting to these practices, the paralysation of the public conscience, and the ever overhanging dread of what the future may bring. Modern civilization hit ignorance of the masses through the means of popular education. What has it done but turn ignorance into anarchy, socialism, strikes, hatred between poor and rich, and universal discontent? In like manner, modern philanthropy hit at suffering and disease through asylums and hospitals; it prolongs the sufferers' lives, it is true, but is, at the same time, sending down strains of insanity and weakness into future generations. My philosophy of life is this: make yourself as happy as possible, and try to make those happy whose lives come in touch with yours; but to attempt to right the wrongs and ease the sufferings of the world in general is a waste of effort. You had just as well try to bale the Atlantic by pouring the water into the Pacific."

This tremendous flow of serious talk from a man I was accustomed to see either gay or taciturn so surprised and overwhelmed me that I could not frame a reply. He left me thinking over what he had said. Whatever was the soundness of his logic or the moral tone of his philosophy, his argument greatly impressed me. I could see, in spite of the absolute selfishness upon which it was based, that there was reason and common sense in it. I began to analyse my own motives, and found that they, too, were very largely mixed with selfishness. Was it more a desire to help those I considered my people, or more a desire to distinguish myself, which was leading me back to the United States? That is a question I have never definitely answered.

For several weeks longer I was in a troubled state of mind. Added to the fact that I was loath to leave my good friend was the weight of the question he had aroused in my mind, whether I was not making a fatal mistake. I suffered more than one sleepless night during that time. Finally, I settled the question on purely selfish grounds, in accordance with my millionaire's philosophy. I argued that music offered me a better future than anything else I had any knowledge of, and, in opposition to my friend's opinion, that I should have greater chances of attracting attention as a coloured composer than as a white one. But I must own that I also felt stirred by an unselfish desire to voice all the joys and sorrows, the hopes and ambitions, of the American Negro, in classic musical form.

When my mind was fully made up, I told my friend. He asked me when I intended to start. I replied that I would do so at once. He then asked me how much money I had. I told him that I had saved several hundred dollars out of sums he had given me. He gave me a cheque for five hundred dollars, told me to write to him in care of his Paris bankers if I ever needed his help, wished me good luck, and bade me good-bye. All this he did almost coldly; and I often wondered whether he was in a hurry to get rid of what he considered a fool, or whether he was striving to hide deeper feelings.

And so I separated from the man who was, all in all, the best friend I ever had, except my mother, the man who exerted the greatest influence ever brought into my life, except that exerted by my mother. My affection for him was so strong, my recollections of him are so distinct, he was such a peculiar and striking character, that I could easily fill several chapters with reminiscences of him; but for fear of tiring the reader I shall go on with my narration.

I decided to go to Liverpool and take ship for Boston. I still had an uneasy feeling about returning to New York; and in a few days I found myself aboard ship headed for home.

CHAPTER X

Among the first of my fellow-passengers of whom I took any particular notice was a tall, broad-shouldered, almost gigantic, coloured man. His dark-brown face was clean-shaven; he was well-dressed and bore a decidedly distinguished air. In fact, if he was not handsome, he at least compelled admiration for his fine physical proportions. He attracted general attention as he strode the deck in a sort of majestic loneliness. I became curious to know who he was and determined to strike up an acquaintance with him at the first opportune moment. The chance came a day or two later. He was sitting in the smoking-room, with a cigar, which had gone out, in his mouth, reading a novel. I sat down beside him and, offering him a fresh cigar, said: "You don't mind my telling you something unpleasant, do you?" He looked at me with a smile, accepted the proffered cigar, and replied in a voice which comported perfectly with his size and appearance: "I think my curiosity overcomes any objections I might have." "Well," I said, "have you noticed that the man who sat at your right in the saloon during the first meal has not sat there since?" He frowned slightly without answering my question. "Well," I continued, "he asked the steward to remove him; and not only that, he attempted to persuade a number of the passengers to protest against your presence in the dining-saloon." The big man at my side took a long draw from his cigar, threw his head back, and slowly blew a great cloud of smoke toward the ceiling. Then turning to me he said: "Do you know, I don't object to anyone's having prejudices so long as those prejudices don't interfere with my personal liberty. Now, the man you are speaking of had a perfect right to change his seat if I in any way interfered with his appetite or his digestion. I should have no reason to complain if he removed to the farthest corner of the saloon, or even if he got off the ship; but when his prejudice attempts to move *me* one foot, one inch, out of the place where I am comfortably located, then I object." On the word "object" he brought his great fist down on the table in front of us with such a crash that everyone in the room turned to look. We both covered up the slight embarrassment with a laugh and strolled out on the deck.

We walked the deck for an hour or more, discussing different phases of the Negro question. In referring to the race I used the personal pronoun "we"; my companion made no comment about it, nor evinced any surprise, except to raise his eyebrows slightly the first time he caught the significance of the word. He was the broadest-minded coloured man I have ever talked with on the Negro question. He even went so far as to sympathize with and offer excuses for some white Southern points of view. I asked him what were his main reasons for being so hopeful. He replied: "In spite of all that is written, said, and done, this great, big, incontrovertible fact stands out—the Negro is progressing, and that disproves all the arguments in the world that he is incapable of progress. I was born in slavery, and at emancipation was set adrift a ragged, penniless bit of humanity. I have seen the Negro in every grade, and I know what I am talking about. Our detractors point to the increase of crime as evidence against us; certainly we have progressed in crime as in other things; what less could be expected? And yet, in this respect, we are far from the point which has been reached by the more highly civilized white race. As we continue to progress, crime among us will gradually lose much of its brutal, vulgar, I might say healthy, aspect, and become more delicate, refined, and subtile.

Then it will be less shocking and noticeable, although more dangerous to society." Then dropping his tone of irony, he continued with some show of eloquence: "But, above all, when I am discouraged and disheartened, I have this to fall back on: if there is a principle of right in the world, which finally prevails, and I believe that there is; if there is a merciful but justice-loving God in heaven, and I believe that there is, we shall win; for we have right on our side, while those who oppose us can defend themselves by nothing in the moral law, nor even by anything in the enlightened thought of the present age."

For several days, together with other topics, we discussed the race problem, not only of the United States, but as it affected native Africans and Jews. Finally, before we reached Boston, our conversation had grown familiar and personal. I had told him something of my past and much about my intentions for the future. I learned that he was a physician, a graduate of Howard University, Washington, and had done post-graduate work in Philadelphia; and this was his second trip abroad to attend professional courses. He had practised for some years in the city of Washington, and though he did not say so, I gathered that his practice was a lucrative one. Before we left the ship, he had made me promise that I would stop two or three days in Washington before going on south.

We put up at a hotel in Boston for a couple of days and visited several of my new friend's acquaintances; they were all people of education and culture and, apparently, of means. I could not help being struck by the great difference between them and the same class of coloured people in the South. In speech and thought they were genuine Yankees. The difference was especially noticeable in their speech. There was none of that heavy-tongued enunciation which characterizes even the best-educated coloured people of the South. It is remarkable, after all, what an adaptable creature the Negro is. I have seen the black West Indian gentleman in London, and he is in speech and manners a perfect Englishman. I have seen natives of Haiti and Martinique in Paris, and they are more Frenchy than a Frenchman. I have no doubt that the Negro would make a good Chinaman, with exception of the pigtail.

My stay in Washington, instead of being two or three days, was two or three weeks. This was my first visit to the national capital, and I was, of course, interested in seeing the public buildings and something of the working of the government; but most of my time I spent with the doctor among his friends and acquaintances. The social phase of life among coloured people is more developed in Washington than in any other city in the country. This is on account of the large number of individuals earning good salaries and having a reasonable amount of leisure time to draw from. There are dozens of physicians and lawyers, scores of school-teachers, and hundreds of clerks in the departments. As to the coloured department clerks, I think it fair to say that in educational equipment they average above the white clerks of the same grade; for, whereas a coloured college-graduate will seek such a job, the white university-man goes into one of the many higher vocations which are open to him.

In a previous chapter I spoke of social life among coloured people; so there is no need to take it up again here. But there is one thing I did not mention: among Negroes themselves there is the peculiar inconsistency of a colour question. Its existence is rarely admitted and hardly ever mentioned; it may not be too strong a statement to say that the greater portion of the race is unconscious of its influence; yet this influence, though silent, is constant. It is evidenced most plainly in marriage selection; thus the black men generally marry women fairer than themselves; while, on the other hand, the dark women of stronger mental endowment are very often married to light-complexioned men; the effect is a tendency toward lighter complexions, especially among the more active elements in the race. Some might claim that this is a tacit admission of coloured people among themselves of their own inferiority judged by the colour line. I do not think so. What I have termed an inconsistency is, after all, most natural; it is, in fact, a tendency in accordance with what might be called an economic necessity. So far as racial differences go, the United States puts a greater premium on colour, or, better, lack of colour, than upon anything else in the world. To paraphrase, "Have a white skin, and all things else may be added unto you." I have seen advertisements in newspapers for waiters, bell-boys, or elevator men, which read: "Light coloured man wanted." It is this tremendous pressure which the sentiment of the country exerts that is operating on the race. There is involved not only the question of higher opportunity, but often the question of earning a livelihood; and so I say it is not strange, but a natural tendency. Nor is it any more a sacrifice of self-respect that a black man should give to his children every advantage he can which complexion of the skin carries than that the new or vulgar rich should purchase for their children the advantages which ancestry, aristocracy, and social position carry. I once heard a coloured man sum it up in these words: "It's no disgrace to be black, but it's often very inconvenient."

Washington shows the Negro not only at his best, but also at his worst. As I drove round with the doctor, he commented rather harshly on those of the latter class which we saw. He remarked: "You see those lazy, loafing, good-for-nothing darkies; they're not worth digging graves for; yet they are the ones who create impressions of the race for the casual observer. It's because they are always in evidence on the street corners, while the rest of us are hard at work, and you know a dozen loafing darkies make a bigger crowd and a worse impression in this country than fifty white men of the same class. But they ought not to represent the race. We are the race, and the race ought to be judged by us, not by them. Every race and every nation should be judged by the best it has been able to produce, not by the worst."

The recollection of my stay in Washington is a pleasure to me now. In company with the doctor I visited Howard University, the public schools, the excellent coloured hospital, with which he was in some way connected, if I remember correctly, and many comfortable and even elegant homes. It was with some reluctance that I continued my journey south. The doctor was very kind in giving me letters to people in Richmond and Nashville when I told him that I intended to stop in both of these cities. In Richmond a man who was then editing a very creditable coloured newspaper gave me a great deal of his time and made my stay there of three or four days very pleasant. In Nashville I spent a whole day at Fisk University, the home of the "Jubilee Singers," and was more than repaid for my time. Among my letters of introduction was one to a very prosperous physician. He drove me about the city and introduced me to a number of people. From Nashville I went to Atlanta, where I stayed long enough to gratify an old desire to see Atlanta University again. I then continued my journey to Macon.

In thus travelling about through the country I was sometimes amused on arriving at some little railroad-station town to be taken for and treated as a white man, and six hours later, when it was learned that I was stopping at the house of the coloured preacher or school-teacher, to note the attitude of the whole town change. At times this led even to embarrassment. Yet it cannot be so embarrassing for a coloured man to be taken for white as for a white man to be taken for coloured; and I have heard of several cases of the latter kind.

All this while I was gathering material for work, jotting down in my note-book themes and melodies, and trying to catch the spirit of the Negro in his relatively primitive state. I began to feel the necessity of hurrying so that I might get back to some city like Nashville to begin my compositions and at the same time earn at least a living by teaching and performing before my funds gave out. At the last settlement in which I stopped I found a mine of material. This was due to the fact that "big meeting" was in progress. "Big meeting" is an institution something like camp-meeting, the difference being that it is held in a permanent church, and not in a temporary structure. All the churches of some one denomination—of course, either Methodist or Baptist—in a county, or, perhaps, in several adjoining counties, are closed, and the congregations unite at some centrally located church for a series of meetings lasting a week. It is really a social as well as a religious function. The people come in great numbers, making the trip, according to their financial status, in buggies drawn by sleek, fleet-footed mules, in ox-carts, or on foot. It was amusing to see some of the latter class trudging down the hot and dusty road, with their shoes, which were brand-new, strung across their shoulders. When they got near the church, they sat on the side of the road and, with many grimaces, tenderly packed their feet into those instruments of torture. This furnished, indeed, a trying test of their religion. The famous preachers come from near and far and take turns in warning sinners of the day of wrath. Food, in the form of those two Southern luxuries, fried chicken and roast pork, is plentiful, and no one need go hungry. On the opening Sunday the women are immaculate in starched stiff white dresses adorned with ribbons, either red or blue. Even a great many of the men wear streamers of vari-coloured ribbons in the buttonholes of their coats. A few of them carefully cultivate a forelock of hair by wrapping it in twine, and on such festive occasions decorate it with a narrow ribbon streamer. Big meetings afford a fine opportunity to the younger people to meet each other dressed in their Sunday clothes, and much rustic courting, which is as enjoyable as any other kind, is indulged in.

This big meeting which I was lucky enough to catch was particularly well attended; the extra large attendance was due principally to two attractions, a man by the name of John Brown, who was renowed as the most powerful preacher for miles around; and a wonderful leader of singing, who was known as "Singing Johnson." These two men were a study and revelation to me. They caused me to reflect upon how great an influence their types have been in the development of the Negro in America. Both these types are now looked upon generally with condescension or contempt by the progressive element among the coloured people; but it should never be forgotten that it was they who led the race from paganism and kept it steadfast to Christianity through all the long, dark years of slavery.

John Brown was a jet-black man of medium size, with a strikingly intelligent head and face, and a voice like an organ peal. He preached each night after several lesser lights had successively held the pulpit during an hour or so. As far as subject-matter is concerned, all of the sermons were alike: each began with the fall of man, ran through various trials and tribulations of the Hebrew children, on to the redemption by Christ, and ended with a fervid picture of the judgment-day and the fate of the damned. But John Brown possessed magnetism and an imagination so free and daring that he was able to carry through what the other preachers would not attempt. He knew all the arts and tricks of oratory, the modulation of the voice to almost a whisper, the pause for effect, the rise through light, rapid-fire sentences to the terrific, thundering outburst of an electrifying climax. In addition, he had the intuition of a born theatrical manager. Night after night this man held me fascinated. He convinced me that, after all, eloquence consists more in the manner of saying than in what is said. It is largely a matter of tone pictures.

The most striking example of John Brown's magnetism and imagination was his "heavenly march"; I shall never forget how it impressed me when I heard it. He opened his sermon in the usual way; then, proclaiming to his listeners that he was going to take them on the heavenly march, he seized the Bible under his arm and began to pace up and down the pulpit platform. The congregation immediately began with their feet a tramp, tramp, tramp, in time with the preacher's march in the pulpit, all the while singing in an undertone a hymn about marching to Zion. Suddenly he cried: "Halt!" Every foot stopped with the precision of a company of well-drilled soldiers, and the singing ceased. The morning star had been reached. Here the preacher described the beauties of that celestial body. Then the march, the tramp, tramp, tramp, and the singing were again taken up. Another "Halt!" They had reached the evening star. And so on, past the sun and moon—the intensity of religious emotion all the time increasing—along the milky way, on up to the gates of heaven. Here the halt was longer, and the preacher described at length the gates and walls of the New Jerusalem. Then he took his hearers through the pearly gates, along the golden streets, pointing out the glories of the city, pausing occasionally to greet some patriarchal members of the church, well-known to most of his listeners in life, who had had "the tears wiped from their eyes, were clad in robes of spotless white, with crowns of gold upon their heads and harps within their hands," and ended his march before the great white throne. To the reader this may sound ridiculous, but listened to under the circumstances, it was highly and effectively dramatic. I was a more or less sophisticated and non-religious man of the world, but the torrent of the preacher's words, moving with the rhythm and glowing with the eloquence of primitive poetry, swept me along, and I, too, felt like joining in the shouts of "Amen! Hallelujah!"

John Brown's powers in describing the delights of heaven were no greater than those in depicting the horrors of hell. I saw great, strapping fellows trembling and weeping like children at the "mourners' bench." His warnings to sinners were truly terrible. I shall never forget one expression that he used, which for originality and aptness could not be excelled. In my opinion, it is more graphic and, for us, far more expressive than St. Paul's "It is hard to kick against the pricks." He struck the attitude of a pugilist and thundered out: "Young man, your arm's too short to box with God!"

Interesting as was John Brown to me, the other man, "Singing Johnson," was more so. He was a small, dark-brown, one-eyed man, with a clear, strong, high-pitched voice, a leader of singing, a maker of songs, a man who could improvise at the moment lines to fit the occasion. Not so striking a figure as John Brown, but, at "big meetings," equally important. It is indispensable to the success of the singing, when the congregation is a large one made up of people from different communities, to have someone with a strong voice who knows just what hymn to sing and when to sing it, who can pitch it in the right key, and who has all the leading lines committed to memory. Sometimes it devolves upon the leader to "sing down" a long-winded or uninteresting speaker. Committing to memory the leading lines of all the Negro spiritual songs is no easy task, for they run up into the hundreds. But the accomplished leader must know them all, because the congregation sings only the refrains and repeats; every ear in the church is fixed upon him, and if he becomes mixed in his lines or forgets them, the responsibility falls directly on his shoulders.

For example, most of these hymns are constructed to be sung in the following manner:

> *Leader*. Swing low, sweet chariot.
> *Congregation*. Coming for to carry me home.
> *Leader*. Swing low, sweet chariot.
> *Congregation*. Coming for to carry me home.
> *Leader*. I look over yonder, what do I see?
> *Congregation*. Coming for to carry me home.
> *Leader*. Two little angels coming after me.
> *Congregation*. Coming for to carry me home. . . .

The solitary and plaintive voice of the leader is answered by a sound like the roll of the sea, producing a most curious effect.

In only a few of these songs do the leader and the congregation start off together. Such a song is the well-known "Steal away to Jesus."

The leader and the congregation begin with part-singing:

> Steal away, steal away,
> Steal away to Jesus;
> Steal away, steal away home,
> I ain't got long to stay here.

Then the leader alone or the congregation in unison:

> My Lord he calls me,
> He calls me by the thunder,
> The trumpet sounds within-a my soul.

Then all together:

> I ain't got long to stay here.

The leader and the congregation again take up the opening refrain; then the leader sings three more leading lines alone, and so on almost *ad infinitum*. It will be seen that even here most of the work falls upon the leader, for the congregation sings the same lines over and over, while his memory and ingenuity are taxed to keep the songs going.

Generally the parts taken up by the congregation are sung in a three-part harmony, the women singing the soprano and a transposed tenor, the men with high voices singing the melody, and those with low voices a thundering bass. In a few of these songs, however, the leading part is sung in unison by the whole congregation, down to the last line, which is harmonized. The effect of this is intensely thrilling. Such a hymn is "Go down, Moses." It stirs the heart like a trumpet-call.

"Singing Johnson" was an ideal leader, and his services were in great demand. He spent his time going about the country from one church to another. He received his support in much the same way as the preachers—part of a collection, food and lodging. All of his leisure time he devoted to originating new words and melodies and new lines for old songs. He always sang with his eyes—or, to be more exact, his eye—closed, indicating the *tempo* by swinging his head to and fro. He was a great judge of the proper hymn to sing at a particular moment; and I noticed several times, when the preacher reached a certain climax, or expressed a certain sentiment, that Johnson broke in with a line or two of some appropriate hymn. The speaker understood and would pause until the singing ceased.

As I listened to the singing of these songs, the wonder of their production grew upon me more and more. How did the men who originated them manage to do it? The sentiments are easily accounted for; they are mostly taken from the Bible; but the melodies, where did they come from? Some of them so weirdly sweet, and others so wonderfully strong. Take, for instance, "Go down, Moses." I doubt that there is a stronger theme in the whole musical literature of the world. And so many of these songs contain more than mere melody; there is sounded in them that elusive undertone, the note in music which is not heard with the ears. I sat often with the tears rolling down my cheeks and my heart melted within me. Any musical person who has never heard a Negro congregation under the spell of religious fervour sing these old songs has missed one of the most thrilling emotions which the human heart may experience. Anyone who without shedding tears can listen to Negroes sing "Nobody knows de trouble I see, Nobody knows but Jesus" must indeed have a heart of stone.

As yet, the Negroes themselves do not fully appreciate these old slave songs. The educated classes are rather ashamed of them and prefer to sing hymns from books. This feeling is natural; they are still too close to the conditions under which the songs were produced; but the day will come when this slave music will be the most treasured heritage of the American Negro.

At the close of the "big meeting" I left the settlement where it was being held, full of enthusiasm. I was in that frame of mind which, in the artistic temperament, amounts to inspiration. I was now ready and anxious to get to some place where I might settle down to work, and give expression to the ideas which were teeming in my head; but I strayed into another deviation from my path of life as I had it marked out, which led me upon an entirely different road. Instead of going to the nearest and most convenient railroad station, I accepted the invitation of a young man who had been present the closing Sunday at the meeting to drive with him some miles farther to the town in which he taught school, and there take the train. My conversation with this young man as we drove along through the country was extremely interesting. He had been a student in one of the Negro colleges—strange coincidence, in the very college, as I learned through him, in which "Shiny" was now a professor. I was, of course, curious to hear about my boyhood friend; and had it not been vacation time, and that I was not sure that I should find him, I should have gone out of my way to pay him a visit; but I determined to write to him as soon as the school opened. My companion talked to me about his work among the people, of his hopes and his discouragements. He was tremendously in earnest; I might say, too much so. In fact, it may be said that the majority of intelligent coloured people are, in some degree, too much in earnest over the race question. They assume and carry so much that their progress is at times impeded and they are unable to see things in their proper proportions. In many instances a slight exercise of the sense of humour would save much anxiety of soul. Anyone who marks the general tone of editorials in coloured newspapers is apt to be impressed with this idea. If the mass of Negroes took their present and future as seriously as do the most of their leaders, the race would be in no mental condition to sustain the terrible pressure which it undergoes; it would sink of its own weight. Yet it must be acknowledged that in the making of a race over-seriousness is a far lesser failing than its reverse, and even the faults resulting from it lean toward the right.

We drove into the town just before dark. As we passed a large, unpainted church, my companion pointed it out as the place where he held his school. I promised that I would go there with him the next morning and visit awhile. The town was of that kind which hardly requires or deserves description; a straggling line of brick and wooden stores on one side of the railroad track and some cottages of various sizes on the other side constituted about the whole of it. The young school-teacher boarded at the best house in the place owned by a coloured man. It was painted, had glass windows, contained "store bought" furniture, an organ, and lamps with chimneys. The owner held a job of some kind on the railroad. After supper it was not long before everybody was sleepy. I occupied the room with the school-teacher. In a few minutes after we got into the room he was in bed and asleep; but I took advantage of the unusual luxury of a lamp which gave light, and sat looking over my notes and jotting down some ideas which were still fresh in my mind. Suddenly I became conscious of that sense of alarm which is always aroused by the sound of hurrying footsteps on the silence of the night. I stopped work and looked at my watch. It was after eleven. I listened, straining every nerve to hear above the tumult of my quickening pulse. I caught the murmur of voices, then the gallop of a horse, then of another and another. Now thoroughly alarmed, I woke my companion, and together we both listened. After a moment he put out the light and softly opened the window-blind, and we cautiously peeped out. We saw men moving in one direction, and from the mutterings we vaguely caught the rumour that some terrible crime had been committed. I put on my coat and hat. My friend did all in his power to dissuade me from venturing out, but it was impossible for me to remain in the house under such tense excitement. My nerves would not have stood it. Perhaps what bravery I exercised in going out was due to the fact that I felt sure my identity as a coloured man had not yet become known in the town.

I went out and, following the drift, reached the railroad station. There was gathered there a crowd of men, all white, and others were steadily arriving, seemingly from all the surrounding country. How did the news spread so quickly? I watched these men moving under the yellow glare of the kerosene lamps about the station, stern, comparatively silent, all of them armed, some of them in boots and spurs; fierce, determined men. I had come to know the type well, blond, tall, and lean, with ragged moustache and beard, and glittering grey eyes. At the first suggestion of daylight they began to disperse in groups, going in several directions. There was no extra noise or excitement, no loud talking, only swift, sharp words of command given by those who seemed to be accepted as leaders by mutual understanding. In fact, the impression made upon me was that everything was being done in quite an orderly manner. In spite of so many leaving, the crowd around the station continued to grow; at sunrise there were a great many women and children. By this time I also noticed some coloured people; a few seemed to be going about customary tasks; several were standing on the outskirts of the crowd; but the gathering of Negroes usually seen in such towns was missing.

Before noon they brought him in. Two horsemen rode abreast; between them, half dragged, the poor wretch made his way through the dust. His hands were tied behind him, and ropes round his body were fastened to the saddle horns of his double guard. The men who at midnight had been stern and silent were now emitting that terror-instilling sound known as the "rebel yell." A space was quickly cleared in the crowd, and a rope placed about his neck, when from somewhere came the suggestion, "Burn him!" It ran like an electric current. Have you ever witnessed the transformation of human beings into savage beasts? Nothing can be more terrible. A railroad tie was sunk into the ground, the rope was removed, and a chain brought and securely coiled round the victim and the stake. There he stood, a man only in form and stature, every sign of degeneracy stamped upon his countenance. His eyes were dull and vacant, indicating not a single ray of thought. Evidently the realization of his fearful fate had robbed him of whatever reasoning power he had ever possessed. He was too stunned and stupefied even to tremble. Fuel was brought from everywhere, oil, the torch; the flames crouched for an instant as though to gather strength, then leaped up as high as their victim's head. He squirmed, he writhed, strained at his chains, then gave out cries and groans that I shall always hear. The cries and groans were choked off by the fire and smoke; but his eyes, bulging from their sockets, rolled from side to side, appealing in vain for help. Some of the crowd yelled and cheered, others seemed appalled at what they had done, and there were those who turned away sickened at the sight. I was fixed to the spot where I stood, powerless to take my eyes from what I did not want to see.

It was over before I realized that time had elapsed. Before I could make myself believe that what I saw was really happening, I was looking at a scorched post, a smouldering fire, blackened bones, charred fragments sifting down through coils of chain; and the smell of burnt flesh—human flesh—was in my nostrils.

I walked a short distance away and sat down in order to clear my dazed mind. A great wave of humiliation and shame swept over me. Shame that I belonged to a race that could be so dealt with; and shame for my country, that it, the great example of democracy to the world, should be the only civilized, if not the only state on earth, where a human being would be burned alive. My heart turned bitter within me. I could understand why Negroes are led to sympathize with even their worst criminals and to protect them when possible. By all the impulses of normal human nature they can and should do nothing less.

Whenever I hear protests from the South that it should be left alone to deal with the Negro question my thoughts go back to that scene of brutality and savagery. I do not see how a people that can find in its conscience any excuse whatever for slowly burning to death a human being, or for tolerating such an act, can be entrusted with the salvation of a race. Of course, there are in the South men of liberal thought who do not approve lynching, but I wonder how long they will endure the limits which are placed upon free speech. They still cower and tremble before "Southern opinion." Even so late as the recent Atlanta riot those men who were brave enough to speak a word in behalf of justice and humanity felt called upon, by way of apology, to preface what they said with a glowing rhetorical tribute to the Anglo-Saxon's superiority and to refer to the "great and impassable gulf" between the races "fixed by the Creator at the foundation of the world." The question of the relative qualities of the two races is still an open one. The reference to the "great gulf" loses force in face of the fact that there are in this country perhaps three or four million people with the blood of both races in their veins; but I fail to see the pertinency of either statement subsequent to the beating and murdering of scores of innocent people in the streets of a civilized and Christian city.

The Southern whites are in many respects a great people. Looked at from a certain point of view, they are picturesque. If one will put oneself in a romantic frame of mind, one can admire their notions of chivalry and bravery and justice. In this same frame of mind an intelligent man can go to the theatre and applaud the impossible hero, who with his single sword slays everybody in the play except the equally impossible heroine. So can an ordinary peace-loving citizen sit by a comfortable fire and read with enjoyment of the bloody deeds of pirates and the fierce brutality of vikings. This is the way in which we gratify the old, underlying animal instincts and passions; but we should shudder with horror at the mere idea of such practices being realities in this day of enlightened and humanitarianized thought. The Southern whites are not yet living quite in the present age; many of their general ideas hark back to a former century, some of them to the Dark Ages. In the light of other days they are sometimes magnificent. Today they are often cruel and ludicrous.

How long I sat with bitter thoughts running through my mind I do not know; perhaps an hour or more. When I decided to get up and go back to the house, I found that I could hardly stand on my feet. I was as weak as a man who had lost blood. However, I dragged myself along, with the central idea of a general plan well fixed in my mind. I did not find my school-teacher friend at home, so I did not see him again. I swallowed a few mouthfuls of food, packed my bag, and caught the afternoon train.

When I reached Macon, I stopped only long enough to get the main part of my luggage and to buy a ticket for New York. All along the journey I was occupied in debating with myself the step which I had decided to take. I argued that to forsake one's race to better one's condition was no less worthy an action than to forsake one's country for the same purpose. I finally made up my mind that I would neither disclaim the black race nor claim the white race; but that I would change my name, raise a moustache, and let the world take me for what it would, that it was not necessary for me to go about with a label of inferiority pasted across my forehead. All the while I understood that it was not discouragement or fear or search for a larger field of action and opportunity that was driving me out of the Negro race. I knew that it was shame, unbearable shame. Shame at being identified with a people that could with impunity be treated worse than animals. For certainly the law would restrain and punish the malicious burning alive of animals.

So once again I found myself gazing at the towers of New York and wondering what future that city held in store for me.

CHAPTER XI

I have now reached that part of my narrative where I must be brief and touch only on important facts; therefore the reader must make up his mind to pardon skips and jumps and meagre details.

When I reached New York, I was completely lost. I could not have felt more a stranger had I been suddenly dropped into Constantinople. I knew not where to turn or how to strike out. I was so oppressed by a feeling of loneliness that the temptation to visit my old home in Connecticut was well-nigh irresistible. I reasoned, however, that unless I found my old music teacher, I should be, after so many years of absence, as much of a stranger there as in New York; and, furthermore, that in view of the step which I had decided to take, such a visit would be injudicious. I remembered, too, that I had some property there in the shape of a piano and a few books, but decided that it would not be worth what it might cost me to take possession.

By reason of the fact that my living-expenses in the South had been very small, I still had nearly four hundred dollars of my capital left. In contemplation of this, my natural and acquired Bohemian tastes asserted themselves, and I decided to have a couple of weeks' good time before worrying seriously about the future. I went to Coney Island and the other resorts, took in the pre-season shows along Broadway, and ate at first-class restaurants; but I shunned the old Sixth Avenue district as though it were pest-infected. My few days of pleasure made appalling inroads upon what cash I had, and caused me to see that it required a good deal of money to live in New York as I wished to live and that I should have to find, very soon, some more or less profitable employment. I was sure that unknown, without friends or prestige, it would be useless to try to establish myself as a teacher of music; so I gave that means of earning a livelihood scarcely any consideration. And even had I considered it possible to secure pupils, as I then felt, I should have hesitated about taking up a work in which the chances for any considerable financial success are necessarily so small. I had made up my mind that since I was not going to be a Negro, I would avail myself of every possible opportunity to make a white man's success; and that, if it can be summed up in any one word, means "money."

I watched the "want" columns in the newspapers and answered a number of advertisements, but in each case found the positions were such as I could not fill or did not want. I also spent several dollars for "ads" which brought me no replies. In this way I came to know the hopes and disappointments of a large and pitiable class of humanity in this great city, the people who look for work through the newspapers. After some days of this sort of experience I concluded that the main difficulty with me was that I was not prepared for what I wanted to do. I then decided upon a course which, for an artist, showed an uncommon amount of practical sense and judgment. I made up my mind to enter a business college. I took a small room, ate at lunch counters, in order to economize, and pursued my studies with the zeal that I have always been able to put into any work upon which I set my heart. Yet, in spite of all my economy, when I had been at the school for several months, my funds gave out completely. I reached the point where I could not afford sufficient food for each day. In this plight I was glad to get, through one of the teachers, a job as an ordinary clerk in a downtown wholesale house. I did my work faithfully, and received a raise of salary before I expected it. I even managed to save a little money out of my modest earnings. In fact, I began then to contract the money fever, which later took strong possession of me. I kept my eyes open, watching for a chance to better my condition. It finally came in the form of a position with a house which was at the time establishing a South American department. My knowledge of Spanish was, of course, the principal cause of my good luck; and it did more for me: it placed me where the other clerks were practically put out of competition with me. I was not slow in taking advantage of the opportunity to make myself indispensable to the firm.

What an interesting and absorbing game is money-making! After each deposit at my savings-bank I used to sit and figure out, all over again, my principal and interest, and make calculations on what the increase would be in such and such time. Out of this I derived a great deal of pleasure. I denied myself as much as possible in order to swell my savings. As much as I enjoyed smoking, I limited myself to an occasional cigar, and that was generally of a variety which in my old days at the "Club" was known as a "Henry Mud." Drinking I cut out altogether, but that was no great sacrifice.

The day on which I was able to figure up a thousand dollars marked an epoch in my life. And this was not because I had never before had money. In my gambling days and while I was with my millionaire I handled sums running high up into the hundreds; but they had come to me like fairy godmother's gifts, and at a time when my conception of money was that it was made only to spend. Here, on the other hand, was a thousand dollars which I had earned by days of honest and patient work, a thousand dollars which I had carefully watched grow from the first dollar; and I experienced, in owning them, a pride and satisfaction which to me was an entirely new sensation. As my capital went over the thousand-dollar mark, I was puzzled to know what to do with it, how to put it to the most advantageous use. I turned down first one scheme and then another, as though they had been devised for the sole purpose of gobbling up my money. I finally listened to a friend who advised me to put all I had in New York real estate; and under his guidance I took equity in a piece of property on which stood a rickety old tenement-house. I did not regret following this friend's advice, for in something like six months I disposed of my equity for more than double my investment. From that time on I devoted myself to the study of New York real estate and watched for opportunities to make similar investments. In spite of two or three speculations which did not turn out well, I have been remarkably successful. Today I am the owner and part-owner of several flat-houses. I have changed my place of employment four times since returning to New York, and each change has been a decided advancement. Concerning the position which I now hold I shall say nothing except that it pays extremely well.

As my outlook on the world grew brighter, I began to mingle in the social circles of the men with whom I came in contact; and gradually, by a process of elimination, I reached a grade of society of no small degree of culture. My appearance was always good and my ability to play on the piano, especially rag-time, which was then at the height of its vogue, made me a welcome guest. The anomaly of my social position often appealed strongly to my sense of humour. I frequently smiled inwardly at some remark not altogether complimentary to people of colour; and more than once I felt like declaiming: "I am a coloured man. Do I not disprove the theory that one drop of Negro blood renders a man unfit?" Many a night when I returned to my room after an enjoyable evening, I laughed heartily over what struck me as the capital joke I was playing.

Then I met her, and what I had regarded as a joke was gradually changed into the most serious question of my life. I first saw her at a musical which was given one evening at a house to which I was frequently invited. I did not notice her among the other guests before she came forward and sang two sad little songs. When she began, I was out in the hallway, where many of the men were gathered; but with the first few notes I crowded with others into the doorway to see who the singer was. When I saw the girl, the surprise which I had felt at the first sound of her voice was heightened; she was almost tall and quite slender, with lustrous yellow hair and eyes so blue as to appear almost black. She was as white as a lily, and she was dressed in white. Indeed, she seemed to me the most dazzingly white thing I had ever seen. But it was not her delicate beauty which attracted me most; it was her voice, a voice which made one wonder how tones of such passionate colour could come from so fragile a body.

I determined that when the program was over, I would seek an introduction to her; but at the moment, instead of being the easy man of the world, I became again the bashful boy of fourteen, and my courage failed me. I contented myself with hovering as near her as politeness would permit; near enough to hear her voice, which in conversation was low, yet thrilling, like the deeper middle tones of a flute. I watched the men gather round her talking and laughing in an easy manner, and wondered how it was possible for them to do it. But destiny, my special destiny, was at work. I was standing near, talking with affected gaiety to several young ladies, who, however, must have remarked my preoccupation; for my second sense of hearing was alert to what was being said by the group of which the girl in white was the centre, when I heard her say: "I think his playing of Chopin is exquisite." And one of my friends in the group replied: "You haven't met him? Allow me——" Then turning to me, "Old man, when you have a moment I wish you to meet Miss——." I don't know what she said to me or what I said to her. I can remember that I tried to be clever, and experienced a growing conviction that I was making myself appear more and more idiotic. I am certain, too, that, in spite of my Italian-like complexion, I was as red as a beet.

Instead of taking the car, I walked home. I needed the air and exercise as a sort of sedative. I am not sure whether my troubled condition of mind was due to the fact that I had been struck by love or to the feeling that I had made a bad impression upon her.

As the weeks went by, and when I had met her several more times, I came to know that I was seriously in love; and then began for me days of worry, for I had more than the usual doubts and fears of a young man in love to contend with.

Up to this time I had assumed and played my role as a white man with a certain degree of nonchalance, a carelessness as to the outcome, which made the whole thing more amusing to me than serious; but now I ceased to regard "being a white man" as a sort of practical joke. My acting had called for mere external effects. Now I began to doubt my ability to play the part. I watched her to see if she was scrutinizing me, to see if she was looking for anything in me which made me differ from the other men she knew. In place of an old inward feeling of superiority over many of my friends I began to doubt myself. I began even to wonder if I really was like the men I associated with; if there was not, after all, an indefinable something which marked a difference.

But, in spite of my doubts and timidity, my affair progressed; and I finally felt sufficiently encouraged to decide to ask her to marry me. Then began the hardest struggle of my life, whether to ask her to marry me under false colours or to tell her the whole truth. My sense of what was exigent made me feel there was no necessity of saying anything; but my inborn sense of honour rebelled at even indirect deception in this case. But however much I moralized on the question, I found it more and more difficult to reach the point of confession. The dread that I might lose her took possession of me each time I sought to speak, and rendered it impossible for me to do so. That moral courage requires more than physical courage is no mere poetic fancy. I am sure I should have found it easier to take the place of a gladiator, no matter how fierce the Numidian lion, than to tell that slender girl that I had Negro blood in my veins. The fact which I had at times wished to cry out, I now wished to hide for ever.

During this time we were drawn together a great deal by the mutual bond of music. She loved to hear me play Chopin and was herself far from being a poor performer of his compositions. I think I carried her every new song that was published which I thought suitable to her voice, and played the accompaniment for her. Over these songs we were like two innocent children with new toys. She had never been anything but innocent; but my innocence was a transformation wrought by my love for her, love which melted away my cynicism and whitened my sullied soul and gave me back the wholesome dreams of my boyhood.

My artistic temperament also underwent an awakening.

I spent many hours at my piano, playing over old and new composers. I also wrote several little pieces in a more or less Chopinesque style, which I dedicated to her. And so the weeks and months went by. Often words of love trembled on my lips, but I dared not utter them, because I knew they would have to be followed by other words which I had not the courage to frame. There might have been some other woman in my set whom I could have fallen in love with and asked to marry me without a word of explanation; but the more I knew this girl, the less could I find it in my heart to deceive her. And yet, in spite of this spectre that was constantly looming up before me, I could never have believed that life held such happiness as was contained in those dream days of love.

One Saturday afternoon, in early June, I was coming up Fifth Avenue, and at the corner of Twenty-third Street I met her. She had been shopping. We stopped to chat for a moment, and I suggested that we spend half an hour at the Eden Musée. We were standing leaning on the rail in front of a group of figures, more interested in what we had to say to each other than in the group, when my attention became fixed upon a man who stood at my side studying his catalogue. It took me only an instant to recognize in him my old friend "Shiny." My first impulse was to change my position at once. As quick as a flash I considered all the risks I might run in speaking to him, and most especially the delicate question of introducing him to her. I confess that in my embarrassment and confusion I felt small and mean. But before I could decide what to do, he looked round at me and, after an instant, quietly asked: "Pardon me; but isn't this——?" The nobler part in me responded to the sound of his voice and I took his hand in a hearty clasp. Whatever fears I had felt were quickly banished, for he seemed, at a glance, to divine my situation, and let drop no word that would have aroused suspicion as to the truth. With a slight misgiving I presented him to her and was again relieved of fear. She received the introduction in her usual gracious manner, and without the least hesitancy or embarrassment joined in the conversation. An amusing part about the introduction was that I was upon the point of introducing him as "Shiny," and stammered a second or two before I could recall his name. We chatted for some fifteen minutes. He was spending his vacation north, with the intention of doing four or six weeks' work in one of the summer schools; he was also going to take a bride back with him in the fall. He asked me about myself, but in so diplomatic a way that I found no difficulty in answering him. The polish of his language and the unpedantic manner in which he revealed his culture greatly impressed her; and after we had left the Musée she showed it by questioning me about him. I was surprised at the amount of interest a refined black man could arouse. Even after changes in the conversation she reverted several times to the subject of "Shiny." Whether it was more than mere curiosity I could not tell, but I was convinced that she herself knew very little about prejudice.

Just why it should have done so I do not know, but somchow the "Shiny" incident gave me encouragement and confidence to cast the die of my fate. I reasoned, however, that since I wanted to marry her only, and since it concerned her alone, I would divulge my secret to no one else, not even her parents.

One evening, a few days afterwards, at her home we were going over some new songs and compositions when she asked me, as she often did, to play the Thirteenth Nocturne. When I began, she drew a chair near to my right and sat leaning with her elbow on the end of the piano, her chin resting on her hand, and her eyes reflecting the emotions which the music awoke in her. An impulse which I could not control rushed over me, a wave of exultation, the music under my fingers sank almost to a whisper, and calling her for the first time by her Christian name, but without daring to look at her, I said: "I love you, I love you, I love you." My fingers were trembling so that I ceased playing. I felt her hand creep to mine, and when I looked at her, her eyes were glistening with tears. I understood, and could scarcely resist the longing to take her in my arms; but I remembered, remembered that which has been the sacrificial altar of so much happiness—Duty; and bending over her hand in mine, I said: "Yes, I love you; but there is something more, too, that I must tell you." Then I told her, in what words I do not know, the truth. I felt her hand grow cold, and when I looked up, she was gazing at me with a wild, fixed stare as though I was some object she had never seen. Under the strange light in her eyes I felt that I was growing black and thick featured and crimp haired. She appeared not to have comprehended what I had said. Her lips trembled and she attempted to say something to me, but the words stuck in her throat. Then, dropping her head on the piano, she began to weep with great sobs that shook her frail body. I tried to console her, and blurted out incoherent words of love, but this seemed only to increase her distress, and when I left her, she was still weeping.

When I got into the street, I felt very much as I did the night after meeting my father and sister at the opera in Paris, even a similar desperate inclination to get drunk; but my self-control was stronger. This was the only time in my life that I ever felt absolute regret at being coloured, that I cursed the drops of African blood in my veins and wished that I were really white. When I reached my rooms, I sat and smoked several cigars while I tried to think out the significance of what had occurred. I reviewed the whole history of our acquaintance, recalled each smile she had given me, each word she had said to me that nourished my hope. I went over the scene we had just gone through, trying to draw from it what was in my favour and what was against me. I was rewarded by feeling confident that she loved me, but I could not estimate what was the effect upon her of my confession. At last, nervous and unhappy, I wrote her a letter, which I dropped into the mail-box before going to bed, in which I said:

> I understand, understand even better than you, and so I suffer even more than you. But why should either of us suffer for what neither of us is to blame for? If there is any blame, it belongs to me and I can only make the old, yet strongest plea that can be offered, I love you; and I know that my love, my great love, infinitely overbalances that blame and blots it out. What is it that stands in the way of our happiness? It is not what you feel or what I feel; it is not what you are or what I am. It is what others feel and are. But, oh! is that a fair price? In all

the endeavours and struggles of life, in all our strivings and longings, there is only one thing worth seeking, only one thing worth winning, and that is love. It is not always found; but when it is, there is nothing in all the world for which it can be profitably exchanged.

The second morning after, I received a note from her which stated briefly that she was going up into New Hampshire to spend the summer with relatives there. She made no reference to what had passed between us; nor did she say exactly when she would leave the city. The note contained no single word that gave me any clue to her feelings. I could gather hope only from the fact that she had written at all. On the same evening, with a degree of trepidation which rendered me almost frightened, I went to her house.

I met her mother, who told me that she had left for the country that very afternoon. Her mother treated me in her usual pleasant manner, which fact greatly reassured me; and I left the house with a vague sense of hope stirring in my breast, which sprang from the conviction that she had not yet divulged my secret. But that hope did not remain with me long. I waited one, two, three weeks, nervously examining my mail every day, looking for some word from her. All of the letters received by me seemed so insignificant, so worthless, because there was none from her. The slight buoyancy of spirit which I had felt gradually dissolved into gloomy heart-sickness. I became preoccupied; I lost appetite, lost sleep, and lost ambition. Several of my friends intimated to me that perhaps I was working too hard.

She stayed away the whole summer. I did not go to the house, but saw her father at various times, and he was as friendly as ever. Even after I knew that she was back in town, I did not go to see her. I determined to wait for some word or sign. I had finally taken refuge and comfort in my pride, pride which, I suppose, I came by naturally enough.

The first time I saw her after her return was one night at the theatre. She and her mother sat in company with a young man whom I knew slightly, not many seats away from me. Never did she appear more beautiful; and yet, it may have been my fancy, she seemed a trifle paler, and there was a suggestion of haggardness in her countenance. But that only heightened her beauty; the very delicacy of her charm melted down the strength of my pride. My situation made me feel weak and powerless, like a man trying with his bare hands to break the iron bars of his prison cell. When the performance was over, I hurried out and placed myself where, unobserved, I could see her as she passed out. The haughtiness of spirit in which I had sought relief was all gone, and I was willing and ready to undergo any humiliation.

Shortly afterward we met at a progressive card party, and during the evening we were thrown together at one of the tables as partners. This was really our first meeting since the eventful night at her house. Strangely enough, in spite of our mutual nervousness, we won every trick of the game, and one of our opponents jokingly quoted the old saw: "Lucky at cards, unlucky in love." Our eyes met and I am sure that in the momentary glance my whole soul went out to her in one great plea. She lowered her eyes and uttered a nervous little laugh. During the rest of the game I fully merited the unexpressed and expressed abuse of my various partners; for my eyes followed her wherever she was and I played whatever card my fingers happened to touch.

Later in the evening she went to the piano and began to play very softly, as to herself, the opening bars of the Thirteenth Nocturne. I felt that the psychic moment of my life had come, a moment which, if lost, could never be called back; and, in as careless a manner as I could assume, I sauntered over to the piano and stood almost bending over her. She continued playing, but, in a voice that was almost a whisper, she called me by my Christian name and said: "I love you, I love you, I love you." I took her place at the piano and played the Nocturne in a manner that silenced the chatter of the company both in and out of the room, involuntarily closing it with the major triad.

We were married the following spring, and went to Europe for several months. It was a double joy for me to be in France again under such conditions.

First there came to us a little girl, with hair and eyes dark like mine, but who is growing to have ways like her mother. Two years later there came a boy, who has my temperament, but is fair like his mother, a little golden-headed god, with a face and head that would have delighted the heart of an old Italian master. And this boy, with his mother's eyes and features, occupies an inner sanctuary of my heart; for it was for him that she gave all; and that is the second sacred sorrow of my life.

The few years of our married life were supremely happy, and perhaps she was even happier than I; for after our marriage, in spite of all the wealth of her love which she lavished upon me, there came a new dread to haunt me, a dread which I cannot explain and which was unfounded, but one that never left me. I was in constant fear that she would discover in me some shortcoming which she would unconsciously attribute to my blood rather than to a failing of human nature. But no cloud ever came to mar our life together; her loss to me is irreparable. My children need a mother's care, but I shall never marry again. It is to my children that I have devoted my life. I no longer have the same fear for myself of my secret's being found out, for since my wife's death I have gradually dropped out of social life; but there is nothing I would not suffer to keep the brand from being placed upon them.

It is difficult for me to analyse my feelings concerning my present position in the world. Sometimes it seems to me that I have never really been a Negro, that I have been only a privileged spectator of their inner life; at other times I feel that I have been a coward, a deserter, and I am possessed by a strange longing for my mother's people.

Several years ago I attended a great meeting in the interest of Hampton Institute at Carnegie Hall. The Hampton students sang the old songs and awoke memories that left me sad. Among the speakers were R. C. Ogden, ex-Ambassador Choate, and Mark Twain; but the greatest interest of the audience was centred in Booker T. Washington, and not because he so much surpassed the others in eloquence, but because of what he represented with so much earnestness and faith. And it is this that all of that small but gallant band of coloured men who are publicly fighting the cause of their race have behind them. Even those who oppose them know that these men have the eternal principles of right on their side, and they will be victors even though they should go down in defeat. Beside them I feel small and selfish. I am an ordinarily successful white man who has made a little money. They are men who are making history and a race. I, too, might have taken part in a work so glorious.

My love for my children makes me glad that I am what I am and keeps me from desiring to be otherwise; and yet, when I sometimes open a little box in which I still keep my fast yellowing manuscripts, the only tangible remnants of a vanished dream, a dead ambition, a sacrificed talent, I cannot repress the thought that, after all, I have chosen the lesser part, that I have sold my birthright for a mess of pottage.